CUPID'S RUIN

*Ten Twisted Tales to Challenge
those Romantic Sensibilities*

CUPID'S RUIN

Ixidorr Hack

Contents

Introduction by the Author

Been a while...

Care to experience another Hack Attack?

Because the Hack is back with a third instalment of tales, this time focusing on the darker aspects of love.

Love. Ah, that unstoppable force of nature that binds our lives together and chooses courage and chivalry over cowardice and cruelty. A source of energy that will either make us or break us, elevate us to our loftiest or leave us weeping in the aisles. The subject of a million poems, songs and paintings.

This book is actually a companion piece to my upcoming anthology of dark, twisted love stories and should give you a fair idea of things to come. A rose motif understandably runs through both books. I, of course, take these tales in directions you will not be expecting.

Some of the stories contained within this book I wrote many years ago and felt needed working on with a wiser mind. It also allowed me to revisit some old characters and themes. Other stories are based on personal experiences – don't they say you should write what you know? – a *roman-à-clef* in some respects, against the infuriating distraction of certain events in the news. The book may or may not be a silent advertisement for visiting France – judge for yourself – and captures any narratives that began to form during the course of each holiday. And I must also warn you that when your wife has a degree in Fine Art and is a painter herself, don't be surprised if there is a lot of paintings in this book. This collection consists of ten novellas, dealing with cats and witches and haunted paintings, Valentine's Day and the King and the state of the world as well as a trilogy of Gallic romance, which together represent the perfect love and all that.

The whole thing is bookended by a wraparound tale and, as usual, the Hack tracks complete this little package, a soundtrack to the book, with songs that inspired me to write and which serve multiple functions, add new layers to the work. A double celebration in some respects, this book reflects my writing since getting married and also brings my tally of published stories to fifty.

So, sit back, put on your reading glasses and see if Love will save the day.

Because this is for all you Lovers out there. Or just Lovers of the Macabre. This is where it all goes wrong . . .

Ixidorr Hack
February 2019

Acknowledgements

Impawsible: A Cat's Tale was inspired by Merlin, our own magical cat and sweet little, furry-purry, lovely man, whose life as a kitten I have recounted in loving detail. I never thought cats could be so playful, energetic and sociable. These days, I refer to him as our 'middle-aged kitten'! XXXX

Having once ignored his music but later discovered and actually come to appreciate Elvis Presley as the greatest male vocalist of all time prompted me to write **Long Live The King.** Remarkably, it has been forty-two years since he died, aged forty-two.

Disgusted by world events, I derived great satisfaction from proving the power of the pen is mightier than the sword in **Paris Avant Le Printemps.** Boys, you have no idea what I've done to you!

Georges and Caroline deserve a special mention for making our honeymoon all those years ago very special, the source material for **A Honeymoon in Normandy.** I hope you guys are doing okay.

And, once again, I express my everlasting thanks to Hannah, to whom this book is dedicated, for granting me permission to borrow different facets of her personality as a template for some of my female characters. Thank you for being my Beautiful Wife and giving me a beautiful life. Thank you for your enduring affections and making me look good. Thank you for loving me for who I am and making me a better person. Thank you for keeping me in line . . . and keeping me *alive*. Thank you for sticking with me through thick and thin and I hope I have made as much a difference to your life as you have mine. Even through the challenging times, it has been an absolute honour being your husband all these years. I cherish your continued support and unfailing devotion. You truly *are* the One I Love, my Adorable One and my Babydoll – because they could make a doll out of you and it would look as unique as you! You shall always be my Muse.

> '*Doubt thou the stars are fire.*
> *Doubt that the sun doth move.*
> *Doubt truth to be a liar.*
> *But never doubt I love.*'

List of Tales

Valentine's Kiss: A thirtysomething woman, keen to start afresh on the dating circuit, is swept off her feet by a tall, dark, handsome stranger – but is he really the right man for her?

Impawsible: A Cat's Tale: A newlywed couple acquire a kitten as a trial run to parenthood, but it soon turns into an object of obsession for the wife and a thing of paranoia for her husband.

Long Live The King: Hoping to impress his girlfriend by writing an essay on Elvis over the summer recess, a schoolboy discovers he knows his subject matter better than he thinks.

A Honeymoon in Normandy: Fascination with an old, derelict Norman farmhouse tests the relationship of a couple on their honeymoon.

Paris Avant Le Printemps: A couple spend Valentine's week in the City of Lights in a last-ditch effort to save their crumbling marriage, but the wife is not quick to forgive.

Hebe on the Make: An English teacher at an all-girls' boarding school in Provence faces a tough decision when senior staff demand he give extra tuition to a schoolgirl who desires to become a writing sensation.

The Girl in the Mirror: After discovering a painting in an old curiosity shop, a horror writer slowly succumbs to its strange, seductive influence.

Harlequin Unmasked: A new college boy, obsessed with taking photographs, strives to capture the heart of one of his fellow students by any means, fair or foul.

Painted Devils, Vaulted Heavens: The Hour of Revelations approacheth against the backdrop of a developing relationship between a Catholic and a Jehovah's Witness.

Indescription II: Caerdroia on the Hill: An invitation from his uncle sees a horror writer learn the deepest, darkest secrets about the Welsh villagers – and himself.

A Loving Wraparound...

I sit in my exclusive, Parisian apartment, taking a break from my usual scribblings to explore the pile of handwritten poems and love stories you have kindly sent me. Twilight bathes the world outside. The windows mute the hustle-and-bustle in the streets below.

I wonder what the hell I am doing here. Love is not my thing, but it is at the forefront of my mind.

It can't be that time of year again, surely? The Day for Lovers. Valentine's Day. *Roses are red, violets are blue . . . and all that jazz.*

There is a reason why I peruse through these love letters and accounts of love lost. It feels like a lifetime since my own Love left me . . . but I know she will return.

The actual skull of Saint Valentine, crowned with daisies, and a winged, chubby statue of Cupid, clutching a bow and arrow, rest atop my writing bureau to celebrate the occasion. A vase of ten red roses sits on the table beside me, their petals glistening with dew and their texture possessing the lustre of velvet. Ten roses to represent a 'perfect ten' for the 'perfect love'. The iPod quietly plays a Mark Ronson-produced cover of an old Smiths' classic in the background, further enhancing the sombre, scholarly atmosphere of the room. I make sense of the material in my possession, put this day into perspective.

For those who don't already know, Saint Valentine was a former Roman priest from the third century who, after converting to Christianity, flouted a ban imposed by the Roman Emperor Claudius II, strictly forbidding young men to marry, thereby bolstering the number of conscripts into the army. By performing marriages in secret and for his unfaltering Christian beliefs, Valentine was executed in 270AD – on February the Fourteenth. According to legend, he is said to have restored the sight of his jailor's blind daughter through his prayers in prison. And, on the day of his execution, he supposedly left her a note signed 'Your Valentine'. He would eventually be martyred for his faith, centuries later, and a feast day would be dedicated to his name in celebration and remembrance.

But, just like Halloween, Valentine's Day has murkier origins, dating even further back to

Lupercalia. The roots of the Lovers' Holiday can be traced to this annual pagan festival when naked men, drunk on wine, ran around with goatskin whips, spanking young maidens desperate to conceive before ravishing them in the hope of optimizing their fertility and spiking the birth rate. That is until it was superseded when that world-renowned spoilsport, Constantine, having legalized Christianity, commandeered this Roman festival and bequeathed it to the somewhat more sobering legend of St. Valentine.

Since St. Valentine had only advocated courtly love, it was only during the fourteenth century, at the time of Chaucer when the feast day of February the Fourteenth became associated with romantic love. This medieval poet first connected Valentines's Day with romance in A Parliament of Fowls when 'every fowl cometh on Valentine's Day to choose his mate'.

Taken prisoner by the English at the disastrous Battle of Agincourt in 1415, found unharmed under a pile of corpses and held captive in the dreaded Tower of London, the French nobleman, Charles, Duke of Orleans, composed five hundred poems, many to his wife, Bonne of Armagnac, including one of which would supposedly become the first Valentine's Day poem.

I pat my statue of Cupid on the head and ponder how he came to be an icon of this special day. Despising chastity, he is the Greek child-god of erotic love. Whomever person or deity he shot an arrow to would be filled with uncontrollable desire. He is a winged figure because Love can be flighty, fickle and fleeting. He is a boy because love is irrational and impulsive. He was also once associated with the Cult of Dionysus, promoting fertility and wine and theatre, ritual ecstasy and madness. As it goes, Cupid would suffer his own ordeal of love when he himself developed an erotic attraction to Psyche, culminating in their sacred union. Who hasn't dreamt of Cupid's passion-provoking arrow striking their Object of Desire?

Exchanging handmade greetings cards, made from lace and featuring cupids and hearts, as a token of one's affections, became common practice on Valentine's Day in civilized English society by the 1800s, eventually spreading to the rest of Europe and the American colonies.

Even today, we follow the deep-seated cultural traditions of Valentine's Day, the expectation people place on making special plans, envisioning the 'perfect' romantic celebration. She has put on a flawless face of makeup and a pretty dress, coiffured a nice hairdo, and her perfume sends the fragrance of love wafting through the air, as she hopes to be swept off her feet in a Nicholas Sparks-style, swoonworthy moment. What most girls want, I suppose. Caught up in the puppy love, he will raise mountains for her, swim the deepest ocean, give her the Sun, Moon and Stars. As corny as you like. Roses on the doorstep like a scene out of a romcom, an expensive prix fixe dinner at a fancy restaurant, followed by a moonlit stroll on the beach or a trip to the cinema or a chance to cuddle up on the couch with your crush or a golden opportunity to take a hot, romantic bath together, even if it destroys the fella's sperm. Images of Barber Quartets and singing telegrams or of lovers singing karaoke in a bar, dancing the night away. Heart-shaped balloons, trite, tasteless jewellery and plush, larger-than-life teddy bears and other such folderols, as cheesy as a fondue. A pair of scissors cutting reams of paper hearts, each scrawled with the legend: I LOVE YOU. A mix-CD of romantic songs, all coming from the heart. Obscene amounts of chocolate, a staple of Valentine's Day, since certain Aztec emperors believed it was an aphrodisiac, able to improve virility and make them better able to serve their harem. Chocolate, of course, contains chemicals found in people who are either aroused or in love: tryptophan, for example, is a substrate of serotonin, our natural 'happy' drug, and another is phenylethylamine, a stimulant released by the brain when people fall in love.

Is it any surprise that Valentine's Day has become an excuse for sex, a license to 'mate'? The three stages of mating, for those uninitiated, driven by the systems in the brain, are the awakening of the sex drive, secondly romantic love (infatuation, obsession, passion) and finally attachment (peace and security with a long-term partner). We all follow the same ritual, dance to the same tune, as though universally blessed by Cupid himself. We all want to be loved.

But what of Shakespearean unrequited love? Dare we talk of V-Day horror stories, of hopeless humiliation and heartbreak, that ill-advised blind date or everyone in the restaurant giving you looks of sad pity for being stood up, those poorly-timed blazing rows, bust-ups and break-ups? When Cupid's arrow points straight towards disaster and even his own downfall. Love-wounds that will never fully heal. When you could wish you could donate your heart to someone else. Misery likes company.

Think of those poor souls whose divorce papers arrive in the post on Valentine's Day.

How awkward would it be if your train home isn't until the next day and you're forced to stay at his place overnight – after dumping him?

Imagine baking a cake for your boyfriend that says 'Happy VD' – and you never have sex with him again.

What if you were to receive a card with the congratulatory words 'You're having a Boy!' and it is only then you know your boyfriend is cheating on you – because you're not even pregnant?

What about the poor, old couple, who go to bed after a lovely Valentine's evening, only to be woken up by their neighbour who has drunkenly made his way into their apartment and, butt-naked, decides to pee on the bed – with them still in it?

Maybe the candlelit dinner was fantastic, and everything went according to plan – there's even rose petals on the restaurant table – and you head back to his place only to see him pull out a condom and, brandishing some whipped cream, he utters the oh, so romantic words, 'I'm really stoked up for Vagina Day' because he is firm believer of 'safety before romance'! Yes, he lives by the code that, for one day in the year, he has to be nice to the girl, because sex is an entitlement. You spend the rest of the evening alone, watching The Vagina Monologues at the theatre.

You get a weird text from a number you don't recognize, telling you how pretty you are and how hard he's fallen for you. You're dying to figure out the identity of your secret admirer, even though he's staring at you in class the whole time. He reveals himself and, after some extensive wooing, he asks you to be his Valentine. You say 'yes', of course, since he's cool, super-cute and kind of goofy, even if you might think he's possibly out of your league. Surely, this is the start of something beautiful. All of a sudden, as the two of you walk home after a night on the town, these guys corner you down an alley and take out knives. Mortified, the next thing you know, your date pushes you against them and runs off as if he has a rocket up his arse!

Or maybe you hail from some liberal-arts' college and, being somewhat liberal-minded, you want to surprise your new boyfriend with your signature move, following a marijuana-fuelled Valentine's night of passion and romance. As daylight breaks and he starts to stir, you decide to go for it. He's hard down below and only gets harder in your mouth . . . when, all of a sudden, he wakes up with a start, sits bolt upright and, in one lightning-fast strike, punches you in the face, breaking your nose. At that moment, it dawns on you that, no matter what pornography may teach, some men don't react all that well to being woken up by a blowjob. You eventually decide that a handjob, with seriously intense eye-contact, might be the best way forward.

This self-proclaimed French playboy spends his spare time chatting to women online and he soon begins to fall for one particular woman he has been corresponding with for several weeks. She reciprocates his feelings and they decide to meet up in person and arrange a romantic rendezvous. Excited he is about to hook up with the girl of his dreams, he receives the shock of his life when his online date arrives. She turns out to be his mother!

A young man wishes to purchase a Valentine's gift for his sweetheart and, since they haven't been dating very long, he decides a nice pair of gloves might be just the thing because it demonstrates his romantic feelings without being too personal. Accompanied by his own younger sister, he buys a pair of leather gloves for his sweetheart while his younger sister purchases a pair of panties for herself. During the wrapping, the shopgirl mixes up the items and the sister gets the gloves and the sweetheart gets the panties. Without bothering to check the contents, the young man seals the package and posts it to his sweetheart along with this letter:

My Dearest --------,

I selected these because I noticed that you are not in the habit of wearing any when we go out in the evenings. If it wasn't for my sister, I would have chosen the longer ones with buttons, but she wears short ones since they are easy to remove. The lady I bought them from showed me the pair she had been wearing for the past three weeks and they still smell divine. I hope you don't mind, but I had her try yours on for me to make sure they fitted perfectly. I wish I were there to put them on you for the first time as no doubt other hands will come in contact with them before I get a chance to see you again. When you take them off, remember to blow gently into them before putting them away since they will naturally be a little damp after being worn. Just imagine how many times I will kiss them during the coming year. Please wear them for me on Valentine's Day so I can check if they look pretty on you, otherwise I can exchange them for another pair.

Yours Truly,

PS: They say it is fashionable to wear them slightly folded down, showing a little fur.

A seriously funny Valentine, *I think, exploding into roaring gales of laughter, putting down the love letters I have been reading.* A classic of its kind. Now that's what I call Love! *How to ruin a perfect Valentine's Day – doesn't it just make you want to open your mouth and scream silently in public? Yeah, rather embarrassing – don't you just want to die?*

You need not doubt the sincerity of the storyteller for, at all costs, the tale must be told.

What do I suppose you will make of the stories I am about to share with you? Will you be able to withstand the assault on your sensibilities? Can you quantify *love?*

I have arranged an impromptu get-together with someone I invited here, someone I once knew . . . and loved. And, perhaps, still *love.*

Sure enough, as the hour approaches, I hear a knock at the door.

Perfect timing.

I get up and open the door . . .

Valentine's Kiss

> *"When we two parted*
> *In silence and tears,*
> *Half broken-hearted*
> *To sever for years,*
> *Pale grew thy cheek and cold,*
> *Colder thy kiss;*
> *Truly that hour foretold*
> *Sorrow to this."*

When We Two Parted (1816)
Lord Byron

A single rose: Love at first sight...

I: The Affections of the Heart

Madelaine Henshaw declared without resorting to melodrama that she was hopelessly in love. And just because today fell rather conveniently on February the Fourteenth wasn't the sole reason for her bursting confidence, although admittedly it did make the occasion all the more special. No, circumstance aside, her feelings for a certain gentleman were practically inscribed on her heart in block capitals, indelibly etched as deeply as a parishioner's love for the Lord's Prayer.

She was in love! El-Oh-Vee-Ee. *LOVE! True, Unconditional Love!*

Impossible! the skeptic inside her argued. *Romance is dead!*

Not so, she countered defensively, *there are those among us who still take romance very seriously. I should know – I speak from experience.* But, in all honesty, she could see where the argument came from.

Consider the sanctity of marriage for instance, an institution founded under the eyes of God. The way marriage was treated with such disrespect nowadays, contempt even, was it any wonder the divorce rate had risen to a phenomenal one-in-three? Or, in more general terms, how about the proportion of singles who thoughtlessly threw themselves into intimate relationships with no conception on earth what was expected of them to make the whole thing work? *Oh, we just did it for the fun of it. You know, the thrill of the chase, sharing the forbidden fruit, two ships passing in the night, and all that figurative nonsense. Anyway, what's there to lose? A little rumpy-pumpy never did anyone any harm. It's all a part of growing up, broadening your horizons. Think of it as a necessity. We'd be poorer off without it, go crazy.*

Point taken, but sex in itself does not a relationship make, marital or otherwise. As neither party was prepared to face up to his or her responsibilities, the relationship was ultimately doomed from the outset with not a hope in hell of lasting a week, let alone a lifetime. The only way they knew of rectifying their mistake was by pulling out of the relationship when there was nothing left to say and engaging in another equally frivolous venture. *The fickleness and superficiality of relationships these days. The clear short-sightedness of those who claim to be broad-minded. Living in the moment. You can boast as many partners as you like, but those of us who know 'True Love' think of you as nothing more than mindless savages, slaves to your genitalia, capable of satisfying only a dumb, baser instinct, without giving a second thought to direction in life or future happiness or the obligations of parenthood. Whether you be a streetwalker or you're in it for the alimony, there's not much differentiating you. You can dress yourself up in as much wealth as you like and pretend to be someone important for the day, but, darling, who're you really kidding? A living, breathing, walking inflatable doll is what you are, will always be, nothing more, nothing less, unless you can find the courage to change your permissive ways. How would you prefer to be remembered on your tombstone? Respected as the penitent hooker, who took the time and trouble to be born again as a lady, or terribly reviled like some widowed millionairess, who comports herself in the vulgar manner of a slut? The Elizabeth Taylors and Zsa Zsa Gabors of this world, please take note.*

Such was the sorry state of society that shamelessly encouraged every person to behave like sweaty hogs in the rutting season, in relationships that were only skin-deep, a poor excuse for love, a shallow imitation at best, not to mention a not-too-endearing reflection of romance, where the philosophy was one of 'love is the same as sex'.

How could anyone, barring the most ignorant, confuse love with sex? What klutz compares the grunting and moaning of casual sex with the fond affections of lifelong lovers? *Sex* is the *act* of coupling, whereas *Love* is an *artform* that has to be carefully nurtured and maintained, lest your skills grow rusty. After all, it's this thing called Love that makes us humans different from animals. There again, even chimps show commitment and fidelity on successfully procuring a mate.

You always gain something beautiful when the love you discover is genuine, whereas you lose a precious part of yourself, piece by piece, from every pointless relationship you enter into. Until there is nothing left.

Ask that exceptional, happily-married couple, who are on the verge of celebrating their Fiftieth Anniversary, what has kept them together all these years despite one of them being unable to conceive or still sticking together even in the absence of any sexual relations? And they'll tell you: their love for one another, the deep, unbreakable bond they share, that mature (almost psychic) understanding of their spouse's loves and hates, their strengths and weaknesses, their mannerisms and foibles, no matter how annoying or downright peculiar. Love is rarely a 'Roses over the Door' affair. In any relationship it won't be long before the cracks in the marriage begin to show. But it's about seeing each other's imperfections and flaws no matter how disappointed and frustrated you might be, talking about how you feel instead of bottling it up, letting your partner know so you can both work on some changes, learning to love 'in spite of' and not 'because of'. If their love is as strong as the day they first met, who can possibly doubt they have not gained from their glorious union? They have learned to harness the secrets of romance, tapping into its rich vein whenever the need suits them; romance, dear folk, is what keeps their love alive.

For *Romance* is an expression of the finer points of Love, as integral and inseparable to Love as paddle-steamers to the Mississippi.

What value do people give to St. Valentine's Day when they buy their loved ones plastic roses that cost a paltry $1.99 or tacky Hallmark cards with banal, manufactured messages moulded in on the inside? *Ah, but it's the thought that counts,* claims the 'enlightened' lover. *I'll give her a tastier surprise later, between the sheets . . .*

This Hallmark Holiday reinforces the entitlement of desire, validating the idea that if somebody desires someone enough to buy them chocolates or roses, they should expect to be desired, also. But does the person whom you've bought a fancy romantic dinner before taking them home really owe you sex in return? Are you really that *stupid* to believe it to be the case?

If love is supposed to be such a private, personal thing, is it really in your best interest to scour bars and clubs and cheap motels for your ideal partner? What guys do you expect to find in a bar except those with the sole intention of picking up girls? Doesn't anyone know that searching for love in the gutter only brings out the rats? Gets you *bitten?*

Not that Maddie was innocent of such crimes. On the contrary, how many junkies, jailbirds and violent drunks had she exceeded, the number of one-night-stands she'd participated in or the string of short-term flings she'd blindly leapt into? Relationships that were based purely on sex. A lot of mistakes she had made in her time, for which she could blame nobody else but herself. Maddie certainly knew how to 'pick 'em'. The associations of her younger lovesick sisters, Minnie, Missie and Maisie, too, had reached a melting point where their scandalous liaisons with unfavourable men had severely jeopardized their reputations, much to the embarrassment of their Christian parents, who could do little to protect their wanton daughters from themselves or from the hurtful remarks directed at them by the sanctimonious locals, accusing the girls of being 'Jezebels' or 'strumpets' or 'women of easy virtue'. There could be no debating the Henshaw sisters' greatest shortcoming: blessed in looks, unlucky in love.

So was Maddie being abruptly dismissive when she proclaimed that romance was a thing of the past, that romance was *dead?* Not entirely. Despite her promiscuous past and lack of direction in life, she was a traditionalist at heart, an old-fashioned romantic, who like all romantic die-hards firmly believed that romance was like a fine wine that matured with age.

Moreover, Maddie was no quitter. A thoroughly resourceful woman, she reinvented herself.

She thanked her lucky stars that she hadn't lost her looks, a cute, blond thirtysomething, who with the appropriate makeover, could still convincingly pass herself off as a teenage temptress. Her present position as assistant salesgirl behind the perfume counter at a plush Baton Rouge department store was fair comment to her lingering looks. Yet she was fully aware that time was not on her side, her body-clock her biggest enemy, and the window of opportunity was bound to close on her sooner or later. Aside from buying a humungous dildo and giving it the name 'Dr. Wankinstein', she never compared herself to those high-powered, female execs who often sacrificed family over career, but a hankering desire to find a suitable match explained why, like her sisters, she should suddenly switch channels: to dating agencies and Lonely Ads' Columns and the suchlike, where privacy was guaranteed and romance an added bonus. *And success only a heartbeat away.*

For Maddie found her man.

Luc was his name and romance his game.

This wasn't like before. As she told her friends at work: *Sometimes you meet someone and you know from the first moment he's the One. Can you imagine the sense of fulfilment you get when you meet the man of your dreams?* There was no rhetoric in her remark, only the delight that came with realization, a coming-together of everything she'd always firmly believed in. She had struck gold in the shape of Lucius Robideaux, or Luc as he preferred to be called. She was smitten from the moment she first set eyes on him. He was the literal definition of the tall, dark, handsome stranger . . . and the perfect gentleman. What more could she ask for? Never having met a real gentleman in her time, she could not but feel privileged. He bore her seal of approval, a stamp of distinction, possessed the pedigree of a perfectionist and seemed by far the hunter in the pack. His profession? *Did he say altruist . . .?* Maddie couldn't be sure. *Something about being a principal benefactor?* He might have said, *Patron to a charitable medical research programme*, whatever that entailed.

Maddie was completely overawed, smitten by him as any girl would be.

After answering Maddie's personal ads' column, Luc had swept her off her feet by wining and dining her in the most upmarket restaurant in Baton Rouge, DES POINTES. A welcome change from the Creole cuisine (Cajun chicken, shrimp jambalaya or seafood gumbo with cornbread) that Maddie was so accustomed to. There, sitting under a textured pool of candlelight, tucking into the hors d'oeuvre of chilled oysters, the main course of smoked monkfish in dill-and-tomatillo sauce and, by way of dessert, fresh strawberry-and-kiwi-salad with crème fraîche, drinking Cristal from fluted glasses, Maddie realized that she was not alone, that Luc had the same romantic inclinations as her, that romance was *not* dead, that she wanted to spend the rest of her days with him, that he understood her, *really* understood her (unlike the deceit of most men before, who only took advantage of her feelings), that she could speak to him openly, frankly and quite unequivocally about anything and he would respond without being either judgemental or demeaning. *His uncanny ability to draw you in like a magnet. His voice, soft-spoken, utterly captivating. His aristocratic attributes that were neither pompous nor patronizing.*

He told her that he was a widower, that his wife had died young a long time ago and he had never got over his loss, hoping that some day he would meet a girl who would help him overcome his sorrow. *There will always be a first true love. The one who taught you how to love. The one you measure any subsequent love against whenever you love again*. Maddie was moved, instantly determined to be that girl. To measure up to his first true love. Widowers, in her opinion, were always sexier than divorcés; there was something sad, romantic and tragic about losing your loved one to the grave as opposed to being partly to blame for any break-up. He told her he had a thing for history: that he was a well-travelled man, fully acquainted with the customs of every country in the world and capable of casting a commemorative eye on the countless civilizations of the past. He told her of his trips to Europe and why France was his most favourite place on the Continent and how Paris wasn't that much different from Baton Rouge or New Orleans, recounting its abundance of theatres, galleries, cathedrals, cafés and boulevards. He told her about the diversity of Parisian culture: from the existential teachings of Sartre to the Spirit of the Resistance, from the pavement artist in Montmartre to the treasures of the Louvre, from the selfless, puritanical ways of the convent schools to the inexhaustible licentiousness of the bordellos. In the manner that Europe fashioned the Americas, he explained, Paris was where the history of New Orleans began. He used Hemingway as a fitting example, comprehensively describing why the celebrated novelist rejected America and sought Paris' Moveable Feast for his later works. He went on to discuss the merits of Gauguin not as a philanderer but as a Post-Impressionist painter. He recited a few stanzas from Baudelaire with such unerring precision that Maddie might have been forgiven for thinking that he wrote the words himself.

This is what she wanted to hear, not some tanked-up trucker trying to enthuse her about the details of the latest baseball season and demanding that she fetch a few more cold ones from the 7-Eleven down the road, or an addict boyfriend complaining that his welfare cheque's late and if he can borrow, no, *take*, another fifty dollars from her purse for a quick fix. Oh, she'd seen her fair share of dregs, wastrels, riff-raff and no-hopefuls, but through the thick and thin of it, the mistakes and the heartaches, she had at last found what she had been looking for all her life. The tide had turned, and Maddie was no longer the loser in love. No more Blanche DuBois, she hoped. This guy was quite a catch and definitely one-in-a-million. *Self-assured as well as sensitive. Rich, handsome and unattached. Humble, not one to flaunt his wealth or play the field.* His bulging bank balance wasn't his only great asset, although a little money on the side wouldn't go unappreciated, thought Maddie. *Foreign and mysterious and enigmatic.* His reconditeness to particular personal issues like his age, origins, past romances and painful moments only intrigued Maddie further. He embodied the kind of irresistible charm that most romance writers seemed incapable of translating convincingly to the written page, and Maddie was desperate to know him a whole lot better. She didn't mind it if every night was the same as this night. The connection they made, the unspoken chemistry between them, the sense of closeness she had felt on that single date was astonishing, considering how little they had in common. Perhaps that age-old saying of 'opposites attracting' was true after all, as was that constantly recurring myth, 'love at first sight'.

At the end of the evening, as Luc announced, "Your chariot awaits, m'lady!" and took her home wrapped up warm in an open barouche, Maddie was sure their love would develop into something extraordinary. Then, pecking her on her cheek, he requested on the doorsteps of her tenement building she join him at his lakeside retreat in New Orleans this weekend. She accepted his invitation gladly, without hesitation. And since the weekend coincided with St. Valentine's Day... *well, what more can a girl ask for?*

Oh, she was as thrilled as a schoolgirl with a schoolgirl's crush! That was less than a week ago. Now having finally arrived at the place of the weekend rendezvous – or 'lovers' tryst', the verve of schoolgirl vocabulary – she wasn't quite sure what to think.

What she had been expecting was a log cabin in the woods or an old colonial mansion in the affluent Middle Garden District. Instead, what she got was a country house that was both devastatingly beautiful and manifestly ancient. Luc's secret hideaway was a grey-stoned, monastic building which, at first glance, evoked comparisons with the fictional castle of Otranto. The windows were tall and arched, centuries of dirt caked on the lateral embrasures, intricate traceries and notched quatrefoils. Deformed, twisted gargoyles spread their batlike wings from the roof, looking down on the edge of the coastal bayou like gloating birds-of-prey. The gothic architecture appeared strangely out of place with the heady surroundings. Lake Pontchartrain lay beyond, a shimmering mirror of water that reflected the diorama of sunset, the lower layers of warm russets gradually dispersing under the oncoming violet of dusk.

Winters are always mild in Louisiana. The spread of frost is gone, the land laid bare for the renewal of the natural world. In the ground, seedlings are taking hold, a sure sign of spring. The ospreys, brown pelicans, belted kingfishers and snowy egrets are returning to the swamplands that are within easy reach of the Mississippi delta. Alligators are not unheard of in these parts, but, like the bats, are seldom seen. Maddie often imagined what it must be like to watch the moonshine across the banks of Pontchartrain, listening to the rustling of reeds, the muskrats, water shrews and other creatures of the night foraging for food, the dull drone of the dragonflies and the chirring call of the cricket. Tonight, she thought, she just might get to find out.

She'd never been this far south before though had dreamed of being here many times. No, the nearest she'd ever been was the famous Mardi Gras festival, the spectacular procession that embellished the streets of New Orleans annually. People of every age, creed and colour mixed and mingled, drank and smoked, and, from noon to midnight, grooved and partied to the rich, riotous rhythms of the samba-beat, many extending their celebrations into the small hours of the morning. Fancy dress, exotic dancers, passing floats of strange, mistick krewes. It had been quite an experience back then, and Maddie never got the opportunity again. Baton Rouge had its own version, a pageant of music and dance that was, in many respects, similar if not inferior. Even a funeral procession through New Orleans beat any Irish wake.

Let the good times roll, as the legend went.

Maddie went further back, remembering with much fondness, how she and her sisters had done the whole length of Highway 61, all one-and-a-half-thousand miles of it, during their late teens, two summers' running. Stretching from Wyoming to the Big Easy, Highway 61 was a road sacred to musicians and college kids alike. You could almost trace the history of popular music southwards to its roots along the Blues Highway: folk-rock, rhythm-and-blues, soul, jazz, ragtime. Along the way, your musical odyssey might take you to the infamous crossroads at the junction between Highway 61 and Highway 49 where the legendary musician, Robert Johnson, supposedly sold his soul to the Devil in exchange for the gift of guitar-playing greatness. For many, New Orleans was regarded as the birthplace of jazz. Many of the exponents of the early jazz movement started out their working lives playing in the saloons and brothels of Storyville, the city's lakefront and foremost red-light district. Even Duke Ellington emerged from humble beginnings, carving out a career through the speakeasies of New York. Living in Louisiana, it was therefore not inconceivable that Maddie's sisters should hold a close affinity for the likes of Louis Armstrong and Lonnie Johnson. In fact, Maddie owned an impressive assortment of their recordings, including some rare collectibles, which she was proud to admit she had paid top dollar for. *But you don't have to be an all-out jazz fan to understand its appeal*, she frequently explained. *You must let your senses guide you. There's something smooth and sensual about the sound, like the feel of silk on skin or the first mouthful of real banana split, blended from fresh fruit and ice-cream and covered in maple syrup. Believe me, listening to a great jazz combo is like having your ears erogenously massaged. Nothing short of* erotic.

Yes, Louisiana, and New Orleans in particular, had always been a progressive place, a city genuinely like no other in America, a society based on French-Spanish-Cuban-Creole cultural influences. Think of the Quadroon Balls of the Antebellum era, where white European men met free women of colour, who would become their mistresses and bear them children of mixed heritage, these particular children destined to be gentlemen, or ladies, enjoying a life of education, opportunity and luxury; *plaçage* operated in a time when interracial marriages were strictly forbidden. Despite the ongoing atmosphere of white privilege and black oppression, could plaçage still be viewed as exploitation or was it the first step towards liberation, the pulling-down of the barriers between race?

Maddie had tried only this morning to contact her sisters, to give them the good news, but she had not been able to reach any of them. Which was indeed odd considering how close she was to them and how they liked to keep in touch with one another as often as they could. *Probably out with their respective boyfriends,* she was forced to conclude, *on this very 'special' St. Valentine's Day. Who can blame them? When it's a day like today, it's worth savouring every minute.* Maddie decided to try them again tomorrow, eager to catch up on all the latest goss where poss. Her drive down to New Orleans had been an uneventful affair, a perfect opportunity to reflect on the future as well as delve into matters nostalgic and romantic.

And now that she was here, Maddie slowed down her blue Chrysler in the circular forecourt, unable to articulate her unaccountable feelings of apprehension. She felt distinctly intimidated by the dark, stilted edifice that was Luc's lakeside retreat. There was something not-quite-right about the house, a cold, conscious undercurrent that called to mind the enduring spook-stories of Shirley Jackson. The setting was pure American Gothic, she supposed, the haunted Southern mansion, but certainly not without its charm, potentially exciting save for the sense of brooding menace she could not shake off, radiating from those grimy windows, as though the house concealed dread mysteries best left undisturbed. The preambling presence of redwoods, cedars and tamaracks did little to soften her growing unease, nor the picotees and poinsettias that clustered about the walls. Reluctantly stepping out of her car, clutching the small, nondescript box, which contained Luc's Valentine's gift, tighter in her fist, she caught a glimpse of a raccoon scurrying into the undergrowth, apparently premature in its quest to scavenge the garbage cans. When a magpie came to rest on a patch of grass by the trees, Maddie was taken by surprise, her startlement almost that of someone who is confronted by a particularly evil-looking crow. *Where's the other one?* she thought, looking around frantically for its mate. *It* has *to be here* . . . To Maddie, a single magpie spelled bad luck, an omen of romantic ruin, whereas a pair communicated impending success. *One for sorrow, two for joy.*

Get a-hold of yourself, woman! her rational self interjected, furious at her for succumbing to the same brand of schoolyard superstition as plucking the petals off a daisy, one by one, in the hope of discovering whether or not your boyfriend truly loved you. As a schoolgirl, this had become something of a compulsion with her. Tying blades of grass together had been another particular favourite: if the grass remained knotted, your relationship would prosper, but if the knot came undone, expect to break up pretty soon. When having a really bad day at school, Maddie took to wearing her bra inside-out and back-to-front in a bid to reverse her luck. (The fact that she sometimes looked as though she had sprouted an extra pair of breasts on her back did not bother her at all, although it did manage to cause some alarm amongst her friends initially!) This inverted-underwear quirk developed into one of her mother's pet peeves. This wasn't proper conduct for a young lady! Martha May Henshaw would scold. Far from sensible, it was downright heathen! Even back then, Maddie never paid much mind to Old Ma's constant nagging. So, like her sisters, she never quite succeeded in outgrowing her superstitious tendencies. *Didn't you read today's horoscope?*

Does it matter?

AIRES: Why is love so complicated for you, a hurdle that you must stumble over? Fear not the future nor regret the past, for those seeking a long-lasting relationship, courage is required to seize the day. Be assertive and your outlook will change permanently.

Yeah, but what if he doesn't want to see me anymore? the tiny voice in her head contested. *What if he's no longer interested or stands me up or tells me that he's got someone else or—*

—Or what? Of course he wants to see you! He has your number, doesn't he? He'd have let you know if his feelings had changed in any way, wouldn't he? He's a gentleman! So stop torturing yourself for no good reason!

God, she was a mess! A nervous wreck! Maddie supposed it was perfectly normal for a person to experience doubts before meeting someone they fancied from the first: 'pre-date jitters' as some people called it. But it just wasn't like her. Not at all. She'd been dating since she was fifteen, always taking every new encounter in her stride, always able to cope with the pressures of any relationship. She couldn't remember ever feeling *this* stressed, so damned insecure. Why should she doubt herself now? Was it because of Luc she felt thus? Luc, who had swept her off her feet with one incredible date and further hinted at the possibility of a whirlwind romance. Luc, who made the powerful male leads of the Arthur Hailey variety seem positively insipid, the racy creations of Harold Robbins look just plain ordinary. Never before had she felt this way about anybody, not even when the college quarterback had chosen her above all the other cheerleaders (and, boy, was he hot!). She had taken an irrefutable shine to Luc, and so she hoped, he to her. *Yes, perhaps Luc is the reason why I feel like I do . . . Luc, oh, Luc. My love. My sweet prince. My last, true romantic.* That one, glorious date just summed him up. *I'll do anything he asks me to do. I promise never to let him down.*

Or maybe it's the damned house!

Will you knock it off? You're feeding your head with all kinds of nonsense about ghosts! Do you really want to blow this?

No, I don't . . .

Then think happy thoughts!

Replaying that heavenly evening at DES POINTES with the man for all seasons, being serenaded through the moonlit streets on a horse-and-carriage ride home, the subtle warmth of his lips upon her cheek as he kissed her goodnight, the promise of future happiness in his expression, unspoken but inferred, what might be, what was yet to come, crushed any subversive feelings that lingered and helped calm her down. "Make it happen," she told herself. *He's probably waiting for you right now, waiting to hold you in his arms, waiting to tell you how much he loves you.*

Her perkiness partly restored, she strode up to the front doorstep and stood there, looking at the thick-panelled door, thinking. She'd made an effort to look her most elegant: caramel-coloured suede jacket, white jacquard blouse, sable hipster leather skirt, black high heels, all pricey items from Chanel. The yellow crocus in her button-hole (more superstition) provided the finishing touch. After bending down to adjust the tilt of her left high heel, she straightened up, composed herself, and whispering, "Here goes..." rang the doorbell.

[Bon chance . . .]

The noise of the bell echoed through the corridors and depths of the house as though voicing indignation at its deployment, protesting like some wroth, fell beast prematurely roused from ancient slumber. Each toll was an elegy in itself and seemed to add its own measure of creepiness to the proceedings. The clangorous surge of sound caused Maddie to shudder, rekindling some of her earlier fear.

A tomblike silence descended, then. The silence, as loud and interminable as her announcing her arrival at the door, afforded no peace to her tension-ridden thoughts. She waited with bated breath, listening for any footfalls, any signs of life. She sensed none. Her finger went for the doorbell again, but at the last instant she snatched her hand back, not particularly wishing to relive that infernal racket. Besides, any person or persons present, unless stone-deaf, would have surely heard it the first time round. Sensing only vacancy within, she deliberated whether to leave.

There's nobody ho—

Without indication, the door opened. Suddenly, Maddie was face-to-face with a man whom she'd never seen before. A strange old man. Old, very old, *extremely* old. Possibly an English butler-type, judging by his formal attire? Manservant, butler, gentleman's gentleman, old family retainer. But his ancient appearance otherwise failed to salve her fear. For, as they locked gazes, Maddie noticed how unnaturally pale he looked, the colour of wax. He stood tall and gaunt, wrinkled, almost withered, as if he had been recently embalmed. She saw no warmth in those eyes, eyes that were dull, detached, unseeing, and a dreadful wave of terror washed over her. 'Pre-date jitters' exploded into the 'heebie-jeebies', only one short step away from the 'screaming meemies'. In that awful moment, she heard the jingle of wind chimes nearby, felt the gargoyles glaring down at her from above and perceived a faint, sinister thud somewhere in the house.

"Can I help you?" he asked in a tone that was as expressionless as his eyes.

I've come to the wrong address. Please tell me I'm at the wrong address! she thought, hoping against all hope that this was all a big stupid mistake on her part. *I'll just apologize for my intrusion and be on my way.* Except it didn't come out quite like that. "I do beg your pardon," she said, unable to disguise the wobble in her voice. "but does a . . . does a Monsieur Luc Robideaux live here?"

A pause, a suspension of time, during which Maddie could have sworn life was filtering into his eyes, slowly but surely and quite visibly. "And you are . . .?"

"Miss Henshaw."

Another hush, fraught and frangible.

"Ah, Miss Henshaw, my master is expecting you," he said, now entirely harmless and ordinary. Thrusting open the door wider, he added, "Do come in."

"Thank you . . ." *Oh thank you, Lord!* Relief. Unreserved relief – and enormous gratitude. She crossed the threshold onto the mosaic floor of the lobby. "Is he in?"

"I'm afraid my master has a prior engagement elsewhere, but I trust he will be home after dark. He has, however, left strict instructions with me to show you to the guest room, where you can freshen up and wait for him. He has a gift for you...*a token of his affections*, I believe is how he put it."

Maddie scolded herself for being so scared, for bending to her overactive imagination or ever doubting Luc's sincerity. Luc was expecting her and would be here soon – that's all that mattered now. "And here's a little something from me to Monsieur Robideaux." She handed the old man the lightweight box she'd brought along with her which contained rhinestone cufflinks from Lafont Paris. *What else could I have got him?* she thought anxiously. *Anyway, how does that old saying go: what* do *you get the man who has everything?* "Please give this to him when he arrives."

"As Mademoiselle wishes." He gave an appreciative nod, then introduced himself. "In case you were wondering, my name is Hargreaves. I am entirely at your disposal for the duration of your visit."

They shook hands and Maddie became convinced that he must have terrible circulation; it was like clutching a frozen fillet of fish. His grip too felt surprisingly weak, almost fragile. Any firmer, she thought, and she might have taken his whole hand away with her. Again, she laughed at how someone as polite, personable and punctilious as Hargreaves, who was very likely well past pensionable age, could so easily have upset her. *It's me . . . I've really got it bad, haven't I?*

"Now that we're fully acquainted . . . this way, please." Hargreaves took her coat and led her through the large lobby into the vast hallway. His gait was stiff, ungainly, almost lumbering, a consequence of both his tall frame and the twinges of rheumatism that quite frequently accompany the onset of old age.

Maddie was astounded by the interior of the house, which she felt could have been a museum in its own right. Marble pedestals boasted a dazzling array of Moroccan vases and Rococo sculptures. An outstanding collection of oil paintings by Boucher, Delacroix and Cézanne hung from the walls. Lucky charms, foreign amulets, strange talismen, Chinese puzzle-boxes, adorned every showcase. She spotted a warrior's helmet, purportedly of Merovingian origin, in one such corner showcase. Climbing the grand, winding staircase, Maddie marvelled at Luc's exquisite tastes, certain that altogether the exhibits in this house must be worth a small fortune. She wondered not inappropriately how many other properties like this one he owned and whether as a business tycoon of tremendous gumption he qualified for the *Forbes* Top 100 Rich List. Somehow it wouldn't surprise her if he did.

I could live here, she thought, suddenly hearing the distant peal of wedding bells in her head. *What's wrong with being ambitious? A little optimism never hurt anyone.*

The guest bedroom was more of the same, a tribute to both equity and antiquity. Rich, resplendent and totally atmospheric, just the way Maddie had come to like it in her short time here. A promenade of candlebra was lit like tiny beacons, complimenting the vibrant décor of the walls. Logs burned merrily in the huge, ornamental fireplace, casting a warm, dignified glow across the chamber. A teak bookcase stood against one wall, its tomes dusty and cobwebbed. Beside it were a pocked writing bureau and a large drinks' cabinet. The pendulum of an authentic Wolfenden clock swung back and forth, providing confirmation of the early evening that showed through the gap between the drawn velvet curtains. A chaise-longue rested beneath the windowsill, a Chesterfield sofa behind the bedroom door. At the far corner of the room, past the dressing table, a connecting door led to a secret, inner sanctum, which Maddie presumed was the coat-closet. She noticed it was locked and bolted but thought nothing more of it.

The enormous bed was made of brass, its bedposts and railings engraved in strange, intricate designs like ancient runes which Maddie could not decipher. Although she'd been anticipating a four-poster, the bed nevertheless looked old and expensive and extremely inviting. Like the walls, the bedsheets were again the same shade of red. On the voluminous covers were placed two boxes, fully wrapped, the smaller one stacked on top of the larger, with a white envelope arranged alongside. These, she suspected, must be the gifts Luc had selected for her. She realized she wanted nothing more now than to open them. She held back despite herself, pausing instead to finish her appraisal of the room.

Her eyes travelled upwards, her attention drawn towards the unlit chandelier and, in particular, the ceiling from which it hung. The ceiling was dome-shaped, like a cupola, and painted with religious depictions of the Afterlife in meticulous, technical detail. The frenzied use of colour lent the mural a strange, shimmering kind of vitality. Unlike the famous Sistine Chapel, there were no saints or angels to speak of. Just files and files of grieving, naked, manacled humans led by grotesque archdemons to the black, fiery heart of the Inferno, a vivid pictorial obviously inspired by Rodin's *Gates of Hell*. Disconcerting to a degree, but it also strengthened her belief of Luc as a man of exceptional vision. From what she had seen of the house so far, who else could have pulled off this remarkable blend of two completely separate styles, this perfect fusion of Art Deco with the Neogothic? Her enthusiasm undented, she went on to speculate where he could have acquired such fine taste.

"I shall bring you up some light refreshments," suggested Hargreaves.

Maddie, who'd forgotten he was there, jumped when he spoke. "No, there's no need," she said. "Honestly. I'll be fine, thanks."

Hargreaves looked slightly astonished as though he'd been requested to forgo a particularly important duty. Reluctantly, he replied: "Very well. If there is anything you need, do not hesitate to pull the cord."

He withdrew presently, and Maddie was suddenly alone. She let herself go. Wearing a schoolgirl's smile, she plumped down on the bed and let out a long, whooshing sigh, unable to contain her joy.

YESSSSSS…!

Maddie could scarcely believe her luck. It was with pure fate, karma, serendipity, happenstance – call it what you will – that she was *here*. In the bedazzling throes of her fancies, in the midst of old yearnings never before fulfilled. *I mean what growing girl hasn't secretly dreamt of such a date?* Maddie hoped she could put aside the frustrations of the past and concentrate on the true promise that lay ahead. Premature or not, she felt her search was over. This was every girl's wish-come-true, for the lonely majority a once-in-a-lifetime experience: to be treated like a lady, a VIP, a queen, an *empress* in the highest lap of luxury, champagne and crystal and candlelight. She could see her whole life unfold before her very eyes, a life of unimaginable wealth, happiness and grandeur. *The sound of those distant wedding bells again.* All of a sudden, she wanted to call up Hargreaves and persuade him to tell her everything he knew about his master, the gossip, the family secrets, the insider information. But she quickly shrugged off the idea, debating that she'd only be prying, taking liberties of Luc's generous hospitality. No doubt she would learn all about him soon enough.

Make it work, Maddie, you've got to make it work. You're old enough to know what's right. And you know Luc defines what's right. He's exactly what you've dreamed of all your life. Don't screw this up like you've screwed up all your other relationships.

She sniffed solemnly. *I won't,* she promised herself. *Not this time.*

Not having stopped off at any of the rest rooms along the Innerstate, she helped herself to the en-suite bathroom. As predicted, it was another work of art. Marble bathtub with jacuzzi, marble shower-unit, marble sinks, marble *everything*. She had never felt so regal whilst answering a call of nature.

More impressed than ever, Maddie returned to her room and decided to check out her presents. Tremulously, she tore off the paper that enclosed the smaller of the two boxes . . . to uncover a jewellery box from Tiffany's. *Earrings . . .? An engagement ring . . .?* No, the box was too long and rectangular for that purpose, only slightly larger than a novelty pen-case. She snapped it open. What she thought at first was a bracelet turned out to be something not too dissimilar when she assessed the size and shape of the item.

It was an anklet.

Oh, not just any anklet . . . As the inlay card described, a *twenty-four-carat* anklet, a concept that was virtually unheard-of in all her experience as a salesgirl. *You're playing me, right?* Tougher, thicker, and studded with tiny diamonds along its entire length, it sparkled iridescently in the candlelight. The five-hundred-and-fifty-dollar necklace she wore was a bargain-counter bauble by comparison.

"It's beautiful . . ." she whispered.

She tried it on, leaning over, slipping the chain around the shapely curve of her right ankle and carefully fastening the hooks at the back. When she was done, she could only stare dumbfoundedly at the anklet, waggling her toes inside her high heels to make the diamonds glitter. *Just needs a matching toe-ring,* she thought. Anklets and toe-rings, not only being the rage these days, were the utmost 'sexy cool' of jewellery.

The second, bigger box, next. She undid the ribbon and, removing the wrapping paper with the excitement of a little girl opening her birthday presents, took a wild, random guess. Was there a cake inside? *Come on, surely not. Clothing? Had to be. Lingerie? Lavender lace. Turin taffeta. Pink chiffon. Fuchsine organza. Cyan shantung. A see-through négligée cut from white viole – now that'd be naughty! Girl, behave yourself!* She lifted the lid. Label: Yves Saint Laurent. She was right about the clothing. Except it was far more *beautiful* than she could ever have imagined. A dress, ruby-red in colour, with matching stole and heels. She felt the material. *Peau-de-soie.* Satin-silk. She raised the dress, overwhelmed by emotion. *That's the nicest thing anybody's ever gotten me. And that ain't no lie!* She would *wear* it, she acceded, wear it now for Luc, who had invested in a dress that probably cost more than her annual salary. *In appreciation of his kindness.*

Then she opened the envelope and pulled out the Valentine's card. Again, beautiful. Embossed, embroidered, tricked out in lace. She read the message:

To my dearest MADELAINE,

"She walks in beauty, like the night
Of cloudless climes and starry skies;
And all that's best of dark and bright
Meet in her aspect and her eyes."

Yours Affectionately,
LUC

Maddie looked at it again, closely, curiously, and realized what had struck her as odd. *Oh, my God* . . . The card was dated 1813 (she could just about make out the numerals in the still of the margin) and faded, erased, scratched (onto which Luc had carefully caligraphed his own name) was the identity of the original poet and sender: Lord Byron.

Buying her a Valentine's card that had *actually* once belonged to Lord Byron was, in Maddie's eyes, the ultimate expression of erudition and romantic sentiment she had ever come across, a gesture that captured the moment perfectly, and gave her the resounding proof of how seriously Luc felt about her. She tried to work out the lettering that underlaid her name, couldn't, considered as to where he could have snagged this priceless relic – *an auction?* – and sought to grasp the magnitude of it all. *The perfect card, perfect jewellery and perfect dress upon the perfect bed of the perfect room in the perfect house of the perfect man on the perfect day. Everything was just* perfect . . .

Was she going *crazy?* Or was this the *greatest* day of her life, the *best* Valentine's Day ever? Was she wistfully counting unhatched fledglings or was there *just* the slightest hint of a *proposal* heading her way? Was Luc about to pop the question?

So soon?

And why not? *Isn't Valentine's Day supposed to be a time for romance, a celebration of love? And what better way to declare your affections than by proposing to the one you love?*

But that old, irksome inner skeptic intervened: *The guy's too good for you. What the hell does he see in a hopeless case like you?*

Must you go pooping on my parade? she argued back. *Can't he love me for what I am?*

Oh, pur-leeze*! Girl, you be trippin'!*

Well, wouldn't you be? It's not as far-fetched as you might think. I feel for him. He's lost the love of his life and he's never quite come to terms with it. It's not pity he wants, but someone who can help him make peace with his tragic past. The amount of interest he's shown in me tells me I'm not some good-time girl he's picked up in a bar for a night of fun and games. He's found the cure. I am *the answer to his prayers.* I am *the special someone he has singled out to assist him in his healing. So please don't ever accuse me of being out on the make! My feelings towards Luc hide no deceit.*

Maddie never thought a man of honour, a man of such consistently high standards as Luc would look twice at someone as ordinary as her. Not once in a blue moon. Yet here she was on the cusp of realizing her dreams. She had an opportunity to rectify old wrongs, a chance to silence her whinging parents and the flagrant bigotry of her neighbours alike. How she would love to see the look on their faces when she told them she had stolen the heart of a rich aristocrat.

She relished the prospect of proving her parents wrong and understood now what it must be like to feel delirious with excitement. Her eyes blazed like those of an opium fiend and her head swam in a waking swoon. Somewhere in the clouds she could hear a church organ ringing out the opening bars of the *Wedding March*.

She kicked off her high heels and began to undress, peeling off her garments with the pace of groping lovers in the dark about to forge a night of forbidden passion or, perhaps with a less than preferable analogy, an escort girl consenting to her client's naked summons as he beckons her to his hotel-bed. She wriggled into the new red dress, tested the fit . . . *Beautiful, perfect.* Nonpareil.

Then, glancing around the room for a mirror, she discovered, much to her surprise, there wasn't one. The dressing table was inexplicably missing a mirror. It suddenly occurred to her that she hadn't passed a single mirror on her way up, either. Nor could she remember seeing one in the bathroom. *So what? Perhaps my perfect man is afraid of seven years' bad luck (or does that have something to do with breaking a mirror?) or maybe he is expecting delivery any day soon or . . . WHO GIVES A DAMN? Why am I thinking about such minor, trivial things as mirrors when I ought to be celebrating? I'm in heaven, for chrissakes!*

The shortage of mirrors wasn't a problem; she could improvise. She extracted her compact from her handbag, applied a dab of lipstick, a whiff of Givenchy, then preening herself, appraised the overall outcome.

Time had been kind to her. She'd always been proud of her well-proportioned figure, which in the past had been a delight to so many lovers, and, now, even on the wrong side of thirty, the clinging, low-cut dress did sufficient justice to her slim waistline. The dress was worthy of her admiration, superb, exquisite, and yet at the same time, eye-catching, provocative, risqué. She looked deliciously accessible, felt dirty and decadent, swathed in its silky elegance. And rid of the 'tramp', which was often the concern with her wardrobe of Friday-wear back home.

Despite this romantic foray being only their second date together, the temptation to skip the customary peacock-peahen ritual of human courtship straight to the carnal pleasures of consenting adults came almost spontaneously to her. In fact, the thought had crossed her mind several times over the past week. What purer means could there be of expressing her gratitude than by giving herself freely to him? she now considered. She would repay him unstintingly for the faith he had shown in her and for all those fabulous gifts he had generously imparted. It also gave her the perfect excuse to satisfy a basic need in her, a need that had existed since the first moment she had laid eyes on him. Provided, of course, Luc was as willing as her.

Are you cupid or stupid? He'll never agree—

Why should he refuse? Ever thought that maybe gentlemen do *prefer blondes?* Besides which there was more to Luc than met the eye, perhaps even a touch of the wild stallion kept in check beneath that polished exterior. After all, he had supplied her with such exquisite objects of desire that if he did refuse, it would truly be going against the grain. Luc could *never* refuse – of this she was certain. Luc, who was totally understanding and undemanding and whose unassuming manner could be used to her advantage. She'd oblige him, let him admire, explore her own personal trove of private treasures. Fast-track their relationship together, expedite the physical connection. *Now that wouldn't be ladylike, would it, Miss Juicy Lucy, if you're already thinking about Sexy Time?* she thought wickedly. *Conduct unbefitting a young lady,* as her mother would have called it. *Love, romance, marriage, sex – that's the natural progression of a relationship. Shortcuts are for sinners.*

That's oh, so passé! *You can't expect me not to bend the rules where Luc and I are concerned. A friendship such as ours does not depend on tired conventions. We were supposed to meet. To marry. Make love and have kids. Does it really matter in what order we do things when all we want from life is the same as anybody else? To find* True Love? *To meet that perfect somebody to whom you may bare your soul and entrust your deepest feelings, and they would think nothing less of you? With whom you can share your most intimate dreams, set the bedsheets on fire, with all the passions of the world? I believe I have finally found him. The man I am destined to wed and live out the rest of my days with. Touch wood, we'll still be together when we're old and grey.*

Girl, seeing all that wealth has warped your thinking!

But I swear it hasn't! *It's not as if I'm some kind of low-down, scheming gold-digger. Luc realizes as much. Or else he wouldn't have invited me to his weekend getaway, agreed for us to meet again. For that reason alone – his gift of a second date – I'm going to love him the best I can.*

You don't waste any time, do you?

Abstinence was never my strong suit.

I thought you wanted to turn over a new leaf. Doesn't sound like it though. Who exactly are you aspiring to be? The slutty millionairess or the repentant hooker?

But the overriding desire was too great, just too impossible to ignore. Screw her self-doubt, screw her personal cynic and screw her mother's censorious opinions! This was the only way forward! In the words of one Billie Holiday: *A girl can wait for the right man, but in the meantime that doesn't mean she shouldn't have a wonderful time with the wrong ones. When the right man does come along, she can dazzle him with her body and all the experience she's gained.*

Her mind was set. Today constituted a red-letter day in her diary.

Maddie pushed aside her clothes and lay barefoot on the king-sized bed, propping herself up on an elbow, like a model posing for a blank canvas, her skin the colour of sand, her body bathed in candlelight. Her neck and bare shoulders suffused a soft, radiant glow, her golden fleece of hair flowed gently down her lithe back. Her dress, a frenzy of red, accentuated the rising swell of her round, voluptuous breasts, traced the dipping crescent of her sides before riding, no, *hugging*, her heavenly hips. Below the diminishing hemline, she draped her slender right leg artfully over her left knee, showing off the ample firmness of her smooth, shining flesh and, of course, the anklet.

And she waited . . . Waited . . . Waited . . .

The portrait of a lady obsessed, feminine wiles poised.

Prepared to surrender a piece of her heart, the kind of thing Janis Joplin had once sung about against the spiky strains of a guitar riff.

To seduce her man.

Her perfect, perfect man.

Luc.

II: The Labours of Love

Now there's the look of a man who's hopelessly in love, Monsieur Jouvet the florist declared, looking up from his newspaper towards the tall, stately gentleman who had just entered his store in the fashionable French Quarter of the city.

There was no debating the observation. *No-one just walks into a flower shop on a day like today for any other purpose than to buy their paramour a piece of nature's choicest.* The newcomer's demeanour was another dead giveaway, undeniably that of someone on their way to a date. The newcomer was certainly dressed to impress, immaculate in appearance, clean as the Board of Health and sharper than an ice-pick. He wore a black three-piece ensemble by Valentino Couture over a white, stiff-collared shirt, rounded off by a striking silk-red Hugo Boss tie. Together, he brought with him class, sophistication and an air of romantic intrigue.

He was curiously different from the usual clientele that frequented the FLEUR-DE-LIS. Whereas most customers considered buying flowers a regrettable inconvenience, there was something deep and thoughtful about the manner in which the newcomer was examining, almost analyzing the floral displays as if this were the single-most important decision of his life. He embodied the strong, silent resolve of a man on a mission, who would sail to the ends of the earth to prove himself worthy of his lady's love. Furthermore, whoever the flowers were destined for must be a tremendously lucky woman, Jouvet thought, and exceptional, too, to have won over the affections of such a dashing beau.

His very presence filled Jouvet with a sense of joy and, one must confess, a little envy. It revived memories of his own days of misspent youth. Those days gone by when Nouvelle Vogue was just breaking through and every boy thought Roger Vadim was the coolest guy on earth and all the girls wanted to look like Catherine Deneuve. What Jouvet would give to be in the full flush of youth again, in the blossom of first love. Stealing kisses behind the sofa, making out in the backs of cars, any place he could find where he could be alone with Bettina who had been, in his view, the best-looking bridesmaid at Auntie Amelia's wedding. There, he had asked her if she would be interested in going out with him and, to his delight and astonishment, she accepted. Despite knowing who her father was and what he would say if he found out about their little secret, a young Jouvet couldn't help but wonder how far Bettina was willing to go. The risk, the danger, the excitement. How could he forget that extraordinary incident in the girl's washroom some months later when the Principal stormed in, red with rage, demanding that he stop knocking off his sweet, chaste daughter, who suddenly didn't appear all that sweet and chaste, sitting spread-legged on the sink in a state of partial undress, her skirt eagerly raised, the young Jouvet standing shocked and speechless in front of her, his trousers pulled right down to his ankles? Thoroughly humiliated, the Principal was forced to revise his own high opinion of his daughter's virtuousness, expelling her boyfriend post-haste in a disciplinary act that smacked of desperation and revenge. But it wouldn't stop Jouvet from seeing Bettina again. He just could not keep away . . . . *And so, mes amis, begins the next phase of the love-cycle. You're stepping into new unmarked territory called* True Love. *Its advent signals a change in attitudes, where the affections of the heart become a more mature, profound matter for consideration. No longer is there a need to imitate your peers, act the part of the wild one or impress the girls in the downtown clubs, the reckless hormones of adolescence having run their course. Your sleep is shot, and your appetite's gone to hell. You're hooked; you crave her company when she's not there, as though she were a drug. And there is nothing else on your mind except how much you want to see her and make her happy.* Forever. *The sensation is as clichéd as two pining lovers on a matinée screen sprinting towards one another across a rolling, sun-drenched meadow, their arms outstretched, their faces alight with acute anticipation, their jubilant voices drowned out by the absurd overkill of sentimental music, the sequence itself deliberately slowed down so as to feel languid and dreamlike. Poignant is the moment when they find each other, a relief to the audience, who can identify with the emotional release shared between the embracing couple, a familiarity and an understanding that is almost empathic in nature.* The respected poet and romanticist, Vigny, likened Love to an addiction, Flaubert as a hard-nosed realist called it the 'Great Affliction'. Jouvet could vouch for either definition through personal experience, as well as attest to the universal belief that Love transcends all known boundaries and always brings out the best in everybody. Bettina had, in her own sweet way, certainly lent his life balance and harmony and a wealth of meaning. Yet could he himself honestly say with his hand on his heart that what he ever felt towards her while they were together was the exact same indomitable True Love celebrated by centuries of poets? . . . *Back in the real world, marriage surely follows, that inevitable union between two inseparable people. You wine and dine, dance and romance, and, before you know it, you're planning your future together, saving up for the Big Day, making all the necessary concessions. You marry, you honeymoon, you have a coupla kids . . . then Fate vomits in your general direction and things just don't work out the way they're supposed to.* You're stuck with her! *You're stuck with her for the rest of your goddamned life, Till Death Do Us Part! Like a curse, middle age sets in. Where once she was a pretty young thing, your wife has undergone a gradual transformation into someone with all the seductive charms of a pregnant buffalo. You can't stand the sight of her and you're repulsed by her very touch, sickened by her occasional advances. You even begin to hate sleeping in the same bed as her. A cruel observation, no less, and totally uncalled-for, but at the same time horribly true. You despair, you feel like you're drowning, trapped like a rat in a sinking ship. There seems no easy way out. So you look for love elsewhere: the street corners, your young assistant, your nephew's new girlfriend.* And that's when the shit really hits the fan and you're found out one scandalous afternoon!

The aftermath was a period that only worsened his midlife crisis, a truly sorry state of affairs. The guilt, the shame, the self-condemnation made all the more painful by a messy divorce, outright criticism from his grown-up children, who disowned their father altogether (*Le Grand Bâtard*, their new moniker for him), and of course the real reward for his advancing years: a rapidly receding hairline, an accumulating paunch and a lot of leaky prostate problems. The upshot of Jouvet's infidelities was a social life that had fallen into permanent ruin.

But not all of it.

He still had his business, and not without occasion considered himself an enlightened spirit in the noble art of romance, an expert on *l'affaires d'amour*. The flower shop provided him with that very avenue of expression, a means by which he could educate some of the courting couples on the essentials, advice that was free and readily available and user-friendly. Over the years, it had developed into a labour of love for him. He was proud of his work, proud of the simple fact that many countless young people may have benefited from his know-how and his well-intentioned lessons in love.

Some might have described it as 'romance by proxy', perhaps, but he didn't care.

Business had been good as it always was on St. Valentine's Day, despite the constant dribs and drabs of customers. Not accounting for good taste, mind you, or a sense of adventure, but Jouvet wasn't one to throw a fuss. Presently, though, he forsaw a serious purchase heading his way. Maybe even a rare opportunity to speak with someone who might know more about love and life than even himself. Oblivious to the florist's watchful eye, the stranger continued to pore over the seasonable selection of bouquets. His attention shifted from a basket of pink and white orchids to a bowl of water lilies, an elastic string stretched around the rim, from which dangled a blank, generic tag, ready to be personalized, upgraded into a *billet-doux*.

"Perhaps I can be of assistance?" Jouvet offered politely.

The man glanced up sharply, causing the florist to release an involuntary gasp at that handsome, chiselled face. Not only did the gentleman appear exceedingly well-off, but he was also endowed with the classic looks of a movie star or a tennis pro. His hair was long, black and slicked back. Every inch of his face was flawless, the nose, the cheekbones, the line of the jaw, as though sculpted by aesthetic hands. His eyes were the most striking feature of all, dark and deeply penetrating, as though capable of seeing into your soul, yet somehow far from disconcerting, conveying only an impossible reassuring softness. Then he spoke with a voice that matched his bearing, eminent and refined and as engaging as that of an aristocrat. "Yes, perhaps you can . . ." He strode over to the counter, ducking his head momentarily to avoid a floating cluster of red, helium-filled hearts. "I'm looking for a particular type of flower."

"Well, Monsieur, you are in luck," Jouvet assured, gesturing proudly to his wares. "We have a very good selection. There is something here for everyone and for every occasion. What will it be? Roses, tulips, carnations, chrysanthemums, geraniums, lupins, racemes, narcissists . . .?"

"How about *Amaranthus caudatus*?" interrupted the stranger. His voice was low, measured, as if he were choosing his words carefully. Was there the faintest trace of a foreign accent? Maybe not French or Spanish but definitely European. *Balkan?*

"We have some in stock, Monsieur, though I cannot imagine why you should be interested in such a flower on a day like today," Jouvet replied, mildly puzzled. "Who are they for? A ladyfriend, perhaps?"

The gentleman merely nodded.

"May I be so bold as to suggest a fresh bouquet of roses fringed with a few carnations?"

"I think you misunderstand me. I *do* wish to buy roses, but I had a different arrangement in mind. A dozen red roses, entwined with wisteria, complimented by a slip of *Amaranthus.*"

"Ah, a man who knows what he wants – I like that in a person!" the flower-vendor remarked, positive that it would be a great pleasure serving this new gentleman. His days of buying flowers were long since over, which is why he now catered for the likes of others. "Forgive me for asking, but why this particular arrangement?"

"It is the custom where I come from, a mere contrivance. It is meant to symbolize full and everlasting devotion to the one you love. In my language we call it: *esti iubirea mea veşnică.*"

"A commendable attitude, Monsieur! I'm sure the lady will be delighted. You have much knowledge of flowers?"

"A little on their importance. Say it with flowers and you will never disappoint."

"*Exactement!*" Jouvet said, laughing. "Practical and to the point!"

The gentleman smiled, then elaborated. "There is a definite beauty about fresh flowers, don't you think? The exquisite fragrance, lustre like velvet, the glisten of morning dew, nurtured by sun and soil, petals that blush and bloom like a sweet young girl coming of age, the colourful configurations as if plucked from God's very own garden. It bears no wonder why flowers are the most popular theme with the artist and why they have always been a gratifying sensation with the ladies. As Shelley once reported of the simple flower: *The Arcturi of loveliness that enslave the eye and tug at the heart-strings.*"

Jouvet was deeply impressed, astounded. "Wonderfully-put, Monsieur, music to my ears!" He had never before, in his thirty-four years as a florist, heard such an eloquent, finely-worded defence of a flower's worth and value. At least he knew now that he wasn't in the wrong line of business. These were exactly the kinds of moments that made the whole thing worthwhile, rewarding, kind of special. It was nice to be appreciated. "Claude Jouvet at your service."

"Luc," the gentleman announced, extending a small, courteous bow. "Glad to make your acquaintance."

"*Enchanté*, indeed . . ." Jouvet said with equal *bonhomie*.

"Did you know that Cleopatra once received her beloved Marc Antony in a room knee-deep in rose petals?" Luc continued educating. "Roses have been sacred since Ancient times, representing Aphrodite to the Greeks and Venus to the Romans. It is claimed that a rosebush grew from the pool of blood spilled from Aphrodite's slain lover, Adonis. Similarly, within the Christian faith, a rosebush is said to have sprouted up at the site of Jesus's crucifixion. Thus, together, one can say that the rose symbolizes immortal love and the ultimate sacrifice. But, for me, the most beautiful legend of all has it that originally all roses were white. Then, one night, a nightingale saw a rose and fell deeply in love with it, inspired to sing a song. Overtaken by passion, the nightingale pressed itself against the flower, and when the thorns pierced its heart, the rose was coloured red ever after."

"You are indeed a man of exceptional knowledge . . . I could listen to you all day." Jouvet went on: "I do not seem to recall seeing you around these parts before. Are you just visiting?" Not wishing to sound too presumptuous, he quickly added: "I am told I have a gift for faces."

"The reason you have never seen me before is because I am new here. I only recently relocated from the Old World."

"And your ladyfriend?"

"From Baton Rouge, but dreams of living here in New Orleans. Persuading her to stay should not pose a problem."

"Monsieur has tender feelings for her?" Jouvet asked as though Luc might volunteer a brief résumé of his relationship.

"Indeed. She is a fair damsel, a sad soul to whom life has dealt many blows. She sees me as a saviour, a way out of her troubles, and why shouldn't she? Her earnestness is for honest romance and mutual affection, pure and forthright, and not, as is so common the case these days, for my circumstances. I sense no pretence, no affront in her ambitions, no plan for self-willed manipulation, her mind and motives an open book beckoning to be read. After one respectable encounter, she is smitten with me as I likewise with her. And I shall do all I can to provide for her future happiness. In short, I love her."

"As it should be," Jouvet concurred amicably. "*We think of women at every age: while still children, we fondle with a naïve sensuality the breast of those grown-up girls kissing us and cuddling us in their arms; at the age of ten, we dream of love; at fifteen, love comes along; at sixty, it is still with us, and if dead men in their tombs have any thought in their heads, it is how to make their way underground to the nearby grave, lift the shroud of the dear departed women, and mingle with her in her sleep."*

Luc recognized the author of the quote immediately. "Gustave Flaubert."

Jouvet was, once again, impressed by the man's vast knowledge of romance. *"Vous avez raison!" You are correct.*

"Love is like a rare and precious stone," Luc continued contemplatively. "It must be handled with the utmost care, polished to make it shine like the midnight sun and worn upon your sleeve in full attendance of the Holy Celeste. Love always trusts, protects and perseveres." Luc paused, thoughtful, knowledgeable as ever. "Maybe I should offer her one-hundred-and-eight roses, suggesting she should marry me. Or one hundred exactly, hoping for a happy union between two loving souls till death separates them. Nine-hundred-and-ninety-nine roses, to signify one's love for someone till the end of time. Or one-thousand-and-one roses, consolidating a faithful love that will live on forever – an Infinite Love, surpassing even Death and Time."

Jouvet listened intently, seized by Luc's veneer of sensibility. "Please accept my heartiest congratulations, Monsieur, and pardon me when I say that I hope you and your lady-love will be awakened some day by the patter of *petit* footsteps on the bedroom floor . . ."

"That will come with time," Luc said, amused. "Still, I thank you for your encouragement, my friend. No, today, we will keep it simple. Let us do twelve red roses: *Be Mine, Sweetheart.*"

The florist set to work, brisk and businesslike. "We must not keep Mademoiselle waiting, must we?" He folded the *Times-Picayune* he'd been reading and placed it on the counter.

Luc caught sight of the headline and an expression of vague discomfort crossed his forehead. *TWELFTH GIRL GOES MISSING: New Orleans Police Department Baffled by Spate of Disappearances.* "What is your opinion on such matters?" Luc inquired, referring to the headline, his voice reflecting both curiosity and an uncharacteristic uncertainty.

Jouvet, who had already begun clipping the stems of the roses, glanced at the newspaper absently. "What is there to say?" He appeared unusually cheerful and unperturbed. *"These* modern girls! *Eux, elles sont stupides, non?* They have an argument with their boyfriend over the tiniest little thing and – *poof!* – up and away they go. Their papas are worried sick, and their boyfriends are implicated. What can you do? Happens all the time."

"I hear the authorities have called in the FBI. They suspect foul play. You do not agree?"

Jouvet chuckled, remained dismissive. "*Non*, Monsieur. Mark my words. These girls will probably come back when they realize how foolish they have been for scaring everyone half to death."

"Perhaps you are right. It is still worrying though."

"Why worry? *Zut alors, non, non, non* . . . it will *not* do! If there is one thing that can be said about the way of the world, it is there is no news like bad news. Crime is with us all the time. It is a part of everyday life, but why should it concern us if we stay out of harm's way? Let the troublemakers go to jail, let them pay their dues to society. We are not philistines. We have our own lives to lead and we can lose ourselves in our finer feelings when the ills of the world become too great for us to bear. Take my advice: *entre nous*, do not let the juvenile tantrums of foolish young girls spoil your evening, or even the worst dreaded possibility that they are now the victims of a lunatic. Go to your ladyfriend, go to her with a song in your heart and a soft spring in your step."

Although his comments held a strange kind of satisfaction, Jouvet sounded neither sinister nor insensitive. He was only speaking his mind. One might have even called his words inspiring, *inspiriting*. Luc, nevertheless, seemed to shudder at the thought of the multitude of horrors hot off the printing presses. Still, he knew Jouvet was right, absolutely right. *The less said, the better.* Luc had more immediate matters to contend with, namely Madelaine Henshaw and her aching desire for a sweet, sentimental evening. *What other auspicious dreams has the night in store, I wonder?* he deliberated inwardly. *What prospect of everlasting devotion am I to expect? What fires of passion shall surrender to my touch? What blissful, late-night excesses await me? . . . In short, I love her*, he had said. There *were* no regrets, no reasons to contest otherwise. His capacity to love had been reawakened with a vengeance, that elusive spark of felicity that had lain dead in a desert of broken dreams, a nadir of sad sorrow. Through the depths of his despair, the bitter tears of what felt like countless, untold centuries, and the silent, unspoken insurrection against God's cruel, petulant ways, he had *found* her. The nostrum for his pain. *Madelaine*. And she would be waiting . . . waiting for him in all her angelic glory to revive the love he had lost so long ago.

He watched the florist set the flowers in the specified arrangement, fluff them up to give them body, treat them with a light sprinkling of water before finally wrapping up the Valentine's wreath in a leaf of crisp, latticed cellophane. The style of the bouquet was curiously avant-garde and reminded Jouvet of a floral cake. The small, pale flowers of the wisteria weaving around the hectic profusion of roses represented the icing on the cake, the red pendant-chain of the *Amaranthus* the cherry on top. *Good enough to eat*, Jouvet thought. *I should start using this arrangement more often.*

Luc paid for the two-hundred-dollar sale in cash, personally throwing in a gallant, very generous hundred-dollar tip.

"*Merci beaucoup . . .*" Jouvet gasped, rendered almost speechless. Kindness of this magnitude deserved the utmost gratitude.

"Pleasure doing business with you, my friend," Luc said, turning to go.

"No, the honour was all mine," Jouvet mustered, but Luc was already at the door. "*Au revoir*, Monsieur. Err, drop in any time!"

"You can count on it!" Luc acknowledged as he departed the FLEUR-DE-LIS.

Outside, the night was young, the air cool and bracing, the delicatessens and confectioners, cafés and restaurants embroiled in the early evening preponderance of customers. Luc crossed over to the opposite sidewalk and, carrying the expensive bouquet of flowers, caused quite a stir. People turned their heads as Luc made his presence felt without even trying.

Sat on a park bench, away from the hooting and hollering of little kids, two elderly widows exchanged knowing glances with each other, contemplating secret wanton thoughts they had not harboured since the Second World War. *Takes me right back, Yvette, to those hot, heaving nights with those Canadian Fusiliers at Normandie . . .*

A group of chic-looking teenage girls standing at a nearby bus stop challenged Luc with a loud, hoky wolf-whistle. He tamed them instantly with a wink and a smile, reducing them to a fit of bashful giggles. *Wow, did you see that? He actually winked at us! Friggin' hell, he's made my panties moist!*

Emerging from BARON SAMEDI'S, Mama Bouvier, as she preferred to be addressed, bumped innocuously into Luc who was coming the other way. He apologized immediately, stepped graciously aside for her before heading coolly onwards. She gave a momentary start when she saw his face, apparently struck by its enormous beauty, looks that could have belonged to a god. The larger-than-life Tarot queen mumbled an apology of her own, watching him go. *Mmm . . . mmmh! Guy candy! I sure got to get me some of dat! Yassir, you look so fine, I could cover you in granadilla sauce and gobble you right up!*

A young man walking his Shih Tzu, looked back as Luc passed by, admiring eyes drawn down towards one particular aspect of that fabulous physique. *Great tush! Nice and tight and homey. Firm as a couple of peaches. An ass like that could make a straight man forget himself!*

Another man, older, bespectacled, meek-mannered, returning home from a disastrous day at the office, too paused for a moment, sighed as Luc clambered casually into a flame-red Lamborghini Diablo. *I guess, some guys have all the luck! Me, I just lost my job, I still live with my mother, and my car's about to get a visit from the Repo Man! He's out there exciting the chicks while I'm stuck at home at the mercy of my right hand. I tell you, suicide never looked so good!*

Such was the general impression of the tall, stately gentleman with the flowers. A stranger he might be to some, but it was as if he were known to everyone, he was *that* transparent. He seemed to be surrounded by a mesmerizing aura that defined everything that was right about Valentine's Day. The promise of ripe affection. A propensity for earthly love. The look of someone who lived forever by the story of Aucassin and Nicolette.

From the FLEUR-DE-LIS, Jouvet watched his last customer of the evening drive off down the street and disappear into the gridlock of traffic. The florist was well-pleased. The man who had graced his humble establishment had definitely made his day. Jouvet had met a gentleman whose motives not only matched his own but bettered them by a thousand degrees. *Whoever says that romance and chivalry are dead should be shot dead where they stand!* The gentleman in question had proved himself a deserving champion of the cause, in the process earning Jouvet's absolute respect and highest praise. *Monsieur Luc, ah, how I wish I were like you. To be so handsome and charming and to know all there is to know. A man of class, of fine breeding, a man of the world, and most of all a true ladies' man, fluent in the language of love. I cannot but envy you.* Smiling contentedly, the florist turned the sign in his shop window from OPEN to CLOSED.

III: The Sins of the Flesh

They were truly, madly, hopelessly in love, and there was no denying it. Nobody apart from a pathological liar would make you believe otherwise.

Maddie frolicked about on the bed, rolling this way and that, relishing the luxuriant feel of the silk-spread, the sleepy warmth that slowly snuck over her. She moaned dreamily, a soft, wordless praise to opulence and ennui, her lids heavy, taking little notice of her quarters, including the weird, painted ceiling, which had ceased to fascinate her.

"I bid you welcome."

Maddie jumped.

He stood deep in the shadows of the doorway, watching her.

Terror twisted Maddie's guts and a dreadful, incomprehensible surge of hysteria threatened to engulf her as she tried to make sense of the unrecognizable figure that lurked in the doorway. Light itself seemed to shun him, leaving him shrouded in an almost impenetrable state of darkness, a mute-black silhouette. His utter stillness resembled that of a sepulchral statue, except for his eyes which seemed too alive, too *real*, too bright for comfort, like feral eyes in a dark cave, that were watching her with a sharp, avid intensity.

Her mind dredged up strange stories, stories half-remembered as a child, bedtime stories told to her by her dear, departed grandmother about haunted woods, of treacherous swamps crawling with unspeakable things and of old Injun' curses which had the power to raise ancient spirits, in particular an evil spirit called a 'manitou', capable of taking any shape or form, summoned forth by the shamans to scare away the settlers and strike terror in every young maiden's heart. Could the presence at the door be the same manitou-spirit that frequently visited her grandmother's imagination?

Maddie was convinced it was so. Despite understanding the absurdity of her fears, she knew it had to be the case. Superstition dictated it.

That is until the intruder spoke. "I did not mean to startle you," he said and stepped duly forward. His face became wholly apparent by the flickering glare of the log-fire, conveying only the impossible good looks of the tall, handsome stranger Maddie had fallen in love with and not the fearsome, fairytale monster from her childhood dreams. His eyes were wide and round and irresistible, [*eyes are the windows to the soul*] eyes that you could literally fall into.

Gone from her was that irrational instant of panic, quickly replaced by a healthy force of attraction, as paralyzing as it was pleasurable.

He was the reason she was here. *He* was *why* she had come.

"You didn't startle me," Maddie squeaked, lying, suddenly self-conscious. Her hair was outrageously tangled, and she felt overexposed, flaunting way too much flesh. *Definitely not ladylike!* She tried to cover herself, pulling the bedspread over her legs. "I'm . . . I'm sorry if I don't look decent."

"*Au contraire*, there is no need to apologize," Luc Robideaux replied, gently reassuring her. "It is I who is at fault. I should have knocked before I entered."

"What time is it?"

When Luc told her, Maddie was surprised. "You mean I've been here four hours? I never noticed. I must have been in a trance or something."

It was at that moment he produced the extravagant floral bouquet just purchased from the FLEUR-DE-LIS he had been concealing behind his back. "Here, a peace offering . . ." He advanced towards her and gave her the flowers, then retreated a few steps, allowing her a moment to admire them.

The cellophane crinkled as she touched the half-closed petals of the roses and brushed her fingertips against the entwining wisteria. The decorative sprig of *Amaranthus* was a stroke of genius. "They're beautiful . . . *perfect*."

"As indeed are you." He was watching her again and, this time, Maddie didn't mind one bit. She sat on the edge of the bed, her left leg curled beneath her, only the rounded nub of her knee showing through the ruffled hem of her dress, her right leg drifting lightly, coquettishly downwards, the tips of her toes flirting with the floor. Fire and candlelight reflected from her taut, nubile flesh. Luc could see she was a living jewel, as unique and flawless as the sparkling, diamond-studded trinket that embraced her ankle.

"You decided to wear it," he said in a low, puzzled murmur.

Maddie put down the flowers and ran her hand slowly, smoothly down the polished curve of her leg, reaching down to twirl the anklet between her fingers. "Of course. The dress too," she said, looking up from her hunched, provocative position. Her bosom became firmer, more rounded, deliberately more pronounced, two luscious mounds half-glimpsed above the low neckline. "You're spoiling me." *And, ooh, turning me on-on-on* . . . she thought but refrained from adding this. From the start she'd been certain Luc was giving her the 'come-on', something she desperately desired and the thought of which drove her giddy with excitement. But now, reading his expression, was she wrong in her assumption?

How can I be wrong? she countered. *He bought me all this stuff. He's bound to expect me to wear it.* No, Luc's expression was one of admiration and innocent amusement and hardly one of embarrassment or disgust.

"You deserve to be spoiled," he said, setting her doubts at ease. "*For she was beautiful – her beauty made/ The bright world dim, and everything besides/ Seem like the fleeting image of a shade.*"

Maddie was charmed, remembered the Valentine's card. "Lord Byron?"

"Shelley. But close."

"I bet you say that to all the girls."

"Not if I can help it."

"This is a nice place you got."

"It used to be a nunnery, centuries ago."

"A nunnery? So what happened to all the nuns?"

"Unfortunately, the sisterhood turned wicked and disbanded. Quite a scandal for the Church, as you can imagine. I do not exactly know what became of the Holy Order, but the land was eventually sold off. It has changed hands many times since."

A story, Maddie concluded, as remarkable as the house itself. "I like what you've done with the place. You have this thing for red."

"Red is the colour of life, of love and war, of laval passions stirring the blood and quickening the heart. The sky at dawn, at sunset. Earthshine when the conditions are right. Perhaps, the gaze of Mars on the horizon. I could go on, but I have no wish to bore you. If you look closely, you will notice the colour scheme I have so diligently employed is a precise shade of red called 'vermilion'." He turned from her, took off his jacket and draped it on the chaise-longue. "I have booked us a table at the finest eaterie in town, CHEZ ANTOINE. But first, I think, a drink and some light music . . . to get us in the mood."

"What about your servant, Hargreaves?" Maddie asked. "Will he be joining us?"

"It is his night off. We shall not be disturbed." A smile crossed his lips. "Before I forget, I must thank you for the cufflinks."

"From me to you with oodles of love," she piped, beaming.

"I shall wear them always." And he was, indeed, already wearing them which pleased Maddie no end. He moved to the large drinks' cabinet, peered inside. Next to an antiquated gramophone rested a silver tray laden with empty apothecary bottles and a crystal decanter, which contained a green liquid. "Absinthe," he told her. "It's main ingredient: wormwood. A prelude to the pleasure principle. A philtre, very potent. The green fairy. Much sought after by the traders of the High Seas in the days when it first came on the market. A prohibited drink these days, but I have my sources." He poured some into two tumblers, added a good measure of water, louching the emerald green to a milky shade of green, and offered one to Maddie. "*The aphrodisiac of the soul,* as our mutual interest, Lord Byron, once referred to it."

Aphrodisiac of the soul? regarded Maddie with the mischief of experiment. *Now that sounds like fun! And what was that thing you said about the pleasure principle?* She tried it, let the liquid glide down her throat, warming her insides. The taste was spicy, unfamiliar – *ginseng? agave? aniseed?* – probably because it was not the kind of drink you could normally buy at the local liquor store. "Whoa . . . .! That stuff packs one helluva a punch!" she marvelled out aloud, spluttering. "Oh, I approve!" She downed the remainder of the contents and grinned devilishly at her host.

"More?"

She didn't have to be asked twice and proceeded to sink the following shot of absinthe with even greater gusto, already feeling its mild sedative effect. "You sure know how to entertain a girl! You do this kind of thing often?"

Luc didn't answer, instead placed the gramophone-needle on a black vinyl.

"Bob Dylan! I love Bob Dylan! I absolutely *adore* Bob Dylan!" she squealed, delightedly, as she recognized the classic number, *Lay Lady Lay*, a torridly tender tune from her early teens that ran deep in her family circles and in particular with her Daddy, whose usual routine it was to play it around bedtime in the amorous hope of attracting her mother's attention. The 'wild mercury' sound of a conceptual folkie, Bob Dylan was certainly many things. Accomplished musician, singer-songwriter, brilliant poet and modern-day, travelling troubadour. How did he know? How could Luc possibly know? *You sure know how to entertain a girl, treat her right.* Could he read her mind? Was all this one big, elaborate set-up? Or was he the world's damnedest, smoothest operator? He was only just playing her all-time, favourite track! *I want to have your babies*, she thought, suddenly sure of this one fact pitted against a tidestream of emotion. She had to be slightly drunk for she was unable to make out the direction where the music was coming from. There was no sign of any speakers, yet it seemed to be all around her, as though conjured up by will alone. The sound quality too was surprisingly crisp for a cranky old gramophone, a perfect clarity of sound one would normally expect to hear in a recording studio.

The music subsided a fraction, magically, dial-lessly, apparently of its own accord, enough for Maddie's ears to catch Luc's supreme question. "Do you love me?"

The question came as a shock to her, not because she'd taken their relationship for granted (*Well . . . yes*, she had, *but so what?*), but for the simple reason that it was a question that Maddie thought he would never ask, a question that she longed to answer with every bit of her heart, to tell him how much he meant to her, how much she would sacrifice to stay with him, how much she was willing to die for him (*Well . . . that's stretching the truth a bit, but it sure damn sounds good!*). "I love you like no other," she declared with the honest, submissive voice of worship, like a sultan's young bride on her first night of wedlock.

Her inner skeptic resurfaced. *Girl, who you kidding? How can you possibly love someone when you don't know the first thing about them?*

What's there to know? she argued back. *He's rich, he's handsome, he treats me with respect, more than any other man ever did, and he just asked me if I love him. Maybe I'm jumping the gun, but doesn't his interest in me suggest a two-way thing? Love at first sight, remember? Instinct?*

Of course, she loved him. *She loved him like no other.* She needed him, wanted him and yes, *worshipped* him if it were to seal their destinies together. She would do anything for him. *Anything at all.* Anything to be his only beloved. Theirs was a match made in heaven, had to be.

Luc's unconquerable smile informed her that he appreciated and respected her attitude, that these deep, passionate feelings applied to him also, and that perhaps now *was* the time for him to set the wheels in motion, to consummate their relationship, a time for love and commitment, for release from her many disappointments of the past, for that special moment she'd been waiting for all her life with the man of her dreams, for–

"What say you to spending the night here?"

"Don't I get a Valentine's kiss first?" Under ordinary circumstances, Maddie wouldn't have been so bold, but something in her the drink had accentuated. The absinthe had certainly got to her and she felt relaxed and strangely disinhibited, something wild and free. Moreover, she was concerned about giving her host a simple demonstration of her feelings, hasten him to stop stalling and make good on his promise, act upon that very suggestion of naked unity. She yearned his contact. *And then comes the morning, the sunlight streaming into your bedroom . . . Waking up by your lover's side, a brand new life ahead of you . . . The beginning of a love odyssey . . .*

Luc smiled again, Jean Anouilh flashing to mind. "I see you practise the philosophy that love is the gift of oneself."

"Why not?" Maddie pouted in feign innocence. "Did I do wrong?"

"Not at all. You wear the face of an angel but inside hides the designs of a naughty little devil." Luc, who had until now kept a reasonable distance between them, moved equanimously towards Maddie. "How could I refuse such an invitation from one so fair? You are indeed the Belle of the Ball. If a kiss is what you desire, then a kiss is what you shall get . . ."

He knew she was entitled to it. Barefoot as a courtesan, adorned in silk-satin as vivid-red as a pot of purest passion, she could not have made her motives any clearer, safe from misinterpretation. Although physically she was endowed with the firm, fruity form of maturity, her cascade of blond hair and the look of sweet longing in her big, blue eyes gave her a luminescent, almost virginal purity. She looked incredible, divine yet ravishing, her beautiful body begging to be explored with complete thoroughness and conviction. Maddie might have been a sorority girl after a homecoming dance, eager to learn, to lose her flower, to discover the joys of sex, at last giving her boyfriend her wholehearted consent to take her by the hand and lead her lovingly to her parents' bedroom . . .

Luc undid his shirt-collar, loosened his tie and honoured her request: he leaned down to meet her lips with his own. Yielding to temptation, Maddie settled back and slipped her long, tanned legs around his waist. He mounted the bed, mounted Maddie, pushing himself more firmly against her parted hips, both hands sliding simultaneously upwards beneath the silk hemline to thrill, tease, titillate her inner thighs, fondle and feel the full roundness of her hips. Their kiss was the height of sensuality, as profound as the erotic practices of the East, their tongues glorying in the delicious juices of the other's mouth, and as he withdrew, Maddie was still submerged in its stirring intimacy. So lost was she in the Moment that she felt as if Luc had swallowed her up whole, that he had kissed, tasted every inch of her salted body with that one, single kiss, setting off a chain reaction inside her. All her nerves tingled like a mass of live wires, awaiting the next surge of sexual current. A sensation born of sweet shock, it left her breathless. Luc's lips caressed her left cheek, his nose brushing lightly against her ear. Maddie moaned, enraptured, loving every minute of it. He coursed his way down her neck in a series of delicate kisses, halting halfway momentarily as if to admire its lissom form or perhaps merely tormenting her before delivering the next tender touch. He shifted to her heaving bosom, which was rising and falling with renewed expectation, her round, voluptuous breasts pressed together, the dipping valley between enticingly exposed above the thin fabric of the dress. Luc cradled her right breast and smothered its unseen tip with his mouth, causing Maddie to shudder, arch her back, to stifle an excited, exclamatory cry. Oh, she was in Seventh Heaven! *No, make that* Eighth *Heaven!*

[*love is not the same as sex*]

If ecstasy were a concrete thing, she would be made of the stuff. Her right leg rode his shoulder and Luc stroked the gleaming flesh, the glittering anklet, in one slow, sleek gesture, drawing his mouth down her comely foot. He stopped to felate her succulent toes, continuing to pleasure her. Maddie gasped, utterly overwhelmed, her passions on fire. As Luc retraced her leg, this time with his tongue as though licking off rainwater, she grabbed his back, pulled him onto her selfishly. And felt his *manhood* . . . crushing herself against it, opposing it with equal force, encouraging it. She was wantonly aware of the huge, gorging hardness rubbed up against her growing impatient, insistent, demanding entry, a way in, passage to her already slavering pink precipice of pleasure. Undergarments notwithstanding, now only the damp, creased resistance of his trousers and the lower portion of her dress and her underwear separated flesh from flesh. She was prepared for there to be nothing in the way, prepared to receive him, taking the experience beyond frottage. She wanted him,

[*her perfect, perfect man*]

wanted him more than ever,

[*he turns me on-on-on*]

wanted him inside her,

[*on this very special St. Valentine's Day*]

right here, right now.

[*it's never been like this before*]

A crescendo of crazy, uncontrollable desire crying out for instant fulfilment,

[*Give it to me, you beast, give it to me harder!*]

that mindless, chasteless release.

[*Fuck me! FUCK ME GOOD!*]

Luc lifted her head, sought a soft spot on her neck, then sank his long, pearl-white fangs into her pulsing veins.

Here's a Valentine's kiss to remember me by . . .

Maddie squirmed in his arms, struggled to break free, to scream, confused, powerless, his hold on her viselike, his mouth clenched firmly on her throat, glutting on the copious, scarlet warmth that gushed effortlessly out of her. From somewhere, faraway, in a remote corner of her mind, echoed her mother's unforgiving voice: *Once a tramp, always a tramp!*

Luc drank her as though drinking from a running faucet. Flavoured with her carnal sins, her blood was like red ambrosia.

"Sleep, child, sleep . . ." he whispered, his voice as dark and ageless as the shores of the Black Sea. Maddie stopped struggling. His hand glanced gently down her face, and her lids fluttered, closed.

Reality came crashing down like the walls of Jericho as she succumbed to the terrible knowledge of what her dream-lover really was, a creature that had maligned her trust and lured her to her final reckoning – the bitterness underlying the sweet. And for all the revulsion of the experience, she felt a wonderful languorous intoxication, coddling her mind and closing off her thoughts. Unbreakable, the sweet torpor carried her down a river of ethereal endarkenment. She did not care, did not want him to stop, wanted him only to kiss her, to love her forever.

The fire in the hearth exploded into a roaring funnel of flames. And in that single, short-lived illumination, Luc Robideaux saw the mural on the ceiling writhe with Dantean life as the enslaved, screaming masses, abandoning all hope, entered the scorching pit, where the grotesqueries of the damned feasted upon their burning souls. He did not turn away from this Grand Guignol of Pain, for it did not repulse him.

It was a way of life for him.

In fact, the beseeching shrieks of the burning masses overhead, horribly punished by the hungry hordes of Hell, aroused him. A gathering euphoria rushed through him like a mad drug as the doomed roll call of sinners howled his name over and over, pleading with him to release them from their misery, their suffering, their infinite torments. The flames rose higher, a furnace on full, the chamber ablaze. Luc withstood the heat, did not even flinch. The yellow, fiery tentacles reached out for him, licked his skin. He felt close to orgasm as he drank deep from God's blood.

Did the earth move? Did the angels weep? Did God have wet dreams?

The sweet unconsciousness soon became a creeping coldness that benumbed every bone, muscle, nerve, blood vessel in Maddie's body. As her natural processes shut down, her senses sank deeper into the black river of nowhere. She was fading fast, nearly everything already lost, part-forgotten: desire, meaning, thought, being,

[*romance is dead*]

the memory of existence. Then she was no more. Her body gave one last agonizing gasp. Her muscles convulsed, then jerked slowly loose. She slid onto the coverlet of the big, brass bed, limp, unresponsive, a study in emptiness.

Consigned to the sleep of the dead.

The flowers tumbled to the floor, spilling open. The roses, wisteria, the *Amaranthus*, or to call it by its more common name: *Love-lies-bleeding*.

Except Maddie wasn't bleeding. Luc had drunk her dry. All five litres . . . *literally*. Blood dribbled down his chin and he wiped it off with his sleeve, refreshed, replenished, his bloodlust fully sated.

He looked down at the pale, peaceful form of Madelaine Henshaw, at the two frayed puncture-marks on her neck, and felt a moment's stab of pity, of remorse. He had read her thoughts, tasted her sins, reinforced her sequacity. She had been beautiful – and intelligent in her own right – and all she had ever wanted from him was the promise of future happiness. But was it really his duty to provide it for her when in fact she made a much more satisfying kill? *I should have brought fifteen roses: I'm truly sorry, please forgive me.* Of course, he had been tempted to Turn her, let her drink of his blood, but after some deliberating had elected not to. Only a select few he would grant vampire status, not her. When he had bitten her, he had been oddly regretful of her babes-in-the-woods innocence to the presence of Evil, her unshakable faith in a world where the living lived and the dead remained dead, her incomprehension and disbelief to who he was, *what* he was.

A dead thing that walked and talked. A creature that endured endless nights, perpetual darkness. Scourge of humanity, author of countless plague-stricken towns and uncovered cemeteries. Vampire flesh that breathed preternatural life with an unquenchable hunger for living blood – the food of the gods. An immortal whose very existence bespoke a cosmic war that had been contested since the Dawn of Man and would rage on till the End of Time, the eternal conflict between Heaven and Hell, the Hierachies of Light pitched against the Armies of Darkness, Ultimate Good confronting Absolute Evil.

He was the Duc de Devereaux, nearly two thousand years old, the oldest and greatest 'living' vampire in known history, with a myriad of names, a variety of guises. 'Luc' served as an alias yet was not so far from the truth, whereas 'Duc' was his official, aristocratic title.

Duc was the son of Mary Magdalene. Lethseme, her first-born.

It was no secret Mary Magdalene had been a woman of many lovers. Her religious conversion could not have come at a better time. Languishing on an ensemened bed, she was heading towards the irredeemable when a wandering prophet showed her a light seldom glimpsed and she solemnly repented all her sins. She had never told Lethseme who his real father was, but he had always suspected it was the man who had once cured her of 'seven demons'. He was still unborn, floating in her womb, when the Romans led his father up the hill, crowned his head with thorns and nailed him to the cross, to the cheers of the masses. They say Jesus died for the Sins of Man, but Lethseme knew better. God had been angry at Christ's mortal indiscretion, that one, well-intentioned illegitimate union with Mary Magdalene, and, making an example of him, had punished him. For Christ would suffer The Passion, for Lethseme it would mean Eternal Damnation, the truth kept carefully concealed from the world. Afraid of the scandal, Mary had given Lethseme up for adoption. A Roman family took him in, a couple desperate for a child. They called him Lucius and raised him as a Roman. Except, even at an early age, Lucius knew whose blood flowed through his veins. Something inside him told him he was different, cursed, destined for terrible things. And, as a direct descendant of Christ, he would be empowered with a lifespan of many lifetimes, worshipped like a god, his unspeakable secret, protected throughout the centuries under sentence of death by the Desposyni. Lucius rose to the challenge, renounced his human origins the day he murdered his adopted parents and drank their blood. Thereafter, he would sail through the annals of time as a silent witness to history at the forefront of both progress and decay.

The saga of Valentinus would follow, during the third century, at a time when Christianity was still establishing itself as a religion. Claudius II – Claudius Gothicus – was the Emperor of the Roman world, Valentinus the Bishop of Interamna. Claudius believed that married men made poor soldiers, because they were loath to leave their families or fiancées for battle. The Roman Empire needed unattached young men of soldiering age to maintain its military might, so Claudius, never one to fear public outrage, abolished marriage. Valentinus saw great injustice in this decree, so invited young couples to come to him in secret, where he joined them in the sacrament of matrimony. The news, however, could not be kept from the Prefect of Rome who, on hearing of this blatant transgression of the law, had Valentinus arrested and condemned to death. When brought before Claudius, Valentinus tried to convert him to Christianity. Claudius would have nothing to do with it and Valentinus was sentenced to death, condemned to be clubbed, stoned and finally beheaded. His execution was held on the Fourteen of February. Whilst in prison, waiting for the sentence to be carried out, Valentinus befriended the jailer's blind daughter, Cessira. Valentinus cured her blindness, converted her to Christianity, and on the day of his execution, left her a note signed: *From Your Valentine*. The responsibility of carrying out this sentence fell on Lucius, who was then passing himself off as a little-known centurion. The fact that Valentinus had defied an edict issued by the Emperor cancelling all marriage by wilfully conducting clandestine wedding ceremonies was not the reason Lucius volunteered. No, he had a different motive. Valentinus, while locked in the dungeons, had managed to seduce Cessira, Lucius's only love, by claiming to have restored her sight. Consumed by jealousy, Lucius gladly volunteered to torture and execute the man. Learning of her lover's execution, Cessira poisoned herself shortly afterwards. *It was the last time Duc shed a tear.*

Valentinus would gain martyrdom for his Christian teachings and alleged miracles with a special day reserved in the year dedicated to his saintliness, replacing the feast of Juno and festival of Lupercalia, whereas Lucius would lose his only chance at True Love with the one person who could have saved his soul from damnation. Instead, she too would be damned. Eternity beckoned, where new gods would be born and worshipped, without his future bride by his side.

Cessira . . .

His vengeance was great, a seething, bubbling maturation of evil, a cornucopia of crimes bred from his insufferable grief for the woman he loved and lost all those centuries ago.

Terrorizing Eastern Europe as ruler of the Huns. Count Estruch. Torturing and impaling tens of thousands of Turkish invaders. Corrupting the integrity of Jeanne d'Arc while riding alongside, plunging her into insanity, leading to her arrest for heresy. Introducing the bubonic plague to London that would soon be consumed by the Great Fire. The popularization of vampire lore. Lord Ruthven. Being regularly invited to the nightly orgies of Shelley at his estate in Geneva. Giving Bram Stoker a hand in his composition. Surviving with his business intact during the Opium Wars. Seducing the Tsarina, using his blood to 'heal' her son. Feeding off the Bowery's starving desolates at the time of the Great Depression. Witnessing two World Wars, the rising popularity of the internal combustion engine, the Cold War, the Space Race, and, in this new age of technology, he was embarking on a business venture that would take vampirism into the twenty-first century, with BATHORY INDUSTRIES, to be the leading transporter of blood and blood products for medical and pharmaceutical purposes. Could youthful blood stop, or even *reverse*, the aging process? Forget about blood-borne diseases; ever heard of the vampire in your drip?

Perhaps his secret admirer, who brought Lestat into being, would care for one last, definitive goodnight kiss.

Duc de Devereaux. The Giaour. The Devil's prince. The Blood God. The Master of Vampires. One of the Undead, their highest-ranking Dignitary of the Damned, cursed to walk the night in shapes and forms unimaginable, compelled to drink society to the very last drop.

But not *without the capacity to love.*

Duc's capacity to love was as powerful as his impulse to kill. But it was reserved for one woman, and one woman alone. The reincarnation of his beloved princess, Cessira. His One, True Love. Even as a vampire, Duc had not Turned her into his own kind because she had loved him regardless of his monstrous birth. She had not deserved his corruption; her faith in his love had been pure. Until the day she was stolen from his arms by a defiant, soon-to-be-martyred fool.

He would find her. There was no doubting it. Century upon century Duc had spent in search of her and now he was certain his search was nearing its end. She was here. In New Orleans. For the first time in aeons, he could hear her waking thoughts whilst he slept in his coffin during the daylight hours. She'd know him from the first moment on and they would be together for the rest of their lives, *die* together as mortals. Salvation would be his, an escape from his vile, lonely existence, the Hell's clarion of heartache. How much the undefeated Master of Vampires would give to be human again, only if his Beloved were to come back?

As they say, *Love is eternal.*

Despite the centuries of blushing maidens he had converted into very able demonesses or, in more recent times, the Avon Ladies and Jehovah's Witnesses he had willed into drinking your blood on the doorstep, he had somehow failed to find her on the last few consecutive nights, since his grand arrival in New Orleans. But he knew she was here, knew he would find her soon. How he had been convinced Madelaine was *her* – he had been *so* sure. Imagine his disappointment...

He opened the coat-closet and three stiff, bloodless corpses toppled forward like bowling pins. They thudded to the floor, one after the other. Duc surveyed them, with an air of cool detachment. From their slight builds and the neglected but expensive, identical red dress each wore, there could be no mistaking they had once been women. Now, though, they were dried-out husks, their identities impossible to determine at first glance. Their skin was flaking and wrinkled, shrivelled like flowers without water, and riddled all over with tiny teeth-marks, as though their meagre, desiccated flesh had been gnawed on by hungry rats.

[*In short, I love her.*]

He would store Madelaine with her sisters overnight and command his ghoul to dispose of their bodies in the morning. They would have to be taken elsewhere since Lake Pontchartrain was getting a little too crowded. Duc was not too keen to leave it too long, particularly with what the police might find if they were ever to dredge the lake. Maybe feed the exanguinated bodies to the alligators in the swamps.

Ah, ma chérie, it was not to be . . .

Duc patted his stomach. He had dined well, supped long and deep from the fountain of eternal youth. That last girl had been particularly satisfying.

His face suddenly grew stern, soulless.

He picked up the newspaper, flicked through the pages to the Lonely Hearts' Column (or 'The Bleeding Hearts' Club' as he cruelly referred to it, a hopeless band of women crippled by constant insecurities and hang-ups and destined to be romantic failures). The list was steadily shortening, only a handful left to meet. He perused through the column before selecting an ad, one not scrubbed out from a previous encounter.

What if it wasn't his reincarnated love, Cessira?

Then another girl, another soul, another dumb romantic. Looking for love. To be serenaded under the moonlight. Unaware that here was a man who preferred *Nosferatu* to Rudolph Valentino, *A Kiss Before Dying* to *Love Story*, a suitable victim to a suitable match. A girl to sustain his need for living blood and whom he also hoped would be enough of an incurable romantic to stroke his prodigious ego.

Love-lies-bleeding.

The bitterness underlying the sweet.

For promises are like hearts, *meant* to be broken.

November 1997-February 1998

Impawsible:
A Cat's Tale

"Cats are a mysterious kind of folk — there is more passing in their minds than we are aware of."

Sir Walter Scott (1771-1832)

Two Roses: Such is our deepest, mutual love and affection...

Prologue

Please define your general opinion on cats. Do you appreciate *Felix catus* . . . or is it a serious case of dislike?

Whether you love them obsessively or hate them with a passion, you cannot deny cats make a fascinating species for study as well as currently being the most popular household pet in the world.

You see, I know a little something about cats. Although I never actually owned a pet of my own whilst growing up in the Yorkshire Dales, our neighbour at the time, Walter Ames, a self-confessed ladies' man in his younger days — but never actually officially marrying — deliberately chose female cats to keep him company shortly after retiring from the Merchant Navy, perhaps because they made a suitable replacement for his lifetime of women. I'd known his three cats since they were six-week-old kittens, curious, playful and rather naughty: Cleopatra the gorgeous, white, long-haired Persian, Boadicea the stippled, fiercely-ginger tabby with a fiery temperament to match, and his mysterious, satiny-black British Bombay cat named after the Haitian goddess of love, Erzulie. I played with them, watched them mature under Walter's close fatherly gaze into intelligent, adorable things, fully domesticated, lounging leisurely around the house as though they inhabited Kubla Khan's Pleasure Dome. Walter treated his beloved kitties like little princesses, was deeply protective of them, safeguarding them against any randy neighbourhood toms and the risk of breeding. It didn't entirely end well for his cats, though, as his darkest fears were eventually realized. One moment's complacency, leaving the kitchen window open one hot summer's day while out shopping, allowed admittance to a crafty stray tom, whom Walter arrived home to find, to his utmost horror, mounting his beloved Cleopatra, her climactic yowling torturing his ears as her mate withdrew from her, Walter's other cats, Boadicea and Erzulie, washing their paws contentedly and wearing the self-satisfied expressions of pussycats – no different from the scores of women Walter had gone through in his lifetime – who have already been serviced. My family left Yorkshire for the sunnier climes of Cornwall, relocating at the request of my father's expanding law firm, myself aged eleven at that time, and I never saw Walter or his beloved cats again, who by now were heavily pregnant. Or perhaps it didn't end too badly for them after all, depending on *their* point of view. All animals have an innate desire to procreate, more so the female of the species, to bring the wheel of life full circle, and Walter's cats had certainly acknowledged their biological clocks.

Neither was Anthea Pettifer, my better half for eight years, a stranger to cats. On her sixth Birthday, her parents had taken her to the Battersea Cats' Home, where she instantly fell in love with a handsome, one blue- and one green-eyed, pure-white Siberian named Balthazar. Her parents' primary quibble was that he possessed only three legs, the other leg apparently lost during a lawn-mowing accident, the result of a kitten's natural inquisitiveness as well as carelessness on the part of his previous owners, who had summarily abandoned the poor thing at the animal shelter either out of disgust or to keep up their upper middle-class appearances. It soon became apparent that Balthazar was also deaf, since genetically there is a strong association between white fur, blue/green eyes and deafness. Anthea's heart was set on the deaf, odd-eyed, three-legged cat, and her parents, despite their understandable concerns, were forced to buy him as a Birthday present for her. After all, according to the wisdom of Charles Dickens: *What greater gift is there than the love of a cat?* Anthea loved her little Balthazar, all the more *because* he was special, and maybe partly out of pity, and he certainly did not disappoint. He was a gentle, sociable creature, who followed Anthea around wherever she went almost with a child's fear of abandonment. He wasn't as disabled as he looked, could do all kinds of physical activities despite his obvious adversity. Her parents' original concerns, however, had been well-founded. Balthazar didn't make it past his third year. One day he went out in the dark and never came back. A middle-aged woman came a-knocking on the door of the Pettifer residence at midnight, distraught and fearful, carrying a cardboard box. She was very sorry to inform Anthea's company-director father that she had accidentally run over their cat – he had zipped out into the road without warning, and she hadn't been able to hit the brakes in time. Answering to her conscience since she was an animal-lover herself, she had taken the poor dead thing to the local emergency vet, and the cat's collar identified him as belonging to this address. Indeed, in the box rested the abject carcass of Anthea's dear cat, his abdomen unspeakably crushed and flattened. He did not suffer, according to the woman; death had been instantaneous. Humbled beyond compare, wracked by the worst guilt possible, she offered the family her sincerest condolences and took her leave. When Mr. Pettifer broke the terrible news to his daughter in the morning, she was inconsolable. It took her several weeks to deal with her grief and return to school. In fact, Anthea later told me that she never completely recovered from her loss. Let it be a lesson to all cat-lovers. Balthazar's lack of hearing had meant he could not entirely assess and negotiate the dangers of the outside world, including traffic. The road outside the long Pettifer driveway was an extremely busy one and, having claimed the lives of countless crazy foxes over the years, had now added Anthea's cat to its tally of roadkill. Balthazar was buried in a plot at the bottom of the family garden, where his consecrated remains lie even to this day.

Having lived together now for five years, Anthea and I decided to get a cat of our own, which we agreed would be a suitable stepping-stone to an actual baby. That was how Presto came into our life.

1

Both Anthea and I were singletons. As only childs to our respective parents, we often tried to seek out other people's company, since our career-driven parents did not always have time for us, nor were our friends always available. We had therefore developed independence from an early age, devising new ways of occupying our time, to avoid lapsing into boredom. I met Anthea at Chertsford University, where she had been studying Fine Art. She progressed to a successful art dealer; I remained at this prestigious seat of learning to become a University Lecturer in Medieval History, eventually gaining Tenureship. My name is Professor Simon Higginbottom, the dreaded scourge of the lazy, underachieving student. Now Anthea and I had each other, self-sufficient individuals though we were. We moved into a nice Georgian townhouse in Upper Nasebury, with its three floors and three bedrooms, and planned for the future. Marriage was a formality rather than a necessity due to the pressure our respective parents put on us to legitimize our relationship and pave the way for grandchildren. I proposed and Anthea accepted without hesitation, even though she didn't mind if we never wed, and we got married in the local parish church with a good contingent of family turning out for the Reception.

It was Anthea's idea to get a pet not only for company but also as a trial run to raising a family. A case of testing the water, seeing what it's like to have a baby. I suppose the original suggestion also arose from her natural maternal instinct. *Yes, let's get a baby cat*, I concurred. *Why not?* The old pontiff may have advised the world to focus on having children, warning us not to waste our energy and love by transferring our affections on to any pets, but I didn't much care for his advice. Neither did I accept that crap about when an animal passed away, it went to Limbo, not Heaven, because it lacked the cognitive ability to worship God. However, we weren't particularly keen on a mangy, flea-bitten dog fouling the neighbour's flowerbeds, since we considered ourselves 'cat people'. *Cats* happened to be our favourite trip to the theatre; together, we'd seen the Andrew Lloyd Webber musical three times at the London West End. Anthea explored the foremost, up-to-date pet website, Preloved.co.uk., and fell in love with the photo of a white, eight-week-old kitten, just as she had done with Balthazar decades ago.

At the tail end of the winter snows, Anthea drove hurriedly to Netherton, and bought the kitten, a Turkish Angora, who would become our 'baby round man' for the moment. I clearly remember idling away my time, listening to *Lotus* by REM on my headphones, preparing to welcome the new arrival to the family, when Anthea stepped into the house, a white furry, purry thing moving within the shadows of the cat carrier she brought in with her. She opened the cat carrier and laid the kitten on my chest. At that time, he looked like the loveliest thing in the world, so small and sweet and vulnerable. Anthea described what amounted to a horror story from where she had procured the cat. Both owners smoked heavily, suffered from chronic bronchitis, and the entire council flat reeked of tobacco smoke and cat pee. The mother cat, only two years old herself, had looked haggard and exhausted, her litter of two remaining kittens suckling on her teat.

The other half-a-dozen kittens had apparently already been sold. Anthea selected her kitten and left. Once again, pity must have played an important part looking into the sad, waif-like eyes on his plaintive face and a burning need for redemption, a second chance to rectify the fate that had befallen her childhood feline friend as well as save this particular kitten from his current appalling living conditions. But, most of all, it had been love at first sight. I am not a sentimental person, but Anthea had a tender, passionate aspect to her personality, in keeping with the soul of an artist.

When Anthea brought the kitten home, I knew he was unwell. *Very unwell.* He appeared lethargic, his fur was badly matted and stank of tobacco, his eyes were swollen, one weeping, the other encrusted over and closed shut, and his nose was severely congested and snotty, resulting in frequent sneezing fits. Afraid for his well-being, we welcomed him to his new home and let him sleep in our bed that night. He slept soundly all night, with Anthea periodically checking on him to make sure he was still breathing. The following morning, we had no choice but to take him to the vet's, transporting him in the cat carrier. The vet at PALAISOFPAWS admitted he'd not seen a white cat in a long while but was amazed we had bought him in this sickly condition and advised we take him back and demand our money back or exchange him for his healthy sibling. Anthea, however, refused to part with our Very Important Pet. Accepting her absolute, slightly irrational decision, the vet proceeded to diagnose our new kitten with cat 'flu – a chlamydial infection in this case – and prescribed eye ointment and a short course of oral non-steroidals and antibiotics. We followed the medication regime to the letter, administering the eye ointment without receiving any resistance, and crushing and mixing the tablet medication into his food without raising his suspicions.

There was a noticeable improvement within seventy-two hours, and Presto made a miraculous recovery within the week. His appetite picked up, his energy levels increased until he was now running around the apartment, and his symptoms of cat 'flu resolved: the periorbital swelling subsided and his nasal congestion, with its worrying sneezing attacks, cleared up.

We were able to see our new kitten, now restored to full health, for what he was. People often describe female cats as 'beautiful' and all male cats as 'handsome'. They also say that male cats are friendlier than female cats. And our new white kitten was certainly a friendly, handsome little man, with all the classic hallmarks of a Turkish Angora. Presto was limber-bodied, fine-boned and perfectly-groomed, sporting a glossy coat with a soft, silken sheen and a foxbrushlike tail. He possessed expressive amber-green, almond-shaped eyes and pink, oversized ears on his wedge-shaped head, with its medium-sized muzzle, moist pink nose and long whiskers, as sharp as bristles and as wide as his body to help him negotiate tight spaces. He exhibited high intelligence, a refined, natural grace and a lovely, sociable, easy-to-manage temperament. Only two months old, he had already been weaned, grazing on the wet, taurine-supplemented kitten food without complaint as well as lapping up all his taurine-rich milk. He ate with neat, little jerks of his head. Having fed, he would lick his coat and paws with his hairbrush of a tongue, instinctively washing himself all over to supposedly eliminate any food scents that might linger and attract imaginary predators.

I had initially been worried he might spray everywhere or leave poo prints on the parquet floor, kitchen counter or draining board, but cats are legendarily clean. Even at his young age, he was fully litter-trained. We showed him his litter tray with its layer of highly-absorbent Catsan crystals, and he did his business consummately, sometimes trying to fastidiously bury it – no mess, no accidents. As hygienic people, we wiped his bum once he was done and we removed his firm, healthy spoor from the litter tray, an easy task since it was a simple case of just picking up the clumped stones on which he'd deposited his excreta. Evidence of our kitten's cleanliness came from the lack of any wayward trace of yellow/greenish stains of cat pee, which normally fluoresces under UV light.

We learned early on he was deaf – those pesky genes again! We knew he was deaf from the simple fact that when you creep up on a sleeping cat and clap loudly, it should jump through the roof, startled; our cat didn't even stir. We knew within the hour we received him. Anthea told me she would not make the same mistake again by letting him out of the house; he would become a housecat. He was Anthea's cat in many respects, and I thought of getting a black female kitten – black, since I had a predilection for black fashionwear, come snow, rain or shine – to provide companionship when we weren't around. A black cat, perhaps, going by the name of Tituba after the black servant girl implicated in the witch trials of colonial Massachusetts. But, ultimately, we dismissed the idea. Because our cat was deaf, the other kitten would probably wonder as to his oddly quiet nature and why he was ignoring her whenever she tried to communicate with him verbally. Besides, it would be unfair on her if we restricted her solely to the house, too.

His name became a matter of debate. We consulted Anthea's paternal grandmother, who had been a stage actress in her heyday before training as an English teacher when she bore children. She could boast that Laurence Olivier had once been in the audience, watching her perform. She loved animals, particularly cats, and had gone through a number of cats over the decades, having given each a powerful Shakespearean name: Hamlet, Romeo, Brutus (who was incredibly well-behaved,) and Julius Caesar (who surprisingly turned out to be an absolute devil, anything but noble). Now retired to Gibraltar, she possessed an eleven-year-old mackerel-brown tabby called Shylock.

I don't know where 'Presto' came from, who first suggested the name; I suspect it might have been Anthea's grandmother. Nothing absurdly exotic, but there was a strange, magical ring to it, befitting magicians and wizards and sorcerers, and we felt it defined our lovely man perfectly. Not that he would be able to respond to his name due to his congenital deafness. Still, it consolidated his place in our lives.

I did not realize the singular appropriateness of his name until much, much later.

2

A part of our family now – our little 'baby-man' – we gave Presto the full run of the house. He initially sniffed his way through every nook and cranny with the typical curiosity of a cat, trusting nothing, as the French philosopher, Jean-Jacques Rousseau, once commented, until he had fully examined and made his acquaintance with everything in the room. Once sufficiently acclimatized to his surroundings and feeling relatively safe in the hands of his new parents, satisfaction brought him back, and he was soon racing around house with a grace and agility that had to be impossible for something so young, poetry in motion, careening off the walls, his legs carrying him faster and faster, able to scamper up each set of stairs in a couple of bounds. Kittens can clock an astounding thirty miles an hour, leaping three times their body length and seven times their height. In the early days, he would claw at the carpets, curtains and cushions until we provided him with a scratching post. Scratch-damage to furnishings is a cause of frustration for owners and a consideration for de-clawing their cat, but we never once contemplated de-clawing our little friend, since this radical and rightly-outlawed surgical procedure, essentially a form of amputation, can often result in chronic pain and disability. Instead, we gave his nails a careful trim every fortnight.

Browsing a few manuals on cat care, including a terrific read of anthropologist and acclaimed author, Desmond Morris, called *Catwatching*, I learned, in keeping with my general observations, that cats are naturally crepuscular creatures, coming alive at dusk and dawn as well as generally being nocturnal animals, with Presto roaming around our townhouse at the darkest hours of night. Kittens are born deaf and blind. But within weeks they develop an incredibly acute sense of night-vision, capable of detecting the faintest rays of light, better than one-sixth of the light-level that human sight requires, the dilated pupils giving the impression of eyes shining in the dark. It is reported that a cat's eyes enlarge on the waxing of the moon and contract when the moon wanes, and I can vouch for this well-documented phenomenon from studying Presto. Cats can see pretty much perfectly in pitch-blackness.

Presto walked in that precise, surefooted manner common to all cats, apparently the only known species to hold its tail vertical whilst walking, like a tightrope walker uses a pole as a counterweight for balance – hence the origin of the phrase 'catwalk' when applied to the fashion industry. He was incredibly active. He loved playing with my tie when I returned home from work as well as his toy balls even if he couldn't hear the tinkling of the bell inside the toy. He'd roll the balls around the room with his paws, like a hockey player. Sparkling, lighted toys kept him occupied, as did the crinkly feel of plastic bags. He would swat at the furry little animals on the television screen, even bat at sunbeams. He liked leaping in and out of cardboard boxes, which he used to create his own little world in the conservatory. He enjoyed spinning round and chasing his tail, like a puppy. Boredom never struck, nor habituation to his toys. As with most cats, he moved with the flowing grace of a dancer, possessing a strong, supple body and quick reflexes. However, with teeth adapted to kill small prey, his play had an inborn tendency to mimic hunting. Our hunting games involved the use of fishing-pole-type toys, at which he would make athletic leaps to snag the toy, pawing and chewing at it playfully. When I would dangle a fake, cloth mouse, he would lie in ambush, stalk his 'prey', jiggling his hindquarters before pouncing, neatly seizing it in mid-leap and carrying it off between his teeth to victimize in a quiet corner somewhere. He demonstrated a cat's self-righting reflex, able to twist his body round in mid-air and land perfectly on his feet, his hyper-flexible spine aiding escape from dangers high-up and other potentially life-threatening situations. A half-an-hour's vigorous workout, letting him stalk, chase, catch and finish off his 'kill', complete his hunting excursion, would culminate with him resting, open-mouthed, pink tongue hanging out, huffing and puffing, panting like an exhausted dog. Then, his mouth would widen into a satisfied yawn, tongue curling delicately around his sharp, tiny fangs, and he would experience a nap attack, sprawling in a lion-cub repose and dropping off to sleep for a couple of hours. *He's certainly proving to be a bit of a sleepy man,* as our former GP might have described. Presto slept for around eighteen hours every day, which was apparently normal for a cat of his age, sometimes snuggling up in the strangest, unlikeliest of places: under the radiator, atop the windowsill, in the airing cupboard, etc. We felt highly privileged when he decided to honour us by sleeping next to us. In these instances, we could not move, forced to remain absolutely still, lest we disturbed him from his slumber. Some people allude to cats as lotus-eaters.

The first two months of life are a critical period for any cat; if they are unable to socialize, they display more feral behaviours in later life. We got Presto when he was only eight weeks old. Presto attached very quickly to us, particularly Anthea, showing us great consideration and affection. He purred contentedly every time we gave him attention – purring at twenty-six cycles per second, according to the books, the equivalent to an idling diesel engine. He liked being scritched behind his ear. He accepted the indignity of being tossed in the air and caught like a baby and smothered in kisses. He would roll on to his back in a submissive gesture and allow us to softly stroke and tentatively tickle his fluffy warm belly; he always appreciated a tummy rub. Belly-up, at his most vulnerable, he would gently nibble our fingers. Other times, I would get on my hands and knees, and we'd rub cheeks together in greeting and touch noses, his nose as pink as his paw pads. Bunting involved him intentionally leaving behind a subtle signature scent as he similarly did when he rubbed against objects at head height, hence the invention of the soothing plug-in mist diffusers, mimicking the cat's natural facial pheromones and artificially conveying a sense of comfort, familiarity and safety to the cat's territory; it was also something akin to a case of Presto deliberately brushing against an object and claiming it as his own. Presto took to licking Anthea's feet with a soft audible rasping of his rough tongue, which she thoroughly enjoyed, nibbling her toes like he was tackling knotted fur. Cats can accurately gauge the prevailing mood of their human keepers, and Presto would read my expression whenever I approached him to determine what kind of mood I was in. Pets are also associated with the release of oxytocin, the 'cuddling' hormone, in their owners, improving the person's mental well-being and strengthening their closeness with the animal, proven to increase longevity of life in both. Unless you're allergic to cat dander – in fact it's the saliva on the cat's hair which is the prime culprit – even children growing up with pets have better immune systems than those in a pet-free household. Would it surprise you to know that cats are the unofficial mascots of the Internet? Cats are the most viewed content on the Web since their pictures make Internet users feel warm and fuzzy, a form of pet therapy and stress relief.

His food consisted of a fish pouch in the morning and a meaty pouch in the evening, whisker-lickin' good. He almost always seemed to be in the cupboard before I'd even opened it.

Misbehaviour, as opposed to ordinary rambunctiousness, while seldom a problem, required instant action. Like the time Presto went to town on my new leather blazer with his claws. It was important that Anthea and I did not give Presto confusing, mixed messages but sang from the same hymn sheet, remained consistent in our approach. Deaf cats cannot hear your voice, let alone the *tone* of your voice. They rely predominantly on sight, touch and smell. As he lacked the entire dimension of sound, we had to be visual with him as best we could. The occasional biting and scratching outside – and sometimes even inside – the forum of play, or knocking things over which the deaf cat does not hear but only interprets as interesting movement, required grabbing Presto by the scruff of his neck like his mother cat would have done, lifting him up, looking him directly in the eyes with a stern expression, maybe wagging a finger at him, then placing him on the floor to reflect. Equally relevant, I suppose, is a humorous observation by Charlotte Gray: *After scolding one's cat, one looks into its face and is seized by the ugly suspicion that it understood every word and has filed it for reference.* Our visual cues seemed to work, for Presto soon learned not to freeze or run off in shame. Good behaviour thereafter would be positively reinforced with a quick pat on the head and a treat.

We would give Presto a few catnip drops as a daily reward for his consistently good behaviour, above and beyond his cupboard love. Cats go crazy for catnip. Catnip is a naturally-occurring herb which imitates the pheromones of a dominant female cat in oestrus, and Presto would gobble it up greedily like a vampire drawn to blood. Cats can detect less than one part per billion. Any male cat, Presto included, catching the scent, will become completely docile or have a wild, clumsy, reckless moment of madness, rolling around crazily to impress the 'invisible' female cat. Catnip is harmless even in large doses, but for the cat it is the psychotropic equivalent of cannabis, not that I intended to be Presto's drug-dealer. Its *nar-cat-ic* 'high' lasts a few minutes, and the cat crashes when the effects wear off, fatigued but contented, suddenly dropping off to sleep. I suspected there might be a knock-on effect, some craving, no matter how short-lived the catnip experience. Be wary not to give too much or too frequently as cats develop a tolerance for it and catnip itself irritates the stomach, causing vomiting and diarrhoea. I tried some catnip drops –

they did nothing for me. Another buzz is apparently valerian root, a natural relaxant and sleep aid in humans, but a stimulant in cats, sending them into the throes of ecstasy, even if it does smell a little like cat pee. Silvervine, too, has a similar euphoric effect on cats.

And as the day drew to a close, Presto would be bouncing around the rooms in a brief, manic, energetic spell of nocturnal acrobatics. Overstimulated and he would bite us; bored, understimulated, looking for variety, things to do, and we got the 'kitty crazies', with him running around the house like a lunatic. And once we'd retired to bed, he would join us, sometimes instinctively kneading the duvet to release endorphins and de-stress (just as he might have once kneaded his mother's belly to stimulate milk production), curling up at the end of the mattress, instantly falling asleep. He might open his eyes midway through, momentarily, to make sure we were still there. His paws and ears and tail might twitch, indicating dreaming. More often than not, he would have left the comfort of our bed by sunrise, prowling the apartment, playing with his numerous toys, waking us up just before the alarm clock went off in order to remind us to feed him.

Presto was an affectionate, boisterous thing, very, very clean, who possessed a strong love of play, a highly intelligent and deeply curious nature, eager to hunt and explore. He was unusually well-behaved, with hardly a mischievous, wilful bone in his elegant little body. The intent, trusting eyes of our pet could not be ignored and demanded a kiss and a cuddle or maybe an edible treat.

James Herriot once described cats as the 'Connoisseurs of Comfort'. How true! Someone else joked dogs have 'owners' and cats have 'staff'. Again, I must agree. But we never regarded cleaning up after him, feeding him or playing with him a chore. He was never hard work, and we encouraged his independence and self-reliance, although it is a common fact that when humans act as surrogate parents, cats often experience an extended kittenhood. He was, by all accounts, low maintenance, appreciating such simple fascinations and tastes. Simple distractions kept him occupied. He never asked for much.

Anthea would often sing to him, even though he couldn't hear a single word. The popular rhyme, *Soft Kitty, Warm Kitty*, soon became a ritual at bedtime:

> *Soft kitty, warm kitty,*
> *Little ball of fur,*
> *Sleepy kitty, happy kitty,*
> *Purr, purr, purr...*

Cradled like a baby, I'm sure our little furry-purry thing appreciated the gesture, his body probably sensing the gentle dulcet vibrations arising from Anthea's chest, his lids heavy. I composed my own short ditty, *An Ode to Our Cat*, deliberately sung in silly, infantile tones:

You're my little man,
My lovely little man,
I just want to be your friend!

You're my little man,
My handsome little man,
I will love you till the end!

Mine, I think, was cuter.

Another was, in the spirit of Monty Python, a re-wording of the chorus of the *Lumberjack Song*:

He's the Lovely Man and he's okay,
He plays all night and he sleeps all day!
He's the Lovely Man and he's okay,
He plays all night and he sleeps all day!

Or how about a similar reworking of the House of Pain classic, *Who's The Man?*, from my Uni days?

He's The Man, He's The Man, He's the Lovely Presto Man . . .

I began to wonder what was happening to us and hoping we weren't emasculating him when we took to using trite, nonsensical turns of expression like 'Yum-Yum Time' for his designated mealtimes and 'Sleepy-Bobos' for his bedtime routine, although Anthea was quick to remind me that Sleepy-Bobos should be applied to a dog; she advised that 'Sleepy-Meowmeow Man' was far more apt for our kitten. Even the soubriquet 'Darling Baby Man' we contracted to 'Darling Man', uttered in ridiculous Tweety Pie-esque babyspeak. Soon he became our 'Lovely Man'.

Presto IS the Lovely Man!

I know, I know. More cutespeak, but you need to be in that moment to really appreciate it.

Nauseating, isn't it?

Okay, barf, barf . . .

Sometimes, we would find Presto sitting on his haunches, ears pricked up, alert and all alone, looking out from the windows of the conservatory doors into the back garden. From behind the glass, avidly watching and stalking the pigeons congregating in the garden as they picked up the crusts of stale bread Anthea crumbled up and scattered on the lawn. Birds were a particular fascination with him. Presto might have been content in either greeting them or eating them, sometimes chattering at them in frustration. He watched the birds like a regular feline Attenborough or Oddie, making me think of Petula Clark singing about that cat in the window. The swirling leaves outside also kept him interested, and sometimes he would go chasing after a particular leaf. Perhaps he realized there was a whole other world out there, containing actual live, moving prey, an apparently exciting, novel place on the other side of the pane of glass, a land yonder he was categorically prohibited from accessing and investigating, clearly not understanding why it should be off-limits. Which raised probably the saddest point of all: living in a silent world, Presto could neither hear my voice nor could he respond to his own name. He didn't say much, either. Experts claim that cats can utter up to one hundred distinct vocal sounds, dogs only ten. Presto, however, rarely spoke. So we did our best to acknowledge his meows. There was something diminutive, inchoate, almost wobbly, about his meows, comparable to how a congenitally-deaf human learns to produce speech sounds. Stationed like a sentry, he would greet us from the cardboard box by the front door when we entered the house. He had loads of these cardboard forts around our townhouse, including the conservatory, where he had created another landscape. Occasionally he would pass by, meow in greeting and wander off. *So sweet!* Anthea would say in adoration. *He has to say what he has to say,* I would tell her. Since he could not hear and doubtlessly did not appreciate the concept of sound, we assumed he had very little need to speak. However, he must have realized he was missing something, watching our facial expressions as Anthea and I communicated with one another. His prolonged silences were a mystery to us both, inexplicable and compelling and poignant, just as they say the soul of a cat is considered to be inscrutable to human beings.

It made me sad because he was deaf and restricted to the house and we were all he knew, so dependent was he on us. Rather demonstratively, I wanted to cuddle him and kiss him and fuss over him all the time. He didn't have much of a life. It's like he was in prison; all he had to look forward to were his meals, his playtimes and the view outside. It must have been hard on him watching the black tom from next door, Sooty, another lively and lovely man, invading our garden every day, looking for some mutual 'cat chat', treading territory that should really have belonged to Presto. But we dared not let him out.

Don't forget us and our love for you, Presto my Lovely Man. We're your family now.

3

Kittens grow eighteen times faster than human babies, reaching sexual maturity around six months. Presto was discovering his own sexuality by the time the summer months arrived, washing his paws and fur and rapturously licking his tiny, aroused, conical pink penis. I remembered the sexual adventures of the stray tom, who had opportunistically impregnated all my old neighbour's pedigree pussies when I was growing up, and I suggested neutering Presto, often regarded as the done thing to do, since it ultimately leads to a calming effect in an otherwise overactive, sexually-frustrated cat. Anthea refused, though, claiming it was a cruel procedure, involving extracting the testicles through the surgical incision, and I did not broach the subject further. She preferred keeping the option of Presto siring a few litters of kittens some day. Yet she also admitted that if she ever saw Presto humping another cat, she may never be able to look at him in the same way again. At least, Presto wasn't a shambling, smelly hound who'd be habitually shagging our legs.

As a reputable art dealer, Anthea managed to acquire a number of cat paintings, which she enthusiastically hung around the house: primarily some expensive reproductions of William Hogarth's portraits of cats as well as cat-themed prints of the Dutch painter, Sal Meijer. She ordered a film poster of *Le Chat* and the classic poster art for the famous Parisian establishment, *Le Chat Noir*. *La Dolce Vita* and *Breakfast at Tiffany's* she had always loved partly on account of the cats. I even bought Anthea a rather pricey first edition of *The Cat Who Went to Heaven*, a famous children's novel by Elizabeth Coatsworth, a literary re-telling of an old Buddhist folktale about the relationship between a penniless Japanese painter and a noble Calico brought home by his housekeeper. Anthea loved the Birthday gift. She had already read everything Doris Lessing had written about cats. She also had a vintage copy of T.S. Eliot's collection of whimsical poetry exploring feline behaviour: *Old Possum's Book of Practical Cats*. She even discovered a French song from the days of Yé-yé: *Fallait Pas Écraser La Queue Du Chat* by Clothilde. *Do not tread on the cat's tail.*

At five months, Presto coughed up his first hairball. He'd been intermittently retching for days, resisting the urge to upchuck, until he was completely overwhelmed and out came a small splatter of clear bilious fluid and the culprit itself: a spongy, sticky, rather innocuous-looking lump of cotton, the size of a walnut. Anthea suffered sleepless nights in the days leading up to this inevitable biological evacuation, catastrophizing that her cat might be dying. We took him to the vet on two separate occasions, who reassured us our cat was in fine health, and we should let Nature takes its course – the furball would be expelled in good time. *He's turned into a bit of vomity man*, as our old GP might have joked; Presto's puke-up was the first in a series of furballs. Anthea missed work, a disproportionate reaction to the actual health scare. When the hairball did finally make its appearance, the relief Anthea experienced was tantamount to a mother who learns that her newborn baby's ten-hour, heart-and-lung transplant operation was a resounding success. I suppose that was when I first noticed things with Anthea might not be quite right. I also wondered if I would develop enlarged cervical lymph nodes, since cats weren't as clean as they made themselves out to be, or cough up a furball of my own, considering how much I kissed our little kitten, our *baby*, who seemed to be moulting his thick, winter coat. His fine white hairs were everywhere, floating up from his hide like dustmotes. But what else could we do except give his coat a good brush?

By six months, Presto hated being cut off from certain parts of the house, meowing earnestly in front of any closed door – even a familiar door – perceiving it had been closed for a special reason, as though something magical lay beyond. He patrolled the house like any good guard-dog, covering its entirety a hundred times a day, making sure the place was safe and sound before any nap; I remember joking that our meow-meow-man might not be able to challenge an intruder, but at least he'd be safe in the knowledge that he'd secured the house.

He had a real talent for inducing sleep – yes, actually *forcing* himself to sleep – always checking out his environment first, making sure it was safe, then washing himself, as though preferring the smell of himself before he slept. It was a fascinating ritual to watch, a young cat only being true to his nature. He enjoyed different sleeping experiences, but these days our Royal Sleepymeowmeowness would often curl up and dream on my bathrobe.

I continued to play with our growing cat while Anthea spent increasing time with him at the expense of her job and our relationship, but I presumed it was just a phase she was going through and that it would soon pass. I thought she might be overcompensating for the cat she lost in childhood, but it eventually dawned on me that there might be more to it than just that. I played with him, making sure I offered a variety of play activities and the play didn't grow predictable. *He's turned into a bit of huntery, stalkery man*, to use our former GP's vernacular. Presto expected me to let him stalk his prey: on this occasion, the laser light. The laser pointer I used during lectures became the new plaything for Presto, who would lie in ambush, wriggle his hindquarters in preparation to strike before pouncing at the red dot, chasing it everywhere, darting and dashing at breakneck speed, leaping and gambolling like an accomplished gymnast at their professional peak. I don't think he knew I was creating that red laser dot at first, but rather it was a ghostly manifestation or a UFO that appeared and reappeared on the ceiling every so often, always whenever I was around, and vanished at will . . . or maybe Presto grew wise and made that connection. Me in one corner and Presto, with his feline smart, in the other. Male bonding over the laser light, like father and son. He was such a proud little thing, always puffed himself up when I stroked him after the hunt was over, and I would reward him with catnip. *Because, like England, Presto* Expects. For a cat confined to the house, this variation on the hunting game provided him with enough intensive exercise to keep him in perfect shape and fitness. And another first in the curiosity stakes was his genuine fascination with the beam of light generated from the laser, instead of the laser dot itself, cutting through the smoky air and now clearly defined after I half-burnt the burgers – how smart is that?

A natural-born predator he soon became an absolute terror to the ants that managed to crawl their way into the house. He protected the house from the flies and bugs, chasing moths, clapping his paws in mid-air to catch them. Anthea's arachnophobia meant she always engaged Presto on any stray spiders. He killed spiders with a ruthless efficiency, but not before toying with them first, sometimes gobbling them up then coughing them out. We got worried our spider-catcher would get sick from eating too many spiders.

At mealtimes, Presto deliberately drew attention to himself by sitting upright on the kitchen bin and rattling the steel lid with his weight, meowing loudly and repeatedly as though singing for his supper, a sight and sound too hilarious to describe.

Presto toddled around everywhere Anthea went. I suppose the reverse would have been true if it had been a female cat. Presto would attack her ankles if I were to 'attack' [kiss and cuddle] her from above. Whether it was sexual aggression as a result of seeing me kiss her, imitating a kiss in his own way or just wanting to play I couldn't be sure. Either way, it was meant to be attention-grabbing, and it worked. The rest of the time he ate and slept, normally in close quarters to Anthea, who doted on him incessantly, as though she'd physically given birth to him.

Once again, we considered getting him a playmate, another white, deaf cat in this instance, male, perhaps, of equal age and footing, ideal company in a buddy-buddy mould – *two lovely men* – but Anthea reneged on the promise without explanation, apart from claiming that Presto was 'the most *im-paws-ible* cat in the world'. I thought with 'impawsible' she meant 'incredible', 'special', 'unique'.

This is my beautiful wife and my beautiful house and, of course, my beautiful cat.

We had such a lovely cat, so companionable, playful and affectionate. Smart, too, even if he had a tendency to repeatedly bat away his plastic bottle tops, after working them like a hockey puck, under the sofa, out of reach, while not quite grasping the moral of the story: don't knock your toys *under* the sofa! We raised him well. I know of a lot of cats that are selfish and too independent, rude and totally wild. *Not Presto*. I thought that if we were ever to have kids, they would turn out to be just as lovely as Presto.

But enough of the niceties. Things were about to change.

Me and the girl I married were soulmates, without resorting to soppy sentiment. Our affection for one another had been transferred to our cat. Increasingly so.

I did not question Anthea's interminable devotion to her precious cat at this stage, the unhealthy amount of attention and affection she lavished on him, pandering to his every whim, but it gradually became apparent that she might be behaving out of character. I confronted her about the disquieting eccentricities of her behaviour much, much later, knowing I should have acted sooner, before the situation escalated into the nightmare I would be forced to deal with on my own. I learned – although I didn't know it then – that Presto was more than just an ordinary domestic cat, and it gradually emerged that I, too, had been negatively affected by his very presence, except in an entirely different way to how he'd influenced – no, *harmed* – Anthea.

I got my first suspicious inkling at a dinner party we held to celebrate the return of Anthea's longest friend, Deanna Cheung.

It was at that stage that things took a sinister turn.

Deanna Cheung (née Li) was Anthea's oldest and dearest friend and confidante. They had grown up together, studied at the same schools, gone to the same University. I first met Deanna whilst a student myself at Chertsford University, after I had begun dating Anthea. Deanna was a lovely person, outgoing and intelligent, excelling in Mathematics. Their ways parted when she decided to go and live in Hong Kong where her husband, Greg, of Chinese extraction like herself, had been appointed the Deputy Director of IT at an international casino syndicate. Deanna maintained her role of housewife and mother to their three-year-old son, Kelvin. She kept in close touch with Anthea by Skype, e-mail and, more commonly, text message. The number of texts they exchanged was phenomenal. Sometimes Deanna would leave fifty-plus texts, many with a picture attached, for Anthea to sort through on waking up in the morning, the sheer volume frequently depleting the battery of her Blackberry and proving ridiculously expensive when the telephone bill came round. It had been nearly two years since Deanna had last visited the UK and, by that time, her existing son was approaching six and she and Greg were expecting another child.

Hugh Fleming, my closest friend and fellow lecturer in English Literature, would also be joining us for dinner with his latest girlfriend and his eight-year-old brown Saluki, Samson. Hugh had met the Cheungs before, knew them through me but had been accompanied by a different girlfriend last time.

Anthea had been excited all week over Deanna's impending visit, arranged for that particular Saturday evening in late July, and had turned herself into a proper domestic goddess, making the house spotless and putting the finishing touches to the guest bedroom as well as preparing a veritable feast for our friends.

Anthea busied herself that particular afternoon while I sat, dressed in customary black, in the garden drinking a nice, cool bottle of Stella, and as five o'clock ticked closer, she grew more distracted and apprehensive. Presto followed her from room to room, mooching for food, idly watching her hoover the floors, dust the shelves, fluff the pillows, etc. The vacuuming raised dust and caused him to sneeze. Then, Anthea went to work in the kitchen, making dinner. By the time I came back into the house, she was slightly grouchy towards me. When the doorbell rang at five, she was in quite a state. "How do I look?" she asked me nervously, catching her reflection, removing an imaginary piece of lint from the cute pink, knee-length Versace dress she wore and straightening her long hair in the hallway mirror.

You may not know, but Anthea is half-Swedish (on her mother's side) and very blond and tans gorgeously. I looked into her bright, blue eyes and saw she was stressed-out, exhibiting a great deal of anticipatory anxiety. Pretty in pink, and despite recently turning the wrong side of thirty, she seemed to have regressed to an insecure teenage girl whose date has just arrived. At that precise moment, she looked like the most beautiful woman in the world, and I fell in love with her all over again. "You look utterly ravishing," I told her and kissed her sensuously and lingeringly on her lips, as a means of diverting her from her butterflies as well as raising her confidence.

Then, taking a deep breath and composing herself mentally, regaining some faith in herself, she threw open the front door and there they were: her greatest friend of all time and her friend's husband and friend's young son all the way from Hong Kong.

The moment Anthea clapped eyes on Deanna, her fears and worries evaporated and the two exchanged hugs and kisses, jumping up and down and screaming in true uncontained girly-girly excitement, like they must have done during their University days. It was as though they had never been apart. The exchange of greetings between Greg and myself was a slightly more sober affair. Deanna was dressed in a long Oriental cherry-blossom dress and, in my opinion, had put on a little weight all over, but when Anthea spotted the slightly noticeable bulge on the belly, she and Deanna began jumping and squealing all over again, thrilled, jubilant. *Five months,* Deanna informed us, *a girl!* We congratulated her and her husband. Kelvin, too, had grown several inches taller and was dressed like his father in a white shirt and beige chinos, looking smart and mature for his age. I slapped high fives with Kelvin without raising even the twinkle of a smile on his fresh, young face. Anthea introduced our cat, and Deanna looked benignly down at Presto, scooped him up, cradled him in her arms and rained spectacular kisses all over his face and warm muzzle, rumpling the snowy-white fur on his forehead, blowing raspberries on the angoran softness of his belly. Presto appreciated the gesture and reciprocated, pawing playfully at her face, scratching her gently, nibbling her fingers, producing a loud vibrating purr from deep within his throat to express his gratitude and contentment. By now, Presto was nearly seven months old and was taking on the definitive shape of a cat, even if some of his facial expressions reminded me of when he was a tiny thing – I suppose he would still be classified a kitten until the age of three years. *Ah, they grow up so fast!* Anthea told Deanna. It turned out that it was Deanna who originally suggested to Anthea we get a cat as a prelude to a baby. Like ourselves, Deanna loved animals and had recently bought a Shih Tzu, a lively, sociable (albeit greedy), black-and-gold Chinese 'toy' dog, who was now ten months old and whom they had named Foo-Foo. He was currently being looked after by Greg's mother back in Hong Kong.

Our townhouse had a long, reasonably-sized garden with an ample patio, complete with wooden furniture and a stone barbecue pit, perfect for alfresco dining. We welcomed them in and retreated to the garden, which smelled sweet with summer flowers and was flooded by July sunshine. The torturously searing afternoon heat had given way to the first cool wind of the evening. We nattered for a short while: Greg's promotion to IT Director another cause for celebration, Kelvin's ambition to become a nuclear physicist and the Cheungs' month-long holiday schedule which involved taking in the culture of London, including the Proms and the West End, and visiting family and friends in Durham and Somerset. *I like what you've done with the place,* a genuinely impressed Deanna told Anthea, *particularly all those domestic French touches.* Anthea would disappear into the kitchen every so often while I entertained our guests. Presto pranced and rushed around on the lawn, chasing the insects, savouring his rare shot at freedom to roam the world outside. He would adopt the hunter's stoop, crouched down low, body tense, preparing to pounce upon spotting a pigeon. At intervals, he stood, taking a breather – curved tail, curious cat, raised tail, cat inquiring, wagging tail, cat deciding. His light olive-hued eyes when caught in the sun turned golden.

Hugh was fashionably late as usual, a conscious practice at social functions, in complete contrast to his outstanding grasp of timing in the seminars, tutorials and lecture halls and castigation of students for any discourteous lateness. His brains, knowledge and excellent time management skills aside, he was self-assured, never descending to the point of arrogance, and together with the fact that he looked substantially younger than his age, meant it frequently made him the object of various student crushes as well as the envy of his male colleagues. He maintained his professional boundaries at work, never dated his female collegians, but after hours managed to attract girls ten years his junior. Keeley Farrell was a prime example, a pouty, perfume-counter brunette on this occasion, whom he had picked up at the BARRACUDA night-club. Nothing serious, all fun and games. Keeley may have looked and sounded chavvy in her white, curve-hugging mini-dress and thick Essex accent, but she could have still given Anthea a run for her money in the desirability stakes. Hugh looked as good as his current trophy girlfriend, tanned golden and modelling this season's French Riviera look.

Us men sat in the garden, swigging Stella, with sparkling elderflower pressé for

Kelvin. The women wandered into the kitchen, gossiping and helping Anthea with dinner. Presto went round all the guests one-by-one and socialized, meeting and greeting everyone in proper civilized, grown-up fashion. A *prop-purr* little gentleman. The Lovely Man. After receiving a lot of 'oohs' and 'aahs', he returned to the garden and began to proudly preen himself. All seemed well until he encountered Hugh's Saluki, Samson.

The Saluki, also known as the Persian greyhound, is one of the few breeds of dog Muslims accept as 'clean' and lives up to its reputation as the Royal Dog of Egypt. Essentially a sighthound, it is regarded as an efficient hunter and the fastest dog over long distances, getting up to an impressive forty-five miles an hour at full pelt. Samson stretched slender and graceful with a long face, big eyes and droopy ears, a curved, feathery tail and fur silky to the touch and the colour of wheat. He was a friendly dog, affectionate and even-tempered, with a love of the outdoors and a hunter's natural instinct, if called upon. But when he saw Presto, something came over him and he bared his teeth and began snarling and growling at the cat. Presto sat up, ears flattened, hackles raised, frozen in a heightened pose of alertness, sensing the imminent threat but not able to hear it. The cat's hypervigilance and reluctance to scoot caused Samson to up the ante, increase his level of intimidation, taking to barking at Presto in a ferocious manner. Credit to Presto, he held his own, stood his ground, against an older animal, four times his size and a dog at that. Presto raised his fur as far as it would go, arching his spine, making himself appear significantly bigger, claws unsheathed and extended, ears pointed down and back, and, turning diagonally and flashing his fangs, hissed back venomously, in open challenge. It was a reaction none of us expected and I'm sure Samson did, neither. Understandably spooked, Samson redoubled his efforts, his barks rising in noise and pitch . . . and menace. We watched the whole thing in silence and awe, but it was Hugh, a man not accustomed to messing around, who intervened and terminated the cat-dog confrontation, sure that Samson was on the cusp of physically attacking Presto, whether or not his dog would have been able to catch the accursed cat in a straight one-on-one chase.

"Samson, what the devil are you doing?" Hugh scolded sharply, shaking his tawny-furred dog and tying the lead tightly around the nearest table leg. "Quit your yapping!" Turning back to the others, Hugh apologized on behalf of his dog: "I don't know what's got into him. He's normally a passive, placid fellow."

"Maybe it's a territorial thing," I offered. Samson's behaviour made me think back to the day Presto went in for his jabs a few months ago. I remember the other dogs in the vet's waiting room had become suddenly restless and begun to bark agitatedly as though sensing the coming of a storm, their individual owners lumbered with the undesirable task of bringing them to heel. Presto had watched the entire chaotic scene from his cat carrier with quiet fascination. I had never thought anything of it at the time – I had just assumed all cats have a kind of strong, perhaps unnerving, presence – and the vet himself had downplayed the incident, regaling us with the tale of the woman who called the pet-care helpline wanting to know what size litter-box she needed to keep her cat comfy [ha-ha!], but looking back to that day at the vet's and now Samson's restlessness, the entire episode took on a whole new significance. Particularly taking into account the way this garden party would ultimately conclude.

"There's that old English proverb: *In a cat's eye, all things belong to cats*," Hugh replied, settling back in his chair. "A cat thinks humans are just big cats. A dog is constantly striving not to be excluded from the pack."

"Puppies are a lot harder work than kittens," I said, watching Hugh's dog. Tied to the table, Samson continued to pace restlessly within the limits of his leash, panting, showing signs of frustration. Meanwhile, Presto trotted off with his usual feline elegance, corkscrewing his tail, his head raised in supercilious and smug fashion, a behaviour not commonly witnessed in a human child aged between seven and eight years, which Presto was the cat equivalent to. *Now, Samson, you know your place here*, he seemed to gloat. Presto had teased him, tested him, seeing how far he would go, shown him who's the 'top dog'. *That's my boy*, I thought, *my lovely man, my little dandy!*

"There's a reason why dogs are regarded as a man's best friend," Hugh said, looking into poor Samsung's dejected eyes, adding distastefully: "A dog is the only creature on earth that loves you more than he loves himself. No matter what it's done wrong, a cat will always try to make it look like it was the dog's fault. Dogs will faithfully come to the rescue of their human masters regardless of danger and death – you can trust them with your life. Cats can be sneaky, selfish, disloyal and cruel – they can leave you cold. Dogs want to be human; cats believe they're gods."

"I guess it must depend on the circumstances," I commented.

Hugh continued in full flow. "You've heard of Pavlov's dogs. But never Pavlov's cats. Whereas dogs are eager to please, cats are indifferent. The bell rings. The cat walks off. *I ate earlier*, it tells the experimenter. The bell rings again. *Don't disturb me*, the cat moans, *I'm napping.*"

"Strangely magnetic animals are cats, believe me, with an equally strong power to fascinate or repel, depending on the individual."

"If you die, a dog will slowly starve to death by your side. A cat will chew your face off."

"That's pretty morbid even by your standards," I commented drily.

Hugh resumed his cat-bashing. "In today's PC-crazy society, cats have been called all kinds of things, including extortionists, rug re-decorators and wildlife control experts. No disrespect, but, to me, a kitten is nothing more than a small homicidal muffin on four legs, committing the absolute wildest and most ruthless acts of cruelty and wanton destruction yet paradoxically manipulating human sensibilities into seeing their behaviour as 'cute'. They regard humans as mere automatic door-openers. And what is it with cats when it rains? It will be raining on all sides of the house and it shouldn't be necessary to check every door. Another great pearl of wisdom: I shall not eat spiders and hallucinate giant dragons from behind the toilet!"

I said nothing, unwilling to inform Hugh that dogs were generally smelly and pretty thick and would rather attempt to eat the laser light that Presto chased. They also allegedly had a taste for cat poo, referring to a litter tray as a 'snackbox'. If cats could speak, they would tell you: *You threw the stick, you fetch it!* Eventually, I decided to impart some old-school philosophy. "An anonymous fella once said: *There are many intelligent species in the Universe. They are all owned by cats.*"

"If that's what he thinks, I'm not bleeding surprised he stayed anonymous!" Hugh exclaimed. Hugh's near-ailurophobic dislike of cats was nothing new and a general source of both amusement and annoyance for me.

I wasn't about to give up just yet. One more grenade in my ammunition box. "Who do you think would win in contest between a cat and a cobra?"

Hugh's smile told me he already knew. "I'm guessing the cat because you wouldn't have asked, otherwise? But pray do tell why?"

"Like a charmer, the cat keeps the cobra focused on the movement of its tail, swinging it hypnotically from side to side, before the cat goes in for the kill."

"Clever. Very sly."

The ladies brought out our meals and we started eating. Anthea had prepared an appetizer of chargrilled whole quail with herb salad, followed by a main course of pan-roasted breast of duck with puy lentils, spring onions, baby carrots and spiced citrus sauce. Dessert consisted of summer berry compote with vanilla Chantilly cream. We alternated between Chardonnay and Chianti, with elderflower pressé for our pregnant guest and her pre-teen son. The chef in question, my wonderful Anthea, received a flurry of compliments for her game-themed cuisine. We caught up on old times in what amounted to be a perfect get-together in a perfect venue (even if I might say so myself) on a perfect summer's day. The cool evening breeze was as agreeable as the food, dispelling the heat that had come before it. The sky was gradually losing its shades of sunset-red as dusk approached.

With our meals polished off, all those partaking satisfied and full, we moved on to the Cognac and coffee and cigars and after-dinner conversation. Samson had tucked into his share of duck ravenously, but he remained strangely restless and unsettled, pacing around in circles, tied to the table. Every so often, he spied the subject of his angst, i.e. our cat, and would growl, for which he would receive a stern reprimand from Hugh. Apart from unintentionally (or maybe deliberately, surely not!) inciting Samson, Presto settled back on his haunches and went about his usual ritual of bathing himself, even washing behind his ears, before preparing to sleep off the large meal. Hugh was quick to inform me that far from disguising their own scent, cats in fact transferred the scent of their food onto their fur while washing themselves, thereby making themselves more conspicuous to any predator. "Not exactly well-thought-out," he summed it up. "Maybe cats are so insecure that they must repeatedly cover themselves with their own saliva as a constant, reassuring reminder: 'This body belongs to me'." Of course, neither was this a reason why cats washed themselves – just another stab at mockery. I decided not to honour his mickey-taking with a response.

I had instead been particularly fascinated by Kelvin throughout dinner, studying him without anybody cottoning on. He hadn't said much, not unusual for someone who's the only kid among a group of adults. But any attempts to engage him in conversation were met with simple, perfunctory answers. Nor had he shown any interest in playing with either Presto or Samson, which any normal kid might want to do. And it couldn't just be boredom. Kelvin demonstrated very little eye-contact and a kind of emotional detachment out of place for any kid. He seemed strangely preoccupied, almost lost in himself. Closed-off in his own little world. One of my nephews behaved similarly and he was later diagnosed with Asperger's syndrome. I didn't want to spoil the evening by communicating my observations to his parents, suggesting that Kelvin might be on the Autistic Spectrum. Some other time, perhaps.

Instead, I focused on Hugh's conversation piece, which had somehow drifted round to Anthea's grandmother. "A smashing lady, your Phyllida," he was telling Anthea, puffing on his stogie. "A real looker and a woman after my own heart."

He had met Anthea's grandmother several years ago and they had really connected. Maybe because they both taught English. As I mentioned earlier,

Phyllida Pettifer had given up being a stage actress when she had got married and had kids to become an English teacher in a Secondary School. Hugh was right. I had seen a professional headshot of her in her heyday and she had been an absolute stunner. Even now, aged eighty-four, a widow and with Diabetes and kidney problems, she was still an attractive lady. Shame she had never transferred from stage to celluloid.

"Thanks," said Anthea, beaming. "She would certainly appreciate the compliment. I'll tell her you said 'Hi'."

"One thing I don't agree with, though," Hugh declared, getting into his stride. "I agree that Laurence Olivier was the greatest Shakespearean actor who ever lived, and Kenneth Branagh is a pale shadow of Olivier's brilliance, a pretender to the throne, no matter how enthusiastic. But I believe that Olivier was badly miscast as Hamlet and Heathcliff. Don't get me wrong, he gave a workmanlike performance in both roles, but I don't think he was capable of playing the rogue, which both roles demanded in their complexity. He was just too much of a gentleman. It was only later in life – *Marathon Man*, *The Boys from Brazil* – that the old darling learned to shine as the villain. The things he got up to in *The Betsy* . . ." Hugh trailed off, a dreamy look in his eyes, as though reliving those tawdry scenes.

"Don't let Phyllida hear you say that," I replied jocularly. "She absolutely loves Laurence Olivier. Did I mention her greatest moment on stage was playing Ophelia when Laurence Olivier was once in the audience?"

"Every time, but it never loses its entertainment value." Hugh continued to intellectualize, changing subjects. "I picked up the newspaper the other day. Makes depressing reading. Unregulated corporate profiteering, global austerity measures, family-value pushers who can't resist divorce, endless dating sites that hide behind a banner of love in order to promote empty sex, the growing acceptability of prostitution and people-trafficking, other unthinking morons who keep banging on about the legalization of drugs, crooked computer-supply companies fleecing schools out of millions with the approval of the banks, increased autonomy of kids when all they need is boundaries and guidance. Murder and terrorism and genocide, that's all you hear about these days. How stupid are human beings?" He addressed Keeley in afterthought. "No offence, my dear."

"None taken," she replied somewhat vacuously, probably not comprehending her boyfriend's snide, disparaging apology. I suppose Hugh wasn't going out with her for her stimulating conversation.

You could easily mistake Hugh's opinionated brand of pessimism for wisdom.

Or perhaps he was the last True Great Realist. Either way, he was a man who took no prisoners. I pretended to stake out the moral high ground. "But how can you ignore what the world religions teach us about the basic goodness of Man?"

"Just a myth, baby, just what we tell ourselves to feel better about ourselves. You're forgetting about Original Sin. Big money is to be made from the God Racket, you know. Organized religion is as evil as the politicians in power and the crimes of the giant corporations. These butt-speaking people try and make us believe we can't have Democracy without Capitalism, but that couldn't be further from the truth. We've destroyed the planet and killed off half the species, so why don't we just finish the job by shooting each other in the head? Believe me, the human race won't last much longer. Extinction beckons."

As the debate continued, Deanna excused herself and disappeared into the house to take a comfort break. Presto must have followed her, probably discovering a new friend. I did not know this, because when I last glanced down, he was still dozing on the ground next to me. It was only when Deanna came out of the patio doors and Presto ambled out after her with a cat-ate-the-canary grin on his face that I realized he must have woken up and wandered off while I wasn't looking.

Greg was the first to notice the stunned, remote expression on his wife's face. "Darling, what's wrong?"

Anyone would have recognized that it was shock, the dissociated look of trauma. Deanna moved robotically, slowly depositing herself in the seat next to him. His inquiry did not seem to register, so Greg repeated his question with greater perturbation, putting his arm around her shoulders. Kelvin looked on with an aloofness and a quiet lack of concern I had never seen any son give his mother. Reality filtered into Deanna's eyes, and she snapped wide awake, shaking off her confusion. "Greg, Kelvin, we're leaving! *Right now!*"

"That's a bit sudden, isn't it?" I said, mystified. "You planned to stay over. Anthea especially prepared your rooms."

"No, we shan't . . ." Deanna responded coldly, pointing a trembling finger towards Presto, who yawned and stretched and lay down on the ground, returning to his characteristic reclining pose of a sphinx, pupils slit-like and constricted, mood complacent, now nothing more than the relaxed, purring cat we were accustomed to. "Not with that *creature* in the house!"

"What the hell happened in there?" Hugh demanded to know.

Deanna's eyes glazed over again briefly with shock and fear, as she seemed to relive an experience which was yet unspoken. "I was a-a-assaulted . . . by that *cat!*"

"Don't be ridiculous!" Anthea challenged, outraged, leaping to our cat's defence. "How dare you accuse our little darling man of doing something so abhorrent! He's just a baby!"

"*Well, your damned baby attacked me when I saw him for WHAT he is!*" Deanna elaborated, screaming back at her. "I only managed to get away by flinging the bastard against the wall!"

It was at that moment I saw the light scratches on her left cheek. There had been a tussle. Deanna sported superficial injuries as confirmation. "I'm so sorry, Deanna, if our cat did this to you. He was probably only being playful. A bit of rough and tumble. Please let me attend to your wounds . . ."

"*Stay away!*" Deanne blasted me. "I don't want anything more to do with the both of you *or* your cat! If *that* is what he is!"

"Are you mad?" Anthea yelled at her friend, gathering up Presto in her arms like a protective mother. "You okay, my sweet one . . ." she fussed over him. Presto just looked surprised at the sudden display of attention. He looked unhurt. Back to her friend, Anthea gave her an ultimatum, on the warpath. "You either immediately apologize to our cat for striking out at him or you can kindly *leave!*"

"Anthea, please, let's be civilized about this . . ." I tried to mediate, but Anthea was having none of it. Neither was Deanna for that matter. *A wise man never argues with a woman,* I had always been taught, *let alone two.*

"Apologize to that-that *thing?*" Deanna spat out, raving. "*Never!* He's the Devil, your cat! He's *not* even a cat! Come . . ." she addressed her husband and son, "we're leaving!" With that, Deanna stormed off. Greg made a hasty apology for his wife's bizarre behaviour and departed on her heels, taking their son with him.

Anthea did not even try to go after them. She was furious. For the first time and possibly the last, she had fallen out with her oldest and dearest friend and confidante.

"Sorry for bailing out on you so early," Hugh declared, "but I think we should go as well. You and Anthea have probably got stuff to sort out." He added, reflecting on the unsavoury scene. "I've never seen Deanna lose it like that. What the hell did she mean Presto's *not a cat?*"

Then, Hugh too was gone, taking his embarrassed girlfriend and anxious dog with him, bringing our dinner party to a premature end. I promised to call him soon with an update.

I stood in the deepening twilight, feeling the breeze caress my skin. Night was almost upon us.

He's not even a cat, Deanna had outright alleged. *I saw him for what he is.*

Presto still in her arms, sensing the rumble of a purr, Anthea went inside the house. I followed her. I could clear the plates up later.

I found Anthea crying on the bed, and when she saw Presto next to her, her mood brightened up a tad. I tried to talk to her, including during the days that followed, but she refused to discuss the events of that evening. I looked down at Presto, who was watching me with the keen innocence of a medium cat, no longer a kitten but neither yet an adult. He would not have caught the brutal verbal exchange between Anthea and Deanna, nor would he have been aware that he had been the centre of the dispute.

The story didn't end there, though. A distraught Greg rang me a week later to inform me that Deanna had suffered a miscarriage on the flight back to Hong Kong and had subsequently died in hospital from the complications of Toxoplasmosis. I was stunned, could only mumble my condolences. I could picture the scene vividly in my mind: the plane in mid-air, a hysterical Deanna trapped in the tiny toilet as she aborted her five-month-old foetus in a thick, explosive gush of blood and amniotic fluid, being rushed to hospital once the plane had landed, later dying from Septicaemia. I remembered Deanna freaking out over our cat when we last saw her, at the time very much alive and enjoying her pregnancy. Her untimely demise represented a prosperous and fulfilling life cut short in the cruellest way possible. Because Presto was an indoors cat and had received all his vaccinations, I could not understand how Deanna could have possibly contracted Toxoplasmosis from him, one of the few zoonoses seldom transmitted from cats. Never disease-free, mind, since a cat's mouth is a reservoir of germs despite their obsession with cleanliness. I asked Greg what day the funeral had been arranged for and stated we would try and attend.

When I broke the sad news to Anthea, she did not even flinch, her only words being: "Good riddance!" Her starkly pitiless and unforgiving, unfeeling reaction scared me greatly as did the inordinate amount of time she was now investing in Presto in terms of attention, bonding and play. Maybe she was processing her grief in her own way, managing her loss by using the cat as a distraction, in a similar way to how she had been overcompensating for the loss of her childhood pet, Balthazar. When asked why she was spending so much time with Presto, she would just nod to the cat and reply matter-of-factly: *Because he's my little man.* Cute but odd. It appalled me when Anthea chose not to attend the upcoming funeral point-blank. Her decision not to pay her last respects to her oldest and dearest friend made no sense whatsoever and I considered it indefensible. Even when I decided to put my foot down, I could not persuade her.

And, all the while, Deanna's astounding remark kept ringing in my head: *He's not even a cat.*

5

We now know that the human-cat relationship has survived since the Neolithic period, dating back nearly ten thousand years. But cats grew to prominence around three thousand years ago when they were first endowed with the archetypal powers of the Egyptians gods, in particular with one of the most esteemed of deities, Bastet, half-feline daughter of the Sun god, Ra. Bastet, the goddess of cats, gave rise to an orgiastic cult that sprang up in the delta city of Bubastis, housing a necropolis where thousands of mummified cats were interred in sacred receptacles. Incantations were spoken with the hope of speedily carrying their owner's message to the goddess, since it was widely believed that cats enshrined the souls of ancestors, such that when people died, their souls would be transferred into cats. The Temple of Bubastis would reveal awe-inspiring images of the white cat deity, the immortal, self-begotten source of Light and All Life, liberator of the oppressed and helper of the underprivileged and impoverished, a nurse and healer capable of strengthening the powers of recuperation in the sick. Some of the earliest feline images were captured on the walls of caves, statues made of stone, charms and amulets, and papyri containing magical formulae and symbolic representations of the sacred cat assembled for use by priests for the purposes of the Afterlife. The people strove to emulate the ideal beauty of the cat, wearing eye makeup to give them a mysterious cat-like look. It was also during the sanctification of the cat in Ancient Egypt that the Trinity of Trinities – the Number Nine – first became associated with cats.

The beliefs of the Celts asserted that the cat formed a bridge between Good and Evil, and between Man and the Gods, linking and separating the outer world of the Living from the inner, invisible world of the Dead. They claimed that a cat's eyes were windows through which humans could see directly into the Faerie Kingdom and from which faeries could look out. Cats were psychopomps, messengers like Hermes, ferrying men after mortal death into the Underworld. The Norse goddess, Freyja, was often depicted riding a cat-drawn chariot across the midnight sky, ruling over those slain in battle in the Afterlife, deemed unfit for Odin's Halls of Valhalla. Numerous wild cat cults have existed and still exist across the New World; cats were considered powerful totemic symbols and familiars of shamans, who could purportedly transform into a cat and be gifted with its powers. Even in hoodoo tradition, cats were always seen as supernatural entities conjured up by witchdoctors, but these days they are thought of as bringers of good luck, particularly for gamblers. In Burma, Sinh the Golden-eyed Cat was revered by the Priesthood of the Temple of Lao Tsun for his oracular powers: foreknowledge of future delights or presentiment of disaster. The Chinese weather prophet was the Winking Cat, predicting the approach of rain. Menike-neko, the Beckoning Cat, is still considered a symbol of good fortune in Japanese culture.

According to Hebrew legend, cats did not exist before the Great Flood. A couple of lions were among the animals on Noah's Ark, though. Afloat on the swelling waters, the Ark became infested with rats, which almost ate all the food reserves. Beside himself, Noah prayed to God for a solution. God consulted the King of the Beasts, who obediently sneezed out a pair of ready-made cats. The cats immediately set to work, fulfilling their natural instinct as 'verminators'. When the flood waters receded and the Ark reached dry land, the cats walked out at the head of the great procession of animals, which is why, as the legend concludes, all cats are proud to this day. The cat was then to suffer a meteoric fall from grace, as bespoken elsewhere in Hebrew teachings. Accused of eating the last fish of a poor, destitute family, causing the family to starve and perish, the cat displeased God so much with its act of selfishness, it was promptly banished from Heaven, but not before it was granted nine lives before death would find it, one life for each life it took. Its descent from Heaven lasted nine days before it landed feet-first on Earth.

The cat would suffer an even greater earthly penalty during the infamous Catholic witch-trials of the fifteenth and sixteenth centuries. Witchcraft was running rampart, according to the unfounded hysteria of the times, and the cat was denounced as being the envoy of the Devil and supernatural servant of the Witch, helping her in her magical workings. Countless women were suspected of witchcraft just because they acted a little odd or happened to own a cat. Witches were thought to have the ability to shapeshift into a cat nine times over or fly into their cat familiars, as referenced in the infamous *Malleus Maleficarum*. Their sleek, agile movements, eyes that seemed to glow in the dark and sparks of green fire thought to emanate from their fur meant that cats were hugely feared. The black cat deity in particular was believed to feed on the sacrificial flesh of hanged men and unbaptized children and blamed for producing hail, gale and storm, destroying crops, killing livestock and rendering humans sterile. It was accused of poisoning people's minds, spreading disease and inflicting blindness. It was an omen of ill-fortune, bringing poverty to otherwise prosperous villages, oppressing and torturing, swindling and lying. It was the centre of mysterious hillside gatherings on dark moonlit nights, integral to the sexual orgies at the witches' sabbath and the nefarious ceremonies of black magicians in celebrating Black Mass and attempting to reveal the Devil. The Embodiment of Evil, paintings of the Black Cat showed it to be seated at the foot of Judas Iscariot. In a holocaust where millions of mostly innocent women died, cats were burned, hung or drowned alongside their ever-faithful mistresses. Following the mass burning of cats, rats proliferated, decimating food sources and carrying fatal diseases, and a time of great plague befell Medieval Europe, claiming one-third of the population.

Even to this day, superstitions about cats persist. A cat in the cradle portends a safe birth. To kill a cat brings seven years' bad luck. Conversely, a cat boiled in oil is good for dressing wounds and thought to cure Consumption (Tuberculosis), still a common practice in some parts of the world. If you encounter a cat at a crossroads at midnight, you should be able to summon Lucifer. A cat seen sitting on the bed of a sick man portends his death. If a cat jumps over a coffin, the corpse will turn into a vampire. The seafarers of the seventeenth century were a particularly superstitious bunch, seldom leaving port without a cat on board, since the ship's cat could control the rodent population, supposedly predict the weather and generally bring good luck to the ship and crew. (It has long since been proven that cats have a coat charged with static electricity that can detect the minutest electrical changes in the air.) The ship's flogging device, the cat-o'-nine-tails demonstrates again the association between cat and the number nine. In the American Deep South existed an old superstition, practised even today, about what to answer to a marriage proposal. The potential bride plucks three hairs from a cat's tail, folds them in a piece of paper and places them on the doorstep overnight. In the morning she will retrieve the envelope and respond to the proposal depending on whether the hairs resemble either a Y or N.

What of those cats immortalized in literature? From Poe's *The Black Cat*, a darkly cat-themed companion piece to *The Tell-Tale Heart*, to gentler fare, such as Aesop's tale where the cat turns out to be more cunning than the fox. Or Kipling's *The Cat That Walked by Himself*? Or the brave, dashing Puss-in-Boots? Or how about the character who set off to sea with the Owl in a pea-green boat? Or T.S. Eliot's Growltiger, or Graymalkin, the cat mentioned in Shakespeare's *MacBeth*? The Cheshire Cat from Wonderland, or Simpkin of Beatrix Potter fame?

The poetic descriptions of the Rainbow Bridge, a purportedly celestial place where a pet goes when it dies, only to be reunited with its owner? The story of how Pussy Willows got its name: when the kittens fell into the river and were saved from drowning by the long reeds consciously bending over for the kittens to grab onto and pull themselves up to the safety of the riverbank? Cats make popular characters in kids' cartoons from the smart-alec Garfields and Top Cats to the not-so-resourceful Toms and Sylvesters.

And continuing with cat lore, taking it into the modern age, I will recount what I consider to be twelve of the most interesting urban legends relating to cats, in no particular order. Urban legends, as you might be aware, are those stories that were once rooted in reality but have become exaggerated and distorted over time, handed down to successive generations as pieces of sensationalist fiction.

Perhaps the oldest and most persistent myth, dating back to the Middle Ages, is the superstition about an evil or jealous cat leaping into the crib, sitting on a sleeping baby's chest and stealing their breath, maybe suffocating them in the process. In truth, cats tend to be attracted to the scent of milk on the baby's breath and have, in rare instances, been known to inadvertently smother the infant, hence their longstanding, somewhat misconstrued reputation as a thief of a baby's breath.

There is the more recent stand-alone yarn of a cat-owning couple who keep receiving massive water bills and they can't figure out how they could possibly be using so much water. One day, the husband is forced to stay at home, too unwell to go to work, and, while resting, he unexpectedly hears the sound of running water. He investigates the noise and discovers the cause of the high water bills. He finds their cat on the lavatory, entertaining itself, by repeatedly flushing the toilet and watching the water swirl down the pan.

Maintaining the relationship between cats and modern technology, you occasionally hear of stories of cats that develop a fascination with vacuum cleaners, and the suction of those Dyson multiple vortex jobbies is so powerful that it attaches to the rear end of the poor animal and sucks the innards out through the rectum, practically eviscerating it. Speaking from experience, televisions prove to be a great source of fascination for cats, causing them to paw and chase the animals on the screen. One particular owner would leave her TV on to the Wildlife Channel to keep her cat occupied while she went to work. One particular evening, she returned to find the whole house had burned down. The poor animal had apparently tried to get inside the TV to get at the birds, chewing on the electrical cables, electrocuting itself in the process and consequently setting fire to the house. In some stories, the cat is the only thing that survives the blaze unscathed.

A couple moves into their dream house to encounter strange footsteps, scratching sounds under the floorboards, unpleasant smells, unearthly night-time wailings and a pungent liquid trickling down the walls, all Amityville Horror-style. It turns out that the previous owner's Siamese cat had gone missing before the move. When the floorboards are lifted, a thin and miserable Siamese emerges from inside the structure of the house, where it had survived on mice and gone about its business between the floors, having got trapped in the loft.

The Tranquilized Travelling Cat relates the tale of an owner who is preparing to go on holiday. He knows from experience that his cat turns into the Devil Incarnate in his car, so this time he goes to the vet and requests his cat be tranquilized for the duration of the trip. The attending vet turns out to be a recent graduate and he administers an injection of morphine. On the drive up, the cat goes berserk, screaming, clawing the carrier and generally turning into a wild thing. The owner completes the journey, nearly crashing the car, his nerves shot. Back at the vet's, the senior partner delivers a stern lecture to his junior: *Are you crazy? Didn't they teach you in veterinary school, that, unlike in humans, morphine doesn't sedate cats? It makes them highly excitable!* Some weeks later, the junior vet bumps into the cat's owner by chance. The owner describes the terribleness of the journey, then adds: *But I'm extremely grateful to you. Just imagine how much more of a total maniac my cat would have been if you* hadn't *sedated him!*

At one time, photos of the Incredible 'Cabbit' circulated on the Internet. The owner claimed that their cat had mated with their bunny rabbit and spawned cat-rabbit offspring. The photos were obviously doctored. Just because cats and rabbits share the same number of chromosomes doesn't mean they are capable of interbreeding and producing hybrid young. Genetically impossible – there is no DNA evidence to support such a far-fetched claim. If you thought that the idea of 'cabbits' was preposterous, what about the pictures of 'squittens'?

Animal Rights' activists have always been the bane of vivisection companies, who were falsely accused of sending out unmarked vans onto the streets to pick up strays or paying large sums of money to catteries for their unclaimed or unadopted cats in order to conduct their supposedly inhumane animal experiments. The cosmetics industry has been frequently implicated in animal-testing their products.

If the suggestion of experimenting on cats wasn't bad enough, what about Bonsai Kitten E-lore which promotes the art of putting a kitten into a flask so that the growing kitten's bones adopt the shape of the flask. Or those cat-skinning ranches you hear about in the Far East, where cats are farmed for their fur. Their prized hide ends up in trinkets and furry figurines which are eventually sold to animal-lovers in the West.

What about eating cat-flesh? Tales of cat-eating have existed for hundreds of years. In Charles Dickens' *The Pickwick Papers*, Sam Weller tells Mr. Pickwick that he's heard about pies made from kittens being sold on the London streets posing as ordinary meat pies. Public Health Inspectors recently closed down an Indian restaurant in Birmingham for using Whiskas in their seekh kebabs. That's nothing compared to the anecdote of the University student who strides into a Cantonese restaurant in Manchester, marches to the front of the queue and plonks a dead, stiff cat on the counter, announcing: *That's the last one I'm getting for you tonight!* China and Korea have received a bad press for their centuries-old, cat-eating culture.

Cats have also been thought of being home wreckers by some cat-haters. One revenge tale involves a wife who adores her cat to the absolute exclusion of her husband – a little too close to home. The husband buys a parrot to keep him company and tries to tolerate his wife's cat until he comes home one day to find the cat has eaten his pet bird, evidenced by the parrot feathers protruding from the cat's mouth. Controlling his anger, he cooks a delicious casserole for dinner. His wife appreciates the candlelit dinner and wine but remains preoccupied with the whereabouts of her sweet, adorable Tiddles, whom she hasn't seen all evening. The husband triumphantly reveals the secret, main ingredient of his cuisine, and the wife's horrified eyes are drawn slowly to the bones on her plate . . .

Finally, I will tell you the freaky tale of a cat who falls foul of traffic. The driver gets out of the truck and finds the cat stuck beneath the front wheel, its head crushed and virtually decapitated. However, to his amazement, he hears a miraculous rasping sound coming from the cat's severed windpipe. He can't believe it's still breathing and takes the near-headless body of the cat to the local vet. The vet supposedly informs him that the hindbrain was left intact for the body systems to still function.

I have digressed to a large extent from my narrative, but as a Professor of Medieval History, I understand the mythology surrounding the Cat.

People have spent a lifetime observing and interacting with cats. They believe cats possess powers we can only dream of, whether you call them 'magical', 'supernatural,' 'paranormal,' or simply 'cats being cats'. There is scientific evidence to suggest they have a remarkable talent for predicting plagues and earthquakes and a death in the family. Cats have even been known to pinpoint cancer from the death-breath of a person. Cats can wail at the same frequency as a crying human baby so that the person is forced to respond to the noise. There are even tales of cats dying, only weeks later for their owners to feel little ghost paws patting their cheek or to suddenly hear purring when there is no cat in sight. Pet psychics and animal afterlife experts believe that dearly-departed cats can *choose* to reincarnate and return to us in another feline vehicle to watch over their owner, to resume that spiritual connection with their loved ones, manifesting previous patterns of behaviour and character traits, a soul *imprint*. You cannot read these stories without feeling a chilling sense of fascination, along with a renewed appreciation for the unique psychic abilities inherent to cats, whether they are thought of as divine or demonic. It's that old saying: *Thousands of years ago, cats were worshipped as gods. Cats have never forgotten this.*

Whether Faerieland shines from its eyes or it forms a bridge between the inner and outer worlds of gods and man, once a sacred idol of the Ancient Egyptians and later rumoured to be a diabolical consort to the Witch, reputed to being a clairvoyant and soothsayer, no other creature has been an object of worship and pilgrimage and ritual sacrifice than the Cat, exciting people's imaginations and attracting a rich plethora of myth and legend, fable and folklore and fairytale literature. It is either honoured and loved or feared and condemned, treated with either respect or dread.

I had a cat in the house. When discussing his feline companion, Marlon Brando once joked: *I live in my cat's house.* I was beginning to feel the same. Except, as Anthea and I approached another critical juncture in our relationship, I would soon start to feel threatened by Presto and, in fact, begin to fear him.

6

That pivotal, make-or-break moment in our marriage occurred a month later. We made love less and less until eventually we stopped doing it altogether – *no boom-boom tonight, my adorable one?* Despite our busy lifestyles, we had always taken time to have sex, which we had thoroughly enjoyed, and we were great together in bed. It was a nice way to unwind last thing at night, to express our affection and passion for each other, bringing us closer together, cementing our love in physical form. Marriage might have made our love legitimate in the eyes of God and the

Law, but our nightly acts of naked unity provided us with a good enough release of our feelings towards one another. Lovemaking is regarded as an essential ingredient in the bedrock of any long-lasting relationship, and although there can always be exceptions, its lack of can often result in the failure of a marriage.

Neither of us attended Deanna's funeral. Anthea did not speak of Deanna, and when I broached the subject, she carefully deflected the conversation to another, more neutral topic.

Anthea had stopped cooking for me. Then the lovemaking dwindled away, and she stopped going to work altogether, relying on her assistant to organize the first exhibition of an up-and-coming artist by the name of Heidi Schilling, supervise Grand Opening Night.

I don't know how it happened. The change in our relationship had been gradual, insidious. Were we growing apart or was there something more sinister at work?

I did not masturbate to channel my sexual frustrations even if wanking is something that men do. Why should I when I've got a beautiful woman in the house?

So, while I grew ever-more frustrated and anxious, Anthea grew ever-more preoccupied with her cat. I say 'her' cat because Presto was rarely spending time with me anymore, not even chasing my LED laser in hunting mode, but fast becoming a permanent fixture in her life. He mooched around the house as if he owned the place, generally ignoring me, and continued to monopolize my darling Anthea, hardly ever out of her sight. I got the eerie and somewhat unpleasant feeling that she belonged to him, rather than vice versa. I remembered the roomful of dogs he had spooked out at the vet's many months back, Samson's unexpected fearful reaction to him and Deanna's peculiar final words to us, claiming that Presto was *not* a cat after accusing him of assaulting her. Then, subsequently hearing the awful news of her demise.

Our world was making less and less sense to me. A dark foreboding took root in my head and, as time went on, began to grow.

We slept in separate beds now, in different rooms, a strange state of affairs. I did not formally question our sleeping arrangements, just considered it a phase we were going through and dearly hoped our crisis would pass soon. I would sometimes wake up in the middle of the night, hearing the sounds of coupling coming from Anthea's room. It was faint at first, but as I got up and went to investigate, the noise – Anthea in the unmistakable throes of carnal pleasure – would grow louder until I flung open her bedroom door, and the sound would instantly disappear wherein, by the weird, middle-of-the-night lighting from the bedside lamp, I would find Anthea under the duvet, sound asleep, and her gentle feline bedfellow fanned out at the foot of the bed, tail curled neatly, sleeping fitfully. Maybe I imagined it, I would tell myself, but as I kept being awoken from my slumber in the nights that followed, I could have sworn I could hear the distinct moans of Anthea in sexual congress. But, as always, my suspicions yielded nothing out of the ordinary when I went to check: just mistress and cat sleeping undisturbed on the bed. Some truth, I suppose, in the saying that the owner soon takes on the characteristics of their pet. Anthea was indulging more and more in Presto's favourite pastime: sleep.

Then, the unthinkable happened. They say that a cat makes all the difference between coming home to an empty house and coming home. Jean Cocteau, the French film director, stated that he loved cats because he enjoyed his home, and bit by bit, they would become its visible soul. I would have agreed with these old chestnuts once but not after I arrived home from work one wet, late September day to encounter a sight I thought not possible outside of those sick, online shock-sites you sometimes hear about, peddling Porsche Girl-style photos or videos of actual suicidal people jumping off motorway bridges or degenerate sexual acts involving someone shitting into another's willing mouth.

Anthea had grown increasingly lethargic, apathetic even, refusing to get out of her night-clothes, as though her spirit were fading away. She didn't look good: her blond hair was tangled, her face pale and filled with stark lines of tiredness, dark circles under her eyes. She neglected her work, calling in long-term sick, delegating all her responsibilities to her assistant, who was more than capable of holding the fort in the boss's absence. She was still asleep in bed, with Presto tucked up alongside, when I headed off to University that morning. I missed her dearly, yet all the while she was in the same house as me. Amidst our disintegrating marriage, I had begun to gravely question my wife's sanity.

After what I saw on returning home that evening, it left me with little doubt.

Getting home, I turned the key in the front door and drifted in. The house was in darkness, except for the kitchen, light shining out from the slit under the closed door at the end of the hallway. I wandered down the hall, hoping that Anthea might be busy preparing dinner. I opened the door . . . and I dropped my satchel where I stood, out of sheer shock.

Anthea had certainly prepared dinner: she was sitting on the floor, wearing a day-old pink négligée, back pressed against the cabinet beneath the kitchen sink, legs spread wide, panty-less, Presto's face buried in her crotch, licking off the gourmet cat food liberally smeared on her euphemistic catflap.

I didn't speak for a whole minute, succumbing to the profane surrealism of the scene. Men have been known to go crazy at the sight of a woman's breasts or the smell of cunt in the morning, but before me was a sexual image so far past kinky and obscene, so far beyond the barnyard, that initially I thought my mind was playing tricks on me again. Then, as I began to process and *believe* what I was witnessing, that the woman I loved had actually persuaded her cat to dine off her private parts and, being an obedient cat, Presto had accepted without protest, like bees attracted to honey, I felt my stomach rise and I fought hard to hold down its contents that threatened to spew out.

Somehow my voice came back to me, albeit shakily at first. "What the fuck are you doing, woman?"

For the first time, Anthea noticed I was standing there. She looked up, but there was no shame or embarrassment in her dull expression, nor did she make any physical attempt to hide her modesty. The cat continued to feed off her contentedly, the sound of his tongue softly scraping against her pubic hairs, without acknowledging my presence. "Hi there, Si," Anthea uttered, looking and sounding faraway, as though lost in a reverie or an opium haze. "Hard day at the office, hon?"

"Have you gone completely gaga?" I exclaimed, incredulous and incensed.

She glanced down momentarily at the undisturbed feeding tom, finally realizing what I was referring to, then looked back up at me. "Oh, don't mind Presto. He's hungry. I thought paté."

"But why . . .?" I responded, unable to find the right words to express my disgust and revulsion at Anthea's mindlessly laidback explanation for her perverted behaviour. It wasn't just plain weird, but downright *insane*, probably warranting detention in a mental hospital. Worse, I wondered how long it had been going on for while I'd been at work. I remembered the time, not so long ago, when Anthea told me about Presto climbing onto the toilet cistern behind her and peering down, full of curiosity, to inspect her deposit in the bowl.

"I told you he's famished . . ." she justified, devotedly and dementedly.

I stared at her, seeing the absurdly serene smile, the perturbing vacancy in her eyes, and realized I just might be looking into the eyes of my ex-wife, that we might have finally crossed the point of no return. A surge of anger flared through me and I reached down and grabbed the perplexed cat by the scruff. I booted the bewildered animal across the kitchen. Presto howled loudly and bounced off the wall, self-righting before landing on the floor perfectly. He glared at me balefully, baring the tips of his fangs and hissing, back arched high, his fur stiff in spikes, making him look rather punk. I was taking no shit from this animal, which had come between me and my wife, somehow bewitched her, bound her to his will, turned her into someone crazier than those batty ladies you hear about who keep a clowder of cats in their pee-stinking house and admit to breast-feeding them. As I began to advance towards him, Presto knew what was best for him and scrammed out of the kitchen door, disappearing into the darkness.

"Why did you have to scare him off like that?" Anthea demanded to know, her thinking and voice regressing, sounding as hurt and offended as a little girl. "I was enjoying that!" She remained seated on the floor, spreadlegged, re-focusing her attention on her cat, the only thing that seemed to matter to her in her ever-decreasing universe, trying to call him back, despite being well-aware of his inability to hear. "Presto . . . puss-puss-puss . . . *come and get it!*"

I could only gawp at her stupidity, her wanton lunacy. Then, standing over her, I yelled down, "Get it together, you *crazy* bitch!" and stormed out of the kitchen but not before grabbing a bottle of Glenfiddich.

I tramped down the hallway, sensing Presto skulking – and sulking – in the shadows. Without switching on the light, I took the stairs and found myself in the guest bedroom where I collapsed onto the bed. The fury in me leeched out in an instant, replaced by sorrow, and I choked back sobs. What on earth had happened to our love? How had it come to this?

Choosing to sit in the dark and assess my life, I took a large gulp of scotch. I needed to talk to someone, and steadying myself, I gave Hugh a ring. Hugh knew I was aware he was currently on vacation with his Essex girl in the Canary Islands, but he still answered his mobile. He must have realized I would not be ringing him at the risk of a huge phone bill unless it was absolutely urgent.

I apologized for calling him on holiday and asked how it was going, what he was up to. Informing me he was drinking Sangria at a beach bar, he didn't waste any time in asking me what was wrong. He had detected the distress in my voice. I confided in him: the feeling of apartness from Anthea that had spiralled into actual separation and madness in recent weeks, culminating in her unorthodox way of feeding her cat. I broke down, crying, and he consoled me over the phone.

"The cat is taking its toll on your relationship," Hugh explained. "It sounds as though it has enchanted your lady. You have to get rid of it."

"How?"

"Give it away, dump it in a cattery . . . but I suspect he'll come back. People do claim there is something supernatural about cats. I don't know why, but the Count of Saint Germain springs to mind."

As a History Professor, I was familiar with the fellow. "You're saying he's got something to do with it," I asked, mystified. "That's quite a leap. The man's been dead for two hundred years."

"Perhaps . . . Perhaps not. He claimed to be able to speak to the animals, Dr. Doolittle-style. Some people even claimed he was capable of transforming into any animal he chose, his favourite animal allegedly being the cat. Others claimed he had mastery over the power of reincarnation. In the meantime, I would take Anthea to the doctor and get her assessed."

"If she'll agree to it . . ."

"Do you want me to cut short my holiday?" Hugh offered, concerned. "I could take the first flight out."

"No, it's okay. Please enjoy the rest of your holiday. I'll handle it."

"You sure?"

"Yes."

"Fine, I trust your judgement. But if there's anything else, please do not hesitate to ring me, night or day . . ."

I thanked him for his time and support, he wished me luck and I hung up.

I lay in darkness for the next couple of hours, swigging straight from the scotch bottle. The scotch warmed me up, relaxed me, pushed aside my misery. I didn't even bother wondering what Anthea was doing downstairs. I reflected on my conversation with Hugh and recalled his mention of the Count of St. Germain. Why not St. Gertrude of Nivelles, if it had something to do with cats, considering she was supposed to be their patron saint? How was this enigmatic figure from history, Count St. Germain, involved in all this? I pledged to do some research on this fellow tomorrow.

I must have been tired or relatively drunk because I don't remember nodding off. I must have nodded off because I dreamed . . .

I dream everything is back to normal – or so I initially think – and I am making sweet love to Anthea. She looks fine again, miraculously so, not the bedraggled, unglamorous madwoman of late, fixated on her damned cat. "I didn't mean to neglect you, Si," she gasps with apology . . . and promise.

"Guess we need to make up for lost time, my sex kitten," I whisper back into her gleeful eyes, thoroughly aroused.

The full moon shines down through the window, illuminating the bedroom floor in ethereal tones, adding to the romance. My hands clutch the sides of her naked, beautifully-contoured body – her trim hips, her exposed stomach, her generous bosom with their attentive nipples – as she straddles me, rising and falling over the shaft of my rigid penis. We maintain our penetrating rhythm as ivory moonlight bounces off our glistening, excited flesh, and we intensify our exertions as we draw closer to climax. Sliding harder and forcibly deeper, I am unable to hold back, and I catch my breath at the apex of orgasm, erupting into her dripping delta, our love-juices mingling, while Anthea synchronizes with me with masterful precision, like she has done a thousand times before, enthusing me with a sharp, sated cry and a grimace of blissful anguish. A sensation of swelling euphoria emanates from my groin and radiates up through the rest of my being.

Somewhere nearby, perhaps from a neighbour's window, I hear Ted Nugent's Cat Scratch Fever start up, a rock classic that either refers to cat-borne diseases in plain-speak, or sexually-transmitted infections picked up from a succession of loose women, or maybe not a sign of promiscuity but the animal scratches sometimes sustained across the back in the heat of passion – interpret it as you will.

Anthea climbs off me, releasing a wild ecstatic yowl as my peculiar barbed penis – I never noticed my penis was barbed before – rakes her moist vaginal wall. She licks her lips desirously and bends silently forward, intimating she is unfinished with me, her golden hair cascading over her face like a provocative waterfall. Seconds later, I feel her mouth close over my deflating penis, her tongue wrapped exquisitely around the sensitive helmet, tasting the milky cum still oozing spasmodically out of my one-eyed snake, making me quiver all over, tingle with a zillion, infinitesimal electric shocks.

From the corner of my eye, I see Presto enter the room soundlessly. Master of All That He Surveys, he finds my wife astride me on all fours feverishly sucking me off, slaking her own concupiscent thirst, and his rapt, lambent-green stare causes spidery feelings to crawl along my back, and I smile hesitantly, nervously. With a twitch of his whiskers and a swish of his tail, he gives me a long, knowing look before slinking back into the shadows. Having retreated into the darkest corner of the bedroom, his eyes continue to gleam with a gold-green omnipresence, taking in my measure, my pleasure, my superstitions, my secrets within.

Now you shall kneel before the immortal Comte de St. Germain, I hear the fiend in my head, as though this particular loving session represents some unspoken rite-of-passage.

Yes, you're the boss of me, I think, almost in a trance. When I finally do manage to rip my gaze away from those blazing, mesmeric eyes, I see my darling Anthea has vanished and her place taken by three cats I instantly recognize from my childhood: the white Persian, Cleopatra, the ginger tabby, Boadicea, and the black Bombay, Erzulie. They carry on from where Anthea has left off, gathered around my crotch, their tongues flicking tentatively, delicately, across my semi-erect member, lapping up my spent semen . . .

The glow-in-the-dark, emerald eyes seem to sneer, to mock: Cat got your tongue . . .?

The unnatural ministrations of those familiar pussycats revolt me greatly, and I scrabble backwards against the headboard and shoo them away with an unintelligible yelp and a stricken *sweep of my arm, and–*

–I bolted upright, wide awake, checking my bearings. The bedroom was bathed in bright morning light, and I was still wearing yesterday's clothes. The whisky bottle was empty. Presto was nowhere to be seen.

"*Oh fuck . . .!*" I muttered, vividly recalling those erotic – and later *sick* – images in my mind. I realized I must have got drunk and dreamed it all. Cats, it seemed, were very sexual creatures.

You cannot escape me . . . I heard a mysterious whisper from somewhere afar, then sinister chuckling, fading away to nothing. Perhaps the last vestiges of my dream.

Sex on the brain, I rationalized. *My subconscious must be trying to make sense of the events of last night as well as reminding me of my own sexual frustration, a burning desire to reconnect with my wife on an intimate, physical level.*

There are two means of refuge from the miseries of life: music and cats, Dr. Albert Schweitzer, regarded by some as the Mother Teresa of Medicine, had once philosophized. I begged to differ.

Coming home yesterday evening and seeing what Anthea was doing, I had, in a figurative sense, aged twenty years. By the morning, experiencing that deeply-disturbing perversion of a dream, I was ready to pick up my pension. Hell, I was talking bestiality. And my back stung. When I checked myself in the dressing mirror, the scratches on my back turned out to be real.

And, yet, what did the centuries-dead Count of St. Germain have to do with any of this?

I had to determine the measure of the man and the temperature of the threat.

7

Most modern historians consider the Count of St. Germain to be one of the most intriguing figures in history with conflicting accounts about his life, rumours documented as fact and wild tales about his age. I do not intend to paint a very perplexing portrait but wish to winnow out what I can and keep it simple – let me tell you what I know and what I think.

One evening, in 1740, a stranger dressed in black arrived in Paris. From the dazzling collection of diamond rings he sported and expensive black, silken clothes he wore, the upper echelons of society took him for a nobleman and welcomed him into the fashionable circles of Parisian life. In the distinguished company of writers, philosophers, scientists, freemasons and aristocrats, the Count proved to be a charming, witty conversationalist, qualifying as a true raconteur, full of regal aplomb, and coming across as an all-round genius, displaying remarkable knowledge and an incredible plethora of talents. He was a gifted singer, an accomplished pianist and a virtuoso on the violin and harpsichord, a fine artist and classical sculptor, and a multi-linguist who spoke fluent French, English, Spanish, Portuguese, Dutch, Italian, Greek and Russian, even Arabic, Sanskrit and Mandarin. Admired by the gentlemen and adored by the ladies, he recounted his many adventures, including visits to the court of the Shah of Persia, where he had learned the secrets of the jeweller's craft. Insinuating links to the Rosicrucians and the Kabbalists, the Illuminati and the Knights Templar, he demonstrated an impressive understanding of arcane matters and hinted towards occult powers, suggesting control over the elements and lower, intelligent species of life, a whisperer of animals. But what divided his awestruck listeners was his extraordinarily blasphemous claim, once the course of conversation turned to religious matters, that he was nearly two thousand years old. He confessed to being the Jewish shopkeeper, Cartaphilus, and revealed to have known Jesus of Nazareth personally. He described in minute detail the miraculous wine-into-water feat at the wedding of Cana, as if it had happened only yesterday. He had always believed that Jesus had been a troublemaker, prophesizing that Jesus would 'meet a bad end'. He claimed he had been a prosecution witness at the trial of Jesus in the judgement hall of Pontius Pilate. As Christ halted for a moment's rest from dragging his cross through the streets of Calvary, Cartaphilus had mocked him, demanding he hurry up. Christ had apparently replied, 'I will carry on my journey, but thou shalt wait for my return...' and, with those rather cryptic words, Jesus, escorted by the Roman soldiers, continued on his way to his crucifixion. It was not until decades later that Cartaphilus realized what Christ had meant when he saw his close friends dying of old age while he had not aged at all. The Count of St. Germain had learned that his punishment was to wander the earth without aging until Christ's Second Coming. He would be the one people would come to call the Wandering Jew.

He spoke of his passing encounters with various famous historical figures during his countless travels and, as the skeptical historians tried to catch him out on trivial details, he would always reply with such unerring accuracy as to leave the person quite baffled, beguiled by his inexhaustible knowledge of science and history. Old Countess von Georgy immediately recognized the black-clad nobleman as the same individual she had met fifty years previously in Venice, where she had been ambassadress, confused by how he still looked the same age now as he had then: about forty-five. It wasn't long before the stories of the mysterious, self-styled Count of St. Germain attracted the attention of the King of France, Louis XV, who invited him to attend the Royal Court. The Count accepted the invitation and succeeded in captivating the King and his courtiers, as well as Madame de Pompadour, the King's mistress. Voltaire was deeply impressed, calling the Count 'a man who knows everything and never dies'.

Count St. Germain lodged in London from 1743 for two years, setting up a laboratory and conducting closely-guarded experiments of an alchemical nature. He had already claimed earlier that he had once taught Nicholas Flamel the secret of the Universal Medicine, the ability to transmute base metals to gold. His mastery over Nature allegedly went as far as discovering the Philosopher's Stone and the rejuvenating Elixir of Life. The ladies, flattered by his private musical performances of the sonatas and arias he composed and the recipes he prescribed for the removal of facial wrinkles, felt he meant 'everything to everybody'. In the evenings, the Count was a frequent guest at the prestigious Kit-Kat Club, mingling with members of the highest nobility. Here, the Count astounded people by talking of an invention he was working on, the steam train, twenty years before James Watt put together his crude prototype of the steam engine and almost eighty-five years before George Stephenson's Rocket of 1829. In 1745, when English xenophobia was at its peak during the Jacobite rebellion, the Count of St. Germain was arrested on suspicion of espionage, suspected of being a Jacobite sympathizer. Both Horace Walpole, the son of Sir Robert Walpole, Britain's first Prime Minister, and the Prince of Wales became involved. Yet, instead of being imprisoned, the Count was released. Just why this occurred still remains a mystery. One curious report circulated claiming that the Count had used hypnotic suggestion to 'persuade' his detainers that he was innocent. Anton Mesmer, who is credited with the discovery of hypnotism, had stated years before that the Count possessed a 'vast understanding of the workings of the human mind' and had been directly responsible for teaching Mesmer the art of hypnosis. There was even an unsubstantiated rumour floating about that claimed the Count of St. Germain was in fact deaf and he communicated solely by psychic means.

History records that King Louis XV employed the Count of St. Germain for a series of diplomatic missions. In 1760, the Count was sent to the Hague to help settle the peace treaty between Prussia and Austria. In 1762, the Count took part in the deposition of Peter III of Russia and took an active role in bringing Catherine the Great to the throne. After the death of Louis XV in 1774, the Count warned the new monarch, King Louis XVI and the Queen, Marie Antoinette, of the approaching danger of the French Revolution, which he described as a 'gigantic conspiracy that will overthrow the order of things'. Of course, the warning went unheeded, and among the final entries in her diary, Marie Antoinette recorded her regret at not having taken the Count's advice seriously. In his memoirs Giacomo Casanova recalled several meetings with the celebrated Count of St. Germain, and how the Count was 'in spite of his manifold eccentricities, learned in all matters of love . . . I thought him an astonishing man as he was always astonishing me'.

On 27th February 1784, Prince Charles of Hesse-Cassel, Germany, announced the news that the Count was dead, having caught pneumonia in his draughty laboratory, with plans for him to be buried at the local church in Eckenforde. Among the crowd attending the funeral service were many prominent occultists, including Cagliostro, Anton Mesmer and the philosopher Louis St Martin. As the coffin was lowered into the grave, many of the mourners sobbed at the unbelievable: the death of the immortal count. A death as profound as the news of the death of Pan might have once seemed when received by the pagan world. However, rumours persisted that the Count of St. Germain was not buried that day, and countless witnesses have come forward, testifying to having seen the supposedly dead Count after the funeral. Cagliostro was suspected of being the Count in disguise for some time. Myths, legends and speculations continued to abound. It is alleged the Count was seen in Egypt during Napoleon's campaign.

In 1896, Russian theosophist Madame Blavatsky claimed the Count had been in contact with her, and she proclaimed that he belonged to a race of immortals who lived in a subterranean country called Shambhala, north of the Himalayas. He was seen in the Russian court during the First World World. In 1919, Aleister Crowley claimed to have met the Count, who foresaw the rise of a Jewish-born Antichrist almost twenty years before the advent of World War II.

In theosophical circles, the Count of St. Germain was hailed as a supernatural being called a Master of Ancient Wisdom, or Ascended Master, possessed of magical powers, such as the ability to shapeshift, teleport, levitate, walk through walls, communicate by telepathy. According to their esoteric beliefs, the Count had been credited to being various incarnations ranging from High Priest of Atlantis to Merlin the Magician and Counsellor to King Arthur and the key figure in the establishment of the Order of the Knights of the Round Table, to the true author of all the Shakespearean plays revealed by cipher code that the texts supposedly employed, to the incognito king and reincarnated son of Francis Rakoczy II, Prince of Transylvania, in the seventeenth century, to the man who inspired the Founding Fathers to draft the United States Declaration of Independence, as well as providing the design of the Great Seal of the United States, to having been the Forefather of the Scientific Revolution. Guy Ballard claimed the Count of St. Germain was in fact a space tourist, who once introduced him to visitors from the planet Venus during his alleged 1930 encounter with the Count on Mount Shasta in California. The Ballards formed a group called the I AM Foundation, which disseminated many channelled messages from the Count and published a portrait of the Count as a dark, bearded, Christ-like figure, comparing him to God. They identified him as the person responsible for the New Age culture of the Age of Aquarius. The I AM cult took their name from God's profound response to Moses when Moses asked His name. *I Am that I Am*, God replied, almost a refusal of a name, meaning you cannot know My name, that I have been here before Time and will be here forever, without end, to look over My people. Just as theologians speak of 'Impassibility': that God does not experience pleasure or pain, no suffering or temptation, free of all emotions and sin. Existence and essence are identical in God alone. Everything else receives existence. For example, the existence of a caterpillar is distinct from its essence; it participates in existence. In the Gospel of John, when asked, Jesus replied: 'Before Abraham was, I *am*,' which upset the Jews greatly, because Jesus was applying the Divine Name and Eternity to himself. Jesus was therefore seen to be as much of an Ascended Master to the I AM Activity as the Count St. Germain, making it an organization of Christian persuasion.

So who was this ubiquitous man, romantic hero and scientific genius, whose longevity some believed reached back to the time of Christ, appearing throughout history even as recently as the 1970s, never seeming to have aged in all that time? Could the stories of his immortality be dismissed as mere nonsense, that the Count was nothing more than a charlatan or just plain deluded? Or could it be possible that this mysterious dandy really did discover the secret of defeating death through a cycle of earthly re-embodiments, achieving a higher plane of existence, communicating with these questionable messengers in order to guide Mankind out of his self-created darkness and into the Divine Wisdom?

Cults are not my thing. They offer a counterintuitive belief in supernatural entities and Life's intractable mysteries, most bridging the gap between reincarnation, the Abrahamic god and fringe religions.

You may think I'm completely bonkers when I talk about this nonsense and I wouldn't blame you, but I began to suspect that the Count of St. Germain had somehow pervaded our lives in Upper Nasebury in the shape of our cat until I was utterly adamant that this was the case and there could be no convincing me otherwise. I didn't know when the Count of St. Germain became our cat or at what point our cat became the Count of St. Germain, whether his undying soul had taken up residence for whatever unknowable purpose in our cat or Presto was the direct reincarnation of the man. I mean who's to say they weren't one and the same? Perhaps Count St. Germain had been banished from the Spiritual Hierarchy of Heaven for whatever reason, regressing to animal form, trapped between human incarnations. After all, was he not once referred to as the 'Lovely Man of Paris'? What if as the cat's brain developed, the Count's personality and power would become more apparent, causing extreme personality shifts in those he wished to manipulate, getting inside their head, splitting the mind? For he knew that the door would open some day when he would be ready to come back in.

I am mindful that my leap of faith could be described as extreme, preposterous, risible, for a normally grounded, rational and well-educated fellow like myself, but considering how far events had progressed since we'd first taken in the cat, it seemed the only explanation that, despite stretching plausibility, made any [obscure] iota of sense.

8

Now, instead of just ignoring me, Presto began to taunt me. I think he knew that I knew. We had once shared a special manly connection with play. I hadn't realized he shared a different connection with my wife. He had stolen my wife, but I was getting more attention from her cat than her, even if he no longer had quality time for me. Anthea and I had loved each other until we got the cat. 'Hautcature': our dandified cat. He had been a consistent presence in our lives ever since Anthea had dropped him as a kitten on my chest. What on earth had happened to our sweet, furry ball of loveliness?

And there was me feeling sorry for him once, imagining him wondering there must be more to life than the confines of this house, eating and sleeping, watching the birds and playing with the laser light. A sociable, affectionate, energetic little thing, yet deaf and vulnerable. Now, however, our cat had discovered his true meaning in life. I didn't know my cat anymore. And he had suddenly become the most important thing in the house. *Probably runs the world, too, but nobody knows it.*

I loved Anthea, *adored* her, but could not believe what had become of her. But

I knew it was the cat that was the problem. The cat was worth more to her than her estranged husband.

Although he generally maintained close proximity to Anthea, who was now looking inexplicably debilitated and constantly scraggly, languishing in bed when she wasn't tending to her cat as though she had no will of her own, now his complete and submissive mistress, damned near oblivious to the rest of the world except him, he would arrive in my presence at the most unexpected moments.

I would be roused from my sleep in the dark of the night to find Presto perched on my chest, his body puffed up to twice its size, staring down at me with his shining, viridian eyes. I would wake up, startled, and he would leap off and dart out of the bedroom in the blink of an eye. I believed he was planning to smother me. On other occasions, I would feel something brush against my ankles at the top of the stairs, and I would promptly grab hold of the banister to regain my balance. I would then just catch Presto slipping off down the landing, merging with the murky shadows.

The little shitter was trying to kill me!

I, too, called in long-term sick, citing depression as a consequence of domestic strife, and the University was very understanding and supportive of me. They even referred me to Occupational Health, but I didn't attend. My sleep was shot and I barely ate. Hugh rang me every so often to check in on me, wondering how I was getting along and if there was anything he could do for me, but I kept our conversation low-key and superficial, not wishing to give anything away, such as my seemingly-preposterous suspicions around my cat harbouring the soul of a mysterious, eighteenth-century nobleman, alchemist and magician, and come across as sounding mad. In the meantime, Hugh informed me he'd got himself a new broad. I was happy for him. I lied and reassured him Anthea and I were getting back together. He was glad I sounded better, and Anthea and I were working things out. When would I be back at work? *Soon*, I told him, *very soon*.

But I had to do something first . . . a deed, despicable though it may be, I must surely complete.

I suffered a recurring dream the following few nights when I did finally manage to drift off to sleep, no matter how briefly I slept.

I dreamt that Anthea died from a long and painful illness. *I don't know if it's breast cancer or something else. Either way, she has stopped eating and, in her anorexic state, she looks emaciated, a near-skeleton. Her last, dying words to me in the hospital room are:* Please look after our lovely man. *Only Presto, once again a kitten, and myself attend her funeral and, as her angry, bereaving husband, instead of looking after our white, deaf housecat to honour her memory, I open the front door and let him out of house to fend for himself, hoping to never see him again and, in the process, find closure from my grief, break my only physical link with my wife and start anew. Told in fragments, the dream switches to my life without my wife, shortly after her passing. If losing my loved one to a terminal illness isn't traumatic enough, I begin to hear unexplained meowing and purring, the feel of whiskers against my face in the middle of the night, and I soon come to the terrible conclusion I am haunted,* jinxed. *And that's when the really bad things start to happen . . .*

The lights go out inexplicably, thrusting the house in darkness. When the lights come back on seconds later, I discover my house has been ransacked and burgled of every last item of furniture. A huge branch falls on the house, destroying the roof and letting in rainwater, which seeps down the framework and floods the ground floor. I smash my car into a tree to avoid a white cat that suddenly appears in the middle of the road ahead of me. I lose my right thumb after accidentally trapping it in a door jamb, watching it swell up and turn necrotic in a matter of seconds. Sitting in the doctor's office, I am diagnosed with the same breast cancer that killed my wife. How can anybody have such a run of bad luck, like it's Friday the Thirteenth every day? What are the chances those evil eyes tracking my destiny are a blend of golden-green?

The dream always culminated in the same way. I would hear Anthea's sweet voice calling my name and, when I pulled aside the bedroom curtain, she would be carrying Presto, still a kitten, in her arms as she floated across the moonlit lawn, like a wraith, dead on midnight. She would silently mouth the words up towards my bedroom window: *Let us be a family again, my love, together forever.* Behind me, dangling from the bedroom ceiling, would be a noose I did not remember fashioning. I would always awaken from my dream in a dripping sweat.

I should have taken Hugh's earlier advice and got Anthea committed. I might have benefited from checking into the booby hatch myself. Anthea's increasing devotion and obedience to her cat had reached fanatical, patently certifiable, self-abasing proportions, and my own justifiable jealousy and rampaging sleep-deprived paranoia that her cat, a vessel to a phenomenal, eighteenth-century alchemist, was plotting to kill me and take over my life drove me to the only solution I could foresee.

Presto must die.

9

All things must head towards their conclusion, I guess. Just like the months we spent with our cat which totted up to almost a year and which I have recounted as comprehensively as I can. I shall do likewise with the rest of it.

I remained deeply concerned for Anthea, the woman I think I still had feelings for. She grew ever-more listless and lustreless, turning into an outright slob. Except slobs get fat from overeating and a lack of exercise. Anthea was losing weight, having shrunk several dress sizes, wasting away like some anorexic or dope addict. *Fading away* – seeming *not there*. Not content with reducing her into a mindless, utterly servile automaton, Presto appeared to be sucking her vitality, her life-energy. She rested firmly under his paw, so to speak. I wanted to come to her rescue, but I felt helpless. The heart may be willing, but the flesh was weak. Besides, she would probably turn against me.

Madness is catching. By what you might call a tenuous link, I believed that Presto was not just a cat, [*lower, intelligent species of life*] but the spirit – reincarnated or otherwise – of an genius/mystic/alchemist going by the name of Count of St. Germain, who [*And Jesus said:* Thou shalt wait for my return.] had somehow figured out a way to live forever.

After his succession of reincarnations in earthly bodies in order to spiritually ascend to the perfected condition of the saints, why should he have taken the form of a cat all of a sudden? What went wrong? I cannot answer that, not that I give a shit. All I knew, the cat, no matter how impawsible, had to go.

How far are you willing to go? I asked myself during that cold snap of early November. *Can I let him get away with what he's done to Anthea? To myself?* The fuck I would! I thought of ways of killing him. I considered poisoning him (with paracetamol, onion powder or chocolate, all toxic to cats), but I knew he would suss me out, and I doubted he would go near anything I might feed him. Maybe I should cut off his whiskers, curbing his power, like Delilah chopping off Samson's hair whilst he slept. What about pouring bleach over the cat, burning his fur, blinding him? The way to a cat's heart is through its stomach . . . grabbing a kitchen knife and shoving and twisting the blade upwards. Disembowel him, hang him up by his intestines. Most people would see the obvious, that I was killing a cat (and not ridding myself of an immortal magician), a crime punishable by imprisonment and a lifetime of hate-mail from Animal Rights' activists. For once, I was rooting for the mouse, in a manner of speaking.

Wearing my black pyjamas and clutching an empty, medium-sized Hessian potato sack in my hand, I stood in the kitchen at midday which, like the rest of the house, had begun to resemble a pigsty. The counters were filthy, and the sink was full of unwashed crockery and cutlery. Unfinished old food, now blue with mould, released an unwholesome stink consistent with untended toilet bowls, with seepage. Like Anthea, I had skipped work in the last fortnight, citing stress, which was an understatement.

"Twinkletoes, come out, come out wherever you are!" I chimed out loudly.

Presto arrived at high speed in my midst as if he'd heard my call. Maybe he did – it wouldn't surprise me, nothing could surprise me anymore. Far from the cowering cat, he moved with a rigid body, his head held low, ears swivelled sideways, his eyes large, black pools, pupils fully dilated, gaze fixed on me, challenge in his leonine expression: the bloodthirsty predator that means serious business.

He growled at me: *Who dares to disturb my royal nap? Do you not understand the measure of my wrath?*

Except he wasn't in actual fact physically talking; he was speaking to me directly into my mind. It was the voice of a demigod, full of cruelty, arrogance, narcissism and evil, matured over countless centuries.

I remembered the nightmarish amount of stress he had put us under lately, the way he had invaded our home, wrecked our relationship and turned our lives upside-down. "*Fuck you!*" I responded as succinctly as possible.

Do not *mock me!* I heard him broadcast into my head. *Don't you know who I am? I, the Comte de St. Germain, am the One that men Fear and Bow and Pray before.*

I threw my head back and dismissed him with a derisive laugh. "You think very highly of yourself. Then why the hell are you stuck as a cat?"

His telepathic communication continued, compelling in its authority and delivery. *One of God's little jests. Soon, however, I shall be free from my incarceration as a feline.*

"Over my dead body!" I declared confrontationally.

I could tell I was cramping his style because he seemed to grow more irate, glaring at me from across the room as though he planned to rip my throat out. *So be it!*

I was suddenly aware of a dark presence in my mind. It was dread, pure and simple. I felt afraid, *very* afraid. My heart suddenly jackhammered out of rhythm, and gooseflesh broke across my skin. Yet, on an inner rational level, I knew dread – or fear – can be overcome if you do not give it credence or let it rule your life. The problem with phobics is that they let their greatest fear bounce around in their head and, if left unchecked, it amplifies to a certain magnitude and begins to affect every aspect of their life, eventually crippling them. Standing there, not ready to succumb to any defeatist attitude, I went about trying to mentally disentangle myself from this viscous, trapped-in-a-web feeling until the sense of fear, like all anxieties, reached a peak, ebbed away and completely passed. "Your little mind-tricks won't work on me. Is that the best you can do?" *Enough games,* I thought, smile gone. *Showdown at High Noon. Each to his own.*

I advanced towards him, bag in hand. Presto moved, too, diagonally, realizing the time had come when there could only be one victor. I slammed shut the kitchen door so he could not escape. We circled one another, neither of us backing down, glares locked and cocked.

It didn't take long for one of us to deal the first blow. With a swift clean strike, my foot caught Presto squarely in the flanks, like I had done precisely the same thing here in the kitchen when he had been feeding from Anthea's intimate place, producing an abrupt mewl, propelling him across the room. He impacted against the wall, grunting, and dropped to the floor. Shaking his head, trying to recover from his daze, Presto received no breathing space as I seized him by the tail and swung him round and round like a helicopter blade, releasing him in mid-flight. Presto struck the window, cracking the glass, and he slid down into the sink. It didn't break his spine. As he scrambled around the sink, his claws clicking on the metal surface, he knocked over the piled crockery, plates and cups, some of which smashed on the kitchen floor. I decided not to give Presto any respite and went after him again. I reached down for him, feeling the rippled silk of his coat, the lithe, supple frame beneath . . . and my fingers closed around his throat as I began to strangle him, twisting and squeezing his little neck . . .

The cat went into a frenzy, fought tooth and claw, at the same time trying to wriggle free. His needle-sharp claws came up and scratched my exposed face. I ignored the blood dribbling warmly down my face from the superficial lacerations, or the burning pain involved, and continued to squeeze harder, driving him towards the waste disposal unit.

Then, in one last-ditch effort, Presto managed to bite down on my right index finger and wouldn't let go. My scream reflex kicked into gear and I couldn't stop the noise.

He leapt out of my grasp and suddenly attached himself to the ceiling and padded fleetingly across like the spiders he used to catch. I stared, momentarily freaked out, by the absurdness of the sight.

But the ceiling couldn't hold him, and he tumbled down to earth, good old gravity fortunately doing its work, cutting short the impossible.

I caught him in my arms and, despite the riot of claws and scratches, teeth and bites, I didn't let up and shoved the struggling cat into the Hessian potato sack, tightening the drawstring.

I looked pitifully down at my finger, bleeding profusely and already beginning to swell.

Now snagged, gagged and bagged, Presto writhed about inside, and I wished to get a big knife and slit him open from groin to throat or dump him in a vat of bleach. I thought, perhaps, of hoisting the bag above my head and smashing it down with great force, stamping on it repeatedly, crushing his tiny bones underfoot, and taking his damned corpse to the animal crematorium for disposal – to make sure. Then, a better, darker, more morbid suggestion popped into my head.

I trooped up to the kitchen counter, undid the sting of the potato sack and pushed the cat into the microwave, immediately jabbing in ten minutes' cooking time. The microwave whirred to life as its plate turned and turned like a fairground carousel. Presto perambulated on the plate, circling one way then the other, peering out, wild-eyed, realizing his immediate fate.

The much-anticipated gunfight in the town of Tombstone had in fact turned out to be nothing more than a brief scuffle, something of an anticlimax. *Purrfect* in many respects. What else were you expecting? No matter how powerful the ageless Count of St. Germain thought of himself, he was relegated to the body of a stupid furry-purry thing and therefore, wearing such a vulnerable guise, limited in what he could do. Having crammed our cat into the microwave, I felt no pity, no remorse. I might not be able to fit the sundered slivers of my splintered heart back together again, but I hoped my action might at least break the hold he had over Anthea. However, I was soon to learn that the Count of St. Germain, aka Cartiphilus, aka Presto, had left an indelible mark on both our souls.

As I watched Presto staring back at me out of the window, alarmed and frightened and furious, paws scrabbling desperately at the door, my nostrils soon picked up the odour of his internal organs beginning to cook from the inside-out, and I wished I had prepared some popcorn to mark the closure of our Year of the Cat and celebrate the impending death of the little shitter.

THWOCK!

Something hard smashed against the back of my head. I collapsed to my knees, receiving a jolt to the brain, right hand coming up to my neck, touching blood and imbedded glass. I glanced over my shoulder and saw a stark-naked, grim-faced, cadaverous-looking Anthea standing over me with her favourite vase in her hand, its base completely shattered, shards of glass scattered across the floor. I watched the contents of the vase, a dozen red roses, once a hopeful, romantic gesture from a bygone era but now withered and dead, fall through the hole at the bottom and tumble to the floor, crumbling like old parchment.

"That's *my* little man!" she proclaimed, with the frostiest of receptions. I noticed the sunken face, the sagging breasts, the prominent ribcage, the months of foul, putrid sweat begriming her shrivelled skin and thinning, lifeless hair. Except her *eyes!* Yes, her eyes . . . they were alive and dancing with madness and blue murder. "Leave my little man alone!" Then, she stepped around me, around the broken glass, and turned off the microwave. One of my hands swiped vaguely at her leg but snatched only air.

The shock hit me before the pain. When the pain did arrive, it was vast and searing and unendurable, like Hell's clarion banging gleefully against the insides of my skull.

I slumped forward, face-down, clutching the sides of my head. Lying on the floor, I tried raising my head as far as it would go, which wasn't much without aggravating the herd of thundering wildebeest stampeding across the plains of my consciousness.

What I witnessed next, though, you may never accept. I would, neither, if I were you, but I would like you to keep an open mind. What I witnessed while struggling to keep my head up or maybe imagined in my semi-conscious or concussed state, despite the absurdity and indescribableness of it, will stay with me forever.

I saw the cat leap out of the open microwave door, unharmed, and saunter up to my face, favouring me with what amounted to a jubilant, condescending, never-dare-fuck-with-me-again look. I expected some form of retribution and geared myself up for it, but it did not materialize. Instead, Presto followed his now-silent mistress out of the kitchen. Then, her impawsible cat proved his impawsibility. By the natural light in the hallway, I saw his shadow cast down low against the cellar door. I swear I beheld, from my current prone, outstretched position on the kitchen floor, the shadow change form, physically transform, swelling and rising upwards until it now took the shape of something that was a cross between human and cat, crouched low, all sinews and claws, poised to spring – a *werecat*, if you will. This proved to be a transient, intermediate stage in its evolution, however, since I can testify that the shadow continued to develop, to metamorphose, growing ever taller, until it was fully upright and very, very human.

"About time, lover," I heard Anthea say in invitation, brimming with girlish excitement, sounding to be near the foot of the stairs. "You have no idea how long I have waited for this moment."

"The wait is over," spoke a male voice, dark, refined and seductive, as the shadow of the man, formerly feline, disappeared outside my range of vision. "The curse is lifted, and as your Lord and Master, you are now *mine* to do as I please!"

The pain hijacking my wounded head grew too intense to stomach or see sense through, and I subsequently blacked out . . .

Epilogue

How does it end, you may ask? And I will tell you, and you will realize it did not end well. The aftermath does not make good reading for either myself or Anthea. We have not been the same since.

Hugh found me. He had called round to check on me because I hadn't been to work for weeks or answered my telephone calls. He found me unconscious on the kitchen floor, bleeding from a head wound.

I remember waking up in hospital, highly agitated and rambling incoherently, warranting restraint from the orderlies as I ranted on about infidelity and immortality and shapeshifting white cats. My paranoia and distress were such, along with the apparent outrageousness of my tale, that I was promptly committed to Chertsford Memorial Hospital, where I still reside.

Anthea stays on a different ward at the hospital. She suffered a complete mental collapse from which she never recovered. Hugh claimed he found her naked upstairs, simulating sexual intercourse. She does not remember me or our life together and seems to have aged half-a-century. I sometimes visit her and talk to her, but she just sits there drooling or mumbling to herself or cackling like an old crone, lost in her own little fantasy world. I want to remember the gorgeous, vivacious, successful art dealer I had married, not this white-haired, demented hag whom I am obligated to visit more out of moral and marital duty rather than from any residual affection. The Count of St. Germain certainly did a fine job on her, absorbing everything that made Anthea uniquely *Anthea*: her beauty, intelligence and individuality. The mind is sometimes the last bastion to fall.

I did not divorce her. I don't have the heart to. I still care about her. To see her go mad has been utter hell for me, knowing that things will never be the same again.

Even stranger than me and my wife losing our sanity is that Hugh has no recollection of Presto. He claims we never had a cat, as do my side of the family. He recalls being drunk at the fated garden party and Deanna suffering premature labour pains. Deanna is still dead though, aborting on the plane, dying from Septicaemia in Hong Kong. Did I dream the whole thing? In the cold light of day, I cannot be sure whether the version of events I remember really happened, but if I am still awake in my hospital room at night, approaching the witching hour, I pull the covers over me like a kid afraid of the closet monster and think that the Count of St. Germain, to add to his prodigious list of talents, has the power to either cloud men's minds and tamper with our memories or actually affect reality and change the physical world around us. As usual, the doctors don't believe me, preferring to patronize me instead. They cannot make me doubt myself or change my perspective of events.

Because I *know*. In my heart of hearts, I know the grotesque truth. I scour through the newspapers, reading between the lines, for any sightings or reports of the Count of St. Germain. I find the true story of an ASBO cat, who stalked the neighbourhood, breaking into houses, frightening children, confronting dogs and mauling a retired, old army lieutenant. I read other news reports of council-estate kids in Netherton showing unspeakable cruelty to cats, including a spate of attacks involving caustic soda being poured over the victim, instantly melting the flesh and blinding the poor creature. I desperately search for news of another couple like us, who eventually went mad – or worse, *perished* – after they take in a cat, who just happens to be white and deaf with gold-green eyes. Let's call him 'Blanc'. Perhaps, their first suspicions are raised when their baby is crying inconsolably, and they learn Blanc is secretly hurting it or feeding off – no, *stealing* – its soul. But Blanc gets away with his household crimes because he is such a 'cute little thing'. The husband probably comes to despise him, but the wife grows fiercely protective of him, at the absolute neglect of her husband and their baby. And Blanc spreads discord at home to the point when the lighted match will be finally tossed into the figurative powderkeg: the husband comes home one day to find the wife in an uncompromising position with the cat . . . and the rest, ladies and gentlemen, is history. Or history repeating itself.

Some people have a special affinity with dogs or hamsters or lovebirds or even tropical fish. My experience, despite its dreadfulness and the catastrophic end-result, how a seventy-kilo History Professor got stymied by a four-kilo cat, has not diminished my fondness for cats.

But do I not remember our cat eventually progressing to human form?

One thing I never quite figured out, though, was why the hell someone as highly gifted and well-acquainted with the world and cast out from the rest of us by the ability to defy all manner of death as the Count of St. Germain, alchemist and mesmerist, shapeshifter and immortal, an Ascended Master, would want to parade around as a deaf, white cat?

Maybe somewhere in there is a tale in itself.

April 2012 – November 2012

Long Live The King

"Until we meet again, may God bless you as he has blessed me."
Elvis Presley

Three Roses: You cannot imagine how much I love you . . .

GENESIS Chapter 1: verse 1: *In the Beginning, there was bubble-poppin' boredom. And Elvis said, 'Let there be Rock'n'Roll, sweet thang!'*

Jimmy Hutton looked down at what he had half-heartedly scribbled into his exercise-book and took a sharp, indrawn breath. The content of his idle meanderings almost caused him to laugh out loud. It looked promising. More than that, it looked inspired. What the heck, it looked like a work of art! *Holy Crow, I done it! I actually done it!* he thought, thrilled, overjoyed by the all-important breakthrough. *I got me a neat, little opening just like I said I would. How's that for genius? The Scripture According to Elvis Presley!*

But no, wait, not so fast! Any room for improvement? he began to muse. *How about changing the boredom to 'beat-the-butt' boredom or 'beat-the-butt-black-and-blue' boredom or, better still, 'beat-the-*teacher-on-the-butt*' boredom?*

Jimmy paused, considered the full impact of what he was conveying. *Overdo it, why don't you? Why does everything have to be 'butts' and 'asses' with you? You always sound as if you're sitting on the can! There's a term for it, you know: anal fixation.* He chuckled at this morbid leap just as the school bell went.

Yeah, that's what you get when you're Chairman of the Bored. At least I'm no butt-kisser like Queer Quincy over there.

Jimmy got up from his desk, filled his holdall with his belongings and slung it over his shoulder while still contemplating the monumental comparison between high school and the can. *SSDD. Same shit, different day. Ah, the* strain *of it! The teacher'd have both your buns in a sling if he ever figured that one out!*

Whether the boredom was 'bubble-popping', as Ann-Marie usually referred to it, or 'beat-the-butt' in his own enlightened opinion, school was out, and the slack, sultry season of summer stretched out ahead of them as promisingly as the untamed, trackless plains of the Old West had once swept out in front of Lewis and Clark, theirs for the taking, with no glimpse of a fall horizon in sight.

A loud cheer ran through the classroom and their English teacher thumped the blackboard repeatedly with the flat of his palm. "Hush, you barbaric lot!" Mr. Kane bellowed, more the dictator, less the disciplinarian. "I want hush, this *instant!*" The commotion subsided, a few low snickers persisting in rebellion. "You can cause as much hullabaloo outside these walls, but, by God, *not* in my classroom!" Above the horn-rimmed glasses, his mean-tempered eyes scowled at the tense, fidgety faces of his students one-by-one as if selecting which unsuspecting motormouth he should put in detention straight after school. He refrained after a while, satisfied with the descending silence. "Okay, you may leave . . . but remember *quietly!*"

The students obeyed meekly, keeping conversations to lame whispers, careful not to incur the wrath of Mr. Kane, particularly ahead of the much-anticipated summer vacation. They left in an orderly fashion, a practice rigorously instilled by Mr. Kane. As usual, only Queer Quincy remained behind of his own volition to chatter away with Mr. Kane, probably to brag his appreciation for the poem they had been studying, from the pen of Ralph Waldo Emerson, something to do with prophets of the soul. It was customary for Chet Quincy to be as shy as a mite during class and fearlessly discursive and upfront when everyone had gone as though intimidated by the very presence of his classmates. A teacher's pet was he and, like any good teacher's pet, he resolved by every means possible, deceitful or otherwise, to stay on the teacher's good side and obtain extra Brownie points for his enthusiasm and endeavour and the kind of attention commonly reserved for a high-flyer while his fellow students suffered in silence and barely made the grade. He wasn't as gifted as he made himself out to be, either, but knew how to impress his ingratiating nature on any teacher if the situation demanded. That reason alone rendered him open to scorn and ridicule and a sincere lack of friends. It was sickening to watch, to see someone deliberately sucking up to a teacher, especially one such as the Weird and Terrible Mr. Kane (*Jump! Sit! Fetch! Smell my butt!*), but what could you do? Rather fiendishly, Jimmy would try to imagine if there was something going on between Mr. Kane and his favourite pupil, whether behind closed doors they were in fact secret bum-chums, which summoned up an image so outrageous that it always made him shudder inside. Queer Quincy you knew was of that ilk (the creep had once inadvertently confessed his undying love for Tom Cruise, and the label had stuck), but with Mr. Kane it was more difficult to tell, though not entirely out of the question. You couldn't exactly picture him in the company of a woman, so deciding whether or not porky teenage boys did it for him was still a matter of much debate and speculation. It seemed safer to assume the man was asexual.

"What a jerk!" Jimmy declared of Mr. Kane as they joined the mass exodus in the corridor, making absolutely sure he was well out of earshot, his voice carried away by the tumultuous stream of laughter and elation. One had to be wary of Mr. Kane when delivering insults, whose ears were so finely tuned they could detect the fart of a mouse from downtown Memphis. "I bet he was bullied at school. I gotta admit it couldn't have happened to a nicer guy!"

They blinked to the freedom of daylight, like prisoners released from solitary confinement, the afternoon sun a godsend on their faces, the school plaza drenched in its hot, blazing brilliance. The sky was laundry-blue and cloudless, the air still but scented summer floral. They hurried past the Civil War cannons in the quadrangle and the ninety-year-old statue of the founder of BUILE HILL HIGH (it was amazing how very few students remembered the dude's name!) before traversing the walkway to the beckoning school gates.

"He's only doing his job," Ann-Marie commented, clutching her schoolbooks close to her chest. Unlike Jimmy, she had never crossed swords with Mr. Kane. Her 4.75 average said it all.

"What is it? You got a crush on him or somethin'?"

She punched his arm playfully. "Don't be dumb. You *know* he ain't my type."

"Remind me, who is?"

"Elvis," she chirped brightly, and Jimmy fetched a tortured groan.

It wasn't quite the reply he was hoping for, never was.

Elvis . . .! Not him again! Why's it always Elvis? The man's been dead for twenty years and he just can't stop hitting on my girl!

Although Jimmy had officially been dating Ann-Marie for nearly eight months, not once had she kissed him or allowed herself to be smooched, let alone accepted any admission of his love for her. There were occasions when Jimmy had been tempted to impart some of his mannish feelings towards her, only to be denied, leaving him disappointed by her stern disapproval, the way she'd deftly withdraw her head from his roving lips and the manner in which she was prepared to trot out that oft-spoken excuse: that she just wasn't ready for a major commitment. It was frustrating to say the least for Jimmy, who would be left wondering whether keeping up appearances – two people simply being seen together – was a sufficient basis for a relationship. With most boys of his age concerned primarily with losing the big 'V' and half the high-school jocks already two-timing the cheerleaders, how anybody could complain that a single peck-on-the-cheek was a major commitment was quite beyond him. *I mean, you'd think I was asking her to walk down the aisle with me or pose nude for some trucker's calender!*

Despite his rampaging hormones, Jimmy chose to respect his girlfriend's wishes and was more than grateful that the townspeople viewed him and Ann-Marie as an item. Lord knows what the other students would say if they learned of the lack of physical intimacy between the happy couple. Schoolkids had a habit of talking, with rumours inclined to spread like wildfire. It wouldn't be long before Jimmy was greeted with nasty barbs like 'the Celibate Monk' or 'the Love Novice' or 'the Right-Hand Stud' and Ann-Marie herself labelled 'Goody-Two-Shoes' . . . or, if they wanted to be particularly cruel, 'Little Miss Frigid'. Queer Quincy was living proof of the schoolyard rumour-mill at its most spiteful, his reputation muddied beyond rescue. He had learned to his dismay that you should never provide the gossipmongers with the necessary ammunition to leave you the laughing stock of the whole school.

At least Ann-Marie put paid to any stray questions about their charade, sparing Jimmy the embarrassment of lying, by silencing the chatterbitches and muckrakers with the sharpest and severest of comments, *None of your darned business!* Which at least left some room for the entertaining possibility that there was something deep and meaningful between her and Jimmy.

Perhaps there *was* something deep and meaningful, Jimmy hoped, about their jog-along relationship, an affable chemistry, a communion of interests, a ready rapport closer than kindred spirits, compensating for the knowledge that they were still strangers on the physical front. (The latter wasn't entirely true, however. Ann-Marie *did* let him hold her hand once-in-a-while when she was feeling particularly amorous, a pleasant treat on rough days.)

She was the pick of the bunch, the coolest girl at the Hop and the only girl Jimmy felt completely comfortable with. He'd known her all his life – they'd grown up together and their families were the best of friends – and he had to concede there was no-one else with whom he could talk to so openly. Ann-Marie discussed a lot of issues with him, as adept at scrutinizing the cases assigned to Kay Scarpetta as revealing quite innocently that it was her time of the month (which always left Jimmy rolling around in stitches). They enjoyed each other's company, Jimmy's jokey, light-hearted approach a direct – but not entirely conflicting – contrast to Ann-Marie's cute, shoot-from-the-hip seriousness. Together they embodied a balanced universe, Ann-Marie the perfectly-sensible yin to Jimmy's carefree yang. Jimmy supposed they had a good thing going and he pledged never to let the parade pass him by. In consequence, he was afraid of losing her (after all there were too many hunks better-looking than him at school,) but was mostly terrified *of* her.

She kept him in line.

You didn't mess with Ann-Marie. He thought of her blond, blue-eyed petiteness that masked another side to her. He thought of her cool and deadly tongue during squabbles, a fierce little vixen when cornered in an emotional confrontation, her clean, capable will cutting through any opponent with the ease of a kitchen knife. Whereas many girls tended to be either wild party animals or plain, bookish types, Ann-Marie was both homely and street-smart in equal measure. He thought of the time on Prom Night when she'd told him, *I know you fancy me,* to which he'd nodded his head like a kid shown a new puppy in a pet-store window, cracking her up into great peals of laughter until tears were rolling down her cheeks. She won first prize hands down, was voted Prom Queen that night. He thought about her parents, Joshua and Cloris, who were religious, principled folk, yet gentle and generous, lenient even, in the upbringing of their only child, their maturing daughter, in a world that was rapidly changing. He thought about her only single distraction, no, *fixation* with Elvis, his influence having done a great deal in further shaping her wholesome character, her formidable intelligence and ever-so-ample independence.

And he thought about the way she looked at present – sporting a pink halter top, long black skirt and white loafers – and considered how much he adored that sweet caboose of hers. Some men preferred breasts, others claimed to be 'leg-men', but Jimmy could say without reservation or shame that he had a big thing for a chick's rear, especially one so firm and curvaceous and aesthetically-pleasing as the tushie he was presently admiring and wished he had his hands on. It was a source of great mystery to Jimmy, bewildering in its firm beauty.

She'd kill you if she heard you say that . . . Probably would as well!

Yeah, but I love her for it!

Cute. Cool. Clever. Crazy. That defined Ann-Marie Caitlin perfectly. *Not to mention that sweet caboose.*

A cicada buzzed by his head, and Jimmy brushed it away with a flick of his hand.

"What's your project about?" Ann-Marie inquired casually.

"Elvis," Jimmy replied sorrowfully.

"Yeah?" Her reaction was one of sudden intrigue.

"I got it all worked out in my head," he explained. "It's 'bout his life-story. You know like a biography, only shorter."

"Cool." Ann-Marie was obviously delighted, like any regular teeny-bopper. "I'm nuts on Elvis, you know," she added as if Jimmy wasn't already aware of this annoying fact.

Can't seem to catch a break. The man won't quit stealing my girl! It's always Elvis this and Elvis that! To be brutally honest, the whole thing made him feel more chump than champ, in what passed off as their itty, bitty, *sans* titty relationship. He couldn't help but feel rejected in some way . . . and obscenely jealous. *Okay, Elvis was a legend, yeah, a world-class legend, but he's also a dead man! He's out of it! He's stone-cold! He's snuffed it, popped his clogs and he ain't coming back, darling! Unless, of course, you wanna make love to a corpse, Ann-Marie, which I guess you don't . . . So do I have to repeat myself? I guess I do. A DEAD MAN! Been dead for two decades! Don't everybody know it? So get real, girl!*

A thought occurred to Jimmy just then, providing him with a sudden flood of satisfaction. The trace of a smile formed on his lips, small, secret and self-congratulatory. He had found the opening line he had been looking for. *Well, I'll be dog-gone! The King was dead.* That's exactly how I should begin: *The King was dead.* Scrap the blasphemy for the indisputable truth. *Yeah, baby! The King was dead!* How the pleasure of hearing those four simple words repeating over and over in his head like a mantra soothed him beyond rapture. *The King was dead.*

"Yo, Daddy-O, how's it hangin'?" a familiar voice greeted him, and someone squeezed Jimmy's shoulder.

Jimmy jumped briefly, then his startled expression gave way to a slow, suggestive grin. "Short, shrivelled and always pointing north-north-west . . ." Ann-Marie threw him a reproving look and his grin faded instantly. "Carlton, how're you doin', dude?"

"Can't complain, my man," Carlton said companionably. "School's out, summer's here and the sun is shining. Soon to be seniors next semester. What more can a man ask for?"

A girlfriend who's not saving herself for a dead guy! Jimmy was keen to impart but thought better of it. Jimmy really couldn't get over it. His own jealousy, he found, was ridiculous in the extreme, but there was no denying that Ann-Marie's fixation was a far worse thing; it was almost unnatural. He often saw Ann-Marie growing old alone, living out her years of spinsterhood waiting for the erstwhile King of Rock'n'Roll to come a-knockin' at her door. Of course, he would never come, and, with faded hope, Ann-Marie would end her days a sad, broken woman. "Got any plans?"

"Go fishin', help my Pa at the store, *chill* . . ." Carlton looked chilled enough, wearing a Hawaiian shirt, blue Bermuda shorts, brown rubber sandals and a Memphis Redbirds baseball cap turned backwards. The Redbirds were doing well this season, already assured a place in the Minor League Play-Offs, and Carlton was a huge fan.

Jimmy was dressed in his usual casual blacks,

[*The King was dead*]

his favourite colour. Strange choice admittedly on a sunny day like today but nevertheless outwardly stylish.

Carlton's Pa owned HARPER'S SHOP-AND-MART down the road from where they lived and was, in all politeness, the best damned convenience store this side of the river. Jimmy remembered when he had been in desperate need of a part-time job last summer, the clutch of cotton mills around Memphis, the fish-processing plant at the Mississippi port of entry, even Old Burt at the nearby hardware store, had all refused, rejecting his application without just cause. Not discounting the POOL 'N' BILLIARD EMPORIUM and the KINGPIN BOWLING ALLEY. Lionel Harper, on the other hand, had obliged without making a fuss and, in the end, was more than satisfied by his employee's performance, who'd worked industriously alongside his son, their tasks ranging from looking after the till to moving crates from the Chevy Pick-up and stacking them up in the storage bay at the side of the store. No unscheduled breaks. No shirking on the job. No finishing early unless authorized by the chief honcho. The pay wasn't bad, and Jimmy was hoping to do the same again this summer. After all, this was what working was all about: learning the Work Ethic and the importance of money. *Give some to your old man for the housekeeping, spend some on your sweetheart and the rest is all mine.*

The Work Ethic was one of Floyd Hutton's popular expressions and he had done his best to drill its value into both his boys, Frank and Jimmy. Frank had made it, invariably the model son. He was junior partner at a law firm in Lexington, a 'real big-shot suit-'n'-tie exec' with CHADWICK, CARRUTHERS &

KAVANAGH, and his parents had big plans for Jimmy, too. He ought to follow in his brother's footsteps, Floyd always said. There was a place reserved for him there. Law school, then an internship. However, stuffy offices and criminal clients, case citations and legal jargon didn't much appeal to Jimmy, who wasn't exactly sure what he wanted to do just yet. Carlton Harper was keen on political science and li'l ole Ann-Marie aspired to get to med school.

"You decided on an essay?" Carlton asked Jimmy as they were walking down.

"Elvis . . ." Ann-Marie answered before Jimmy could so much as open his mouth, her voice bubbling with excitement. "He's eager to get it started."

Jimmy wasn't exactly eager – *perish the thought* – but he knew he *had* to get the damned thing started at some point. Not for himself or Mr. Kane but for Ann-Marie's sake, who was holding out on him physically because of her terrible obsession with Elvis, prepared to give up everything for Elvis. She was probably already wondering how the damned script would read. Perhaps then, if he played his cards right, he might eventually win her over and get her beautiful bod into bed. And that cute caboose.

"Elvis?" Carlton commented. "That's a first!"

"Ain't that so?" Ann-Marie agreed and flashed Jimmy her sweet, trademark smile, her eyes sparkling like sapphires. At that moment, she didn't look a day over twelve. "There's hope for him yet."

"I suppose." Jimmy gave her a quirky, sidelong glance, unsure whether he should tell her [*The King was dead*] how he was planning to start the essay. No, leave it till later, he decided, when he was well on his way through the minefield of words. "What's yours on?" he asked Carlton.

"I was thinkin' Martin Luther King."

"Not a bad idea."

Carlton shared the same dream as the assassinated Civil Rights' leader, for whom a wreath marked the spot on the first-floor balcony of the LORRAINE MOTEL. Carlton was a staunch activist in the crusade against racial intolerance, an advocate for equal opportunities for blacks and other minority groups. Wherever there was a meeting, rally or demonstration, Carlton was apt to attend without fail. Unless, of course, he was at school or doing a shift at his Pa's store. Otherwise, he would be there with the other protestors, chanting slogans and waving his banner, marching against the surging tides of political and social injustice. Weekends suited him best and, lately, he had started making a habit of joining any old protest march so long as it was friendly and peaceful and they had a *bona fide* cause that he could identify with. The Pro-Lifers were currently in town, and Carlton was intent on going. He'd already accompanied the Abortionists earlier in the month.

Although times had changed, with racial segregation a thing of the past, there were still stubborn pockets of resistance throughout Tennessee. Every place has its bad elements, its own 'Hicksville', its own motley band of illiterate, beer-guzzling rednecks, and the town of Old Shelby was no tall exception. Prejudice and racial hatred were still a matter of great concern, mainly out in the boondocks. The rather fecund Colebank family were one such case, their firm beliefs and generations of membership in the Ku Klux Klan gaining them wide publicity and a notoriety that they positively wallowed in. Despite the ever-changing attitudes of the Deep South, the Colebanks continued to abide by the extinct Jim Crow laws and participate in the kind of 'niggerhunts' that had plagued America in the late 1950s. *Damned shoe-shine boys are running the show these days. Ain't it a cryin' shame what's happenin' to our once great nation? White is white and black is black, and never the twain shall meet.* Things had come to a head quite recently, after the gang-rape and strangulation of a pregnant black lady. It caused quite a stir in the community and led to some dozen arrests. Most of the Colebanks and their trailer-trash accomplices were implicated in the killing and were eventually handed down life-sentences after numerous unsuccessful appeals. They were now rotting in jail, where they belonged, unable on this occasion to escape the long arm of the law. The newspapers had applauded the verdict, calling it a great triumph for justice. *Good Riddance to the Scum of Society!* read one newspaper headline. *Let Them Suffer, Suffer, Suffer!* Because of the cold-blooded nature of the crime, the general public still voiced their discontent with the Court's ruling, insisting the murderers deserved the electric chair. The people's signed petition demanding blood for blood failed to convince the Governor of Tennessee, who clung to his decision that the use of the death penalty was not appropriate in this case. Others suspected he harboured sympathies with the white supremacists. The Colebanks had finally gotten their just desserts, he went on to explain, and their use of intimidating tactics, ranging from their frequent practice of placing burning crosses on the lawns of decent coloured folk to straight, full-blown arson attacks on those homes, were hopefully at an end and could only serve as a deterrent for those who found it particularly amusing to incite racial hatred.

However, old Willard Colebank, the real instigator behind this supremist terror-campaign, had remained totally unrepentant throughout the trial. *The black bitch had it comin'*, he said on the stand, *always dressin' like some classy socialite, actin' all high-and-mighty as if she owned the place. But we showed her for what she really was! As they say: you can't polish a turd. The Yankees fought for black freedom, and the coon-lovin' Yankees won, don't we regret it? Slaughtered our Great White Fathers on the battlefields, and for what? So's we could get niggerhoods of drugs and guns and disease-spreading whores. Breed like shithouse rats and steal good tax-dollars 'cos they're too dumb-ass lazy to work. They should be janitors and stay janitors, is all I'm sayin'. We was just teaching them not to get above their station, that's all, and that's the darn thanks we get!*

"Elvis, B.B. King and Luther King, the greatest men ever to walk in Memphis," Carlton said contemplatively. "The Three Kings! Brought blacks and whites together." Then he gestured to Ann-Marie ". . . And you? What're you gonna write?"

"I ain't decided yet," Ann-Marie replied. "Maybe Elvis. Me and Jimmy could compare notes. He could use my expertise. I'd be interested to read his take on the King."

"Don't you reckon you've had enough of writin' 'bout Elvis?" Jimmy said in an is-that-all-you're-good-for? tone.

"Yes, sure, but–" Ann-Marie giggled, sounding like a child delighting in a game of tic-tac-toe. "–isn't Elvis great? Don't you think he's great?"

"Yeah," Jimmy said, his voice trailing off. "Just great." *Real* kick-in-the-nuts *great!*

"Howdy, Missie. Afternoon, fellers. How y'all doin'?"

The trio turned, took a gander at the person gatecrashing their party.

"Oh, no, it can't be . . ." Ann-Marie groaned.

But it was.

A cop-cruiser was pulling over, crawling alongside the sidewalk. Within rode two boys-in-blue, one of them her cousin. *To serve and per'tect.*

"Hi there, Sheriff," Ann-Marie returned, feigning surprise, forcing a smile. "What can we do for you?"

Merle Brubaker was your definitive small-town sheriff, an uncouth slob-of-a-man who constantly chewed tobacco, spat a great deal, tucked into T-bone steaks on a regular basis and blew his fuse with anybody he didn't like – which was with nearly everyone. His specialty was patronizing the public and bullying the new, emerging generation of officers. Politeness was outside his jurisdiction.

Beside him sat Pete Lawson, as inexperienced as any deputy could be. He was tall, scrawny and not particularly bright as Ann-Marie had often remarked of her cop cousin. Apart from looking as though he'd just stepped out of kindergarten, his buck teeth and sappy smile gave him the vague resemblance to a domesticated woodchuck.

"You folks wanna hitch a ride home?" Deputy Lawson asked, one hand resting on the steering, the other arm dangling from the rolled-down window. "The Sheriff don't mind."

Ann-Marie declined the offer graciously. "No, we'll be fine, thanks."

"My, you look purtier ev'ry day," the Sheriff complimented from the passenger side, casting an admiring eye on Ann-Marie. "Ain't that so, Jimmy?"

"I guess," Jimmy replied, surprised that the Sheriff was more approachable than usual. *Must be his Birthday.*

Ann-Marie's cheeks flushed, her fake smile frozen on her face, and again she reminded Jimmy of a girl of twelve. "Why, thank you, Sheriff, but flattery won't get you anywhere."

"No flattery, Ann-Marie," Deputy Lawson said. His Adam's apple bobbed up and down like a shuttlecock each time he spoke. "Sheriff's jus' makin' an obs'vation is all."

"Ay-uh," Sheriff Brubaker admitted, then shifted to the matter in hand. "Now if you kids'll do sumpin' for me . . ." His wheedling terms of endearment had a price.

"What's that?" Jimmy asked.

"As you guys rightly know, it's the Elections soon . . ." Lawson began, got glared at by his superior and chose wisely to close his mouth.

"Yeah, it's the mayoral 'lections comin' up," Sheriff Brubaker drawled in explanation. "We was hopin' we could count on your folks' votes." He pulled out a handful of fliers from the glovebox and passed them over to Jimmy. "If you'd be kind 'nuff to dist'bute these."

"It'll be a pleasure," Jimmy said as diplomatically as he could muster. His lie went unnoticed. He read the political slogan: VOTE GAINES FOR MAYOR. GIVE LAW A SHOVE IN THE RIGHT DIRECTION.

In Jimmy's enlightened opinion there was only one thing worse than Sheriff Brubaker and his pompous idiocracy, and that was Dudley 'Flash the Cash' Gaines, as detestable an individual as J.D. Hogg from *The Dukes of Hazzard*. With plummeting popularity in the polls, the chances of his re-election were, realistically-speaking, slim. His campaign was complete cheesecorn (crack down on crime, more power to the unions – you know, the usual bullcrap!), and his previous indictment on corruption charges (involving a number of financial scams, chiefly embezzlement and accepting bribes and the unsubstantiated allegation of money-laundering, hence the nickname 'Flash the Cash') didn't help his cause. Neither did recent photos of him snapped romping with a couple of hookers in a hotel room make his shit smell any sweeter. Even more astonishing was how he'd nearly got away scot-free, receiving only thirty hours' community service for his illegal activities (just because he happened to be on good terms with the Judge, the cynics claimed). His tearful 'plea for forgiveness' speech afterwards, including a very personal televised confession to the local pastor, only made him look more guilty; it simply highlighted his dishonesty and now threatened to rip his already dwindling support at the grassroots' level, to effectively bury his career once and for all. His reputation would never recover. The real scandal — the absurdity of it all — was the fact that the man didn't have the dignity to resign and, despite an intense mauling from the Press, was preparing to run for another term in office.

What a team they made: Brubaker the foul-mouthed sheriff and Mayor Gaines the fat, oily sleazeball. There couldn't have been a more rounded argument against them. Their abysmal track-record had left them wholly unelectable, but their downright pigheadedness would not allow them to see it. If Tweedledumb and Tweedledumber thought they had an outside chance of winning, then they were liable to be extremely disappointed. No fooling the voters. The pairing of Delaney-Shapiro was a cleaner, safer bet. The sad, far-reaching truth, however, was that nobody had yet managed to take the Corruption out of Politics. An honest politician came along once in a blue moon, but they didn't last long.

"How'll you handle the rise in crime?" Jimmy inquired.

"Give those goddamn sumbitches an assful of holes, is what!" was Sheriff Brubaker's impartial response.

Give those goddamn sumbitches an assful of holes. Nice to see the mayor's chief law enforcement officer speaking his mind. Just about sums up their chances of re-election.

"These are dangerous times, kids," continued Sheriff Brubaker, swearing and cursing as usual, "and you can't afford to be soft on jackasses who think they're above the law. Believe me, now'days the world's chock full of weirdos, punks and homosexshuals to be a safe place, what with the heat an' all. Heat can make a man do all kindsa crazy things!"

He was abruptly interrupted by a female voice on the police radio, breaking through a sizzlepop of static: "Calling Unit One . . . Calling Unit One, do you copy, over? . . . Unit One, please respond . . ."

Sheriff Brubaker jumped to order, lifted the radio-mike from its prongs. "This is Unit One. We're receivin' you loud and clear, over. What's the problem?"

The woman at the police switchboard handed them their instructions: "Proceed to *Joe's Country Diner*, Kenton Street. We've got a ten-ten: fight in progress. Reports of a barroom brawl. Over.”

Sheriff Brubaker spoke into the mike businesslike: “I think we can handle it from here, but please have Unit Three on standby, just in case. Over and out.” Leaving those instructions, he replaced the mike with a critical shake of his head. “Tearing up a family joint like that. Looks like we got them goddamn troublemakers by the short-and-curlies, Pete.” Full of confidence and hubris, he delivered a quick gesture of his authority. He unholstered his six-shooter from his Sam Browne belt, spun the barrel to check that it was fully loaded, then snapped it shut. *There's nobody faster than Quick Draw McGraw! Give those goddamn troublemakers an assful of holes!* “Gotta go,” Brubaker told Ann-Marie and her two friends hastily. *Yep, got some* actual *work to do: flip on the cuffs and haul some asses into the slammer!* “Give my regards to your folks...”

“Will do, Sheriff,” Ann-Marie declared with the brightest of innocence.

“And remember: keep your noses clean,” the Sheriff advised. As if to emphasize his last point, he hawked up his sinuses and spat a great gloop of tobacco juice onto the sidewalk. It was a needless spectacle, too gross for comical effect. Brubaker’s full attention was now directed at his deputy. “Now let’s go kick some ass!” he retorted – straight from the horse’s mouth.

“Yes, sir,” Deputy Lawson affirmed . . . and unintentionally stalled the car.

“*What in God's name d'you think y'doin', boy?*” Brubaker demanded, whacking Lawson over the head with his stetson, the three onlookers instantly forgotten. “Was you born in a barn? Get your ass into gear, slowpoke.”

“I was just–”

“I don’t care what you was *just* doin’, you dufus!” Brubaker barked back. “*Get goin'!*”

Mumbling apologies, Lawson re-started the ignition, set the squad car into transmission and both Sheriff and Deputy drove off, leaving a trail of dust in their wake. *The posse's on its way, hoss.*

As the Badge disappeared down the street, Jimmy went back to examining the fliers that Brubaker had given him. That crooked tub of lard, ‘Flash the Cash’ Gaines leered up at him, a large cigar clenched between his teeth. “What d’you reckon?” Jimmy asked Carlton.

“Are you my huckleberry?”

“Are you my Bubba?”

“You *know* the score, dude,” Carlton enunciated, hinting towards the only possible solution to municipal matters and political wrangling.

Jimmy gave a go-devil-go grin. “You bet, homie,” he said and dumped the campaign leaflets into the nearest trashcan, then slapped palms with Carlton in a high five.

They grabbed a hot dog each from a hamburger stall and stopped off at the nearest drugstore for some ice-cream-and-soda before heading homeward.

Their neighbourhood in Old Shelby was a picture of hometown America as it always had been and always would be. Although somewhat more upbeat and less impoverished than the urban ghetto, it was nonetheless a racially-mixed, blue-collar area, a place where you locked your door when you went out without encountering dope dealers on the street corners or hobos drinking from brown paper bags. Its railroad depot was a proud reminder of its place on the Memphis and Charleston Railroad.

They dropped off Carlton first, Lionel Harper standing at the convenience-store entrance puffing on his corncob pipe, listening to the radio. He wore a red chambray shirt, his slacks heavily oil-stained having finished repairing the blue Jalopy. The old Chevy pick-up stood nearby. Ma Harper, Della, was inside the apartment above the store, breast-feeding Carlton's two-month-old baby sister (The Baby with the Big Bib, in Jimmy's words), Eliza. Business was slow, Lionel told Jimmy, probably on account of the heat. Carlton invited Jimmy to stay for a movie. Him and his Pa were going to put their feet up and watch *Malcolm X*. "A chance to hang out with the homeboys, what do you say?"

Jimmy and Ann-Marie declined, saying they had things to do at home. "Seen it. Still prefer *Jungle Fever*," Jimmy said, a cheap, wayward shot at triggering another debate. Their differing opinions meant little to Ann-Marie, who as appointed referee and bubble-poppingly bored out of her skull, often declared their bull sessions a draw, much to their dismay. No favouritism if Ann-Marie, the hanging judge, was to have her way.

Nor was Ann-Marie up today for another meaningless tussle on another totally meaningless topic. She had to pull Jimmy away quickly before he stepped into the ring with Carlton again. When it came to man-talk, once they got going, there was no stopping them. They were apt to go the distance, like two intellectual heavyweights, leaving Ann-Marie largely in the lurch.

Jimmy understood Ann-Marie's eagerness to scoot and shook hands with Carlton, rather reluctant to leave. He wouldn't have minded sticking around, but if Ann-Marie wanted some lone time with him, then how could he possibly deprive her of that luxury? It was a blessing for him, also, because it wasn't often she asked for his sole company. Just lately, she seemed a bit too involved with Elvis to bother. So if the chance beckoned for Jimmy to have her all to himself, he wasn't exactly going to jeopardize what precious moments they shared together. She was his girlfriend after all, the best thing that ever happened to him. Carlton would have to wait. Jimmy promised Carlton he'd pop his head round tomorrow, check what was going down. Ann-Marie gave Carlton a friendly thumbs-up who reciprocated the gesture. They left him minding the store while Pa Harper snatched a short break.

Ann-Marie's place came next, two streets down, the same street where Jimmy lived. Her parents' homestead, like all the other properties on the street, was a whitewashed, split-level house built on a sturdy platform, supported by short, stumpy posts, wooden steps leading up to the porch. Midwestern design, but conservative all the same. He walked her to the door past a well-maintained lawn and a neatly-manicured rosebush. Although he was tempted to pluck off a single red rose and present it to her as a romantic offering, he didn't think her mother, for whom the rose garden was her pride and joy, would take kindly to someone meddling with her beloved flowers. Ann-Marie didn't invite him in; it was getting dark and her mother wouldn't approve of male visitors at this time. She and Jimmy ended up talking a while outside, about general stuff mostly: their plans for the summer vacation, who did and did not sign their High School Yearbooks, slumber parties they'd been invited to, relatives they would be visiting, and the like. And as the sun gave up its dominance for the day, both eventually decided on going to the pictures tomorrow night. Then Ann-Marie disappeared into the house for several minutes, only to re-emerge with a couple of books that Jimmy might find useful. He thanked her for her troubles. Inside the porch, they bid each other farewell. Rather unexpectedly, Ann-Marie actually allowed Jimmy to *hug* her, and he took full advantage of her sudden change of heart. He never mistook her embrace for anything other than affection, but that still didn't stop him from testing the boundaries.

Oh, no, physical contact! Aren't we being sentimental today? Such un-cool, un-sophisticated behaviour, and coming from you, Miss Caitlin, how could you? Looks like I just might well have to kiss you to prove you're not as tough as you like to pretend you are . . .

He shouldn't have kissed her. Maddened her.

Ann-Marie was not in the mood.

Definitely not in the mood.

The No Kissing rule still applied, as Ann-Marie was forced to remind him. She stayed true to her word when she pointed out more indignantly that he also kindly remove his hands from her butt.

*****

Jimmy swaggered down the street, swigging on a chilled can of Coke. The first ashes of twilight were descending upon the reddish haze of sundown, throwing gradually lengthening shadows on the ground. The early evening air held an odd but interesting mixture of smells: from the faint aroma of mesquite-marinated meat being griddled in someone's backyard to the more natural fragrance of cut grass, of earth. Pleasant smells, smells connected with the summer months. There was hardly anybody about, except for the Patterson twins, who were tossing a Frisbee between them across their front lawn. Jimmy tipped them a wink as he went by, and the two little girls giggled back at him before resuming their game. Further down the block, he heard the Grady's collie barking away endlessly as though it were being tortured in some horrible way. A flock of sparrows flew past high overhead, preparing to give up their day's exertions for the simple comfort of their nightly roosts.

Jimmy touched his face, where Ann-Marie had slapped him, and grinned. He had copped a feel and she had dealt with him accordingly. His left cheek stung, but he could live with it. Ann-Marie certainly knew when to draw the line, never hesitated in letting him know if he was treading forbidden territory.

Still, she'd forgive him soon enough when she realized he had only been fooling around.

He let a green Pontiac glide slowly past him before crossing the road.

On the other side, he discovered his neighbour, the ever-watchful Mrs. Conway, peering at him from her window. She stood assessing him almost prudishly, her knobbly knuckles having drawn aside the net-curtain. She was elderly and white haired and a recent widow. Hard to believe she was also a chronic invalid when one considered how much of her waking hours she spent watching the happenings up and down the street, like the world's oldest sentinel. She wasn't branded an empress of the grapevine for no reason. Nothing escaped her prying eyes. Jimmy waved at her. She didn't wave back, merely stared impassively at him with her eagle eyes. What else did he expect from her? Judging by the way her window commanded a perfect view of the whole street, there was no doubt in Jimmy's mind that she must have witnessed Ann-Marie slap a reprimand on him and was probably privately pleased he had been chastised for his ungentlemanly conduct. Her cat sat on the sill alongside her, also in the process of watching him. Jimmy didn't like the look of either the old lady or her fat, grey tabby and hurried on home. There was something deeply perturbing about their synchronized staring, as though both shared a single will, like some old witch and her familiar.

As he approached his own house, he noticed the blinds were drawn, the windows open and the lights on, his father's silhouette cast on the kitchen window. *Probably looking for a cold one or something.* He wondered how his old man could consume vast quantities of beer and still remain relatively sober when everyone else got as pickled as a gherkin. *Know what the secret is, son?* Floyd Hutton had informed Jimmy more than once. *Some folks got it, and I'm the host who can boast the most. A right ole drinkin' phenomenon. Never find me drunk as a coot. No sirree-Bob!*

On trooping up the short driveway upon which reposed his father's pampered pink Cadillac, he saw Mrs. Conway still watching him closely. So too was her cat in exactly the same unblinking manner. He shivered.

"I'm home!" Jimmy hollered, stepping through the front door.

"Hi, Jimmy." His mother was sitting in the lounge wearing a sundress, serenely watching a documentary on the TV about the Oklahoma Land Runs. "Everything okay?" she asked when she noticed his look of exhaustion.

"Couldn't be better." The daily grind of school was at an end – at least for now – and he was as free as a bird. *Yippee-Yi-Yay, Jack can come out play!*

"I kept some supper warm for you."

"That'd be great, Ma. I ate earlier, but I reckon I could still eat a whole cow." The evening was sultry enough, but it was a sauna inside. "Ma, what's with the heat?"

"Oh, the air-conditioning's on the fritz," Darlene explained, rising from her chair.

"Again?"

"So much for your Pa fixin' it."

They were in the kitchen now, Floyd Hutton pouring himself a Jack Daniel's. "Don't blame me, Darlene, I done all I could." His blue shirt was stained by a tree of sweat, the half-soaked vest beneath thankfully hiding his paunch. His braces hung in loops around his waist. He was the kind of man who never classified clothes as either 'clean' or 'dirty' but in subtle *grades* of laundry. He gave a quick snifter of his armpits to check what grade he was at.

"Floyd!" Darlene protested, half-appalled and half-amused. "Jimmy's gotta eat."

"I was only kiddin', son. Old habits die hard, even disgustin' ones."

"I know, Pops."

"How was your day, son?"

"Good, Pops, good."

"Keep it up an' you'll soon be joinin' Frank at the firm."

"That'd be swell, Pops." Law school: the last thing Jimmy was thinking about. Suddenly, he had an awful feeling. He could sense a lecture coming on, not quite what he was in the mood for at that moment.

"The Work Ethic, that's what it's all 'bout," Floyd began to explain with sour, rye breath. "I told you 'bout the Work Ethic before, dint I, son?"

So soon? I just got here, Jimmy sighed within. *Yeah, Pops. Steady on, Pops. Be cool...*

"Just that I don't want you to be like your old man: a lowly postal worker. Invest in your future, that's what I always say. I dint do all the investin' I should have done in my prime; that's why we live here." Floyd rambled meditatively on, trying to embrace all that he himself had achieved, what he liked to call his Long-term Plan. "But I guess, in some ways, we ain't doin' so bad. We got a roof over our heads and no mortgage. And I got two fine boys with bright futures, one who's already a smart lawyer. Allow me to retire comf'tably when the time comes...Anyhow, that's all I'm gonna say on the subject for now, son. Make the most of the Work Ethic. Invest in your future." He sounded as solemn as someone administering the last rites, delivering a dying declaration or pronouncing that it was the end of the world.

Jimmy nodded, not liking the route this conversation was taking or the way the atmosphere had suddenly taken on the quality of a deathbed confession. *Lighten up, dudes, I only just started my summer vacation.* His parents could be so serious sometimes, particularly his father after a few drinks, when Jimmy felt obligated to listen. Jimmy decided to talk about something cheerier. "I got some books today on . . . guess who?" He dumped his holdall on the floor, rummaged through it and lifted out the bunch of books he'd borrowed from Ann-Marie – or, more precisely, Ann-Marie had thrust upon him. "Elvis. His life's the subject of my summer essay."

"Elvis, hey?" Floyd Hutton said, warming up in a flash. He drained the glass, poured himself some more bourbon. He no longer sounded as though he was at the Last Chance Saloon, ordering a whisky-sour and waiting for the Big Showdown with the evil Clanton Gang. "About time! I can tell you ev'rythin' you need to know about Elvis."

"I knew you'd be thrilled . . ."

"Thrilled, you shittin' me? I'm not thrilled. I'm *ek*-static! You see, I used to think liquor came in bottles. Then Elvis came along, and I realized it came in words, too. We was raised on Rock'n'Roll, your mother and me, and Elvis was the staple diet of Memphis. Ain't that true, hon?"

"Sure takes me back some," Darlene agreed. "Can't beat the Million Dollar Quartet. Perkins, Lewis, Cash and, of course, the undisputed King of 'em all: *Elvis*. My hero."

"I thought I was your hero, jitterbug," Floyd humoured her.

"Well, I s'pose . . ." Darlene murmured, shrugging off a slight tinge of embarrassment. She removed a plate of Southern-fried chicken and home fries from the oven and set it down on the kitchen table in front of Jimmy. She placed a jug of homemade root beer next to the meal. "There's pecan pie for dessert."

"Yeah, we was *real* hung-up on Elvis," Floyd enthused. "The greatest man that ever lived. He was the talk of the town, the toast of Tennessee. He was a legend. He was a god. He was *Elvis*. The One and Only . . . the All-time Great."

Common ground, Jimmy thought dully, not expecting such an animated response to one of his all-time *hates*. That mixture of jealousy and frustration resurfaced, succeeding the initial exasperation. *At last, everyone's happy: my parents, Carlton . . . Ann-Marie. God, what I would give to conquer Ann-Marie! You look purtier ev'ry day. I wonder if she'll ever let me get inside her pants.*

Perhaps, now's my chance. With her passion for Elvis and hopefully my project, I'll probably be able to make love to her without her even noticing.

All of a sudden, making out with Ann-Marie seemed not so unthinkable a notion as Jimmy had always been led to believe. On the contrary, it began to feel like a real possibility, attainable somehow, so much so that Jimmy had to caution himself for feeling horny at such an inconvenient moment. His approach was the actual problem; her slap provided the confirmation he needed. Elvis was the one, vital key to gaining Ann-Marie's absolute trust, and Jimmy was making a real hash of it. *Daydreaming again. Mustn't daydream. Now's not the time nor the place. Remember your report card – what do you think Mr. Kane's been telling you all your life? Pay attention. Learn to keep your mind focused on the here and now. Take his advice for once and you can't go wrong. It might mean the difference between sex and no sex. Incentive enough.*

"Eat up, son, and I'll give you the full rundown on Elvis, the whole story." With that eager promise, Floyd disappeared into the lounge.

"I had a crush on Elvis myself once, you know, before I met your father, that is..." Darlene remarked. Then smiling knowingly, she added: "Actually I still do, but don't tell your father that!"

Floyd Hutton gave his son the full rundown on Elvis with the enthusiastic march of an Amtrak nostalgia-express sliding out of the station, gathering speed, climbing the hill of old sorrows, perking up again at the top, then hurtling downhill, spilling its freight-load of reminiscences all over the tracks. There was very little in the way of information for Jimmy, who salvaged whatever nuggets of gold he could find, as meagre as those settled on a prospector's pan once the silt is washed away. However scant his scribbles were, he was sure they were sufficient enough to get him started.

He was a legend. He was a god. He was Elvis . . .

The All-Time Great.

My All-Time Hate.

Except, even if the man had turned into a cliché in every sense of the word, Elvis couldn't be his all-time hate, surely not. Elvis was utterly unique, loved by the youth of past and present, a man who singlehandedly changed the face of popular music forever. He was the original Rock'n'Roll star, the prototype to all those other rockabillies who came after him. Jimmy *had* to like something about Elvis if he was preparing to compose an essay on the guy, surely.

Am I right and the rest of the world is wrong? Am I the only one who thinks Elvis was way overrated?

Jimmy sat in his bedroom, under a splash of desklight, deep in thought, staring hard at the Smith-Corona typewriter, afraid, as if it might be a ticking parcel left on the doorstep. Beads of sweat glistened on his forehead. The blank page looked back at him with staid indifference.

His room was spacious, décored in lime-green. A hi-fi resided in a shadowy corner, away from the bed, beside a stack of *Rolling Stone* magazines. On the walls hung posters of Axel Rose and Kurt Cobain. Now theirs was the kind of music you could really sink your teeth into. Bands apart from Elvis. But Jimmy knew with an awkward acceptance that even they owed Elvis a huge debt of gratitude. If it hadn't been for Elvis, none of it would have ever been possible.

From the open window, the breath of a breeze drifted in. From somewhere down the street, the Grady's dog barked on and on. *Ruff-ruff. Ruff-ruff-ruff.*

Jimmy had heard it all before – everyone spouting on about how amazing Elvis was – and it was getting to be a constant bee in his bonnet, wearing him down. If it wasn't for Ann-Marie and her crazy obsession, then he wouldn't have to work himself into a lather over Elvis every time. Elvis could stay buried, his interred bones providing refuge for the bugs, and Jimmy wouldn't have to care diddlysquat one way or another.

But life is never easy. It has a habit of biting you in the ass when you least expect it.

Ann-Marie *had* to be tamed, made more accessible. *So did Elvis.* Unbearable though it sounded, it had become a necessity, as overwhelming as the need for some drunken old-timer forced to do his duty in the woods. A necessity that couldn't be put off any longer.

Which is why Jimmy had gotten wise . . .

If truth be known, he hadn't been entirely idle in his spare time. He had actually taken to learning some Elvis. He'd spent the last few weeks doing exactly *that*, practising to sing like him, trying to establish whether he could match up to Elvis. Like some sad Elvis aficionado, Jimmy had remained in his bedroom singing to a run of Elvis records his father had lent him. Except it had turned out to be an unusually uplifting experience. Jimmy's singing had been loud, but the deck-speakers had been louder. Yet nobody had complained so far. Should they have? Maybe it was because his folks wanted him to understand why they held Elvis in such high regard or perhaps they simply yearned for him to appreciate what they had listened to when *they* had been growing up – what would be deemed 'culture' in their time – which might explain why they had tolerated the racket coming from his room thus far. Hell, Jimmy wouldn't be at all surprised if they were listening against the door, quietly proud of him and his newly-acquired taste in music. He could even imagine his father boasting to his friends at work: *Finally proved himself a Memphian through and through.*

Although Elvis had proved a hard act to follow, Jimmy had made significant progress, much to his satisfaction. After weeks of sweat and toil, he could now safely say he'd mastered the voice, an achievement in itself. Within reason, of course, but it didn't deter from the fact that Jimmy could do a pretty mean Elvis if needs be. He now carried a fairly wide-ranging repertoire of Elvis hits locked inside his head in case the opportunity ever arose for him to perform. He hoped it wouldn't . . . but, then again, another part of him wished it could, even if only to prove he wasn't as blind-ignorant of the Elvis myth as most people suspected.

Although he could quite comfortably string a few chords together on his rhythm guitar, Jimmy had never really regarded himself much of a composer, even worse a lyricist. But now, remarkably, there was the sound of guitar music coming from his room, as though he was the new, consummate Guitar Man, the notes and chords swelling into sheaves, while he sang along to the King's records at the top of his lungs. Jimmy could sing, a knack he'd picked up from Elvis. Jimmy had come to the definite conclusion – rather begrudgingly, mind – that Elvis was probably the greatest male vocalist in the history of music. Perhaps the King wasn't all that bad, considering. He'd taught Jimmy how to sing, for one. Made Jimmy more adorable to Ann-Marie, for another. And it went some way in explaining the King's enduring appeal. The man practically invented Rock'n'Roll. Jimmy considered even singing for Ann-Marie some day, maybe even composing a song especially for her. She was a sucker for cheap, trashy songs.

What of the essay? The query lodged in his head like a large, unwieldy axe. Now here was a matter for real concern. *Surely singing's a cinch compared to writing.*

Whereas Ann-Marie was definitely in the ballpark, Jimmy didn't know shit from Shinola when it came to writing. Writing had him walking on shaky ground. His parents gave him more credit than he deserved because he wasn't particularly literate and even letter-writing was a bother, although in the end he got by. So it wasn't inconceivable that writing, let alone writing an abridged biographical account on Elvis, should give him the willies. After all, a person goes through a million events in the Theatre of Life and selecting all the relevant moments can be an extremely time-consuming experience for somebody not entirely *au fait* with the person's life story. But if he managed to pull it off, it would be the crowning piece in his attempts to woo Ann-Marie, making her more amenable to his advances. He could see it already: her finishing reading his masterpiece on Elvis, falling into his arms in a breathless swoon, then asking him dreamily to do whatever he wanted to her. Hope springs eternal.

Anyways, how do you begin a tired, old subject in a new and refreshing way?

The King was dead.

That's how, *don't you think?* The brainwave from earlier on. That's where he ought to start.

Already, he had something here – something good, something eye-catching. That's exactly what Mr. Kane would have called a 'sensational' opening sentence. Like sundogs on the horizon or a hail of meteors scratching the night sky. Spectacular. Sensational. *Tempt the reader and draw them in. Then the rest is as plain as rain.*

He typed:

```
The King was dead.
```

"Someone beat me to it," he muttered, chuckling at his own wry wit. Then his eyebrows beetled into a strenuous frown as he continued:

```
The King was dead.
1977 was the year it happened, as representative of the
```

scene as the rest of the decade. The climate was one of chaos over order, madness over sanity, experimentation over conformity, and its uncensored sexual liberation and mindless glitz surpassed even the free, disinhibited, drug-crazed Flower Power generation before it. The Sham Glam era as it was to be known saw the birth of ephemeral fashion trends like airplane collars, dinosaur ties and flared bell-bottom pants in a period of disco, transvestitism and political unrest.

Post-Saigon, post-Watergate, the moderates were in power, Jimmy Carter securing a year in office. The Cold War was at the crest of an iceberg adrift in a sea of paranoia and Commie-phobia, nukes on standby. The diplomats still considered Fidel Castro a cancer on the face of humanity. Across the Atlantic, the emergence of punk rock was seriously undermining the Silver Jubilee celebrations of a dowdy monarch. In the east, almost every country was either under martial law or on the verge of a coup d'état. In Hollywood, the renowned neurotic, Woody Allen, swept away the Academy Awards for *Annie Hall*. And the King of Rock'n'Roll, Elvis Aaron Presley, died of heart failure in his Graceland bathroom from a life of excess.

A case of irrevocable heartbreak for his *hoi polloi* of devoted fans, a worldwide billion-strong following: fans in every nation, on every continent, of every age. From the sunsets of the Serengeti, where native elders hummed to the long-distance buzz of boogie on the wireless, to the sprawling metropolis of Tokyo, where a family might be sitting down to a supper of sushi, unaware that their big, bouncing baby is jiving in his crib to the sound of Elvis singing on the T.V. screen, Elvis-mania was everywhere.

In Memphis, Tennessee, August the Sixteenth would be a day of mourning. Shopping malls closed early, banks kept business to a bare minimum, gospel rang out from the crowded churches, and local and national radio stations broadcast hourly bulletins. The week that followed saw the arrival of hundreds upon thousands of Elvis fans from around the globe, flooding the gates of Graceland to keep vigil and sing funeral dirges by candlelight. The subsequent funeral was fit for a king, and the world of showbiz paid its last respects as Elvis was finally laid to rest in Graceland.

The shock of Elvis's death would continue to generate intense public interest even when the furore did eventually die down: rocketing record sales, a troupe of teddy boys and Elvis lookalikes and impersonators, and a mountain of Elvis memorabilia and franchises, including

Elvis perfumes and pizzas and playing cards. Wild theories abounded claiming Elvis to still be alive, having faked his own death, in the eyes of those who had never accepted it in the first place. Or the others who assumed that the CIA had done the dirty on Elvis in the name of national security.

Then there were some who were convinced they had seen him supposedly after his death...

Jimmy's father owned a '75 Cadillac convertible, which he had always kept in mint condition. He had traded in a rundown Coupe de Ville for it some eight years ago and had never looked back. A classic in practically every sense of the word, its body was long and sleek and shiny-pink. Tail-finned, fenderskirted, chrome-grilled, with a resplendent leather interior, a Hurst gearbox, a behemoth twin-exhaust and four whitewalled, gangster tyres, it had all the trimmings one would expect with this particular custom-made model. To go with its beautifully-crafted shape, a reliable, high-octane V-8 engine rested beneath the bonnet – unquenchable in its thirst for gas, accepted, but, ah, what awesome power!

Car maintenance came second nature to Floyd Hutton. In his capable hands, his faithful Caddy never fell into disrepair. He looked after it with meticulous care, almost lovingly, like a trainer looks after a champion racehorse. Unlike other owners who balk at every chance of driving their vintage saloon and prefer instead to leave it on display in their garage to cut down on costs and general wear-and-tear, Floyd took every opportunity to drive his pride-and-joy which also meant he was prone to fret over it more than was commonly necessary. Although he took it in for a complete overhaul every few months, he spent the rest of the year labouring over it himself, endeavouring to keep it as roadworthy as best he could. He washed it, polished it, checked its oil, made absolutely sure it remained in tiptop condition – a fully-functional mean machine with a healthy regard for the admirers. So new and gleaming was its appearance by the time he finished, it might just as easily have driven off the production line only yesterday. A remarkable feat for a car with four previous owners and an odometer that clocked over one hundred thousand, thoroughly confirming that old workman's adage about Cadillacs being built to last. He continued to employ it as often as he could, driving it to work or when taking his wife out to meet some friends or on a routine trip to the shopping mall.

Yet, the most outstanding aspect of Floyd Hutton, the absolute clincher, was his generous nature, since every Saturday night he would borrow his car to his son. As long as he contributed to the extra insurance (which didn't amount to much) out of his own pocket-money (of which there was more than enough) and filled up the tank by the end of the evening, Jimmy could take it out for a quick spin whenever he felt like. It would have horrified the average automobile collector, but not Floyd Hutton. He had his reservations, of course, a protectiveness for his car, but he also valued it highly enough to believe it could act as a useful teaching aid for Jimmy by hopefully instilling in him a real sense of responsibility, so marking another milestone in his maturity.

Jimmy thanked his father for trusting him with the car and swore never to let him down. Moreover, Jimmy went on to tell his father how he was the World's Best Dad and if there was anything Jimmy could do in return, he only had to ask. Unaccustomed to such heartfelt sentiment from his son, Floyd found the moment somewhat awkward, not unlike most men who are just plain hopeless at expressing their feelings. *You're a chip off the old block, Jimmy, a good kid, which is what we've come to expect from you. So we've decided to give you free rein of the car because we think you've earned it. Just act grown-up from now on, and everyone will always be right behind you,* was Ray Hutton's final advice, doing his demonstrative best. Jimmy promised he would on a day that promised not to disappoint: passing his driving test first time round, taking the Cadillac out with only himself at the wheel, and of course that rare case of male-bonding with his father.

As with any new, fully-licensed driver, Jimmy felt most grown-up on Saturdays when he had the car at his disposal. He loved the car, but not nearly as much as he loved his father, whose kindness would not go unappreciated. The car looked the part and certainly drove like a dream. An exquisite design, coupled with an impressive stock of horsepower and a dynamic manoeuvrability, made it fly like a demon in the wind. Jimmy relished its smooth handling that seemed to defy every known convention – its potentially crippling age, which should have seen it destined for the chop-shop, and its inordinate size, which made it almost as wide as a boat. On most nights, he would knock on for Ann-Marie and Carlton and they would drive around together, maybe take in a late show at the local Drive-In. Sometimes they would just cruise the freeways up until the City Limits. Other times, they'd go beyond and ride up to Liberty Heights, where they'd sit for hours in sweet solitude, talk and watch the earthlights of Memphis twinkling away in the distance.

Tonight, however, was strictly Movie Night. As planned, Jimmy picked up Ann-Marie with plenty of time to spare, and they headed straight for the RIALTO DRIVE-IN. They had invited Carlton along earlier, but he had politely declined, saying he was 'indisposed for the evening'. Him and his Pa (both of whom had mastered male-bonding to a tee) were going to crash out in front of the TV and watch, among other things, *Soul Train*; 'The Word On The Street' was that tonight's special guest star would be Antonio Fargas, aka Huggy Bear. An episode of *Starsky & Hutch* was expected to follow, the one in which David Soul gets possessed by hoodoo magic and tries to kill Paul Michael Glaser. There was also Richard Roundtree's super-cool detective to look forward to later on in *Shaft's Big Score!* A criminally funky, spunky night was up on offer on the box, compulsive viewing for those who were somewhat Blaxploitation-minded.

Viva Las Vegas was playing at the Rialto, and although Ann-Marie had seen this particular film over fifteen times, she and Jimmy nevertheless settled back in their respective car-seats to enjoy the flick, one of the better Elvis efforts. And, as Jimmy hoped, learn some Elvis in the bargain.

Whereas Ann-Marie always rooted for the relationship between Elvis and his leading lady, Jimmy's primary concern lay with the fabulous sights and sounds of Las Vegas, a location he himself dreamed of visiting one day. Stupendous shots of rich folk in long cars milling up and down the bright, colourful Strip past a mad kaleidoscope of neon signs and studded lights and blazing billboards. The casinos and the gambling joints, the nightclubs and the luxury hotels. Millions of dollars exchanging hands each night. The kitschy wedding chapels. Sunrise over the Hoover Dam.

Trip Central. Sin in Paradise. The City That Never Sleeps.

Las Vegas held a certain dangerous allure, making you come back again and again until it eventually destroyed you. Look what it had done to Elvis. Where once Elvis had set the concert halls of Memphis on fire and emerged a decade later as a Hollywood golden boy, he had quickly withered to nothing more than a cabaret act in Las Vegas. Although still performing to packed audiences, Elvis had effectively become a tragic lampoon of his former self. The lure of Las Vegas had been far too great for him to endure, and he had finally succumbed to its endemic madness. Las Vegas was where the high-rollers came to show off their wealth, but it was also a place where the foolhardy came to commit financial suicide . . . *or the real deal*. They didn't call it 'Gambler's Ruin' for nothing. Las Vegas laughed at you when it robbed you of your riches, whether it be your savings or your talents, leaving you crawling in the gutter, stumbling broke, unable to afford even a cup of coffee. Las Vegas made you feel big and important before sucking you dry.

Jimmy loved the motor-race through the Nevada Desert towards the end of the movie. Secretly aside from this, he had taken to admiring the *Terr-rific!* Ann-

Margaret. He shouldn't have (wasn't it enough he was in the company of his sweetheart?) but couldn't help it. Fast cars and gorgeous gals: the universal craving of all men. He wondered, quite confidentially he hoped (Ann-Marie would kill him if she knew. Probably will as well!), what Ann-Margaret looked like under that tight-fitting red dress, then speculated on a more ordinary note what Ann-Marie would look like bare-breasted and butt-naked, sucking on a soda-pop. His hard-on speculated with him, and it took a lot of will-power to keep the hungry mutt at bay, tucked away and out of sight. Almost as a guilty gesture, he tried putting his arm around Ann-Marie's shoulders, only to find her stiffen to his touch, shrugging him off. He promptly withdrew his arm from the passenger seat, altogether discouraged, and let Ann-Marie get on with the picture without any further interruption on his part. He glanced around at the other hot rods parked at the Drive-In and saw they were full of necking teenagers. It didn't take him long to feel he was missing out on something big with Ann-Marie. Perhaps he *ought* to be satisfied with her presence alone, but did she have to be so impersonal about it, so parochially platonic? Her stubbornness sometimes left him wanting to tear his hair out from its roots.

Gotta keep your girlfriend happy, particularly when she looks as cute as a chickadee, he later supposed of Ann-Marie, *even if it caters for her Elvis addiction.*

For Jimmy, there was, apart from the bright lights of Las Vegas and Ann-Margaret's feisty performance, something to be *had* from the movie itself, particularly towards the purposes of his essay, a deeper understanding of the actor playing the leading man. Since he had begun taking an interest in Elvis, Jimmy had gained valuable insight into the accomplishments of the King. It was intriguing to experience Elvis in a different context. Music was what Elvis would be remembered for, not his B-movies, yet Jimmy could clearly see where the attraction lay. The camera loved Elvis. Elvis had image. Elvis had star quality. Elvis had a photogenic presence and a sexual magnetism which women obviously went for. In a word, Elvis possessed a certain X-Factor which most men could only dream of. He smouldered on screen, fashioned a very believable hero: the man of action who was just at adept in the art of seduction. Elvis was almost too perfect for the role. Jimmy didn't claim to be a critic, but he thought Elvis could have progressed to a film star of some higher standing if the scripts had been remotely decent.

By the closing reel, Jimmy was rearing to go, confident of writing. He had made a good start to his project the previous night, the best thing he'd ever written. It had flowed out of him as naturally as an underground spring. Indeed, his work was coming along nicely, and he was keen to maintain the momentum.

Next week's main feature was *Grease*, but Jimmy wasn't intending on going. He'd seen John Travolta and Olivia Newton-John singing and dancing their way through *You're the One That I Want* too many times to really bother with it again. When the time came, Ann-Marie might persuade him otherwise, if there was nothing else happening, but as far as Jimmy was concerned, next Saturday sat blank in his calendar.

It began to drizzle, and Jimmy was forced to raise the car's hood. The cinema-goers vacated the parking lot in their respective cars. Jimmy was one of the last to leave. He took his time, once again marvelling at the clean rumble of the engine and the smooth, graceful response of the steering. In the few weeks that he had been driving his father's Cadillac, Jimmy was at last beginning to get a feel of its personality. '*Kick-ass elegant*' was how he'd describe it.

On the way back, making conversation with Ann-Marie was a near-impossible task. She appeared unusually reticent as though preoccupied. Her replies were short and perfunctory. She kept staring ahead to somewhere beyond the lighted streets, her mouth puckered small, her lips pursed. She was giving him the silent treatment.

"What's wrong?" Jimmy asked her, as he chased the Fuelly headers in the dark. The windscreen wipers swished back and forth, warding off the spats of rain.

"Nothing."

"Doesn't seem like nothing to me. Is it because of what I said?"

"No!" she snapped, causing him to flinch and nearly lose control of the car.

He quickly swerved back into the outer lane, narrowly avoiding a brown Buick that was speeding past. The driver of the Buick honked a long, furious warning before flipping Jimmy the bird and roaring on ahead.

"Then what is it?" he ventured more cautiously when he'd reassured himself that he was cruising within the speed limit and inside his own lane. He was still shaking from the close call with the Buick.

Ann-Marie didn't appear to have noticed how dangerously close they'd come to side-slamming the other car, for she had hardly budged in her seat. Now she turned to face him, exclaiming with unexpected venom, "*You know damn well what it is!*" Jimmy realized with growing dismay that Ann-Marie, who was normally sugar and spice and all things nice, was seized by a murderous rage. He saw flint in her eyes and hellfire, damnation, the fury of a woman scorned in her expression. Given a gun, she would have gladly shot him with it.

What did I do? Jimmy didn't like it when she became this way. It didn't bode well for the future. He should have known something was up ever since they'd left the Drive-In. He could sense an argument coming on. It had all the ominous signs: first the sullen silence, followed by the hateful accusations. He suspected he knew why she was behaving like she was, but he wasn't willing to remedy her feelings of humiliation just yet. They had last had a bit of a falling-out during the Fourth of July parade when he had innocuously commented on how good-looking Jennifer Love Hewitt was. He had apologized to Ann-Marie but not before she made him feel like some kind of adulterous, two-timing snake-in-the-grass.

Probably caught me checking out Ann-Margaret and that's got her rattled. Jealous, are we? Why not? Can you blame me if Ann-Marie isn't prepared to give me any? I mean what do you expect me to do? Shut my eyes each time I see a beautiful woman? I'm a man! I have needs! But does she understand? At least now she knows what it's like when she goes on about how amazing Elvis is. Like he was her long-lost lover or something. So how does it feel like to have a taste of your own medicine, punkin-dearest? Yeah, sulk away. I got better things to do with my time. I got me a story to write . . . strangely enough, about your dead idol, Elvis. You'll certainly be more forgiving when it's done!

"I love you," he murmured lamely. He didn't know what else to say.

"You don't love me!" Ann-Marie declared, rebutting the sentiment with cool, deadly resolve. "You think you do, but you *don't*."

How would you know? Do you love me? Have you ever once expressed that you love me? Because you're too wrapped up in your beloved Elvis to even admit it! "Suit yourself..." Jimmy muttered, feeling a little irritated himself.

The remainder of the ride home was a tense, unpleasant affair. Neither spoke nor made any attempt at reconciliation. Jimmy might have if he knew Ann-Marie were willing. But, as he recognized from past experience, no-one could get through to her when she was in one of her moods. Not that the wet weather helped matters; the rain beat harder as though sensing the deep animosity between them. Jimmy dropped Ann-Marie off and wasn't at all surprised when she omitted to offer even a cursory goodnight. Jimmy drove on without bothering to see if she got into her house safely, hoping to give Ann-Marie the impression that he was just as sore at her as she was at him.

He slipped the car competently into his driveway, a few houses down, and remained there for a couple of minutes, reflecting glumly on how a potentially wonderful evening had gone spectacularly wrong. A fight with Ann-Marie was never a good thing, but neither was he going to accept her tantrum when she didn't see it fit to take their relationship past token friendship. Frustrated like most teenage boys, his hunk-hunk of burning love could not be pacified so easily.

Maybe he *was* growing up. Maybe he needed something stronger, less neutered than the prosaic attentions of a family friend. Maybe he should do like some of the other students did and play the field, satisfy those hungry desires that plagued every horny teenager and, in his case, seemed so unfulfilled by his so-called girlfriend . . . Then again, maybe Elvis was all he really needed to ultimately convince her. He cut the engine, switched off the headlamps and clambered out wearily. He checked to make sure all the doors were locked.

It occurred to Jimmy what Carlton had mentioned out of passing only yesterday. They were all seniors now. It was a sad, scary thought. Scary because Jimmy could go one step better and already picture himself beyond the countless lunches on the football bleachers, the peephole appeal of the girls' locker room and the smell of dry chalk in history class to the mortar-board hats and billowing, silk gowns everyone would be expected to wear at the high-school graduation ceremony. College thereafter, then possibly University before pledging allegiance to the corporate greenback. Your years of reckless youth are far behind you and all you have to look forward to are the emotional crises of middle age and the brittle frailties of old age until death befalls you, sooner than you expected. You breathe your last breath, giving up a life you finally realize was too short for hollow arguments and needless worries.

There was also a terrible sadness enmeshed into this frightening, fatalistic future, for wasn't it always the case that the old gang splits up in the end? The drifting-apart was almost an inevitable part of life. Few were those personal friendships that stood the test of time. Different paths meant different friends, *new* friends. *Out with the old, in with the new.* Would Ann-Marie still mean as much to Jimmy when they finally embarked upon their different prospective careers? Would they still meet up or were they simply destined to lose touch? Was the time they had now their last chance at developing their affections for each other or was it already too late? How would their friendship pan out as they both took their first tentative steps towards adulthood?

Enjoy what you have now, son, make the most of the moment, because you'll find it may never come again. Here was another piece of advice, courtesy of Floyd Hutton, and it couldn't have made more sense to Jimmy standing there in the rain and gloom, delving on thoughts of estrangement and his own glaring mortality.

Life is all about making difficult choices and hard decisions in the hope of leaving a decent legacy for the ones you hold dear. It might well involve making a few sacrifices along the way, which may even be for the greater good.

For the greater good . . .

Ray had struck a crucial note. Jimmy considered this more deeply.

How would he like to be best remembered?

Law was simply out of the question; Jimmy neither had the brains for such an undertaking nor did he subscribe to the notion that real-life legal eagles got up to anything noteworthy outside the novels of John Grisham. No, cinema and music were where his sole interests lay. Elvis had got himself remembered through both mediums. James Dean for his handful of movies. And the equally-doomed Janis and Otis through their own distinctive contributions to music, as officially commemorated by the ROCK 'N' SOUL MUSEUM in Memphis. Some might even call them pioneers in their fields. No doubt they would all be remembered for a long time to come. Probably forever.

If they can do it, why can't I?

What was the secret of immortality? Fame, fortune and a tragic death? *Not quite,* Jimmy postulated. *Too messy, too unpredictable.* Fatal car crashes, drug overdoses, drownings and assassinations? Lives cut short in unpleasantly painful ways, most victims of their own stupidity and excess. *What vaguely notable fool in their right mind would prefer to die a horrible death in order for their lifetime's work to be preserved and celebrated by the generations yet to come? Unless you're enormously talented, an originator or innovator, you're liable to end up T-shirt of the Week or, if you're lucky, make Flavour of the Month, after which it's a given you'll slip into certain obscurity. What was it Andy Warhol said about the fickleness of fame?*

No, there had to be a quicker, easier route to lasting prominence. Jimmy had read about it somewhere. It was suddenly becoming quite clear. The book was still in his bedroom, gathering dust. He hadn't touched it since . . . since the Harpers had given it to him as a Birthday present almost five years ago when Jimmy had been deeply into that weird stuff: swapping horror comics with Carlton on a daily basis, never missing late-night repeats of *Night Gallery, The Twilight Zone* or *Tales from the Crypt.* Pa Harper even went on to claim that Haitian blood flowed in his veins, that some of Carlton's distant ancestors had been practising witchdoctors. Looking back, Jimmy could clearly recall being fascinated by such dark, esoteric knowledge, a phase he gradually grew out of, much to his parents' relief. Thinking about it now, this absurd lateral slant on reality, this twist on the supernatural . . . was it possible? Did such things exist?

The answer when it came was obvious. Crazy though it sounded, there was only one way to find out. *It's worth a try at least, I can tell you that much.*

[*For the greater good*]

If it doesn't work, what's there to lose?

Jimmy decided to let the matter rest there. Ann-Marie would regret her outburst in due course. Best to be standoffish – let her come to him. She'd soon come round from whatever grudge she was harbouring. Not out of some sinister intervention on his part but of her own accord. She was bound to. *Teenage angst, don't you just hate it? Add a pinch of PMT and you've got yourself a lethal concoction.*

He walked up to his house, mildly aware that Mrs. Conway was spying on him again. She would presumably have followed the events outside the Caitlins, seen Ann-Marie leave the Cadillac in a foul mood. More juice for the underground gabblers, except Jimmy didn't mind so much. He had more pressing things to worry about than the dubious connections of a twittering old lady. Like how he should go about the next, enthralling chapter in the Elvis saga.

His father was up when Jimmy returned home, drinking as usual and laughing out loud to *Saturday Night Live* in the lounge. His laughter had a genuinely sincere ring to it which Jimmy found rather comforting. His mother, who had heard the car approach, had dutifully set a steaming bowl of pigs' trotters on the kitchen table. Jimmy was famished. He wolfed it down, not really tasting it, more concerned with filling that grumbling emptiness in his belly. At the same time, he avoided any questions related to Ann-Marie that strayed in his general direction. He didn't feel his parents needed to burden themselves with the few trifling problems he was currently experiencing with Ann-Marie, so he retreated to his bedroom just as quickly.

Once in the solitude of his room, Jimmy went about his business as conscientiously as he could. The drum of the rain on the window disturbed him not. The incessant barking of the Grady's dog in the distance he barely took notice of. His mind was engaged elsewhere. By the buttery glow of his desklight, Jimmy gleaned up on Elvis's life and hit the typewriter like an investigative journalist trying to beat an important deadline:

Elvis Aaron Presley was born on 8th January 1935 near Tupelo, Mississippi, the son of a sharecropper and a part-time seamstress. His twin brother, Jesse Garon, was stillborn. They were a poor but pious family, and Elvis was always the apple in his mother's eye. Gladys took him everywhere, shopping, to religious meetings, their closeness growing during Vernon Presley's three-year spell in jail for forging a cheque. Elvis worshipped his mother and shared her bed until he was nearly nine years old.
Money was so tight in the Dust Bowl during the Depression that their diet regularly consisted of sweet potato, cornbread and possum, or deep-fried squirrel if

they wanted to treat themselves. They were eventually forced to move to East Tupelo after their house got repossessed. Because their new neighbourhood had no running water, Elvis showered outside when it rained.

Even from an early age, Elvis was a natural-born musical wonder. From only two years of age, he would accompany his mother to the First Assembly of God Church and join in the hymn recitals with her, which meant an early, extensive exposure to white gospel. From six years onwards, he went on to absorb a good deal of R&B from his black neighbours.

The U.S. entered the war in 1942. In the Philippines, 36,000 G.I.s surrendered to the Japanese. Rationing of coffee, sugar and tinned food hit America. People were allowed only three pairs of shoes a year, not that it affected the Presleys, since Elvis walked barefoot in the summer and wore hand-me-downs in the winter.

At the age of ten, he sang 'Old Shep' in school. His teacher was so impressed she entered him in a talent contest at the Mississippi-Alabama Fair and Dairy Show where he came second, winning a $5 cash prize.

Unable to afford a bicycle, his parents bought Elvis a guitar for his eleventh Birthday. A tad shy, Elvis only played his guitar in his bedroom when no-one else was watching.

When work dried up for Vernon in Tupelo, he moved his young family to welfare housing in Memphis. Elvis would get through his formative years at Humes High without achieving any formal qualifications. He tried a number of jobs, ranging from interstate trucking to working for a tool-company, but none of them suited him more than his favourite pastime: learning the guitar and singing the delta blues. Loew's State Theatre, where he worked as a grip in 1950, provided him with an outlet for self-expression, but Elvis ended up losing his job after a fight over a girl. There, the last building blocks of his personality would be moulded together: a quiet defiance, a greased-back quiff 'like the truckers used to wear it', and a timid, fish-out-of-the-water relationship with the opposite sex.

Opportunity knocked, and a seventeen-year-old Elvis got the crucial break he needed when he recorded a demo in 1953 at Sun Studio, 706, Union Avenue. Evidently, the promoter and founder of Sun Studio, a shrewd businessman named Sam Phillips, had been looking for 'a white singer with a black voice' and Elvis fit the bill perfectly. Phillips battled to get airtime at the local radio station. Phillips took a chance, risked everything, and Elvis solved all his problems. Then they would all come running: Cash, Orbison, Jerry Lee. 'My Happiness' was a purely private recording from Elvis, meant as a Birthday present to his mother. His first official Sun record was a track titled 'That's All Right Mama', which Phillips took to the local radio station, WDIA, the first black radio station. However, on July 14th, 1954, a DJ on a rival station, WHBQ, played Presley's 'That's All Right Mama' on a continuous loop for a whole hour. Before Elvis knew it, it was a local hit, the most requested record on the radio, and a legend was born. That was Memphis in those days, a community shaken by racial strife, a time of segregation, but coming together on the radio waves, playing records in the car with the windows rolled down. Rather than being a white man with a black sound, some people would accuse Elvis of being a white man who 'stole' black music. Elvis believed all culture should be shared. Elvis sang the blues, did not sing about the blues, because he had lived it growing up.

Elvis's next efforts in the coming year included other R&B standards such as 'Blue Moon of Kentucky', 'Good Rockin' Tonight' and 'Baby Let's Play House', all of which guaranteed him live dates throughout the South, including at the Levin Shell, an open-air theatre, where he gave one of his first concerts, as well as a regular spot on KGRI, confirming once and for all Elvis was here to stay. He released one, final Sun record, a slick, pulsating cover of 'Mystery Train', before deciding to move on. 'Colonel' Tom Parker, an indomitable figure but at the mercy of the Mob because of his gambling habit and shady business deals, became his personal manager and struck a hard bargain with the record companies. Those were the days when the businessmen tried to figure out the music and the musicians tried to figure out the business.

RCA signed him up in 1956 after some stiff competition from the Columbia label. From then on, his publicity only grew, steamrolling to mythic proportions. 'Heartbreak Hotel' was the definitive breakthrough, with 'Blue Suede Shoes' and 'Hound Dog' following close on the heels, all number ones, driving his fans delirious with delight. His live performances caused something of a scandal. Elvis stated that while some people tapped their feet, some people snapped their fingers and some people swayed back and forth, 'I just sorta do 'em all together, I guess.' However, the dyed-in-the-wool critics nailed him for his supposedly lewd, improper, 'negro' dancing routine, nicknaming him 'Elvis the Pelvis', claiming his kind of devil's music could only lead to an outbreak of juvenile delinquency and corruption of the white youth. Make good girls bad . . . so bad. Even Frank Sinatra expressed his dislike for the growing influence of Rock'n'Roll, calling it 'a vulgar, rancid-smelling aphrodisiac' and Elvis, one of its champions, 'a third-rate punk'. On the silver screen, 'The Wild One' and James Dean's 'Rebel' were making waves, notorious greasers drinking Wild Turkey.

Elvis survived the hoopla by taking photo-opportunities and making several guest appearances on numerous prime-time shows, including 'The Dorsey Stage Show', 'The Perry Como Show' and 'The Ed Sullivan Show', to improve his image and bolster his charismatic profile. This carefully-chosen national promotion paid dividends. Soon the seething critics packed their bags and went home, admitting defeat, among them Ole Blue Eyes, who now felt suddenly obligated to invite the third-rate punk to his show.

The Rock'n'Roll craze continued to sweep the nation. By his increasing popularity, Elvis triumphed and was soon crowned the 'King of Rock'n'Roll'.

At the age of only twenty-one, he bought Graceland for $68,000, a semi-derelict mansion on the edge of Memphis, and moved in with his parents and grandmother. And there was no holding him back as his film career took off. Elvis Presley would come to be the ultimate embodiment of the rag-to-riches ideal, a parvenu exemplified. For Elvis, fame happened so fast that he thought he was dreaming. On the pitfalls of finding stardom, Elvis once commented: 'If you let your head get too big, it'll break your neck.'

They say Elvis grew up too fast. Or maybe he never did.

Ann-Marie was upset like she was sometimes after an Elvis flick.

I know tear-jerking's uncool and unsophisticated, but what can I do? I need him. I love him. I worship him."

She'd seen Elvis at the Drive-In and was now even more crazy about him than ever. All she could think about was Elvis. He haunted her waking thoughts. He aroused her deepest desires, like the rekindling of the bittersweet memories of a former Casanova in an old flame. Elvis was why she was here, on this earth, and in such awful turmoil. To revel in his past glories and suffer his tragic loss. Her anguish and burning passion for Elvis corresponded with a hard, implacable contempt for Jimmy. Jimmy, good old Jimmy, *horny* old Jimmy, who often pictured himself as some modern-day interloper in the rye, possessed all the subtlety of a brick through a window.

Joshua Caitlin was working the night shift at MARRIOT'S FARM. Cloris was downstairs entertaining guests: the Wives' and Daughters' Bible Group, made up mostly of the same members as the Quilting Circle. Ann-Marie would be expected to join her shortly in preparing the cheese-and-wine supper.

But presently Mother's Little Helper sat in her bedroom, weeping away, moping over the countless singles and LPs she possessed of the King, her tears and lipstick marks staining a fair number of the record sleeves. The room was a shrine to Elvis lore; posters, books and mementos of Elvis were everywhere, some of them rare collector's items.

What was the point of being President of the Buile High Elvis Presley Fan Club, she sometimes wondered, when everyone on the planet knew she could never get to meet the legend himself?

She stared down at her greatest treasure, a priceless, specially-signed photograph of Elvis from his days of military service:

To my Darling,

Eyes like buttercups, lips like cherries,
The face of a sweet, white dove;
Your smile lives on in my garden of memories,
As I cry for your love from the Heavens Above.

ELVIS XXX

God only knew who the 'Darling' [*Priscilla?*] in the poem was, but Ann-Marie liked to imagine that he was referring to her.

If only it were true.

Was it wrong for her to care so much for someone who had died well before she was even born? Was her dependence on Elvis irrational? A *sickness*?

No, she assured herself, *a lot of folk feel like I feel, even now. Just go out into the street and ask them. They'll explain how much Elvis meant to them and their families, and how much he still does. They might even tell you it's no great crime to want him as madly as I do.*

He'd be in his mid-sixties today, probably chasing after Britney Spears, and Ann-Marie would still have loved him.

Why did he have to die?

The world was a sadder, duller and oh, so lonelier place without him.

It hurt. Hurt like hell. The Lord had given Elvis a gift, then taken the man away from his people. So, for the time being, she could curse the Lord for killing the King. That at least made the hurt go away.

Dead.

The King was dead.

Thank you for reminding me, Jimmy Hutton. Exactly the kind of information I could have done without. Rub salt into the wound – why dontcha? – while you lust, tongue hanging out after Ann-Margaret, you dirty lech! Don't you think I noticed the way you were ogling her, undressing her with your eyes? Try telling me you weren't about to cream your jeans, Mr. Randy Handy! You might as well have had a sign tattooed across your forehead saying: SPERM BANK DONOR.

Never again would Elvis be able to inject his own brand of magic to the sphere of sound that is music. Never again would his listeners draw strength from his unique vocal ability – countless times his voice alone had saved the day even if the songs were significantly inferior. Never again would the Baritone of Ballads tug the heartstrings with a pitch and depth unmatched by any artist since. Never again would the Voice croon to a multitude of adoring fans, except in those timeless recordings of yesteryear. Never again would the Master Performer adorn the stage, sing his lines to mellifluous perfection, then deliver a blistering encore to an enraptured live audience. Never again would the snake-hipped Dancehall Supremo, like some self-stylized marionette, send the crowds, especially the young ladies, into states of screaming frenzy. And never again would they see the sweat dripping from his brow in sheets as he gave it all he got.

Because one might say that the rehearsal for the next act was over before it had begun.

The King of Western Bebop was long gone. But not forgotten. Not in this house. Not in Old Shelby. Not in Memphis, Tennessee. Not in the world at large, even if he had never performed outside of the United States.

These days people were subjected to all manner of musical nobodies – from the cheap, saccharine-saturated popsters to the mindless, repetitive pap dished out by the techno-heads, from the gangsta-rappers glorifying sex, drugs and violence to the raucous, ear-bleeding mayhem of the trash metallists – none of them fit to kiss the shoes of Elvis. They were pretenders to an unreachable throne and came and went a dime-a-dozen. Elvis, on the other hand, twenty years in his grave, would outlast each and every one of them till the End of Days. *The King rules and will always rule.*

His greatness would live on.

Ann-Marie gave Elvis's photograph another emotional kiss and held it tightly to her heart. She sniffed again as she put on one more record before slipping under the bedsheets and dreaming of him lying next to her.

Elvis was well-established by now, even more so since he had started appearing in feature films as the lead role. His film debut was the horse opera 'The Reno Brothers' which was later re-titled 'Love Me Tender' for commercial reasons. It proved a tremendous hit with the cinema-goers, and Elvis's adjustment to the silver screen was complete. 'Loving You' ran next with its memorable soundtrack, including the hit single 'Teddy Bear'. 'Jailhouse Rock', too, was a stomping box-office success, then what is regarded by some as his best film, 'King Creole'. Tracks like 'All Shook Up', 'Party' and 'Trouble' were also storming the U.S. Hit Parade.

Such was his success that Elvis forked out a Cadillac for each of his faithful entourage, and soon went about getting a home.

In 1957, Graceland came into being on 3764, Highway 51 South (Elvis Presley Boulevard, as it would be later known), a grandiose colonial mansion that deserves a quick mention. The twin gates have an impressive cluster of musical notes welded in perpendicularly. A long, tree-lined driveway leads up to the main residence. A red carpet stretches down the main hallway. There is a lavish dining hall to the left, a projection room to the right and a living room straight on ahead that houses a white, grand piano and a trove of statues and foreign vases. The draperies are pure white corduroy as well as purple velvet with gold trim. A cream colour scheme is deployed to the living room, music room and hall. Stained-glass peacocks are set in frames in the music room. Beyond the projection room extends the kitchen, giant conservatory and swimming pool. Also, on the ground floor is his parents' bedroom, complete with poodle-print wallpaper in the en-suite bathroom. The garish basement television room, in acid yellow and black, is dominated by a lightning-bolt mural emblazoned with the letters TCB, which stand for 'Taking Care of Business'. There are three TVs in the room because Elvis liked to emulate Lyndon Johnson by watching three network news shows simultaneously. At the top of the gold-and-white grand staircase hangs a blue curtain with gold-fringed swag across the top. Beyond runs an endless concourse of guest bedrooms and private quarters and, of course, the fabled Jungle Room, a den with a vivid-green shag pile on the floor and a ceiling that is apparently excellent for the acoustics; the room would later become his recording studio. Graceland overlooks 14 acres of land, wherein lies the meditation garden - the site of Elvis's grave.

Elvis took a short hiatus from his movies when Uncle Sam called, and although he was regarded as a popular anti-establishment figure, he did not attempt to dodge the draft, Personnel Number: 53310761. His trademark hair and sideburns were cut off in a Press event, but apart from this he was treated like any ordinary soldier. He received no special favours from his commanding officers and worked 'just like everybody else'. He spent a fair chunk of his national service with the 3rd Armoured Battalion posted in the bleak Hessian winter, where he was eventually promoted to the rank of sergeant. He was given compassionate leave on account of his mother's failing health. She was to later die from cirrhosis of the liver (she had always had a weakness for margaritas), and Elvis, who doted on his mother, would be forever wracked with grief. It was one of the lowest points in his life.

Relieved of duty after this difficult two-year period, Sergeant Presley returned to the movie circuit and churned out a number of notable films like 'G.I. Blues', 'Flaming Star', 'Blue Hawaii' and 'Viva Las Vegas'. When Elvis was offered the lead in 'West Side Story', Colonel Parker would not let him take it, since three low-budget formula films could be made in the same time while proving more profitable overall. In the recording studio, Elvis remained King, his talents pouring out hit after hit, topping the charts, beating the competition. His style saw a shift towards bigger ballads such as the breathtakingly tremulous 'It's Now or Never', a deeply-moving revival of 'Are You Lonesome Tonight?' and the lush, sensuously exotic 'Can't Help Falling in Love'. There was still the pleasure of enjoying the vibrant, more uptempo numbers, in particular 'A Little Less Conversation', '(And Marie's Her Name) His Latest Flame', '(You're The) Devil In Disguise' and 'Guitar Man'. Surprisingly, the only million-selling single for Elvis, at a time when songs had taken second place to his films, was 'Return to Sender'. However, box-office successes meant chart-topping soundtracks, with Elvis soon becoming the highest-paid actor in Hollywood, commanding a million dollars per picture. However, Elvis admitted that he lost his musical direction during his Hollywood years, his songs nothing but the same 'conveyor belt mass production' as his movies.

The British band, the Beatles, were on the march, touring America, and Elvis sent them a congratulatory telegram. He would later invite them back to Graceland for drinks, dinner and some light jamming. That must have been one hell of an encounter. Somewhere in the world, there is preserved a priceless recording of that impromptu jamming session...

Interest in his love-life was growing when Elvis admitted that, while stationed in Friedberg, Germany, he had met a certain Airforce Colonel's fourteen-year-old daughter with whom he was still in close contact. There was a ten-year age difference between them. She would officially move into Graceland under the care of Elvis's granny in 1966. She would become his constant companion on film sets, and there surfaced rumours of an engagement. In December that same year, Elvis proposed. And on May 1st, 1967, he would tie that very knot with Priscilla Beaulieu, who was by then aged twenty-one, at the Aladdin Hotel, Las Vegas. They would honeymoon in Palm Springs and be rewarded nine months later with a child, christened Lisa-Marie. Now a devoted family man, things were looking exceedingly cosy for Elvis. Life surely couldn't get any better.

Some say he had reached his peak, and it was only a matter of time before his career hit the skids. Others said Elvis had never been stronger with still so much to give. Whatever the public opinion, whether he was past his shelf-life or still a dominant force in music, the happiness was not to last.

His fusion of gospel, blues, rock and country-and-western continued to flourish, but stories began to circulate of domestic problems, his growing erratic behaviour and his decline into drugs...

At a quarter to midnight, Jimmy stood by the telephone on the kitchen wall and dialled the number for the Caitlins. He was consumed by guilt. He felt he deserved a hundred lashings like some servant caught plotting to poison his master. He had derived no peace of mind from his angry confrontation with Ann-Marie, and although it had been less than two hours since they'd last quarrelled, Jimmy already felt he should rectify the situation.

Aw, shucks!

He'd screwed up royally. He'd offended her, wounded her pride. He'd checked out Ann-Margaret, and Ann-Marie had sussed.

But his other self, his bruised ego, wasn't prepared on letting go so easily. *So damned what? You can't fault me for being a man. Don't know what she's bitchin' about! It's not as if I was cheating on her or acting like a hunk of spunk like Elvis. Every couple goes through their ups and downs, it's a known fact. Make up and break up, break up and make up, sometimes for all the wrong reasons. Anyway, why is it always me who ends up apologizing?*

The essence of it was he'd got carried away, that's all. Ann-Marie would understand. She would have cooled down by now.

But that wasn't important now, was it? What was important was smoothing things out with Ann-Marie and finishing off his essay on Elvis. The latter he was particularly excited about. It was going so well, better than expected. He had spent a productive few hours and it was shaping up nicely. The best stuff he'd ever put down on paper in his life. Now it was a matter of maintaining the quality and flow of the thing.

After a couple of rings, someone picked up the phone on the other end. Jimmy took a deep, steadying breath, ensuring his voice didn't betray his nervousness. There followed a short, polite exchange: "Evenin', Mrs. Caitlin . . . I'm okay, thanks . . . They're okay too. Is Ann-Marie about? . . . That'd be great, Mrs. Caitlin. I promise I won't keep her long . . ." He waited, wondered again whether or not he should apologize for

[*The King is dead*]

his insensitive opening line and his apparent indiscreet appraisal of Ann-Margaret. *What d'you think of her, Ann-Marie?* his bad self sneered back. *Don't you reckon she's All Woman and much more?*

Screw it, Jimmy backtracked, feeling rather aggrieved. *I'm not apologizing. She ought to apologize to me for teasing me all these years, the selfish little hypocrite. I really shouldn't have called so soon. What was I thinking? I'm hanging up . . .*

Then, Ann-Marie was on the line. "Hello?"

Too late. Shut your butt and deal with it.

"Hi there, sweet pip, how y'doin'?" Jimmy asked cautiously, bracing himself, expecting short shrift, gearing up for her to cook his goose.

But the argument didn't materialize. "Not so good," she replied in a small trembling voice, not like Ann-Marie at all. "How are you?" Ann-Marie, whose mind was usually as level as shaved wood, sounded depressed and dejected. No doubt tears had been shed.

Jimmy had *definitely* upset her. All of a sudden, he felt the greatest remorse. He kicked himself for being so stupid, entertaining such cold, callous thoughts. He promptly pushed these earlier rankling emotions aside. How could he be so utterly oblivious to Ann-Marie's needs? He loved her, he respected her, was willing to die for her. Hell, he'd surely die *without* her. It was Elvis he hated, not Ann-Marie. All-in-all, Ann-Marie was a thoroughly decent girl, worth her weight in gold . . . just right for Jimmy. One girl you could never think ill of when she was at her most vulnerable. He was thankful they were no longer at loggerheads. *Why so glum, sweetheart? You know what's past is past. Just a whole lot of water under the bridge.*

"Desp'rate to see you," he admitted with total honesty. "I really didn't mean to offend you or hurt you in any way. If it's any small cons'lation, I'm sorry for acting like a mean and uncaring nitwit. Forgive me."

Ann-Marie interrupted him. "No, it's not you. I'm sorry for being such a grinch. I can take your wacky sense of humour. Believe me, it's me and my crazy obsession. I still get so worked up over Elvis."

That sinking feeling again and another faint tug of resentment. *Slam. Bam. Thank you, Ma'am.* A different breed of monster stirred inside him, scattering the troublesome scourge of guilt-gremlins. Jimmy realized at that instant why people thought of jealousy as a repulsive, green-eyed bug. It infested your scruples, sought out your baser instincts, then proceeded to feast upon your dwindling humanity with relish, perpetuating a cycle, ultimately bringing out the worst in you. Murder had been committed for less. "Do you wanna talk about it?"

"No, I don't think so . . ."

"You know, I miss you."

"I know you do."

"I don't s'pose you wanna see *Viva Las Vegas* again tomorrow night?" Jimmy suggested hopefully. "We'll do it prop'ly this time. If you catch me peekin' up the teacher's skirt, you can banish me to a monastery, you have my permission! I'll become an Amish or a Quaker or somethin' until you think it's alright for me to return to civilization. Or if you like, alternatively, you can lay me across your knee and spank me till I'm black and blue." Conspiratorially, he humoured: "Person'ly, between you and me, I prefer the spankin'. Is that a deal?"

Ann-Marie managed a small, husky laugh at the compromise. "I don't know..."

"Please, I'll make it up to you. You have my word as an officer and a gentleman. If there's somethin' I can do to make you feel better . . ."

"I don't think anyone can."

The hollowness of her reply didn't sound encouraging. His charm didn't seem to be having any effect on her. He bowed down, pleading, hating himself for having to resort to begging, the indignity and shame of it, but frankly having no other choice. "Come on, we're insep'rable." *No, Elvis and Ann-Marie are inseparable. I'm just a bystander caught between their love for each other.* "Partners-in-crime, remember? You Bonnie, me Clyde . . . You *know* I can make you feel better."

"Sometimes."

But not often enough. The man keeps making moves on my girl. "Don't sell yourself short. Elvis might be closer than you think."

"Don't tease . . ."

Jimmy was struck by a suggestion, possibly a way to kill two birds with one stone. It might serve as a fitting apology and yet cater to her love for Elvis. "How's about I sing you a song?" he ventured.

Ann-Marie immediately warmed to the novelty. "I'd like that," she whispered rather daintily, and Jimmy detected a slight improvement in her, a perceptible brightening of her mood. This was more like the Ann-Marie he knew. It was precisely that cute, bubble-popping innocence of hers that made her so adorable to him. At least they were in agreement for once. They could have both used a hug right about now.

"There was nary a voice as fine as mine," Jimmy bantered breezily on.

"Stop exaggerating, silly."

"You never know, you might be pleasantly surprised . . . What'll it be?"

She deliberated for a brief moment, then told him.

This time, Jimmy was sure there would be no disappointing her. "Anything for my special girl."

With his new-found singing skills, he took it from the top, ready to put on a good show for his girlfriend down the phone line. Jimmy sang. A sad, old number by Elvis.

He certainly impressed her that night because, afterwards, she didn't feel quite so lonesome again.

Sweet dreams or horrid nightmares, on which side of the dreamline are you sleeping?

He is at a concert, a congested, cram-packed, sell-out concert. He is but one of hundreds of people, mostly screaming teenage girls, who have turned out in force to watch a legend perform. Although it is a perfect vantage point from where he is at, standing closest to the stage, there are so many bodies jostling him, pressed against him, he is in danger of being crushed. He already feels half-suffocated by the heat and noise. What the hell he is doing here, he doesn't know. All he is aware of is that he has somehow found himself smack-bang in the middle of a concert with no idea how he got there.

Up on stage, Elvis is performing his heart-rending rendition of Are You Lonesome Tonight? *He croons into his mike with consummate professionalism, his voice a powerful vibrato that rises above the elated screams of his fans. His cool, starkly handsome face never ceases to amaze, capable of turning every woman weak at the knees, every man green with envy. His dark hair cascades across a sweat-soaked forehead above blue eyes that blaze with fiery passion. To Jimmy, he looks both rich and ridiculous clad in a cape and white jumpsuit. The rhinestones studded on his extravagant costume wink and glitter under the glare of the spotlights. A profusion of red roses is strewn across the stage, completing the image.*

Where is this place? *Jimmy wonders.* Birmingham? St. Louis? Carson City? *There is no way of telling. It certainly isn't the 'Elvis Lives 2000 Tour' when his former bandmates hooked up old footage of Elvis on the big screen and beat out all his hits as if he were there in person.* Clever concept, *the critics had called it,* but sacrilege all the same – why can't they just let the dead rest in peace?

Except Elvis isn't dead. Jimmy can see him from where he is, as clear as daylight. Elvis is alive and well, here at this concert.

How–?

Elvis strides casually to the front of the stage, removes the white silk-scarf from around his neck and drapes it upon the wrist of one of his screeching fans, like a king bestowing a precious gift upon a particularly loyal subject. The lucky recipient, a red-haired girl of about fifteen, shrieks in swoony disbelief as she shows the scarf to her friends. Elvis moves on, still crooning away magnificently into his mike with that sublime, rhapsodic voice of his. From stage left, a roadie appears, slips an identical scarf around Elvis's neck, then retreats into the shadows. Below centre stage is a strange sea of faces, some pale and nondescript, others streaming with tears, weeping away at the raw emotion of the song. Groping hands reach out to touch the King like paupers begging for scraps, hoping to be the next in line for another prize, a small souvenir apart from their ticket-stub that will allow them to relive this glorious night forever, something they can tell their children and grandchildren about in years to come. This scarf once belonged to Elvis. I swear I was there, that night, when he gave it to me.

Elvis drifts along the edge of the stage, and his roaming eyes suddenly fix upon Jimmy. His upper lip curls in characteristic laconic style, casting a conceited knowingness in his expression that causes Jimmy to shudder inside. Elvis has picked Jimmy out unerringly from a surging mob of adolescent girls and is actually smiling *at him – there is no mistaking otherwise. Elvis, who has somehow sprung back to life,* [Why don't they just let the dead rest in peace?] *is watching Jimmy with an interested gaze. A close, friendly,* entre-nous *kind of gaze.*

"Well, ladies and gennelmen," Elvis announces, digressing from his song, "hope y'all doin' mighty fine because we have a special surprise for you tonight . . ."

The crowd roars its excitement.

In the background, the rhythm section maintains the unchained melody.

"There is someone among us who is not from the State of Mythic," Elvis continues, watching Jimmy more intently than ever. "Someone who has come from the outside to join us in our hour of resurrection. Let me intra-duce you to a very special fella. Give a big, neighb'ly welcome to... James Hutton!"

Then the King is beckoning Jimmy into the limelight. Summoning him up on stage as the Boss once rallied a then-known Courtney Cox to dance with him. "Come on up, son."

Jimmy, who can't understand what Elvis could possibly want with him, let alone how he could know him by name, freezes up, too shocked to respond. For a moment, the shock overwhelms him. Then he sees the crowd are showering him with applause, pushing him from behind, nudging him forward. He gets a few admiring glances from the ladies, warm support and congratulations from the men. They are all urging him on as though he were a decorated war hero finally returning home from enemy territory where his plane was shot down over sun-scorched desert and he was presumed 'Missing in Action'. Stepping up to receive the Congressional Medal of Honour or perhaps a Purple Heart.

He *must honour*

[the President's]

the King's wishes.

The paralysis releases him, and Jimmy climbs on to the platform with flushed awkwardness, eventually encouraged up by a helping hand from Elvis.

Elvis shakes hands with Jimmy on stage and wraps an accommodating arm around his shoulders as if they are soul brothers or close drinking buddies. "Nuthin' to be afraid of, son," Elvis whispers into his ear.

Jimmy isn't sure whether he should be afraid or not. He is still recovering from a daze. The crowd cheer him on regardless. Elvis raises his hand, gesturing for hush, and almost instantly the noise quietens down. The band carries on in abiding, mellow tones.

"Where you from, Jimmy?" Elvis asks him.

Jimmy finds the words on his tongue huge and cumbersome. It is almost impossible to talk, standing next to the King in the brilliant spotlight, with so many attentive eyes focused on him. His shoes trample roses with impunity. "O-O-Old Shelby, sir."

"Old Shelby, huh? Twenty miles from Memphis. Memphis – that's where I'm from. One swell place is ole Memphis. Ain't that so, folks?"

"YEEEAAH!" the audience agree with a good-natured cheer.

Elvis becomes thoughtful, contemplative. "Yeah, been a long time since I last stepped foot in Memphis. Don't think I can ever go back in my condition . . ."

What condition? Jimmy wants to ask, but he is unable to do so because the answer is right in front of him. For the first time, he notices the smell emanating from Elvis. Beneath the clean smell of sweat and fresh aftershave is a peculiar undersmell: the slow, turning smell of corruption, the low, sickening reek of a small animal that has crawled into a cellar and died.

". . . *unless our friend Jimmy can lend a hand,*" Elvis muses, patting Jimmy on the back. "*I really miss good ole Southern hospitality. Are you game?*"

Game for what? Jimmy demands, suddenly suspicious. He feels a horrible uncoiling in his stomach. He senses nothing is as it seems.

"*Thank you for comin'. We all appreciate it. Don't we, folks?*"

The crowd go wild, roar their approval. They treat Jimmy like a celebrity.

Elvis is addressing Jimmy again when the commotion has subsided a little. "*So, son, are you prepared to lay down your life to help me win back mine? Be the vessel of my rebirth? Are you game?*"

Jimmy now has a firm handle-hold on what is going on. He doesn't like it one bit. He has suspected all along that he has been deliberately brought here

[Never heard of the State of Mythic before]

from the outside to fulfil some single, dread purpose,

[The Hour of our Resurrection?]

and he realizes with frightening clarity what Elvis and probably the damned audience are after. He recognizes perfectly what this little exhibition is in aid of.

They want him. They want Jimmy to sacrifice himself. Sacrifice himself in some nameless, godless way.

But Jimmy isn't so forthcoming. The idea of possession – which is what Elvis is hinting at, right? – is a non-starter. He's getting out of here before it's too late. If Elvis thinks he can lull Jimmy into a false sense of security, then he is gravely mistaken. "*I'd love to help, Elvis, but you know how it is,*" Jimmy counters candidly. "*You're not real. None of this is real. You're dead. You're all dead! And you're feeding on my dreams like-like . . . mindworms.*"

"*Excuse me?*" murmurs Elvis, momentarily taken aback.

The audience is stunned, the sounds of teenage hysteria completely silenced. Even the band has stopped playing. The people stare and the spotlights glare. They can hardly believe it! The shameful disrespect! The King has been refused, flat-refused by this miserable, uncooperative excuse of a boy. How can this happen? How could such a lesser mortal deprive the King of new life?

"*Uh-huh-uh,*" Elvis says, nodding slowly, moving away from Jimmy. "*I like your honesty, son, but I'd like you to reconsider. I thought we were friends.*"

"*No way, José!*" Jimmy cries adamantly. The decision is made, and no amount of persuasion will sway him. He is not about to sacrifice his whole existence just to let Elvis live again. He can't, he won't and he mustn't. He has never liked Elvis in his entire life, and his views aren't about to change now that he has met him. On the contrary, this bizarre, surreal encounter *has only served to strengthen his dislike. Elvis has displayed all the obnoxious traits that have accompanied him to his death – arrogance, vanity, bombast – and Jimmy has learned a couple more. They hardly enhance the King's appeal.*

Incredulous gasps from the audience, followed by a few vindictive boos.

Must wake up. Must get out of here . . .

"Then, I guess I'm just gonna have to convince you," Elvis explains regretfully. "This ain't gonna be a pretty sight . . ." Right there on stage, standing a few feet away from Jimmy, Elvis has begun to grow old. "In fact, this is gonna be mighty unpleasant . . ."

His blue-black hair turns white, and countless wrinkles storm across his once-handsome face, humbling those impressive looks, etching deep merciless lines into his skin. Within seconds, his flesh has taken on the texture of dried prunes.

"Will you do it, Jimmy, will you? Are you game?"

Jimmy doesn't want to look, but the temptation is just too great. He stares in fixed horror as the aging process races on as though caught on fast-lapse camera until Elvis has reached the outer limits of old age . . . and beyond. *If Elvis had lived to be a hundred in real life, this is what he would have looked like: stooped, gaunt and ancient, the skin on his lined, shrivelled face cinched tight across his high cheekbones, his pate visible through a fine, white gossamer of hair. Milky cataracts cover both eyes, the corneas already yellowed.*

"Are you game? Are you game? Are you game?"

But the physical degeneration doesn't stop there. Surface tumours erupt all over his face. The skin splits open in crusty, suppurating sores. The nose erodes and drops off. The lips decay, revealing brown festering teeth. Those eyes, those bewitching blue eyes that have been one of the King's finest features, sink back into their sockets. The flesh moulders and sags with minute, crawling things. Bone gleams through in various places. Even his costume thins, stretches and frays. Jimmy is now looking at a living corpse dressed in dirty, shredded rags.

The stench is thick and all-encompassing like the high, gassy, gagging stench of open graves and recently-exhumed bodies.

Jimmy turns away from this hideous spectacle only to discover the rest of the band have aged as well. He swings his head the other way and sees the audience too are rapidly decomposing into the same mummified abominations. Jimmy is trapped in a concert hall, surrounded by a plague of zombies like something out of Night of the Living Dead. *They shuffle towards him from every direction, all pointing accusing fingers at him.*

Jimmy moans, cringes when Elvis – or what has become of Elvis – puts another brotherly, albeit skeletal arm around his shoulders. "Are you game?" the lipless, tumour-raddled face jabbers. "Are you game?"

Please, no, this can't be happening!

The last of Jimmy's self-control breaks down, and he starts to scream, scream like a lunatic, into the farthest reaches of this corpse-laden nightmare . . .

A dull gunmetal dawn is creeping across the eastern sky as Ann-Marie moans in her sleep, rolls over and nudges against—

—Her eyelids fly open like shutterblinds.

Something is wrong, different, out-of-whack.

Terror flares through her, and she leaps from the bed, her reaction like that of someone who has just woken up in a nest of scorpions.

Her sudden movement disturbs the other occupant beneath the bedsheets, a breathing man-shaped lump that stirs sluggishly.

There is someone in bed with her. *Sound asleep by the looks of it.*

Her own sleep completely shot, she tries to make sense of the situation, distrusting what she is seeing almost to the point of complete denial. Except she can't dismiss the admissible evidence snoozing away peacefully under the sheets.

Christ, there's someone in my bed . . .

She went to bed alone last night. Okay, she'd played with herself, but she remembers going to bed alone. Ann-Marie, who has never ever taken a lover or shared her bed with one, is greatly upset and understandably disgusted.

So who has gotten into her bed? Who could do such a despicable deed? Who—?

Jimmy.

The name just pops into her head.

No, not Jimmy, surely. He is a fine, young man, one whom she intends on marrying some day. Jimmy could never climb into someone else's bed like that, not even on a prank.

He loves me too much.

Is that a reason? Sentiment can be so uncool, unsophisticated sometimes.

She rebuffs the possibility of it being Jimmy. Besides she has Jimmy wrapped around her little finger. Jimmy knows the restrictions. He would have to be crazy to pull a stunt like this.

What if it's a total stranger? Snuck in through the window, slipped into my bed?'

It is a far more troubling thought, yet more plausible, and it brings on a fresh wave of panic. It sloshes and splashes around inside of her like liquid in a watering can.

Unlawful entry. Attempted assault—? The charges are very serious, indeed.

She feels sickly scared and too exposed for comfort. She tries to address some of her modesty, desperately stretching the length of her white T-shirt to hide her pink panties.

Who could do such a thing? Sneak into a young girl's bed like that, without asking?

Not that she would have let him in anyhow.

How long have they been there?

She stares at the somnolent mass hidden beneath the sheets, the grey pre-dawn light giving no indication as to their identity.

Who is it?

'Pervert' comes to mind. More disturbingly, so does the word 'rapist'.

Stop shitting yourself and do something, *her thoughts pedal, round and round, faster and faster.*

What do you expect me to do? Run? Call the cops? Scream across the hallway for help?

No, she must determine [Are You Lonesome Tonight?] *who the intruder is before she takes any further course of action.*

Composing herself, she tiptoes nearer, each step a conscious effort. Her throat feels as dry as a flannel, her stomach a tight knot. Her heart is a runaway threshing machine in her chest.

She reaches forward nervously, grasps a handful of the coverlet . . . and, holding her breath rigidly,

[lonesome are you lonesome lonesome are you]

she snatches it away, instantly unmasking the mystery guest . . . then lets out a long shuddery gasp. "Oh, my God . . ."

"I guess I am."

It isn't Jimmy, neither a stranger intent on rape.

It is the last person on earth she is expecting to see.

He is naked, apart from a pair of black dungarees.

A man of powerful iconic presence. A man voted the world's greatest sex symbol of all time. A man whose artistic courage was an inspiration for generations to come. A man much talked about and revered by the TV stations, newspapers and magazines, more than any other Rock superstar. A man largely captured by the eternal posters, photographs and publicity stills plastered around these very walls.

The same man, who is presently in Ann-Marie's bedroom . . .

Dead but not forgotten. Not in this house, not in Memphis, not by all the populated world.

As his sleepy, bedroom eyes meet hers, a sly sardonic smile spreads across his face.

"Elvis . . ." Ann-Marie croaks in a mixture of fear, joy and genuine bewilderment, trying to grasp the meaning of it all. Here she is in the company of the boppin', bubble-poppin' man of her dreams. It's almost too good to be true.

I've waited for this moment all my life, *she thinks, suddenly immensely proud and a little bashful. She's not looking her best for her white knight. The embarrassment, however, is short-lived. Happiness prevails, as soulful as it is sweet, sending her to new dizzying heights of utter bliss. She feels blessed. She's in her own heaven.* How many girls can say they've woken up next to Elvis? How many? Elvis, the King, has chosen me above all others. He has shown himself to me – and *me* alone. It was meant to be.

They look at each other longingly, lovingly, *as if they are bride and groom after the wedding reception about to embark on their torrid, intimate honeymoon. At last, they are alone, together. That's all that matters now. Everything else be damned.*

"Are you just gonna stand there, sugarpie," Elvis asks her softly, coaxingly, "or are you gonna give me a li'l lovin'?"

There, he said it! He wants me. He's calling for me.

This is too much. I think I'm going to faint . . .

We must sin before we seek salvation. So quit dithering.

The hot-bloodedness inside her triumphs, crushing any lingering fears. I can't let him down, surely. He is the King. Oh, *anything* for the King . . .

"I'm coming, darling," Ann-Marie, who has never in all her sixteen years surrendered herself to any man, whispers back. "Please be gentle with me." She is about to hop into bed with her dream-lover, planning on giving him more than just a li'l lovin', when the unexpected happens.

It brings her back from her private fantasy with terrifying speed, ripping through her eager confidence and blind, aching desire as cleanly as cougar claws through warm flesh.

His face flickers, changes like a wet-wired cable transmission, like the prints of two different people superimposed on one another. Becomes transparent, less vital, less there, *and at that moment Ann-Marie is staring down at an apparition of Jimmy, fighting for control, his expression twisted in a rictus of mortal agony.*

Sinister crawlings run up and down her spine.

Not only can she see through him, she can actually see into *him. Through gauzy, glassy flesh, the bulb of the brain pulses within the casing of the shiny, X-ray skull. Perfectly spherical eyeballs roll around in their dark sockets, and his tongue lolls behind a discorporate Reaper's grin to convey a low, stricken murmur, "Help me . . ."*

Ann-Marie stands dumbstruck, petrified, unable to move or break free from the sight of this unearthly manifestation.

Then to her relief, the image dims, ebbs away as though fading out of reality . . . and is gone, leaving only a faint imprint on the bedsheets where the phantom figure has lain.

When the alarm clock rings out its shrill tune, Ann-Marie screams.

The hot, humid spell continued into the next day, evanishing every last drop of rain that had fallen the night before.

The streets shimmered beneath the late morning sunshine, the sky above blue and clear and unclouded. Leaves hung limply from the trees, and dogs basked, frazzled and panting, in the ninety-degree shade. The National Weather Service predicted temperatures to soar even higher.

At the FIRST BAPTIST TABERNACLE CHURCH, Reverend Vincent Brooks was in the throes of his Sunday Service. He was sermonizing on the wicked ways of the world, in particular the evils of idolatry. This was where one normally found the neighbourhood any given Sunday, here chiefly out of plain Christian duty and partly because the good reverend expected as much from them. Unless the condition was life-threatening, Reverend Brooks did not take kindly to undue absenteeism. The parishioners listened patiently, fanning themselves now and again with their hymn books to ward off the oppressive heat.

"It feels like *weeks* since our hearts were ravished by the Glory of God," Reverend Brooks was preaching, his voice loud and commanding, "*months* since a hymn was sung with abandonment, *years* since tears trickled down the cheek of any worshipper." He leaned forward, clutching the sides of the pulpit firmly until his knuckles turned white. "We're guilty on that barren orthodox front, sitting here with our Bibles open, with all the theology known, and somehow completely *in-different* to the Spirit of Worship.

"Why? What is the 'Spirit of Worship', you may well ask?

"It is a fundamental question about the *appli-cation* of faith and one that I will answer without gildin' the lily. It involves worshippin' the Lord in Spirit from the *in-side*, glorifyin' God from *with-in*, using every scrap of devotion, filling thy heart with thy praise until it bursts forth and gushes His divine light. You must surrender yourself *absolutely* to its supreme power. And it is precisely that *resident* Holy Spirit that prompts your heart. If you don't have a spirit of God to summon, you *can-not* instruct . . . moti-vate . . . cleanse . . . purify your heart.

"I see that some of you, good folk, are ponderin' this very question. And so you should. Nobody, I repeat, *no-body* can escape the *enemies* of true worship: the *fake* religions and the *false* idols. They are among us everywhere, in every corner of society, open to every race, creed and colour. We *worship* Money, *em-brace* Science, *praise* Rock'n'Roll, *exalt* movie stars . . . then we claim there is no room left in our hearts for the Spirit of Worship," Reverend Brooks boomed, looking down upon his flock with a look of melodramatic contempt. "We put our trust in the sinners of our age, the graven images and the pop culture prophets, all those who have turned their backs on God, then wonder why we cannot find the righteous path, like sheep that have lost their way to the grazing pastures. Broad and paved with gold is the road that leadeth to everlasting damnation for, as Psalm 135 points out, *the idols of the heathen are silver and gold, the work of human hands.* Do you not *re-member* how God punished the people of Babel? Did not the Lord visit his judgement upon Nebuchadnezzar? Is it not written in Exodus: *You shall have no other gods before Me?* Does not Deuteronomy state that if you choose to serve other gods, then the anger of the Lord will be kindled against you until He *des-troys* you?"

Jimmy Hutton sat in the back pew, beside his father, getting increasingly bored. Five minutes into the sermon, Jimmy was already finding it difficult keeping his eyes open; by fifteen minutes, he had almost lost the will to live. He really didn't think much of evangelical ministers as a whole, a bunch of Bible-bashers, egotists, seducers, fornicators, confidence tricksters and very occasionally apocalyptic suicide-cultists, except in this instance he had to concede Reverend Brooks wasn't such a bad crop. At least Reverend Brooks didn't criticize or hypocritize, steal from the church fund or impregnate his women followers in the name of God. No, his heart was in the right place, and Jimmy considered him one of the better members of the God Squad. His oratorial style came straight from the school of Swaggart (Praise the Lord!), he listened to Johnny Cash whenever he could (naturally) and he was an extremely close friend of the Caitlins (confirmation enough of his good character). Unlike some of his brethren, the tireless old stalwart did as he preached and commanded plenty of respect from his fellow man.

Jimmy looked two rows ahead to where Ann-Marie sat. He had caught her sneaking glances at him throughout the service and he had smiled at her. She did not smile back. He noticed how unusually pale and strained she looked as though she had slept badly. He knew why. He recalled the incredible 'mind-meld' (for want of a better word) they'd shared last night on the only thing sacred to his darling dreamboat and wondered if she realized just how far he had progressed.

I love Elvis secretly, so secretly I don't even know it myself.

Little did Ann-Marie know, Jimmy had been *touched* by Elvis.

He had screamed into the night, the scream not only frightening himself awake, but also bringing both his startled parents rushing to his door. He was strangely disorientated and rambling on incoherently in his bed, his body slick with sweat, his eyes wild and dancing.

His father, who had been wearing just a blue bathrobe, had come carrying his shotgun, expecting trouble. His mother, dressed rather inappropriately for her age in a flimsy pink night-dress, had shook Jimmy by the shoulders to calm him down. "What is it, Jimmy? What's wrong?"

Jimmy stopped gibbering, looked at her uncannily and said: "Ma, I just seen the ghost of Elvis."

Floyd had blamed his son's strange behaviour on a bad dream, culminating from the essay he had been working on so diligently.

"Or p'raps you're comin' down with somethin'," Floyd added on a more serious note, downstairs. Jimmy took a sip from his milk-and-honey before munching on a cookie. "We might need to call in Doc Merrill in case you're catchin' a fever." Floyd had already hunted for a fever, found none, finally concluding it might be early days yet.

Was it not conceivable that Jimmy's old man was right? That Jimmy was experiencing the first signs of an infective process?

Perhaps . . . *perhaps not.*

However, was there not a constant stream of sightings of the King every so often? Didn't the newspapers put this phenomenon down to mass hysteria, born of fantasy, the product of wishful thinking?

Jimmy didn't think so, at least not in his own personal case. That magical concert. The scene in Ann-Marie's bedroom. Were these just figments of his imagination? A lucid dream, the kind where the person knows they're dreaming? Except Jimmy did not agree with his father's summing-up and remained convinced otherwise. The Elvis concert, he supposed reluctantly, could be attributed to a nightmare, even if inside he believed as surely as day follows night he had been there, *actually* there, in that mysterious place called Mythic. *Some nightmare!* He could still smell the atmosphere, still see Elvis strutting about on stage, still hear the amplified music and the gratified roar of the crowd, still vividly recall how the party had suddenly turned nasty. The face of Elvis, prune-wrinkled, warped with age. Okay, let's suppose he had been asleep and dreaming then . . . but certainly not when he returned to his room after that little talk with his parents.

That time, he was very much awake – *cock-a-doodling* awake – when it happened.

What happened, exactly?

Astral travel? Telepathic communication? A dip into the collective unconscious, like the cross-connection between two telephone conversations?

Jimmy couldn't explain it. All he remembered from this second experience was that he found himself floating

[*born of fantasy*]

in someone else's dream. He wasn't himself, either. There was a struggle going on inside, and he was losing. It was like he had brought something back with him from his previous nightmare. A *presence*. A restless presence that he could neither see nor hear – nor feel – but only sense. Inside him, drawing psychic energy, growing steadily in size and strength, like a cancer. He couldn't altogether remember what had occurred there, in Ann-Marie's bedroom. The harder he tried to remember, the vaguer became the specifics of the episode, like someone was deliberately blocking him.

But he knew somebody who might remember. In fact, he had scared the living bejesus out of her. She sat just two rows ahead, probably still unnerved by the whole thing.

The book had done the trick, all right. Something odd and inexplicable was going on. In some way Jimmy hadn't felt this good since he and Carlton had smoked their first doobie last summer under the school bleachers. After the initial coughing and hacking, the gathering euphoria had been amazing, the colour and contrasts of the world around them brighter and sharper, motion slow and dreamlike, the sounds so perfectly defined you could hear a pin drop.

Admittedly, he also felt mighty peculiar. When he'd got up this morning, he had noticed his eyesight had improved, the contact lenses now redundant. His hair had somehow changed, sprouted thicker from the roots, as dense as horse-mane. And the skin on his face tingled all round as if anticipating the onset of a nervous rash. Even his father had commented on his appearance on the way to Church: "I don't know what it is, Jimmy – I can't quite put my finger on it – but you look kinda different . . . *fresh*."

"Just a boy's natural growth spurt," Jimmy lied, trying to act nonchalant.

Something was happening to him. Something beyond the normal constraints of nature, something weird and wonderful and out-of-this-world.

A miracle, perhaps, assisted on by the guiding hand of God?

Elvis spoke to me. Give your sweetheart what she desires most. That defines my purpose.

Later that day, Jimmy would consult the books, resume his research and finish his comprehensive guide to Elvis undisturbed, purely for the sake of the miracle in progress. For all miracles must be allowed to run their course, like a secret, subterranean river, unseen by the citizens above, winds its way to the tidal mouth. *Let's see where it takes me . . .*

In Elvis's own words: *You can do and be anything you want to in life as long as you have faith in God, faith in yourself, be willing to work for what you want and never let anybody tell you that you can't accomplish your dreams, because if you believe totally in yourself, there is nothing you can't achieve.*

I have found my calling, Jimmy thought contentedly. *Not long left before the grand unveiling.*

The sermon was nearly over, except for the hymns, which was exactly what Jimmy was waiting for.

". . . And worship *not* the false idols for they *de-value* that very part of us that is immortal," thumped Reverend Brooks, "strengthening the grip of darkness. Human nature is tainted by Original Sin. War, greed, hatred, pride, lust. Satan is in all things, and we must combat his artifices of vice and *temp-tation* with ev'rythin' our hearts can muster. Be not conformed to the heroes of this world – the secular idols – but be transformed by the renewing of your mind. Do not give the Devil access to your heart or the rights to your soul. The Devil says you should have the time of my life before you die, but do not let him steal that immortal part of you. God tests Man to see if we are worthy of His mercy. Let us be God's right hand to strike down those who put their faith in false miracles. Sometimes a 'miracle' is nothing more than a vulgar illusion – a *magic trick* – conjured up by the Father of Lies with the deliberate designs to *de-ceive*. Heed the words of our Maker. If our hearts are full of His praise, we shall triumph. If our hearts are lacking, then we will suffer Now and in the Hereafter. We are *all* of us God's children and only the glorious Spirit of Worship, brought to us by Jesus Christ our Lord and Saviour, can weaponize our hearts and deliver us from all Evil. *Amen.*"

"Amen!" repeated his flock in clamorous unison.

"I'm afraid, that's all for today," Reverend Brooks declared somewhat solemnly. "May you take with you the Spirit of Worship and its true meaning. God bless you all and God bless America."

The congregation paid tribute to Reverend Brooks's call for spiritual awareness with a long, hale round of applause. It seemed Reverend Brooks never disappointed.

The gospel choir took over proceedings from that point on, striking up some ecstatic gospel singing, beginning with a joyous rendition of *What a Friend We Have in Jesus*. The rest of the packed church joined in, one voice rising above all the others: that of Jimmy testing out how far he had advanced vocally since taking up singing. Since taking up Elvis.

Pout those lips, swing those hips! Move to the music, the groove's at your feet! We're kickin' and revvin', rockin' and reelin'! Sing it, white boy, don't miss that crazy beat!

Jimmy sang without even trying. He flowed like a tenor, a natural-born musical wonder. The Spirit of Worship? Or the power of Elvis?

Holier than Jesus.

*****

Attention was focusing sharply on Elvis's private life. With the dawn of a new decade, rumours were rife of discontentment amongst his crew, a collapsing marriage and an affinity for drugs, both prescribed and illicit.

Perhaps it was due to his mother's loss that his attitude to women was so odd, somewhat concerning. Elvis got into a habit of dating underage girls from early on in his career. He often engaged in pillow-fights, would tickle, wrestle and kiss the girls. Romantically obsessed with virtue, he preferred heavy petting to mature sex and loved only to cuddle up next to a beautiful girl without offering anything deeper. At the height of his career, a constant stream of girls was invited to Graceland to spend a night in Elvis's king-sized bed, and the majority left the following morning, dissatisfied and confused. A prime example would be his relationship with Priscilla.

On the wedding night, it's been alleged he asked his bride to wear a schoolgirl's outfit and pose for some photos so that he could 'preserve her innocence' on film. For the first three weeks after returning from their honeymoon, they locked themselves away from the outside world. They kissed for long periods, went skinny-dipping, had pillow-fights, played hide-and-seek and watched T.V. And, during that time, they never once made love. Not until the odds swung Priscilla's way. They'd been kissing torridly when Elvis suddenly got up and told Priscilla in an almost fatherlike manner that he couldn't go on anymore, claiming he didn't want to corrupt her innocence, wanted her to remain pure and untouched. He disappeared into the bathroom and was there for quite some time. Hot under the collar and annoyed at Elvis's lack of sexual commitment, desperate to consummate their marriage, Priscilla followed him and banged repeatedly on the bathroom door, demanding he come out. He refused, stating he wasn't finished yet. Overcome by curiosity, she went outside, stood on the ledge and peeked through the bathroom window . . . only to discover Elvis beating himself off.

Priscilla was frequently quite maternal towards Elvis who was, in many respects, naive and infantile, a throwback to his Oedipal love for his mother, subconsciously reflected in the movie 'The Trouble with Girls'.

However, there was also another, darker side to him that

effectively wrecked his marriage. Priscilla learned to laugh when he laughed and deliberately avoided him during one of his black moods, most commonly caused by his intemperate intake of drugs.

His dependency on drugs, which began when he was posted in Frankfurt, Germany, taking amphetamines to keep himself awake on guard duty during the wintry nights, partially contributed to his inability to get a proper, grown-up grip on life. He threatened his own personal physician, Dr. Nichopoulos, with a gun because he'd confiscated his 'sweeties'. After that particularly nasty incident, Dr. Nichopoulos gave him whatever he needed whenever he needed it.

Two of his bodyguards, Sonny and Red, highlighted some of his erratic behaviour in their telling book on the King. The book was out of pity and not betrayal, the pair pointed out, the story of the consequences of a celebrity losing control. They too described his black moods and mean temper. If he didn't get his way, he would pitch a fit at anyone, even girls, who disobeyed him, sometimes punching them in the face. He was the boss, surrounded by lackeys who pandered to his every whim.

At home, he gained a reputation for shooting T.V. sets if he didn't like a particular show, his Ferrari if it misperformed and the toilet because it was just there to be shot.

Elvis learned karate, read books on religion, took up numerology and Scientology. He claimed he saw a UFO over Nashville. He sat and spoke to his own shadow in memory of his stillborn twin. He dressed absurdly, donned bizarre, garish, laughable costumes. Dressed outrageously in a cape-and-jumpsuit, he even visited the White House and talked Nixon into recruiting him as an undercover drug enforcement agent. How's that for unfettered lunacy?

He gave up on the movies, claimed their silly scripts always revolved around the same, dumb plotlines, so as to concentrate on his music and concert-touring. He needed to regroup, re-launch his career. Insulated from the progressive music scene for much too long, he decided to host a nostalgic one-hour Comeback Special, where he chugged out his old hits in front of a live audience, his first live performance for seven years. It was well-received, a return to form for the old showman, Elvis the hottest draw on television. This happened back in 1968 when things were still ticking along nicely, the show itself dedicated to his newborn daughter, Lisa-Marie. His Hawaiian concert in 1973 was another scintillating moment of musical history, watched by over a billion people in 36 different countries. Even to this day, there is no other musician who could boast such phenomenal success in the popularity sweepstakes.

Elvis and Priscilla divorced in 1973 when Lisa-Marie was only four. The painful break-up took matters to a new, all-time personal low. Elvis kept touring to numb some of the heartache. His diet was appalling: he consumed fried-egg, bacon and sausage breakfasts, fried chicken and meatloaf dinners, a casual mountain of cheeseburgers, éclairs filled with whipped cream, and possessed a prodigious appetite for jam doughnuts and the classic, calorific fried peanut-butter-and-banana sandwich. He took drugs to meet his punishing touring schedule (200 concerts in one year), and it wasn't long before these excesses took their toll. He collapsed during a concert in 1974 from over-exhaustion and was rushed to hospital in a semi-comatose state, not the first time he'd accidentally taken an overdose of barbiturates and painkillers. He recovered fast and returned to the stage. He now slept during the day and toured and partied all night. After a while, he was only getting up to go on stage and sleeping fourteen hours a day. Gradually he began to lose his looks.

The songs too had started to take on a grim, fatalistic quality. Scratch the surface of 'If I Can Dream', 'Suspicious Minds', 'American Trilogy', 'Always on My Mind' and 'Moody Blue' and you will find the succinct, tormented, 'last-stand' eulogy of a man, who is slowly losing the will to live. It doesn't mean he couldn't let rip some good old-fashioned Rock'n'Roll numbers once in a while. Tracks like 'Burning Love' and 'Way Down' are exactly of that jaunty variety, albeit examples of ribald rock.

But the downward slide had begun long ago and, as Las Vegas became his scene, his decline was fast heading towards a horrible conclusion.

In the end, Elvis was a sad, sorry sight: lonely and depressed despite his huge entourage, addicted to prescription drugs, morbidly obese, suffering from poor eyesight, high blood pressure and an irregular heartbeat, and incoherent. There were moments when he would be barely intelligible on stage. He was forgetting lines, drifting off in choruses and mumbling apologies to the audience. One of his last recorded conversations, three weeks before his death, saw him contemplating his own mortality while expressing his deep admiration for his childhood hero, Jesus:

ELVIS (in his Las Vegas hotel room after a concert): You

know, Jesus died for our sins.

JOE ESPOSITO, Road Manager: There you go again, makin' no sense. We all know about Jesus. (laughs)

ELVIS (angry): Don't mock me, you steamin' pile of horse manure. I might only be the Kingly kind, but I'm talkin' 'bout the King of Kings.

JOE: We're not mockin' you, man.

ELVIS: You're all conspirin' against me, but Jesus is gonna save me from you disrespectin' curs. He spoke to me last night whiles you was out.

JOE: What're you sayin', man? We're all buddies here. We're not plottin' against you.

ELVIS: He promised me He'll come back. An', He reckoned if I seek His Love strong 'nuff, so will I.

JOE (worried): Look, man, you're scarin' me.

ELVIS (triumphantly): Gee, golly, gosh, you scared of death, boy?... Well, I ain't... 'Cos I'm comin' back when I die. (nods slowly) Yeah, I'm comin' back when the time is a-right... Comin' back like our friend, Jesus, some day... Got the message, boy?... Just you wait and see...

Ann-Marie descended the stairs to the dining room, where her parents were sitting down to breakfast. Her father was back from his night shift and presently attacking his generous portion of bacon and grits-al-dente, along with a basketful of cinnamon rolls on the breakfast table. Cloris stood by the stove, making coffee. In the background, *Good Morning America* was on, recounting the haunting of the Bell family in 1818. *Highway to Heaven* was scheduled to follow, religiously anticipated.

"Mind if I skip breakfast?" Ann-Marie said hurriedly. She appeared as pretty as the day, wearing a sunny-yellow blouse and long, summery-blue skirt. A rose-red headband kept her corn-coloured hair in place. "I gotta knock on for Jimmy . . ."

"Why?" Cloris asked with a look of concern. "Is somethin' the matter?"

"No, nothing like that, Mommy. Just that Jimmy needs my help on his essay is all. We planned to go to the library Monday morning." Although lying didn't appeal to Ann-Marie, she was glad her parents bought her indiscretion without another word.

"Okay, but studyin' don't work well if you're runnin' on empty."

"We'll get something on the way, I promise." She produced one of her sweetest smiles.

"That's my girl, always thinkin' ahead," Joshua said over a mouthful of bacon. "Have a good day, sweetness."

"I will, Daddy." She kissed her father on the cheek, gave her mother a hug, and hastened to the front door.

Outside, the sun blazed bright and unchecked by the tattered remnants of cloud, promising another hot, sticky day.

Ann-Marie looked down the street at the Sheriff's patrol-car that had been parked outside the Huttons all night. She'd seen it through her bedroom window ever since its arrival just past midnight. Sheriff Brubaker and Deputy Lawson had gone into the house briefly, then returned to the car. From where they hadn't moved. It sat there, flashers off, siren silent.

Is something the matter? her mother had asked.

Darn right there is! Ann-Marie had hardly slept a wink last night through constant worry.

Ann-Marie headed towards the Huttons, a deep, dark dread rolling around in the pit of her stomach.

When exactly had things gotten weird? Sunday Service when Jimmy had shone brilliantly as a young Elvis soundalike? Or before that, on Saturday night, when she had dreamt of waking up next to the ghost of Elvis?

Jimmy had deliberately brushed her off after Church, claiming that he was too tied up with his essay to see her, focused only on completing a tale befitting the King. Neither could he spare any time to take her to the pictures again that weekend; he had cancelled their date rather abruptly and inconsiderately, without regret.

When did an essay take precedence over your girlfriend's company? All that after they'd patched things up between themselves on the phone the night before.

He had even given his best pal, Carlton, the cold shoulder, which was so unlike him. Ann-Marie had been frankly astonished by Jimmy's remarkable flair for Elvis, whom he had regularly despised, but what had worried her the most was how different he had looked at Church.

As if he were changing . . .

Hard to explain and insane though it sounded, it seemed like he was lugging two different people under the same skin, himself and an outsider, the other stamping their own distinct personality on Jimmy's physical appearance.

His hateful, wild-eyed look – the look of a man who means to chop up his wife – had frightened her. Nevertheless, she had managed to pluck up enough courage to call for him now.

Jimmy was precious to her, and she dared not lose him for all the pain it would cause her.

Has he took sick? Somehow she doubted that. There was something going on with him, of which she hadn't a clue.

She approached the dormant cop-car, peered in through the open window. "Pete . . .? Sheriff . . .?"

The nightwatchmen sat still and inanimate and, for a terrible moment, Ann-Marie thought they were dead. Then slowly, almost creakingly, Sheriff Brubaker turned, his eyes failing to appraise her, remaining eerily empty and faraway, his round features drawing in the faintest trace of a smile. "The darnedest thing I ever saw," he murmured to no-one in particular . . . and fell silent, went back to staring ahead, reverting to his trancelike state.

Had they got tanked? Drunk on something? They certainly looked drunk on something other than moonshine. *Drunk on the good stuff, fool!*

Might this be the effects of shock, perhaps?

Snap out of it, please!

"What's happened? Why're you waitin' here? What did you see?" Ann-Marie asked earnestly. Nothing else was volunteered from the stagnant police officers. Not even the usual cuss words from the Sheriff. She passed a hand over their faces. Got no reaction. Just blank, unbroken, unblinking expressions, frozen like department-store dummies. "Won't you tell me . . . pleeease?" she continued, pleading hopelessly.

Ann-Marie was suddenly aware of how unnaturally quiet it was. She felt as though she had stepped onto an otherworldly replica of her street. No pedestrians or passing vehicles. No whippoorwills twittering in the eaves. Even the Grady's dog, the loudest creature on God's green earth, come rain or shine, was uncharacteristically mute.

She was spooked.

And where was Mrs. Conway? Mrs. Conway, who made it her habit to watch the comings and goings of the street from her window, was remarkably nowhere to be seen. (Unbeknownst to Ann-Marie, Mrs. Conway lay dead in her bed, her heart having seized up at the exact moment Jimmy finished his essay. She would remain undiscovered until about a week later when her niece would pay her a visit and find her cold and stiff and stinking of decomposition, gathering flies by the summer heat pouring in through her bedroom window. Dogs would rather die with their owners. Her cat, terribly hungered, would have tucked into most of her face.)

Her own heart way up in her throat, Ann-Maire crept up the Hutton driveway past the pink Cadillac and ascended the steps leading up to the house, where both

Jimmy's parents sat on the veranda, Floyd on the rocker, Darlene on the love-seat. Their glazed, catatonic expressions

[*snap out of it please please snap out of it please*]

resembled those of the cops . . . and at that instant Ann-Marie didn't want to go in. She wanted to run from here and keep running until she got home safe and sound. But a part of her – a curious, unflappable part – insisted she investigate.

What the hell is going on? Someone PLEEEASE tell me!

Reluctantly, she crossed the porch and slipped into the house.

"Jimmy!" she called out. "Where are you, Jimmy?"

Again, she was greeted by a suffocating silence.

She crept upstairs, slowly, cautiously, her will draining out of her like water down a culvert.

Jimmy's bedroom. She knocked and entered.

"Jimmy . . .?"

There was no-one there.

The hi-fi was on, quietly playing *Black Velvet* by Alannah Myles.

She glanced round the room, saw nothing of interest . . . then caught sight of the sheet of writing sticking out from the top of the typewriter. She went over, pulled out the paper, read it:


```
On his last night, Elvis was far from well. Exhausted,
pouring sheets of sweat, speaking in slurred tones, his
breathing laboured, Elvis retired early to his quarters.
    It would be much later, around two the following
afternoon, when his latest flame and fiancée, Ginger
Alden, would find him dead in his Graceland bathroom. His
final, immortal words had been: 'I'm going to the bathroom
to read.' She would find him lying face-down with his gold
pyjama-bottoms around his ankles, amidst a pool of bloody
vomit, fixed-eyed, his face grey and mottled, his tongue
grotesquely enlarged, protruding, deep purple. He had
fallen off the toilet. The book he had been reading was
not far away: 'A Scientific Search for The Face of Jesus'.
Wrappers from over thirty pills and nine injections were
strewn around the bathroom.
    His daughter, Lisa-Marie, bawled her eyes out when she
couldn't rouse her unresponsive father, a terrible image
that would give her nightmares for years to come. Vernon
wept with the knowledge he had outlived his son.
    Last-ditch attempts to revive Elvis came to no avail,
and Dr. Nick was called for. He directed the ambulance to
the hospital, rather than the morgue, in order to clean up
```

the bathroom and so avoid a full-scale investigation. Elvis was pronounced dead at 3.30pm, August 16th, 1977. He was only 42 years of age.

The world was devastated and went into a state of mourning. People flocked Elvis Presley Boulevard in a colossal traffic jam.

The King was dead.

An autopsy determined the cause of death: Heart Failure as a result of Polypharmacy. His heart had apparently been twice its normal size and composed largely of brown flab. His body weighed 25 stone. He was in the advanced stages of cardiovascular disease and his bowels were twice their length, containing stool that was almost four months old. A toxicology screen revealed at least nine different substances inside his bloodstream and a list of his drug intake (drugs used to function with, drugs to boost his performance and drugs used for sleeping) was compiled, including demerol, quaaludes, valium, codeine and pentobarbital. He had been addicted to powerful painkillers that would normally be used to treat terminal cancer patients. Dr Nick would take the fall.

Elvis was initially buried in a granite mausoleum at Forest Hills cemetery in Memphis, until his casket was removed and re-buried on the grounds of Graceland.

Memphis remains a musical crossroads, where Rock and Soul, Jazz and Blues, Gospel and the Music of the Bayou intersect. Rhythm is everywhere in the crisscross of the street grid, where there are no level crossings, and marks a merging of light and shade. Its irresistible lure can be both vibrant and welcoming and wistfully nostalgic and kitschy, and sometimes dark, as though the Devil lurks in its shadows. The musicality of the city seamlessly links the puritans with the hedonists. Here in Memphis, you can find the Peabody Hotel, opened in 1869, as much an iconic landmark as the Ritz in Paris and the Savoy in London. It has periodically hosted celebrities, from US Presidents to showbiz stars - Elvis came here regularly to have his suits tailored at Lansky's inhouse clothing store, which continues to perpetuate the past with its endless line of blue suedes shoes, sequined jackets and stylish loafers. The Orpheum Theatre remains Memphis's performing arts venue. Shangri-La Records remains a mecca for lovers of Blues LPs, Bakelite, delightful rarities and forgotten gems. Stax Records now serves as a museum of American Soul Music, with its impressive array of historic artefacts and fascinating curios. Take a guided tour of the Gibson guitar factory. Step into Sun Studio, where the legendary songs of American music were recorded between 1950 and 1960. Now it's a tourist attraction, and although it might be tiny, it has not lost any of its emotional clout. But no pilgrimage to Memphis would be complete without paying your respects to Elvis Presley. Explore Graceland, the second most-visited home in America, after the White House. The King's house has stayed unchanged since the 1950s. Surprisingly, it's not as big as one imagines and no two rooms are quite the same. Nevertheless, it's like a trip back in time: the T.V. with the oval screen, the cocktail table, the cushions and couches and curtains, the mirrored staircase, the Jungle Room. Check out Elvis's cars at the Presley Automobile Museum and even climb aboard the King's custom jet. A must-see, reverential experience, the sentimentalism, the glitz. Remarkably, the King's private rooms on the upper floor have remained closed since 1977, as though the King might be secretly hiding out in there...

Of all the enduring mysteries of his death, the most popular remains that of Elvis faking his own death and living out the rest of his life on a tropical island, perhaps somewhere in the South Pacific, keeping away from civilization, out of History's way. Cherishing the peace and solitude of his new existence.

For the obituary, Elvis was a remarkable man, a phenomenally gifted genius, a shy country boy who singlehandedly revolutionized the shape of popular music, united blacks and whites in a segregated world and frequently contributed to charitable causes, such as the Dallas Evangelical Mission and the Mississippi Wheelchair Welfare Fund. He had eighteen number ones in the US charts alone, starred in over thirty feature films and left a legacy worth five billion dollars. He remains the most imitated artist of our era. His myth endures and will forever live on.

It is the artist we should remember and not his lifestyle or his ignominious end.

His voice never let him down even when he was ravaged by multiple health problems.

Whether Teen Rebel or G.I. Hunk, Leather-clad Lothario or Bejewelled Jumpsuit Junkie, he always believed The Show Must Go On.

Elvis was a national institution and each and everyone took a piece of him with them. For many, celebrity is toxic to creativity and, sometimes, fame can become too powerful a force to handle. Elvis was uable to protect himself from his own fame. It is a tragedy he never belonged to himself, otherwise things might have turned out differently. Perhaps, even now, he's up there singing his heart out in Hog's Heaven, waiting for his next major

Cut! That's wrap!

Ann-Marie put down the paper and exhaled deeply. Jimmy had done it. He had *actually* done it. He had finished his factual account on Elvis during the weekend. No question about it. *Lordy, Lordy, the boy might as well be whistling Dixie!*

But what of the cost?

Resting by the typewriter, on top of the numerous Elvis biographies she'd borrowed him, was a book, an obscure, slim volume, entitled: *Psychopomps and the Transposition of Souls*. She picked it up and noticed Jimmy had highlighted various passages he thought relevant in phosphorescent yellow. Ann-Marie didn't need to read any of the pages to know what Jimmy had been trying.

Had he succeeded? If so, what had this little experiment cost him?

In her mind's eye, Ann-Marie visualized an image. A supernatural vision of Carlton whose dark skin was a helter-skelter of pink, vitiligo-like patches. His neat, curly hair grew straight to comb. A ghastly intermediate stage that reminded her of a botched skin graft.

What's happening to me? Carlton, the great polemicist, was demanding, terrified. *Oh, my God, I'm becomin' white, bleach-white! I'm turnin' into Wacko Jacko!*

The discoloration spread, the bony structure of his face reshaping, reforming.

Except it wasn't Carlton who had physically transformed, taken on the visible attributes of someone else. It was Jimmy. And Jimmy himself had winked out of existence.

Sacrificed himself to honour his girlfriend.

To keep her happy, feed her obsession, fulfil her dreams. Give her what she wanted at his own expense.

A grinding, rattling noise came from the bathroom down the hallway.

She wasn't alone . . .

Someone yanking the chain, the flush of the toilet. The sound of a door opening, then closing. Footsteps on the landing.

Ann-Marie knew who it was long before he halted in the bedroom doorway and leaned relaxedly against the door jamb.

"Where's Jimmy?" she asked with teetering authority.

He looked at her, amused, that sly, old smile sneaking across his face. That same heavy-lidded look, that same sleek, greased-back hair she remembered from the catalogue of films she owned. "Ain't no Jimmy here, ladybird . . ." he replied in rich, resonant tones formed round that characteristic Southern twang. "No use a-lookin', either."

"What have you done with him?"

"Nuthin' he dint want doin'," he said, clicking his fingers to stress Jimmy's permanent disappearance. *Abracadabra, whoosh!* "And he ain't comin' back, honeybunch!"

Ann-Marie was nearly at a loss for words. "But how–?"

"He was just the right fit," came the reply, as if it explained everything.

Ann-Marie pulled herself together. Could it be divine intervention? "You mean this is for good?"

"Damn straight! If you're looking for trouble, you sure came to the right place..."

Speak of the Devil and he shall appear before you.

[*Sometimes a 'miracle' is nothing more than a vulgar illusion – a* magic trick *– conjured up by the Father of Lies with the deliberate designs to deceive.*]

Ann-Marie stared at the presence before her, wondering how sometimes things worked out just peachy. It might all be at the consequence of poor old Jimmy, but hadn't Jimmy wanted this? That book on the occult certainly confirmed his desperate intentions. Their arguments aside, Jimmy had come through for his special girl in the end, given her what she had always wished for.

Elvis was back. Back from the dead. Not the potential pensionable veteran supposedly eking out the remainder of his existence in some secret hideaway, nor the bloated forty-two-year-old who'd choked on his own vomit and suffered a heart attack, but the younger, fitter post-adolescent version, who was yet to discover the thrills and spills and pills – and *chills* – of fame and fortune all over again, unexpectedly granted an impossible new lease of life. Rebel-teen, duck's-tail hairdo, crushing good looks, dressed in fashionable black, cool wraparound shades, blue suede shoes, eagle's wings engraved into the chunky belt-buckle. The quintessential Elvis. Alive and in the flesh.

Jimmy had somehow brought him back

[*Elvis might be closer than you think.* Psychopomps and the Transposition of Souls. *One of the dead for one of the living.*]

as a full-time replacement.

The Second Coming, no less! Hallelujah! People of the world, rejoice! Elvis lives! Hail to the King! The star attraction of the Greatest Show on Earth is back by popular demand! The King rules and will always rule! Long Live the King!

All because of [*cute cool clever crazy*] Ann-Marie's love for one man – one special, *unique* man – who had died well before his time. Maybe there was a measure of

Jimmy still left inside, some trace imprint of his soul.

Jimmy, you're really something! This is the best present a girl could ever ask for! How you did it, what you had to go through, I cannot even begin to thank you . . .

"I get the picture," Ann-Marie said, her firmness melting away, readily accepting the newcomer's fabulous presence. She felt liberated. Hanging hours with her svelte god promised to be a thoroughly wicked experience. She would be the envy of the school . . . heck, no, the world! "So where do we go from here?"

He hooked his thumbs into his belt. The rings on his fingers glinted in the shafts of morning light. He moved towards her, stopping a few feet short of her, his walk partway between a swagger and a stagger. His voice dropped to soft, syrupy tones. "I dunno, sugarpie. How 'bout cuttin' a record?"

"Sounds like a plan."

"Said I'd be back before the year 2001."

Thank you very much, thank you very much! You've been a wonderful audience, you really have!

LIGHTS OUT. ELVIS HAS LEFT THE BUILDING . . .

April 2001–August 2001

A Honeymoon in Normandy

"At last she was going to know the joys of love, the fever of the happiness she had despaired of. She was entering a marvellous realm where all would be passion, ecstasy, rapture: she was in the midst of an endless blue expanse, scaling the glittering heights of passion; everyday life had receded, and lay far below, in the shadows between those peaks."

Madame Bovary (1857)
Gustave Flaubert

Four Roses: As we will celebrate our new life together, built on the foundations of Love, nothing will do us apart...

Everything from the wedding vows to the bridal toast went off without a hitch, and the newlyweds, Marc and Daphne Hulin, set off on their honeymoon. They had considered honeymooning in lovely, romantic Paris or staying in a turreted, fairytale château in the Loire Valley once belonging to the Plantagenet monarchs. The suggestion that they should rent out a cottage in Normandy came from Marc's grandfather, Maurice [still living]. The man was a decorated veteran, having once fought the Nazi evil during wartime. He had stormed the heavily-machine-gunned beaches of Normandy during the D-Day landings and survived, eventually settling down here with a French girl, Amélie Dupont, before their grown-up children returned to Old Blighty. Besides, Daphne loved France. *Where else can you buy some cheese and a bottle of wine and call it a meal?*

Marc last stepped foot in France, aged fourteen, on a school trip to Boulogne-sur-Mer. They had taken a hovercraft over. He had been so sleep-deprived that weekend, he sleepwalked to the front of the coach and tried to open the door at

60mph and, when redirected back by his puzzled teachers, subsequently seated himself down on his best friend's lap. He remembered his classmates never let him live it down. On this present journey, over a decade later, a ferry would provide them with the means of transportation, Cherbourg the port-of-call. Marc marvelled at its buoyancy, considering the bays of cars and lorries it contained as well as carrying over two hundred people on board. Yet, somehow, the ferry stayed afloat. He half-feared a cock-up on par with Zeebrugge, but it never transpired. He kept thinking they were going to make several stops on the way to pick up passengers, but that was just plain silly. He caught Daphne smiling at other men on the boat, but he let it go, since he knew she would be getting over the fact that she was no longer a mademoiselle.

The Viking raids of the ninth century soon produced its own influx of settlers, intermarrying with the local inhabitants and quickly adopting the Gallo-Romanic language. They became known as the Normans, derived from the word 'Norseman' or 'Northman'. Their descendents would continue to expand their fiefdoms, leading to the Norman Conquest of Britain in 1066 and the composition of the Domesday Book in 1086. The Channel Islands were once part of the Duchy of Normandy until, with the exception of Chausey, they came under the British Crown in the late eighteenth century.

Marc and Daphne arrived in Cherbourg, which at first glance proved to be an impressive sight. At the northern tip of the Cotentin Peninsula, the harbour was surrounded by sea defences built in Napoleonic times. There was kayaking on display and boat trips to various enchanted islands, replete with old smugglers' paths ideal for walking. The fishing and maritime history could be captured in the sunken century wrecks that languished on the ocean bed. A transatlantic port of some note since its seagoing expeditions to the Americas, the Titanic supposedly stopped here in 1912 to let its passengers embark before its fated maiden voyage. Marc read somewhere that Cherbourg boasted a remarkable public garden and a Museum of Natural History that showcased a diverse collection of fossils, minerals, insects and stuffed animals. One might even stumble upon prehistoric cave paintings along the coastline.

Normandy, in the department of La Manche, appeared to be everything Maurice Hulin had described. The amount of open space was staggering, breathtaking. France was well over twice the size of the UK and supported a population of sixty-eight million compared with a sixty-million figure for the UK, with ten million residing in London alone. Paris was only three hours by car from where they would be staying. It took Daphne some getting-used-to driving on the opposite side of the road as though caught up in some mirror universe, with roundabouts that seemed back-to-front. Charles Trenet accompanied them on the journey, providing the background music, including his happy, happy *Douce France*, before their stereo travelled up the years to Jean-Louis Murat and Carla Bruni's *Ce Que Tu Désires*. Along the way, Daphne discovered Françoise Hardy and her hauntingly beautiful *Bâti Mon Nid*. It would be Daphne's song and, yes, she hoped she and Marc would have children one day and be able to build a solid life together. Marc promised to give his wife whatever she desired.

The sat-nav directed them along the autoroutes, passing the signed exits to Omaha Beach and Utah Beach, and the roads that branched off grew steadily narrower and quieter, their traffic sparser, until the country lanes were practically devoid of any traffic, aside from the occasional chugging tractor herding pied cattle. Field upon field of wheat and linseed and corn were intermittently interrupted by small hamlets predominantly comprising cottages and farmsteads. The couple surveyed the idyllic beauty of sleepy, rural Normandy in stark wonderment. The general absence of cars, the rustic stone dwellings and the vastness of the land gave the overwhelming impression they'd been transported back to an earlier period in time. Not an unpleasant sensation, mind.

They were destined for Hameau Périgueux and a certain GÎTE JOULINES, which they soon discovered was located down a copse-hedged, meandering country lane. Daphne parked the red Mini beneath a sycamore tree and, switching off the radio, clambered out, as did her husband. Gîte Joulines turned out to be a traditional country farmhouse of imposing stone, bearing a slate roof and casement windows, done up in the decorative half-timbering of the Romanesque style. Once again, Daphne got that sense they had slipped back to the medieval period.

They approached the farmhouse, their sneakers scrunching pebbles. Marc lifted the latch for the gate and entered. "Hello, there," he said to the grey-haired gentleman in the white, granddaddy shirt, khaki pants and brown sandals carefully manicuring the hedge. A slim, middle-aged woman wearing a blue summer dress was crouched down behind him, de-weeding the flowerbeds. There were irises, azaleas, bougainvilleas and a variety of two-toned roses still in bloom, along with lavender and wild rosemary. A brown, floppy-eared cocker spaniel trailed behind them, sniffing the flowers.

"*Bienvenue, Monsieur et Madame,*" the fellow replied, taking off his gardening gloves and offering them a hand by way of greeting. "You must be our new guests. Grant us the opportunity to introduce ourselves: I am Gilbert Chalfont, and this delightful creature is my better half, Mirielle." He gestured to his wife, who had stopped what she was doing and was hurriedly removing her marigold gloves.

She came over and shook their hands. She was a fine-looking woman for her age – deep blue eyes, curiously-unlined face in contrast to the greying hair that had been tied back into an elegant bun and the distinct lack of makeup. The Frenchman wasn't bad-looking himself, his skin as olive-tinged as his wife's. "Pleased to make your acquaintance."

Their mooch was called Francis, at age fourteen, looking old and lethargic. He wasn't averse to a good pet from the newcomers.

Daphne made the necessary introductions. "Call us Marc and Daphne."

"I hope the journey over was not too stressful."

"On the contrary, it was a feast for the senses," Daphne responded, suitably impressed. "You have a beautiful country." She did another once-over of the exterior of the farmhouse. "And a beautiful home."

"Thank you for your kind words, Daphne," Mirielle said humbly. "We have been living here since we married thirty years ago. It suits us being so close to Nature."

She led them indoors. It seemed Marc and Daphne would be occupying the adjoining annexe, a barn conversion attached to one end of the farmhouse. It was compact and cosy, fully-furnished, the essential mod-cons, including microwave and DVD player, all inclusive. Exposed stone walls accompanied by original crossbeams, terracotta flooring, a granite fireplace with a wood-burner, and a hard-wearing jute carpet and wrought-iron balustrade on the stairs and landing leading up to a stand-alone WC, a bathroom with an oil-fired boiler, fitted shower and deep, free-standing bath, and a single bedroom with a king-sized bed, spread with an exquisitely-designed patchwork quilt. Above the bed hung a reproduction of *The Kiss* by Théodore Géricault, masterfully depicting the naked anatomies of a pair of lovers at close quarters at the height of a devastatingly passionate kiss while employing a technique of charcoal and gouache, combining the elements of Classicism with Romanticism.

Daphne summed up her opinion of the domicile and the painting. "Nice. Very bijou."

Mirielle was delighted. "I'm glad you like it."

As Gilbert bemoaned the European economic crisis, the fact that the ordinary French taxpayer had to forgo fifty percent of their income as tax, with millionaires forced to fork out a whopping seventy-five percent, Daphne meanwhile broached the reason for their vacation: she finally told them they had just got married.

Congratulations were heartily delivered and received. "It would be an absolute honour for us to have you spend your honeymoon here," Mirielle said with pride.

Marc reciprocated the platitude. "No, the pleasure is all ours."

Mirielle's thoughts went back to the painting. "Strange coincidence that we should have acquired that Géricault nude during our own honeymoon, and now we have you, honeymooners, also, to enjoy it."

Daphne studied the perfect, naturalistic outlines of the two lovers, the fall of light upon their intensely passionate embrace. "It shall be our talisman, hopefully bring us good luck."

"If there is anything you need, do not hesitate to knock," Gilbert said, deciding to take his leave. "We are just next door." He winked at them. "*À bientôt, mes amis*...We hope you have a wonderful stay."

When their hosts had excused themselves, Marc held Daphne in a tight embrace and kissed her tenderly on the lips. "Does it bother you if I keep telling you how much I love you every ten seconds, my adorable one?"

"Not as much as if it were every five seconds, honey bear."

"I shall adore you always until I draw my last breath." Marc decided to postpone the unpacking. "What I desire most right now is a Big Kiss."

"Anything else?" asked Daphne.

"Some Hot Love?"

'Hot Love' was an affectionate term Marc used to describe the physical, intimate relations between two consenting adults, something akin to 'steamy sex', while feigning the look of someone who is sex-starved. The phrase and the lust-struck manner in which he delivered it always made Daphne smile and, even now, it brought on a glimmer of a smirk . . . except there was something she had been meaning to tell Marc. "I think we'll just stick with the Big Kiss for now." Dutifully, Daphne planted a wet smacker on his cheek. "*There*, now isn't that better?"

Marc sounded disappointed. "Not really . . . How about unlocking your chastity belt and giving me some Hot Love?"

There was never a good time to offload what she was about to offload.

"I don't know how to tell you this, Marc, but I can't have your willy inside me because I'm surfing the crimson wave . . ."

For a moment Marc looked at her blankly, not comprehending the euphemism. Then, realization filtered in, which changed to outright incredulity. He could not believe his new bride was at her time of the month at the commencement of their honeymoon, as though the very prospect of making love (which they had done so many times in their two years together before they decided to tie the knot – *and what fun it had been!*) had induced a period in the girl. "My God, woman, why didn't you tell me? We could have postponed our honeymoon by a few days!"

She tried to hug him in an attempt to soften the blow. "Really sorry, Marc, I will make it up to you in some way, promise. We could always make out as much as you like."

"But in France everyone's having sex!" he said, bitterness and anger creeping into his voice. Menstrual jam or no menstrual jam, he could still demand sex from her, and she might comply, but he knew she would not be happy. Adding a rubber johnny into the equation would not sway her, either. She would most certainly think less of him if he insisted on intercourse whilst she was bleeding, and he did not want to risk going down that road. Aunt Flow was such a mood-killer! *This is oh so messy!* What choice did he have but to go along with prolonged foreplay, like a pair of college kids exploring each other's tonsils in the back of a car? "*A honeymoon should be like a table. Four bare legs and no drawers!*" he told her emphatically as a reminder. "*A husband may forget where he went on his honeymoon, but he never forgets why!*" He felt on the verge of quarrelling. But what would that possibly solve? "I give up! Happy periods, sweetheart!" He released himself from her embrace and went about attending to the suitcases in a sullen mood, the emptying of which he had previously deferred, hoping presently to distract himself from his grievance. "Is it a sin to lech over your own wife?" he thought out aloud. According to one Pierre Corneille: *Desire increases when fulfilment is postponed.* Marc reminded Daphne of her aunt, who was left in the company of her tabby as consolation after her own husband cheated on her and skedaddled out of town. Could it be that her aunt was not giving the husband any sex? *If not, then good on him!*

Daphne did not reply. She gave him space. It was a reaction most people would have come to expect under similar circumstances, but, in this instance, he was managing his disappointment and frustration better than expected. It wasn't as if she was being selfish, inconsiderate. It wasn't her fault, after all, merely a woman's curse. The distasteful agony of bleeding out of your private parts every month. He knew it, too. Arguments can emerge from nothing and spin out of control. Neither wanted that kind of start to their honeymoon. He would soon come round. He always saw sense in the end. In the meantime, it was okay for him to stew awhile. Understandable.

In this case, Daphne hoped, patience would prove to be a virtue. A test of his undying love for her.

Just go with the flow, she advised herself, *please pardon the pun.*

They decided to spend the rest of the morning cramming in as much as they possibly could, exploring the lay of the land, so to speak. Before setting off from England, they had devised a travelogue, itemized an aide-mémoire they intended to follow outside the lashings of their lovemaking, but with Daphne's beautiful body now out of bounds, they got on with it somewhat in earnest.

The first stop set down in their formalized schedule was Barfleur with its seafront marina, gift shops and tourist office. The mob of large, hungry seagulls owned the harbour, purportedly known to carry out vicious attacks on the unwary visitor. Not on this occasion, mind. Daphne half-expected to see Captain Cod, foot propped up on the side of the boat in a hardy, sailorly stance, elbow resting on the knee, puffing away thoughtfully on a corncob pipe, such might be, she supposed, a common sight in most fishing towns. But she was not in luck. The numerous cafés dished out mussels fresh off the fishing boats in the form of a traditional stew called *Moules à la Normandie*. If Marc and Daphne were being adventurous they might have feasted on fished crab, lobster or shrimps, or gulped down some chilled oysters in the name of romance, since this region was renowned for cultivating and harvesting *fruits de mer*, but they were working on a deadline and *soupe de poisson* sufficed for now, washed down with a small glass of very inexpensive but palatable white plonk. Perhaps another time. Their stroll along the quayside, breathing in the salt tang of the ocean, took them to the pier, from where the lighthouse was starkly visible, white and resplendent, a feat of mid-nineteenth-century structural engineering, the second tallest in France.

They tracked slightly south to Saint-Vaast-la-Hougue, a former lazaret and another coastal port not that much different from Barfleur, a gathering place for the trawlers, freight carriers and pleasure boats, except for the presence of MAISON GOSSELIN department store on its shop-lined streets, with its famous, all-in-one delicatessen, gift shop and wine cellar, not only an epicurean paradise but a nostalgia trip back to the 1950s, probably the highlight of their visit.

They drove back towards Hameau Périgueux as the sun continued its glorious ascent and the day grew hotter still on this exceptional September day. But not before stopping off at a sleepy village in the opposite direction called Saint-Pierre-

Église. Presently, its popular, lively country market ran all day once-weekly, falling conveniently on today. They late-luncheoned on grilled Toulouse sausage in a baguette with fries, a gastronomic delight. One of the things that Daphne discovered while passing through the village square was that the French respected their bread, eaten as religiously as if it were the Body of Christ. They may not have a post office in all the sleepy villages the couple drove through, but they certainly had a boulangerie, offering lovingly-prepared brioches, croissants, baguettes, chunky country-style breads – the list was endless – while the inhouse pâtisserie/delicatessen displayed the quiches, delectable tarts and cakes and sablés. And so utterly divine was the aroma of baking bread. The all-in-one boucherie/charcuterie, just as important, provided both fresh meat and the cured variety, the saucisson sec and garlic sausage most people have heard of. Many of the shops completed their business for the day after lunch, preparing for afternoon siesta. It was a different lifestyle here, laidback, relaxed, contented. It was fascinating how the individual histories and cultures of Olde England and Olde France had diverged since the Middle Ages. Aside from the lower cost of living, something as simple as the price of the wine exemplified this disparity. The refined palates of the French appreciated the taste and texture of their wines, an accompaniment at mealtimes or drinking for pleasure, at peace with their lot; the English drank because they were miserable, finding no other escape from the painful hustle-and-bustle of their daily lives. Marc intended to take a dozen bottles of wine back to the UK; even if at three euros each, they were still better quality than the overpriced swill in most British supermarkets.

There were many stalls at the country market, selling homemade terrines and pâtés, a wide range of smelly cheeses, farm eggs, bottles of vinaigrettes and flavoured oils. Lower Normandy – or Basse-Normandie, as the locals referred to it – was largely agricultural, and Daphne learned that bee-keeping, butter-making and cider presses were staples in these parts. In fact, Normandy was famous for its cider, not so much its wine, and she hoped to inspect the apple orchards as well as partake in a little strawberry-picking later in the week. They bought quality gigot steak and wild mushrooms and seasonal vegetables from the vendors, essential ingredients for the beef bourguignon Daphne was planning to cook this evening. She hoped to try out the resident Crueset cookware.

They made a slight detour to the nearby CARREFOUR hypermarket to pick up some exquisitely-scented shampoos and shower gels – the French were big on perfume for obvious historical reasons – and dropped by a chemist's to buy tampons (instead of condoms) before the couple headed back to their self-catering holiday retreat. House-proud, Daphne spent a good one hundred euros on her perfumed toiletries and household cleaning products. Marc did not know how it was possible, but it was, and he was none-too-impressed.

Aside from that, Marc commented peevishly on Daphne's dippy dress sense, and, justifiably some might have said, the implications of wearing red stockings and carrying a baguette under one arm, even if unintentionally, but she laughed it off with her usual Goldie Hawn scattiness. *Enough of the filthy talk, you naughty man!* she chided him lightly. *It's chic, Bohemian . . . Yé-yé! I'm just entering into the spirit of the place, the fashions, blending in!*

Ooh là là!

Once the pot was bubbling on the stove, they went for a ramble up the lane to get a feel for the local geography. Marc had been moody and quiet all day, but Daphne got a sense that he might be coming round to the idea that they might not be undertaking any Hot Love for a few days. She felt sorry for him but hoped he could still have a good time, regardless. It wasn't easy for her, either. They had lived together for almost two years and entered into this matrimonial alliance under increasing pressure from their respective Catholic parents. They did not know what to expect. People claimed that marriage could make or break a relationship, and there were all those unkind jokes she and Marc had chuckled over in the lead-up to their nuptials: *Love is blind, but marriage is an eye-opener!... Marriage is a tale of romance in which the hero dies in the first chapter! . . . Marriage is an institution in which the husband loses his Bachelor's degree and the wife gains a Master's!... During marriage, a wife has the last word in an argument and anything a husband says after that is the beginning of a new argument! . . . The honeymoon is over when the husband rings home to say he'll be late for dinner and the answering machine tells him it's in the refrigerator!... The honeymoon is over when she starts wondering what happened to the saint she married, and he starts wondering what happened to the angel he didn't!*

People could have made jokes over their – or more precisely, *her* – current predicament, but it didn't bear thinking about.

Presently, they walked awhile in silence, Daphne slightly ahead, Marc dawdling behind, hands in his pockets, head bowed in a sulk, less than conversant.

Ironically, despite having some French blood in him on account of Amélie, his grandmother, who was born and raised in Le Havre, Marc had failed his GSCE French. Still, it didn't preclude him from becoming a schoolteacher, with an aptitude for the Basic Sciences. So bad was his French he would probably have gone into a coiffure's and asked for coffee. *Parlez-vous français?* (instead of *anglais?*), which he had repeatedly asked the locals during the course of the day before realizing his blunder, Daphne had found amusing without openly ribbing him, lest he should feel more embarrassed and self-conscious than he already must be. Instead, he grew comfortable with the words, *Mon français est terrible*, which prompted the other person to feel sorry for him and speak English just because he'd made a genuine effort in speaking French. Daphne worked as a legal secretary, and her long blond hair, waist-deep, gave her the appearance of a maiden dancing around the maypole which Marc adored.

The weathercasters didn't know the first thing about the weather. *Might as well consult a soothsayer,* Daphne thought. Rain had been predicted, but the sky was anything but indicative of rain, the soft, sepia tones of sunset proving once again they were in the grip of a sultry Indian summer.

The road continued to slope upwards, and they came to a crossroads, marked by a statue of the Crucifixion. Erected on a pedestal of antique stone, it rose seven feet tall, cast entirely from classic bronze, kept polished and relatively pristine by generations of care and attention. Nailed to the Cross, Jesus gazed down compassionately over the hamlet, his divine presence a reassuring, protective influence on the spiritual wellbeing of the local community. The bronze plaque, worded in French, Daphne roughly translated as: *On a hill far away stood an old rugged cross,/ The emblem of suffering and shame;/ And I love that old cross where the dearest and best/ For a world of lost sinners was slain.* Daphne recognized it as the first verse of a popular hymn from Sunday Service.

Up here, the lane forked, producing a belvedere view of the bocage landscape, the rolling fields on either side unbroken as far as the eye could see. Nature, even during this season of peatbogs, had never looked so picturesque, so grand. In one particular pasture were some horses and donkeys. Daphne, an animal lover like her cousin, Anthea, took to them immediately. She wished she had brought along some carrots to feed them. Still, she was at least able to snap a few lovely photos of them on her mobile. They were of the shaggy variety, the jack slightly stockier than the jenny, but both were equally friendly, docile. Daphne tried to talk to them in soft, affectionate tones by the gate and the two donkeys responded appropriately, appreciating her company, letting her stroke their manes and chestnut-coloured, tangled hides, braying contentedly. Flies buzzed indolently around their heads, the donkeys swishing their tails to ward them off. The two darker, brown horses, elegant of physique, sleek of coat, kept their distance, maintaining their position at the far end of the enclosure, eyeing the intruders with frank suspicion. Pleased that she had made two new friends, Daphne left the Poitou donkeys to it, as dusk fell, making a mental note to visit her furry friends again tomorrow.

In readiness for their dinner, the couple made the return journey down the lane, passing the neighbouring cottages, when Marc, who had said very little during their short hike, uttered a sharp, exclamatory cry. He stopped in his tracks, and Daphne, who had been following close behind, bumped into him.

"What is it, Marc?" Daphne asked her husband, puzzled.

Marc pointed towards the old, two-storey farmhouse that had attracted his attention. She seemed surprised she had not noticed this building on the journey up. The farmhouse certainly appeared old, even from afar, constructed from sturdy granite blocks, moss-covered and conveying a look of sheer abandonment, some of the tall, rectangular windows cracked and broken, the roof on one side having caved in. There were no vehicles in the vicinity, All Quiet on the Western Front.

The place warranted a closer look, and Marc stepped over the empty flowerpots that had been lined up to cordon off the entrance.

"I don't think this is wise . . ." Daphne began nervously, but Marc had nearly crossed most of the cobbled courtyard. She ran on behind, afraid they were trespassing on private property. She eventually caught up with him.

Marc took a quick gander into the adjoining stables, which were disused, padlocked. He redirected his focus on the house itself. The arched front door, made from sturdy oak, was chipped and bolted. The large windows were caked in dirt, adding to the sense that the house had been left neglected for a number of months, perhaps even years. Peering into one such grimy window, eyes adjusting to the prevailing gloom within, they saw a vintage dresser, patinated blue in shabby chic, against the roughly plastered far wall. The scuttle next to the dormant antique fireplace was piled up with wood. There were bits of masonry on the stone floor, along with a stepladder and a table bearing a number of paint-pots and rolls of wallpaper. It seemed the house was undergoing renovation, but there was no sign of the painters and decorators. Maybe they had finished for the day. After all, it was almost past twilight. Marc was tempted to break in, investigate its brooding secrets, but he resisted the urge in case someone still lingered in the house. He, like Daphne, could not shift that perturbing, unshakeable feeling most people get when checking out a derelict, old house and thinking they're being watched.

Something dark leapt up onto the sill inside, making them jerk back from the window. Once the initial shock had abated, Marc realized what had startled them. Luminous green eyes peered up at them, separated from them by a single pane of glass. It was a black cat and it was watching them intently. So the place wasn't quite as unoccupied as it seemed. Somebody must surely be around to feed the cat.

"Are there any ghosts in Normandy?" Daphne asked, strangely unnerved by this feline presence. She remembered that song from her childhood: *How much is that kitty in the window?*

Marc remained distinctly fascinated by this dark house, transfixed by the black cat that was now yawning lazily, revealing its pink mouth and tongue and tiny, white fangs. "There are no ghosts anywhere in the world, my adorable one."

Gilbert popped his head round that evening to see how his guests were settling in. The beef bourguignon and French bread had been an instant hit, and they had moved on to the red wine. They offered a small glass to Gilbert. He did not decline.

"So how are my honeymooners?" he asked jovially.

"Your honeymooners are very happy to be here!" Daphne piped, with equal good cheer.

"You know it was your English gentry in the 1820s who first decided to celebrate marriage by honeymooning in secluded, exotic places. The custom became popular during our Belle Époque era. Or so the tradition goes . . ."

The newlyweds welcomed this little tidbit from their host, a retired history teacher, who informed them that his wife, Mirielle, was presently entertaining their daughter, Lisse, from Lyon. She was visiting with their grandson, Didier, who was apparently a very fat baby and now in the throes of the Terrible Twos. However, Didier was getting on swimmingly with Francis, their very aged dog. Daphne briefly recounted the day's adventures and their plans for tomorrow: Rouen, Bayeux. Her narrative soon led to their discovery of the mysterious, deserted farmhouse they had fortuitously stumbled across.

Gilbert seemed only too glad to be called upon in enlightening the couple of the history of the local community. "That house has been empty for a long time. It belonged to an elderly spinster, Henrietta de Mares, who died five years ago. It has been inherited by her niece, Hettie, who is in the process of renovating it." Gilbert paused, frowning, thoughts turning to darker matters. "We in Hameau Périgueux refer to the house as *Maison Noir* because of the witch who lived there once, many centuries ago."

"A witch?" said Marc, surprised.

The word brought up all kinds of connotations for Daphne, but most of all, made her think of Black Annis, that grotesque, grinning, hooked-nose witch of English lore, tanning the skin off children and cooking their flesh in a cauldron. She shuddered at the image.

"Yes, her name was Héloïse."

"I thought witches didn't really exist," replied Marc thoughtfully, "and the witch trials of Northern Europe were just religious hysteria fuelled by the Inquisition, poisoning the minds of naive and gullible people, leading to the mass persecution of innocent women, who were either a bit strange, or perhaps, mad."

"Maybe . . . maybe not," Gilbert continued. "Modern Wicca is a harmless religion centred around Nature's protective influence and New Age remedies, but in those dark days of the witch hunts of the late Middle Ages, witches were genuinely seen as evil consorts of the Devil, possessing supernatural powers."

"And what is your take on the matter?"

"Our country is steeped in superstition and folklore, this region more so. Here, people believe that seeing something as ordinary as a tortoiseshell cat foretells your death in an accident. We have legends of *Fées* in these parts, such as the *Dames Blanches* who would haunt ravines and bridges, torturing the male passersby to the brink of madness if they refused to dance with them. The *Fourolles* were supposedly the souls of scorned, hateful young women, taking the shape of a will-o'-the-wisp, who would seduce and lead recently-betrothed travellers astray, in a malicious act of love sacrilege. The Ankou is the personification of Death, a tall, haggard stranger in a black, hooded cloak and hat with long, flaxen hair, wielding a scythe, haunting deserted crossroads and forests, watching over cemeteries at midnight, a collector of lost souls. Then there is the historic case of *La Bête du Gévaudan* . . ."

"This one I know," said Marc, excitedly. "A monster terrorizing the Langogne region, ripping out the throats of a number of locals, resulting in a national panic and the King sending forth a hunting party to track down this elusive, savage creature. It turned out to be a vicious man-eating wolf, but it was originally mistaken for a werewolf. Before the beast was eventually captured and put down, many men were executed, suspected of indulging in lycantropy."

"You are well-informed," Gilbert explained, impressed. "Monsters fill our canon of myth to the brim. What is a monster but an aberration of Nature, or a creature born of legend or allegory, designed to bring dread into the hearts of men? There are written accounts of monsters dating as far back as the Sumerian epics, the Viking sagas and the works of Ovid. Throughout the ages, the definition of 'monster' has changed, constantly evolving, shifting through time in any given society. Octave Mirbeau once claimed there was no such thing as a monster but only a superior form of life or a form beyond comprehension. Otherwise, we would be accusing gods of being monsters, or men of genius, or even those who live beyond our social norms. As a historian, I am tasked with understanding monstrosity in a French context. Our society also has the *Nain rayée*, a Norman hobgoblin full of mischief, revenants, corpses brought back from the dead, and tarannes, gnomes that were once the souls of unchristened children. I could go on, tell you what each one signifies, represents . . ."

"Tell me about Héloïse."

"She lived in that farmhouse. People were afraid of her. She had lost her unborn child after her lover ran off with another woman. She lived a life of quiet solitude. However, rumour spread that she was a witch. The locals believed that she could cast spells and curses, jinx humans, blight crops and spoil harvests, make the livestock sick by contaminating the water of wells, send forth plagues of rats and toads and snakes, control the undead spirits of the night and govern the weather. As the crops failed and famine and drought struck this region and the people suffered a sudden outbreak of St. Vitus dance, they rounded up a lynch mob one night and ransacked her house while she was out collecting herbs during the witching hour. They found the discarded remains of over a dozen men who had gone missing in recent months: skulls, ribcages, long bones . . ."

Daphne imagined the angry lynch mob advancing by moonlight, their flaming torches in the dark casting demonic shadows over their features, stressing the hate and murder in their rabid eyes . . .

"The corpse of her lover was found in the cellar, petrified like stone. The place slithered with snakes. When Héloïse returned from her nightly trip to the woods, the mob arrested her and beat her and set her on fire with their torches. Still, she survived their retribution. The community decided that the law should take its course, and she was eventually delivered to Rouen in her weakened, horribly-burnt condition, somehow still alive, and sentenced in the infamous *Petits Sorciers* trial, accused of the crime of witchcraft. She was incinerated at the stake like the others of her kind to purify her soul and the land, but not before she cursed the Christian Church and threatened to come back from the grave and seek revenge on the people of Normandy. It is rumoured that Salvator Rosa's painting of *The Witch* was based on her."

"That's quite a story . . ." said Marc, engrossed. Daphne had to agree. She thought of Black Annis again and shivered.

"But there is a twist to the tale," Gilbert lectured on, in his element. "It is recorded that as the fire was lit and began to burn her flesh, she changed into a huge snake – her true appearance – before the flames rose higher and consumed the rest of her. Most eyewitness accounts are sketchy, conflicting, unreliable. But a respected diarist of the time claimed he saw it happen. *Tres outré*. Soon after, some people began to suspect that she might be an incarnation of the one and only *Vouivre*, a French wyvern, or dragon, the type once supposedly vanquished by the feudal knights, or *wyrm* in Anglo-Saxon, all interchangeable terms. She is usually portrayed with the head and upper body of a voluptuous woman and the lower half of a snake. She is meant to have a ruby set into her face between the eyes, or maybe the eyes themselves are rubies, guiding her through the Underworld. She is supposedly the Guardian of Treasures, protecting her Aladdin's cave of infinite riches, and any robber who stays too long in her lair risks the monster returning at dawn and the rock to her cave entrance closing up, and the unhappy person serving as nourishment for the serpent woman.

"*La Vouivre* is also connected with the medieval tale of Melusine, a lady born of fae and mortal pairing, married to a nobleman. Once a year, Melusine retreats to her bedchamber, refusing her husband entry until the next day. Inevitably, the husband grows suspicious and drills a little hole in the door and spies on her as she bathes in milk. She is revealed to be half-woman, half-snake. Finding herself discovered, Melusine shrieks and transforms into a giant python, swallowing up her prying husband and many men thereafter, whole. People claimed Héloïse's lover must have discovered these very unearthly origins about her, so she promptly got rid of him.

"Other scholars date her even further back to Echidna of Greek legend and Apophis from the pre-Coptic language. Some people hold that Héloïse was nothing less than an incarnation of Hecate, the Ancient Goddess of Necromancy. *That, Monsieur et Madame*, is a *monster*, or the Mother of All Monsters, even deserving a brief mention in *De Vermis Mysteriis*."

"And you don't believe in the existence of such monsters, right?"

Gilbert glanced over his shoulder and crossed himself, which startled Marc. Sweat beaded his forehead. "Are you asking me whether Héloïse is Melusine – or Hecate? That Héloïse managed to unlock the secrets of Magick and the Dead? I am only telling you what I know. Even as a scientist you must know you should never assume that what you cannot measure is not true. You can only disprove the null hypothesis."

Marc was not a religious man, and as a science teacher he was a rationalist, a believer in evidence-based practice, and the strange colloquy they had participated in did not hold as much weight as Gilbert might have intended. After everything he had heard this evening, witchcraft, or the *Vouivre* for that matter, he speculated, all should be reserved for that dubious space between ignorance and myth.

The cock announced the dawn. But Marc and Daphne remained in bed, making the most of their lie-in together.

Daphne played a lot of Cliff Richard on their honeymoon, a throwback to her sheltered upbringing in Chertsford, sometimes ringing in the day with the soundtrack to *Summer Holiday*, passable at first, but Marc soon grew weary of it since he did not hold this lifelong Peter Pan in high esteem: those strong Christian values and the mystery surrounding his sexuality, including his self-imposed bachelorhood, that seemed curiously at odds with the whole Rock'n'Roll image. Was the man terrified of women or just plain queer? Or was he hiding a more sinister secret – maybe an inclination towards something truly dark and ugly? Might be something, might be nothing. Whatever the hell was wrong with the man, Marc found, in his own musical opinion, only *Devil Woman*, which was of course not on offer on this occasion, vaguely interesting, thinking of it every time Daphne kept torturing him with Cliff Richard songs. It was, Marc considered, probably also Cliff Richard's most honest composition.

However, the morning emerged bright and unblemished, promising lucid blue skies and another sweltering day. Sunbeams fell through the partially covered curtains in a golden dazzle, causing the dustmotes to dance and swirl. The stark, naturalistic beauty of Géricault's *The Kiss*, hanging over their cosy, wedding bed, may have served as a catalyst in redefining the purpose of this vacation – their honeymoon – and strengthening Daphne's feelings for her husband, for she seemed more amorous than usual, friskier even, maybe dwelling on missed opportunities, and she led Marc to the bathroom where they proceeded to shower together.

As the steamy torrents dispelled the last dregs of sleep and warmed their desperately-wanting bodies, their questing hands worked on each other's exposed, highly-aroused flesh. Daphne decided to let him in. It hurt below, and she tried ignoring the discomfort as best she could, but it was difficult, near-to-impossible, and he withdrew at the right moment, considerately, the domestic waterfall washing away the flood of blood that accompanied his painful exit.

Did this act of belated passion constitute complete consummation of their wedlock or merely to a degree, an extent? Did it matter? Regardless, he was no longer sore at her. "What changed your mind?" Marc asked with open tenderness.

"I want us – *you* – to be happy," she responded softly. "Forever."

Marc had no choice but to relent. She had always been that little girl who dreamed of meeting her Prince Charming. And he had proudly stepped into that role without the slightest hesitation. "I forgive you, my adorable Princess Bride," he whispered, satisfied they had made sufficient progress in observing their conjugal rights and consolidating their affections for one another. He held her tightly, silently, in the cascading waters for several minutes, each cherishing the other's nakedness and closeness, bathed in a rose light of the love they had shared and physically expressed. An 'infinity of passion' contained in that single moment, as Gustave Flaubert, author of the then-notorious *Madame Bovary*, might have put it. A moment so poignant as to be considered sacrosanct. Marc was satisfied Daphne had done her best under difficult circumstances in abiding by her wifely duties. Thankfully, their relationship was back on track. "You are my beautiful wife," Marc whispered, matter-of-factly, "and anyone as adorable as you deserves to be loved and cherished all the time, even after I am long gone. You cannot stop me from adoring you. You are my guiding light when the days are dark and life not worth living . . . as well as being an absolute dynamite in the sack! No contest!"

Both were partial to the great French writers. Voltaire believed Love was a canvas furnished by Nature and embroidered by imagination. Flaubert considered Love like a plant from India, requiring a prepared soil and a particular temperature, as fertile as sighs in the moonlight and long embraces, and all the fevers of the flesh and languors of tenderness. If one quoted Flaubert's protégé, Guy de Maupassant, Love meant the body, the soul, the life, the entire being. We felt Love as we felt the warmth of our blood, breathed Love as we breathed the air and we held Love in ourselves as we hold our thoughts. How queer it was to love only one person in the world, to have only one thought in our minds, only one desire in our hearts, and only one name on our lips – a name which rose up from the depths of our souls to the lips, a name which repeated itself over and over again, whispered ceaselessly like a prayer.

One particular quote Marc once whispered to her, again from the library of Flaubert, she had committed to rote memory: *I will cover you with Love when next I see you, with caresses, with ecstasy. I want to gorge you with all the joys of the flesh, so that you faint and die. I want you to be amazed by me, and to confess to yourself that you never even dreamed of such transports . . . When you are old, I want you to recall those few hours, I want your bones to quiver with joy when you think of me.*

Oh, she loved him so, so much!

They dressed and hung out and ate breakfast together: croissants and café au lait. It put them in good stead to explore the other Norman sites listed on their itinerary.

It was Marc's turn to drive, and he took them to the famous and historic city of Rouen, the final resting place of one Joan of Arc, that enduring folk heroine, who guided by self-reported communications from God, led the French army to many victories over the English. She was later arrested and convicted of heresy by the Inquisition, then put to death and burned at the stake in 1431. The Roman Catholic Church sainted her in 1920. Daphne thought back to their discussion with Gilbert, and his mention of the *Petits Sorciers* trial, Héloïse the witch in question.

The couple visited Rouen Cathedral, the seat of the Archbishop of Normandy. The church – or an earlier version of it – had been around since the fourth century, but the real work on it began in the twelfth century. The gothic architecture encompassed towers, spires, side chapels, stained-glass windows, statuaries and various high-profile tombs. William the Conqueror was buried here as well as Richard the Lionheart, his heart entombed. There was a sense of something profound here. Daphne found peace, which was the closest she felt of ever attaining a state of grace.

Rouen had much else to offer, in particular the Musée des Beaux-Arts and the Jardin des Plantes. The MUSÉE DES BEAUX-ARTS DE ROUEN hosted a league of original works that somehow defined the history and progression of French Art. As they wandered around the galleries, Daphne and Marc came to learn the periods through which Art had evolved. The Romantic movement, whose strong passions dominated their works with Théodore Géricault as much a figurehead as the other Norman artists like Jean-François Millet and Eugène Boudin, preceded the Impressionists, founded and influenced greatly by Claude Monet, whose water lilies were as striking as his depiction of Rouen Cathedral, making Daphne think they'd gone full circle. Other Impressionist canvases they inspected belonged to Pierre-Auguste Renoir and Alfred Sisley, expressing their perceptions before Nature *en plein air*. The Post-Impressionist era followed, serving up the likes of Paul Gauguin and Georges Seurat, exploring emotionality in Nature, dynamic in the delivery of their brushstrokes. Some Cubist paintings were provided by Georges Braque, and the Fauvist works by Raoul Dufy, forerunners to the Surrealist school of art. It was an education; Daphne felt she had learned so much she might as well have gained a scholarship in Norman Art History. And still no sign of the *Painter's Honeymoon*.

Famished, Daphne snacked on baked Normandy camembert with hot breadsticks while Marc plumped for woodcock, slow-cooked in shallots and white wine and served on top of chargrilled *pain de campagne* at the JARDIN DES PLANTES DE ROUEN, a botanical garden of some distinction. After consuming a homemade mille-feuille by way of dessert, they each tried a cup of Verveine tea, an altar plant, which legend had it was supposed to ward off vampires and werewolves as well as protect humans from bewitchment. They strolled down resplendent gardens of fuchsias and irises, gave pause to a herb garden of medicinal plants. They saw the biggest Venus flytraps, first-hand. They passed through a tropical greenhouse of assorted palms and other botanical treasures. They nervously touched the bust of the pagan god Pan, strangely warm on contact, inconsequent of the fine weather, as though generating its own source of secret energy.

After lunch, the couple left Rouen, and instead of exploring the other towns of Haute-Normandie such as Le Havre, where Marc's grandmother hailed from, they made a conscious decision to return to the familiar grounds of the lower regions. Maybe they could visit his grandparents another time; their visit was already scheduled into the tail end of their trip. Maurice had suggested popping round the day before they return to England, perhaps the perfect end to their honeymoon. The problem was one of time – or perhaps not so much a problem. It was so easy to get lost in the beauty of the place that time became an irrelevant constant. Once again, that comparison between Olde England and Olde France, and their parallel histories and contrasting cultures, occurred to Daphne. The French led a contented life in their enchanted land, in a country that was self-contained and self-reliant, without any need for dependence on the rest of the world; the British were just too stressed and depressed, constipated even, caught up in the daily rat race, always eager to start wars. Daphne felt an affinity with the French. Even at this time of year, the people did not suffer from closed-shutter syndrome. Normandy remained a paradise for hikers, bikers and nature-lovers as well as art-world scenesters and those keen to experience the original chanson-and-café society. The more she thought about it the more she wished to buy a small cottage in Normandy (or Brittany) some day and call it their holiday home, if they ever got fed up with life in England, or struck gold and hopefully never had to work again.

Wife in tow, Marc proceeded to Bayeux. Just like Rouen, no street performers here or vagrants or kids high on weed. The French motorists did as they wanted, as usual, construed by the world over as 'crazy' drivers. Marc parked up next to a beat-up, old Peugeot sat diagonally in two spaces. French cars were the norm here; the domestic car industry flourished. And bicycles. Despite being so far up north, the local women were dressed in Parisian fashions, fetchingly so, and all the country gents tailored out in provincial dress, casual yet deceptively dapper.

Bayeux was the obvious choice for the tourist. It was very Roman in its design, and it was the first French town to be fully liberated from the Nazis during the Allied air and sea offences of coastal Normandy, as Maurice Hulin once told his grandson, paving the way for the liberation of Paris and the rest of the country. It summoned up images of old Maurice, then in his twenties, charging at the nests of machine-gun fire on the beaches, the Nazis lying in deadly wait inside their well-concealed bunkers. The astounding acts of valour from the Allied military effort unfurled from the shores of Normandy would forge a battalion of heroes to whom society owed a massive debt, forever uniting in remembrance.

However, it was the Bayeux Tapestry Marc and Daphne had come to see.

Kept in a museum of its own, the Bayeux Tapestry was a visually-arresting series of fifty scenes in embroidered crewel, colourfully illustrating everything from King Harold's coronation ceremony in the wake of Halley's comet (considered a bad omen at the time) to his eventual demise amongst the slaughter of his troops on a bloody, corpse-strewn battlefield during the Battle of Hastings. Marc had to admit it was incredibly well-preserved for something that was a thousand years old and so very dramatic in its depiction of the times that it was a masterclass in pictorial storytelling.

Daphne decided to defer their visit to Ludiver's planetarium and astronomy centre to another day, where she might observe the stars through its powerful telescopes and learn about the finer workings of the Universe. Not too much of a disappointment for a science teacher like Marc, who had already had the good fortune of visiting Jodrell Bank in his teens. No, they were too tuckered-out from their travels, and another stop might have proved too much. Tomorrow they would stick to somewhere more local: Quettehou, Valognes, Bricquebec, or perhaps even take a trip down to Saint-Lô, where the nearest MAISON DU MONDE store did its business. Maybe take in the religious grotto at La Pernelle and dine in the Michelin-star PANORAMIQUE restaurant.

So back home they journeyed in the last of the late-day sunshine, back to their romantic getaway for a night in, and maybe the promise of love.

But not before Marc told her of something he had read somewhere, long ago. This particular item of trivia had presented itself during their trip to the botanical gardens in Rouen, standing there in that sanctuary of herbal plants cultivated to cure all manner of ailments. He had spotted wolfsbane and the mandrake plant which were considered lethal poisons with no medicinal value, but frequently used in occult practices. Hemlock was once used for its sedative properties, but because it was also a major paralytic, it had grown out of favour with the medical community. Digitalis was used even today to treat heart conditions. But it was deadly nightshade, also known as belladonna, which he focused on, coupled with their conversation with Gilbert the night before. Belladonna in small doses keeps asthma at bay, but, in a historical context, it was also the drug the medieval witch smeared on her broomstick, which she would subsequently sit upon, wearing nothing underneath, of course, and as she rubbed against it, and it absorbed through her mucosa in higher concentrations, it would bring on vivid hallucinations, including a perceived sensation of flying. Thus sprang the myth of the mad witch riding on her broomstick, flying into the night.

Their morning shower together and their enjoyable yet enlightening travels during the course of the day had gone more than partway in restoring their faith in one another, their belief in their nuptial union. A psychiatrist will tell you that when it came to spousal matters, women have more emotional depth than men, but men will always see the bigger picture. So, ergo, a psychiatrist is a person who will give you expensive answers that your wife will give you for free. While Marc was stuck in fondly-adolescent, 'emergency' mode, demanding a 'Big Kiss, Big Kiss', Daphne remained the sensible one, albeit amused, and complied with his request before deciding what they should have for dinner. *Cassoulet à l'oie* was easy to prepare: scoop the contents from the tin into a Crueset pot and pop in the oven for half an hour. Another preamble in their rural locale was called-for first, however, another chance to take in the countrified air before she started the actual process of cooking.

Their early evening stroll took them past the various cottages and farmhouses, aiming for the field where Daphne hoped to see those lovable donkeys, again. But she was about to be seriously disappointed.

A few of the local inhabitants were around, knocking on doors, looking distressed in typical Gallic fashion. The man who approached them was dressed in farmer's attire, middle-aged and ruddy-faced, probably the owner of the paddock.

From what little Daphne gathered from his loquacious manner, language being the stumbling block, some ne'er-do-well had unbolted the gate to the paddock, and the donkeys and horses had fled. Nobody had seen hide nor hair of them since, and the farmer was wondering whether he should rustle up a search party to find his lost animals. He was understandably worried that some harm might have befallen them or that they might even have been kidnapped.

The news upset Daphne, sharing his concern for the welfare of the Poitou donkeys – after all, they had taken to her immediately, such had been their sweet, placid nature – but she reluctantly accepted Marc's firm view that this was none of their business. They were on holiday here. On their honeymoon, in fact. There was no need to butt into the affairs of other people – let the locals deal with this matter themselves – since they might otherwise jump to conclusions. No matter how friendly country folk were perceived, everyone knew they were also a mistrustful bunch, particularly when encountering outsiders. The animals would turn up eventually, safe and sound, and the community could return to its peaceful existence.

As they made their way back down the lane, far from leisured, Daphne still fretting over her four-legged friends, Marc paused again at the same farmhouse they had stumbled across the evening before. It brought Daphne out of her anxieties, and she, too, looked in the direction of the farmhouse, soon realized what was distinctly different about it.

Night had descended, and a low-lying gibbous moon rode, pale and ghostlike, in the nocturnal sky. The North Star shone brightest of all in the scintillating canopy of the heavens. An owl hooted. From somewhere nearby, a dog barked.

The farmhouse, also known as *Maison Noir*, had been restored overnight to its former glory. Even from where they stood at the entrance to the courtyard, its row of flowerpots now absent to allow access, they could see that the stable door had been fixed, new windows had been fitted to the main house, and the section of roof that had previously collapsed had been miraculously repaired.

Maybe not so miraculously. Marc and Daphne had been away all day, and it looked as if the builders and decorators had been ridiculously busy. They had done a bang-up job restoring the place, finishing off all the repairs to the house. Dare anyone accuse the French of being lazy should come and see the refurbishments, completed in one day, for themselves, thought Daphne.

Yet, it wasn't the hard work on masterly display, the extraordinary dedication in which the house had been splendidly – and *lovingly* – restored.

No, the lights were on, suggesting occupancy.

The front door was suddenly thrust wide open, on either side of which antique confit pots had been placed as a decorative gesture, and a dark figure stood in the doorway, silhouetted against the light from the hallway.

"*Bonsoir, ça va?*" came a silvery female voice from the doorway. Whoever was standing there had spotted them.

The branches of the oaks and osiers soughed in the light evening breeze. The cold eye of the moon stared down at them. A cicada buzzed shrilly by.

Despite his hesitation, Marc had no choice but to respond to this friendly greeting. "Sorry . . . We didn't mean to disturb you."

"You are English?" the woman said, surprised, and stepped into the moonlit courtyard to take a closer look at them. She was no longer the sinister, indiscernible silhouette but a rotund, middle-aged woman, clad in a green dress and open-toe sandals. A brown shawl was thrown over her shoulders.

"Yes," replied Daphne, pleasantly enough.

"I like the English," complimented the woman, delighted. "A very noble people...May I seek the pleasure of your company?"

"How do you mean?"

"Why don't you come in for a few minutes? We can – *how do you say?* – shoot the moon."

"We really wouldn't want to impose," said Daphne. "Besides, we have to make dinner."

"Don't worry, my little one," the woman reassured her. "I have dinner on the stove. Plenty to go round. I would love it if we could get acquainted. Only for a short while, please, then I shall bid you goodnight, I promise. I really do not wish to inconvenience you for too long."

"Come on, let's do it," Marc whispered to Daphne, but his eyes remained firmly fixed on the fat Frenchwoman. "What's there to lose?"

Daphne expressed her reservations. "I don't think it's a good idea . . ."

Marc tried to put her mind at ease. "Nothing to be afraid of, my adorable one. This is what vacationing's all about, getting to know the natives, sampling the local culture. She's inviting us in with the goodness of her heart for simple, honest companionship, and she did say only for a short while, didn't she? She's practically begging. Let's make it worthwhile for her."

"I don't know . . ." Daphne was still undecided, but Marc had already begun walking across the courtyard towards the house. Daphne went after him, hurrying to catch up. The nearer she got to the house, the more she experienced a dark sense of foreboding. The façade of the house somehow reminded her of the candy house Hansel and Gretel chanced upon in the woods. *Welcome, children. I have so many wonderful treats to show you, you will never want to leave* . . . Daphne could not quell the disquiet sitting in the back of her mind. But she followed Marc, anyway, not wishing to appear like some Nervous Nerys.

As Marc approached the house, he pulled out his hand in greeting which the woman promptly shook. "We decided to accept your kind invitation."

Daphne did likewise and noticed the woman had a strong, almost manly, grip. Daphne recognized her name, Hettie, as that belonging to the niece of the erstwhile spinster, who had once owned and died in this house.

"You have made a lonely woman very happy," Hettie said gratefully. "Thank you for gracing me with your presence. Shall we go in?"

The woman led the Hulins across the threshold, the hallway adequately lit by a single light fixture. The walls were adorned at regular intervals by framed, nondescript charcoal sketches of landscapes, of bucolic life. She took her guests into her kitchen.

Daphne had to admit the kitchen was the kind of kitchen advertised in holiday brochures most people yearned for if they ever wanted a taste of Old Normandy, a kitchen that Time forgot. The enormous, eat-in kitchen was as rustic as its surrounds, complete with exposed walls and stone flooring, wooden cupboards, a deep enamel sink and cast-iron oven. Daphne saw the bundles of kindling piled up in the corner to light the wood-burning stove. The illumination was provided by islands of candles, nestled in pewter-holders, room-wide, giving the place a homely, almost romantic feel. The atmosphere was further enhanced by the aroma of cooking blended with the soothing scents of lavender and clove. Enchantment fell around them to such a comfortable degree that Daphne nearly missed the wooden crucifix on the far wall, uppermost part of which had slipped out of its mooring and seemed to be dangling crookedly, almost upside-down. She was tempted, out of Christian duty, to put it back the right way up but thought the better of it in case Hettie should take offence if Daphne suddenly got up and started rearranging the place.

Hettie invited them to grab a chair at the round, oak dining-table while she attended to the cooking pot. A wooden vase rested on the table, filled with red roses. "I saw you watching the house the other night . . . it *was* you, *non?*"

Marc was taken off-guard. "Guilty as charged. We didn't realize anybody was in."

Their hostess carried the pot over to the dining-table. "I was upstairs. I heard your voices outside."

"We apologize if we were trespassing. We were just curious." [*like Hansel and Gretel*]

She brought three pewter bowls and spoons to the table along with a crusty loaf and a breadknife. "Not at all. Everyone who comes here is curious about this house. There is *legend* to the house."

The odd manner in which she emphasized the word 'legend' caused Daphne to look at her more closely, and for the first time, she was able to study her face. One might have called it round and seasoned, but there was a strange beauty to it, a vitality. Her chin and jowls might be sagging and her greying blond hair tied into a bun, like Mirielle the other day, but her nose was elegantly-sculpted, sharp and alluring, and her bright, green eyes were that of a much younger lady, captivating to behold but forever vigilant. Daphne concluded Hettie must have been very attractive in her prime. "We heard. Gilbert Chalfont told us about its reputation."

Hettie smiled, as though reliving some private joke. "Ah, you're staying with Gilbert Chalfont. I bump into him sometimes. How is he . . . and Mirielle?"

"They're doing great."

She lifted the lid, sniffed the result. With the ladle she dished out its steaming contents into each bowl.

The aroma that wafted up to Daphne's nostrils was strong and gamey but very appetizing. "Smells divine. What is it?"

"Rabbit stew, cooked with the finest morels."

"Morels?" asked Daphne.

"Wild mushrooms . . ."

The couple tucked into their meals. Marc complimented the food and the red wine which they drank from pewter goblets, old-school. "This is very kind of you."

"Not at all. I could do with the company."

"I love your house," Daphne said, remembering how the homestead was in a state of disrepair only yesterday. "It's so full of charm. I can't believe how it's been fixed up so quickly."

"I rely on a reputable firm of building contractors. They're expensive but very efficient."

"Sorry to hear about your aunt," Daphne said with gentle consideration. "Our sincerest condolences."

"I am grateful, but please do not trouble yourselves. Henrietta was a frail old lady, a recluse, but she lived a long life. Unfortunately, she could never find love." There was a note of sadness in her voice. "It breaks my heart to see a young couple in love like you because I cannot find a man who will stay with me long enough. Good men are so hard to come by. Maybe my aunt and me were never cut out for love"

Daphne tutted sympathetically. "I think it's just a case of trying. One will soon come along and adore you for the rest of your life." Daphne talked a little about herself and Marc, how much they themselves were socially awkward when it came to romance, how after months of loneliness on the dating circuit they had connected on their very first encounter, almost naturally.

Hettie listened with interest, nodding now and again, maintaining the flow of conversation. "It should always be seen as a joyous occasion when two people start out on the long road together as a married couple, a call for celebration."

Dinner was consumed with gusto, and Daphne thanked her hostess for a lovely meal. Hettie poured each a small measure of an amber liquid in a liqueur glass.

"What do we have here?" Marc asked, intrigued.

"Calvados."

Marc had heard of it: apple brandy. Here, a traditional digestif on par with Cognac. He took a sip, nodded his approval, then gulped down the rest. "You people do such amazing things with apples."

"One for the road, as you English say."

Daphne sipped hers more slowly. It produced a warm, fuzzy feeling, not unpleasant, in her stomach, spreading outwards. Something brushed against her leg, making her bolt upright. Daphne looked down and saw it was the black cat that had spooked them yesterday. Green eyes peered up at her, bespeaking only friendship. She stroked it, and it brushed its cheek against her hand in appreciation. She watched it wander off, disappear into the shadows. She thought of how the flag of Normandy depicted *les trois chats*. Her eyes travelled back up to the downturned cross on the wall. Daphne suddenly got an ominous sense that perhaps Hettie hadn't put it back up deliberately. That it was inverted for a reason.

Yet she felt so relaxed, so lethargic, like being hypnotized. *Bewitched*.

Hettie spoke directly to Marc. "Your name suggests French heritage."

"That's very perceptive of you." Marc replied. He told her of his grandmother from Le Havre.

"But your bloodline stretches even further back."

And Daphne thought she saw her twitch. Just under the skin. It was only a fleeting impression and it was gone in a flash. Was it her imagination? Tiredness? The effect of the burgundy, the brandy? She gestured to the goblet. "This stuff's gone straight to my head."

Marc bypassed Daphne's comment. "Bloodline?" he said, referring to Hettie's original observation. "How do you mean?"

Hettie's stare grew more watchful, hawkish. "Your ancestry dates back to the time of the Inquisitors. You are descended from one of the judges of the *Petit Sorciers* trial: Édouard Arundel was your forefather!"

The unexpectedness of the exposition astonished Daphne. She did not know where it had come from. From what source could Hettie have possibly made such an audacious leap? How could she pretend to know anything about him unless she had done some background checking? Marc was rubbing his temples. "I don't feel all that well . . ."

"You sentenced me and my coven!" Hettie bellowed abruptly, like a bull. "So I shall now condemn you!"

The sudden impact of the threat, or curse, or whatever it was, jolted Daphne out of her reverie. Unforeseen by either of them, the mood had changed, and things had suddenly turned nasty. Fear swelled in her like a creature rising up, dripping, from a swamp. "I think we should go . . ."

But Marc seemed to be in no fit state to move. He was swaying drunkenly in his chair, a perfect, imbecilic look on his face.

"*Not so fast, fools!*" declared Hettie with hate-congested rage.

Daphne was thrust into panic mode. The vaseful of roses shrivelled up in an instant, as though the withering process she was witnessing were through a fast-lapse camera. The bread turned mouldy, blue, gathered flies. Oh God, there were maggots crawling in the pewter bowl she had just eaten from! She tried to scream, but her throat was locked. Instead, she knocked her pewter bowl off the edge of the table, nauseated, revulsed. It clattered loudly on the floor, spilling its contents, the heap of tiny maggoty things writhing blindly. The stink of rancid meat pervaded the air. She attempted to bring up her dinner, but all she could produce were a few dry heaves. *Now she was really seeing things.* Hettie was twitching madly, with more than just rage, and this time there could be no mistake. Her face contorted as individual groups of muscles convulsed separately from one another. It was like Hettie was wearing a mask of human skin and whatever lay beneath, whatever underlying form she possessed, was striving to break free.

The terror ramped up inside Daphne. She tried to get up, make a beeline for the door, but she stumbled to the ground, her legs unable to bear her weight. That was when she noticed the five-pointed star etched into the floor beneath the table – a pentagram, a cabalistic symbol of esoteric power. The lure of the candy house sprang again to mind. Daphne struggled against a rising tide of dizziness, the world around her spinning like crazy. Whether their drinks had been spiked or there was magic in the mushrooms they had consumed, she could not be sure. There were toads coming in through the open kitchen window in brown unassailable numbers, bounding towards her as though their legs were powered by tiny pogo sticks, goggling at her, thick-lipped mouths seeming to croak out her name . . . the latter of which, like everything else she was experiencing, was ridiculous, surely. They flopped next to her, their repellent, warty bodies buffeting and bulging against her exposed skin, and that urge to upchuck occurred once more. Why the age-old association between frogs [and snails] and the French? Could it be that Charlemagne had borne frogs on his coat of arms long ago . . . or could it have something to do with frogs' legs? Was this insight relevant at all at a mad time like this? Her clumsy attempt at maintaining a grip on reality did not diminish the horror.

The word 'familiar' floated up to the surface of her disorganized thoughts. A glance back at the far wall, and she witnessed two white snakes coiled around the upended crucifix.

And where the hell was the cat?

She began to crawl towards the doorway in a desperate bid to get away.

Hettie's voice grew more hissing, snakelike. "*Abandon all hope, any who dare enter here! Les conneries de la Immaculée Conception! There is nothing divine about the Virgin Whore who was fucked by your so-called God! I deny the one they call Jesus, who was born of sin, and rejoice in his Suffering! I serve only Prince Lucifer, the one, true god, pledge allegiance to him and prostrate myself before him! Make your presence known this night, O Goated One, and fill me with your fiery essence, so I may trample on the Cross, burn the Book of Lies and desecrate the souls of my accusers, bind one of their last, living descendants to my will!*"

While Hettie spewed her repugnance of Christ, Daphne called out Marc's name. Her voice sounded unreal, as if it were coming from somewhere faraway. Her husband appeared unable to respond, face-down in his bowl, out cold.

Hettie was now less than human. Her flesh rippled horribly, assuming a scaly, reptilian cast, slick with slime, and her eyes glowed, sparkled luridly like polished rubies. [*snake, worm,* wrym, Vouivre] Still, she continued to pour out her vitriol in a tirade of obscene blasphemies, the unholy profanities of a very angry witch reaping her revenge, now speaking in full, sibilant tones. "*And let usss rape nunsss and slit the throatsss of newborn babieesss! Let every cunting Christian whore ride the Goat and slide down the snake to the blessed, bottomlesss pit! The serpent grows mightier with each rebirth—"*

[*Are there any ghosts in Normandy?*] What were the chances the spinster and her niece were the same person? *Héloïse . . . ?*

"You're not real . . ." murmured Daphne, trying to fight the sedation.

"I'm as real as I wish to be . . ." Hettie informed her mercilessly. "My gift to you on your honeymoon, sissster . . ."

As the toads flopped and pressed their unnaturally-plump, clammy bellies against Daphne, leapfrogged and tumbled and piled over her with the feel of cold jelly, her shoulders could no longer support her head, and as her enfeebled arms yielded beneath her, she collapsed on the stone floor. Daphne's eyelids grew heavy, and her mind felt confused, scratched, ripped. Blackness staked its claim, her consciousness seeping away.

Going, going . . . *gone.*

It was the sound of sex that roused Daphne from her slumber. As the real world filtered back through her senses, she found herself lying on the floor of the kitchen. The candles had long since tapered away into a thousand tallowed globs. She felt terribly tired, exhausted as though her body didn't know whether to rest or stay awake, and a part of her mind seemed to be missing. She sought to recall the events of the previous evening – Hettie ingratiating herself into their company, Daphne and her husband being invited in to dine with her in her house, being drugged and incapacitated, being witness to all those *crazy* things, the pentagram, the toads, the snake-hag – and she could not be completely sure any of those things happened . . .

But the sound of coupling that awoke her dispelled any doubts, the faint noise of carnal moans. Daphne got to her feet, groaning. Outside the window, she saw the approach of dawn, a primrose hue on the horizon. She walked out of the kitchen and followed the sounds up the stairs. On the landing, she saw a series of closed oak doors on either side, except for the farthest one. The open door cast an oblong buttery light in the hallway. The sounds were coming from within. Daphne walked down the corridor, her mind imagining terrible things. The lewd noises grew louder, grunting, moaning male and female voices in sexual congress. Sure enough, she recognized the male voice in the midst of coitus, and an ice-pick of dread stabbed her heart. A loud ecstatic shriek emanated from the occupied room, causing Daphne to pause in her tracks. No second guesses to what that sound signalled. Daphne felt sick and confused. But she forced herself to get to the doorway, each step a prodigious effort, driven on by more than just basic necessity. She knew full-well what she would find.

The bedroom had the same rustic décor as the rest of the house, the walls painted mustard-yellow and barren, dusty and cobwebbed. The furniture consisted of a cherrywood armoire and a dressing-table and chair, distressed in hunter-green and on which rested possible heirloom pieces and junkyard treasures Daphne could not fully discern in the muted lighting the candles shed, and a pewter bed. And on the bed was her husband, head turned away, right leg flexed ninety degrees, buttocks tight and muscular and on display above the blanket. He had developed a tattoo just above his right hip, of a slither of snakes not unlike a caduceus. His skin glistened with a coating of something, a substance stickier than morning dew. No, her eyes were not deceiving her; she was actually staring at the naked body of her husband in bed with another woman. And what was he covered in . . . moisture, sweat, [*snake*] slime?

"Marc!" she called out, beginning to sob. But he did not hear her, did not respond, remained still, his chest rising and falling with each breath, immersed in a deep sleep. Daphne didn't want to believe it – there was no use denying it – but it appeared that Marc had succumbed to the desires of the flesh and had consummated their marriage by sleeping with someone else.

That someone else lying by his side emerged from the coverlet or, more precisely, *slithered* out of the bed, her body scaly, slippery and serpent-like from the waist-down, that of a giant anaconda, only for a transient spell. It quickly transformed into a woman's pair of smooth, silky legs, and the illusion was gone. Hettie or Héloïse or Hecate – or whoever or *whatever* the hell she was – slipped into a red kimono and, like the madam of a burlesque house, padded over to Daphne, very much human and black-haired and shapely. *Young and beautiful.* Radiating a Siren's dark, irresistible lure. "I prefer to copulate with another than conjugate with myself."

In spite of the emotions tumbling around in her head, Daphne told her straight. "He's spoken for."

Héloïse addressed Daphne, woman-to-woman. "You love him?"

Tears gushed down her cheeks. "Yes."

"He has given me a memorable fuck," Héloïse said callously, wickedly. "So ripe for seduction. But there is no hope for him now."

"I want him back."

"You should be rewarded for bringing to me the kin of Judge Arundel. For that, I shall spare your life. But there will be no end to your suffering. Get out while you still can – leave us."

"Not without my husband."

"You are nothing! He will always be married to *me*! I can give him so much more than any woman can give! His punishment awaits him. Do *you*, too, wish to be punished?"

Daphne persisted bravely, held her ground. "I don't know what you've done to him, but he needs me more than ever."

She tried to push past Héloïse, but she could not somehow get through the doorway. Her attempt was impeded by a barrier, statically-charged, rubbery in texture and invisible.

"You cannot enter." Héloïse picked up a challis, half-filled with a dark red liquid, which had been sitting in the doorway previously unnoticed by Daphne. "In here lies your blood."

My blood? Then it occurred to her. Daphne's hand reached down to her crotch and touched the damp, sticky patch that had formed on the fabric of her dress. The challis must contain her dead blood, the lining of her womb sloughed off in clots. *Menstrual blood.* The thought that Héloïse might have evacuated the blood from her down below while Daphne had been unconscious caused her to feel unmitigated disgust, a sense of feeling horribly violated, and that urge to vomit returned with a vengeance. Héloïse had not only got to know Daphne's husband in the Biblical sense – no, *infernal* sense – and marked his flesh as a sign of ownership, but she had also used Daphne's menses to cast a spell that barred access to him, keeping Daphne outside the door.

"Marc, wake up! Marc, come with me!" Daphne began punching the barrier furiously, emitting sparks, her fists bouncing off the flexible, electric membrane. All the while her husband lay soundlessly in bed, either asleep or perhaps paralyzed. At the mercy of a glamour wrought by the witch, who had seduced him with a philterous potion and was slowly drawing energy from him, feeding on his youth.

"Do not test my patience," Héloïse warned. "If you value your life you will leave."

Daphne spoke to Héloïse, woman to witch, continued to challenge her, "You're not hearing me, sister! I don't care what the hell you are, but I am not leaving here without my husband!"

The time for talking was over. Daphne was about to discover that the peculiar things she had witnessed so far, what she had rationally put down to her imagination working overtime, was nothing compared to what was about to come.

Héloïse's eyes blazed lantern-red and upon opening her fanged mouth, she sprayed a jet of venom from the back of her throat into Daphne's face. For a moment Daphne's eyes burned and she could not see. "You should have left when I gave you the chance! Let's see how you fare against the minibeasts I invoke upon thee!"

And Daphne felt something crawl across her ankles. As the stinging in her eyes slowly subsided and her vision gradually restored, she saw that the floor of the hallway was moving. Then she realized what was causing it to move.

Bugs.

Lots of bugs.

The hallway was a churning river of bugs. Flightless, sightless beetles bearing hard carapaces, black-armoured scorpions equipped with claws and a sting in their deadly, curled-up tail, fat, wormlike, multi-segmented millipedes, and spiders – oh yes, lots of hairy, long-legged, silk-spinning spiders, and spiderlings – boiled up from the floor, skittered over each other, vying for position, and swarmed around her ankles in a bid to climb her bare legs. And the sensation of their tiny feet across her skin was awful.

Daphne had never been much of a fan of insects and arthropods, less so of arachnids, and momentarily rendered immobile by this flowing, seething horde of tiny terrors, she was forced to make a tough decision, fuelled by the surge of adrenaline dumped into her muscles and spiking her heart rate. She pushed aside a disturbing mental image of Héloïse eating her lover, metamorphosing into a giant ophidian horror and encircling Marc's vulnerable form, wrapping him in her coils, crushing him and gobbling him up head-first, with the same hideous efficiency as a black widow consumes its mate or a wolf spider eats its young, and fled. Daphne retraced her steps, half-ran, half-stumbled back the way she had come.

It was a horrible sensation underfoot. Her plimsolls crushed the undulating carpet of creepy-crawlies with a palpable, unpleasant squelching, mixed with a sound vaguely reminiscent of crushed eggshells. Daphne somehow managed to keep her head and her stomach in check; she didn't know how.

Aside from the same beasties infesting the stairs, the walls had suddenly acquired a hundred warped faces that protruded out like living bas-reliefs. Daphne knew they were the faces of the men lured into the lair of the serpent woman over the centuries, their souls somehow fused with the material of the walls, held captive within the foundations of the house, their misery and despair made quasi-immortal by some diabolic practice of high sorcery. Their forever-tortured screams matched Daphne's own raucous shrieks as their arms reached out from the animated walls to snatch her. And as Daphne reached the bottom of the stairs and raced past the kitchen, her sneakers squashing the bugs to goo, herself consciously making sure to avoid the grasping spectral arms, her ears suddenly attuned to a familiar voice calling out above the cacophony of desolate wails.

"Daphne, I am so sorry for what I've done."

Daphne stopped in her tracks. "Marc? Marc, is that you?"

"Yes, my adorable one . . ." The voice came from one of the faces on the wall. It was a rudimentary version of Marc's face, blank and unseeing, and he looked to be in the hellish depths of agony. It seemed he had become an unwilling part of the house. "Please let me out."

The sight of him – what had become of him, Héloïse's prize prisoner in this place of hell – threatened to rob her of her sanity, but Daphne held it together, even though she wanted to cry. But all manner of putrid bug-life mounted her feet, flooded up her legs, perhaps lured by the smell of her period blood, and she could feel sharp pincers sinking into the flesh of her calves. "I'm coming back for you, my darling . . . Promise."

She shook the bugs off her legs and ripped herself away from the heart-crushing vision of her perpetually-suffering husband, who went back to the screaming hell, the wall filled with the frightening, writhing emanations of those doomed for possibly eternity.

"*Please don't leeeeave meeeeeee . . .!*" was the last thing she heard Marc say, his pleas intensifying, before his voice was drowned out by the other residents.

But her long ordeal was not yet over.

Out through the oak door, the courtyard ran amok with more of Héloïse's minions. The heads of vipers emerged from the confit pots, hissing, their mouths open, fangs poised to strike. The ground slithered with salamanders and snakes. There were newts and toads . . . and *rats*. Whatever witch's spell had conjured up the bugs in the house had surely summoned these meaner creatures of the night from whatever hell they languished in.

The toads abnormally large, bloated, all orb eyes and webbed feet, hopped sluggishly, their throats together forming an echo of ugly, croaking sounds. The black, beady eyes of the huge plague rats remained unblinking, glared up at her. The twitch of whiskers, the patter of tiny paws, sleek black hides, jumping with fleas, their collective squeaks magnified to execrable screeches.

Daphne steeled herself for the onslaught and pelted through the abhorrent swarm of vermin, serpentine and batrachian life, little demons conscripted to the witch's cause, prepared to do her bidding. Under Daphne's feet, the ground heaved uneven and wet and slippery, and those wild creatures trodden on were crushed to a noisome, ichor-squirting pulp. The gagging stench of liquefaction accompanied their demise. She slipped, regained her footing, legs pumping harder as she cut a swathe through this legion of the damned. She fought against her rising gorge, stifled her screams. The snakes, rats and toads demarcated the entrance to the courtyard, almost magically. As Daphne ran, bats, the furry rodents of the flying world, suddenly swooped down from overhead and their tiny claws nicked her cheeks and entangled in her hair . . .

Behind her, the dark granite of the farmhouse writhed and rippled, as though composed of black, animated flesh.

Daphne limped, staggered down the lane, back of Gîte Joulines and began hammering violently on the door of the Chalfonts.

The sight of their guest, cut and bruised, dirty and dishevelled, screaming hysterically of snakes and sigils and shiny-eyed demonesses, produced only alarm and the grimmest, gravest fears. Gilbert and Mirielle called the police. The police took down a statement from Daphne who, at the advent of dawn, led them to the place.

Except there were nothing to see, nothing out of the ordinary.

It was still the same old, stone farmhouse, the roof of which had fallen in. Daphne frantically reiterated how the house had been fixed up and tried to explain what had happened, but the police would not accept her mumbo-jumbo as evidence. They were of the opinion she was suffering from shock, possibly even madness.

Only Gilbert knew that what she was describing was the truth, and it was not the product of a malady of the mind. For this was not the first time this had happened. The fugitive dragon had claimed another victim. His talk the other night had meant to serve as a warning and not to be taken as a cue to revisit the house. Black House, whose very name indicated its dark legend, was home to an unspeakable monster with a gory past and a legacy of collecting unfortunate souls. An ancient creature of the slithering type, deity to the cult of snakes, destroyer of crops, befouler of men's minds, desecrator of love. Although Gilbert dearly wished for the banishment of this sublime evil from this land, he could not tell the authorities or anyone of what he knew. *Not ever.* He had once entered into an affair with Hettie and would have ended up the same way as Marc, if he hadn't managed to flee the house in time. He too had seen all manner of crazy things which he did not wish to relive. *Never again*. It had since strengthened his marriage, and he never informed Mirielle of his indiscretion. She didn't need to know. It was a French thing. And he knew of all the other men who had disappeared in the area. His heart went out to Daphne.

Then there was the coincidental finding at the Jesus statue, posted like a sentinel, up the incline, overlooking the hamlet. The missing Poitou donkeys were discovered, their throats slit, their bellies cut open, their blood pooled over the marble platform of the statue. Mercifully, Daphne never learned of the dead donkeys, whose gruesome discovery would have made her more distraught than she already was. Up on the hill, Christ wore a wounded expression, of sadness and anger. Someone had replaced the original plaque with another that read in translation: *For, behold, the Lord cometh out of heaven to punish the inhabitants of the earth for their iniquity: the earth also shall disclose her blood, and shall no more cover her slain.* Isaiah 26:21

So far Daphne had been keeping it together, but now on thinking that it might have just been in her head, she let it all out. She collapsed in a sobbing heap and wept.

She remembered an old quote from *Jane Eyre: Our honeymoon will shine our life long: its beams will only fade over your grave or mine.*

Daphne went back home without her husband.

In the clear light of day, those events seemed like they happened a lifetime ago, like the residue of a dream that lingers upon wakefulness before gradually fading. But she had the ruins of her heart to contend with. Daphne returned to England a broken woman. She never recovered. Utterly traumatized by her experience, encumbered by the knowledge of what she had witnessed, she suffered panic attacks and nightmares, complicated by guilt, shame and self-blame. It was not helped by the angry recriminations and a lack of forgiveness she received from her in-laws, including Marc's war-veteran grandfather, for losing her husband on her honeymoon. The doctors could do nothing initially except sedate her. In her grief, she thought of killing herself and she was hospitalized. As Michel de Montaigne, probably the greatest essayist of the French Renaissance, put it: *Nothing fixes a thing so intensely in the memory as a wish to forget it.* Even the words of Voltaire could not comfort her: *If the people we love are stolen from us, the way to have them live on is to never stop loving them. Buildings burn, people die, but real love is forever.* She received bereavement counselling without success. No more would Marc refer to her as his 'adorable one', his physical presence sucked into the very fabric of those walls, a lost, lamented spirit in a house of hell, consigned to the nether-plane by spell or potion. Marc was never seen again, his case remaining open to this day, declared 'Missing'. But that wasn't the worst of it. No, the worst of it [*just go with the flow*] was her damned period. Héloïse, who had the power to bestow misfortune on others, whether disease or death, had woven a malediction upon Daphne, a promise of no end to her suffering: a period that never stopped, a constant, heavy menses, despite the doctors' best efforts to understand the cause. She required weekly blood transfusions for the remainder of what little life she had left, for she continued to bleed, bleed, *bleed* . . .

June 2014-October 2014

Paris Avant Le Printemps

Five Roses: A message of love and admiration to the one I truly cherish and care for, more than words can ever describe...

This tale begins in a cemetery and ends in the catacombs, or maybe slightly after, but the middle third could be described as a pleasant, if not somewhat peculiar, account of our journey through Paris. I think our experiences, no matter how pedestrian or rambling at times, are still worth recording for the sake of posterity.

Hayley and I – Emmanuel Foster – were in the City of Lights to repair our relationship and, perhaps, rekindle our romance. Looking back, I felt I did what I did because Hayley did what she did. My actions had caused a serious rift between us, jeopardizing our marriage. So why not spend Valentine's Day in Paris? We mutually agreed that if these romantic few days together did not work out, then we would gladly call it quits and begin divorce proceedings.

One might consider PÈRE LACHAISE CEMETERY being an odd, almost macabre place to kick off one's sightseeing. But we were both keen to experience the past at the earliest opportunity, commune with Paris's celebrated dead in a manner of speaking, adopting an enthusiasm that for us was uncharacteristically morbid. We had got into the GARE DU NORD the night before, checking into the four-star ASTORIA HOTEL in the Opera district. Setting off from St. Pancras station, the Eurostar had proven to be considerably cheaper (only twenty-five euros each, can you believe it?) and way more comfortable (an *honest* service, always bearing the customer in mind) than Network Rail's ruthless profiteering tactics, unscrupulously exploiting the public by demanding extortionate fares for cramped, second-class trains and delivering untruthful, third-rate excuses for disrupted or cancelled services. We took the Paris Metro to the eastern, somewhat rundown part of the city on that damp, misty Sunday morning.

Père Lachaise was a veritable piece of Parisian history, the most-visited graveyard across the globe, largely for the extraordinary heritage of human talent interred within its high stone walls, a burial ground for the famous. This one-hundred-and-eight-acre necropolis had buried an estimated million people since it was first opened by Napoleon Bonaparte over two hundred years ago and currently accommodated an astonishing seventy thousand gravesites. Being a sucker for quotes, I thought of Alfred de Vigny, who once penned: *France, for example, loves at the same time history and the drama, because one explores the vast destinies of humanity, and the other the individual lot of man.* The map posted at the gated entrance, where there was attached a security hut, helpfully counted off paths and avenues and walkways from which one was supposed to access the graves. Despite the clearly-numbered divisions on the map, Hayley and myself must have trudged aimlessly in the chilly morning air for a good three-quarters-of-an-hour without locating a single grave of interest, not a criticism of my navigational skills, mind. For that short, unproductive duration, regardless of the simple elegance of the cemetery's geographical layout, the vast repository of family mausoleums and chapels, alongside the generic, moss-covered gravestones, must have seemed like any cemetery, anywhere in the world. The graves were as grey and forbidding as the dreary, sullen sky against which the leafless, centuries-old chestnut trees, lining the labyrinth of sloping, uneven cobblestoned lanes, were silhouetted, awaiting the rebirth of Spring. It was not until we were on the cusp of giving up and turning back that our luck changed, I hoped, for the better. I never expected otherwise at the time. That was when we actually got to see the place for what it really was, what we had come here for in the first place.

"I can't do this anymore," Hayley said, already out of breath. "I'm getting tired,"

"You're saying we should head back?" I clarified.

"I think going on would be a bad idea, a futile exercise. We've done our best, and at least I've exercised my legs today." Hayley surveyed our wet surroundings and the limited presence of visitors so early in the day, a few random couples like us, the occasional group of tourists, the occasional passerby, strolling the promenade of the dead, both in leisurely fashion and yet with a goal-directed purpose. "Or maybe we can stop somebody who might be able to help us—"

It was at that exact, fortuitous moment that a man came striding down a steep incline between a number of tombstones. "I heard that!" he announced in a distinct French accent, having spotted us. He marched over to us. "Monsieur *et* Madame is lost?"

He spoke to us with a pressing concern unheard of from any stranger, and the joviality in his voice was almost infectious. Hayley was instantly taken by him. I suppose I was, too. "How did you guess?"

"Tourists, speaking English, looking for the exit," the stranger said. "The cemetery is big. Very easy to get lost."

"And there was I thinking, no *hoping*, someone—"

"—Might show you around?" said the man suddenly. "It will be a pleasure."

I studied the man, who had somehow overheard us at such a critical juncture and appeared before us like a miracle – or an apparition. He was short in height, slim to the point of scrawny and clad in a black leather reefer jacket, white open-collar shirt and blue jeans. He'd compensated for his completely-bald pate by growing his hair long from the back of his head until it was shoulder-length and fixed in a ponytail. The dark colour of his hair was inconsistent with the lines and wrinkles on his face, suggesting he might be approaching sixty. He was missing a few teeth here and there and the remaining teeth were stained brown from decades of smoking and neglect. Aside from his friendly, easy-going manner, there was a wiliness to his expression, almost fox-like, enhanced by his small, shifty eyes peering at us from behind his round, orange-tinted glasses. "We could probably do with someone who knows the place."

"Julien Étrange at your service," our new friend said amicably, "but people call me 'Jules'. I shall be your guide."

My wife and I introduced ourselves. I reflected on his surname for a moment. I wondered if that was his real name. It made me think of the Rue Morgue. At least he didn't claim his name was 'Effrayant'.

The sky remained grey and drizzly, our breath condensing into mist.

"Where to first?" Jules asked eagerly.

I looked at him again, taking in his leather jacket and the fashionable, tinted shades, the long hair on his sides and back which he had stylishly fashioned into a ponytail, despite the utter baldness of his crown, and I thought him reminiscent of a biker or a rocker or a roadie. A rocker, perhaps, who might also be as cunning as a fox. "Jim Morrison's grave," I requested. Hayley nodded in agreement.

"Ah, always a favourite!" Jules said, pleased. He grabbed our hands and led us through the graveyard. His memory was excellent. He told us he'd done this for nearly twenty years so knew the location of all the graves like the back of his hand. He also apprised us of what kept him going: he produced a cigarette packet from his jacket pocket which he opened to reveal . . . The secret to his success, his high stamina levels and inexhaustible supply of energy? No, not cigarettes or drugs... but pieces of chocolate. "Keeps my mind mellow," he told us, "and my body full of pep." He weaved this way and that, surprisingly nimble, and, within a couple of minutes, we'd arrived at Morrison's grave, amongst the most popular at the cemetery and admittedly the tackiest, touristy thing to do. There were a few visitors gathered at the barrier.

I had to admit I was disappointed. I could have described Jim Morrison's final resting place as very ordinary, unremarkable, *unimpressive*, the gravestone itself discoloured, the lettering of the epitaph faded, all strangely out of keeping with the tomb of a Rock god, if it were not for the endless bouquets of flowers and incense candles and sheets of poetry that had turned his rather modest tomb into something of a shrine. The Greek inscription on the headstone translated as: *True to his own daimon*. I imagined that his grave had once been solitary, until people got wind of his burial place and acquired their own plots in close proximity to his in order to bolster their own reputation by association, selfishly or vainly get themselves noticed in death. So the other graves I felt made the whole area look crowded, cluttered, *common*. You remember I mentioned security earlier? Jules informed us that Jim Morrison's was one grave that warranted the presence of security due to it having endured graffiti and other deliberate acts of vandalism over the years, outside of its natural wear, by the sheer number of people visiting it, including being a place of pilgrimage for hippies, holding candlelight vigils to commemorate the Summer of Love, or a hot spot for drug parties run by American gap-year students, who had crossed the Atlantic for the express purpose of seeing the Rock legend's grave. The recent theft of yet-another precious bust of the dead musician prompted a further increase in the security detail. Oscar Wilde's was another grave needing protection from the public.

"Morrison died young," Jules tried to enlighten us. "Too much drink and drugs." Truly the understatement of the year.

"You don't say," I replied. By the end of his life, aged only twenty-seven, the Doors' frontman was downing two bottles of bourbon a day and had taken to using heroin regularly while continuing to binge on a cocktail of marijuana and cocaine and hallucinogens, such as peyote, acid and 'shrooms. From the Doors' eponymous first album, released in 1967, pioneering a kind of psychedelic rock greatly imitated since, to their last, Jim Morrison's influential career spanned a mere four years, but the Man, the Myth and the Music will be forever remembered for changing the face of popular music, even encouraging the Beatles to experiment. In that ridiculously short time, going by the law of diminishing returns, that included exposing his penis on stage during a concert in Miami, Morrison, now grossly overweight, had knackered out his heart, making it so enlarged it could pump no more and it went into failure while he ought to technically still have been in the prime of his life. Morrison embodied the ultimate, clichéd tale and oft-told, tragic consequences of Sex, Drugs and Rock'n'Roll. *I'm sure the Lizard King wouldn't mind a group of beautiful maidens with flowers in their hair, barefoot and high on weed, dancing provocatively over his grave.*

From one musician to another. Jules, our new-found guide, quickly wound his way through the tombs and took us to Chopin's grave within a matter of minutes. People were gathered here, too, whom Jules explained were mostly Poles, from Chopin's homeland. "We probably get over a hundred Poles a day who come to the cemetery for nothing more than visiting Chopin's grave when there is so much more to see and experience in Paris. Most of his remains are buried here, except for his heart, which was removed and sent over to his home town in Warsaw."

Indeed, it was a tomb befitting a virtuoso pianist, whose genius had composed some of the greatest piano concertos in history. Worthy of attention, the statue of Euterpe, the muse of music, surmounted the tomb, mourning over a broken lyre.

We got into the spirit of the immortal poet, Baudelaire, who was not even buried at Père Lachaise but at West Montparnasse and who stated beautifully: *To the solemn graves, near a lonely cemetery, my heart like a muffled drum is beating funeral marches.*

We walked to our next notable resident of the cemetery, whom Jules informed us was the greatest mime artist in the world, Marcel Marceau, and who performed professionally for sixty years before eventually dying of old age – *makes a pleasant change* – having enjoyed a clean, wholesome life. Marceau created that iconic character, Bip the Clown, whom Michael Jackson allegedly acknowledged as the inspiration for his signature 'moonwalk'. Marceau rested peacefully in a simple, unobtrusive grave that captured his humble, unassuming nature.

Next up: Molière. The stage name of a comic playwright, master of the French farce, who wrote such great works as *The Misanthrope* and, of course, *The Hypochondriac*, where Molière plays a man suffering illnesses he does not have. Ironically, during his final performance, Molière went into an uncontrollable paroxysm of coughing, ultimately making his actual terminal illness known to the audience, having long since been stricken with TB. He died later that evening. In the play, *The Love Doctor*, Molière spoke of 'Orviétan', a mythical cure for all ills, maybe even a cure for love itself, says the doctor in spite of himself. Molière once claimed: *Writing is like prostitution. First you do it for love, and then for a few close friends, and then for money.* I suppose there was a certain truth to it. We paid our respects to the Gallic 'Shakespeare', interred beside the fabled writer, Jean de La Fontaine, who famously said: *A person often meets his destiny on a road he took to avoid it.* He also claimed that every journalist owed tribute to the evil one. Moliere's stone sarcophagus was raised on small columns in contrast to La Fontaine's plinth, enclosed within a wrought-iron fence to deter trespassers.

Where to next? I thought. The resting place of Honoré de Balzac? Or Marcel Proust? Maybe Stendhal or Sartre?

More talking, more walking, escorted by this strange, little man, and we arrived at the big one, by far the most famous tomb at Père Lachaise, belonging to one Oscar Wilde. And, indeed, it was a spectacular piece of artistry, eye-catching, unforgettable. Aside from the rich offering of flowers, love letters and trinkets that garnished his Art Deco tomb, it was immediately obvious that the elaborately-carved sculpture of the Modernist Angel gracing the tomb was missing an important part of itself; an ardent admirer had snapped off its erect penis and run off with it. The cemetery officials had therefore decided to contain the monument within a perspex façade, but that did not prevent generations of adoring women from kissing the tomb, covering it in a legacy of lipstick.

"He died of a broken heart," Jules said, poignantly.

The epitaph said it all. Engraved on the tomb was an excerpt from *The Ballad of Reading Gaol*: *And alien tears will fill for him/ Pity's long-broken urn,/ For his mourners will be outcast men,/ And outcasts always mourn.* Wilde had, in life, greatly struggled with his homosexuality, carrying on an affair with the Marquess of Queensberry's son, Lord Alfred 'Bosie' Douglas, who got away scot-free due to his aristocratic connections, despite his obvious penchant for Uranian poetry, while Wilde got convicted for 'gross indecency', suffering incarceration in Pentonville prison, a tale as heartbreaking as that of Abelard and Heloise. Lord Alfred Douglas's ancestry had suffered tragedy and misfortune – the 'Queensberry curse' – dating as far back as 1298, when his ancestor, Sir William Douglas, died in the Tower of London after joining William Wallace on the battlefield against the English. And the curse would continue to strike down his descendants, even to this day. Paris was where Oscar Wilde went into exile after eloping with Bosie in Venice. Paris was also where he had come to die, succumbing to meningitis. Paris was where he finally found eternal rest. RIP.

We reverted to the theme of French culture. Édith Piaf, the world-renowned, diminutive cabaret singer, took the spotlight. Piaf endured an impoverished upbringing, even spending part of her childhood in a brothel, suffering a miscarriage in early adulthood, before her talent for singing, marked by an incredible, soaring voice brought her fame and immortalized her stage-name the world over. But Jules reminded us that, like Jim Morrison, it was Édith Piaf's lifestyle that led to her eventual downfall: her severe alcohol abuse and addiction to morphine. Although Piaf had been a frequent performer at Nazi social and bordello gatherings during the Occupation, therefore considered by some of her fellow countrymen to be a traitor, nearly one-hundred-thousand people attended her funeral ceremony at the graveyard. We noted she was buried in a family plot marked FAMILLE GASSION-PIAF, adorned with numerous red roses, alongside her father as well as her second husband, who had been many years her junior.

"Where to next?" Jules inquired, preparing for the next grave.

"I think that's enough for one day," said Hayley wearily. "We've seen enough."

"As you wish . . ." Jules said, sounding disappointed, and immediately stuck out his hand, palm-side up.

Hayley did not comprehend his gesture initially, but when it did finally dawn on her, she was horrified. "You expect us to pay you? Are you not with the cemetery staff?"

I knew the answer to that one even before she finished asking the question. The man was unlicensed, working illegitimately. He was not an employee of the cemetery. However, in my book, he had carried out a service. *Commendably*. He had effortlessly escorted us to some of the most important and well-visited graves in the cemetery when it would probably have taken us hours finding the damned things. He had also demonstrated a certain expertise on the life-story of each departed person. The man had been extremely knowledgeable and helpful in a non-existent job. "Pay the man!"

"Why should I?" Hayley protested furiously. "He's exploiting tourists. What does he think we are? A charity?" She addressed him directly with the look of a woman who might commit murder at Père Lachaise Cemetery. "We did not come to Paris to get robbed."

Jules went quiet for a moment, possibly offended by her unkind words. When he next spoke, he spoke calmly, rationally. "You should only pay me what you think I am worth."

"I think that's fair," I said to Hayley. I felt obliged to pay him. It wasn't as if he was driving a hard bargain . . . or *Tartuffying* us, so to speak.

Hayley didn't speak, merely shrugged her shoulders.

"What do you do for a living?" Jules inquired.

I was a former music journalist with the *Chertsford Echo* who had, early in my career, written an award-winning account of the unique tale of Heath Axton, lead singer of the Rock band, the Mind Rippers. I planned to catch up with the Rocker, who was never short of scandal, for a follow-up book. I understand the Mind Rippers were planning to record a final album together in the coming year before scheduling a farewell tour. "I'm a successful author. Non-fiction. Music, mostly."

"And you, Madame?"

"An illustrator. I provide Emmanuel's books with the essential artwork they need. But that doesn't put enough bread on the table so I work part-time as a nanny."

"So what is the problem? You are clever, artistic people – a *beautiful* couple. A *team*. You should not be worrying about money. Money is an invention to make someone feel artificially superior to somebody else. Money is the root of all evil. Imagine a world without money. The billionaires and the bankers would be useless, fit for nothing." He quoted La Fontaine: "*Neither wealth nor greatness render us happy.*"

Hayley was still holding out. "I would have expected you to have helped us with the goodness of your heart." We stood in the fine, misty rain at an impasse. I heard the sinister caw of a crow. Jules did not move, kept looking into our individual faces expectantly. Then, Hayley relented. A tad. She produced a coin. "Okay, just to get you off our back, here's one euro."

This became the new sticking point. Jules was appalled. He considered the payment for his services inadequate, paltry. "Madame, this is insulting . . ."

Hayley shot him down in flames. "Now who's worrying about money? The root of all evil, right?"

I stepped in at this stage. I had to. This dispute over money – a few measly euros – was getting beyond ridiculous. I did not want it to get ugly. I did not know this contradictorily bald yet long-haired, little man with the missing teeth, crooked nose and the orange-tinted shades that hid the natural colour of his eyes. Rather than exuding the craftiness of a fox, or maybe even the deviousness of the weasels in *The Wind in the Willows*, Jules could very well turn out to be batshit crazy. "My sincerest apologies for my wife. She's been under a lot of stress lately. Here's another five euros. One for each grave."

Jules accepted the five-euro note graciously, slipping it into his pocket. "*Merci beaucoup*, Monsieur. You are a gentleman." He glanced at Hayley who was staring furiously at me for my timely intervention, for not conferring with her and for my generous tip. "Perhaps I can show you one more grave for free. On the house. *From the goodness of my heart.*"

His last remark was spoken with such deliberate irony and a verbal sideways swing, throwing Hayley's words back at her, that it caused her to briefly glance at him with a spiteful expression, all narrowed eyes and pursed lips. She did not say anything.

I took Jules up on his offer. "That would be lovely. Much appreciated."

"Any graves particularly in mind?" he asked me.

Maybe old Bonaparte himself. Or maybe not. "Surprise me."

Jules grinned, revealing the horrible state of his teeth. "As you wish . . ."

We began moving again. He walked quickly, with an unthinkable fleet-of-foot and agility, which made me think of foxes again. Despite his brisk pace, I managed to keep up with him. Hayley trailed far behind us, sulking, stewing.

Crisscrossing various graves, traversing along cobbled footpaths, the hilly, uneven pavement, Jules took us to our mystery gravesite. One for the road. He had chosen the grave of Colette, best known for her novels, *Chéri* and *Gigi*, the latter turned into an Oscar-winning musical extravaganza and leading to the discovery of the then-unknown actress, Audrey Hepburn. Colette had brought the *Claudine* series of novels to the world, thinly-disguised accounts of her own life. Colette was not free of scandal, secretly sharing the same women as Willy, her selfish, philandering first husband, but also openly admitting she wrote all the books originally published under his name. Like her very sexual novels, Colette was a very sexual woman, leading a very unconventional love life, comprising countless dalliances with both men and women, including an affair with her second husband's son. Jules explained that Colette became the first woman in France to receive a state burial, paving the way for more women being seen as national heroes.

Colette's grave was wreathed in flowers, apparently changed daily. "But she is regarded as the original cat lady," Jules explained. "She even wrote a novel called *La Chatte*, about a man's helpless devotion to his Chartreux cat, Saha, a creature based on a Chartreux Colette once owned during childhood. Just as she was a lover of cats, the cats that lurk behind the tombs are rumoured to gather at her grave at midnight. Probably to celebrate the special bond Colette shared with their noble race."

A black cat emerged from behind her headstone and peered at us with emerald eyes. Its sudden appearance caused me to jump. It was as though it had been listening to Jules and had decided it was its cue to make an entrance. It was a tom, sleek of fur, and in perfect physical health, not malnourished or scraggy as one might expect of cemetery cats. I tried to ignore him. Hayley had caught up with us and was staring at the black cat slightly fearfully.

"It is a great prestige to be buried at Père Lachaise," Jules continued. "As long as you have lived in Paris for one day – your holiday counts – you are entitled to buy a burial plot."

"How much is a standard burial plot?" I asked him, more out of curiosity than anything else.

"Twelve thousand euros for one plot, twenty-five thousand euros for a family tomb." he replied helpfully. "Are you interested?"

Hayley spoke up then, unable to contain herself. "Let's go, Manny. This no-good chiseller's trying to swindle more money out of us. He's probably the type of person who'd try and sell snow to the Eskimos."

"Very well, Madame," Jules responded, not taking her comment personally this time. "I know when I am not welcome anymore. It was a pleasure to meet you both."

"Likewise," I said, shaking his hand, genuinely grateful he had shown us around for only a nominal fee.

"I envy you, Monsieur. I wish I could have your life. But I am needed here. To help others like you."

I took his comment as a compliment, but there was something slightly odd about it. I could not put my finger on it.

He turned to Hayley. "And you, Madame, do not be hard on me. I only wish you well. You have a great husband, a good man. But please do not fight over money. It is not worth it."

Hayley's expression softened. "The root of all evil?"

Jules smiled. "*Exactement!*" He added: "Love is more important. Love is all you need. *Love is the great master. Love teaches us to be what we never were.*" After Molière, he rounded off with a quote from Balzac: "*One should believe in marriage as the immortality of the soul.*" He then did something that neither myself nor Hayley was expecting. He touched Hayley on the head with his fingers, momentarily tapped her hair. "You say you are a nanny? And you shall have twins!"

Hayley was frozen for a couple of seconds, taken by surprise. I, too, was taken aback. The moment was eerily atmospheric, enhanced by the black tom watching us with an avid curiosity and the sound of crows cawing loudly in the stark, high trees.

"Look after yourselves," Jules finally said, the moment passing. "*À bientôt.*"

Then, the strange, little man, who had found us at an opportune moment and taken it upon himself to be tour guide, not without an element of deception some might say, wandered off in search of fresh prey. He grew transparent, losing colour, and for a moment I thought I could see right through him, like he was a ghost. I thought I imagined it. Surely, the effect a cemetery can have on a person's mind, suggestible or otherwise. Then, he disappeared into the misty rain. Like a genie, he was gone – had he granted us the wishes we requested? "I wonder what all that was about."

I thought of how he had touched my wife on the forehead, as though bestowing a blessing . . . or a *curse*. Had he hexed her? Was he not so much a rocker but actually a gypsy? Had he delivered some sort of gypsy curse? Twins, he had said. But I did not want to misconstrue an innocent gesture, a simple platitude, into something dark and sinister and supernatural, even though he seemed to temporarily fade out of reality. Just my imagination playing silly games with me, I supposed.

"You okay?" I asked my wife.

She nodded. "Glad he's gone. Let's blow this joint."

We started walking again, following the tree-lined, cobbled avenues. We were trailed throughout our journey back to the main entrance by the black cat from Colette's grave. Hayley asked him to scram, but he refused to do so, seemed unafraid, maintaining some distance behind us. It was a rather disconcerting experience, spooky even, not that I'm a superstitious person, walking with a black cat on my tail, like we'd been *marked*. I thought again of the manner in which Jules, if that was his real name, had touched my wife's forehead and how he seemed to drain of colour and vitality. Maybe the cat was hungry and wanted us to feed him something. Yes, I went with that explanation.

Soon, we had negotiated the maze of celebrity graves, gothic tombs, family vaults and other sepulchral monuments and, before long, we were striding down Principal Avenue, the chequered flag in sight. But Hayley was not going to let our encounter with Jules rest quietly. Despite my best attempts to tell her to let it go, not to be vindictive, she was adamant that the security guard at the entrance hut needed to be warned of this 'evil' man, to be on the lookout for him. The security guard, a woman of thirty, listened politely to Hayley ramble on about this man without understanding a single word of English. I duly thanked her for hearing my wife out. I looked behind us. The black cat was thankfully no longer following us and nowhere to be seen.

We had begun our holiday by paying homage to Paris's open-air museum of the celebrated dead. The ghost of our marital rift would haunt us throughout our stay in Paris, compounded by our indelible encounter with that peculiar man from the cemetery, whose memory would hang over my head like a black cloud, waiting to burst. I suppose, with everything that occurred before, we just wanted to make the most of our holiday by bypassing the usual touristy spots, such as the Eiffel Tower, the Champs-Élysées and the Louvre, and experiencing the artistic, quirkier side of Paris.

And the weirder the better.

Even if Hayley had resoundingly proved she could have her cake and eat it too, we decided to forgo visiting the Place de la Bastille just ten minutes down the road, where the remains of the former prison, stormed and destroyed during the French Revolution, still stood. No, we were famished, and a stop-off at a nearby café/restaurant proved a much better bet, instead. The inevitable duck confit with Parmentier potatoes for myself and roast poussin with herby frites for Hayley, beginning our culinary journey with the more traditional fare, went down well with a glass of white wine. Amazing how French cuisine, mostly organic, has flavour; you can actually *taste* the meat. No factory farming, either, or meat pumped full of antibiotics or growth enhancers. Conversation between us was superficial, focused only on planning our next tourist landmark. But I knew we would talk once we'd done enough sightseeing and felt comfortable and ready.

Once pleasantly full, we travelled back on the Metro, dropping by the hotel to pick up a few odds and ends before starting off on a long walk. Our hotel, the Astoria, was in a prime location, practically in the centre of the city, perfectly situated to allow us to walk to the major attractions on our itinerary within half-an-hour-to-one-hour radius in any direction. Our wander took us first to the

TUILERIES GARDEN, separating the Louvre from the Place de la Concorde and created, on the authority of Catherine de' Medici in the sixteenth century, by the same architect who designed the Royal Gardens of Versailles, further added to and enhanced by generations of monarchs since. Every arrondissement in Paris had some description of a *parc, jardin* or *bois* to retreat to, forming one quarter of the overall land, thereby making Paris the greenest city in Europe. The Tuileries Garden, was, by all accounts, the most culturally-significant green space for Parisians and tourists alike, who came here to promenade and rendezvous and serenade. People flocked the parkland in their droves, happy to take a stroll, to play chess or read a book, to sit and chat with their friends and family on the plentiful chairs and benches. We saw a fair number of young couples kissing, unabashed public displays of affection apparently the norm in France. We kept our gander through the vast, beautifully-landscaped gardens to a minimum, passing among the walkways, terraces and patios as a way of a short cut to the River Seine. If we'd had more time we might have immersed ourselves in the magnificent splendour and grandeur of the gardens, relaxed by either of the ponds, appreciated the water-fountain features, ridden the carousel, admired Maillol's provocative statues of nymphs on the same grounds as Rodin's sensuous sculpture of *The Kiss*, borrowed from his own infamous *Gates of Hell*. Here, near the entrance of the MUSÉE DE L'ORANGERIE, visitors could enjoy Monet's fascination with water lilies as well as paintings by the likes of Cézanne, Renoir, Matisse, Picasso and Rousseau, or more contemporary and somewhat odd photographic displays at the nearby GALERIE NATIONALE DU JEU DE PAUME. The day had brightened up considerably, the drizzle had cleared and the sun had come out, but we knew the exotic flowerbeds of the Tuileries Garden, temporarily accommodating some of the floral pillars of Chanel perfumes, including jasmine, iris and rose geranium, were not quite yet in full bloom as we walked in Paris before the Spring.

We followed the chic promenade, lined by chairs for taking a break and resting on. We beheld the spectacular vista ahead of us in the distance, a line of perspective between the endless parade of chestnut trees that took us as far as the Arc de Triomphe. But we effectively deviated from this sight, under instruction of my mobile mapping system, and clambering down some stone steps, we stepped onto normal pavement, the boulevard which it belonged to running parallel to the cobbled banks of the River Seine, with its preponderance of boat-tour operators.

We walked for a short while until we arrived at our destination, PONT ALEXANDRE III, the first of the two famous bridges we planned to walk across.

And it certainly was a more awesome sight in real life than when featured in such flicks as *Midnight in Paris*, *Forget Paris* and, perhaps my favourite Bond film, *A View to A Kill* (just for Christopher Walken's super-villain). The city had, within its limits, an extraordinary thirty-seven bridges spanning the River Seine, and by far the most sumptuous and grandiose of them was Pont Alexandre III, voted also as one of the most beautiful river crossings in the world, connecting Champs-Élysées on the right bank with the Invalides – the site of Napoleon's tomb – to the Grand Palais on the left bank. It had been built at the turn of the nineteenth century, during the glorious Belle Époque era, and named after Tsar Alexandre III to symbolize the diplomatic relationship between France and Imperial Russia, who had shared a nervous, mutual mistrust of Prussia. France was flourishing during the Belle Époque, building one icon after another, signalling a watershed moment in the Arts whilst further popularizing the Art Nouveau-style, reflected by the elegantly-ornate lampposts and lavish sculptures of cherubs and nymphs and water spirits and sea monsters. Four high granite pillars, crowned by magnificent, bronze-gilded statues, provided stabilizing counterweights for the single span of the bridge. These statues, called 'Fames', watching over the bridge and bringing the winged horse Pegasus to heel, represented the Sciences, the Arts, Commerce and Industry. On the base of the pillars sat further allegorical sculptures representing France from different eras: King Charlemagne, the Renaissance, Louis XIV and Modern Times. Lions adorned the banks of the bridge. The Beaux Arts and Art Nouveau décor ran across the single, low, long arch, continuing the Belle Époque theme, an era looked back fondly upon by the French people and yearned to be revisited, its end marked by the outbreak of the First World War.

We walked across the bridge – and back. Indeed, it was a magical experience, offering endless romantic views. We watched the Bateaux Mouches tourboats float by on the shimmering, sun-mirrored waters of the Seine, a spectacle in itself, the sheer diversity of tourists aboard and on the bridge wishing to experience the illustrious history and incredible beauty of Paris from every conceivable angle. One of the nymphs atop a fish was giving me the eye, so I winked back at her. Dude, she was gorgeous, and I would have given her my number if she weren't just mythical and if I wasn't married to Hayley! Hayley caught me and asked me what I was doing. I told her. She smiled.

Good. At least we were now reconnecting. I was incredibly grateful that Hayley had changed her mind and decided I should come to Paris with her after our recent marital difficulties and the extreme course of action I'd been forced to take. But it was still too early to start hooking love locks to the Pont des Arts. We could explore our relationship, what went wrong, and rectify things. It should be a lesson to the both of us. Once we had saturated ourselves with the spectacular views from the bridge, snapped enough pictures for posterity, we decided to move on. Onwards and upwards.

A half-an-hour's pleasant stroll later and we arrived at the PONT DE BIR-HAKEIM, constructed in the early twentieth century, but given its present name in 1948 to commemorate the victory of the Free French forces against Rommel in the Libyan desert during the Battle of Bir-Hakeim. Made of steel, the two-tier bridge was used by motor vehicles on the lower level, with a bicycle path down the middle as well as access for pedestrians, whilst through the upper viaduct ran the Metro. Metal colonnades, lined with Art Deco streetlamps, supported the railway viaduct throughout its length, except when crossing the Île aux Cygnes, where it rested on a masonry arch. The elegant central arch of the viaduct at the level of the island was decorated by four monumental stone statues in high-relief: the allegorical figures of Science and Labour, upriver, and Electricity and Commerce, downstream. The road level of the bridge extended out into a belvedere, where it passed over the tip of Île aux Cygnes and where stood the bronze equestrian statue titled *La France renaissance*. Visitors following the walkway from the middle of the Bir-Hakeim bridge could admire the Statue of Liberty, a quarter-scale replica of the time-honoured original in New York. And, of course, one could enjoy a superb view of the Eiffel Tower.

More people, more photo-taking, more profound awe at the epic monuments gracing the city. I mean compare the sheer opulence of French design to the lame ostentatiousness of the English effort!

Hayley was more open to conversation, no matter how light. She indicated she'd done a lot of thinking lately and she would want to begin the process of discussing recent events – discussing *us* – wherever we decided to eat this evening. Being a film nut like myself, she also reminded me, out of passing, which movies had utilized the Bir-Hakeim bridge.

The mind-bending *Inception* was filmed here. But I guess what sticks most to mind is the opening scene of *Last Tango in Paris*, where a bloated, middle-aged Marlon Brando clutches his ears, like that tormented figure in that famous Munch painting, to drown out the roar of a passing train and, expressing his wretched distress skyward, bellows, *"Fucking GOD!"*

I'm a pig, she's a monkey. Yes, all shall become very clear soon.

HARD ROCK CAFE. I don't know why we chose to have dinner there, but I reckon it had something to do with the fact we bumped into it on the way back to the Astoria and it turned out to be a mere ten-minute walk from the hotel. Why not check out the Parisian branch of this popular Rock 'n' Roll diner, I suppose?

It wasn't too dissimilar to its counterparts in London and Manchester. Low lighting, big television screens, set on the walls at intervals, playing an endless parade of Rock tracks, a Hall of Fame of Rock memorabilia, including autographed guitars and photographs and posters and costumes from legendary world tours as well as Classic Rock gold and platinum records, showcased across the restaurant, the usual gift shop selling overpriced T-shirts so as to make your visit unforgettable and make you feel part of the Rock establishment. But you got the feeling the owners of this Rock-themed restaurant chain had sold out a long time ago, the original inspiration behind this Celebration of Rock lost in the corporate fine print and buried under bucketloads of big bucks, as dead as Morrison, Lennon and Hendrix. *Shame.*

Like with pizzas, *nobody* should be forced to pay more than ten euros for a piece of glorified dough; same with burgers, customers should *never* have to spend eighteen euros on a burger. The state of the world. Everybody, including the pitiless princes of the financial world, scrabbling for pennies, like pitiful paupers. I remember my father who earned only ten thousand pounds a year as a school caretaker with which he always paid his taxes and mortgage on time and supported a wife and four children and still had enough money at the end of the month to treat his family to dinner in a nice restaurant. Compare my father to those bankers, who earn millions to blow on drugs and whores and then expect handouts and tax breaks when they gamble away your pension funds on the stock market. The bank shakes your hand and takes you out to lunch when you owe them two million pounds unlike threatening foreclosure or a visit from the bailiffs if the ordinary person has defaulted on two hundred pounds. There's an old saying which states that if you really want to know the personality of someone, give them money and power. I thought of our trip to Père Lachaise, this morning, and how the mysterious Monsieur Étrange had referred to money as 'the root of all evil'. I was, however, quietly satisfied with that Biblical quote: *it is easier for a camel to go through the eye of a needle than for a rich man to enter the kingdom of God.* So, if you believe in that kind of thing, those worthless bankers, who've chosen money-holing, mother-whoring greed over moral, social and intellectual betterment, must be praying that God does not exist.

I appreciated the social atmosphere of lively chatter and the drool-worthy aroma of grilled meat on an optimally-amplified background of hard rock classics. Through the notes and chords and riffs that flowed into our ears, of melodious, highly-recognizable Rock numbers, Hayley stated plainly she was now open to talking. "Okay, where do you want to start?"

At what point did the decline in our marriage begin? Should I cite last weekend, when the incident occurred, or should I talk about three months ago, when our relationship difficulties began to pick up tempo, or should I start right at the beginning and tell you how I met Hayley?

There is not much to say about the first time we started dating, except I was besotted with her like no other before her, practically soon after our second date. Hayley's a pretty cute girl, who looks much younger than her thirty years, me being on the wrong side of thirty-five. I might even be so bold as to call her a 'dappy' blonde, daffy, ditsy, etc., you get the drift. But endearing, nonetheless. Also, a girl who spent most of her life 'worrying about things that never happen', to bring Molière into her character. Another descriptive, this time from Baudelaire, would be: *I barely conceive of a type of beauty in which there is no Melancholy.* Although she had a degree in Fine Art, she lacked commitment to paint and the only time she dabbled in any creative art these days would be when she illustrated any books I might write. Instead, she worked as a nanny for well-to-do families, who were more concerned about making money than spending time with their own offspring, when she met me at the *Echo* through her father, my boss. Our appreciation of Art brought us together, but once she realized I had branched out into book-writing and was on to a potential winner with the crazy story of the Mind Rippers, she was mine forever. I might have left the rag I worked for behind me, but I never stopped being a journalist. These days, most bestsellers don't make millions. But, at least, we were comfortable now. I shared my spoils with Heath Axton, who had kindly chosen me, above all others, to interview him. Hayley and I got married shortly after, a little too hastily. I think it was her expectation that I would one day become a money-machine. Because, you see, Hayley *loved* money. I didn't know that at the time, only after we got hitched. But then it was too late. I was such a disappointment to her when I didn't financially hit the jackpot with the story of the Mind Rippers, regardless of the rave reviews, accusing me of wasting my time probably because the band had fallen out of favour with the public a long time ago. Hayley would pester me some days, particularly after a night on the town and a good few bevvies, about how 'poor' we were; that's crap, of course, since we could now afford to move to the posher part of Chertsford. I suppose it makes sense when you think about how she treated that unfortunate gypsy in the celebrity graveyard, crying over a few euros when the man had obviously done us a great service. Our physical relationship suffered when she perceived me not to be loaded, and I got a sense she began window-shopping for newer models. Not that she was ever unfaithful to me. I can vouch for that. I should know – I'm a former newspaper man, after all. She often threatened to go down the local pub and grab herself some real 'cock' during our ever-frequent rows, but she never made good on her promise. I know she would *never* do it. Because, you see, she had hypochondriacal tendencies and was afraid of catching an STD . . . can you believe it? She also repeatedly expressed a desire to have children – her biological clock gradually ticking away – complaining about looking after other people's children when she had none of her own – yet we were nowhere near having enough sex these days. In her frustration, she blamed me for us being childless, when it could so easily be her, and spoke of borrowing some sperm from the local pub. But it was ambivalence on her part. If she really wanted a baby, I would have fully committed to it. *One hundred percent.* Except Hayley didn't wish to lose sixteen years of her life raising a child, lose her own fiercely-guarded independence, because, yes, once you have a baby, the life you once knew would be 'over'. So right now, she had a love of money, a childless, sexless marriage and a fear of getting ill and dying. Now add real *stress* to this. I can tell you I had not slept properly for the past three months since Hayley's father, whom Hayley was very close to, dropped dead from a massive stroke, aged fifty-nine, a day before officially retiring. He was Chief Editor at the *Echo* and a functioning alcoholic, a boss who expected his employee's articles yesterday and not this afternoon. He was prescribed warfarin after suffering a near-fatal pulmonary embolism several years back, and ironically it was the warfarin that was seen as the catalyst for his fatal brain haemorrhage. Although I had seen Hayley cry, she bottled up her grief inside of her and never attempted to vent her feelings, talk through those feelings with her own hubby, even though I broached the subject numerous occasions, made it easier for her to come to terms with her loss.

The situation became untenable when we spent a week in Stratford-upon-Avon. The highlight should have been a playing of *Two Noble Kinsmen* at the SWAN THEATRE; I mean that's the whole purpose of going up to Shakespeare country, isn't it? The play proved to be an excellent piece of theatre, except within minutes of it commencing, Hayley was bored and restless and fidgety, disturbing the punters around her with more than three hours still left to endure, and by the intermission, she was making very tactless, unkind and hurtful comments about various theatre-goers, calling them 'fat' and 'ugly' within earshot. I did my best to rein her in, chastising her for her behaviour and her fat-shaming remarks, and you cannot imagine how many discreet, grateful looks I received from the people around us, some of whom had been targeted by my wife and who had just kept quiet. Except the row that followed in the hotel room afterwards was too much for me. I abandoned her in Stratford-upon-Avon that night and returned home. Don't worry, I took the train; I left the car with her so she could drive back whenever she felt up to it. Or not at all, if she so chose. Hayley returned a couple of days later, remorseful but stipulated that what I'd done – deserting her like that – was unforgivable. We made up in the days that followed, superficially, however. Oh, how the French music channel in our hotel room playing Nouvelle Vague's Bossa-nova cover of the Buzzcock's *Ever Fallen in Love* last night made me think hard and ask searching questions. Yes, the woman was dealing with her father's death, without letting me – her own husband – in. And her distress spilled over into her day job, getting tearful in front of and offloading her distress on her young charges, until she was promptly fired. She was a blubbering mess but at other times pricklier than ever, and it was like walking on eggshells. Our fights grew more intense, more ferocious.

Things came to a head the last weekend before Paris. I was pissed off with her outright disrespect to me, hurling insults at me and her continued refusal to talk to me properly, so I went out into the garden to smoke a cigarette so I could at least feel vaguely better about myself. Except smoking was a habit she'd made me give up when we met because her grandfather died from lung cancer aged eighty-five, yes, *eighty-five*. Hayley went spare. She flipped. *I hate you! I HATE YOU!* she screamed at me like a six-year-old girl in the throes of a temper tantrum. Her volatility reached a new peak. In a volley of unrepeatable abuse, she lunged at me and her hands went around my throat. She tried to strangle me. I grabbed her hands and pulled them off my neck. She was strong. And crazy as hell. Then her hands went for my face, trying to gouge my eyes out, nails scratching my cheeks. I pulled her off me a second time. We struggled for a few more moments until I informed her I was calling the police. She stopped physically assaulting me but continued to call me names, including calling me 'schizophrenic' and 'a mad bastard'. Two female police officers arrived early on that Sunday morning. They took a statement from her, but I think they must have realized from her hysterics, calling me all kinds of hateful things in their presence, that she wasn't in any fit state. When I spoke to the police officers, I was calm and rational. They must have seen the lack of sleep in my eyes. I told them about the strain my wife had been under – worrying about money, children, illness, losing her job, the death of her father – but I could not just stand by and do nothing when she attacked me. This was the third incident of its kind. I'd accepted it previously without acting because I'd been naively expecting things to get better. This time, however, I had been unable to contain her distress *and* she had actually tried to strangle me. Give her a simple caution so it's a lesson to her, and please don't take it to the Crown Prosecution Service so it won't get recorded on her DBS for future employment. But when the police officers saw the bruises on my neck from her stranglehold and the scratch-marks on my cheeks, they were going to arrest her there and then. It took a lot of bargaining, a lot of negotiating and persuasion on my part for them to kindly reconsider. We needed some time apart, a chance to think things through. The police officers wisely informed us they would use their discretion in our case; after all, there was a world of difference between our circumstances and a domestic disturbance involving some malingering, welfare-scrounging couple, who warranted repeated callouts for their drug-fuelled, antisocial behaviour. A criminal record could impact greatly on her professional standing, particularly in the area of childcare. I watched a hugely-upset Hayley pack some belongings and be escorted out of the house by the two police officers, who had threatened earlier to arrest her. I wondered if I'd done the right thing calling the police.

We'd already booked the Valentine's getaway to Paris months ago and, now no longer in her good books or on speaking terms, I expected Hayley would go there by herself or with her sister, whom she was staying with. And I should be going down the route of initiating divorce proceedings. Yet, remarkably, she finally decided I should go with her, as originally planned. It was an extraordinarily brave move on her part for which I commended her. It would be a risk, but hopefully an example of positive risk-taking. The aim would be to work on our problems in the hope of saving our marriage. I wanted reconciliation, but the ultimate decision rested with her. Most crises, whether political, emotional, medical, etc., passed, I knew, but if our arguments persisted, spilled over into Paris, we would automatically know that it was time to pull the plug.

Thus far, we had not argued and we were hugely enjoying our time in Paris. But now was, as we sipped our watered-down cola and waited for our extortionately-priced burgers, a convenient time to open discussions.

"I think the starting point should be the police taking you away."

"I felt humiliated, treated like shit," she replied.

I thought of Marcel Proust: *People who are not in love fail to understand how an intelligent man suffers because of an ordinary woman.* I decided not to mention it aloud. "You have been humiliated and I have been greatly humbled."

"I know I shouldn't have overreacted, but you, too, lost your sense of proportion. You didn't need to get the police involved like that.

"You gave me no choice. You took your rage too far, and my response was proportionate to the risk. I mean if I had let this one go, you might grab a knife next time. It had to stop there and then."

"But still . . ."

"I mean look at it this way. If the roles had been reversed, can you imagine what you, your family, the Law and the Press would have done to me?"

Hayley could see it. "So you're the man who calls the police on his wife?"

"I guess I am and I am certainly not proud of it. At least they've let you off. Next time, though, you won't be so lucky."

"If you're looking for a full pardon, there won't be a next time."

I stared hard into her period-drama face, a face that would look adorable in the Blitz – or wartime Germany. There is one thing I haven't told you about Hayley, another facet of her personality that defines her. She is an incredibly spiteful woman. Jealousy, spite, vindictiveness, you name it. She told me how jealous she was, when she was nine, of her four-year-old sister showering with her mother. She told me how, in school, there was a girl whom she was friends with, and she made damned sure nobody else could be the girl's friend. She expressed her envy of her friend's newly-refurbished kitchen and wanted one exactly like it. She reminisced on how greater a catch her ex-boyfriend, a small holdings' business manager, was compared to me which I shouldn't have taken lying down. She was the kind of woman who would go straight for the hair and eyes in a catfight. I suppose I could compare Hayley to the Furies, those chthonic goddesses of vengeance, such was her temperament, quick to self-perceived grievance, harbouring a grudge at the slightest provocation, snowballing into an intense, burning desire of exacting wild justice, at the cost of even her own existence. Indeed, to quote *Cyrano de Bergerac*: *Perish the universe, provided I have my revenge!*

"You shouldn't feel slighted so easily," I advised her. But I knew she was a woman who would *always* be unhappy.

"You think you calling the police on your own wife is a case of me feeling slighted?"

"As I said, I had no choice. I couldn't contain you."

"You should have tried *harder*!"

I felt her anger bubbling below the surface. "Curiously enough, I'm just waiting for my punishment, *your* retribution."

"Why should I want to get back at you?" she said, guiltily averting her gaze, as though I had cottoned on to precisely what she was thinking.

"I got you pegged. It's who you are. You find it difficult to let go."

"What's happened has happened," she replied, with a shrug. "I can't change the past."

"I'd be really impressed if that is your current stance. If we get through Valentine's week unscathed, I still want you to tell me how you would have punished me when I least expected it, hypothetically-speaking."

"I'll try my best not to disappoint you," she mustered quietly, "even if familiarity breeds contempt."

"The reason I had asked the police to spare you was because you are still adorable to me, so cutely insecure. For what it's worth, I still consider you a sweet girl even if you're the kind of woman who wants to throw dog poo through our neighbour's letterbox because they're contesting the boundary between our respective gardens or you wish to deform your pregnant best friend's baby just because we haven't yet managed to conceive our own child." She was the kind of woman I could imagine building an eyesore of a spite house, like those from centuries ago, just to get back at her enemies – *how very Hayley!* I paused for a moment before quoting Molière: "*It's not my fault I love you . . . It's yours.*" I smiled engagingly. "Do you think we can work it out?"

She sprung it on me. "We have a fifty-fifty chance."

"You've calculated the odds?"

"Yes, our love match or compatibility rating according to the Chinese zodiac."

"I didn't know you took an interest in astrology. You have more?"

"Our star signs are very close to our personality traits. You're a pig and I'm a monkey."

"Fair dos . . ."

Hayley fed back an outline of what she'd read. "The male Pig is happy and honest, and compassionate and sincere, sometimes too trusting and caring for his own good. The female Monkey is generally cheerful, confident and creative, full of energy and enthusiasm. Whereas the Pig is educated and attains his wealth and good fortune from extreme hard work, demonstrating tremendous endurance, the Monkey is very selfish and egocentric, prone to being snobbish and materialistic, achieving the fruits of her labours from the emotional manipulation of others. The Pig and the Monkey can be respectful of one another, drawing out the strengths of the other, but if they don't put enough effort into their relationship, they will lack communication, deep love and cohesion. The Pig will help the Monkey see through her projects as she has a persistent habit of leaving them unfinished due to her restless nature and short attention span. The Monkey, who likes to be the centre of attention, will encourage the Pig, who prefers the quiet life, to get out and socialize a bit more, while the Pig will teach the Monkey to focus on her sentimental side and emotions. The Pig will forgive the many small transgressions of the Monkey, who has something of a wandering eye, but he must be inventive enough to hold her interest or, since she is economical with her affections, she will leave their relationship without bother. As the Pig could never think about hurting anyone, always empathizing with the less fortunate, his gullibility, if not kept in check, can be easily exploited by the Monkey." She paused before delivering the final verdict. *"The Monkey's quick temper and aggressiveness will hurt the Pig's gentle self-esteem."*

The silence between us spun out, seconds seemed like minutes, the background music and the chatter of the customers around us momentarily muted. I digested the salient points, put them into context, applied them to recent events back home, my wife attacking me, the police escorting her away. "Very canny," I finally said. "Chinese wisdom. Who'd believe it? They seem to have captured our relationship perfectly and the difficulties therein." Or was this, like any astrological reading, all down to ambiguity, interpretation and suggestibility? Still, whether there was any credence to her claims, it had relaxed us enough to start talking on ways in which to rectify our relationship. As Victor Hugo put it succinctly: *The greatest happiness in life is the conviction that we are loved – loved for ourselves, or rather, loved in spite of ourselves.* Yes, worth another shot, a concerted effort to repair things, address our shortcomings, ease the friction between us.

Our burgers arrived. We ordered more drinks, Kronenbourg 1664 this time.

On the television screens, Yodelice took on the timeless challenge of *People Are Strange*. The Doors but with French swagger. It brought to mind Jim Morrison's grave among others, my wife's sour exchange with the dodgy stranger at the cemetery, the watchful crows, the black cat following us to the gates, Marlon Brando's blasphemy on the Bir-Hakeim Bridge, the summary of our personality traits in Chinese astrology. All in one day.

Can the rest of our adventure in Paris get any weirder?

You bet it can.

And, yes, I'm a pig and she's a monkey!

We got back to the hotel and decided to unwind on the comfy leather sofas in the lobby with free tea, a slice of decadent lemon drizzle cake and a newspaper. Never a major tea drinker, I discovered lapsang souchang, a palatable, wood-smoked pick-me-up, for the first time at the Astoria. I was also on course to discover lavender tea that same evening, at bedtime, as an aid to good mental and physical health; once you get past the initial taste resembling munching on a bunch of flowers, it grows on you, alleviating all manner of stress, insomnia and bowel problems. I was amazed this miracle tea was not even available in English supermarkets. Renowned for their lavender and garlic, no wonder the French lived long and were one of the happiest and healthiest people in the world. Unlike the poor, old Americans.

Indeed, it was an American couple, Theodore and Margot Freemont, who befriended us, fiftysomethings, both tenured Professors at Boston University, of Political Science and Social Studies respectively, and visiting Paris to decide whether it might be worthwhile to relocate here for good, like their erstwhile fellow countrymen, Hemingway and Scott Fitzgerald. They were not liking what was happening in their country. Professor Theodore Freemont had spotted me perusing through the International Edition of *The New York Times*, laid out neatly in the lobby for the guests, a somewhat respectable read, admittedly. After we made our acquaintance, we spoke about the state of his country over deliciously-smoky black china tea. Theodore was impressed I was a newspaper man.

Following on from the shock result of Brexit last summer, championed by the obnoxious likes of Buffoon Boorish and Wobblegob Fartrage and I-hope-he-was-bullied-and-humiliated-in-school Gove, there was a similar, bizarre kind of perversity to Donald Trump's victory in November last year, a truly strange event. I was about to ask the obvious question about the fellow, whose absurd antics had entered into the political consciousness, but Theodore beat me to it: "What do the Brits think of Trump?"

"Do you want the long version or short version?" I asked him.

"Let's start with the short version and go from there . . ."

"El Trumpo is a flick of toss on the arsehole of humanity, pardon my French."

"That's quite the sweeping statement," Theodore laughed. "Okay, how about the long version?"

"You heard what I think. Let me hear your opinion. After all, you have to live with him as your President."

"Trump is a populist, a terrible thing in the field of politics," Theodore responded critically. "The Presidential election somehow ended with a victor, who scored higher negative ratings than his opponent and garnered three million less actual votes. Trump's opponent would always be the lesser of the two evils, but he won by the slimmest of margins through the Electoral College system and, like George W. Bush before him, by restricting voting rights through jerrymandering and disqualifying a noticeable proportion of the African-American vote. And from the moment he was inaugurated, blatantly exaggerating the inauguration numbers in attendance, he has been the focus of the world media – and not in a good way. Yes, Trump is a 'gift' that just keeps on giving. Signing a stream of Executive Orders in favour of the rich, giving them monumental tax breaks, using the feeble excuse that it would benefit the working classes, whom he despises. Feed the needy *not* the greedy, I say. On the same note, Trump is actively trying to repeal Obamacare, which if he succeeds would leave his Health Insurance buddies better off and millions of low-income earners without any access to healthcare. He continues to redistribute wealth from the honest, hardworking, tax-paying middle classes to beef up the already absurdly-funded Military and to spend on insane policies like building that goddamn wall between Mexico and the US."

"If he really wants a wall," Margot mocked, "he should build one around him, keep him away from the rest of the world!"

We chuckled.

"And someone *please* take away his mobile phone!" Theodore added. "He's like an internet troll at three a.m., capable of only using *ad hominems* towards his critics, with his administration at a loss on how to manage the aftermath of his early morning Tweets, forced to perform damage control. He just has *nothing* worthwhile to say. Makes empty, preposterous statements without ever supporting them or resorts to degenerate words that no president has any business speaking – or Tweeting, for that matter."

I gave my opinion. "You'd think for someone who supposedly wrote *The Art of the Deal*, you'd expect better social graces from him, not offending old, trusted allies with insensitive, undipomatic comments."

"*The Art of the Deal?*" Theodore exclaimed incredulously. "The man's an absolutely *terrible* businessman! He makes himself out to be a self-made entrepreneur, but in fact that's what his father was, and Trump has constantly lived – and will *always* live – in the shadow of his father. Trump has always used the idiots in the media to promote a myth of savvy business sense when there has never been any real substance or truth to his claims. He is the worst dealmaker in American history and the media should do more in injecting a stringent dose of economic reality into Trump's make-believe world. He might actually learn something, but I think I'm being a little too hopeful. He has always believed that little voice in his head about how successful he is, and any attempts to question this have been met with lawsuits; he's had over four thousand lawsuits in his lifetime, most of which he's lost miserably, including that one involving his ultra-crooked enterprise of 'Trump University', its unsuspecting students graduating with Mickey Mouse degrees. If he'd just rested the money he'd inherited from his father in a bank account for twenty years, gaining compound interest, he'd actually be richer today than him investing it in his worthless business ventures. I mean the man's defaulted on his bank loans so many times, he's filed for bankruptcy four times! Even his casinos have gone tits-up shortly after opening – how is that even vaguely possible? And he's had to dip into his father's account to paper over his own financial disasters. Anything he touches turns to *shit*!"

"That's so whack!" Margot concluded. "I guess with his tax cuts to the rich alongside his feeble understanding of the mechanics of the business world, he'll probably saddle our entire nation with decades of debt. Just goes to prove that *The Art of the Deal* was a self-perpetuated myth all along and is now finally, truly *dead*! I think I'll stick to the Johnny Depp film. It's probably closer to the truth!"

"Wealth or money does not buy you brains or talent no matter how much you delude yourself to soften the blow," I added.

"The Supreme Court judges were sensible enough to tell him where to go with regards his travel ban which used the bullshit excuse of national security," Theodore explored. "His aim has always been to control the media, militarize the police, sabotage the democratic process, chip away at civil liberties and abolish the Constitution, create a mass exodus of perceived 'undesirables', thereby creating a fascist state as a springboard for world domination by his Neocon masters."

I agreed with him. "Yes, there already seems visible signs of him governing a dictatorship rather than a democracy."

"Don't even get me started on the Republicans," Theodore said, "all of them suffering the great Christian delusion that it's acceptable to wield one's faith like a sword of self-righteousness to justify war and every act of military aggression, including torturing one's enemies and laying waste to entire cultures, while allowing the richest corporate devils to make fortunes in one's wake."

"Shame," I said, peeved. "They should read *Catch-22*, one of the seminal novels of the twentieth century, demonstrating how war has a way of concentrating power in the hands of those most likely to abuse it."

"I know it well," agreed Theodore dreamily, his mind probably drifting back to those unputdownable pages. "The absurdity of war. Poor old Yossarian, the sanest man in the book, forced to keep up with crazy Colonel Cathcart, who keeps raising the mission counts."

"I reckon Trump's refusing to release his taxes," Margot opined, "probably because he doesn't want people to know that he isn't as much of a billionaire he's made himself out to be. Maybe check his financial records to reveal the secret flow of dirty money to and from dubious Russian businesses."

"Why not actually subpoena his financial records and trace the extent of his dealings with the Russians?" I suggested. "I'm sure the FBI have enough legal justification. Then they've got their man!"

Theodore continued to lay it on thick. "He's borrowed Putin's approach to get into power, generating fake news and untruths every which way, then accusing the media of fabricating the news, threatening to shut down whole news organizations he does not like, deflecting his own wrongdoings on those around him, making controversial statements he refers to as 'alternative facts' otherwise known as *bullshit*, as he continues to clumsily and *transparently* gaslight the public."

Margot agreed with her husband. "Yes, cries of 'fake news' when presented with the facts, just like the Israeli politicians cry 'antisemiticism' when accused of murdering Palestinians. We seem to be living more and more in a world that silences the truth and amplifies misinformation. Trump *is* fake news! He feeds the cosseting far-right media like 'Faux' News his fabrications every day, often multiple times a day, all easily disprovable and, for the most part, utterly *pointless*, and they broadcast it as the gospel truth. His spread of toxic, divisive lies in his attempts to normalize fascism is not much different from the propaganda used by the Nazi party in the build-up to the Second World War."

Theodore continued: "The problem is he lies ceaselessly, even needlessly when he doesn't have to."

Margot suggested a simple solution. "My advice? Apply reverse psychology to everything he says and that will be closer to the truth."

Theodore drove home his point. "Trump may be a pathological liar yet he's so damned socially-inept and childishly-bad at lying. 'Egregious' might be a suitable descriptive."

"He *is* like a child," Margot interjected. "Trump blurts out every dumb thought that comes into his head and acts on everything he thinks. He's just a bundle of id, impetuous and immature, spewing bullshit most of the time without thinking, and *believing* his own bullshit, while behaving like a pig-ignorant, preschool bully in any contretemps. But it does tell everyone how maladjusted his personality and his underlying beliefs are as he goes about showing off his own stupidity and lack of scruples."

I interjected: "El Trumpo emboldens the racist apologists into believing they can spout the same racist chants as him without reproach, only for these far-right imbeciles to watch their own lives unravel as they're hauled off to the clink for hate speech, at which point he completely distances himself from them, claiming he has nothing to do with their predicament. Absolutely priceless! I don't know who's more stupid, him or his lily-livered leg-huggers!"

"And the only people who believe his garbage have serious issues of their own," Theodore continued. "Does he think the American people are stupid? Have none of the sycophants in his employ told him that decent Americans see him for the idiot that he really is? Trump's like Liberace, who denied he was gay all his life, challenging any allegations of homosexuality, despite evidence to the contrary, and eventually dying of AIDS, at which point all his gay ex-lovers suddenly appeared out of the woodwork."

Margot agreed with her husband, adding: "I guess the Truth sounds like Hate to those who Hate the Truth. Trump is so thin-skinned and petty and insecure he can't admit error or acknowledge his own failings – of which there are countless. Every one of his screw-ups is somebody else's fault. And yet he claims credit for everything positive that occurred before him, living off the success stories of the Obama administration." Margot laughed. "I bet Trump considers himself one of our Founding Fathers and bears the right to change the Constitution!"

The professor continued the ribbing of his president. "You betcha . . . but please don't make fun of him! If Trump says it's true, it *must* be true! Dintcha know he *wrote* the Declaration of Independence? *And* he's got proof coming 'next week' or 'soon'! *Proof* I tell you!"

"Just when I was hoping that El Trumpo would break the Bush-Clinton dynasty's monopoly over the Presidential office, and he might actually turn out to be a fine President," I said with mock sorrow, "but I must be dreaming of a parallel universe."

"I'm not holding my breath." Margot remarked. "Do you reckon the malignant narcissist would ever be interested in helping other people? Sadly, he is a clowning, posturing, lying, trigger-happy oaf who aims to drag everyone down the rabbit hole where 2+2=5. Obama will always be regarded as a *sui generis* politician for advocating multiculturalism, a true Statesman, whereas Trump will be a worldwide joke, a liability and embarrassment to the office of US President, with our once-great nation of America the laughing stock of the world."

I took her comment one step further, smiling. "That's what happens when you run an idiocracy. Indeed, his entire administration should paint their faces with makeup, wear red noses, oversized shoes and a water-spraying flower in their lapels and squeeze themselves into an impossibly small car."

Theodore offered a different kind of hope. "I guess once Trump's Neocon masters have used him for their own unscrupulous financial ends, they will happily give him up for impeachment themselves, anything to save face, no matter how much he tries to openly obstruct the official investigation into his alleged ties with the Russians, whom the public full-well know interfered in the democratic process of last year's Presidential election. Just need to find the smoking gun. I'm certain the FBI will. Just a matter of time."

"Yes, I'm sure the Russians are blackmailing him for him to openly lie to and sell out the American people," I observed. "Quite the pair, Golden Shower Boy and Dobbie, the Malfoys' House Elf. Both *are* fake news, but at least Putin's got some brains, even if he doesn't have any shred of moral decency in his bones. Putin's taught him everything of what little El Trumpo knows about politics. El Trumpo is nothing more than Putin's Apprentice!"

"That's quite the epiphany," observed Theodore.

"I bet the Secret Service are chuffed they have to protect Golden Shower Boy whilst endangering their own lives. Might as well hand in their resignation or step out of the way of the assassin's bullet. The man's not worth dying for."

"Pleeeaze, make America *sane* again!" remarked Margot. "Trump should be ousted from office before he can undo every humane decision of Obama's administration. Before his Kremlin Klan, quietly working behind the scenes like some demolition crew while Trump shows off his own stupidity as a distraction to the public, completely dismantles the Office of Ethics and every aspect of democratic government."

"Don't worry," Theodore reassured his wife, "he won't get much of his controversial legislation through, and he'll get his comeuppance in good time. If his cronies have any sense and don't want to be tarnished by the same brush, they'll bail out on him as the *prime facie* evidence builds up against him. Only the absolutely dumb would want to go down with the sinking ship. I mean the man would betray his own son in order to save his own hide."

"They should be worried about hanging around with El Trumpo too long," I added, "in case his shit sticks to them!"

"I guess to make his billions," I considered, air-quoting the word 'billions', "El Trumpo must have done anything he could for personal gain, no matter how unsavoury and criminal, *always* getting his own way. He's probably never done an honest day's work in his life. Now, as President, he's discovered he's completely out of his depth, a fish out of water, since he's meant to serve the people for a change, *not* line his own pockets. *Welcome to the real world!*"

"Yep, his ineptitude is staggering!" replied Margot, astonished. "Trump's probably stupid enough to withdraw from the Paris Climate Accord Agreement, ignoring hard evidence in favour of enriching his petrochemical buddies. He's also the kind of moron who would pull out of the UN Human Rights' Council because he thinks it will give him license to indulge in some seriously illegal, inhumane practices."

"Yes, he's definitely compensating for something," I said, smiling. "A psychiatrist will tell you that a superiority complex is actually an inferiority complex in disguise. Turn a deaf ear to his persuasions, cut off the narcissistic supply to this attention-whore and see what desperate measures he takes to grab the limelight. El Trumpo's also the kind of guy who would probably resort to demanding his cabinet members openly praise him and insisting it be filmed."

"I can imagine him doing just that . . ." said Theodore, conjuring up the image in his head. "What a hideously embarrassing scene that would be . . ."

"I know: pathetic, cringeworthy . . ." I added. "Might as well pull his pants down and each one from the line-up takes turns sucking him off, pardon my French."

"The traditional definition of a Tea Bagger, I guess . . ."

Margot revived the memory of the leaked videotape that emerged during the Presidential campaign. "Don't you remember Trump boasting that he could get away with sexually assaulting women? I think his exact words were: *When you're a star, they let you do it. Grab them by the pussy. You can do* anything! And didn't this inadequately-endowed, sexual violence-promoting blowhard describe his thick-as-a-brick daughter as 'a nice piece of ass'? He has the gall to criticize true American war heroes and patriots like John McCain when Trump's idea of a personal Vietnam, after using the lame, cowardly excuse of bone spurs to exempt himself from military duty, was to copulate the 'Sixties away and not catch an STD!"

"Makes me want to cut off his tiny balls and shove them up his huge arse," I said frankly, "shut him up from where he communicates from!"

"He's one to boast," continued Margot. "Trump vaguely passes off as a human being, let alone a man. Wig and dentures and mushroom dick, I bet. More like a snake who's crept into the Garden of Eden, his Evangelical Christian supporters be warned. I mean have you seen his dumb, gerbil-faced expression as he tries to look intelligent and wise? Such is this recrudescence of a Republican victory, you wouldn't have thought there could be a dumber shit than George W. Bush. Well, think again! Trump actually makes that intellectually-challenged George W. Bush sound like a goddamned genius!"

"Yes, El Trumpo and Dubya," I observed, "the Republican Presidential candidates get thicker with each election. I guess it's just morbid curiosity, like watching a car crash in slow-mo. El Trumpo wants the world's attention poised on him. *Always*. He doesn't give a crap if it's bad publicity because so far gone is his narcissism. Should be entertaining stuff. At his expense."

"America was built on slavery, whorehouses and the blood of gunfighters," Margot said fiercely, impassioned, "but our ancestors fought hard to move on from those days of violence and puritanical hypocrisy. Now we stand on the cusp of a true idiocracy, as you referred to it earlier. Typical, hypocritical Republicans: one rule for themselves and one rule for everyone else. No transparency. Always standing in the way of human progress. Of everything that comes out of Trump's mouth, people already know the reverse is true. Decent Americans are certainly not going to let this unmitigated shit-of-a-man take us back there. He rightly deserves the world's contempt. Mr. President, my *ass*!"

I thought it was an extraordinary situation. "It's like he's stepped out from an alternate reality – and a *fucked-up* reality at that!"

Theodore looked mystified. "So tell me . . . we elected this man – or he got into office by means fair or foul. Is there *anything* he is actually good at?"

We looked at each other with blank faces. No-one could think of anything. *Hopeless at business, holding office, public speaking, personality, looks, women. A Know Nothing yet totally deluded into believing his own greatness. No redeeming qualities. A failure of a human being. A trumped-up, little shit. Yep, shitly does it. Useless, worthless. A loser. A* nobody. But it turned out he *was* good at something. "The man's a confidence trickster," Margot declared. "A scammer. A flimflam man. And, like any conman, he preys on the confidence and hopes and dreams of others without any intention of ever delivering on his promises."

Something occurred to me. "Following Brexit and El Trumpo, I wouldn't be surprised if Marine Le Pen wins the French election. It's like the world is lining up for something, and whatever that something is, it's not good . . ."

Margot poured us each more tea. "The French may prove smarter than you Brits and us Americans, yet!"

"What is the world coming to?" mused her husband with a sense of sadness. "Everywhere you look there are tyrannical regimes that enslave their people or corrupt governments looting their own country or populist leaders practising toxic politics, deliberately deceiving their own voters and promoting conflict. Trump manages to be all three!"

Margot followed through, "He makes such an excellent horror character, a grotesque, reprehensible villain, with no hope of redemption!"

"Strange times we live in," I thought out aloud. "It may just be incidental that the President your countrymen voted in, during a rigged election, happens to be a pathetic, vulgar, callous, hateful, amoral, unethical, sexist, misogynistic, racist, socially-inept, self-aggrandizing, draft-dodging, politically-incompetent, nepotism-practising, dunce-of-the-class, most undeserving and utterly detestable, narcissistic orange shit with clear psychopathic tendencies, but don't you get a sense that El Trumpo might be part of something bigger, maybe something more sinister? That El Trumpo is President by design? That there was a *purpose* to El Trumpo coming to office?"

"What do you mean?" Theodore asked, adjusting his spectacles, frowning.

My sincerest apologies to the word 'shit' for using it in the same breath as El Trumpo! He's an insult to 'shit'! "What if the whole point is to gradually wear him down, make him feel more and more paranoid, unpredictable as he is to begin with, until he reaches breaking point, and as the net closes in on him and he feels cornered, he is meant to trigger off World War Three, with Europe the battlefield, expediting the coming of the single world government? And so, from the ashes of human civilization, emerges the long-prophesied New World Order of the super-rich and the über-elite? How's that for the mother of all political conspiracies?"

"You mean all this is preparation for the annihilation of mankind and the subsequent creation of a society governed by self-elitist cowards?"

I nodded. "Maybe Trump *doesn't* even know the masterplan and is only meant to serve as pawn and instrument of the Apocalypse. It will definitely end badly for him. Maybe for all of us, too. Let's see where we are in five years' time . . . *or less than a year.*"

I saw Theodore shudder while his wife just stared at me with a perturbed expression of dawning realization. It was a chilling theory, true, the idea of this unstable moron with his pulse on the nuclear button, but not entirely outside the realms of remote possibility. "I wonder how much of what you've said will prove correct."

On this sobering note, we bid our American friends goodnight and headed to our respective rooms but not before I finished our rap session with a parting shot, which caused a few guffaws: "If I had the nuclear codes implanted in me, I certainly wouldn't let El Trumpo come near me, so he wouldn't be able to initiate the Fisher protocol! It wouldn't surprise me if that interminable orange shit puts in an Executive Order to surveil and assassinate me on foreign soil with one of those military drones!" Or, without being too unkind to Hayley, if that interminable orange shit wanted to bump me off, he could do it through my wife with lies, bribes and the false promise of amnesty. "Hopefully Trump will resign first, like Nixon did. I don't really care for that fat, orange prick. He doesn't deserve my time . . ."

"Neither ought he ours even if the idiot's in the Oval Office," agreed Margot.

"Except if he destroys the world . . ." I uttered in a mock-maniacal tone. They both shuddered again, maybe not quite seeing it as a joke. The seed had been sown.

Yes, 2016 was already proving to be the Year of the Fat, Ugly, Dumb, Orange Shit! El Trumpo deserved the same derogatory language and to be treated with same contempt he showed everybody else – give him a taste of his own medicine. There *was* something else, I concluded, that El Trumpo was good at: giving the Devil a handjob!

It was a lovely hotel. The staff were courteous and very professional, bending over backwards to help address any enquires the guests might have. The modern trompe-l'oeil wallpaper murals of open doors and long corridors were an ingenuity of design, adding an extra dimension to the bedroom, giving it the illusion of depth, of space. Immaculately-clean, our room was charming and cosy, accommodating a generous wardrobe and decadent furnishings, a Holly Golightly hat lampshade from the ceiling as opposed to the Jeeves and Wooster pendant lighting in the lobby, and the en-suite bathroom was equally impressive, the temperature and pressure of the water of the bath-cum-shower spot on, and, as a nice, personal touch, the hotel had provided us with complimentary His and Hers bathrobes as keepsakes. I raided the free, non-alcoholic minibar. I still cannot understand why mineral water was so ridiculously expensive in French restaurants – cheaper to just drink beer. I considered myself a Volvic man and Hayley an Evian lady. And why the hell don't they stock Vittel water in the UK?

I got ready for bed and made myself some lavender tea. Yes, it proved a hit, a revelation, promising a restful night. Hayley, who'd hardly spoken during our deconstruction and well-deserved slagging-off of El Trumpo in the lobby, accepted a drop of lavender tea. I touched her shoulder, hopeful.

"I'm not ready yet . . ." she murmured.

"Take a load off, baby."

We called it a night.

So ended our first full day in Paris.

The other thing I discovered about the lavender tea was that not only did it give me a fitful sleep, but it also gave me dreams – *vivid* dreams.

I recognize the place and the people. I am dreaming of the Oval Office, occupied by only two individuals.

"You know why I'm here?" Vladimir Putin confronts his American counterpart, unbuckling his belt and unzipping his fly. "Bend over and take it like a man, BITCH!"

"Again?" protests President Trump to Putin's unambiguous demand. "Will I never live it down, Putain?"

"I told you never to call me that! You and your sloppy American accent! The name's Putin!" Trump sees Putin's stern, steely expression and realizes he has no choice but to pull down his pants and assume the position across the Oval Office table, fawning. "Yes, Lord and Master, receiving. Your wish is my command."

Putin shoves his overrated manhood into Donald Trump's posterior and starts moving rhythmically back and forth. "You're my bitch! You're my bitch!"

"I'm your bitch! I'm your bitch!" Trump yells in agreement, taking it up the arse, feeling loved. Neither of their 'sex faces' are a pretty sight, the strained look of two men competing in a constipation contest, seeing who evacuates first. "It feels so snug! I don't think Melania will approve of this, but who's going to find out? She's stopped giving me sex and I think she's starting to dread the obligatory Valentine's Day handjob!"

"And you do not tell the proletariat I like men!"

Trump raises his hand in a solemn pledge. "On my oath of office . . ."

"As if that means anything . . ." Impassioned, Putin runs his hand through Trump's fox-coloured hair, which easily goes away in his hand, revealing a less-than-attractive, shiny pate. "Der'mo!" Putin throws the orange wig to the floor in disgust and rams Trump harder, causing Trump's false teeth to fall out. "Ah, time for fellyatsiya!"

I watch them perform this subsequent homosexual act in the Oval Office – certainly gives a new meaning to the term 'Oval Office' – *in graphic detail, Putin the dominant of the two, Trump initially the reluctant recipient, now on his knees, knob-gobbling. I feel they lack the homoerotic prowess of Alan Bates and Oliver Reed wrestling naked, but at least Putin and Trump have each other, when the whole world hates them both, and their gay love seems curiously natural–*

–The next second their hands are holding me down in the President's chair, as Trump rummages around painlessly inside my blood-soaked chest, and pulls out the Fisher code, a small rectangular piece of bronze, inscribed with a numerical sequence–

—Then Putin returns to backshafting Trump over the Resolute desk, as if I was never there, and as Putin orgasmically explodes inside Trump, a nuclear missile launches itself from the White House lawn and roars up into the sky, headed towards China, heralding the advent of World War Three . . .

My eyes jerked awake. It was morning. Suddenly, El Trumpo's puckered, toothless mouth transmitted his vaguely-coherent voice inside my head: *Fake dream . . . Sad.* The vestiges of my explicit dream, more chucklesome than homoerotic, as audaciously envisioned in glorious Technicolor. "Holy shit!"

I had to take my mind off my crazy nightmare, recycling that old fear of thermonuclear war, cobbled together from my conversation with our American guests in the hotel lobby. I cared not for the idiocy of the edentate, comb-over caudillo or a desire to dwell on the black-is-white bullshit of his fugly, house-elf master. It took a short while for its darkly-comic absurdity to wear off. Dreaming is such a weird business, don't you think? The older you get, the weirder it gets.

My wife lay by my side, sound asleep. I was instantly attracted to her, although I would not call her instantly attractive at that moment. Most mornings, she looked doughy and frumpy, and when she stirred presently and slowly opened her eyes and saw me watching her adoringly, her grump was up: "Why're you acting so crazy?"

"Rise and shine, baby!" I said cheerfully. "Another glorious day in glorious Gay Paree!"

"What's got into you?" she complained and pulled the duvet over her head. "You know I'm not a morning person. I *actually* enjoy my lie-ins."

"Well, light of my life, *enjoy!*" I said jovially and kissed that single, visible fist that clutched the duvet that cocooned the rest of her. I got out of bed to use the en-suite bathroom and prepare myself for the day. "Just a gentle reminder, though, we do have a city to explore. Next stop: Montmartre."

The Astoria really was thirty minutes from everywhere, and Montmartre was no exception. After breakfasting on a basket of freshly-baked croissants and sliced baguettes with fruit preserves and café au lait, we took a tough, uphill walk from the milling city below to the twisted, cobbled streets of one of the most charming neighbourhoods in Paris. *The Village on the Hill.* The arduous climb on this wet, blustery day sent a rush of blood to our brains and our muscles, and we felt a euphoric lifting of our moods as we wandered past elegantly-aging apartments, with their ivy-clad walls and brightly-painted shutters, and up the steep, gaslampbedecked stairways of RUE FOYATIER that could make your head spin. Art seemed to permeate every wall of Montmartre, relaying profound messages left by strangers: *J'EXISTE*.

Montmartre was talked about by Parisians in the same way New Yorkers talked about 'the Village'. Montmartre captivated bohemian artists during the Belle Époque and continued to delight tourists today. Artists' workshops began to flourish by the end of the nineteenth century, nurtured by the likes of Toulouse-Lautrec, Renoir, Degas, Matisse and Picasso, turning Montmartre into the hub of the Art world from when it had since retained its status as one of the most famous artists' enclaves in the world. Montmatre was also the birthplace of Cubism and Surrealism.

And, in the heart of the village itself, in a quiet corner of the Butte Montmartre, just west of Sacré-Cœur, a stone's throw away from the mythical PLACE DU TERTRE, we would be rewarded for our efforts by arriving at a little gem of a museum, an intimate space that celebrated the legacy of the flamboyantly-moustachioed inventor of whimsical, soft watches. Although it could easily be mistaken as just another nondescript residence, the ESPACE DALÍ was deceptively bigger on the inside, like a Galifreyan's time machine, and presented the only permanent exhibition in France entirely devoted to the Master of Surrealism. The museum showcased a memorable retrospective of three-hundred original works of Salvador Dalí in a progression that spanned nearly half a century and beautifully told the tale of his life, his inspirations and his place in the tapestry of Montmartre, after his expulsion from Spain.

Surrealism is a form of art depicting the artist's vision while in a sort of dream state, completely free of rational control and, certainly, stepping into the Espace Dalí was like entering a waking dream, a phantasmagorical universe of extravagant, impossible Dalínian concept art. Each artwork was numbered and signed by the artist himself. The artistic endeavours that populated his fantasy world – paintings, watercolours, drawings, etchings, sculptures, collages, engravings, lithographs, short films – ran the gamut from the dreamlike, erotic and theatrical to the droll, poetic and irresistibility humorous, all incarnations of his favourite themes, given carte blanche by the curator.

After paying the entrance fee at street level, we descended a flight of stairs to the subterranean depths of the museum proper, where we were immediately greeted by the extended claw-like hand of the strange sculpture of *Woman with a Head of Roses*. It was relatively quiet inside the museum, peaceful, a huge contrast to the busyness of outside. Music played unobtrusively in the background. Hayley and I strolled around the various exhibits, some of which prompted gasps of mind-blowing awe, as Dalí invited us to explore his encyclopaedic fascination with literature, mythology, religion and science. The *Space Elephant* with spindly legs while supporting a glass obelisk on its back, defying gravity and evoking weightlessness, represented St. Anthony's battle against the power of temptation. Limp, melting watches draped over branches, portrayed the omnipresence and fluid nature of Time, and how it is perceived differently from one person to the next, depending on the circumstances of the situation, Dalí yearning to control the passage of Time itself – who cannot identify with the tyranny of the clock in our lives, how it would outlast all of us? Minotaurs – and even the Venus de Milo – donning drawers, depicted memory and the maze of the unconscious, of its infinite mysteries, of hidden sexuality. The juxtaposition of a lobster with a naked, female crotch. A snail spreading its wings. Ants symbolized decomposition and the ephemerality of life. Lithographs illustrated the fantastical world of Alice in Wonderland, the dreamlike influences of which were a constant preoccupation for Dalí. Freudian influences, depictions of eggs, urchins, ants and bread, contrasting a hard shell with the soft inside, consistent with psychoanalytic notions that individuals developed hard defences around their vulnerable, flexible and fragile inner psyches. Moses and Monotheism. Angels penetrated the heavens, communicating with God, defining purity. The infamous Mae West Lips Sofa. Dalí's love for Gala, his wife and muse, whom he called his 'Oxygen' inspired some of his great illustrations: Romeo and Juliet, Ovid's *Art of Love*, Tristan and Isolde. His passion for science and mathematics was exemplified by a number of artworks that bordered on knowledge and belief, optics, atoms, DNA, Newton, the Alchemy of the Philosophers; Dalí always believed an artist should possess a respectable grasp of science to achieve unity in their work. The collection struck a chord with me, moved me in a powerful way. But, in my exposure to this eccentric artist and his iconic style, it was the bronze sculpture of the *Surrealist Eyes* that truly got me, creeped me out good and proper. I have a thing for eyes, just like Hayley has a certain dislike for holes, the lotus seed pod making her particularly squeamish. I got the sense the lattice of alien eyes, stacked up on one another in a near-cuboid shape, were fixed on me, peeking into my soul, learning my secrets, controlling me . . .

Luis Buñuel's 1929 masterpiece, *Un Chien Andalou*, and its 1930 follow-up, *L'Age d'Or*, played in one of the chambers. In conventional cinema, the desires and terrors of the audience were transformed into empathy or hatred for the characters in the film. Surrealist cinema, instead, displayed a sequence of objects and disparate images, whose vicissitudes generated laughter or disgust, the extremes of Humour and Horror, Buñuel and Dalí particularly interested in the audience's reaction. The image of a donkey. Of two grand pianos, side-by-side. Of the moon and a passing cloud. A pair of lovers walking joyously on the beach, only for them to be suddenly buried waist-deep in the sand, rotting. The equally-visceral pairing of a razor and an eyeball made me think of the *Surrealist Eyes* and I shuddered. It was the bizarre, raw texture of the film that separated it from the ethereal unreality of Hollywood, but avant-garde cinema would soon enter the mainstream, just as Georges Méliès' technical wizardry once captured the world's imagination. Probing the Freudian depths of the Psyche, Alfred Hitchcock consulted Dalí on the surrealistic dream sequence for the movie, *Spellbound*, in which Gregory Peck plays a mental patient and Ingrid Bergman his doctor. The Monty Python team, too, were famously inspired by Dalí and changed the face of comedy forever. The most recent French movie we watched, *The Strange Colour of My Body's Tears*, was more an extraordinary piece of surrealistic filmmaking than a straightforward homage to Giallo cinema. Even the prominent dream architecture of David Lynch took its cue primarily from Dalí, in which weirdness had become an aesthetic in its own right, an expressive frontier, and where the physical world was so violent, erotic and shocking that it no longer relied on a logical or coherent narrative structure.

At the end, there was a room where one could purchase limited-edition prints of Dalí's work and back up the stairs was located the gift shop and exit.

Dalí would probably have agreed with Théophile Gautier, who said: *Any man who does not have an inner world to translate is not an artist.*

Back out in the open, we meandered the hilly, winding streets, once again amongst the quaint, sidewalk cafés and crêpe stands and artisanal shops, the old-fashioned carousel and the lively plaza of Place du Tertre, packed with street-artists – painters, portraitists and caricaturists – who exuded the ongoing creative spirit of Montmartre, hoping to cross paths with the ghosts of Van Gogh and Toulouse-Lautrec. The stoned-paved square rested at the foot of the neighbourhood's stunning, pilgrimage-worthy Byzantine basilica, SACRÉ-CŒUR, the highest point of Montmartre where Saint Denis was buried following his decapitation atop the hill in 250AD to be subsequently martyred.

We hopped on board the tourist funicular railway at the Place du Tertre which would assist us in our sightseeing, passing numerous landmarks as it carried us down the hill of Montmartre. We passed the double windmills of the MOULIN DE LA GALETTE, a former flour mill, now a chic restaurant.

MUSÉE DE MONTMARTRE, where the artist, Maurice Utrillo, lived and painted, the mansion at the back once owned by Claude de la Rose, the actor who replaced Molière on stage, later occupied by Renoir. LE BATEAU-LAVOIR, the former workshop of Picasso and Moglidiani, now regarded as the most famous art studio in the world. CLOS MONTMARTRE VINEYARD – the last vineyard of Paris – just past the MAISON ROSE restaurant. LAPIN AGILE cabaret. And soon we had weaved our way down to the bottom of the hill, the *'petit train'* stopping off at the BOULEVARD DE CLICHY in the red-light district of Pigalle where we could not miss the sight of the infamous MOULIN ROUGE cabaret, founded in 1889 and the spiritual birthplace of the can-can. It was an establishment adored by the lowly artist and the haute-bourgeoisie alike and immortalized by Toulouse-Lautrec, whose posters and paintings referencing it secured its international fame early on. Its Voluptua of cabaret singers and dancing girls and courtesans cemented Paris's reputation as a city of decadent and hedonistic pleasure, of sensationally sensuous orgies and sophisticated sex. It was ironic how something that had once served as a critique of decadent society had become a symbol of decadence itself. Its windmill and distinctive red paint did not indicate 'painting the town red', as some people suggested, but supposedly represented the private, blood-gorged lips of a woman when aroused. We had considered taking in one of its erotic revues but decided we would do so the next time we were in Paris – if there was a next time.

We disembarked on Boulevard de Clichy, where the crowd grew edgier and cagier. The dregs of Parisian society – entrepreneurial misfits and crooked underworld types and sleazy pimps leaning against neon-flashing doorways – operated from here, adding a picaresque slant to Montmartre's picturesque street scene. For, alongside the kebab shops and stores specializing in rock music instruments, our eyes were bombarded by sex shops and peep shows we pretended not to notice. From one den of vice to another, the never-ending offer of cheap sex. The writer, Henry Miller, had been the most outspoken in his ambivalence towards Paris: *It is no accident that propels people like us to Paris. Paris is simply an artificial stage, a revolving stage that permits the spectator to glimpse all stages of the conflict. Of itself Paris initiates no dramas. They are begun elsewhere. Paris is simply an obstetrical instrument that tears the living embryo from the womb and puts it in the incubator.*

But it was further along where we would luncheon, in LE CHAT NOIR 1881 restaurant, above which towered its hotel. It may not be the original site of the famous nightclub-and-restaurant, first founded by a group of radical writers and poets and painters called '*Les Hydropathes*', who had a self-professed 'rabid' aversion to water in favour of drinking cheap wine, but it was still a hip place to stop off for a spot of fine dining and fashionable drinking in Montmartre. Théophile Steinlen's instantly-recognizable poster design of the scraggy black feline was as iconic as the establishment itself, reminding me of the black tom that followed us at the old cemetery.

The interior was plush and cosy, with a running, black motif, including the presence of a black grand piano in the corner staging area, currently shut, silent. The place was busy, the service customer-centred and first-rate, leading to a quick turnover of tourists. I sat facing the window and, across the road, one of the outlets was advertising its wares with the overhead shop-sign, PORNO SHOP – *I mean how subtle is that?* I wondered if Hayley might be interested in visiting one such sex shop in search of kinky underwear or a French maid's outfit, but I refrained from asking her to devise a Naughty List, lest she misconstrued my wicked request as me perving over her; Hayley did not like being perved over. The mix on the street was more cosmopolitan, including more Arabs and Africans amongst the everyday folk and the smut peddlers.

We both went for roast coquelet with potato-and-celeriac dauphinoise, washed down with refreshing beer. Hayley was discussing film actresses with her usual spirit. "I can understand why men might fancy Naomi Watts, but Juno Temple...? No, Juno Temple looks like a smelly person, absolutely mingin' . . ."

So very Hayley! I tried to remember what had given rise to this particular line of conversation, couldn't. Instead, I quoted Voltaire: "*Men will always be mad, and those who think they can cure them are the maddest of all. I should like to lie at your feet and die in your arms.*"

"No, give me Isabelle Huppert or Catherine Deneuve any day," she said, a faraway, wistful look appearing on her face. "My mind goes back to *Belle Du Jour* sometimes . . ."

I wondered what was going through her mind. *Belle Du Jour* was a respectable later effort from the same surrealistic filmmaker who had wooed the world with *Un Chien Andolou*. The film involved Catherine Deneuve in the role of a bored, sexually-dissatisfied housewife, who pursues more excitement in her life by moonlighting as a prostitute. Hayley had watched the film repeatedly. Was Hayley hinting at something? Was she intending to switch jobs? Swap over from being a nanny, as she couldn't stand looking after those 'rich, spoiled, *ugly* babies' [In her own words: *Enough bloody kids in the world . . . it annoys me!* And my honest observation? *Doesn't bode well if we're thinking about conceiving, dear!*] to working as a high-class hooker from home? Sadly, I couldn't put it past her. But I left her interest in it unspoken since I hoped that the whole STD thing might put her off the idea. Another thought occurred to me. I prayed she hadn't tried to seduce the rich father of the kids she was nannying and was carrying on an affair in typical gold-digging fashion . . . "Always about money, isn't it?"

"Money makes the world go round," she reminded me.

"Unfortunately," I said quietly. "Why can't we just go back to the days of good, old-fashioned bartering? A worthier system of financial transaction."

Hayley ignored me. "I think I would make a great actress. I really would look good on stage . . . or in a Hollywood blockbuster!"

"My darling, you couldn't sit through a Shakespearean play in Stratford," I reminded her. "You told me it was 'boring'!"

"We're back to that then, hey?" she said, suddenly cross with me. "Just let it go..."

"I thought it was you who wasn't letting it go."

"Let's not raise the dead right now," she advised. "I'm talking about me attending drama school in Paris."

"Where did this suddenly come from?"

"I've already applied to the Cours Florent drama school in Paris . . ." she informed me. "They accept foreign students and run courses in English while teaching you French. I start in September."

I was utterly gobsmacked. For a moment I didn't know what to say. It was news to me. Still, I could imagine her, a thirtysomething acting against ambitious, aspiring actresses in their late teens and early twenties. Imagine the bitchiness and jealousy and the sense of feeling slighted. Imagine being forced to play mothers or other mature roles against these young actresses' heroines. Or, worse still, I wouldn't put it past her to do sexual favours for a film director to get a part in the film and then accuse the said-director of taking sexual advantage of her when the said-role was eventually offered to someone else. I dared not think about it. But I did not plan to dampen her enthusiasm. No point reasoning with her once her mind was set on something and with her having after all sent through the application behind my back. Otherwise she might resent me for not giving her the chance to prove herself. Let her make her own mistakes. "Good luck to you! You have my full support! You know it is claimed that while Hollywood makes movies for a world audience, French cinema is aimed purely at Paris."

It brought a smile to her face, a genuine smile of pleasure, and she reached out and touched my hand on the table, as the after-dinner cappuccinos arrived. "You won't regret it . . ."

Knowing that she liked posh things, I said: "You are the Evian lady to my Volvic man, I guess . . ."

She appreciated the running gag and lifted my hand and kissed my knuckles. "Thank you . . . but why can't I be the Vittel lady, mind me asking?"

Even if she was correcting me on a stupid, sentimental comment I was making, it was the most affectionate we'd been on holiday so far and I hoped things could only improve.

With lunch sorted, we departed this latest incarnation of Le Chat Noir and resumed our day out, continuing to focus on Paris's art treasures. We left Montmartre by foot. Next stop: the POMPIDOU CENTRE. On the other side of town.

The Pompidou Centre was a high-tech architectural marvel, named after Georges Pompidou, former President of France, who had commissioned the building to decentralize art and culture while revitalizing the Beaubourg envions. Thus, this popular social, artistic and cultural hub officially opened in 1977, costing nearly a billion francs to build.

Its architects broke with convention, creating a design that was revolutionary; indeed, I thought it looked like a giant spaceship of glass, die-cast steel and tubing, colour-coded to denote function, that had unexpectedly landed in the historic heart of Paris. Extraordinary still was how the building looked strangely inside-out, its utilitarian facilities – air conditioning, elevators, pipework, electric cables – on its façade, like an exoskeleton, freeing up the interior space for exhibitions and events. This must-see attraction was largely disliked by the French people, who compared it to a boiler house or an oil refinery, but this fact did not deter the quotidian twenty-five thousand visitors.

On the west front, the PLACE GEORGES POMPIDOU was noted for the presence of street performers – buskers and musicians, sketch artists and skateboarders, jugglers and mime artists – while on the south aspect of the building was the PLACE IGOR STRAVINSKY with its fanciful mechanical fountain and several kinetic sculptures, incorporating skeletons, hearts, treble clefs and a pair of ruby-red lips, objects that could have dropped straight out of a nursery school or Pixar film. Next door, adjoining was IRCAM, the centre of music and acoustic research, a popular place for classical composers hoping to bridge the gap between classical and modern, experimental music.

Inside the Pompidou, many strands of culture intertwined with art, design, literature, music and cinema. The Pompidou Centre brought together an extensive library and a popular bookshop, art galleries with cutting-edge exhibitions, hands-on workshops and adaptable performance spaces and a repertory cinema.

The BIBLIOTHÈQUE PUBLIQUE D'INFORMATION took up part of the first floor and the entirety of the second and third floors. The Public Library in its enormity housed half-a-million books. Escalators zigzagging through transparent tubes up the front of the building afforded increasingly extraordinary views of Paris.

Not to be confused with the Musée d'art moderne de la Ville de Paris, which would be a sin not to visit and see the psychedelic, chamber-wide mural by Raoul Dufy, *La Fée Électricité*, recounting the history of electricity from the Olympian gods with their lightning bolts to the one-hundred-and-ten scientists and inventors who brought electricity into modern usage, the MUSÉE NATIONAL D'ART MODERNE, was accommodated on the fourth and fifth floors, the most important modern art museum in Europe and one of the most renowned in the world. Its collection of paintings, sculptures, drawings, photography and video and installation art, featuring only a fraction of its 50000-plus artworks, exhibiting only five thousand works at any given time, covered the entire spectrum of the twentieth century, including the movements of Primitivism, Fauvism, Cubism, Dadaism, Surrealism and Abstract Expressionism in progressive fashion, chronologically over two sections. Level 5 housed the modern period, from 1905 to 1960, capturing some of the masterpieces of Matisse, Picasso, Kadinsky and Miró. I guess lots of oohs and aahs. The eccentricities of Dalí were well in abundance, and the photography of Man Ray was characteristically as weird as ever. And Marcel Duchamp's urinal – I guess it must have been ahead of its time. But the revelation for me – and a macabre revelation at that – was Otto Dix.

Otto Dix was a German Post-expressionist who once stated: *Art is exorcism. I paint dreams and visions, too; the dreams and visions of my time. Painting is the effort to produce order; order in yourself. There is much chaos in me, much chaos in our time.* As a member of the New Objectivity movement, he is best remembered for the *Portrait of the Journalist Sylvia von Harden*, concerned not with the outward beauty of women but the psychological and emotional turmoil within. He was also a war veteran, haunted by his traumatic experiences on the Western Front, and a harsh critic of the grossly-decadent Weimar Society, with some of his darkest and most enduring work spanning that period from the end of the First World War to the accession of the Nazis. In fact, his hellish visions of the Trenches – skulls wearing gas-masks and dead, maggot-riddled brains of soldiers, rats roaming among human body parts and convoluted intestines, the tragic, partially-rotting carcass of a horse

– and his grotesquely satirical portrait paintings of the celebrities and notable intellectuals of the Weimar era – of drunk customers with vagina-shaped disfigurements, of witchy prostitutes entertaining top-ranking German officers, of frightening psychiatrists with mad, glittering eyes that reveal the demons of their mind – gained a certain notoriety in his day, later cast off as 'Degenerate Art' by Hitler himself and summarily banned in contrast to Arnold Böcklin, whom Hitler embraced for creating the much-imitated *Isle of the Dead*, a painting the Führer claimed he could dream to. I suppose Dix was Goya's true successor, where the order of the day was nihilism with the power of ugliness employed to remarkable satirical effect in an unforgiving indictment of corruption and immorality and the senseless waste of human life. The hyper-real quality and credibly-morbid strangeness of Dix's work blew my socks off and would stay with me for a long time to come.

Level 4 covered the contemporary period, from post-1960 onwards, encompassing the figurative art and Pop Art movement and, yes, all the usual suspects were in attendance. Warhol in drag. The extraordinary explosions-in-colour of Edith Torony's *Junkyard Symphony*. Ralph Steadman, the social caricaturist and illustrator of Hunter S. Thompson's books, had been given some floor space to display his unique craziness. However, Jeff Koons' college yearbook headshots were unfortunately as uninspired as found-footage films or reality TV – his balloon dog was slightly more creative – this from a man who once held the world record for the most expensive work sold at auction by a living artist. Even Damien Hirst made an appearance, but I was unimpressed, remembering an article that stated he no longer produced his own work, paying others to create it. Most of his art was no longer art anyway, like some of the ordinary furniture by other so-called artists that was pretentiously scattered around the exhibition classified as 'Art'. No, Hirst had stopped doing his job, and, in my opinion, that made him a world-class sell-out. He had somehow managed to demonstrate that his creativity was a perishable skill, not a lifelong talent as it should be. But it was also the critics' fault for not taking him to task. The critics had lost their rigorous objectivity, pandering to the has-been artist like brown-tonguing sycophants, not telling him how his work now plumbed the depths of laziness. *Obsequious fucks!* Of all the modern art on display, one of Jenny Holzer's truisms on a wall-mounted plaque caught my attention: YOU CAN MAKE YOURSELF ENTER SOMEWHERE FRIGHTENING IF YOU BELIEVE YOU'LL PROFIT BY IT. THE NATURAL RESPONSE IS TO FLEE BUT PEOPLE DON'T ACT THAT WAY ANYMORE.

In addition to the permanent collection, internationally-renowned temporary exhibitions were organized every year on the uppermost, sixth floor. Cy Twombly, Lexington's own, was the guest of honour on this occasion. We paid tribute to his artistic expression, but I admit I was disappointed for the most part. I had to agree with public consensus that he was nothing more than a graffiti artist – a child could do better. I thought his abstract work lacked the method of Pollock's dripping fractals. But it wasn't all bad. Once Cy got colour into his works, the final product noticeably improved. The big, deconstructed flowers of *Blooming*, dripping with fiery colours, like huge bouquets of blood on white canvas, was simple and genuinely stirred romantic sentiments.

I suppose I came to an epiphany that day. After visiting Montmartre and the Pompidou, I concluded the painting would always belong to the artist, living or dead, and the museum or private collector or buyer – an undiscerning collector with lots of money but no taste – would only be caretaking or babysitting the work, like our souls supposedly only belonged to God and our human bodies served merely as their vessels.

Our whistle-stop tour of the Pompidou ended with dinner – a light supper of hake grenobloise for Hayley and sole à la meunière *pour moi* – at LE GEORGES restaurant, also on the top floor. We admired its sweeping, rooftop panorama of Paris, including the Sacré-Cœur Basilica at Montmartre and the Eiffel Tower twinkling at dusk. The Parisian skyline was breathtakingly laid out before our very eyes in the dying of the light, evoking fairytales, the stupendous sense of spectacle. I thought of Rousseau and the perfectibility of man. I considered Man's artistic and architectural accomplishments encapsulated by one city. Self-actualization, in a word, without a place for God.

All tuckered-out, we retired early to bed, cuddling up for a change. Valentine's Day on the morrow.

In the meantime . . . *Bonne nuit!*

Another undisturbed sleep with lavender, full of strange dreams.

I dream of that same black cat at the famous cemetery as he tails us to the gates, keeping a safe distance, not respecting any of our constant attempts to shoo him away . . . until I stop and decide to approach him. The black tom halts in his tracks, does not run off. Instead, he actually allows me to pick him up, sensing my friendliness, and rubs cheeks with mine proudly, and I feel his moist pink nose against my skin and his soft, warm breath. So, as I hold him purring cradled in my arms, I take out the electric shaver, somehow in my pocket, and switch it on. With a loud buzz, I shave the damned thing, avoiding his claws, hearing his desperate high-pitched meows, his dark, lopped-off fur floating to the ground like mowed hay. Then, I dump the cat onto the footpath, as he tries to make sense of his circumstances.

"Don't ever follow us again?" I warn him, getting a thumbs-up, wicked grin from my wife, fully supportive of my act of cruelty, "or next time I shall be skinning you alive!"

The cat, now all naked-pink and pathetically skinny and resembling more the last-turkey-in-the-shop look than one of those naturally-hairless sphinx cats, begins to wail in self-pity and shame, utterly humiliated, robbed of his pride, grieving the loss of his beautiful fur, sitting on his haunches in a scattering of it, like the sheared hair around a barber's chair, and it is the sound of those miserable cries that jerks me awake—

—I found myself in our hotel-bed, still at the Astoria, in the small hours. I remembered the dream, my open cruelty towards the cat, the cat's loud, mournful reaction. Why would I ever want to shave such a handsome creature and reduce him to a bald, skinny, crying thing with the looks of a skinned turkey? I considered the symbolism inherent within, seemed at a loss to interpret it. Regardless, it made me think of Baudelaire: *Common sense tells us that the things of the earth exist only a little, and that true reality is only in dreams.*

Somewhere close-by, I thought I could still vaguely hear the sound of a cat crying. Until those inconsolable wails gradually faded away altogether.

I nodded off again. And drifted off into the privacy of my dreams.

In the second dream, or maybe it is a continuation of the first, I find myself back at Père Lachaise in the grey drizzle and, as I lie on Jim Morrison's modest grave, bound and gagged, with Hayley and Julien Étrange and the black cat (fur intact) gathered and watching me impassively, the earth suddenly rips open and swallows me up . . . literally. I remember wrestling with my bonds, drowning, choking, suffocating . . . as I sink deeper and deeper into the ground as though it is made of quicksand. Then, Jim Morrison's distinctive voice echoes from somewhere faraway, philosophizing: "A lunatic hides in the windmills of the mind . . ."

I suddenly awoke to Valentine's Day, my first in Paris. That special day when all inhibitions melt away, and one half of Paris makes love to the other half. We did just that: we celebrated the ultimate day of amour in La Ville Lumière by making love. I think Hayley and I had by now had our fill of beautiful art treasures. Hayley initiated the lovemaking by kissing me the moment she woke up, and I got the sense of an act planned rather than driven by impulse or spontaneity, like she intended to do this all along. They say the first six weeks of the New Year, up to and including Valentine's Day, are the busiest time of the year for divorce lawyers, which goes to show that lots of people aren't getting that loving feeling as much as Hallmark hopes. During this precious time of love, many, in point of fact, are feeling nothing but complete-and-unconditional *hatred*, just as the homeland of the Catholic faith, Italy, is also the Satanic capital of the world.

"You're very affectionate, my darling," I observed, questioningly, as she separated her lips from mine. I thoroughly appreciated the kiss we had shared.

"I've got to make the most of you before you pop off . . ." Hayley chirped lightly, and the comment, meant to be taken in good humour, made me think of the dream from last night.

I do not wish to sound paranoid, but was it my brain's way of processing the past and extrapolating future events? A sign of things to come? An omen? However, it wasn't difficult giving Hayley the benefit of the doubt, even if her spite might be plotting something, since I was quite sexually aroused.

"Why don't we get it on?" I asked her.

Hayley obliged. "I thought you'd never ask."

"You cannot imagine how much I'm going to ravish you!"

"Is that a threat or a promise?" she teased.

However, I was abruptly interrupted by the need for a whizz. I quickly got up and strode to the en-suite bathroom. "I shall return . . . don't go away." Having answered my call of nature, I made an important observation. "Every time I walk into the room, you're wearing less clothes . . ."

Hayley lay in bed, naked as sin, all yearning, glorious flesh and soft, gorgeous curves. "I hope I don't remind you of the woman from Room 237."

Another dark joke, but I was too turned on. "Not one jot. Let me show you how much I still fancy you." I climbed into bed and we decided to shut the world outside for as long as it took. I went down on her. "Is this doing anything for you?"

"What should it be doing for me?" she whispered, moaning with pleasure.

We were all over each other. And we were on fire, consumed by passion. We made love like we did when we used to date. It had been so long since our last loving session, it felt like I was having an affair with another woman, who just happened to be my beautiful wife. *Is it a sin to covet your own wife?* as Ned Flanders of *The Simpsons* fame once nervously but excitedly asked.

Hayley was dripping for me, and she accommodated my throbbing hardness with her usual juicy squelchiness. We did nothing else, just went at it for hours, like the horny honeymooners at the beginning of *Barefoot in the Park*. In the end, I was pooped – I guess I hadn't done this much exercise in ages. "I think I will just lie here and admire you, my adorable one, make you self-conscious."

Hayley was equally slick with sweat and exhaustion. "I've got what I needed..."

"Indeed," I joked, breathless, "it's my semen, my love. Use it well!"

"Oh, you've got no idea how much I intend to . . ." she said enigmatically, and again I wondered what she meant. Even though we both had performed exceptionally well, like rabbits in heat, I got a strange foreboding she was only going through the motions and our intense lovemaking served only as a means to an end. *We* must *do this. Have sex.* I thought of a black widow devouring its mate. I decided not to explore my gut feeling with her; I decided not to rock the boat. I was just pleased I had satisfied her, multiple times.

"Was I everything you wanted me to be?" I asked her when we were done for the moment.

"Yes, and much more . . ." Hayley replied, smiling a dreamy smile.

"You mean I can be less?" I joked.

We got lunch in Little Tokyo around the corner on Rue des Petits-Champs, wasabi and Japanese curry. We did a bit of shopping afterwards – I bought Hayley a necklace from a nice French jeweller's while she got me a bottle of vintage Chartreuse from an epicurean shop, on-the-spur Valentine's gifts. We drank coffee in a quaint bookshop. Then, we were back at the hotel and still able to manage an afternoon nap, cuddled in each other's arms, ahead of our evening plans. And, upon waking, we were enkindled enough for another round of hot, meaningful sex.

Yes.

Yes!

YES!

We had booked our evening reservations at LE GRAND COLBERT, situated in a tiny street one block away from the Bourse (French Stock Exchange) and five minutes' walk from the hotel. Immediately on arrival, I was witness to an amazing sight outside the restaurant. *Where else but in Paris do you see a posh lady with a mink coat and a silver bob, smoking a cigarette and chatting away to a polite, well-educated tramp?*

The glassine and rather unremarkable exterior of the restaurant nearly fooled us since it hid a one-hundred-seat brasserie that plunged far away into the distance, the magnitude of the deception only becoming apparent upon entering. The gilded, high-ceilinged interior was beautifully decorated in a Belle Époch-style and divided into thirds by etched glass screens. Its doors first opened in 1830 and now open all year round, the place was always packed and today would prove more so. We were greeted enthusiastically by a handsome, smiling waiter and each offered a free complimentary glass of champagne to mark the occasion which we graciously accepted. A bar with a painted frieze ran the length of one side of the restaurant and we took in the swankiness of the rich, velvet curtains and the pastel glow of the copper lights. The walls were adorned with paintings and mirrors, upon the latter of which were tacked old theatre posters.

Talking of posters, there was a reason why Hayley had chosen this particular restaurant. The movie poster of the romantic comedy, *Something's Gotta Give*, in the restaurant window should have been a dead giveaway. The final crucial scene of the movie had been filmed in this very restaurant, and tourists had flocked here ever since. Since Hayley revered Diane and fancied Jack and absolutely and utterly adored the film, able to recite all the quotable exchanges between the two leads, we had only thought it fitting to book the exact table they sat at to honour Jack and Diane for making out like a couple of old turtles. TOUT PEUT ARRIVER, as the tribute read. *Anything can happen.*

Le Grand Colbert promised a glorious romantic dining experience in an atmosphere that could be best described as exuberant and with us seated at the most prized table in the house, embellished further by a vase of fresh red roses. The menu offered a delicious reinterpretation of French bistro classics and gourmet dishes – they might as well have been dreamed up by a Cordon Bleu chef – and I wanted to spoil my fair lady with fare befitting this very romantic of romantic evenings. Amidst the effervescent buzz of the place and the Parisian dash of the waiters, Hayley and I shared chilled oysters and ordered Chateaubriand-for-two to maintain the mood of Valentine's. I even got her to try some garlic snails, which I'd ordered on the side with crusty bread. When the main course arrived, I thought my tastebuds had been catapulted to heaven; the meat was mouthwateringly, melt-in-the-mouth divine and the Roquefort sauce flavoursome, second-to-none. A bottle of Châteauneuf-du-Pape provided essential, round-bodied lubrication.

I educated Hayley on the origins of modern-day French cuisine. The culinary world owed a lot to Marie-Antoine Carême. Abandoned in the street aged eight, Carême's creative spark would see him eventually rise to the position of the world's first celebrity chef by the early nineteenth century and would soon be elevated to the status of a god in the pantheon of pioneering culinary heroes, a reputation he enjoyed even today. It was Carême who invented food as a cultural experience, introduced the concept of the three-course meal and raised cooking into an artform called '*haute cuisine*'. Some of his innovative recipes and culinary creations were being used even to this day. Hayley and I talked about maybe living in Normandy, if I ever made it as a marketable writer, the perfect location for hopping across the English Channel or travelling down to the South of France, whenever we felt like it. Hayley reminded me we could purchase a huge, Norman manor house for the same price as our house in Chertsford, with acres and acres of land thrown in. Then, we were on the subject of acting again and Hayley's dreams of movie stardom. In other words, *money*.

"I was told I use Received Pronunciation," Hayley was saying, her voice full of pride, "but I would love to learn the Queen's English, like the Fox acting dynasty."

"I suppose it takes lots of practice and hard work to talk like a Royal," I replied. "They learned to talk like that from birth."

"Shouldn't take too much effort."

"Psychologists claim that when one's efforts do not match one's ambitions, it generates anxiety and possibly despair."

Hayley blurted out her inner thoughts. "There's so much wrong with Hollywood. I'm fed up of Shakespeare's rubbish!"

"You're fed up of Shakespeare's rubbish?" I exclaimed, astonished where this had come from, "but you want to be a successful actress?"

"Shakespeare's been done to death!"

"You're not interested in new interpretations of timeless Shakespearean characters?" I asked. "You do realize that Shakespeare is the actor's bible."

"If you say so . . . It won't matter once I'm a famous movie star."

I had to be frank with her. "There are very few things in life that are one-hundred-percent certain and other things, like acting, that are one-hundred-percent *uncertain*."

Her expression soured, and I felt bad that I might be hurting her feelings or crushing her hopes. "How do you expect me to get rich? You're not exactly a household name!"

"I'm a giver, not a taker." *So bend over, dear, and take it like a moany cow . . .*

"If you were more of a taker, we'd be wealthy."

"Believe me, money is not worth wasting your life worrying about or fixating over at the expense of everything else."

"Hence your failure to set the book world on fire!" she belittled me. "You write *shittily*! Even your handwriting is a childish scrawl, *illegible*, unlike my neat, joined-up style of writing."

After the fine dining and excellent wine, we were in the process of finishing off the cheese platter and myself polishing off my generous measure of Remy Martin XO, delivered in timely fashion by our whirling, aproned waiter. I think Hayley was always at her most honest – even if in an obnoxious, outrageous and offensive manner – when she had a few drops of alcohol in her. "Does it matter if my penmanship is non-cursive? A little chaos isn't a bad thing. Keeps you alert, on your toes, focused, sharpens the senses . . ."

She grew more hostile. "Rubbish! You're just making excuses for your own inadequacies. You don't even read anymore so how do you expect to write? I've read so many books in the last year . . ."

"You mean you've *started* so many books in the last year! I can't seem to remember you finishing a single book during our entire years of marriage!"

"Throw that at me, why don't you?"

"I've got a proper firecracker of a wife . . . and I really love you for it . . . for still inviting me to join you in Paris, of all places, on Valentine's Day, of all days, after what I did to you." I reached out for her hand, but she snatched hers away. "You shouldn't take things personally. I get the impression that telling you off or telling you how things really are diminishes me in your eyes."

"Blah, blah, blah . . ." she said, pretending not to listen. I didn't think she appreciated me dredging up that incident with the police. "Repeat, repeat, repeat..."

"There again, taking things personally. When all I'm giving you is good advice and preparing you for any disappointments in life." I stopped for a moment, told her how I felt. "You have no idea how extraordinarily patient I've been with you because you're such hard work." But now I was starting to get angry. "You cut my hair short and won't let me wear contact lenses because it makes me more attractive to women . . . as if I don't know?"

"Ha!" she remarked, laughing. "Instead of looking like Harrison Ford from *Blade Runner*, you look like Tom Hanks in *Philadelphia!*"

Wonders never ceased. Hayley bafflingly desisted from resorting to the cruel barbs that defined her and frequently wounded in their savagery. Her mood had suddenly lightened, and she was cracking jokes. Everything was okay again. A good sign, surely. I decided to go with the flow. "Thank you very much! You telling me I look like an AIDS victim? I can't even get away with being Jack Skellington?"

She responded with good humour. "More like *Beetlejuice!* The Char Man in Hell's waiting room!"

"And what about you?" I mock-rounded on her. "Ms. Jill Tyrrell from *Nighty Night?*"

Hayley did not take affront to the reference. Instead, she laughed harder, so uproariously it made the laughter seem forced, put-on. "Shallow, self-obsessed, attention-seeking, am I?" She mock-protested, mock-threatened. "How dare you call me that! And you know exactly what I'm going to do to you!" She looked thoughtfully at me and pulled out a Biblical quote from the hat: "*Eat, drink, and be merry for tomorrow we die.*"

We didn't retreat to the hotel for the night. The night was young, and it was Hayley, in unusually bright spirits, who suggested we visit a jazz club or piano bar. We hailed a cab for the Latin Quarter, part of the first café society and once a mecca for the intellectuals of the literary world – from Voltaire to Rousseau, Camus to Sartre – destined for Paris' most celebrated jazz spot for the past seventy years, just across the river from twelfth-century Notre Dame Cathedral: LE CAVEAU DE LA HUTCHETTE.

Once linked to the Rosicrucians and the Knights Templar before the sixteenth century, the building became a place for secret lodge meetings by the Freemasons in the eighteenth century before operating as a Court room, dungeon and place of execution during the Revolution. Historically, the deep well that existed in the lower chamber and the secret subterranean passages leading off were used to remove all evidence of the horrendous travesties of justice committed here, and, yes, some of the original aspects of that time had been preserved, such as swords and muskets and daggers and instruments of torture, like the guillotine, and, oddly-enough, a fiercely-guarded chastity belt. The Harlem-bred G.I. Joes, stationed in France during the Great War, delighting in the liberal attitudes of the Parisiennes, introduced the jazz scene to Paris. It is claimed that the Caveau inspired the creation of the Cavern Club in Liverpool in 1957 where the Beatles would make their name before achieving worldwide fame.

If we were expecting an old-school jazz club, like Ronnie Scott's in London, we got two basement rooms, each on different floors, instead. Not that it was a bad set-up, mind, since the place purportedly invited a higher class of musician and attracted a particularly savvy, artsy crowd. I walked to the bar upstairs to get us each a champagne cocktail. Most of the space in the downstairs club made up the dancefloor, around which existed a bench-style perimeter of seating, without tables or chairs. The place reminded me of Ali Baba's cavern. Indeed, it smelled like a real cave alongside the smell of tobacco smoke, alcohol and sweat. It was slightly cramped but not claustrophobic. The atmosphere was upbeat, informal.

We didn't dance, just grabbed a bench on the edge of the dancefloor, lounged around, as I did not wish to show off my two left feet. The punters had come to natter, drink and boogie to the consistently excellent live music pumping out from the four-piece jazz ensemble, onstage, for the listening pleasure of regulars and visitors alike, allowing any aficionados to indulge their Love of Jazz. Soulful tunes, mellow melodies – mostly danceable. Aside from the Chansons Française, the jazz band performed a bit of everything: Avant-jazz, Acid jazz, Bossa nova, Soul, Blues and Rock, and I understood the party would continue in full-swing straight into the early hours. I should single out the greatness of the saxophonist, smooth and sensual in his delivery. Many of the punters strutted their stuff on the dancefloor. Some of the older guys cut the rug with some of the younger ladies. I enjoyed foot-tapping to the jamming session.

Time flew by. Hayley got the next round, more champagne cocktails. It was nearly eleven when I was thinking we should head back to the hotel room since we would be leaving early tomorrow morning. Get some kip before catching the Eurostar back to England. A police officer had allegedly sodomized a young black man with his truncheon in a socioeconomically-deprived part of northern Paris and more riots were brewing. Marine Le Pen had already jumped on the bandwagon, using the incident to her own political advantage. I recalled my intensely-surreal, earlier dream of Putin sodomizing Trump and wondered how my mind could have conjured up something so deeply crazy. I thought it prudent to get out of Paris before the nights of public unrest encroached on the Gare du Nord.

All of a sudden, my Spidey sense was tingling. Something was wrong. I suddenly didn't feel well. As the jazz group played on, up on stage, and the punters danced the night away to the beat of the strobe lights, I felt sick, lightheaded, dizzy. Next to me, Hayley was watching me closely, intently, darkly. I saw malice in her eyes, a small, wicked smile on her lips. It bespoke vengeful satisfaction. Behind her, his hands on her shoulders as though giving her a massage, stood the very same man who had befriended us at Père Lachaise. Julien Étrange, leather coat and ponytail and all, seemed to take great pleasure at my misfortune, his lips, too, curled into a faint, triumphant smile. Except he wasn't entirely there. I could see through him, like one might see through a ghost. My vision swam and my mind relinquished its hold on reality.

I don't remember anything after that.

When I awoke, I wasn't at the jazz bar anymore. But I managed to correctly guess where I was.

Beneath this metropolis of twelve million people was a dark, subterranean world holding the remains of seven million of its former inhabitants. As the cemeteries overflowed by the end of the eighteenth century and the locals complained of the strong stench of decomposing flesh and the spread of diseases from the rotting corpses spilling out of the open graves, the long-dead were exhumed and transferred for reburial in the network of old caves, disused quarries and tunnels underneath the city, vaults strengthened, lighting adjusted, their remains blessed and consecrated. The bones of the dead were packed into the roofs and walls of the charnier's galleries, and the underground ossuaries eventually became a visitable mausoleum to satisfy the curiosity of the general public. This winding labyrinth stretched over two hundred miles, with only a small fraction open to visitors at PLACE DENFERT-ROCHEREAU, where one entered via the BARRIÈRE D'ENFER, or the GATE OF HELL. Collectively, this underground burial system was known as LES CATACOMBES DE PARIS.

I knew I was in the Catacombs because my immediate surrounds were filled with centuries of the Parisian dead, a regular bone repository. A collection of bones lined the walls in decorative patterns. I felt odd being so close to people who might have died during the Black Death. And I couldn't have felt more alone down here, like Gaston Leroux's Phantom. Maybe, in Paris, our lives *were*, indeed, one masked ball.

But these subterranean passageways held secrets much stranger than the skulls and femurs stacked in the walls. Once used by the French Resistance as a place of safety, this dark underworld nowadays served as a novel space for concerts and secret society meetings. It was also a frequent haunt for urban explorers known as 'Cataphiles', who accessed the Catacombs through secret entrances, wishing to escape the everyday hustle-and-bustle of city life above ground. These tomb raiders had illegally transformed some of the world below into creative spaces. In fact, where I found myself presently could be described as a 'creative space'. The underground cavern in my midst, regardless of the ornamental arrangement of medieval human bones set into the walls, had been converted into a secret amphitheatre, with a fully-equipped movie theatre. Directly ahead, was a giant, pull-up cinema screen, its projection equipment professionally installed into the ceiling, and I sat in the front row of audience-seating. I discovered the neighbouring area had been revamped into a fully-stocked bar and restaurant, complete with tables and chairs for the absent patrons. The source of the electrical power so far down into the earth remained an enigma. Various powerpoints around the cavern supplied the tripod floor-lamps, deliberately turned upwards so as to illuminate the ceiling in a playful crisscross of beams whilst casting a lambent blush on the rest of the auditorium. But the greater mystery was how my wife could have brought me down here all by herself.

And I realized it was the pain that had woken me up. The back of my ankles hurt like hell, and when I glanced down, I learned my Achilles' tendons had been slashed, my ankles bleeding steadily outwards with no sign of abating. Aside from the intense pain, I could feel the wooziness come on in waves, more a consequence of the extensive blood-loss, the emergence of shock, rather than the after-effects of the mickey Hayley had quietly slipped me in the jazz club. I wondered how much time had lapsed, how long I'd been out.

Then, as if by magic or remote control, the projector turned itself on and shone an image on the huge cinema screen, the image of my wife, wearing the fashionable black dress of this evening and standing in our hotel room. Apparently for my viewing pleasure only. My wife's huge presence on screen, like a beautiful figure from a dreamscape, made me think of Julien Nonnon's audacious street art, *Le Basier*, inspired by Alfred de Musset's timeless observation: *the only true language in the world is a kiss.* Nonnon managed to project long-exposure shots of kissing couples, whether young or old, straight or gay, white or black, across the public buildings of Paris, *Cinema Paradiso*-style, nocturnal screenings of a 'library of love'.

Presently, Hayley looked straight at the camera, straight at me, the single audience. A smile slowly spread across her face. Except there was no love in that smile, no prelude to a kiss, only a malicious look of triumph. The illusion was broken; this was not *Cinema Paradiso*, but the harder, darker stuff of HBO free-style. Even in my groggy state, what I caught in her expression was Schadenfreude: joy at another's misery.

Then, she spoke: "Hello, Manny. Surprised to see me? Surprised to find yourself *six* feet under?"

"What have you done to me?" I demanded to know.

As if she could hear me, she said: "After I spiked your drink with a date-rape drug, you did everything I told you to. You kindly walked down here without so much as a complaint. You protested not when I severed both your Achilles' heels –

you can't get very far now. On my instruction, you swallowed the rest of my father's old vial of warfarin, you know his blood thinner, which means you will either bleed to death or you will be eaten by the rats that are swarming towards you. Let's see what gets you first . . ."

Her words chilled me to the bone. My physical condition was worse than I had first suspected. Either physiological shock would claim me, as the blood continued to pool around my ankles. Or the rats, native to the Catacombs, attracted to the coppery scent of my blood. In a sense she had buried me down here. Very soon, the place would become my final resting place, my *tomb*.

Again, I addressed the screen. "Why?"

She answered my thoughts as though this were a live exchange, not something pre-recorded. Maybe she could genuinely read my thoughts or she had placed a microphone somewhere nearby. "Nobody crosses me the way you did!" she responded with swelling anger. "I *cannot* forgive you for calling the police on me! You cannot imagine the humiliation I suffered! Then, you put down my acting career when you know I'm about to become a famous movie star?"

You haven't even done the goddamned acting course yet, I wanted to scream at her but refrained. These were the truths she was not prepared to hear, living in her own 'Hayley's World'. On the surface, she was a competent housewife, sociable and pleasant if required, even affectionate, but underneath she could be a horrible person, selfish and uncaring, not particularly supportive or understanding of her husband's needs. All *Me-Me-Me*! And ever so spiteful . . .

How had it come to this? *This doesn't seem a fair and equitable solution to me,* I thought grimly. *Smash my car windows, file for divorce, get someone to beat me up, yes! Make a false accusation of rape, like I know you're so goddamned capable of! Are you telling me that wasn't make-up sex at all but hate sex?* I'd always thought I would die a lonely man one day and, before I met Hayley, I had reluctantly accepted the idea. Now I couldn't believe it would come to pass. *Let some other poor sucker suffer your burden and suffering! Always looking for the next best thing. You'll probably turn a blind eye to your next husband's affairs as long as you have access to all his wealth. Sorry I'm not a major success, a millionaire, if that's how shallow you are!*

"And I couldn't have done it without this man . . ." Hayley announced on screen, either not hearing my inner thoughts or deliberately *ignoring* them. The dark figure got up from the chair in the corner and slowly walked forward, eventually standing behind her. I was surprised I hadn't noticed him earlier. But now he could not be mistaken. Modest height. Sporting a ponytail below his baldness and dressed in a black leather jacket. The gypsy from the cemetery who had taken us to the graves of the dead celebrities, prophesized we would have twins and whose harbinger of a black cat had stalked us to the cemetery gates and invaded my dreams. Except, even now, Julien Étrange lacked absolute substance, appearing only as a spectral image, a conjuration. Perturbingly, I could see the outline of the bathroom door through his physical form. Like he was not completely *there*, just like he hadn't been there for that split-second at Père Lachaise. Étrange placed his right hand on Hayley's shoulder in a gesture of unity, but in his other hand rested the bronze statue of Dalí's *Surrealist Eyes*, its cuboid stack of multitudinous eyes, to my further growing horror, alive and moving and seeing. "My new agent-and-manager! Jules has agreed to advertise my talents and manage my impending fame!"

What talents? What fame, *for chrissakes? And weren't you at loggerheads with this man at the cemetery?* The woman sounded deluded. But was my wife really the deluded one? I was seeing ghosts. Figments of emotional unrest, visual manifestations of my dark imaginings. Pope Francis once said: *Wretched are those who are vindictive and spiteful.* I remembered her jealousy about her four-year-old sister getting into the shower with her mother, driving Hayley mad, a jealousy greater than mere sibling rivalry. I remembered Hayley telling how her best friend in school could have no other friends but her. I had wondered how she would get her revenge on me, and now I knew. She had given me a false sense of security, kept her cards close to her chest. And her spite had done the rest, let loose and amplified. So consumed by spite had she been and her desire for revenge, she had given Étrange unnatural life. Magicked him up, made him real. *For Étrange was the personification of her spite.* Her creation, her invention, brought to vivid life. The embodiment of her hatred towards me, whispering venomous opinions into her ear. Hell hath no fury and all that. Indeed, as Hamlet said: *The time is out of joint. O cursèd spite, / That ever I was born to set it right!* Hayley's spite had been festering inside her, mushrooming to monstrous proportions, until it had spilled over into a supernatural force of its own. Maybe it was only I who saw him for what he was. Or perhaps it was all inside my head. I thought of everything that had come before. Were any of her actions without contempt, without premeditation?

Hayley brought the film reel to a close. Whereas Jules remained expressionless, still comfortably carrying the weight of the bronze, alien composite of living, expressive human eyes in the palm of his hand, Hayley offered me a brief farewell wave with a pointed, unmerciful pronouncement. "Just goes to me to say it was nice knowing you . . . and I sincerely hope you *suffer* all the way to your last breath..." Then, the projector shut down of its own accord, and I was once again alone with my thoughts.

My throat was as dry as parchment, my stomach burned with acid and my heart felt light and fluttery. My senses were still intact, but I knew they wouldn't be for too long. Even sitting up was now becoming an effort, particularly with the onset of dizziness. With my strength ebbing away from my body, I gradually slid off the theatre-seat and tumbled to the floor. I tried to rise, stand up, but the pain in my ankles exploded up my calves as my life-blood continued to flow relentlessly out, laced by a potent anticoagulant. Besides, with the ruptured tendons, my ankles were now useless, incapable of carrying my weight.

I cried for help, but my voice only bounced off the walls and echoed back. I began crawling, painfully, towards the bar in the adjoining cavern, hoping to find a cold one to extinguish my thirst.

The rats were coming . . .

Like vampires, they could smell my blood. Rats were still the scourge of Paris, a matter of public health as the authorities tried to unsuccessfully tackle the French capital's growing vermin problem. In recent years, the rats had grown bolder and more aggressive, pouring out of dustbins and attacking refuse collectors, invading school playgrounds. They say there are two rats to every Parisian.

Indeed, Paris had a lot of rats.

Regardless of my blurring vision, I thought I could see them, a mischief of rats emerging from the darkness of the tunnels, tiny paws scuttling across the floor, big, black, beady eyes catching predatory sight of their helpless victim, nose twitching to the enticing direction of my blood . . .

Should I pity her? Should I pity Hayley?

No, she might resent me for pitying her. Neither should I be mad at her. She would always be unhappy, but I genuinely hoped she would find happiness some day. Might I one day make her happy and proud of me and make her more secure about herself? I may have begun our tale in a cemetery, but I certainly did not want it to end in the catacombs.

It dawned to me. *To err is human, to forgive is divine.*

Forgiveness was the sweetest, kindest revenge in any dire, spiteful circumstance.

That was the plan. *And the hope.*

As the rats came in their horde and crawled all over my body and plunged their tiny, vicious incisors into my flesh, jumping at my throat, knowing I was about to die in this cave of bones that doubled as an improbable cinema and would soon become my underground sepulchre, I decided to forgive Hayley. *Absolutely, I forgive you, my darling, with all my heart . . .*

A loving interlude.

I was back in bed with Hayley. On the advent of Valentine's Day. Like the clock had somehow reset itself. I checked to see I wasn't bleeding and if my Achilles' heels were still intact . . . only to discover all was well with the world, again.

Hayley reached forward and kissed me.

"You're very affectionate this morning, my darling," I said, encouraged by her kiss.

"I've got to make the most of you before you pop off . . ."

Her joke should have disturbed me, my memory still clinging on to the catacombs and the blood and the rats. Except it didn't. Despite her flaws – *oh, toxic spite!* – she was the woman I married. The woman I loved. "You're amazing. And you're going to be even more amazing. And I'm going to help you achieve your dreams."

She smiled at my comment, confirming her elevated position in my esteem, and kissed me lovingly. "I keep thinking back to how you proposed to me . . ." she murmured, thinking back to a happier time, a sweet reminiscence. "You were so romantic . . ."

Indeed. One of my finest moments. And I decided to do a repeat of that special moment. Just as I did the first time, I planned to drop Hayley off at the local recreation park in pursuit of clues I had left around the park, a photograph of us together with an item of removed clothing next to each sentimental object until her hunt led her to a gazebo I had set up in a field earlier. She would find me inside, kneeling down on one knee, completely naked . . . and I would propose to her. "Would you like to marry me *again* or shall we call it a day?" And, after our original betrothal, we had made love in the tall grass without getting caught or arrested for public exposure. I hoped she would never forget. I wanted to capture that old magic. "I still am . . . romantic, that is."

I suppose I could do something even more enduring, something that might last even when I'm gone. Maybe I could leave Hayley little messages of love around the house, scribbled on Post-it Notes or gift cards, hidden away for her to chance upon, keeping our romance alive. I sometimes imagine being dead, and Hayley finding an old message scrawled on the bathroom mirror when it mists over: SHMILY. Which stands for *See How Much I Love You.*

Flaubert occupied himself with exploring the deep, inscrutable mysteries of women: *The hearts of women are like those little pieces of furniture with secret hiding places, full of drawers fitted into each other, you go in, break your nails, find in the bottom some withered flowers, a few grains of dust – or emptiness.* I thanked my lucky stars for this second chance, pulled back from the brink, and all I wanted to do was reinvigorate those flowers, bring them back to bloom. Remedy our problems by doing justice to Valentine's Day with acts of generosity and love and devotion that defined the romantic season, with Spring just around the corner. Flaubert further compared Love to a springtime plant that perfumed everything with hope, even the ruins to which it clung. Of Spring, Maupassant described: *When the first fine spring days come, and the earth awakes and assumes its garment of verdure, when the perfumed warmth of the air blows on our faces and fills our lungs, and even appears to penetrate to our heart, we feel vague longings for undefined happiness, a wish to run, to walk at random, to inhale the spring.* Quoting that old stalwart, Henry Miller: *When spring comes to Paris the humblest mortal alive must feel that he dwells in paradise.*

Let's get to the point. Maybe my mission in life was to make my wife happy. Wait for Spring to come, the season of hope, of renewal and rebirth. Let her abandon her acting when she realized it wasn't for her, dropping out of the course after blaming her tutors for constantly and unfairly singling her out. Instead, we celebrated the springtime of our love, our renaissance. Hayley agreed to us renewing our marital vows in church with our closest and dearest family and friends in attendance and took to raising the twins she was destined to give birth to, full-time, with a remarkable commitment and a different, sharper focus I never thought she had. Yes, *twins* as foretold, double the trouble. Hayley proved to be an excellent mother and everything a wife should be, and the birth of our son and daughter on the heels of our second wedding ceremony healed our relationship.

Our marriage had been on the rocks and we had gone to Paris to patch things up. And we had achieved something better than reconciliation. Paris had done more than just reinvigorate our love for each other. *Oh, the magic of Paris!*

I knew, during that miraculous moment of waking up again on Valentine's Day, nothing would ever come between us and we would be together forever.

With the resurgence of my love for her, we never looked back and went from strength to strength, no longer counting the years but making the years count. Our newborns now toddlers, my writing career revitalized, flourished, and my wife rented a gallery for the evening and launched an exhibition with a portfolio of her most surreal paintings. Credit to her, she had learned to successfully sublimate her spitefulness into her art, and the short-statured, leather-clad gypsy from the graveyard haunted her work, his dark presence a recurring theme in her paintings, appearing whenever she felt like saying jaggy things to hurt others she didn't like.

It may feel deliciously satisfying to punish someone we feel has wronged us. But the urge can become so powerful that it can, if left unchecked by reason, spiral to self-destructive extremes.

Because Spite has eyes, *many* eyes, and gazing upon its multifaceted, abhorrent glare, one can see the vile sickness within its victim, permeating the sufferer's very being, demolishing their soul in a ravenous, self-feeding frenzy, as though the person has consciously swallowed a chalice of deadly poison in hateful and mistaken anticipation of the horrible death of the one they most vehemently despise.

Spite's darkest paradox.

JOYEUSE SAINT-VALENTIN!

February 2017-December 2017

Hebe on the Make

'For, like desire, regret seeks not to be analysed but to be satisfied. When one begins to love, one spends one's time, not in getting to know what one's love really is, but in making it possible to meet next day. When one abandons love one seeks not to know one's grief but to offer to her who is causing it that expression of it which seems to one the most moving. One says the things which one feels the need of saying, and which the other will not understand, one speaks for oneself alone. I wrote: 'I thought that it would not be possible. Alas, I see that it is not so difficult.' I said also: 'I shall probably not see you again.' I said it while I continued to avoid showing a coldness which she might think affected, and the words, as I wrote them, made me weep because I felt that they expressed not what I should have liked to believe but what was probably going to happen.'

In the Shadow of Young Girls in Flower (1919)

Marcel Proust

Six Roses: I want to be yours.

1

Provence. Ah, yes, Provence!

Myles Hawking could not believe his good fortune. He couldn't believe he was back here, in Provence, after so many years away. He hadn't been to Provence since he and his older sister were still in primary school, accompanying their parents on a fortnight's holiday. Back in the day when time had no meaning and the summer days were hot and long and seemed to stretch on forever, with no sight of a new term on the horizon. Even then, it was the best holiday he had ever been on abroad, meeting the French people, who were greatly despised by the

English, yet for whom the English also harboured a secret respect for being smarter, more fashionable and way *cooler* than them. France was a self-contained country, its inhabitants self-sufficient, a nation who needed nobody else. And, outside of Paris, Provence was where all the posh, cultured and creative French types went.

From its craggy limestone peaks and salt marshes to its vineyards and lavender fields, Provence was one of the most popular tourist destinations the world over, offering nourishment for the mind, body and soul, a place of good living and the home of the mistral wind, which cleared the sky and dried the air, providing sunshine all year long, with the temperature rarely dropping below sixteen degrees Celsius in the winter months. Provence had a history harking back to the Romans, as evidenced by many of its buildings and ancient ruins. Another constant throughout the region, permeating every town and village, was the food and drink, sun-ripened and full-flavoured. Nothing artificial about the food here, as a lot of tourists would attest and exactly how Myles remembered it from his youth. Provençal, derived from the Occitan language and closely related to Catalan, was spoken only by the very elderly population these days, when it was once the language of the troubadours. Some of the greatest and his most favourite writers, such as Edith Wharton and Somerset Maugham, had lived and set some of their finest stories here. *Tender is the Night*, a semi-autobiographical final novel by F. Scott Fitzgerald, told the twisted tale of a psychoanalyst and his wife, a former patient, who both move to the South of France, their turbulent relationship impacting greatly on the husband, who drifts deeper and deeper into his own insecurities and neuroses, gradually descending into a state of insignificance. Another fine work of literature included Hemingway's posthumously-published *The Garden of Eden*, the story of a couple honeymooning in the French Riviera who end up in a *ménage à trois* with another woman, leading to the eventual downfall of their marriage. Lawrence Durrell authored the Avignon 'Quincunx', a curious and rather odd collection of five loosely-connected novels comprising elements involving Nazi-occupied Provence, Gnosticism, Grail lore and Quantum Physics, bearing the mind-blowing stamp of metafiction while other times containing the controversial patter of explicit sexual language. It would be much later, however, before Peter Mayle truly put Provence on the map. *I think that's what people do,* Myles remembered telling his sister before setting off. *Spend a year in Provence just like in that Mayle semi-autobiography. Rent somewhere cheap and decide after a year whether Provence is the place to live out the rest of your life.*

Provence held a special place in the history of motion pictures, courtesy of the

Lumière brothers, as far back as the first short film of that train pulling into the station of La Ciotat and freaking out the audience who'd seen nothing like it before, believing that the train would leap out of the screen and mow them down. The more recent French films, *Jean de Florette* and *Manon des Sources*, captured the idyllic quality of Provence beautifully as did the big-screen adaptations of the Marcel Pagnol novels, *La Gloire de Mon Père* and *Le Château de Ma Mère*. In Myles' opinion, Provence really was like those films. Provence had also attracted some of the greatest painters of all time, including Cézanne, Renoir, Matisse, Van Gogh, Braque and Picasso, interpreting Provence with their own unique, artistic vision.

Myles had dreamed of living in Provence since those sweltering summer holidays long ago and, as he presently took up his appointment as an English teacher in an international all-girl's boarding school in Mazan, he knew those boyhood dreams were about to be realized.

So, passport and visa in hand, he flew economy class to Marseille-Provence Airport before hiring a small car, a blue Renault Clio, which would take him to NOTRE-DAME DES DOULEURS: *ÉCOLE, COLLÈGE ET LYCÉE INTERNAT PRIVÉS*. The airport was forty minutes from Marseilles itself, but Myles suppressed the urge to visit this sultry metropolis, the second largest city in the country, with its stunning contemporary architecture and boasting one of the oldest trading ports in Europe, colonized by the Greeks two-thousand-five-hundred years ago. Marseilles was home to the French Connection and the unbeatable fish stew, bouillabaisse. No, Myles was focused on getting to his new digs. While his closest friends were honeymooning up north in Normandy, he dearly hoped to sample the cuisine and culture of the South of France. The French radio station, NRJ, chugged out local and foreign dance hits that accompanied him on the journey down. And the weather was typical for this time of year, hot and baking, in the mid-thirties. The summer months had given way to early autumn, but the sun had no intention of letting up.

Speeding through the highways, then taking a much gentler approach through the well-signposted towns and villages, Myles followed the sat-nav to Mazan, nestled at the foot of Mont Ventoux in the *Département* of Vaucluse, a region which embodied all that was good about Provence. It was the weekend before the start of the new academic year.

Located on Chemin de Pied Marin № 3, his place of lodgings was a beautiful, eighteenth-century, honey-coloured stone villa with mature gardens filled with trees and fragrant bushes. It was furnished in a country style, capturing the charm of a bygone era, giving the overwhelming impression that one was stepping backwards in time. The single-storey, rural retreat housed a living room with a cantou fireplace, adjoining a beamed dining room, across from a farmhouse kitchen complete with an Aga. The floors were antique terracotta, and the walls were rough plaster on stone. The rustic décor provided a neutral canvas for the continental furniture and ornaments: bouillottes, confit pots, clocks, bronze statues, framed oil paintings. Myles unpacked his belongings in the bedroom, down the hallway, towards the rear of the property, its French windows overlooking a young, lovingly-tended olive garden. There was even a hammock stretched across two plane trees. The swimming pool down a narrow, steep embankment belonged to the house, but it was currently out of use and empty. The bathroom, with its deep, free-standing bath, seemed to be a haven for tiny, red spiders, which Myles didn't mind. At the front of the house was a wooden veranda where he intended to spend his evenings relaxing, enjoying some outdoor dining accompanied by a glass of Côtes du Rhône. He did precisely that on the Sunday of his arrival, sitting outside, amidst the scent of juniper, rosemary and wild thyme, alongside the shrill buzz of cicadas, in preparation for the day ahead. The school owned the residence and other similar properties along this particular stretch of road, rented out at a reasonable price to those staff who did not wish to lodge in the staff quarters at the boarding school.

Myles hoped to do a great deal of sightseeing outside of work, maybe take weekend trips to the various neighbouring Provençal towns. This *was* a dream come true as he looked back on those endless summers of childhood spent caravanning in the hot, heady climes of Provence-Alpes-Côte d'Azur. Myles felt like his outsider had just won the races.

But first he needed to officially meet his new employers, his colleagues and his pupils, clarify his teaching responsibilities.

Tomorrow, he thought contentedly, *I will get to know them tomorrow*. At the back of his mind a forbidding voice rose to the fore in a warning reminder: *And, please, let's avoid a repeat of your last school posting.*

2

"How's the new job?" Carmain Fiske asked him over the phone the following evening.

"Going great," Myles informed his big sister, at relative peace with the world.

He sat outside on the veranda of the villa, soaking up the early evening sun, having dined on duck confit and lentils. Duck was popular in these parts. Once again, he was amazed how everything here had flavour, unlike back home, where everything tasted artificial and bland. It had been a good first day. Notre-Dame des Douleurs, cradled in the herb-fragranced hills, had turned out to be a converted Cistercian monastery, an impressive fourteenth-century building of international gothic design, with walls of thick stone worn over time, its roof laden with gargoyles. Historically, the monastery had fallen into disrepair when the French revolutionaries had tyrannized the noble families of the region, forcing them to migrate, and closed down the churches and abolished worship, expelling the local priests, forcing them to say Mass in secret, until Napoleon reclaimed the country and re-established Christianity, with the former hard-hit Mazanais flocking back to their prohibited sacraments.

The lobby and main hall were decked with marble floors, the stone walls housing a gallery of paintings by Alexis Peyrotte, one-time painter to the King, as well as a couple of tombs and a host of beautiful statues of angels and seraphim from the masterful hands of Mazan's other son, Jacques Bernus, whose many other works were exhibited in the local Church of Pareloup. Glass cabinets showcased winners' trophies of lacrosse, netball and cross-country. Echoey, high-ceilinged classrooms were the norm at Notre-Dame des Douleurs, the Louis XVI furniture elegantly carved and resting on cabriole legs, and the cells of the former monks transformed into student dorm-rooms. Remarkable how this house of spiritual worship now served as a prestigious seat of academic excellence, and with so many young ladies in attendance, one might have even called it a 'prieuré'. Indeed, it was an impressive place to work, as renowned as any preparatory or international finishing school, with its pupils travelling here from far and wide. Mme. Marguerite Renard, the distinguished headmistress, whose family apparently descended from the old Conseigneuries, some of them as far back as the days of the Comtat Venaissin, introduced the new English teacher at the morning assembly, and Myles' presence was well-received by his pupils.

"I'm definitely getting back into the swing of things after being away so long," Myles told Carmain. "How are you and the little ones?"

"All good," Carmain replied. "Erin has passed the Terrible Twos and is now into the Troublesome Threes. Quite a handful, actually, but very happy. Elena has comfortably settled into Nursery School, but she remains forever jealous of her little sister, always bidding for my attention. Frank's still busy with his police work. He's a detective-in-training now." She decided to tell him about events on her street. "A word to the wise about the bus stop: a pinch point. Police have increased their vigilance in the area. I incurred a fifty-pound fine for making an illegal left turn. Can you imagine I've never had so much as a parking fine *and* my husband's a policeman? The stopping officer pointed out that it was a traffic violation. No idea why the prohibition is there, but clearly someone decided years ago that we need to pollute the atmosphere more by driving another mile or so, instead of a few metres."

"That's life for you!"

"A part of me envies you. The whole purpose of living abroad is to meet new people and experience exciting adventures."

Myles spotted a trail of ants crawling in organized file on the veranda. He caught the drone of a bumblebee as it visited the various potted flowers. Every so often he batted away the chiggers, which were proving a particular nuisance at night. The cicadas buzzed shrilly. "I feel like a kid again. It's like I've been granted a new lease of life. Provence has so much history. Here, everything has a story, a tale to tell."

"Happy travels."

"Thanks."

"How are the students treating you?"

"Incredibly well-behaved and quietly respectful of me."

"I genuinely hope it all works out for you at your new school, and you can put aside that awful business back home . . ."

There, she said it. Myles knew she would mention it at some point. He hadn't worked at any school since he was a young, newly-qualified teacher, almost five years ago, himself a nominal few years older than the students he was teaching. He hadn't had a full-time post or done anything substantial in terms of career development following the scandal involving that Lovemore girl at his last school. Of course, what the girl had alleged had never been substantiated, but his probity and integrity had been called into question, forever logged on his record, a black mark to his name even if nothing was ever proven. The Lovemore girl had sullied his reputation terribly, nearly made him unemployable. The fact that his sister was a shrewd Safeguarding Nurse, able to defend his character, had helped his case immensely. Myles had since survived on the measly earnings from providing private tuition *ad hoc* to those families who were not aware of his chequered past, with every school application rejecting his services until he chanced upon an ad seeking an English teacher at Notre-Dame des Douleurs. He had admittedly been somewhat economical with the truth which is why he'd managed to secure the job. And nobody knew him abroad. Even to this day, the emotional baggage he carried from that vulnerable time weighed down on him greatly. But he was hopeful. "I intend to turn the page, start a new chapter in my life and forget about the nightmare of yesteryear."

"Please do just that and I wish you every success in your new job."

Myles glimpsed a small, green lizard scurrying away into the undergrowth. "Thanks, Carmain." He paused for a moment, wondering how he should express the disquiet in the pit of his stomach. "It's just the syllabus that I'm slightly stressing about."

"What do you mean?"

"Most of the English syllabus is your usual, bog-standard secondary school stuff, except for one aspect of it."

"What aspect is that?"

Myles thought of that old, sinister Matthew Lewis novel, *The Monk*. He could identify with Ambrosio's humble, highly-respected character before his fall from grace and eventual descent into insanity and *hell*, all on the heels of earthly temptation. "God must be testing me . . . or the Devil mocking me. Ironically enough, they want me to teach *Lolita* . . ."

3

Lolita was not one of Myles' favourite books. He knew it well, all its minutiae – any good English teacher should know the book well – but he hardly considered himself a huge fan of its controversial subject matter. Somehow it hit too close to home. He felt uncomfortable with the idea of himself, a male teacher, teaching its very sensitive themes to a classroom full of adolescent girls. Call him a traditionalist, but Charlotte Brontë's *The Professor* would have been a better bet, a more literary work for study, tried-and-tested. But a job was a job and he just had to be professional about it. Psychologists would tell you that avoidance was a bad thing, self-perpetuating any existing anxiety. Besides, Notre-Dame des Douleurs was an international school renowned for its forward-thinking and near-one-hundred-percent Baccalauréat pass rate. Mme. Renard had advised him to teach the book to his students without holding anything back since his charges were in the transition to adulthood anyway and the school prided itself as a centre of progressive learning. Furthermore, a more detailed exposé of the book would have greater impact on their hungry minds and generate a wider degree of reflection and discussion. Analytical thinking and creativity were greatly nurtured and highly-prized commodities in the French education system.

"For those of you who are unfamiliar with Vladimir Nabokov's *Lolita*, and I'll be very surprised if there's any of you who don't know the book,"–which raised a few chuckles–"*Lolita* combines parody and pathos, the comic and the tragic, with the erotic complications of a very dark love story between a grown man and a pubescent girl, chronicling its tender, romantic beginnings to its ruthless, tyrannical extreme, how obsessive love can soon descend into absolute possessiveness in the most disturbing way possible. Yet, there is a chance at redemption in the end, the emergence of insight and remorse. We shall explore the first ten chapters this week. I think a summary of this should set you on your way."

Myles began: "The book opens with a foreword written by a psychiatrist, who has been tasked with editing the manuscript authored by an accused murderer, whom he reports has suffered a fatal heart attack in prison whilst awaiting trial. The psychiatrist defends the content of the manuscript against charges of indecency and claims it will become essential reading in psychoanalytic circles.

"We then proceed with the actual tale, a first-person narrative of an émigré professor writing under the double-talk pseudonym, Humbert Humbert, who turns out to be a very eloquent but ambiguous and unreliable narrator, expressing his regret for and yet celebrating his love for Lolita. These first ten chapters assigned to you, class, will take you from Humbert Humbert's origins – born in Paris in 1910, of Anglo-French heritage – all the way up to his discovery of Lolita in 1947.

"It is revealed that, at thirteen, Humbert experienced his first love affair, with a girl of similar age named Annabel Leigh, who would die a premature death four months later from Typhus. He never gets over his love for Annabel and remains constantly haunted by her memory, of their shared episode of interrupted coitus and his feelings of unfulfilled lust, until he later finds her essence 'reincarnated' in Lolita in small-town America. He continues to describe his early years in Europe, where he studied English Literature and became a teacher, a poet and a dilettante, but he always seemed drawn to young girls of a certain age between nine and fourteen, maidens on the edge of puberty, whom he affectionately refers to as 'nymphets'. However, he chooses a more conventional existence in the hope it will inspire him to develop a more moral character. He marries for the first time, but his wife leaves him for a taxi driver and ultimately dies in childbirth.

"Humbert Humbert moves to the United States, at the start of World War II, and after a short spell in a mental institution, he seeks refuge in a sleepy New England town called Ramsdale, where he rents a room from a pretentious, vacuous widow going by the name of Charlotte Haze but *not* before clapping eyes on her twelve-year-old, gum-chewing, Coke-guzzling, comic-book-addicted, precocious-brat-of-a-daughter, known as 'Lo' to her mother, 'Dolly' to her friends, 'Dolores' on the dotted line, but always 'Lolita' to Humbert. And he soon discovers that his own darkly handsome looks resemble those of some singer/actor on whom Lolita has a schoolgirl crush. And so the story proper begins . . ." Myles paused. "Any questions, ladies?"

The classroom was hot and stuffy. The sun streamed in through the partially-opened, stained-glass windows, splashing rich, vibrant colours on the floor. No pupil raised their hands to volunteer any questions. Myles was satisfied. His synopsis must have proved self-explanatory. "The first ten chapters it is, then. Class dismissed."

After class, Myles strolled across the grounds of the school in the bright afternoon sunshine. The groundskeeper did a thorough job of keeping the lawns well-tended just as housekeeping did a spankingly-good job of keeping the inside of the school immaculate. He passed juniper bushes and a herb garden of rosemary, sage and wild thyme, essential ingredients in the kitchen. The students claimed conspiratorially that grand Artemisia grew there too, which the chef used to cook his own illegal absinthe, allegedly. Myles crossed the sports' field with its athletics' track and passed a field of poppies and bluebells before entering the wilder, wooded aspect of the school estate, replete with stunted holm oaks, plane trees, larches and Atlas cedars, perfect for relaxing walks and picnic lunches.

Somewhere in these woods was a truffle orchard, one of the school's most prized possessions. Sunlight dappled the woodland floor, the air fragrant with floral scents. As he walked on, he heard a female voice call out his name from behind him accompanied by the approach of running footsteps. "Wait up, Mr. Hawking!"

Myles twisted round, took a gander. He recognized the girl as one of the pupils in his class. Her long, platted blond hair bounced up and down as she ran, her blue eyes fixed on him. She was still dressed in her maroon school uniform. "Hello. It's Charlotte Heymans, isn't it?"

"Charlotte . . . but I prefer 'Lottie' best."

"What can I do for you, Lottie?" Myles asked.

She caught up with him. "I just need to ask a big favour from you."

"Which is?"

"Can you give me extra tuition after school?"

Myles hesitated. It was a long pause. He considered her request, formulated a response. "I've looked over your work, assessed your ability. It's more than satisfactory. You have an aptitude for English. Why do you feel you need the extra help?"

They were walking now, the pace more leisurely and relaxed. "I would like to write a book, which I hope to get published some day soon. It takes the form of a diary actually."

"Ah, the old epistolary novel," Myles said, his mind drifting back to pleasanter times. "Some of the greatest works of literature were built around a series of letters and such correspondence, diary excerpts, newspaper clippings, ships' logs, telegrams and other documents to string together a story – *Frankenstein*, *Dracula*, *The Screwtape Letters*, *Fanny Hill*, *The Moonstone*, *The Tenant of Wildfell Hall* and *Les Liaison Dangereuses*, to name but a few – the purpose of which was to provide a greater degree of realism to the story with the inclusion of differing points of view, mimic the workings of real life. The epistolary novel fell out of fashion until it was revived in the 1980s with the likes of Adrian Mole and, more recently, through Bridget Jones. It is still not considered the most popular form of prose." Then, Myles inquired: "What's your story about?"

"It concerns the relationship between a teacher and his pupil."

Myles stopped walking. That disquieting sensation was back in the depths of his stomach. "What made you choose that particular subject?"

"I got the idea from the story that you're teaching in class: *Lolita*. It's along the same lines, except mine would be a collection of Dear Diaries. I have always aspired to be a writer and I was hoping I might use some of your insights into the English language, spend some time with you, *learn*."

Lottie was a likeable girl, good-looking, smart, intelligently-spoken, *ambitious*. It should be his duty to assist her in her noble quest, but it was way too early in his teaching post for him to be providing one-to-one supplementary lessons. He let her down gently. "I'm afraid I don't see a need to see someone as able as you more frequently than is necessary. He added, rather vaguely: "Besides I'm rather busy out of hours . . . got so many things to do . . . ."

"Please, it would help me greatly . . ."

Myles reconsidered, compromised. "I'll see what I can do. I'm keen to set up a weekly Book Club so more girls interested in reading and writing like yourself can join. I will speak with the Headmistress tomorrow." Lottie's face dropped. "Don't despair, just pay attention in my class and you'll turn into a wonderful author!"

The disappointed look did not leave her face. "I'll be speaking with my father..." she said, mysteriously. Myles detected the hint of a threat.

"Up to you. If there's nothing else, I shall be on my way. Keep up the good work."

"Okay, Mr Hawking, have a pleasant evening," she said distractedly and headed back the way she had come.

Myles could not escape the disappointment in her voice. He had a sense that it wasn't the last he'd heard from her on the subject.

4

Myles was one of only two male teachers at the school, the other being M. Alphonse Garance, who bore more than a disconcerting resemblance to Alan Rickman of Slytherin House. Still, all men should stick together. They got talking in the staff-room and the conversation drifted to the history of Mazan.

Myles was able to learn much more about Mazan from M. Garance's musings, and he went out exploring his locale. There were only five thousand inhabitants in the whole of Mazan, suggesting it was more of a village than a town. The old town was protected by a circled wall of buildings, and the gates of its ramparts dated back to the fourteenth century. Mazan consisted, like so many places in Provence, of narrow streets of old houses, most of their windows shuttered against the afternoon sunshine. A unique sight in Mazan was the ALLÉE DES SARCHOPHAGES: a cemetery surrounded by a series of sixty-six Gallo-Roman stone sarcophagi. *A necropolis for vampires*, M. Garance joked in typical Professor Snape fashion. Aside from all the famous lords and consuls who had taken up residence in this neck of the woods, Mazan was also de Sade country. The Marquis de Sade was probably the most famous – and notorious – Mazanais. Condemned for his libertine sexuality, the Marquis de Sade subsequently held private theatrical productions at the Château de Lacoste in the days he was considered vaguely sane before he fled the country following a series of depraved incidents involving local women and ended up being committed to Charenton Asylum at the edict of Napoleon. The CHÂTEAU DE MAZAN, formerly the de Sade family home, now functioned as a very charming and elegant luxury hotel. The Auzon River flowed through the village, its rolling plains providing rich farmland devoted to agriculture and wine-growing. Pine forests offered memorable country walks along its small roads. Agricultural wealth had been achieved by cherries, olives, silkworm, madder, hemp and vine, broken briefly through the ages by plague and famine, which had severely decimated the commune before it found its footing again. The famous Côtes du Ventoux was a cooperative winery of nine private cellars offering guided tours and wine-tasting, of which CAVE LES VIGNERONS DE CANTERPEDRIX was situated in the town centre of Mazan. Of some note, the English actress, Kiera Knightley had got married in Mazan town hall, Myles reminded his sister on the phone that weekend.

Across the fountain in the square, situated diagonally from the Romanesque medieval church was the MUSÉE HISTORIQUE ET FOLKLORIQUE DE MAZAN. It was a small, cosy, unassuming building. Under a beautiful mural ceiling, it housed everything from geological specimens to stuffed birds. There was mining equipment on display, old farming implements and war memorabilia, such as gas masks and helmets. The place captured the religious arts and crafts, showcasing various curios and delicate figurines. Prehistoric artefacts such as old fossils rested alongside stamps and coins. One particular noteworthy archaeological find was a Gallo-Roman skeleton. Such was the gentleness of the mother and daughter, the apparent owners, Myles made a small donation to them for their troubles and a very enlightening tour.

Stepping out into the early evening sunshine, Myles stopped in his tracks when he saw Lottie standing there between the ruins of the low stone wall and the ancient kiln. "Hello, Mr. Hawking."

"Hello Lottie," Myles replied when he had overcome his initial surprise and his speech came back. "Are you following me?"

"Not intentionally. I just wanted to know if you've thought about my request."

"Indeed I have," he replied, nodding slowly. His mind went back to the conversation with Mme. Renard. She had ushered him into her office after class, and informed him that M. Piers Heymans, Lottie's father, had contacted her, gravely concerned that the school wasn't paying enough attention to Lottie's academic needs. M. Heymans had made his wealth from investment banking and had a very formidable reputation. His daughter had spoken to him and informed him, rather distressed, that her English teacher had turned down her proposal for more educational support, and he was not happy about it. Mme. Renard reassured him at great length that her English teacher would take his daughter under his wing. She therefore explained to Mr. Hawking that it was imperative that he spend more time with the girl, work with her and turn her into whatever her father wanted her to be: a young writer of great distinction. She added that M. Heymans was willing to make a sizable donation to the school as well as pay Mr. Hawking handsomely for his additional services. Much as Myles wanted to help her out, it was not his intention to fraternize with the young ladies. *Do you think that's wise?* he asked the headmistress, a genuinely pertinent question. *Our hands are tied,* she had told him. *It is now down to you to teach Mlle. Heymans all the tricks of the trade.* "I will stick with my personal view on the matter, but I think we can proceed with your plan," he told Lottie, presently. "Your father's a very influential and persuasive man, not someone who's used to being declined."

"My father won't take 'no' for an answer particularly where his little girl is concerned. He always gets his way."

"As do you, it would appear."

Lottie didn't respond to the remark.

They wandered down the narrow streets, arrived at LA PIZZÉRIA DE MAZAN, a reputable place to dine, offering lovely pizzas, a choice permutation on a limited selection of pizza toppings, although their grills were also good. Duck was on the menu. The diabolo strawberry syrup and lemonade slaked all thirst.

It seemed Lottie was keen to join her teacher for dinner. "I hope you don't mind," she said, inviting herself to the table.

"Do I have a choice?"

Lottie's smile informed him he didn't. "Promise I won't impose on you again, unnecessarily." She chose a thin-crust pizza, Myles plumped for grilled duck and feta cheese salad.

He decided to find out more about the book he had been strong-armed into helping write. "What's the title of your book?"

"*Hebe on the Make,*" she replied openly.

Myles reflected on the title, frowning. It was a very clever and oh-so-risqué title. Definitely eye-catching. *Provocative.* "How did you come up with the title?"

She told him she was studying Classics as well as English Literature and History. She had gained top marks in her Brevet examinations. She wasn't lying. Myles had investigated her academic record so as to know what he was dealing with. "Hebe was the goddess of youth, representing purity and the innocence of childhood, the keeper of the Fountain of Youth, the personification of everlasting life. She was also the daughter of Zeus and handmaiden to her mother, Hera, preparing the royal chariot and carrying out her duty of being cupbearer to the Olympian gods, serving them chalices of nectar and ambrosia, until she married Hercules, the Protector of Olympus."

Myles was a Classicist in his own right. "I am quite familiar with Hebe. She had the ability to restore youthfulness and renew life. She is always seen in the presence of an eagle – or more precisely, a phoenix. She reminds us to look after the magical child in all of us." He went on to ask: "And the plot of the book?"

"Through a series of Dear Diaries, exchange of letters and emails and texts, we learn that a schoolgirl in a private boarding school is carrying on an affair with her teacher until the affair is discovered and all hell breaks loose."

The notoriety of the plot almost left Myles at a loss for words. *Talk about close to home!* Here he was discussing a story that was bound to raise disapproving eyebrows and sharing a meal at a public pizza parlour with this obviously ambitious and very demanding schoolgirl, who planned on penning it. He suddenly felt very self-conscious. "I would either call you bold and audacious or naive and stupid."

Lottie took his remark as a compliment. "I hope you can help me turn it into bestselling material."

"I'll see what I can do. But don't expect too much."

5

Lottie had proved herself a worthy young lady of letters having completed and scored top marks in the spot comprehension test for the class covering the first ten chapters of *Lolita*.

Myles decided to move on to the next stage of the book, summarizing the key elements: "Humbert Humbert obsessively records his every encounter with Lolita and admires everything about her: her oppositionality and general disobedience towards her mother, her clothes, the way she sunbathes in the garden. The scene where she stretches her legs on his excited lap is described in achingly vivid detail. In the meantime, Charlotte Haze makes plans to send her daughter away to summer camp which distresses Humbert. Then he receives a note from the maid, written in a childish scrawl. It is a confession: *I Love You.* Except he is horrified to discover it is not from Lolita but her vapid mother, who informs him that he must either marry her or move out to avoid a scandal. So Humbert marries Charlotte Haze only in order to be near her daughter. He knows a stepfather would have closer access to Lolita than a mere lodger. At the same time, he plots to get rid of her mother, avoiding physical love as much as possible, even if it means drugging her with sleeping pills. When Charlotte accidentally reads his journal and discovers his contempt for her alongside his paedophilic tendencies towards her daughter, she runs distractedly out of the house and is conveniently run over by a passing car, killing her, before she can expose him and publicize his perversion . . . That, Ladies, takes us to the twenty-fourth chapter . . . I shall set another impromptu comprehension test for the class this coming Friday, so please read the chapters carefully."

That weekend, Myles took Lottie along to the picturesque village of Sault. Lottie had demanded she join him, and although he had wanted to gently decline her request, he had been compelled to bring her, lest he should get more stick from her father. One could at least describe this as a field trip, even if it consisted of a single student. She brought some music with her on her iPod, the songs stored including Alizée's pop-saturated *Moi...Lolita* and Noir Désir's *Lolita Nie En Bloc*, demonstrating, once again, her affinity for Gallic music. When Myles complained about the suggestiveness of those songs, Lottie brushed aside his wariness by stating they provided, among other tunes, inspiration for her writings as much as his English class.

Sault was an old fortified village perched along the top of an elevated plateau at Mont Ventoux, one thousand metres above sea-level, overlooking a wide valley. Deep canyons plunged southwest, officially named Les Gorges de la Nesque. Vestiges from the Bronze Age painted the caves northwest. Along with the ancient buildings lining the high ridge were the remains of a huge feudal castle. Sault housed a natural history collection and antiques dating back to the Barbarian invasions. There was a good selection of cafés and shops which Myles and Lottie stopped off to explore. However, the south of Sault was immersed in lavender fields, a must-see for tourists, the harvested crops of which were transported straight to the distillery, creating a multitude of lavender products: honey, sorbets, syrup, soaps, cosmetics. Lavender famously relaxes the mind and eases insomnia, calms the digestive system and opens up narrowed airways when drunk as a tea. It also kept spiders away. Although the tourist traffic had reduced during these hot autumn months, Mont Ventoux remained a mecca for cyclists and provided numerous hiking trails. In fact, Mont Ventoux was one of the foremost back-breaking climbs of Tour de France fame. The summit of Mont Ventoux was reported to be ten degrees cooler than its base and the limestone gave it the appearance of being snowcapped all year round. M. Garance informed Myles that Petrarch, the Father of the Renaissance and Founder of Humanism, spent much of his early life in the Papal court of Avignon. He is also remembered for his well-documented account of his ascent of Mont Ventoux.

Not that Myles or Lottie did any climbing. Sightseeing and exploring the local vicinity was all Myles was interested in. Lottie just tagged along. Her book raised little conversation between them, despite her persistence to discuss it, since Myles reminded her that today was a day for rest and recreation, going out and about. She accepted his explanation and enjoyed her time with him. She knew that after hours, outside the rigours of the classroom, he would make more of an effort.

She told him about her father, Piers Heymans, Vice President of an international brokerage firm and senior hedge fund manager, through whose unscrupulous practices a lot of people got burned, lost their assets, when the bubble burst in 2008, whereupon he took early retirement in the Bahamas outside the long arm of the law. He kept an eagle eye on his daughter's progress from afar.

Myles kept his opinions about this man to himself even if he knew world politics had regressed into a corrupt platform for propping up corporate greed. The British government, too, had a lot to answer for. It provided a corporate welfare state, a place for tolerating tax evasion and advocating bailouts, engendering a moral turpitude in society. It had forced University students to moonlight as escorts for rich, older men or work as pole-dancers in gangster-run clubs to make ends meet, to fund their studies or pay off their student debts. You rarely saw this kind of exploitation in France, where students were seen as the future and treated with the respect and dignity they deserved, as it ought to be. Even alleged abuse referrals had risen to one-fifth for all children in the UK; it was a damn sight lower, three percent, in France, where the people treated their kids as respectfully as the younger generation looked up to its elders. Myles decided to be a more fitting, morally-centred surrogate parent to Lottie in lieu of her greedy, dishonest father. If Lottie was prepared to put in the effort to meet her ambitions, then why shouldn't Myles be the catalyst in her success as an author? She was only sixteen, a kid with the brains of a potential protégé, and in his care and safekeeping. In *loco parentis*. Like all of us, she was only trying to find her way in life.

He pointed her in the right direction: *If you write every day, consistently, and rewrite where indicated, imagine how much you will have written in six months, a year. A writer writes. Always. If not putting down words on paper, you're writing in your head. And when you're not writing,* read. *Read to learn new words, broaden your vocabulary, improve your versatility and your style of writing.* He advised she read up Shakespeare for the beauty of the English word, Dickens for character study, the concise caricature and the perfect prose, and the Brontë sisters for the cruelty and heartbreak of love but, above all else, for how Love could be found in the most unexpected of places. *I wish that if I died, I could be buried in Poets' Corner at Westminster Abbey*, Myles confided in her, dreaming aloud.

She told him she hoped it wouldn't come to that.

6

Seven kilometres from Mazan lay the town of Carpentras. It was not the richest town in the department of Vacluse, but it was renowned for its truffle market. Its fifteenth-century synagogue was famous for being the oldest in France. The Cathedral St. Pierre and St. Siffrein would attest that Carpentras was a frequent residency for the Avignon popes. The CHÂTEAU DES COMTES DE TOULOUSE had a campanile representing the divine points of the Universe. Bibliophiles were familiar with the HÔTEL-DIEU, a former hospital which had been converted into one of the oldest municipal libraries in the country.

At various points around Mazan there were places to visit and explore. Also relatively close to Mazan, only twenty-six kilometres away, was the town of Orange, its imposing amphitheatre and triumphal arch as old as the Severan dynasty. THÉÂTRE ANTIQUE D'ORANGE was probably one of the best-preserved of the surviving Roman theatres in Europe, periodically staging operas and festivals. Just like with many communes in Vacluse, urbanization surrounded the old town.

That following weekend, Myles' travels would almost amount to a marathon. Once again, Lottie accompanied him to these great places. She was full of boundless energy and enthusiasm – and vitality. Myles admitted there was something refreshing about having an adolescent tag along. As they headed towards their next destination, Lottie told Myles a little about her relationship with her parents. Mother was a gin-soak and emotionally unavailable. Father, too, was more or less absent, always away on business, concerned only with making money and unconscionably cheating his clients. Myles sensed an unconscious yearning on her part, as with any growing child, to live in an idealized family unit. He remembered his sister, Carmain, a Safeguarding nurse, only yesterday in their weekly, long-distance catch-up, informing him that a child's individual needs should always come ahead of their parents – a child's needs were *paramount* – and to Myles it seemed that Lottie's parents had, due to their own selfishness, failed in that department, even though she was a singleton. Carmain had also told him about the mysterious Dark Web, and the notorious Silk Road, a clandestine online drug market, outside any form of official monitoring, through which people had overdosed after buying suspect illicit drugs, whose deaths had allowed the authorities to finally pinpoint its existence and shut it down, prosecuting and sentencing the people who had been operating their illegal trade. But the Dark Web now served another sinister, scarier, even more despicable function: child trafficking and exploitation. That was where the current battle raged. *Imagine how you felt,* Carmain asked her brother, *the first time you fell in love, the emotions you associate with that moment: feeling warm and fuzzy, happy, excited, a sense of feeling wanted, mature, feeling a belonging and a responsibility to the other person, etc. That is* exactly *how the flash-car-and-flash-cash 'grooms' of these child exploitation rings, scouting for girls, make their victims* feel *before ruthlessly passing them on to older men.* Carmain wondered why anybody would want to do something so heinous. What motivated the generic sexual predator to prey on someone so young? *Maybe it's love or lust or loneliness. Maybe it's a chance to relive their youth. Maybe they themselves have been abused in childhood. Maybe they're perverts looking for a steady stream of innocent victims. Add the explosion of chatrooms and easy access to online pornographic material, both parents working, unable to keep an eye on their child. Or just careless parents showing off their child swimming on Facebook – how dangerous is that? And, in this day and age, note the growing phenomenon of older women committing sexual offences.* Carmain told him about a case she'd been working on recently. *A thirteen-year-old girl has been chatting away with an online buddy, a boy of supposedly fifteen years, on one of the popular chatrooms and, after weeks of online communication and friendship, eventually arranges to meet him in person. When she gets there, she's shocked to discover her father standing there with a bouquet of red roses. He is promptly arrested.*

Myles was able to infer how much Lottie felt let down by her parents and how she longed for a father figure. He hoped to rectify that situation in a sensible, constructive manner, provide her with the guidance she so desperately sought. He explained in not too many sentimental terms why he took up teaching high school. *Working with kids reminds me of my own enjoyable childhood and adolescence,* he told her, *makes me feel young again. So there must be something true about your Hebe. I thought I'd give something back to you teenagers, who, like all of us, are only trying to find out what they want in life. Why not equip them with the knowledge and the necessary skills to help them to progress into well-adjusted adults?*

The government had devalued learning. Myles, like many of his contemporaries, believed, without sounding too cynical, there had been a deliberate 'dumbing-down' of the education system in the UK, removing massive chunks of the syllabus and making exams easier in order to raise the pass rate, so as to make the national educational statistics in line with the rest of the EU; in other words, creating an 'illusion' of improved educational standards, a *cheat*. Western civilization could claim that it took better care of its kids, but was that really the case? Teachers had less powers than ever before and any attempt at physical discipline – which had been the norm when Myles had been growing up, and better for it – led to them getting suspended, resulting in classrooms full of unruly kids with no desire to learn. Parents got arrested for spanking their child and risked their child getting taken into care by social services. So we now had a society where our kids were running amok and causing all kinds of merry hell, permanently distracted by street drugs, computer games and cheap Reality TV, gaining top marks for subpar schoolwork, a perennial strategy put in place by those in power to prevent our children from actually thinking for themselves. There was always a political agenda behind the spin, painstakingly hidden from the public eye and normally involving self-invested interests and, if such a thing existed, dictated by the Devil.

Nîmes lay southwest of Mazan. Its sights included the Roman Arena of Nîmes, the best-preserved elliptical amphitheatre in all of Roman Provence, a place of enforced combat between Christians and lions in its heyday, now a venue for concerts and bullfighting. In the centre of Nîmes stood the MAISON CARRÉE, a temple, complete with Corinthian columns, built in the first century by Marcus Agrippa, dedicated to Julius Gaius Caesar. The JARDINS DE LA FONTAINE was an eighteenth-century park built around the old Roman thermal ruins. Around the sacred spring were ancient monuments, including the Temple of Diana. The Roman tower of Tour Magne, built on forested parkland across the hilltop northwest of the centre, provided a great panoramic view of the city. Tree-shaded boulevards traced the foundations of its former city walls. The city seemed to take one back to the time of the Gauls under Roman occupation and made one wonder how its inhabitants lived two thousand years ago.

Looming between Orange and Nîmes was one of the most remarkable, grandest engineering wonders of the Roman world, the PONT DU GARD, an ancient aqueduct bridge spanning the Gardon River valley. It was the highest bridge ever built by the Roman engineers, consisting of three tiers of arches rising to a height of fifty metres and once delivering nine million gallons of water to the homes, baths and fountains of the Nîmes colony daily. It had been operational up until the sixth century, then served as a toll bridge. The spring still existed today and was now part of a water-pumping station.

Travelling farther afield, Myles took Lottie to Arles, a commune dating as far back as the seventh century. Its Roman arena and theatre had become integrated into the houses and buildings. CATHÉDRALE SAINT-TROPHIME D'ARLES stood adjacent to the SAINT-TROPHIME CLOISTRE. The central PLACE DU FORUM, packed with terrace cafés/restaurants, smart shops and boutiques, led to the main square of the old town, PLACE DE LA RÉPUBLIQUE. Here, the fountain was adorned with an Egyptian granite obelisk from the old Roman circus. Outside the former city limits, the ALYSCHAMPS was one of the largest Roman necropolises in the ancient world, with the better-preserved of its sarcophagi housed inside the MUSÉE DE L'ARLES ET DE LA PROVENCE ANTIQUES. Of particular historic interest, Vincent Van Gogh is reported to have lived in Arles between February 1888 to May 1889 during his most productive period, creating over two hundred paintings, including that notable work, *The Night Café*. It was in Arles he would cut off his ear during a frenzy, getting himself committed to an asylum in nearby Saint-Remy. The premises of the old Arles hospital now housed a collection of his many masterpieces. His house and favourite café might have been bombed in 1944, but the surrounding fields were still alive with the sunflowers and olive trees he loved to paint. It was Van Gogh who said: *I dream of painting and then I paint my dream.*

By the end of that weekend, Myles supposed they'd seen everything that needed to be seen in the immediacy.

There was just Avignon to do.

7

"Having laid his wife to rest, Humbert the widower undertakes the difficult task of retrieving Lolita from camp, maybe not such a difficult task being the girl's sole guardian, giving her the excuse that her mother has been hospitalized. He constantly reminds us in his entries of his own handsomeness and how attractive he is to young girls. Rather than return her home, Humbert takes her to a hotel, *The Enchanted Hunters*, and plans to drug her and rape her while she lies unconscious. As he waits for the sleeping pill to take effect, he wanders through *The Enchanted Hunters* and meets a man who seems to know him. Humbert excuses himself from the strange conversation and returns to his hotel room. There, he tries to molest Lolita but finds that the sedative has only partially worked and has left her somewhat drowsy. Instead, she initiates sex the following morning, and

Humbert describes his sexual relations by waxing poetic, comparing the event to painting a mural. Humbert explains that Lolita self-reported that she has been 'revoltingly unfaithful' to him, having had a previous homosexual encounter with another girl at camp but more recently having played sex games with a boy."

He heard tittering. Myles looked around the sun-drenched classroom, the windows thrown wide open to admit the modicum of a breeze and saw a number of girls giggling. There was no embarrassment on their parts, but he fought to hide his own discomfort. He felt he was treading dangerous territory, walking a tightrope, not only with the material he was teaching but also considering his working relationship with Lottie. He hated the idea that her fellow students might be understandably thinking he had singled her out for special treatment, like any teacher's pet. Kids aren't stupid. They can see what goes on, and tongues can easily wag with some spurious version of the truth. Neither did he trust Lottie's two preppy schoolfriends, Gabrielle Bouchard and Bridgette Lémieux, together with Lottie self-proclaimed 'Les Trois Mousquetaires'.

"Ladies, *please!*" he reminded his class sternly. "Let's be grown-up and civilized about this! For those of you studying Psychology, I'm certain you'll be familiar with *Identity versus Role Confusion*. Erikson proposed that adolescence was a time of self-discovery, finding out where one fits into society, including discovering friendships and one's own sexuality. It is not uncommon for teenagers to experiment, be *bicurious*." Even if most of these schoolgirls were sixteen and over, almost adults, he still had his doubts about teaching this particular book. Should he really be telling them this story, considering what was yet to come? The senior school hierarchy had thrust this unenviable task upon him since it was a book apparently on the English syllabus. Again, he reminded himself to proceed with caution, with as much focus and professionalism as he could muster. "Later, Humbert reveals to Lolita that Charlotte, her mother, is dead and blackmails her, giving her the choice of either accepting him as a stepfather on his terms or face foster care.

"Humbert takes Lolita on a year-long tour of the United States, driving from one state to the next, from cheap motel to cheap motel, remaining fairly anonymous. When Humbert first begins his affair with Lolita, she is eager and curious. Soon, however, she begins showing open disgust at him and his unhealthy desires. In order to keep Lolita from going to the police, Humbert reminds her that if he is arrested, she will become a ward of the state and lose all her earthly possessions. He also bribes her with food, money and permission to attend fun events in exchange for sexual favours, although he knows that she does not reciprocate his love and shares none of his feelings. She manages to negotiate a higher and higher allowance for each sexual encounter. After an entire year of wandering around the country, the two settle down in another New England town called Beardsley, where Lolita is enrolled in a respected all girls' school. The school advises him not to think of his daughter as a little girl but as a growing young woman who needs fun and freedom."

Myles thought of the girls here. The thought struck him with the unpleasantness of a flashback. Did the schoolgirls here have the maturity and independent thinking to see the book for the morality tale it was supposed to be? He thought of the movie remake which some of the girls had mentioned watching, despite their tender age and the film's harder-hitting content than the original version. Ironic – and shocking – how Jeremy Irons had given up children's television to star in the film adaptation of the book, to play the pervert who seduces Lolita.

Myles continued: "Terrified that Lolita will fall in love, Humbert becomes very possessive and strict, an 'old ogre', forbidding Lolita, now fourteen, not to under any circumstances take part in after-school activities or attend co-ed parties or to associate with boys. Most of the townspeople see this as the action of a loving and concerned, albeit old-fashioned, parent. Humbert, however, has a roving eye, 'innocently' assessing the promise of Lolita's friends as potential nymphets. Meanwhile, the headmistress of the school, Mrs. Pratt, has noticed how poorly Lolita is doing in class and calls in Humbert to her office. He starts to panic, believing she suspects something about the illicit relationship between him and his stepdaughter. Mrs. Pratt is indeed worried that something is wrong with Lolita, sexually, as she is rude to her teachers and still indifferent to boys, but the headmistress blames this behaviour on Humbert for preventing his daughter from mingling with her peers and dating, hindering her social and sexual development, not allowing the girl to grow up. Reluctantly, he accepts Mrs. Pratt's scathing criticism of his parenting skills, in particular his need to overprotect his stepdaughter from the big, bad world.

"Lolita pleads with him to allow her to take part in the school play, and Humbert reluctantly grants her permission in return for more sexual favours. He personally loathes the theatre, considers the art form 'primitive and putrid', *beneath* him. This particular play is written by Mr. Clare Quilty. Quilty is said to have attended a rehearsal and had been extremely impressed by Lolita's acting. Just before opening night, Lolita and Humbert have a ferocious argument, and Lolita runs away while Humbert assures the neighbours everything is fine. He searches frantically until he finds her exiting a phone booth. She is in a bright, pleasant mood, saying that she tried to reach him at home and that a 'great decision has been made'. They go to buy drinks and Lolita tells Humbert she doesn't care about the play and wants to resume their travels. She starts missing piano lessons, gets mysterious letters. She is growing up – or outgrowing the 'nymphet' stage that Humbert found so attractive and irresistible. She is hiding something; Humbert believes she is plotting something.

"As Lolita and Humbert embark on their second trip and drive westward again, with Lolita showing far more interest in the roadmaps than she did a year ago, Humbert gets the feeling that their car is being tailed and becomes increasingly paranoid, suspecting that Lolita is conspiring with others in order to escape. Then, one day, she falls ill and must convalesce in a hospital in Elphinstone while Humbert stays in a nearby motel. Lolita suddenly disappears from the hospital, with the staff informing Humbert that her 'uncle' checked her out. He knows there is no uncle, and he believes she has been kidnapped. Instead of going to the police, Humbert embarks on a frantic search to find Lolita and her abductor, retracing the thousand-mile journey from Beardsley, even going back there with the intention of shooting her male English teacher, whom he suspects of being involved in Lolita's disappearance but realizes he is only being insane in his suspicions and jealousy. Lolita's trail goes cold and Humbert eventually gives up, falling back on his two-year relationship during this time with a woman named Rita, who approved his search for his stepdaughter while knowing none of the details of the sexual abuse he inflicted on the girl."

The schoolgirls looked at Myles with wide, open eyes, engrossed. Once again, he realized they weren't shocked or fearful but fascinated. It was amazing how many of them identified with Lolita, even the sound, non-flirty ones. Myles felt he had done a sufficiently decent job relating the synopsis to them to hopefully motivate them to read the book, pre-warning them of what to expect in its pages.

"Aside from the weekly mock test of the book, I would like to fire up your imagination and to appeal to the actresses in you. As part of your coursework, I am going to ask you to play a dramatic scene from a genuine literary source – Shakespeare, Agatha Christie, *The Crucible, The Iceman Cometh*, etc – or perhaps just a piece of dramatic reading, whether serious or nonsensical, powerful or trivial. I suggest you pair up with someone you know and rehearse if you *are* performing a scene, because be warned: to make it a real challenge, you will be in direct competition with each other, and the whole class will score you on your performance." His last sentence was met with an equal measure of enthusiasm and trepidation from his students. He started tidying his notes. "Lottie, stay behind class," he instructed, without looking up, as the lesson and the school day wound to a close.

He heard more giggling from the girls at the back of the class.

"I'll have none of that, thank you!" he scolded the culprits. "Class dismissed!"

The schoolgirls dawdled out of the schoolroom in dribs and drabs, leaving only Lottie at her desk. He looked at her thoughtfully and found her beaming back at him. Her smile made him think of the vulnerable position the school and the girl's father had put him in, particularly if one threw the course syllabus, *Lolita*, into the potentially volatile mix.

[*treading dangerous territory, walking a tightrope, dangerous territory, tightrope*]

The temptation to discontinue the extracurricular study sessions was strong, but Myles put up and shut up. The fear of becoming too close to one of his students had been taken out of his hands, the decision no longer his to make. *I talk in a daze. I walk in a maze. I cannot get out, said the starling*, wrote the pen of Nabokov. Lottie tagged along happily, and Myles let her tag along, not out of choice, mind. It was odd how she was yet to let him read any of her stuff, downright peculiar, and preferred only to discuss the details of some of the great English authors, appearing to harbour a commendable passion for the intricacies of the English language. She continued to work on her Dear Diaries secretly, promising him that she would let him have a read of her manuscript soon. Did he trust the girl? Might people perceive her interest in him as being more than just academic? He didn't want to think about it, and he pushed away this rather disquieting thought with some effort, as he prepared to spend more time with Lottie, post-school tuition-wise, and give her a few more pointers.

8

As Provence entered another sultry October weekend, Myles dedicated most of Saturday to exploring Avignon. As usual, Lottie accompanied him on the trip. So too did her two closest friends, Gabrielle and Bridgette. M. Garance, who had already given him the heads-up on the history of the place in the teachers' lounge, decided to, also. One of the Art teachers, the delightfully eccentric, hippie-dressed Mlle. Angelique Bouygues, overheard the conversation between the two men and invited herself on their adventure. Both M. Garance and Mlle. Bouygues knew the city well and neither was averse to a return visit, particularly Mlle. Bouygues, who had a soft spot for its art treasures and never tired of looking at its priceless works. In that rivalry between the value of a painting against the written word, Mlle. Bouygues used Napoleon's widely-held opinion that *a picture is worth ten thousand words*, that a picture should be allowed to flourish and not be burdened, or *suffocated*, with verbal descriptions, but Myles was equally quick to point out Kipling's observation that words were the most powerful drug known to mankind, and cite Herman Hesse, who contended that without words, without writing and without books there would be no history or any concept of humanity. They reached a compromise, plumping for Plutarch: *Painting is silent poetry, and poetry is a painting that speaks.* Myles didn't mind her intrusion; she would represent the necessary adult female presence, who would help supervise the three girls coming along for the ride, the perfect chaperone for the two men. *The more the merrier.* It promised to be a nice day out.

Northwest of the limestone hills of Avignon were the Chauvet caves, their walls skilfully rendered with Palaeolithic paintings of bison, auks, seals, horses, penguins, cave lions, reindeer, rhinos, bears and woolly mammoths, as old and impressive as the rock art at Lascaux.

Myles knew that Avignon and its surrounding region had always been a place of historic and archaeological significance, as evidenced in the novel he was reading at the moment to get himself in the mood, *The Bones of Christ* by the composite author, Jefferson Bass, Dan Brown-esque in its research and telling, but with more substance and less razzmatazz. Also, a million miles away from the stuffy classroom read of *Lolita*. Everybody needed an escape, a diversion from serious, weighty matters, sometimes. *Les Demoiselles d'Avignon* by Pablo Picasso, regarded by some art critics as the most famous Cubist painting of all time, was another piece of work that had become synonymous with this great city.

Avignon was a city with over one-hundred-thousand people, of whom twelve thousand lived in the ancient town centre enclosed by its medieval eight-hundred-year-old stone ramparts, complete with towers and battlements. Before evangelization, it was a place of turmoil and upheaval with multiple raids from the Visigoths, Ostrogoths, Franks and Berber pirates. It remained a Gallo-Roman town until the fifth century. The Black Death in 1348 visited the city, killing off two-thirds of the city's population. Between 1309 and 1377, during the Avignon Papacy, seven successive sovereign pontiffs resided here, rebel popes who broke from Rome, and Papal control persisted until 1791 when, during the French Revolution, it became part of the French Republic. It was now the capital of

Vacluse. The reason the site was originally chosen for development was because Avignon stood high above the plains of the River Rhône and was the strategic point for the whole valley.

Sightseeing boats and riverboat hotels were anchored on the left banks of the river. Fortified medieval walls surrounded the old part of Avignon, within which hid a maze of ancient, twisty, narrow, cobbled streets, courtyards of private mansions and small, leafy isolated squares overflowing with café tables. Visitors to the city could shop at the markets, browse the boutiques, and wander the streets lined with fountains and elegant *hôtel particuliers*. In the summer there would be a performing arts' festival in the streets, citywide. Full of history of life, youth, art and music, Avignon had become a long-established centre of culture. PLACE DE L'HORLOGE was a pedestrian zone of smart shops and hotels, restaurants and terrace cafés, with an authentic, Belle Époque, perhaps *Fin de siècle* carousel at the top end, leading to the PLACE DU PALAIS, with its many street entertainers. The skyline was dominated by the PALAIS DES PAPES, the largest gothic palace in the world, the seventeen-feet thick walls of this feudal fortress built on a natural spur of rock, dwarfing every other building in sight, a monument to piety and grandeur, once the seat of Papal power and the Centre of Christendom in the Middle Ages until the coming of the Great Schism and the antipopes. Its neighbouring attractions included the CATHÉDRALE NOTRE-DAME-DES-DOMS D'AVIGNON, a mausoleum of exquisite gothic carvings, its bell tower crowned by a gilded statue of the Virgin Mary. At the end of the square stood the MUSÉE DU PETIT PALAIS, which served as a museum, containing a collection of paintings from Renaissance Italy and the Avignon school. The picturesque gardens of the ROCHER DES DOMS, its sundial enabling the person's shadow to tell the time, led to the PONT D'AVIGNON – and the Saint- Bénézet bridge. Only four of its twenty-three arches survived the floods of 1670, and on the four-arch pier stood the small Romanesque Chapel of Saint-Bénézet, originally commissioned to commemorate the shepherd, whose saintly visions in 1177 inspired the building of the bridge. The bridge would also be immortalized by a much-loved nursery rhyme.

The University of Avignon was as old as the early 1300s when civil and ecclesiastical law were still the main disciplines of study. Its philosophy and theology departments soon followed, standing side by side with medicine and the sciences. Following the French Revolution in 1792, the University was abandoned and closed before a new university would spring up, much later in 1963, on the site of a former hospital building.

Whereas his travelling companions went for lighter options, Myles dined on tenderloin steak in bordelaise sauce, after an interesting starter of *cuisses de grenouille* – frogs' legs.

Avignon was a genuine cultural experience for Myles, one he thoroughly enjoyed. M. Garance and Mlle. Bouygues had kept him abreast of the history and art of the city in typical tour-guide fashion, and the three girls had passed the day, chattering away in the background, thick-as-thieves, while chomping away on a packet of Haribo Orangina. The temptation to come back the next day, Sunday, to visit the rest of it was hard to resist, but Myles, tired from all the walking and sightseeing and talking, dropped off his colleagues – and the Three Musketeers, including Lottie, who had remained unusually quiet and reserved throughout the course of the day, distant even from her friends – back at the boarding school, thanking them for their company, and he decided to enjoy the rest of his evening with a bottle of Farigoule he had purchased in a quaint liquor store in Avignon.

The evening was sticky, free of any stresses or worries.

Under the Provence sun, he sat on the steps of the veranda, appreciating the sounds and scents of the countryside as well as the gorgeously intoxicating sips of the unique herbal liqueur, replete with the fragrance of wild thyme.

He must have been sitting there for perhaps an hour, relaxed, savouring the pleasant, swimmy effects of the drink, the fading scarlet shades of sunset acquiescing to the approach of autumnal dusk, when he heard footsteps nearby, scrunching gravel. His head followed the direction of the noise and discovered Lottie standing there up the tree-shaded lane. She had changed from her casual jeans and T-shirt into a short, sleeveless navy-blue dress with yellow polka-dots, its hemline riding above her knees. Her feet sported white sneakers.

"What do I owe this pleasure, Miss Heymans?" he asked her, pleasantly enough.

For a moment she didn't speak, as though giving him the opportunity to appraise her. Then, she spoke in a tone that was meant to be nonchalant but came across as absurdly friendly. "I thought I'd surprise you. See you in case you needed some company. Besides, I cannot thank you enough for your most excellent tutelage."

Myles noticed she was wearing pink lipstick and dark eyeliner, which complimented her oval face and golden hair and glowing tan of her bare arms in the dying light of day, the budding valley of her chest accentuated by the low cut of her dress. She had made an effort. "Don't think me remiss, but I value my privacy. I think I would like just to have a little 'me'-time right now, if you catch my drift."

She did get his drift, but she ignored it and sat down next to him. She did not beat around the bush. Her hand stroked his thigh in a gentle, upward caress, producing a very audible, sibilant intake of breath. "I just wanted to be alone with you. I haven't had a chance to talk to you all day. Now that I've got you all to myself..."

Drunk on Farigoule, his vision slowly dimming over, his mind considerably less sharp on the uptake, it only just began to dawn on Myles the ambitions of Lottie's visit and where this might actually be leading to. He responded, struggling to keep a straight head, teetering on the brink of passing out, trying desperately not to slur his words. "And why should you want to be alone with me?"

"Don't you want me, Daddy?" she said suggestively. "I've been such a bad little girl. *Sooo* naughty . . ."

Myles was wracked by a conflict of emotions, panic and confusion and desire. "Whatever you came here for, I cannot possibly–"

Lottie placed a finger on his lips to hush him, stopping him in mid-sentence. "You want–?" she whispered as provocatively as the title of her book or the dress she was wearing. And went to kiss him . . .

9

The last chapters of Lolita, thought Myles, glad he was now cruising down the inside straight. "While in a relationship with Rita, who is petite and girlish, three times divorced and a lush, and whose mayor of a brother pays her to stay away because of her trail of scandals, Humbert lives in despair until Lolita finds him. He receives a letter from Lolita who, now seventeen, informs him she is married, pregnant and in desperate need of money. Humbert leaves Rita, who is drunk and passed-out, forever and goes to the address Lolita has given him. She is older, taller, with spectacles, an expectant mother. Although murder is all he can think about, he cannot hurt Lolita because he 'loved' her. He gives her money in exchange for the name of the man who abducted her. She reveals what really happened: Clare Quilty checked her out of the hospital, posing as her uncle in a carefully-planned plot she was thoroughly complicit in, after following them throughout their travels. His intention was to turn her into a starlet in one of his adult films, but when she refused to be filmed, he threw her out. She worked various odd jobs before meeting and marrying her husband, who knows nothing about her past. Humbert repeatedly asks Lolita to leave her husband, Dick, and live with him which she refuses to do. He gives her a large sum of money anyway. As Humbert leaves, she shouts goodbye in a 'sweet, American' way. Humbert reflects that Lolita never saw him as a romantic partner, but only as a physical inflictor of sex, a molester, an abuser, a criminal. Her *destroyer*. Possessed, insatiable, he could never stop wanting her, but all he ever had was her body. In the end, his punishment matches his crime. Lolita runs off with someone a hundred times worse than him. Yet, despite all her tribulations, she is now an entirely different person, a triumph for the vital force that has managed to make a life out of the rubble that Humbert's sordid, mindless passions created. For once, and possibly for the first time, he learns to be genuinely fatherly towards her when he hands over the money.

"Humbert tracks down Quilty, whom he intends to kill, at his mansion in what soon amounts to a tragicomic shambles. Eventually, Humbert shoots him dead and exits the house. Realizing now that he is both a rapist and now a murderer, he decides he might as well break the traffic laws. Soon afterwards, the police arrest him for driving on the wrong side of the road and swerving dangerously. His crimes are revealed to the authorities. The narrative closes with Humbert's final words to Lolita in which he wishes her well and reveals the novel in its metafiction to be the memoirs of his life, only to be published after he and Lolita have both died. The novel's fictional foreword states that Humbert Humbert died of a coronary thrombosis after completing the manuscript. It also states that 'Mrs. Richard F. Schiller'/Lolita died giving birth to a stillborn girl on Christmas Day, 1952, at the tender age of seventeen."

As Myles scanned the classroom and saw only eager faces mesmerized by his command of the book, his eyes drifted to the desk belonging to Lottie, devoid of its occupant. He did not ask. Despite the consternation fluttering in his stomach, Myles couldn't have been more pleased it was all nearly over. Time now to dissect the work, sharing his own analysis with the class, a little critiquing. "The novel was denounced upon its release, and there were even demands for its censorship and the deportation of its author. It was first published in 1955 in Paris with the other Western countries playing catch-up. The book highlights the hypocrisy and pretensions of family values in 1950s America, and one can argue a clinical and sociological seriousness pervades throughout. The work is written by a virtuoso stronger than Joyce, more subtle than de Sade. Notice the rich prose, its presentation so carefully thought through, some critics have described it as one the finest books of the twentieth century. Nabokov deliberately makes Humbert an unreliable narrator, whose moral atrophy in this sordid tale, justifying his unforgivable feelings and actions, reduces Lolita to an object that must be lusted over, since Humbert never makes an attempt to give the reader the poor, pubescent girl's point of view. Humbert never considers Lolita a human being but some dream figment of his desires. Moreover, what makes Nabokov such an eloquent and manipulative writer is that he coaxes us into sharing all the vulgarity and nastiness – Humbert's perversion disguised as love – so as to make us actually care for this evil man; Nabokov humanizes the monster, someone who ultimately loses the girl to his metaphorical 'doppelgänger', Clare Quilty, a figure so much more perverse than Humbert ever was. Add to this, Nabokov wrote a number of short stories about similar inappropriate relationships between older men and teenage girls, what does that say about him as a person?" Myles deliberately completed his formulation with a rhetorical question. Relevant, germane, food for thought.

There was a rap on the door. Mme. Renard, the headmistress was peering in through the classroom door window.

Myles gestured for her to come in. She entered, followed by two men dressed in standard police uniforms.

"*Bonjour*, M. Hawking," Mme. Renard greeted him, cold as ice. "These gentlemen are here to ask you a few questions."

The first of the police officers spoke up. "M. Hawking, we would like you to accompany us down to the station."

"Why, certainly," responded Myles, unusually brightly. "Do you know what this is about?"

"We'd rather not say here. We can talk more freely down at police headquarters."

But Myles knew what it was about. He glanced at Lottie's empty desk again, one last time. There was neither surprise nor startlement in his expression. From the restless murmurs sweeping across the classroom, he knew his adolescent charges were already talking. "Ladies, please, I have a little business to attend to…"

With that simple announcement, he walked calmly out of the schoolroom, out of the building, flanked on either side by the *agents de police nationale*, as Mme. Renard prepared to continue his class and apply a little damage control. There would also be angry parents to contend with later on.

10

A fly sat next to him, undaunted by his presence. Myles Hawking was hunched forward on the bed under the dim coverage of twilight, swigging from the near-empty bottle of Farigoule, the half-drunken state of his mind turning over the events of the day.

They had let him go. *For now.*

A gentleman never tells.

His word against hers. All circumstantial for the moment until the results came back.

"I need to know what I'm accused of," he requested down at the police station. "Don't you think that's fair? My legal right?"

Inspector Anatole Gaspard and Detective Yvonne Mercier were his interrogating officers in the sterile, white interview room, one length of the wall fitted with a mirror, of, as Myles surmised, one-way glass, behind which their colleagues were probably watching him, judging him. The interview was being taped. The video-recorder rested on a tripod. The air-con was either not working or had been deliberately switched off, since it was as hot as hell in the interview room; Myles was sweating like a pig.

It was Inspector Gaspard who began the cross-examination. "Anything you say may be used in evidence against you. Do you want a lawyer present, or are you confident to proceed with your preliminary statement?"

No, he thought, *a lawyer would be an admission of guilt. I can handle this.* "I can continue without a lawyer. I have nothing to hide."

Inspector Gaspard spoke to the video-camera. "Please note, M. Hawking has declined the offer of counsel." He turned back to Myles. "*Bon*, then let's proceed."

Detective Yvonne Mercier took over. "We are currently in the process of conducting an investigation. Mlle. Heymans has made a disclosure against you of improper conduct . . . of you having sexual relations with her."

Myles expression turned into one of incredulity. "That's outrageous! There's a code of conduct between teacher and student that should always be observed, professional boundaries that must never be crossed! You think I'm one of those guys who pervs over sixteen-year-old girls? Her father granted me permission to spend time with her, against my better judgement don't forget, *coach* her, help her find her own 'voice', turn her into a writing sensation. She's obviously upset about something. Curious, I never pegged her for a troublemaker."

"Are you saying her allegation is false, that intimate relations did not occur?"

Myles went back to that fateful evening. He was drunk. She had visited him, deliberately dressed in provocative fashion. To what end? He had been oblivious to the fact she had been holding a torch for her teacher, an infatuation considerably deeper than a simple crush, and she had come that evening with the clear intention of seducing him. He racked his brains to remember what had happened, but all he got was a black hole where his memory should have been. Had he discouraged her advances, jilted her? He could not remember. It was all a blur. Presently, there was a crucial need to deflect. "She set me up. You must have something more to go on. Otherwise we wouldn't be having this conversation."

Detective Mercier glanced at Inspector Gaspard for instruction who nodded for her to go on. "You mentioned the book she was writing," Mercier said, lifting up a manuscript from the table, the spine bound by string. "I can read you excerpts from it." She flicked through the pages. *"Dear Diary, It was love at first sight, and last sight. He mentioned he kept photographs of girl-children because he values and adores their mortal sense of beauty and fantastic power of youth. He explained that only an artist or a madman can discern the nymphet among the wholesome children."* Detective Mercier read from another page. *"He told me I was a loud echo of a nymphet he once knew, practically a replica, bearing a visual facsimile of her beloved face. In my presence, he thought he would be one of those great sleepless artists who had to die for a few hours in order to live for a few centuries. He promised me I would be* his *nymphet, with the beauty of Venus but the youthfulness of Hebe, his sin, his soul, his* Lottie." Mercier skipped a few sections. *"Dear Diary, We did* everything. *We lived in a world of thoughts, each other's thoughts, coddled in an expression of love. It is not the artistic aptitudes that serve as secondary sexual characters as some shamans have said but that sex is the ancilla of art."* Another extract: *"We perched ourselves on the steps of the veranda. A cluster of stars palely glowed above us between the silhouettes of long thin leaves, that vibrant sky seemed as naked as I was under my summer dress. He looked at me and knew as clearly as he knows he is to die one day that he loved me more than anything he ever imagined. We fell to wrestling again. We rolled all over the floor, in each other's arms, like helpless children. He was naked and goatish when he pulled his trousers down, and I felt smothered as he rolled over me. He groped me intelligently, like a gynaecologist feeling for a tumour. All at once we were shamelessly, hopelessly, agonizingly – madly – in love with each other. He gave me the sceptre of his passion to hold. I pulled back the pistol's foreskin and he opened me wider, as a gynaecologist might do with a speculum, allowing me to accommodate him until I eventually enjoyed the orgasm of his crushed trigger. He, too, reached his watershed moment, a case of internal combustion, a paroxysm of desire physically manifested by the flow of honey, cool and spasmodic. He cast me a dreamy expression, of half-pleasure and half-pain, over my childish features. I was thinking of aurochs and angels, of Shakespearean sonnets, the refuge of art. Our doomed love, designed to destroy adult lives, hastened to alienate the very fates we intended to woo. It was a paradise with skies the colour of hellfire. I mislaid my virginity that day. He had popped my cherry, turned me into a complete woman. Afterwards, he jested that I should change the title of my book to* Hymen. *It does have a certain ring to it, I admit. I was a daisy fresh girl until he interfered with my innocence.* Hebe lives, *he confessed breathlessly, looking as smug and satisfied as the cat that has got the cream.* Oh, and did I tell you I love you? *The Côte d'Azur can wait another day. He promised me minks and diamonds in Antibes, where we would get married soon and declare our love to the world."* Mercier paused. "Shall I continue?"

It made uncomfortable listening, and it was all very damning, particularly the use of those contextual metaphors with growing explicitness. "No need. I've heard enough." But the words . . . the words were so *familiar.* Recognition dawned on his face. This was the book Lottie had been writing, the book she had refused to let him read or discuss until it was finished. Instead, she had been content only in spending time with him. But, oh, she had done her homework! Done it well! Myles could not contain himself. "I give her credit for writing so well. But, persons of the jury, note the *'the Dostoevskian grin, this tangle of thorns'*! For it is a *cheat*! Can't you see what she's done? She has borrowed – no, downright *stolen* – lines from the book I was teaching in class, *Lolita.* There is nothing original in the passages she's summarized, and she cannot use the nonsense excuse that she was only influenced by it or only researching from it, or it demonstrates erudition or revolution. It's unpublishable! Plagiarism is the worst sin any writer can commit. If you don't believe it, get an expert to analyze that manuscript." Why had he not figured that Lottie could not write but only plagiarize? Had she cheated on her assignments, too? Suddenly, Lottie did not appear all that innocent as she had previously led him to believe. With her openly committing the crime of plagiarism, appropriating Nabokov's words like that, could she be as crooked as her father, in order to ensnare her own teacher and tell on him like this? "A schoolgirl's fantasies, nothing more. You must have more than the wishful thinking of an adolescent girl. The title alone, *Hebe on the Make,* barely disguises her intention." Maybe all this palaver was intended to generate public interest in her book as well as access sympathy. It was not uncommon for people to do the most despicable things for fame.

Detective Mercier went on. "Mlle. Heymans refused a forensic examination, but she kept her underwear which she claims is stained with your semen. She handed it to us this morning. It's undergoing DNA analysis."

Myles reeled at the hammer-blow. It took him time to process the news. The girl was clever. "That's very convenient."

"Do you mind if we get a sample of your DNA?"

Myles shook his head slowly. "What if I refuse?"

"Then we have grounds to arrest you on the suspicion of abusing your position as a teacher and engaging in sexual intercourse with a minor, who put her trust in you. If sentenced, you face twenty years in prison and being placed on the Sex Offenders' Register for life"

It was a hard threat, too difficult to ignore, one that demanded he comply. "I guess I have no choice. Take whatever you need."

Detective Mercier rolled the inside of his cheeks with a cotton swab. This sample of his buccal mucosa she placed in a sterile container for the lab.

"Her father is furious," Inspector Gaspard informed him. "He wants results, closure to this investigation."

"He's a fine one to talk!" replied Myles angrily. "There wasn't any affair to conceal. The man granted me his permission to tutor the girl. And now *this*?" He suddenly felt very tired. "Can I go now?"

"At what point did you sleep with her? Tell me, did you *do* it? Yes or no?"

Myles eyeballed the Inspector. "You accuse me of something heinous, of taking advantage of a schoolgirl, and I will respond by saying a gentleman never tells . . ."

It was a furtive, suspicious response, only the best he could come up with on the spur of the moment. There followed a discussion between the two police officers. "I think we've asked all we can for now," said Inspector Gaspard. "We don't have enough evidence to charge you. And, as there is no previous felony that we're aware of, you can leave. We will keep your passport in case we need to bring you in for further questioning."

And so Myles was allowed to leave. Until next time, when the authorities would come calling for him again. Probably soon.

And now here he was back at the villa, in the twilit bedroom, drinking. So far they'd let him off lightly. It had been a fairytale-come-true finding a teaching job in Provence, even if it was in a school for girls. But his entanglement with Lottie which he had pursued as a strictly teacher-student relationship, even a father-daughter relationship, had somehow gone awry. Was she so driven by the idea of fame that instead of crafting the perfect book, she needed to write this sensationalist drivel? A case of art imitating life imitating art? Where fiction masqueraded as non-fiction? Myles hurt over the sense of betrayal, the terrible accusation of hebephilia, the unravelling of his life.

Does lightning strike twice?

[*A gentleman never tells*]

He thought of that song she had played all those weeks ago, Noir Désir's *Lolita Nie En Bloc*. Had she been planning this charade all along?

Once he'd polished off the Farigoule, he slept in the foetal position, dreaming troubled dreams.

By the morning, the same fly, his only company, lay on the floor, its legs curled up, dead.

11

"Did you do it?" Carmain demanded over the phone all the way from Chertsford, beside herself.

Myles had related the events in the lead-up to his interrogation at the police station and the police interview itself. "I really don't want to talk about it." he replied, confidence shattered, morale at rock bottom. "I've got myself into a terrible mess. I thought she wanted to become an accomplished writer. I never thought she might be infatuated with me, be so intent on ruining me. This is entrapment."

"Why didn't you tell me about this before?" Carmain asked. It was her turn to put him on the rack. She was rightfully upset, not just because Myles was her younger brother but because she could cogitate on the situation with the thinking cap of a Safeguarding Nurse.

"I thought it was something that I would be able to deal with on my own."

"This is a *very* serious allegation, Myles. You're a teacher accused of sex with a minor, possibly even rape. You need a lawyer to clear your name. And what about your school, I hope they're being supportive?"

The headmistress and the rest of the school administration had been far from supportive of his current predicament, distancing themselves from him immediately. The French press would be descending on the school in its droves. Myles knew the school would do its utmost to avoid a scandal that might damage its reputation. He had been relieved of all teaching duties and he was no longer allowed to step foot on the school premises until the investigation had been completed, one way or another. "Hardly. I've been suspended."

"I may need to fly over and see how best I can support you," Carmain said, businesslike. "I should be able to help you clear your name."

"There's no need to put yourself out like that on account of me."

A silence followed, a silence that spun out for several long seconds. Myles could hear his sister thinking. Finally, she asked him again, frantically, "They're accusing you of sex with a minor, abusing your position as a teacher. *Did you do it?*"

For a moment he didn't respond, to some a sure sign of guilt. "A gentleman never tells."

"What the heck does that mean?" Carmain burst out, incredulously. "This is not some gentleman's-code-of-honour nonsense! A gentleman never *lies!* Even if the investigation never substantiates the allegation and reports no wrongdoing, the allegation will be logged on your record, keeping in mind your previous run-in with that Lovemore girl. It'll raise suspicions, people thinking there's no smoke without fire. You either did it or you didn't?"

"I can't remember . . ."

Myles knew it was a lame response, but it was all he could offer under the circumstances. After all, it was the truth. He could sense unbridled frustration in his sister's voice as a result of his continued twisting and turning, his ducking and diving. "Being drunk is not an excuse the Judge will let you off on. When I said find a nice girl and settle down, it wasn't a license to seduce a schoolgirl."

"It's just a mistake. A simple misunderstanding." He thought of how the dirty old man of *Lolita* notoriety had transformed, in his sister's astute observations, into the predatory, manipulative woman of *The Reader* and *Notes on a Scandal* in modern literature, a reflection of today's society.

"This is more than just a simple misunderstanding. If her underwear incriminates you, I won't be able to help you." Something occurred to Carmain. "Did you inform the school about your previous chequered record when you applied for the job?" Carmain heard Myles freeze up. His sudden silence spoke volumes. "Please tell me you informed them! *Tell me you informed them!*"

Myles decided to bring the conversation to a close. "I value you as a confidante and friend, not just as my big sister . . . but my mind's made up. I can't go through the same nightmare in another country that I went through with that Lovemore girl. I'm already screwed in my own country, just like Roman Polanski is in America. I'm going to disappear for a while, make myself scarce."

"Don't do anything rash."

"I have to go. Speak soon."

Frustration had given way to screaming despair at the constant roadblocks Myles had erected down the telephone line. "Talk about putting the cat among the pigeons, the fox in the henhouse! *Did you do it? TELL ME!*"

But he had already hung up.

12

Myles Hawking felt it was always a good thing when someone knew when to call it a day. He knew what he was going to do even before he left the police station. Following his preliminary interview, he packed a few essential items and got ready to disappear. He did not even wait for the results of the DNA analysis, which would have proved conclusively one way or the other whether or not he had intimate relations with his student. The bottom had dropped out of his world, and he decided to make himself scarce, shutting himself away from civilization. He went into hiding, but nobody knew where. He knew the previous allegation would catch up with him, and when it did, the police and the public would look at this case in a completely different light. His case turned into an international incident, warranting the attention of the French Interior Minister. The investigation soon took a strange turn and uncovered a conspiracy between Mr. Heymans and the senior school staff designed to frame the English teacher, fuelled by a secret, old grudge the banker still held against the man. Lottie's father had put his daughter up to it. For her to act as jailbait. To befriend, seduce and entrap her teacher, manufacturing excuses for spending time with him. And when people spend too much time together, things are liable to get serious, mistakes liable to be made. Mr. Heymans had never got over the decision made by the English Courts of letting Myles Hawking off the hook over the alleged relationship with Mr. Heyman's niece, Miss Jade Lovemore, and the connection only came to light when the team investigating the Lottie case delved deeper into the affair.

But, by then, Myles Hawking was nowhere to be seen, nowhere near to hear the evidence or the final verdict of the enquiry. Mr. Heymans was held accountable *in absentia*, with calls for his extradition, and Mme. Renard was tried for complicity and perverting the course of justice.

Shut away from the world, Myles Hawking mulled over the timeless words of Nabokov from his not-so-favourite book. *Human life is but a series of footnotes to a vast, obscure, unfinished manuscript.*

Although Myles had survived Hebe, figuratively-speaking, the same question haunted him, wherever he went. Even to this day he did not know if he slept with the girl.

August 2015-November 2015

The Girl in the Mirror

"True love makes the thought of death frequent, easy, without terrors; it merely becomes the standard of comparison, the price one would pay for many things."

Stendhal (1783-1842)
French author and realist

Seven Roses: I'm so infatuated with you...

I: The Girl in the Mirror

The bell tinkled. The door creaked open. Hedrick Savage entered the old curiosity shop, IGNATIUS QUIGLEY'S VINTAGE EMPORIUM: *Antiques & Curiosities*, the rusted sign hanging above the door read.

Hedrick found himself in a dusty, cobwebby old room full of forgotten curios. He stepped forward, wiped dust off a curio cabinet with his index finger and spotted a graveyard of long-dead spiders, web-festooned to the yellow-wallpapered wall. He was struck by the smell of age and must and stale tobacco. Despite the clutter and stillness, he suddenly became conscious of being watched, of another presence in the vicinity.

"I thought you might come by . . ." came a husky male voice from behind the till at the counter.

Although it was not Nell's grandfather who greeted him, the man who emerged from the shadows could have been mistaken for a Dickensian character. His quiff of flaming-red hair was considerably greyed and framed his round face, which sported a dirty stubble that covered his chin dimple and horn-rimmed glasses that had slid down nearly to the tip of his nose. He was dressed in a white shirt knotted with a flowery green cravat, topped off by a natty brown frock coat and waistcoat.

"Do I know you?"

"No," spoke the man, his parting wide lips revealing brown teeth. "But I know *you*. You're that horror writer, Hedrick Savage." Hedrick detected no awe in his voice, not that he considered himself an egotist.

"Guilty as charged."

"Read your last book *The Id and I*. Very vicious, almost as good as your first novel, *Flint & Bones*. No wonder they call you 'The Savage'."

"And you must be Ignatius Quigley . . ."

"The one and the same."

"I didn't know your shop existed. I've been to Church Falls numerous times, searching for inspiration. But I seem to have strangely overlooked this place. Missed it altogether."

"Few people notice my establishment. *It comes and goes . . .*"

It was an odd comment, left unfinished, but Hedrick didn't probe further. He was taken by the exquisite pieces in Ye Olde Curiosity Shop with the excitement of a toddler let loose in a candy store. He would never call them 'junk'. It surprised him that these collector's items didn't belong to a museum. Aside from the various African tribal figures on display, there was a warthog tusk, a symbol of fertility in the Dark Continent. Represented by a dark figure sitting on a crow was a small statue of Shani, the medieval Hindu deity, the bringer of bad luck, full of rage, always getting his revenge on whoever upset him. There was a miniature Terracotta Warrior figurine, made from ceramic, and an early Chinese bronze teapot-and-caddy, with lotus-leaf decoration. Hedrick discovered a Russian three-bolt copper diving helmet *circa* 1930; so incredibly retro. A moth-eaten dreamcatcher hung from the ceiling. A mounted fox skull rested on a cabinet alongside a Louis XVI French inkwell, the statue of a horse, cast in silver, rising up from the lid. Next to it was a silver platter on which stood a Victorian ruby decanter and four crystal glasses. In another section of the curiosity shop, Hedrick was greatly impressed by a perfectly-arranged rodent funeral diorama. Beside it was mounted a dried fruit bat preserved in sleep, hanging upside down, and a gold-plated birdcage containing the skeleton of a parrot. There were crystal balls of various sizes and leatherbound books on witchcraft and Ecuadorian shrunken heads and grinning wood masks and moon-gazing hare sculptures. The Green Man served as a decorative wall plaque. The shop even provided a good selection of medical curiosities, mined from the depths of Time: surgical brews, a wet specimen of a dissected sheep's head in a jar, a plague doctor's costume complete with its bird-like, beak mask, and a box of trepanation tools that once drilled holes into patients' skulls in order to release madness.

Such was Hedrick filled by the mystique of this curiosity shop with its oddities and knickknacks and quirky *objet d'arts*, of olden times remembered, he half-expected it to be hiding one of those cute, furry things that turned into a gremlin if fed after midnight. He wondered what amazing and magical things had been found in curiosity shops the world over.

But it was the sense of being watched that made Hedrick slightly uneasy. He had got this unpleasant feeling since he'd entered Mr. Quigley's warehouse of odds and ends and had assumed it was nothing more than the owner sizing up his new customer. Aside from him and the proprietor, the shop was empty. But that sense of eyes following him around the store was overwhelming, almost palpable and getting stronger . . . and it seemed to be coming from the farthest corner of the establishment. From beneath the dark, dusty cloth that covered a slim, rectangular-shaped object . . .

Hedrick whipped off the cloth to reveal–

He stared at it, instantly captivated. It was an oil painting, framed in wood. It also turned out to be a picture of two halves.

The artist had painted the profile of a beautiful woman, long blond hair flowing down her lithe back, dressed in red satin and barefoot, staring into a cheval glass and, where her reflection ought to have been, was the sharply-rendered figure of a pink, bloated monstrosity, stretching the seams of the dress, the face horribly-deformed and elongated into a proboscis and covered in cobweb-like growths. But it was the eyes that were the most disturbing feature, lantern-red and glowering back at the viewer. It was almost as if it were these very feral eyes that had given rise to the earlier unsettling sensation of being watched and followed around the shopfloor.

"Ah, you have found it," Mr. Quigley announced from afar, breaking the silence, making Hedrick jump. "Or maybe it has found *you*."

Hedrick looked back at the salesman. "What can you tell me about this painting?"

"It's called *La fille dans le miroir* – or *The Girl in the Mirror*, to you and I – and it was created by an artist named Haston Sant-Cassia in Paris in the 1920s."

Hedrick recognized the name of the artist. Sant-Cassia had supposedly painted the supernatural and the macabre. Connoisseurs of canvas horrors had struggled to find much mention of the man, let alone been able to locate his works. The title of the painting, too, was a treat, like seeing just too many faces in a mirror when you're all alone. "Is it an original?"

"There is some dispute as to its authenticity. All I know is that the actual original now belongs to the noted industrialist, Jacob Erlebach. I suspect what you have in front of you is either a reproduction or a lesser-known, supplementary version of the original."

Hedrick surveyed the painting again: the beautiful red-dressed model and her grotesque, reflected image in the looking glass, glaring balefully back. The painting had everything: technique, content, originality, quality. And the weirder the better. "I'll buy it," he declared, excited, picking up the painting and bringing it to the counter. "How much?"

"One hundred pounds," Mr. Quigley replied, fixing a pipe to his lips. He lit it with a match, and the aromatic smoke drifted lazily upwards.

"Will you accept a cheque?" Hedrick asked, pulling out a crumpled chequebook from the inside of his jacket pocket.

"Cash only," Mr. Quigley informed him abruptly.

"But I don't often carry money on my pers–" Hedrick stopped, perplexed, when he retrieved his wallet and opened it. He didn't remember taking any money out from the cashpoint, but somehow he discovered *exactly* one hundred pounds sterling in his wallet. After a moment's pause, during which he made an unsuccessful attempt to understand how he could possibly be carrying the right amount of cash in his wallet, he handed the proprietor the banknotes.

Mr. Quigley accepted the cash, counted the notes. Satisfied, grinning broadly, showing off his mouthful of brown, tobacco-stained teeth, he proceeded to wrap the framed, offbeat painting in brown paper and tied a string around it, completing the transaction. "I hope you enjoy your painting."

Hedrick grabbed the sides of the picture, tucked it under his arm and prepared to leave the curiosity shop. "I'm sure I will."

"I firmly hold the notion that the customer is responsible for assessing the quality of the goods before they leave my premises. *Caveat emptor*, I believe is the legal term."

"No, I'm happy with my purchase."

As Hedrick opened the shop door, the bell above his head tinkling, Mr. Quigley decided to imbue a little theatrics and mysteriousness to the deal. "There is no doubt that paintings can have a profound effect on us. Putting brush to canvas, the artist channels their soul into the image we see, their imagination impacting on us emotionally. We may be moved to tears or be inspired, feel uplifted or disgusted, even experience the entire spectrum of emotions by merely casting an eye on a single painted canvas. But, besides influencing us, can paintings have the power to influence the world we inhabit? Could there be moments when, rather than merely channelling the artist, thus affecting our emotional state, paintings might have the capacity to channel darker, more inscrutable powers beyond our understanding, saturated with the unknown rather than mere paint, reaching out from someplace else to *affect* our reality, going far beyond any work of art . . . to become something far more sinister than the ordinary faculties can conceive? I consider *The Girl in the Mirror* something of a rarity in the antiques' business. It has a very chequered past as you will soon discover and, being a horror writer of your reputation, you may appreciate its remarkable history and relish its sublime beauty. You bought it for one hundred pounds. Now it is worth a thousand nightmares. You have been warned . . .”

II: The Editor

“What do you think?” Hedrick asked his editor.

Hedrick and Leslie Fossington stood admiring *The Girl in the Mirror* in its new home above the dormant fireplace in the horror writer's house in Oaks Fold, HUNTER'S LODGE. Dark leather sofas and armchairs surrounded the antique apothecary-table-cum-coffee-table in the drawing room, giving the painting a wider audience.

“Girls alive, is that what she really looks like?” Leslie exclaimed with a whistle, referring to the blond-haired, satin-clad woman in the painting and, of course, her image reflected unfaithfully back. He examined the painting with his usual sharp eye for detail. “I can certainly see the attraction. Top hole! I'd take it home with me if I could! Beauty and the Beast all rolled into one. The model in the red dress is a piece of art just by herself, full of beauty and grace and poise, and you know how much I love barefoot women! But her apparent reflection is *something else*, the very antithesis of the model looking in, a thing to be greatly feared. I wonder if the image in the mirror is *not* her reflection at all but a visitor at the door – or *gateway* – to another place, inhabited by these monstrous beings.”

“I like that,” contemplated Hedrick. “Gives a new slant to the painting, adds another dimension to the work.”

Leslie continued to critically appraise the painting. "Maybe it symbolizes a monster based on life, and the painting speaks of the dual nature in all of us. The ugliness is a part of us, too. But, being a horror writer, you already know that."

Hedrick accepted the interpretation. "Makes perfect sense, I guess. Lady, lady, quite contrary . . ."

"Art allows us to see what we want to see, like a Rorschach inkblot, but it can make us share a universal feeling." Leslie dwelled on this thought for a moment longer. "Down to business, however," he eventually said, changing the subject, but Hedrick noticed his editor's eyes kept wandering back to the painting. "When do I get to read a few chapters of your new book?"

Hedrick sighed. He might be in between books, but he was suffering the throes of writer's block, a malady that most writers experienced at least once in their lifetimes. "I haven't made a start on the new book yet. I'm devoid of ideas or inspiration."

Leslie Fossington was a disciplined man, almost regimental, as evidenced by his pencil-thin, military-style moustache and brown tweed suit and waistcoat, and he expected results from the writers in his employ at HORRORWORKS Publishing House. He was, indeed, a retired army officer, with more than a passing resemblance to that old dog, Leslie Phillips. *I say, Ding Dong!* Every writer, in his opinion, needed an editor since writers tended to be blind to their own work. Learning, presently, that one of his writers was struggling to put words onto paper was particularly anxiety-provoking for the man. "Should I be worried?"

"Hopefully not." Then, it occurred to him. A light-bulb moment. Hedrick's eyes lit up. He gestured to his new acquisition. "My next foray could be about the painting! A tale about a well-to-do character who happens to purchase a painting, unaware of the painting's terrible history, only to slowly succumb to madness under the painting's negative influence."

"My thoughts, *exactly*!" replied Leslie, and Hedrick detected relief on his face. "Inspired! Pulled an absolute corker from the ideas' factory!"

"The idea was right there all along. I just couldn't see it at first."

"All good things come to those who wait . . . without procrastinating." Leslie picked up his beige overcoat draped over the back of the armchair. He extracted the extendable brolly from the coat pocket. It had begun to rain outside again, fresh, warm summer rain. The scud of dark clouds overhead suggested a thunderstorm waited patiently in the wings. "I shall take my leave of you, good sir, now that the crisis has been averted," he announced jocularly. "I can always rely on my pool of writers to furnish me with the goods, come hell or high water.

Your readers shall wait with bated breath for your next book. But I can safely say you have found the hook that reels the reader in."

Hedrick smiled. It was odd that, just like Liverpool, there should be an over-representation of horror writers originating from Oaks Fold, predominantly based at Horrorworks. Maybe it was Oaks Fold itself that attracted these authors of strange fiction. Hedrick, also known as 'The Savage' for obvious reasons as well as 'The Kill-Murder-Death Man', was one of the vaguely-celebrated 'Triumvirates' according to his respectable readership, alongside Nicholas Haures, who had mysteriously disappeared in the Canary Islands, and Hartigan Strange, who had suffered a fate weirder than his works. As for Connor Holden, from HAMBLEYS PUBLISHING, one could have considered him the fourth musketeer in this intimate circle, a young pretender who had become a legend in his own right. True, Hedrick hadn't quite gone global yet, but there were marketing plans in the pipeline to better his exposure. What separated the Oaks Fold writers from the more mainstream fare was the realism in their dark writings, taking horror to its absolute extreme without having to suspend the reader's imagination. Stephen King certainly was a damn fine storyteller – probably the best, hands down – and he endeavoured with complete conviction to tell a good story – it was always about the story – but there was nothing meaningful or educational about his small-town, homespun yarns. Britain's own James Herbert, when living, had utilized a better, quintessentially English writing style than Mr. King, his prose narrated with calm, clinical efficiency, but he had lacked the range and versatility of Mr. King's imagination. When the modern greats of horror claimed that it's scarier if things *just happen*, otherwise their work might seriously fall down if they ever dared try rationalize the events unfolding in their book, Hedrick considered it a cop-out and a failing of their work, a *cheat*. As far as he was concerned, things happened for a reason, and it had to make sense to the reader for it to be believed; logic was called for even in the realm of the fantastic. Hedrick viewed himself as a pilgrim travelling through this world in search of affirmation, an adventurer exploring the very limits of human nature, the darker aspects of existence, without actually physically daring to experience the horrors life had to offer, because in fiction-writing, as a rule of thumb, he knew that if you can think it, somebody's already done it. He held the notion that the End was near, approaching us both through the brevity of mortal life and, on a global scale, the ruination of the world. *We, Prophets of the Apocalypse,* he often philosophized, *shall prepare the Reader for the Coming of the End.* "If my father hadn't burned the horror stories I used to write for pleasure as a teenager because he firmly believed I should concentrate on my school work instead of wasting my energy on macabre things, I might never have developed the determination to forge a reputation in the very niche he found offensive." He paused for a moment, thoughtful. "The secret is always about telling a good story, doing a damned decent job, blowing the reader's mind, making them feel different emotions . . . and *not* about becoming famous. If it is money or fame you seek or getting laid or making friends, instead of putting in the toil and effort, writing an *honest* piece of work, putting your soul into it, you will never succeed. You write because you love writing. Fame is always secondary, a pleasant consequence."

"You're a damn fine storyteller," Leslie said thoughtfully, "Talent accounts for success, but not all of it. Hard work plays an important role. And luck has something to do with it, too." He took one last glance at *The Girl in the Mirror*, sitting pretty on the wall. Or, when taking into consideration the repulsive creature in the mirror-image, maybe not so pretty. "Here's a pleasant thought . . . What if it wasn't you who was attracted to the painting, but it was the painting that was attracted to *you*?"

III: The Girlfriend

When Hedrick showed his girlfriend, Gemma Wetherby, the painting, the colour drained from her cheeks and her jaw dropped in a look of horror, her mouth forming a silent O expression. It was a completely different reaction to the one produced by his editor.

"It's horrid!" Gemma protested, taking in the reflected abomination in the picture. "But I also fully appreciate why you bought it. I just kindly ask that you keep that *girl-fiend* away from your dearest *girl-friend*."

Hedrick accepted his girlfriend's catastrophic reaction and subsequent request, not altogether surprising, without another word, and led her into the large kitchen.

Gemma was a sous chef at PASCAL'S, and it was her evening off. She had planned to cook them both a romantic dinner. *I prefer Bambi to Peppa Pig tonight*, he joked with her. As she toiled away over the stove, Hedrick popped out briefly with the excuse of 'checking-out'; in other words, to smoke a cigarette. The thundery showers of the afternoon had given way to a gorgeous sunset.

When the food was ready, Gemma laid out their lovingly-prepared meals on the round, pine kitchen table rather than formalizing dinner in the dining room.

The pan-seared venison steak with mixed peppery salad went down a treat with a nice glass of Bordeaux.

Hedrick expressed his gratitude, once he'd polished off his meal. "Thank you for that."

"It was the least I could do for my little Savage," she remarked, smiling. She remembered that Sunday afternoon she first met him at THE SQUIRE'S OAK pub. He had been, as always, dressed in black, his dark, slightly greying, wavy hair shaped into a stylish pompadour, his blue eyes drifting to her table, where she sat with her friend, Josette Barker. He had a deep, somewhat unsettling stare to go with the old scar that radiated up the right side of his neck and corresponding cheek, acquired from a mugging at knifepoint ten years ago in London. The scar gave his face character, just as the scar the *real* James Bond sported, as envisioned by Ian Fleming in the books, was meant to bestow the aura of a sophisticated thug.

Who's that cute guy? Gemma had asked Josette.

Looks like a murderer, Josette responded, not without humour.

I wish he would murder me . . . Gemma said in admiration.

Then, she, like her friend, learned who he was. Hedrick had been down the local for a pint, celebrating the completion of his last novel, *The Id and I.* He bought everyone in the pub a round. At the time, Gemma had thought it amazing to meet a successful, real-life horror writer, but when he had shown a particular interest in her, she was blown off her feet.

Just like the life-story of every individual human being on this planet, I consider every relationship to be unique, Hedrick explained.

Me too, she spluttered.

I suppose we can make our own unique *memories.* Hedrick winked.

They dated and now they were going steady. Even though she hailed from a medical family, she didn't like Horror, found the subject too uncomfortable for her tastes, but this did not affect their relationship. There survived a mutual agreement between cricket-hating wives and their famous cricketer-husbands not to discuss cricket at home. Gemma accepted Hedrick's eccentricities and quirks without complaint, but his vices, namely a fondness for drink and cigarettes, she bore somewhat reluctantly.

Hedrick looked adoringly into Gemma's hazel eyes, set in her oval face and crowned by her long, chestnut curls. "You are as lovely as a Picasso painting."

Gemma quipped: "You mean I look like one of Picasso's painted women – long horsey face, nose and both eyes on one side of the face?"

"Picasso loved all his women passionately, no matter what they looked like."

Gemma grinned. "Good recovery."

"And you thought the Mona Lisa was disappointingly small . . ."

"Well. it *was* . . ." Gemma mock-complained. "It looked way too small in the Louvre compared to the photographs." She sounded as cute as a button, so Hedrick kissed her. "You taste like an ashtray."

"That's probably because I smoked the ashtray," said Hedrick somewhat dreamily. "That reminds me . . . Need to check-out." 'Checking-out' as he called it. Euphemism for smoking. He disappeared outside, lighting a cigarette in the warm dusk, at his usual spot, next to the bougainvillea tree. Gemma cleared away the plates in the meantime. Once done, Hedrick entered the house again through the kitchen side-door. He wrapped his arms around Gemma's waist as she washed the dishes, his right cheek tight against the back of her neck, breathing in her expensive perfume. "Would it turn you on, having sex with a dying man . . . if I had cancer?"

"No, it wouldn't!" she exclaimed, laughing. "Why anyone would want to pay a lot of money to slowly poison themselves to death is beyond me!"

"I don't care if you preserve me or cremate me or jump up and down on my corpse or do filthy, depraved things to me when I die from cancer."

"That's grim, Heddy. I don't do necrophilia."

"But that's so fly!" he mock-encouraged.

She looked back at him expressionlessly.

"Shame . . ." he murmured, but she knew he was only kidding.

"I'm sick of people who don't appreciate life, and when they're about to die, they want to live."

"Good for you, babe . . ." he bantered, "I do hate sick people, moaning on about how sick they are . . ."

"You've certainly set the bar too high tonight."

"Stoners and loners."

"Designer vaginas."

"Multiple penises and cock sleeves."

"Holes . . . plenty of holes."

"Lotus seed pods." Hedrick brought the word association to an end. He grinned, full of juvenile mischief. "My horn is up!"

Gemma laughed. "I'll show you mine if you show me yours . . ."

They made out on the kitchen table. Tarting up his breath with a quick spray of mouth freshener, Hedrick removed his black shirt and partially opened

Gemma's yellow flowery dress and climbed on top of her. She kicked off her white peep-toe shoes and he pulled down his trousers, excited, highly aroused. He penetrated her instantly. She was wet. And soon they were synchronizing their climax in tune with the other's sensitized body. Straight, uncomplicated sex.

When they had concluded their lovemaking and whispered sweet nothings into their partner's ear, Hedrick put on his clothes and prepared to reward himself by checking-out. However, he discovered the cigarette packet was empty. He scrunched it up and wandered down the hallway to access the box of cigarettes from the bottom drawer of the desk in his study.

He passed the drawing room . . . and he stopped dead in his tracks. The door to the drawing room was ajar and Hedrick could clearly see the painting from where he stood. He drifted into the room, walking with slow, conscious steps, and positioned himself directly in front of the painting. Somehow the scene in the picture looked startlingly different from how he remembered it. The red-clad model and her unsightly reflection still occupied the picture, but what had hit him was that *both* figures were now looking at him. Whereas the pink, snouty creature in the looking glass continued to glare straight at him with an avid hatred, the model's face was no longer in profile. In fact, her face was turned ninety-degrees towards him, and she was now looking at him, full-on. No mistake. He could presently see the fullness of her lovely cobalt-blue eyes in more detail, watching him intently.

The strange half-light of dusk had nothing to do with it. And he could not explain it away by saying he hadn't paid close attention to the finer points of the painting when he'd first bought it. Because he remembered scrutinizing it carefully at the time.

The painting had *changed*. Without a doubt. Subtle but definitely noticeable.

He stared at it long and hard, transfixed, his entire being suddenly filled by an unhealthy dread. Gooseflesh prickled his skin. A vein twitched on his temple. *Here's looking at you, kid!*

The model was definitely facing him and, where she had been beauteous in profile previously, her entire countenance was now clearly visible in the finest detail and wholly arresting, an exquisite pleasure to look at, more desirable than he ever imagined, captivating and comely enough to fall in love with. *Yes, indeed, the fun has begun—*

"Uh-hum . . ." a female coughed nearby.

For a split second, Hedrick thought the model in the picture had begun to vocalize too, and the noise made him jump. Until he realized the sound had emanated from beside him.

Gemma stood next to him, looking questioningly at the painting. "What are you looking at?"

"Huh?" mumbled Hedrick, glancing at her with a puzzled look of his own.

"Hello?" Gemma said, trying to get through to him. "Earth calling Heddy, do you read me, over?" She was glad to see reality filtering back into Hedrick's initial blank expression. "You were gone nearly half an hour, so I decided to find you. So what happened? What kept you? What grabbed your attention all of a sudden?"

"The painting . . . it's *differ–*" he began, abruptly breaking off in mid-sentence when his eyes travelled back to the painting. The knowledge he had been staring at the painting for a near-eternity without even realizing didn't even enter into the equation.

The minor alteration to the painting was gone. The juxtaposition of the figures was as it had been all along. The beautiful model in the red dress was standing in profile again, clearly facing the looking glass, and her beastly, demon-eyed reflection threw a hostile, penetrating stare at the onlooker, sufficiently capable of following them around the room.

"Don't worry . . ." Hedrick murmured. "I'll meet you back in the kitchen."

Gemma kissed him on the cheek and wandered off.

Hedrick went back to staring at the painting, drawn to it, looking for signs of movement or life, unable to pull his eyes away.

But the painting, it did not change.

IV: Haston Sant-Cassia

It seemed prudent for Hedrick to gain a little background on the artist himself. After a restless, unrefreshing sleep, filled with troubling, unremembered dreams, Hedrick awoke at the crack of dawn, keen to learn a little something about Haston Sant-Cassia, whose particular genius had created this work of art. Yes, Art was meant to entertain and educate, enrich and inspire – a picture should reflect the beauty of the subject in its various shapes and guises – but sometimes, in the case of Sant-Cassia, it might also be designed to creep you out.

Quickly checking the painting in the drawing room and discovering there was nothing out of place with the scene or the poses of the model and her reflection – was he expecting anything else? – Hedrick went online to read up about the picture's creator.

Surprisingly, there wasn't a great deal of information on the Internet about Haston Saint-Cassia, and admittedly Mr. Quigley, the proprietor of the old curiosity shop, had disclosed as much as he could, but Hedrick managed to glean up a little more about the man. Of course, Sant-Cassia was the tortured-genius type, but curiously enough he had been a *persona non gratis* in artistic circles, during Jazz Age Paris, the well-documented hub of creative endeavours, where the relocated Literati rubbed shoulders with the new Masters of the Canvas. A fiercely private man, Sant-Cassia had shunned and been shunned by his contemporaries. Gertrude Stein had expressed her distaste of Sant-Cassia's repertoire with a cautionary note: *Nobody should dabble in powers they don't fully understand.* Even someone as bizarre as Dalí, during the emergence of the Surrealist movement, had given Sant-Cassia a wide berth, referring to Sant-Cassia's work with almost prophetic accuracy: *Man creates Art. Art destroys Man.* But Sant-Cassia had been unfazed by his own alienation and carried on his labours like a man possessed. Little was known about his origins – where he was born, his family, his childhood, his life during the First World War – and his fate was still a matter of debate.

From his online research, Hedrick learned that Sant-Cassia had eked out a modest existence from his works, most however unsold, and those few who had bought his paintings had allegedly suffered horrible deaths or gone barking mad. After a short, impoverished life, penniless at the end, Sant-Cassia had disappeared in 1927, never to be seen again. He had been only thirty-four. Rumours abounded, from the possibility that he'd killed himself, hurled himself in the Seine in the grip of an alcoholic depression, to the more implausible and frightening notion that the monstrous beings he had been so adept at painting had taken him away. The latter defied explanation, but it was also the most intriguing theory for a horror writer like Hedrick Savage.

The fledgling idea had been trapped in his head since it had first appeared to him in the presence of Leslie Fossington, waiting to be put down on paper, and presently it grew into something more real and workable, ready for flight. Hedrick had even finalized a title for his next novel, borrowed from Dalí: *Art Destroys Man.*

He had a long session of writing ahead. *Yep, that's me again, up to no good!* Throughout the morning, propped up by coffee, Hedrick generated a detailed book synopsis, which he hoped to email his editor later, complete with character study, with the verve of a proto-psychologist, and a detailed plot set-up, to start working on whenever he chose.

I revel in serial killers galore and murders of barbaric intensity, he thought, confidently typing away on his PC. *You just need a little forensic understanding to write that kind of stuff. But this will be a new direction for me. An actual focus on dark art and the dreadful impact it can have on a fragile human psyche.*

But what did become of Sant-Cassia's sketches and paintings? More rumours, more unsubstantiated reports. Distributed to the wider population and the apparent cause of unexplained fatalities and asylum-dwelling madness among the collectors. Switching owners, the cycle always allegedly repeating itself. No museum had ever succeeded in holding on to his pieces, as workers and visitors become unhinged and killed themselves, some even attempting to destroy the works. It is alleged that the Nazis soon confiscated as many of Sant-Cassia's works as they could find, using them for secret ceremonies in order to raise dark forces from beyond this earth or worshipping them in depraved, drug-fuelled, ultra-decadent orgies to propagate the Aryan race of Nazi philosophy, as Hitler's pursuit of occult relics reached fever pitch. Then, as the Nazis were defeated in 1945 and their evil, genocidal officers faced the Nuremberg trial, the entire collection of Haston Sant-Cassia went up for auction behind closed doors which the noted industrialist, Jacob Erlebach, allegedly acquired with a million-dollar bid. And Erlebach was never heard of again, such is the nature of any recluse, and the name of Sant-Cassia dwindled away over the decades, fading from the lips of the public just as he had once disappeared from life.

So, whether Hedrick possessed an original painting or a reproduction did not matter. Authentic or otherwise, it was the content of the picture, in his opinion, that was the true selling-point. It was worth a thousand nightmares, as Mr. Quigley had claimed, and Hedrick just needed to access its full potential for literary means. He was excited about the book he had made a start on. Might even be his best yet, his most sophisticated and grown-up. *His masterpiece.*

Hedrick wondered who the model in *The Girl in the Mirror* was. The act of uglifying her beauty through the looking glass was an interesting choice of thematic deconstruction, but the barefoot, blond, red-satin-wearing girl fascinated him. Psychologists might describe her hideous alter-image as a representation of her inner personality: *beautiful on the outside, loathsome on the inside.*

Lacing his fingers behind his head, resting his heels on the computer desk, Hedrick closed his eyes for a moment to contemplate this very notion when he slowly drifted off. He napped before falling into a deeper sleep . . . and he began to dream.

In the dream, Hedrick finds himself in a dirty, rat-infested studio apartment. There are weird-looking canvases laid out against the walls. Empty wine and absinthe bottles are strewn across the sparsely-furnished apartment. The apartment overlooks the bustling boulevard, the windows glimpsing pigeon-nestling rooftops and chimneys, the glass as filthy as the figure standing in the middle of the studio, wearing a voluminous, stained shirt, palette in hand, applying the final brushstrokes to the easel-propped painting he is furiously working on.

The artist suddenly stops and steps back to admire the finished product. "Voilà," he declares proudly, triumphantly.

No longer trying to peer over the shoulder of the artist, Hedrick is now able see the picture in its absolute glory, made all the more peculiar in the grey light of day, and he recognizes it immediately. The artist has painted The Girl in the Mirror, the same delectable model peering into a cheval glass which reflects back an obscene representation of her, still wet from the paintbrush.

Which means–

"Thank you for coming to see me complete my work," the artist announces matter-of-factly, turning round to face the intruder in his midst, the unexpectedness of the introduction causing Hedrick to start.

Hedrick composes himself. "You can see me?"

"Of course," states the artist calmly, his English slowly and inexplicably losing any trace of a French accent. Although his hair is matted and unwashed and his face gaunt and streaked with paint and grime, Hedrick cannot deny the underlying handsomeness of the man. There is something else that Hedrick cannot yet put a finger on to describe this man. "I've been expecting you."

"You're Haston Sant-Cassia!" Hedrick exclaimed.

"I am he."

This is such a pivotal moment in history, Hedrick thinks, overawed, the crossroads to something monumental, for I have witnessed a past master at work and the completion of the very painting I was destined to own, and I am actually conversing with the very artist underground fables hold dear – and with fear. Hedrick realizes he is in 1920s Paris, either in real time or merely in his mind, and he wonders if he would be able to meet any of those writers and artists and musicians who occupied this classic Années Folles era. Might he bump into the luminaries of the Lost Generation: Hemingway, Scott Fitzgerald, Miller? Despite the wealth of knowledge about the art scene of Paris during this period, little is recorded about the struggling Outsider artist, Sant-Cassia, as though his contemporaries like Dalí and Picasso were ashamed of him – or afraid to mention his name – treating him like a black sheep, until he eventually died a destitute man, vanishing from the world altogether, a controversial figure whom History conveniently buried and spoke no more of.

"I'm–"

"–Hedrick Savage. I know *who you are* . . . You are the man who buys my painting almost a century from now."

Hedrick tries to wrap his head around the situation. He has misplaced his fear somewhere. There is only fascination of the impossible. "How can this be? I must be dreaming, surely."

"There are ways to cross Time and Dimensions – and Dreams," Haston Sant-Cassia explains. "The Mind is a place of easy access under the right circumstances." He is reluctant to elaborate any further and draws Hedrick's attention back to the picture he has duly completed. "You may be wondering who she is . . . and what became of her."

"How did you guess?"

"Her name was Arabella," Sant-Cassia explains, gesturing to the beautiful, barefoot girl in the red satin dress in the painted canvas, the intimacy within. "She was a simple country girl from Rennes, not yet twenty, who came to Paris to seek her fortune. I met her by chance, but I was taken by her. She posed for this painting and was the subject for a series of other pictures, but I could tell she was dissatisfied by my company, yearning for more exciting adventures. I put her restlessness down to her young age. Whatever the motivation, she soon left me to chase her bohemian dreams. Unfortunately, she was passed around by so many men she ended her days in the Parisian bordellos, a putain. She eventually hung herself in a moment of despair."

This sad tale Sant-Cassia relates on the edge of lugubrious emotion, a sucking melancholia, and Hedrick acknowledges how special this woman must have been to the fellow. The painter, who looks as if he is losing the passion for his craft and coming to the end of the road, is so far removed from the whoring ways of most painters of his age, while his only true love ends up a disease-carrying whore. Tragic. "I'm truly sorry . . ."

"No need for pity," Sant-Cassia goes on morosely. "I captured from life a part of her that will stay with me forever. It is that very wildness in her I have imbued into her painting that has the power to drive men mad."

And Hedrick understands what has eluded him so far, the word that has sat on the tip of his tongue to describe Sant-Cassia's general haggard appearance. Sant-Cassia looks haunted – which has nothing to do with being constantly wasted on absinthe when he is not painting. Sant-Cassia may have lost the girl he once loved, but he has sublimated those romantic sentiments by preserving her unique beauty and the grief she caused him in pictorial form. The girl must have been a genuine heartbreaker! "I appreciate your insights into your painting."

"Art is art whichever medium it's set in," Sant-Cassia emphasizes. "Words are as powerful and timeless as any image or sculpture. Arabella will get inside your mind and refuse to leave until you too, mon ami, are surely at her mercy. She was always destined to attract a great number of lovers – and victims. She can make men say or do whatever she wants."

His warning brings a small shiver up Hedrick's spine. Hedrick hears the cooing of pigeons from the rooftops, the hammering of his own heart in his chest. Sant-Cassia continues, "There is no room for complacency," and Sant-Cassia suddenly booms with the husky voice of Mr. Quigley. "Be warned. Arabella is worth a thousand nightmares . . ."

And Hedrick sees, with dawning horror and confusion, that the red-satin-wearing model in the freshly-completed painting, set on an easel in the centre of the studio, no longer resembles the sweet country girl of Sant-Cassia's eternal affections but Hedrick's girlfriend, Gemma Wetherby, with her cascade of chestnut curls, her head turned to face the viewer, hazel eyes fixed directly on Hedrick, her face contorted into the sublime wickedness of the demonically-possessed. "Enjoying your afternoon nap, my love?" the girl-fiend in the painting inquires, grinning contemptuously back at him . . .

–Hedrick screamed . . . and fell, flailing, fingers clutching air. He hit the ground, banging his head. He opened his eyes and the world around him swam for a moment until his vision steadied itself. He found he was safe in his study, albeit lying asprawl on the carpet. He realized he had unbalanced in his chair, where he had been sleeping in a precarious position, and gravity had sent him unceremoniously to the floor. His head smarted, and he rubbed his right temple where it had struck the floor.

When a female voice asked, up close and personal into his ear, "Enjoying an afternoon nap, my love?", Hedrick shrieked again.

V: The Sound of Her Voice

Hedrick discovered it wasn't the girl-fiend but his *girlfriend*. "I didn't mean to frighten you," Gemma apologized, kneeling down beside him. "You must have had quite the tumble."

"Glad it's you," he murmured with absolute honesty, getting to his feet. That peculiar but lucid dream, that remembrance of things past, that journey through time to witness a talented artist, ostracized for investing his emotions and energies on warped, arcane subject matters, putting the finishing touches to one of his dearest paintings, was already fading to a vestigial memory. "I didn't mean to lose my cool exterior like that."

Gemma smiled, amused. "It's not often one sees a man of horror screaming like a little girl confronted by a spider in the bathtub."

"Yes, talking of spiders," Hedrick improvised, thinking of those huge, spindly cellar spiders in the shed. "You go to bed and all the spiders come out in the middle of the night, gather on your bed and look at you sleeping with their countless eyes. How's that for an image?"

Gemma shivered. "No thank you! Not an image I care to think about!"

"What about the image of someone frenziedly eating handfuls of live spiders?"

"You're not winning any sympathy here."

"We shall therefore speak no more of it," Hedrick said, not as embarrassed as he ought to have been. "What brings you to my neck of the woods?"

"I thought I'd check in on you before going off to work," Gemma replied. "I've got a long evening shift ahead of me at the restaurant. I have a Head Chef who bullies his staff because I think he's insecure about his height. He's probably five-foot-eight but wants everyone to believe he's five-foot-ten. Men lie about their height unless they're six foot, in which case they have no reason to lie."

Which meant, if Gemma was heading off to work, it must be just after six. He had slept all afternoon. He had slept and dreamed for nearly seven hours. Outside, through the study window, Hedrick could see it was still light, a reddening, summer evening light. "I didn't realize it was so late."

"I'm guessing you haven't been sleeping well."

"True," Hedrick admitted. "The weeks of writer's block probably got to me. The last few nights have been a sleepless hell. But, good news. I've taken a crack at the new novel today. I've completed the synopsis, which I intend to share with Leslie this evening."

"That really is good news," said Gemma, delighted. "Hopefully you can sleep better tonight. You know a sleep deficit will always catch up with the person. Just have a nice long lie-in in the morning."

"I'll try . . ." he said, greatly appreciating her concern and sound advice. At least, he'd made a start on his new book. Going forward, things could only get better.

Then, out of the blue, someone whispered: *If you don't love me, it does not matter...*

Hedrick jumped. "Excuse me?" he said, glancing at Gemma questioningly.

"What is it, Heddy?" Gemma responded, surprised.

"Did you say something?"

Gemma frowned. "No, I don't think so . . ."

If you don't love me, it does not matter, came the lady's voice, repeating the statement, and it suddenly occurred to Hedrick it had originated from inside his own head. The words were tinged in a soft French accent, giving them a musical sound. *Anyway, I can love for the both of us.*

What the hell . . .? thought Hedrick, somewhat startled.

Gemma saw her boyfriend's face, the look of puzzlement and alarm. "What's the matter?" she asked, mystified.

"Nothing . . . I think . . ." Hedrick replied, trying to play it down, producing a fake smile. He partially succeeded because Gemma's furrowed brow smoothed out.

"Will you be okay?" she asked in a maternal tone.

"I'll be fine," he told her. "Don't worry about me."

A little reassured, she kissed him on the lips. "I've left a case of six bottles of Chateauneuf in the kitchen. I thought the arms of the old lady at the till were about to fall off just trying to lift the case. Why they would want to work at that age, I'll never know. Word to the wise: I know it's reasonably quaffable wine, but please don't drink it all. I wouldn't want you ending up with a strawberry nose like Gerald Depardieu, who can comfortably glug down three bottles a day and still remain relatively sober." She moved to the hallway. "I'll pop by in the morning, Heddy. Rest well." With that, she departed. Hedrick watched her go out of the front door.

Leave her! demanded the delicately-spoken French voice with a vengeance. *She cannot love you like I can! We can be together!*

This time the inner voice was louder, sharper, more insistent, and Hedrick felt a conflict of emotions. Yes, he was hearing the voice from inside his head, undoubtedly, and that should have freaked him out, but the voice was beautiful, full of adoration . . . and yearning.

"Are you for real?" he said out aloud. And kicked himself. He had begun talking to himself. His subconscious was playing tricks on him and he was giving in to it.

I only want us to be together.

"Stop pestering me!" he said to the empty study. "You're making me sound crazy!" He switched on the radio as a distraction, hoping to drown out the voice. Alice Gold sang *Runaway Love*.

The voice went quiet. He hoped, this time for good. He decided to distract himself. He made his way into the kitchen. Sure enough, he found the case of wine Gemma had kindly bought for him on the kitchen counter. He opened the box, pulled out a bottle, applied the corkscrew and poured himself a glass. He felt like a drink right now. But he also felt more in need of a cigarette. He checked-out, enjoying the light buzz of a fresh cigarette by the bougainvillea tree outside, his usual spot, before returning to the kitchen to prepare a quick snack. The triple-decker ham-and-mustard sandwich went down well with a generous glass of quality full-bodied red.

Once pleasantly full and somewhat relieved the intrusive female voice hadn't made a reappearance in the corridors of his mind, he poured himself another glass of wine and rang his editor at home.

Leslie Fossington answered after a couple of rings. "Hello, Mr. Savage," he said mock-formally. "How goes it?"

"Very well, thank you," Hedrick said amicably. "And your health is unchanged since yesterday?"

"Fit as a fiddle," replied Leslie in his usual clipped tones. "What can I do you for?"

"Just to update you," began Hedrick. "I've not been idle. I've managed to make a concerted start on the new book. I've been beavering away conscientiously on the synopsis."

"Splendid!" said Leslie, pleased. "I knew I could count on you."

"I've even come up with a title, borrowed from an uncredited quote by Dalí: *Art Destroys Man.*"

"Sounds like an excellent title! A change of direction for you, methinks. Curiously enough, reminds me of Stendhal's ailment."

"Stendhal?"

Leslie elaborated. "For the benefit of us unfamiliar with the name, there was once a nineteenth-century French writer and philosopher going by the pen name of Stendhal, who visited Florence and was driven temporarily insane by viewing the powerful paintings and statues there, and whose experiences gave rise to a genuine psychiatric condition called Stendhal Syndrome, which is a transient madness brought on by appreciating sublime works of art, be it a painting, an absorbing piece of music, the refined text of a literary masterpiece, etc., in the same way that a psychotropic drug may have a potent effect on the mind. Doctors say that even the dark, terrible beauty of a house can have this impact on a person."

"Definitely worth knowing, thanks. I'll email you the synopsis shortly for your perusal before I send you any new pages. Hope you dig the tale. Tell me what you think."

"How's the painting in question, the picture that provided you with the inspiration to start afresh? Looking after it well, I hope? . . . But is it looking after *you*?"

Leslie's last remark caused Hedrick to recall his recent vivid dream, of the unclean, absinthe-addled figure from a bygone era, whose interest in the macabre had left him friendless and alone, dedicating one of his final paintings to the woman he once loved before she went down the dark, slippery road into prostitution and eventual ruin, taking her own life in the end. And the French-accented female voice surfacing up from his unconscious afterwards, like some spring bloater, which he had kept shtum about from Gemma. Hedrick lied. "All is well." He said hurriedly: "Got to go. Will call you at a convenient time of your choosing, chum, to catch up again." Then, he hung up.

Hedrick was feeling agitated which he could not explain. In the study, he forwarded the synopsis to Leslie's work email address before surfing a little information on Marie Stendhal. Finally, he felt he should check in on the painting in the drawing room.

Even from afar he could tell it had changed. It was *that* obvious.

He strode across the drawing room and stood in front of it.

The picture had changed but not in the way he had expected it to.

The painting had become a full-frontal nude. Whereas the snouted, cobwebby monster in the mirror was still present, still fully clothed and unchanged in stance, its malevolent stare fastened on Hedrick, the blond-haired model, whose reflection it was, had stripped off her dress, shamelessly exposing her well-endowed body.

She was naked. Completely naked.

The red satin dress lay on the floor of the chamber in the painting.

No longer in profile, the nude model faced Hedrick directly in a seductive pose, and Hedrick regarded her naked hourglass physique: the creaminess of her skin, the gorgeous roundness of her perfect breasts with their pert nipples, and the dark thatch of hair between her legs, shaped like the inverted triangle of a road warning sign.

Pigment on canvas, nothing more, Hedrick tried to remind himself. But he knew these magically-changing details of the painting were something more. *Much more.*

He could not escape the bare facts.

She was naked . . . and she was beautiful. Devastatingly beautiful.

The onset of dread gave rise to the first stirrings of desire.

The pleasures of love are always in proportion to our fears, Hedrick thought, citing Stendhal, who had also clearly observed that all religions were founded on the fear of the many and the cleverness of the few.

The golden hair cascaded down her back, her lips were curled upwards, clearly forming a smile, and the lovely blue eyes were now focused on him. He had her complete attention. She had his.

I have been staring at you staring at me. It was that soft-accented voice again – *her* voice.

"Who are you?" he spoke to the painting, himself cognizant of the craziness of it all. "*What* are you?"

You know who I am, she replied, a mental presence co-existing with his conscious mind. Or perhaps it was only his own thoughts bouncing back, taking on the persona of another person.

"Arabella?"

She doesn't deserve you, the voice declared abruptly.

He knew immediately Arabella was referring to Gemma. "She's my girlfriend. I love her."

You need somebody like me. It is our time now.

The moving picture, the ever-changing scene in the painting, a dead woman manifesting as a ghostly voice in the forefront of his mind should have reminded him that nobody was exempt from madness. But he had a different opinion. *The picture is changing. Taking on a life of its own.* Coming alive.

The eyes of the nude model fixed on his, the voice said: *Come, my love. Attend to me. I ache for you.*

Those words were not a warning but a sultry welcome, Hedrick realized. He seemed rooted to the spot, unable to break free from her powerful gaze, mesmerized, sensing her eyes look deep into his soul and his own sins shining back at him. Had he lost all objectivity and his subjective perception of the painting was a form of wish fulfilment? He did not need anyone else to tell him he was engaging with the painting in a very unhealthy manner.

Then he was no longer standing in the drawing room. Experiencing a magnetic, fluttery pull in the pit of his stomach that radiated outwards along all his limbs, Hedrick realized he was somewhere else as the painting proved to be more than just a simple construct of wood, canvas and paint. It opened up a window into the basement of the Universe, outside the range of normal awareness and accepted reality.

Are you man enough to love me?

She invited him in.

VI: A Collection of Haunted Paintings

Hedrick might have expected to find ghosts in foggy cemeteries or old, creaky mansions, but he knew people also believed that certain unearthly entities could inhabit everyday, inanimate objects, such as statues, mirrors and, of course, paintings. Hedrick had done his research well. As far back as Dorian Gray, whose fictional portrait grows ever more ancient in appearance while the man, whose portrait it is, maintains eternal youth, Hedrick was aware the world had produced a collection of cursed and disturbing paintings, like the works of Sant-Cassia, that had a way of becoming all too real. Not for the faint of heart or those sufferers of stress-related illnesses.

The Hands Resist Him is regarded by some as one of the most haunted paintings in the world. Painted in 1972 by the Californian artist, Bill Stoneham, it depicts a young boy and a life-sized, dead-eyed female doll in a darkened room standing in front of a glass-panelled door against which are pressed many disembodied, floating hands. Stoneham claimed the doorway represented a barrier between the waking world and the dream world, and the female doll would guide the viewer into the world of fantasy. The first three people to come into contact with the painting, a gallery owner who first showcased the work, the art critic who reviewed it and an actor who bought it, all died shortly afterwards. The people who looked at *The Hands Resist Him* reported feeling nauseous, dizzy or faint, or being overcome by an irrational sense of dread or even a terrifying sensation of invisible hands touching them, while others claimed that their children would flee from the picture, screaming when they laid eyes on it, or that infants would cry whenever they went anywhere near the painting. Each owner of the painting reported strange happenings in their house after acquiring the art. The painted figures were said to move within the frame at night as well as the boy and the doll disappearing from the canvas altogether. Another reported the painting showed the doll threaten the boy with a pistol. Others even reported experiencing eerie dreams where the boy entered the actual room where the painting hung. Stoneham painted two sequels to the infamous painting, called *Resistance at the Threshold*, which depicted the same characters within the picture forty years later, and *Threshold of Revelation*. He seemed disappointed that both appeared free of any strange phenomena. Of the art of painting, Stoneham stated: *We live in an age of science of revelation and hard realities and hard facts, but we are still drawn to the mysterious. And what is more mysterious than a painting? More than any other object, a painting is a one-of-a-kind thing created by someone using their hands.*

It is uncertain whether Franchot Seville adopted a war orphan found wandering the streets of Madrid, lost and hungry, upon which he based his painting, *Crying Boy*, depicting a boy with sad eyes and big tears rolling down his cheeks. The painting and its many prints have been blamed for inexplicably setting houses ablaze. Franchot Seville's studio is rumoured to have burned down after a mysterious fire broke out once he finished the painting. Since 1985, firefighters have spoken of prints of the *Crying Boy* turning up, undamaged, in the ruins of properties destroyed by fire. In an attempt to understand why this particular painting – and paintings like it – inexplicably survived dozens of house fires, unscathed, advocates of the paranormal claimed that these portraits were haunted by the ghosts of those orphans who had died during World War II.

The Anguished Man has rather gruesome origins. The artist is alleged to have mixed his own blood with oils for the painting and is said to have committed suicide after the painting was completed. The painting gained further notoriety after it was discovered in the attic of the Robinson household a quarter of a century later, and the Robinson family were subsequently beset by a series of chilling occurrences as though a dark force had pervaded their home. Initially instilling feelings of panic, dizziness and unease in the family members, the son was pushed down the stairs by unseen hands, the wife often felt an invisible presence stroking her hair and the grandmother frequently described a shadowy figure lurking near the painting. The family also reported instances of apparent poltergeist activity such as knocks and banging noises and doors slamming shut, the painting falling unexpectedly from the wall and smoke rising up from the painting, a strange mist on the stairs and anguished screams in the dead of night. The Robinsons came to believe the spirit of the tormented artist had come back to haunt them, so they returned the cursed heirloom to its original resting place, the attic.

On the end of a downstairs hallway in the Hotel Galvez, Galveston, Texas, hangs the *Portrait of Bernardo de Galvez*, drawing ghost hunters and paranormal enthusiasts alike from all around the world. The eyes of Bernardo de Galvez's portrait will follow visitors and employees as they pass by, and many have described entering a cold spot when they approach the painting. However, the portrait's real claim to fame is its great dislike of having its picture taken. Peculiar blurs, fogs and orbs are seen in the shots of the painting, and one particular paranormal team's investigation yielded a ghostly skeleton near the painting in one of their photographs, allegedly of the ghost of the Spanish military leader, Bernardo de Galvez, who fought on the side of the American revolutionaries in the War of Independence.

In a different part of Texas, in Austin, hangs a painting in the Driskill Hotel called *Love Letters*. The portrait is of Samantha Houston, the four-year-old daughter of a U.S. Senator, who fell to her death down a flight of stairs while chasing a ball. Guests have reported feeling ill or dizzy or experiencing a lifting sensation if they ever gazed upon the painting too long. Some have gone as far as to say they can see the girl's facial expressions change or her physically shifting positions in the picture.

There was an artist in the mid-1990s going by the name of Laura P., who based her oil paintings on photographs. One unusual photograph, by a commercial photographer called James Kidd, with whom she shared a gallery, she took a particular interest in and reproduced it on canvas. The photo, of an ordinary stagecoach stop in Tombstone, involving an old-fashioned stagecoach and a rusty, old wagon is made all the more eerie when a wispy figure, appearing to be missing its head, suddenly looms out of nowhere and stands on a log at the left side of the wagon. Experts felt the photo was the result of a double exposure. Kidd agreed for Laura, intrigued by the photo, to do a 16 x 20-inch painting of the image. The finished painting, titled *Painting of a Headless Man*, Laura initially displayed in her office until strange things started happening: every morning the painting was hanging crookedly, even though it had been straightened the previous day, papers went missing and appointments in the diary got mixed up. Her office colleagues were so spooked by the painting that, within three days, they asked her to take it back home. Even at home, the mysterious events continued with increasing frequency. The garage roof constantly leaked, despite being fixed a number of times. Other instances included hearing footsteps or strange knocks, doors opening by themselves and objects moving of their own accord, finding a heap of spilled salt next to an upright salt-shaker and a glass that Laura was drinking from broke in her hand for no discernible reason. A clock securely fastened to the wall, fell to the floor, the glass shattering. Visiting friends reported seeing a hazy white figure at the window. On one occasion, dogs gathered at her front door, growling and howling. Laura now regrets ever painting the stagecoach and wants only to destroy the picture. Except it won't let her . . .

Man Proposes, God Disposes by Sir Edwin Landseer commemorates the doomed Arctic expedition, led Sir John Franklin, supposedly being feasted upon by polar bears. The voyage is also remembered for the fact that the survivors cannibalized their dead crewmates. The painting occupies the picture gallery of Royal Holloway College at the University of London, a room frequently used for exams. However, this particular work is said to induce feelings of suicide in those who gaze upon it. It is therefore customary for this fine academic institution to cover the painting with a flag of the Union Jack whenever an exam is held due to the persistent rumour that the painting can drive the students mad or make them fail their exams. It is alleged that when the College first opened, a student sitting an exam was so upset by the painting that she killed herself while still sitting at her desk right in front of the other students by shoving a pencil into her own eye. Psychologists speculate that the fear-provoking properties of the painting operate purely on suggestibility.

Edvard Munch, whose most famous painting remains *The Scream*, also created one of the most infamous. *The Dead Mother* was painted thirty years after Munch's mother and sister died from Tuberculosis when he was only five years of age, and his upbringing was governed by an abusive, religious fanatic of a father, nearly driving the young boy to the brink of insanity. The painting depicts a horrified young girl with her back turned from a bed, on which rests her dead mother, holding her hands against her ears in a wide-eyed expression of shock and despair. Previous owners of the painting have claimed that the girl's eyes have a habit of constantly following them around the room or have heard the bedsheets of the deceased woman rustle. Some have even alleged the figure of the girl will occasionally vanish from the painting altogether. Art critics have often claimed the painting to be a symbolic representation of a lost family or a vision of Munch's own dark soul. And Munch himself once said: *Sickness, madness and death are the black angels who watch over my cradle.*

VII: The Demimonde

"Are you man enough to love me?"

Those words come again, the sweet lure and challenge in them, but they are no longer being spoken directly into his mind by another intrusive personality. He hears those words directly in front of him, spoken by a beautiful, naked creature, in external space. A space he does not recognize, except within the borders of the picture frame, now substantial and tangible and somehow inhabited by himself. Yet, his experience takes on the atmosphere of a dream.

Hedrick has read about paintings in which the subjects can somehow change the expressions of their face or move positions within the canvas or even leave the picture altogether. Maybe the painting has trapped something, and it is now letting it out, giving it free rein. Or perhaps it provides the source of a witch's malignant power and perpetual vitality or serves as a gateway to another dimension, a dark and terrible realm, unglimpsed by the mortal eyes of man. Or all of the above.

Yes, Hedrick is in a room of sorts, but not one in his own house. The place seems consistent with a bedchamber, judging by the canopied four-poster, but his mind soon summons up a more accurate descriptive: a boudoir. A lady's boudoir.

Besides the bed that occupies the corner of the room, the chamber serves a variety of functions, doubling as a dressing room and sitting room, a private room for private talks and private affairs. The walls are painted passion-red and the furnishings in it – the armoire, dressing table, writing bureau – are distinctly ornate and French, like the chaise longue by the window. Outside the window, night has fallen, the boulevards lit up by the mercury-vapour streetlamps, the room itself illuminated by chandelier and candlelight. Hedrick doesn't need any second guesses to know that this particular room is part of a bordello, with Arabella preparing to ply her trade for the evening, servicing her roll call of clients, some prestigious and aristocratic, others not so. The era is undoubtedly the same as that within his dream of Sant-Cassia finishing off the painting. A segment of old life set amidst the brothels of Paris.

These maisons closes *are as relevant to the hedonistic Parisian nightlife of the 1920s as the more straightforward burlesque houses and the underground opium dens. Louis XVI and Napoleon, through to the authority figures of the golden era of the Belle Époque, all deemed the 'world's oldest profession' necessary for the sexual well-being of society and promoted a strong permissive attitude, designed to cater for all manner of lusts, appetites and depravities, leading to people flocking to the French capital from all over Europe to sample the finest wine and enjoy the unrivalled beauty of the girls, specializing in the art of seduction and capable of fulfilling every carnal whim, no matter how wayward, in a background of relative opulence. There was even a Michelin-style guidebook, the* Guide Rose, *in those days, rating the merits and star attraction of each establishment in what amounted to government-sanctioned sex tourism. Teenage boys are typically escorted by their fathers or uncles so they can experience their first meaningful sexual encounter with a professional woman, a coming-of-age or rite-of-passage, their first taste of manhood. The double moral standards of husbands wishing to take a momentary break from marital life so as to satisfy their own sordid desires, secret perverted desires they know their wives will be curiously unreceptive to. These licensed institutions of licentiousness attract even the crème de la crème, creating a gentlemen's secret society as socially important as the Freemason lodges. Visiting foreign dignitaries are quietly slipped a special VIP ticket, officially authorizing a night to unwind and relax in one of the more lavish houses of tolerance, devoted to decadence and debauchery, before sitting down to the mind-numbing monotony of a morning summit with the other Heads of State. Edward VII, also known as 'Bertie' to his chums, Queen Victoria's eldest, very oversexed son, has his own private chamber at LA CHABANAIS, probably the most celebrated and luxurious of these dens of ill-repute, where he bathes in a copper bathtub filled with enough champagne and monetized courtesans as his mouth can royally handle; drunken threesomes are his favourite. Even members of the senior clergy, on a 'sabbatical', are* taken by the fetish devices and naughty 'nuns' of Satan's torture chamber; or shell-shocked soldiers, returning home from the Trenches, will stop off to play out a steamy hospital fantasy with a 'nurse', going the extra mile to care for her 'patient'. Famous painters are no strangers to the red-light district with the likes of Picasso, Gaughin and Henri de Toulouse-Lautrec being frequent patrons, as well as high-society types, sometimes even including the Hollywoodsters, such as Cary Grant and Errol Flynn, until the French government eventually deems these demimondaines illegal and closes them down in 1946.

And Hedrick knows full-well that the apartment building he occupies is a brothel, maybe not as prestigious as the one on Rue Chabanais but nor is it in the least bit shabby, in the heyday of legalized prostitution. In the presence of a woman fully versed in the Art of Seduction.

But it is the single painting on one of the walls, in Arabella's possession, which catches Hedrick's attention, presently. It is a nocturne of the exterior of his own English house, Hunter's Lodge, complete with the bougainvillea tree beyond the side-gate. In the picture, a strawberry moon hangs in the night sky. How can this picture possibly exist, let alone exist here of all places—?

Windows, he tries to rationalize, windows between worlds.

The woman in question, the woman who has, on the last count, paraded herself brazenly in the inscrutably-changing Sant-Cassia painting back in Oaks Fold, confronts him wantonly in the middle of the room, larger than life, standing there completely unclad and proud. The mirror has not corrupted her pulchritudinous form, not reduced it to a glaring, monstrous thing. Her reflection in the cheval glass is unremarkable, ordinary, faithful in every aspect, only her pure, butt-naked loveliness cast back.

"I have waited so long for you," Arabella murmurs in sweet anticipation, "for this moment."

Hedrick cannot deny her extraordinarily-alluring good looks, her concupiscent beauty. Her blond hair flows like silk behind her back, her skin is smooth and unblemished and golden in the candlelight, her face naturally pretty without the application of rouge or lipstick or any other trace of makeup. She moves towards him, closes in on him, presses herself against him, and Hedrick feels the suppleness of her nubile flesh. He can smell her too, actually smell her, the ridiculously-cloying fragrance of cheap perfume masking the immediate smell of her dirty pussy above the smell of other men, and something else . . . a subtle, uncontained scent of gaseous decomposition – and death.

Her finger traces the old scar on his neck. She clasps his hands and they dance the Mephisto Waltz like two courting lovers, whirling around the room twice before coming to a stop at the foot of the four-poster bed. Then it isn't the Mephisto Waltz anymore on the gramophone but Danse Macabre without anybody changing the record.

"Are you man enough to love me?" Arabella repeats, like any good seductress, and pushes him on to the bed and climbs on top of him. She rips open his black shirt, the buttons popping off in all directions. *"Monsieur Sauvage,"* she refers to him. *"Wild at heart."*

Hedrick *deliberates again if he is dreaming or if everything is happening for real. There is just too much detail for it to be a dream. Either way, he is hard as fuck. Pant-explodingly hard.*

Arabella is now crawling all over his chest. Her luscious lips delivering small, sensuous kisses, her tongue circling his nipples, her teeth gently nibbling. Hedrick lets out a gasp, greatly stimulated, more than sexually aroused. Her mouth journeys pleasurably across his chest, and he clutches her firmly on her juicy behind and lifts her on top of him. Again, his nostrils pick up that toe-curling odour of dead, decaying things, more noticeable now in such close proximity, underlying the overpowering redolence of cheap perfume, as though Arabella inhabits a body in which all life has expired. This thought does not dampen his enthusiasm. He tries to kiss her on the mouth, but she pulls away from his roving lips, and his initial incomprehension quickly gives way to understanding: the woman's a prostitute, and prostitutes do not kiss on the mouth.

She has brought him this far, he thinks, so can she not make an exception for him?

Arabella reads the surprise and disappointment in his reaction and seems to acknowledge the subsequent request, not entirely unreasonable, and draws her face towards his. Her eyes are utterly bewitching, intensely blue and sparkling with carnal excitement and longing, and Hedrick feels a slight sad pang seeing all this youth and innocence and incomparable, poetic beauty go to waste, degraded time and time again by countless paying men, clients incapable of having normal, fulfilling relationships but intent on acting out their depraved fantasies, paying good money to debase her. The girl could have lived the life of a princess or a duchess or settled down as a doctor's wife instead of finishing up her days a knackered, prematurely-aged harlot. Can happen to any girl. The number of angels who fall from Friday nights, never to recover their dignity. He wonders how many men she attends to each night. Ten, twenty, a hundred?

Their lips connect, press harder, their tongues exploring the moistness of the other's mouth. His hands travel up to the gorgeousness of her breasts, curvaceous and full and ravishing. Meanwhile, her fingers unbuckle his belt, open the fly-buttons of his jeans and curl round his throbbing erection, grabbing it with a firm grip, before bringing her mouth down on it.

Hedrick gasps again, tremulously, closing his eyes, Arabella's lips and tongue wrapped explicitly round his engorged member, sliding up and down on it rhythmically, the nerve endings tingling exquisitely, the vein on the underside of his penis pulsing wildly. "Where have you been all my life?" *he breaths, hot, enjoying the sensation, completely immersed in the moment.* "Come, baby, let's fuck our brains out . . ."

Arabella stops going down on him for a few seconds, coming up for air. "Gobble, gobble, gobble . . ." *Hedrick hears her whisper, more out of amusement than salaciousness. It provides her with enough encouragement to resume where she has left off. She goes back to gobbling his penis, polishing him off . . . and it feels* amazing!

"You're not going to bite my cock off, are you?" he breathes, eyes still closed on the bed, *relishing the smooth, back-and-forth motions of the warm, moist mouth accommodating the rigid, gloriously-sensitive shaft of his penis.*

She does not respond, continues to pleasure him with her mouth.

[gobble gobble gobble]

He can feel her cram the entirety of his cock deep into her throat until her mouth envelopes his ball-sack, licking, teasing, gently squeezing his testicles. The woman is not only a stunner, able to floor her men with her knockout looks, she is bloody good at her job, accomplished, performing with thorough conviction and outstanding prowess. It is a shame she works in a Parisian brothel and hails from a different day and age. Dream some from me, babe . . .

It is at this stage that Hedrick opens his eyes. It occurs to him that he has got so caught up in the moment, in Arabella's desire to please him, that he has completely forgotten his feelings for Gemma, his actual girlfriend. Fuck, he is cheating on the woman he loves! A conscience must not stand between a man and his dick, *he has selfishly told himself. As he continues to be fellated upon with an expertise he has never previously encountered, Hedrick is suddenly slammed by a combination of emotions: shame, embarrassment and, of course,* guilt, *that last bastion of moral rectitude. "I think you have to stop now . . ." Hedrick mutters, rather unconvincingly, eyes still filled with a dreamy, faraway expression. His feeble command only causes the hooker on her knees to work harder, and he feels so close to coming . . .*

Hedrick's eyes focus on the woman at the end of the bed, lovingly tending to his manhood. Except Arabella has vanished. *She has been replaced by the last thing Hedrick expects to see. It isn't Arabella's mouth, presently, that is working its magic on him but the long, pink proboscis of the same malevolent-eyed abomination from the painting, attached to Hedrick's inflated organ like the nozzle of a vacuum cleaner.*

Hedrick is balls-deep into the tube-like snout, its distal length stretched, distended, moulded into the shape of his erection. The hideous creature is making greedy, truffle-pig noises, somewhere between grunting and sucking.

[gobblegobblegobblegobble]

Her expression, for the first time since Hedrick has acquired the painting, is far from a venomous glare but contented, almost serene, engrossed in the act of going down on him.

What the FUCK? *Hedrick's mind yelps, horribly sickened, until he is finally able to vocalize:* "Get the fuck OFF me!"

As he tries to pull himself away, utterly revulsed, scrabble backwards on the bed, he feels his penis tug from the root, a hideously painful sensation, genuinely risking ripping off if he persists too long, whilst the proboscis clings on obstinately, stretching with a wet, tensile sound but still holding on like a hose attached to a fire hydrant. Eventually, thankfully, Hedrick yanks himself loose, kneeing the monster hard in the face, and the tube-shaped mouth disconnects from his penis with a slimy, popping sound.

Hedrick turns to his side, doubling over, nursing his penis, which suddenly explodes into semen, blood and agony.

It has been an experience. A unique, alternative girlfriend experience. Or ghastly girl-fiend *experience. An experience that has ended badly.*

He was not aware of returning to the real world, his house in Oaks Fold, as he contended with his immediate suffering down below . . . until he noticed Gemma staring down at him with a look of shock and horror.

VIII: Return to Church Falls

Gemma was horrified. She had come to check on him in the morning, as promised, and she had found him in the drawing room, in pretty bad shape. Hedrick looked shattered and, worse, he was near-to-completely naked, his shirt discarded miserably on the floor and his jeans crumpled between his knees. He was sweaty, unshaven and smelled strongly of sex, the evidence clearly visible to her, a glob of slightly blood-tainted jism smeared across his thighs, his penis in a sorry limp, bruised state. She knew he was not one to indulge in an affair, but he'd got his jollies from somewhere else. She hailed from a medical family. Her father was a doctor, so too were her grandfather (retired now) and brother and uncles and cousins; there was presently a nephew going through the paces in medical school. Even if she'd never inhabited a medical world, she could see something wasn't quite right with her boyfriend. As Hedrick tried to maintain his dignity in her presence, hurriedly went about the process of dressing himself, making himself decent, she just needed to glance up at the oil painting above the fireplace, the picture of the red-dressed blond scrutinizing her repellent reflection, to guess that he had acted on his possibly unhealthy, sexualized feelings towards it, beaten himself off over it. "It's the painting, isn't it?" Gemma said cannily, her tone tight and accusatory. "It's got to you. I never liked it in the first place. I sense malice in it. I'm a rational person, but even I know there are things in this world that no-one should trifle with. Either you get rid of it or I will . . ."

"Don't be hasty," Hedrick tried to reason with her earnestly. "Let's talk about this."

"The time for talking is over. I'm getting rid of it, if you're not."

"Are you jealous of the painting?"

"Ever thought that maybe the painting is jealous of *me*?"

"You're overreacting . . ." he replied, but even he knew he sounded weak. "It's not what it looks like."

"It most certainly *is*!" Gemma said angrily. "You're behaving like you've developed a crush on the goddamn picture, like it was a pornographic image. Do you know how crazy – and *creepy* – all this is?"

Hedrick took a mental step back, digesting his girlfriend's genuine worries. They were not accustomed to fighting. Gemma wasn't one to go off on one. It did look bad. His obsession with the painting had taken on a sinister turn. He had begun imagining, dreaming or *hallucinating* receiving a blowjob from the girl in the painting, the situation growing crazier, until the sensory experience had cut to her nightmare, proboscidate form blowing him off. And his penis was sore, very sore. He'd probably gone to town on the damned thing like some permanently-unsated lunatic in an asylum. "I'll take it back," he finally decided, rising to his feet. It was a bright morning outside the bay windows, warm sunshine streaming through. He'd slept all night and dreamed up a sexually-explicit scenario, or so he assumed. Yet, it seemed it had not been a restful sleep; he currently felt exhausted, befuddled. "I will just return it to where it came from. Just for you and for my own peace of mind."

Gemma relented, showed her gratitude by hugging him.

He held her for nearly a minute as though he hadn't seen her for years. He thought of how much she meant to him. Gemma was an intelligent and talented individual, and morally-centred, irrespective of the worldliness of her words, and completely receptive to his emotional needs – and oh so faithful. He couldn't ask for a better woman by his side. She was, after all, only looking out for him. Her heart was always in the right place. She loved him as he did her, utterly and unreservedly. Yes, he should give back the accursed painting to the man who'd sold it to him, considering it was having such a weird effect on him. It was the sensible thing to do. *Besides,* he told himself, *never argue with a woman. She's always right!*

Gemma rustled up a good, old-fashioned English breakfast while Hedrick checked-out and showered before slipping into fresh clothes, black clothes, what he referred to as his 'horror-writing uniform'. Having eaten heartily, chatted about pleasanter matters and drunk plenty of coffee to awaken and sharpen the senses, they both left the house, Gemma heading off to get a minor gift for her boss, whose Birthday her colleagues would be celebrating at a small, private luncheon, while Hedrick grabbed the painting off the wall and sat it up in the back seat of his black Jaguar XJS. Gemma reminded him she was cooking goose legs tonight for the pair of them, well-roasted, alongside asparagus, artichoke and mushroom sauté with tarragon vinaigrette. He told her he looked forward to tucking into the 'Lord of the Marsh'.

The drive to Church Falls was unremarkable, Hedrick presently gigging out to the rock number on the car stereo, *Molly's Chambers* by the Kings of Leon. He reflected on the events of the last couple of days and how madness can slowly creep on a person without them knowing it. Cracks can appear and the mind can slowly fracture like a porcelain vase and splinter into a million jagged pieces. He knew his own limitations as a writer, but also his strengths. He knew how to write 'Crazy'. In fact, he could teach 'Crazy' if ever called upon. 'Crazy' would be his specialist subject if he ever stepped into the *Mastermind* chair. He had made 'Crazy' his own in the horror business. John Milton had once said: *The mind is its own place.* Ne'er a truer word was spoken, contemplated Hedrick. The painting had a way of putting a mysterious hold on whoever gazed upon it, beyond the aesthetic. The painting somehow blurred the lines between fantasy and the real, waking world. Life imitating Art, Art destroys Man. Hedrick had started getting his gratification from the painting. If anyone knew a little something about horror tropes, a horror event always followed close on the heels of a sex scene, enough to kill any hard-on or urge to masturbate. Horror writers commonly expressed Eros and Thanatos in their fiction with an unwavering authority. Sexy and Scary segueing seamlessly. That had been quite an experience, visiting a whorehouse in 1920s Paris, getting laid in such an unspeakable manner, pleasure and pain entwined. A unique, alternative girlfriend experience, he had thought earlier, at the tail end of his waking dream. There was, of course, the distinctly frightening possibility he might actually be losing the plot. *Yep, bring on the 'Crazy'!*

"Baby, you're just too old for me," Hedrick remarked jokily, much more relaxed, as he entered the sunlit village of Church Falls. "It was nice whilst it lasted…" He glanced into the rear-view mirror, at the painting in the back seat, as if to emphasize his point, gauge its reaction.

Hedrick nearly crashed his car.

Not that the roads into the village centre were ridiculously busy, people going about their daily business, breaking for lunch. His attention was held momentarily too long in the reflected image in the rear-view mirror. His thoughts froze.

The back seat was empty.

Yet, when he turned his head round, compelled to do so, taking his eyes off the road fleetingly, he found the painting still physically resting there.

His eyes returned to the road, his mind an incomprehensible daze, and he quickly swerved his car, avoiding a head-on collision, reacting more out of instinct than conscious thought, having drifted into the opposite lane, the responsiveness and manoeuvrability of the Jaguar a testament to superior automotive engineering. The oncoming cars passed by in an angry honk of horns.

Hedrick brought the car to a halt in the village square, finding a suitable parking space. He paused for respite. He was shaking badly. Once he'd gained some control of his body, he looked apprehensively into the rear-view mirror again, fearing the impossible. The painting was not on the back seat. Glancing back again, however, the painting was still sitting there comfortably, unchanged as the day he first bought it.

How is this happening?

This was no illusion of the senses or an elaborate hallucination. This was real. This was really happening. Like a vampire, the painting did not exist in the reflection. It made no rational sense.

Totally spooked now, Hedrick emerged from the car and eventually mustered up enough courage to handle the painting. He picked it up from the back seat with delicate hands, as though it were a bomb. *Gemma was right! I must get rid of it! Pronto!*

I shall prepare for your safe return, Arabella seemed to whisper into his head.

Hedrick ignored the voice and walked briskly on the pavement under the hot, midday sun, weaving through the leisurely throng of passersby, the painting under his arm, with him lost in thought, focused on returning it in one piece to the person who'd unloaded it upon him, complimented with a dark warning that Hedrick had rather naively mistaken for a sales pitch.

[*The painting shall be worth a thousand nightmares.*]

Hedrick hurried his pace.

When Hedrick arrived at the place where he had received the painting, the strength ran out of his legs, and he thought he might collapse.

[*Yep, bring on the 'Crazy'!*]

The eccentric, ginger-haired, pipe-smoking man, who had sold him the painting, was not there. Neither was his old curiosity shop. For, just like the mind-reeling phenomenon Hedrick had witnessed in the rear-view mirror of his car, he discovered that the exact spot where Ignatius Quigley's antiques' store ought to have been was now taken up by one MISS CHARLENE'S DELISH DELI RESTAURANT.

As though Mr Quigley or his curious establishment had never existed at all.

IX: The Mirror in The Painting

Hedrick chain-smoked his way through three much-needed cigarettes in the garden, deep in thought. After checking-out, he returned indoors by way of the kitchen and traversed back to the drawing room where he had returned *The Girl in the Mirror* back to its original place above the fireplace. Hedrick stared at the painting.

The first thing he had done once he'd returned home and hung up the painting again was put a mirror to it. Lo and behold, the painting did not cast a reflection, as though, just like Mr. Quigley's missing, non-existent antiques store, it did not exist. Which implied what?

That it wasn't there at all?

Taking it one step further, could it be a figment of Hedrick's runaway imagination? A paranoid fantasy?

That's nonsense, Hedrick argued with himself. *Gemma and Leslie have both seen it. Unless you're telling me that they've imagined it, too.*

Which leaves us where?

Is this the crazy effect the painting has on people?

He remembered Gemma's words: *There are things in this world that no-one should trifle with . . .* He also recalled Mr. Quigley's earlier odd comment when referring to his antiques' store: *It comes and goes . . .*

A familiar female voice suddenly interrupted Hedrick's train of thoughts. The voice of that same third party who had invaded his life, pervaded his mind. Arabella's voice. *You are the first thing I think about in the morning and the last thing at night.*

There was affection in that voice, whether genuine or otherwise, Hedrick could not be sure. He stared at the satin-wearing, barefoot blonde gazing at her monstrous self in the cheval glass, her reflection absurdly-underdressed, ripping stitches, straining the fabric of the dress to its limits. [*Lady, lady, quite contrary*] Hedrick steeled himself up. *I dare a horror writer of your distinction to go tell her to fuck herself. Because, my good man, that is precisely what she deserves. Do not hold back. Tell the whoring bitch how it really is.*

But, whether Arabella really existed in his mind or not, Arabella heard and responded with pity and remorse. *Please forgive me, I cannot change what I am or what I do. It is too late now.*

Yes, nearly a century too late, agreed Hedrick. Indeed, it was the nature of the thing. Justification enough?

Arabella spoke with a yearning. *I long to be with you, again. To love you.*

And if I don't want to be loved by you? Hedrick asked clearly.

Then, SHE will punish you, Arabella responded darkly, fearfully.

At first, Hedrick was unsure whom Arabella was referring to. Then, it dawned on him. Arabella was referring to her horrible reflection as another person. Could he possibly have been looking at two *different* figures all along? And that *wasn't* meant to be a mirror in the painting?

Hedrick felt an odd, fluttery sensation, beginning in the seat of his stomach, far removed from anxiety-driven 'butterflies', spreading throughout the rest of his torso and limbs until the sensation resembled a tugging as though from an invisible electric lasso, blossoming into a body-wide pulling, and within an instant, he stepped into the picture, into Arabella's boudoir from a bygone era.

Nothing has changed since his last trip. Rose-red wallpaper, French furnishings, four-poster bed, a picture of Hunter's Lodge hangs eerily on the wall. Outside, that same strawberry moon rides the June sky. Candles light the room.

Arabella looks ravishing as ever as she pads barefoot towards Hedrick. She hugs him, and he catches the subtle whiff of death on her again underlying the strong scent of perfume, a sickly-sweet smell masking the corruption of rotting flesh, like bouquets of roses on an exhumed corpse.

Yet, she is so beautiful, so utterly impossible to refuse, so damned accessible.

For fuck's sake! his mind screams, *in conflict with itself, experiencing an all-too-familiar dissonance of thought.*

"Please save me," Arabella implores him. *"Protect me from her."* She points to the cheval glass. *It is just him and her normal reflected image. But Hedrick knows what she is referring to.*

The Thing in the Mirror. Absent from the glass, presently.

"What does she want with us?"

"She feeds off the energy of sin, of lust, thrives off the evil deeds and sexual appetites of man," Arabella explained sorrowfully. *"She owns me. I must do as she commands, otherwise her wrath will be mighty."*

So the Thing in the Mirror is a whoremonger, a madam of sorts, encouraging Arabella to indulge in despicable acts of sexual degradation, the more twisted the greater the source of energy derived, upon which the creature survives. "Who is she? What is she?"

"A Croquemitaine of the Mentaur variety."

It is the best Arabella can come up with. Not that Hedrick expects anything more specific. The umbrella term 'Bogeyman', a thing to be greatly feared, cannot not be debated. But the term 'Mentaur' is new to him. A play on the French word 'menteur'/'menteuse', perhaps, meaning 'liar', 'deceiver', 'falsifier', etc.?

And, when he glances back at the cheval glass, he notices it has stopped reflecting the contents of the room. Its mirrored surface is gone. In its place is an ashen twilight, a scene from someplace else, somewhere beyond, which reminds Hedrick of when he first bought the painting upon which Leslie had raised various theories. One such interpretation seemed too far-out at the time: I wonder if the image in the mirror is not her reflection at all but a visitor at the door – or a gateway – to another place, inhabited by these monstrous beings.

Not now, however. Leslie's shrewd observation is coming to pass. Gateway to another place. And the Thing in the Mirror might turn out to be a separate entity altogether.

If Hedrick thinks his trips into the past (blackouts in the real world) or the actual painting being physically invisible to a mirror or Mr. Quigley's curiosity shop magically uprooting from Church Falls overnight are seriously impressive supernatural feats, then he is about to experience something equally unique. More so, perhaps.

Hedrick detaches himself from Arabella's loving embrace and steps towards the cheval glass, that murky greyness within the glass inconsistent with the warmth and cosiness of the boudoir.

That magnetic pull, a sensation more palpable and corporeal than just a mere mental compulsion, takes hold of him again.

And Hedrick travels through the mirror, beyond *the glass, as easily as if it were an open door.*

The journey is instantaneous. Hedrick finds himself in a large cave on the other side of the mirror.

Dimensions, *he considers.* Realities upon realities.

The tunnel yawns blackly behind him, but he decides to walk on ahead, up to the opening of the cave. Indeed, the world is bathed in a preternatural dusk.

Hedrick stops at the edge of cavemouth, no further ground available beyond the narrow ledge. The cave is cut into a mountain, a single mountain amidst an immense mountainous complex as far as the eye can see, and below the ledge is a dizzying, precipitous drop of thousands of feet, disappearing into the swirling mists of the ravine below. Somewhere, he hears thunder, coming closer.

He does not know where he is. It is cold up here, and he shivers. The wind, too, at this altitude is frosty, biting.

Once again, he has to admit that Haston Sant-Cassia was an extraordinary man. The man must have gazed too long into the abyss and tapped into something beyond reality, taking instructions from the monsters he chased and painted. In turn, his paintings must surely transmit his dark energy as they develop a life of their own.

The twilight continues to deepen, the upper sky approaching purple, bordering on violet, stars beginning to peek through. Except Hedrick does not recognize the crazy, helter-skelter pattern of the stars, and he wonders if he has been transported to a place not of this earth.

Perhaps, a portal to a faraway world. Or a different dimension.

I HAVE you! *Hedrick hears something whisper into his thoughts.* You belong to me NOW!

He spins round, sees the creature emerge from the dark depths of the cave.

She is uglier in person than portrayed in the mirror-reflection in the painting. Even in this half-light, Hedrick feels his bile rise as he takes in her grotesque appearance. She has discarded her ridiculously-undersized dress, revealing the entirety of her repulsive form in all its alien glory. He can now see her for what she really was. An enormous skull, soft and bald and wedge-shaped and framed on either side by pointy feline ears, crowns her generally corpulent, Buddha-bellied figure, her breasts flaccid, sagging sacs of veiny tissue terminating in obscenely large nipples, her general puffy-pink flesh moist and sticky all over with a dusting of spidery-web growths. The hairless crack between her ample thighs, too, is clearly visible, further denoting her femininity, and Hedrick is struck by a fleeting, abhorrent notion that if he enters her, he will slide in easily. Set back from the trumpet-like trunk of a mouth, the hateful glare in her wizened, wrinkly expression that Hedrick has grown accustomed to, from the painting, has relaxed. Gimlet eyes, set within the misproportioned head, watch him hungrily, jubilantly, full of obscene relish, like a whore blowing a kiss to a paying john.

"I belong to no-one!" Hedrick tells her, his voice echoing in the confines of the cave. "I am my own master."

The Mentaur creeps towards him, surprisingly agile for her swollen frame, in a succession of careful, stealthy steps, a predator stalking its prey. She comes to him, telepathically. You cannot deny me. I know what lies in the hearts of men. And your heart – the heart of an author of dark fiction – is particularly sweet, full of the juiciest sins possible.

"Imagination, nothing more," Hedrick reminds her. "I know I'm no saint, but I can distinguish between right and wrong. I will never duplicate in real life the terrible things my imagination concocts, which therefore renders your argument redundant."

But the Mentaur skulks ever-nearer, arms outstretched and reaching for him, pudgy hands ending in claws, open and vicious, her posture suggesting she is preparing to pounce. You exist in my world now – your future is not as distant as you might think – where the Ancient One holds dominion and the Spindle King brings justice. You cannot escape. I will have you whether you are willing or not. *Drain* you.

The future, thinks Hedrick grimly. Not some far-flung world across the aeons of space or an alternate dimension co-existing with our own. But the *actual* future . . . Is this the bleak, dystopian future the descendants of the human race face, ruled over by an all-powerful, multimillennial god and its myrmidons?

"Don't come near me!" warns Hedrick, slowly backing away from the advancing flabby, noisome-pink creature, claws and snout and all. It is the snout he is afraid of and what it can do.

He does not wish a repeat of last time. He isn't sure if it is a dream anymore. But the Mentaur promises to take him by force this time. Hedrick unbalances briefly and nearly falls backwards when his heel strikes the edge of the ledge, stones clattered down the slope. Oh, fuck! *Somehow, he manages to bring his arms out like a tightrope artist and steady himself, keeping himself upright, on hard ground.*

The situation grows graver, still.

The electrical storm rages on. For a fraction of a second, lightning splits a remote section of the dusky sky. Thunder follows the spectacular atmospheric discharge, an ominous rumble like the snore of a slumbering dragon.

And in the wake of the thunderous echo, Hedrick hears the screeching. The screeching grows louder, rising in pitch and intensity than even the high whine of the prevailing wind, until it resembles the night-call of a hundred strix. He glances over his shoulder, skyward, and sees them emerge from the shifting stormclouds, like the Nightgaunts from the Lovecraftian menagerie. They flap and whirl and spin towards him, slender, skeletal things with leathery wings and skulls that have evolved into faceless, eyeless spheres, dominated only by a single, enormous mouth full of rotating, buzzing, hooked teeth like the jaws of a rock crusher. They are coming for him.

Refuse me you cannot, *the Mentaur declares with confidence and cruelty.* You either let me TAKE you or the Doomfliers dine on your worthless flesh.

Less a negotiation, more a blackmail. Of the worst kind. Be raped or be eaten.

Hedrick assesses the helplessness of his predicament. Perched precariously on the edge of ledge, one more inch, and he risks falling off the edge of a mountain.

A vanguard of winged monstrosities, supposedly called Doomfliers, occupy the benighted sky, like a flock of vampire bats, speeding towards him in funnelling, spiralling formation, drawing closer, howling for his flesh and, like mutant, flying piranhas, keen to pick him clean.

The Mentaur has brought him here, to this stark, tragic vision of the future, to this inhospitable, alien world, once Planet Earth, where even the night stars have stopped making sense anymore, when Mankind has become mercilessly enslaved by eternal, multi-cosmic beings. The role of the Mentaurs is to purge the sins of man, brainwash him into conformity and submission, purify him and allow him to worship the Ancient One, unconditionally. Presently, this particular Mentaur, has staked a claim on Hedrick and, like the rest of her kind, is destined to feed on the winter of human souls.

Hedrick does not intend to be zombified by this devourer of sins, depleted of his rich reserve of emotional experience, ultimately reduced to a blind follower of a cruel, unjust quasi-religion. He values his humanity. He also believes that mercy lasts as long as sin pursues man. Does he have any choice, though?

Or can there be, even in his present predicament, a glimmer of hope?

"Come and get me, you fuck-ugly *bitch!" he dares the Mentaur, psyching himself up, relying*

on the tiny smidgen of an idea but more on luck itself. Well, it's now or never!

If the Mentaur has been expecting him to capitulate, the resistance and downright challenge in his voice causes her to hesitate. The features on her wedge-shaped head contort into an expression of dark hate, the mouth at the end of her preposterous snout shrinking and puckering like pursed lips, reminding Hedrick of the petulant expression of a person whose will is not accustomed to being questioned or defied. Enraged, bent on retribution, the pink, bloated thing charges at him.

He closes his eyes . . .

He senses the godless howl of the Doomfliers arrive at the cave, so close now he can hear the whirring and gnashing of their teeth. He hears the whistling strides of the Mentaur close in on him, feels the warmth of her rank, decaying breath brush his cheeks, experiences the tips of her claws graze his crotch—

Silence.

Hedrick opened his eyes, blinking, orientating himself. He was back at his house, Hunter's Lodge, standing in the drawing room, facing the painting. The air was hot and sultry, unchilled by the wind of a mountain pass, from another time and another place. It was summer.

Hedrick released a sigh of relief. *It had worked!*

He had wished himself back.

The power of imagination, pure and simple, he concluded smugly. *That's why I write. Like Milton once said:* The mind is its own place.

Doomfliers and Mentaurs. What an adventure! What wicked, exhilarating hi-jinx!

So damned good to be back home, however, when he'd survived multiple dangers and the prospect of a horrible death, while slipping in and out of dreams, and Time, and he'd genuinely despaired he might never see his house again.

He was collecting his thoughts, getting his sanity back, when he was disturbed by a female voice, speaking to him directly into his head. The sweet, alluring voice of the psychic, pervasive presence of the dead artist's model from the painting, who had long since declared her attachment and devotion to him.

She wishes to destroy me, Arabella said, afraid. *Steal you from me. Separate us.*

"Who?" demanded Hedrick, aloud.

But Hedrick already knew. So focused had he been on Arabella's beautiful satin-dressed form in the picture, his eyes had neglected to notice her grotesque reflection in the mirror.

The mirror was empty.

She's coming for you! Arabella warned urgently. *Do something! It will be your fault if I lose you . . .*

The fact that the Thing in the Mirror had inexplicably vanished from the painting meant only one thing.

The Mentaur had followed him back to the real world.

X: Art Destroys Man

The distant crashing noises in the house brought Hedrick back to absolute alertness.

Something was moving in the house. *Coming closer.*

He needed a weapon. He glanced around. The poker in the fireplace sufficed just fine. He pulled it out of the old ashes, felt the weight of the metal in his hand. He soon realized the explosive smashing sounds were the cough of glass shattering. Again and again. Making its way downstairs. Getting louder.

He was sweating. Not a cold sweat, but because the drawing room was stuffy. Hot as hell. The furnace light of the setting sun that filtered through the westward-facing bay windows made the angles of the room look odd and stilted, as if the walls were about to collapse and unfold on themselves and disappear into some unseen dimension. Even though he felt unreal, there was no fear in Hedrick's flinty expression, staring expectantly towards the open doorway of the drawing room. Only mild, understandable apprehension gnawed at his bones. And *outrage.* How dare she? How dare the fucking Mentaur enter his house? His world. *His reality.*

So it had come to this. This inevitable confrontation. He was prepared . . .

Don't mess with the Crazy . . .!

He stood, poised, poker at his disposal, ready to swing it like a golf club.

The drawing-room mirror abruptly exploded, spraying the hardwood floor with countless fragments of tinkling glass. The thing that had sucked him off with her lengthy oral appendage in that Parisian bordello of former dreams and had threatened to rape him in a not-too-distant future was presently silhouetted in the doorway.

She had left in her wake a trail of broken mirrors, Hedrick knew now. It explained the repeated explosions that had followed her here. Either her image had been too unsightly for the mirrors to bear or she had consciously shattered them as though afraid of seeing herself. Could this be a weakness? A way to destroy her?

No more hyperbole. This was just too much hokey shit for one man to endure alone. He needed to put an end to it

Hedrick could see the definition of her dark, tumid shape in the doorway – and her eyes, yes, her *eyes*, seeming to glow like those of a jack-o'-lantern, seethed with an intense rage, a rage as fierce as the blazing sunset in this crazily-lopsided room. He laughed deliberately, wildly, hoping to infuriate her further: "Is that a pout? An angry pout? Lady, you are one sad, old whore! Lapping up the lustful sins of men must mean you are a major whore! The *queen* whore!"

[*What on earth is going on? What's got into you?*]

Too many fuckers out there, the Mentaur whispered. *Are you a fucker?*

"You know I'm not," replied Hedrick, "although I don't mind pretending to be."

[*Heddy, who are you talking to?*]

Somewhere, a faint voice, like a distant radio communication, vaguely coherent, trying to break through, penetrate. Instead, the Mentaur continued: *Your impulses, your desires, your darkest fantasies, your sickest urges are what I seek.*

"Unfortunately for you, you will not be gaining access to them. I will not be made compliant, diminished to a blethering imbecile for your pathetic god."

You will learn soon enough, the Mentaur snarled. *You will learn never to mock the Ancient One. The Olden Ones have already risen, but when the Ancient One awakens, it will bring its reign of destruction on mankind, begin his universal conversion . . .*

But Hedrick brushed aside her apocalyptic words. He was enjoying himself, enjoying hurling insults at her. "Those girls might be your bitches, but you're *my* bitch now! Bend over and take it like a cunt!"

[*Are you deliberately trying to piss me off? I warned you not to mess with things you don't understand. I'm afraid of it. I'm afraid of what it's doing to the man I love. I'm going to undo the picture, get rid of it. Burn it! Now! It's the least it deserves. The picture never happened.*]

Stop her, please! beseeched Arabella. *If she destroys the painting, the love that binds us shall separate. The world you knew shall be no more.*

Hedrick did not know how she got there – he did not anticipate it – but one moment the Mentaur was by the door, the next, she was digging her claws into the painting, sliding her nails down the canvas, slicing it open. The Mentaur ripped the painting off the wall and threw it into the blazing fire in the hearth Hedrick did not remember lighting. The canvas combusted into flames, curling up.

"No, not the painting!" Hedrick screamed and swung the poker like a baseball bat, too late to make any attempt to save the combusting painting in the fire.

The poker's curved hook impaled the side of the wedge-like skull with a hideous wet crunch, the sound of a knife stabbing a ripe pumpkin, and as Hedrick tried to reclaim his poker, he discovered it was lodged firm. Using all his strength, he yanked back, the curved end of the poker scraping the inside of the skull, crushing the brain within, in a spray of dark blood. Hedrick tugged violently again and this time he managed to wrestle free the poker's grip from the Mentaur's skull in a further grinding of bone. The force of his efforts to extract the metal tip caused the head to deracinate clean off the shoulders and roll abysmally to the floor, as he prepared to take another swing at her. The headless torso twitched, jigged, before collapsing in an unceremonious heap. The decapitated body of the otherworldly creature began to melt like warm tallow, liquefy immediately, as though set upon by concentrated acid, the flesh quickly breaking down, dissolving. The stomach dehisced, essentially opened up, guts spilling out, in a mix of acid, bile and shit. Soon the skeleton of the thing turned to jelly, it too losing its integrity and shape. For a moment the decapitated head remained whole, with its absurdly-prominent snout, but soon even the sockets could no longer hold the eyeballs, which popped out and plopped, still fully intact but trailed by a bundled thread of nerves and blood vessels, onto the floor. The Mentaur was now nothing more than a steaming pool of putrifying flesh soup, frothing and bubbling, stinking to high heaven.

Yet there was movement. Hedrick realized to his utter repulsion she was still alive. The pair of isolated, spherical eyeballs seemed to glare at him wrathfully. She could never die.

We will always have Paris . . .

The sunset was so deep that the drawing room began to resemble the chamber of a heart, fleshy walls that seemed to thump with the beats of his own heart.

"I don't need a woman like you to cramp my style . . ." he muttered, catching his breath. And, as the adrenaline dumped out of his system, as he gained a modicum of composure, the Lords of Reality intervened. He saw it was not the Mentaur he had wasted but his adoring girlfriend, Gemma Wetherby, whose motionless body lay in a crooked, uncomfortable pose on the Persian rug, head slightly askew as if questioning. The radio transmission had finally found the right frequency. Gemma's shattered skull revealed a grisly excavation site from which oozed blood and gore, painting her beautiful chestnut hair in crimson streaks. Hedrick, too, was covered in blood, which was already beginning to congeal, become sticky.

"No, no, NO!" Hedrick wailed, falling to his knees, gathering Gemma up, cradling her head in his lap, trying to revive her. She remained unresponsive.

"Everything will be alright, you'll see."

Gemma had probably come back from her work's jolly, her Chef's Birthday party, and found him hallucinating this shit – an illusion of the senses – and she had tried to help him. She had tried to warn him. The illness had been hidden, but now it was visible, his unravelling mind manifesting in his gruesome handiwork, for all to see. Sanity can fracture. And those cracks can get larger and larger until they swallow a person whole and any loved ones around them.

Love is a disease, an abnormal state of mind, a cancer, Arabella tormented him, her spirit somehow having survived the fireplace. The painting was a charred, curled-up mess, its wooden frame crackling, presently, nothing more than kindling, slowly turning to ash and cinders. *Love is so easy to abuse. Monsieur Sauvage . . . so wild at heart!*

Hedrick was weeping. Arabella had spun a web to ensnare him. She had poisoned him, her malign influence spreading through his mind. [*She can make men say or do whatever she wants.*] He had seen what the picture had shown him, heard what it had told him. Arabella had masterminded his internal disintegration. Everything he held dear to him she had taken from him. *And you only realize what you've got until you lose it.* "LEAVE ME ALONE, *you crazy, cocksucking whore!*"

You are no use to me anymore. She said and disappeared from his life forever, whatever life remained.

Hedrick wondered who had been worse, more deceitful. Arabella or the Mentaur? He didn't care. His relationship with Gemma, the woman he loved, had been undone by the painting. *I'm a horror writer, not a monster. People think we work for devils or monsters. In this case, it just happens to be true.* He understood the full spectrum of life, but his speciality had always been fear, death, disease and madness. *I have sacrificed for my art and, in my arms, behold the final product.* Frederich Nietzsche had once warned those who fought monsters not to become a monster themselves in the process. Certainly, Hedrick had, like Haston Sant-Cassia, not heeded that warning and gazed far too long into the abyss. Hedrick had ultimately lived up to his name, his moniker, and brutal writings, the Savage. He had even found the perfect ending for his book: *Art Destroys Man.* Yet, regardless, this horrendous act he had been tricked into committing had been beyond the scope of his imagination, unforeseeable.

Bring on the Crazy! Psychiatrists don't have affairs. They masturbate!

There's always room for a cannibal! I will eat any policeman who comes to arrest me!

His focus was back on the loving corpse in his lap. "Gemma . . . Gemma . . . Oh God, what have I done?" he wailed desperately.

"I don't think she's coming back," arose a voice from behind him.

Hedrick turned his head round, and Leslie Fossington looked into his eyes. *The lights are on but nobody's home.*

Leslie fired the gun. It proved to be the kill-shot, the quietus.

Hedrick fell forward across the dead body of his beloved, blood dribbling from the small bullet-wound in his forehead.

"Goodnight, dark prince," the editor misquoted, deliberately. "May flights of devils sing thee to thy hell." He remembered that celebrity signatures were worth more when the artist was dead and without the name of the fan they're signing for. A personalized autograph was always the lesser collector's item. Leslie supposed he could pass on the synopsis of *Art Destroys Man* to another author at his publishing house to complete, Edwin Drood-style, one who did not procrastinate. Meanwhile, Hedrick Savage's popularity would surely rise, posthumously.

Leslie took stock of the situation. Hedrick Savage was dead. The crazy sonofabitch had killed his own girlfriend, bashed her brains in, given her a real Savaging. Now the man himself had met a fitting end.

Leslie decided to do what he had come here to do. He went up to the painting, unscathed and untouched, above the mantelpiece, *The Girl in the Mirror*, the blond model with her Siren's looks contrasting disconcertingly with the Medusa's stare of her monstrous reflection in the mirror, full of wordless, inexpressible hate, and gently, lovingly, Leslie lifted it up from the wall. "You have found someone else, someone more deserving. Now, my beauty, we can be together. I shall never part with you."

November 2016-January 2017

Harlequin Unmasked

"A soft air fans the cloud apart; there comes
A glimpse of that dark world where I was born.
Once more the old mysterious glimmer steals
From thy pure brows, and from thy shoulders pure,
And bosom beating with a heart renew'd.
Thy cheek begins to redden thro' the gloom,
Thy sweet eyes brighten slowly close to mine,
Ere yet they blind the stars, and the wild team
Which love thee, yearning for thy yoke, arise,
And shake the darkness from their loosen'd manes,
And beat the twilight into flakes of fire."

Tithonus (1860)
Lord Alfred Tennyson

Eight Roses: Permit me to support you through this tricky time, when the attention I lavish upon you shall secure your love...

I: THE TALE OF HARLEQUIN

A new semester had begun at Pemberton College, following the summer break, and the students reconvened for class. As the afternoon shadows drew long, Mr. Jonty Chivers re-focused the efforts of the class on the subject of Harlequin. Most of his A-Level students held no opinion either way regarding their English teacher while some remarked on the duck's-ass pompadour and greaser's jacket he sported, referring to him as a 'recycled teenager' still clinging to his youth.

"Harlequin is one the principal stock characters of *Commedia dell'arte* from the late sixteenth century, one of the most best-loved *zanni* archetypes," Mr. Chivers explained to his students. "However, he gets his name, in fact, from a mischievous devilish character in medieval French passion plays from the eleventh century. Orderic Vitalis, a chronicler of the times, recounts the tale of a monk who was hunted down by a group of demons when walking at night along the coast of Normandy. Hellequin, as he was called then, was depicted as a black-masked, club-wielding emissary of the Devil, roaming the countryside with his demonic entourage, sending the damned souls of evil people back to Hell. Harlequin later receives a notable mention, referred to as Alichino, in Dante's *Inferno*. But it is in the Italian theatre stage that Harlequin's character develops into a comic servant, taking on the role of a witty and resourceful gentleman, also acrobatic and nimble, acting as a foil to the diabolical plans of his master while pursuing his only love interest, Colombina. He is most notably characterized by a motley, tight-fitting costume chequered with garishly colourful, diamond-shaped patches, spangled tights and a mask. Despite being thought of as the prototype for the romantic hero, Harlequin is still an imperfect being, who is a glutton for food and drink and whose grudge-holding and revenge-seeking nature is eclipsed by his fear of his master and his covetous love for his inamorata. Harlequin's popularity and his physical agility and sly trickster qualities inspired the Harlequinade portion of English pantomime, when in Victorian England, a more sophisticated Harlequin was pitted against Grimaldi's Clown, a brutish agent of chaos."

One week into the new academic year had also brought with it a new student. The other students were far from welcoming towards Roden Quist, and he was having a hard time fitting in. Roden always dressed in black – black parka, black jeans, black woollen jumper – which might have indicated some form of insecurity. Some of the students might have called him a 'stalker', others might have considered him a 'creep' or a 'weirdo'; perhaps they didn't know what to make of him, but one thing was certain: he had taken a particular shine to Cosmina Huggins.

Cosmina Huggins seemed not to notice him at first until Briony Madigan and Micah Walcott, her closest friends, caught him staring at her from the back of the class. Briony nudged a bored, distant-looking Cosmina as Mr. Chivers followed through his verbal study of Harlequin by writing a whole bunch of stuff on the whiteboard. "Pssst . . ." Briony whispered into Cosmina's ear and gestured towards Roden Quist. "I think he fancies you."

The daydreamy expression on Cosmina's face vanished and she turned her head towards Roden, who was taken aback by her unexpected attention, the fact he'd been caught red-handed, and he immediately averted his eyes.

The three girls giggled.

Mr. Chivers went straight down to business. "Your homework today, ladies and gentlemen, is to read up on three romantic heroes borrowed from the same time period as Harlequin for a class discussion and a short descriptive essay next time."

The three girls glanced back at Roden and noticed that, behind his glasses, he was staring stiffly ahead, his cheeks now reddening into two blooming roses of embarrassment.

The girls laughed again.

Pemberton College was the main educational establishment that faithfully served Becton-upon-Sea, a mere doorstep away from the strange goings-on of Oaks Fold and Church Falls. It taught a wide range of students, from those completing salt-of-the-earth apprenticeships in Car Mechanics and Bricklaying to the more academically-minded destined for Law School and Medical School.

Since the College opened its doors in 1976, its library had stayed predominantly unchanged in its architecture, requiring neither renovation nor refurbishment, and remained the principal mainstay of more serious study as well as doubling as a Don Juan's passion pit for some sweaty, frantic groping at the back many students would be averse to admitting. The huge library was circular in design with four entrances, its eight carefully-situated Corinthian columns rising up from the mosaic marble floor to support a cupola, its rounded oculus bathing the entire library in bright, effusive autumn sunshine. During the evenings, when the overhead library lights were turned down low to save on electricity costs, the oculus gave spectacular coverage of the heavens and the stars.

Three hours before the library was due to close for the day, a bespectacled boy approached the lonely girl sitting along one row of tables, reading by lamplight. "Hi there," he greeted her.

Cosmina Huggins looked up from the book she had been perusing through: *The Master and Luna* by Henry Schofield. She appeared startled, not recognizing the voice. It turned out to be Roden Quist, the newbie. "Hi," she reciprocated, gathering herself.

"Mind if I talk to you . . . if you're not too busy?" Roden asked politely.

Cosmina glanced around the dimly-lit library. Apart from them and a handful of chairs, where the previous occupants had forgotten to turn off their desk-lamps, leaving a few random islands of waxy light, it seemed the place was deserted and quiet, eerily so. But appearances could be deceptive. "The library's not the best venue for a natter. It might seem dead at the moment, but I don't trust the formidable Miss Phillimore to be lurking around the corner, preparing to jump out and bite our heads off."

Roden smiled, and Cosmina was able to study him for the first time. He was medium-height, very skinny and looked much younger than his age. His hair was lank and matted, as black as the clothes he wore, and his face was long and narrow and dotted with acne, with a pointy nose and prominent upper incisors. But those polished, jet-black eyes set slightly too close together behind the dark-framed glasses watched her with a dreamy intensity. Cosmina realized what he reminded her of. *Rattus rattus. A black rat, carrier of the bubonic plague. Roden the Rat.* "So where did you have in mind . . . for a chat, I mean?"

There! The awkwardness. The social anxiety behind his friendly words. Then it occurred to her what the puppy-dog intensity of his gaze was consistent with, having experienced it countless times before. *Adoration. You like me, don't you?* Not the first time she had seen it. *I have that effect on people.* Cosmina didn't wish to brush off this pimple-ridden creep who, whilst vaguely resembling a human rat, had also plucked up enough courage to talk to her, even maybe make a play for her, but nor did she wish to lead him on unnecessarily. She had to admit that, despite his overintense presence, there was something oddly appealing about him. No doubt he saw her for the good-looking girl she was: brunette bob, button nose, skin milky-white and untouched by the aging poisons of foundation and cosmetics, eyes huge and round and dark, deep wells one could fall into and never escape from. Damn, she looked fine! "What is it you want to talk to me about? My boyfr–"

"What do we have here?" interceded a booming voice from nearby.

Roden and Cosmina turned round and saw a trio of boys head in their general direction from the south entrance. All wore jeans, suffering different degrees of distress, and rugby shirts, sporting the blue-and-green stripes of the College team, underneath American-style varsity jackets. The huskiest of the three, the only one whose head was covered by a baseball cap, worn backwards, of course, spoke again. "Looks likes someone's making moves on my girl! Are you making moves on my girl?"

Roden seemed to cower. "It's not l-l-like that," he stuttered nervously, obviously intimidated.

"So, if it's not l-l-like that, wh-wh-what you doing, daddio?" Griffin de'Marco demanded to know with a mock-imitation of the stammer, appraising the small, puny, insignificant four-eyed geek, possible closet fag and definite weirdo.

"N-n-nothing . . ."

"N-n-nothing?" Griffin repeated in perfect, falsetto tones. Then, his voice took on a hard, menacing edge: "Well, rat-face, get *lost!*"

Griffin was greeted by a peculiar smile, kindling with bitterness and anger, like the mainspring of a watch slowly being wound to breaking point, and, for a couple of seconds, a shade of uncertainty featured across the bigger boy's face, like an unconscious wondering that maybe he wasn't just messing with the wrong guy, but he might actually get beaten up. Then, the moment passed, as Roden, twitching as though jumping inside his skin, tremulously grabbed his holdall and took his cue to make himself scarce, scurrying away towards the exit.

"Fucking loser!" Griffin remarked, satisfied, as he and his smirking friends watched Roden disappear into the night. He turned to his girlfriend with a mischievous grin. "Well, beautiful, how goes it?"

"You didn't have to be so rude to him," protested Cosmina, leaping to Roden's defence. "Where's your manners?"

"As Captain of the College rugby team, isn't my responsibility to keep my girlfriend away from any dirty dorm rats?"

"Quiet, please!" came a stern admonishment from behind them. Miss Phillimore, forever prowling in the shadows and always looking to administer some of her authority, stood large as life, bespectacled and waspish.

Griffin suddenly looked sheepish, at odds with his macho image. Even he was afraid of Miss Phillimore. "Sorry, miss," he murmured humbly to her. More bravely, he whispered into Cosmina's ear: "Let's blow this joint!"

Griffin, his girlfriend and his two buddies emerged from the library, taking in the early evening. It was already dark outside, and chilly, their breath condensing into mist. Rugby practice was over for the boys and Cosmina had done her fair share of studying. As far as Griffin was concerned, now was the time to ditch his friends for the day and spend some quality time with his girlfriend. He always harboured an inner timetable for sex. In relation to Cosmina, he was always up for it. He could smell it. Sex in the air. He knew that love would be made later on – or whatever passed off as love. With alcohol, perhaps, and without inhibition, of course. Without mind. Clumsily and quickly. A little too quickly, as Cosmina sometimes complained. He prepared to go to her place.

Hidden in shadow behind a large oak, Roden watched them on the library steps from a distance. He was furious. How dare those chest-thumping morons show him up in front of Cosmina! He pulled out a camera from his holdall and, pointing it at the figures outside the library, took a snap.

He would later go home and develop the film in his own, personal dark room, hanging up the paper until it would be dry enough to handle. Although the image of the boys would come out clear, the picture of Cosmina in the snapshot would appear strangely distorted, as though affected by some kind of interference, maybe not enough light exposure or the consequence of an inappropriate shutter speed. Roden would be surprised by his own sloppiness, but he would also presume her photographic image not turning out too good might have something to do with the fact that she was the object of his desire, the focus of his fixation. There were mystical powers at work here, after all. He decided to think no more of it. At least for now.

Whereas Roden always aced the tests and made the grades, those remedial idiots were all brawn and no brains, used to skiving lessons and shooting pool in the student mess, total gym addicts as though compensating for something. He had plans for them and, as far as he was concerned, they would not be missed. As for Cosmina, oh, angelic Cosmina, Roden had to protect her from muttonheads like Griff. Roden fell back to dreaming of her to the faint tune on the radio playing in the background of his dark room, The Delmonas performing *Dangerous Charms*.

Yes, my love, I pronounce my intentions to thee.

"What're we watching?" Tyler McCallister asked Griffin.

"I pulled one out from Dad's secret stash of adult videos," Griffin replied, putting the disc into the Blu-ray player. "*Night Call*. Tits and pussies galore."

"I see . . ." Tyler said, performing a chinny reckon.

Along with Vance Sheppard, the three rugger mates were at the de'Marco residence, a sizeable mansion with acres of land, Griffin's parents away at their country place for a romantic weekend. Taking Cosmina home hadn't quite gone according to plan – or expectations. Cosmina had pushed him away, unhappy at her boyfriend for scaring off the new boy. There was a big difference between being cool and cruel, she reminded him. Her refusal to make out with him this evening pissed him off no end and he had been tempted to take her by force. But he'd held it together rather than go off on one. He so desperately needed her validation – and her love. Griffin decided to teach the new kid a lesson when he saw him next. He knew that Cosmina wouldn't hold out for too long. She'd come round sooner or later. Instead, he'd called up his friends for a proper rave-up.

Disappointed and downright frustrated, always at the mercy of his rampaging, adolescent hormones, Griffin had chosen to kick off the weekend with some porn, an open keg of beer and a bag of weed. In other words, get rat-arsed in true manly fashion. His buddies did not protest. It promised to be a rowdy night. A night of *misbehaviour*.

Within minutes they were high. They chugged down their beers and cheered. Finding that competitive edge had become second nature. Even in drinking.

Vance already looked the worse for wear.

"You're such a lightweight!" commented Tyler.

"What do you expect?" joked Griffin. "The guy gets the munchies just from watching a couple of episodes of *Disjointed*."

"Watch it, mate," mock-warned Vance, "or I'll give you a titty-twister."

Tyler went in for another jibe. "We should be careful of him. He's the only one who plays cricket among us. A game for wussies. I've seen him play. Cack-handed and with two left feet."

Vance did not seem too offended. "Do you want me to carve my name on your balls?"

"Who popped your cherry?" Tyler asked him as they continued to trade insults.

"Which fat, ugly bitch gave *you* a mercy fuck?" responded Vance.

"What, no noddy pics of your babe?" Tyler ventured towards Griffin, in high spirits. "Such sweet eye-candy – imagine her undressed. Twerking, downblousing, upskirting, any which way's good for me!"

"Clean your mouth out with detergent, *douschbag*!" exploded Griffin, drawing the line. True, he used to take pictures of former girlfriends undressed to share with the boys, and he was on a divine mission to devirginize the entire female student body, but Cosmina was different. Without sounding like a sentimental, old fool, she was *special*. "The joke's gone too far! Nobody *disses* my girl!"

His sudden outburst silenced the laughter of his two buddies. When they emerged from their substance-enhanced stupor, they sounded strangely sober. Tyler was remorseful. "Sorry, mate, won't happen again, I swear. I didn't realize things were serious between you two."

"The less said, the better," replied Griffin, shutting off any discourse around his relationship with Cosmina. He nodded to the widescreen television mounted on the wall of the enormous lounge, the sordid scene involving a bored, scantily-clad housewife, who just happens to accidentally lose her negligée in front of the emergency plumber, who has come to attend to a leaking pipe in the middle of the night.

"Now that's more like it!" exclaimed Tyler, getting back in the swing of things, their evening of culture – or lack of. "Nice movie, Griff! The height of sophistication!"

They partied like Frat Boys that evening: smoked weed, drank more beer and watched films of a similar quality as the first while steering well clear of discussing Griffin's girlfriend. Three boys in one room, aroused by the dirty material on the TV. Three stiffies. Three jerks holding off, unprepared to relinquish their cool, unless one of them dictated otherwise. Nobody did.

Soon, Griffin's eyes grew heavy. He closed his eyes, just for a moment . . . when he opened them again, it was already midnight in the aftermath to their party.

The house was quiet, the lights still on. The television screen was blank, the last movie having long since run its course. Only Vance lay stretched out on the lounge-room couch, back turned, out for the count. Griffin did not notice the leather upholstery towards which Vance's head was turned was unusually tacky. Tyler, meanwhile, was nowhere to be seen. Griffin assumed he'd either gone home or he was possibly passed out somewhere in the house.

Griffin got up awkwardly, unsteady on his feet. His head hurt. He realized he was already nursing a hangover. He supposed he'd nodded off like the others. He felt wasted. His bladder was full – he needed to pee. But his throat was also dry, almost scratchy.

He staggered into the kitchen in search of the downstairs toilet further along. Parched, he checked the medium-sized beer keg. It was empty. He was about to pour himself some water from the tap when he noticed the door to the walk-in freezer was ajar. Living in a mansion meant the place was big enough to accommodate a walk-in freezer and a separate larder.

He moved to the shiny, reflective steel door and a small voice spoke inside his head. He didn't know if it was his own thoughts spoken out aloud – or someone else's. *Aren't you scared?*

Suddenly, a sense of foreboding filled him.

Drugs, dear boy, make things particularly easy, the voice at the back of his head explained. *Drugs open the gateway to the mind, make it open to influence . . .*

"Go away!" uttered Griffin with a dull croak.

But the voice persisted, chuckled. *You, Griff, have been a very,* very *naughty boy!*

Griffin realized why. As he entered the walk-in freezer, against his better judgement, the overhead fluorescents lit up the naked body of Tyler, hanging upside down on a hook, pale and frozen like a beef carcass strung up in an abattoir. His throat had been cleanly slit from ear to ear and the blood from the gaping wound had dripped down and pooled, forming a dark, crystallized puddle on the floor.

Griffin dropped his empty glass, which shattered the second it struck the kitchen floor. He stared at the frozen corpse of his friend dangling from a meat-hook, stared at the cold savagery on display in terror and incomprehension, feeling his own skin ice over just like the shiny, swinging human flesh he beheld.

All of a sudden, the inverted, exsanguinated corpse opened milky eyes, fixing them on Griffin. "Why did you kill me?" his reanimated friend demanded, possessed of the deep, guttural voice of a demigod.

The starkest horror crushed Griffin's mind for, in that exact moment, he noticed he was wearing a blood-soaked butcher's apron and he was carrying a slaughterhouse knife in his right hand.

That inner voice from someplace else continued to torment him, whether drug-induced hallucination or otherwise: *Do you believe in things that aren't possible, daddio?*

At that moment, it dawned on Griffin he might have actually gone mental and butchered his best mate.

The horrific deaths of Tyler McCallister and Vance Sheppard rocked the staff and students at Pemberton College. Vance had apparently been murdered as he slept on the couch, his throat also cut with one clean stroke. But the vicious manner in which Tyler had been killed and then his body hung up in the step-in freezer, like a sack of meat, shocked the entire community. With tears came fury and a call for answers, for justice. It was bad enough that the star athletes of the College had indulged in a wild, drug-fuelled evening, but the way in which the party had gone out of control brought the reputation of Pemberton College into question. Worse still, there was no sign of the person who had committed these brutal murders. Griffin had obviously fled, sparking off a manhunt.

Just when you think you know someone . . . Briony had commented to Cosmina. Cosmina understandably struggled to accept the terrible news her boyfriend had done something so abominable and was presently missing, without so much as any earlier indication that he might not be right in the head, but she managed to keep from shedding a tear or descending into fear for her own safety – brave girl. Both Briony and Micah remained wholly supportive of Cosmina in their friend's time of need.

The double funeral at WYCH HILL CEMETERY on that cold, late-September day was well-attended, not only by the grieving parents of both boys but also by a significant number of the College faculty as well as a fair share of fellow students, all solemn-faced and anxious to pay their last respects. The boys had been popular, well-liked by most, even if they had a tendency to rub some of the more timid students the wrong way with their own brand of peer aggression. The cemetery was blanketed in a carpet of autumn leaves, awaiting raking by the groundskeeper. A procession of pallbearers delivered the two coffins to the mounds of wet earth, gently and safely depositing them to the bottom of each respective, open grave. Mr. Pickering, the usually formidable rugby coach, appeared uncharacteristically down in the doldrums, shaken, as eulogies were spoken and tributes paid. Mr. Lerner, the Principal, said a few words, reassuring the public and those gathered that the College was working closely with the police and security on campus would be tightened so classes could reconvene. Accompanied by her two friends, Cosmina held it together throughout. She did not weep, and Briony admired Cosmina for maintaining her calmness in the face of such adversity. Cosmina had even boldly turned down the offer of police protection, volunteered in case her lunatic boyfriend came for her. Let her process her grief in her own way, thought Briony. She, along with Micah, would be there for her in case she did break down and needed a shoulder to cry on.

Inspector Raglan O'Hara, the investigating officer from the Chertsford Police Department, was also present, hoping to catch a glimpse, if any, of the chief suspect. But Griffin didn't show. Was he really expecting Griffin to make an appearance? Inspector O'Hara had already questioned the girls closest to Griffin, but his inquiries had yielded nothing of significance so far. He was at a loss. So too were Griffin's parents, who, obviously in shock, could not come to accept their son having done something so terrible. Inspector O'Hara still couldn't understand how something like this could happen here in Becton-upon-Sea . . . in the College, of all places. Homicides were not a common occurrence in these parts. Weird things happened in Church Falls, yes, but Becton-upon-Sea . . .?

Blame it on the influence of drink and drugs and the violent, unruly nature of growing boys, but he could not ignore his gut feeling that there was more to this case than just some mentally-unhinged kid running amok. The last serious case he'd investigated had been the unexpected death of a teacher in Oaks Fold a couple of years back. Different school, yes, but twenty years of detective work told him there must be some unseen connection between that teacher's death, eventually ruled suicide at the subsequent Inquest, and the murders of these two boys in a neighbouring district eighteen months apart.

The boy kept his distance, watching the funeral procession and graveside service behind his thick glasses. Roden Quist was less concerned with the proceedings in the cemetery than the girl who had awakened his dark heart. Roden had a certain way of dealing with people he did not like. He had a way of making things happen. If he wanted something badly enough, he had his own unique way of getting it. He had comfortably dispatched those goons and now his love rival was conveniently on the run. It paved the way for Cosmina, who would now be at her most vulnerable, ripe for seduction, easy for the taking. Well-pleased, a slow smile crept across his face. It had been a long time since he had felt such strong feelings for a girl. She was the only thing that mattered now. October suddenly stretched out in front of him, full of teenage dreams . . . and promise. *Fear not, my love, I shall make you mine . . .*

II: THE BOY WHO TOOK PHOTOGRAPHS

"Gothic fiction always reflects the anxieties of the modern age," Mr. Chivers was lecturing in English Lit class. "So what can we say about *Carmilla*? What was Sheridan Le Fanu driving at?"

"The fluid nature of female sexuality, perhaps?" Briony, his prize student, hazarded a guess. "A lesbian *ménage à trois* between dominants and submissives?"

"Quite possibly," replied Mr. Chivers. "Le Fanu had that ladies' secret sex thing going on in his characters. Lesbian love and lesbian rivalry. The gothic novel will never go out of fashion. In fact, it has become even more relevant in today's day and age, with the whole LGBTIQ movement, the world of transgender relationships . . ."

"Homosexuals and transsexuals are still being discriminated against in certain circles of society, like the Military," Cosmina reminded the class.

"I guess there's an upside to it," suggested Briony. "Who needs war anyway, except the bankers who make a killing from both sides in a conflict? If you want to avoid being conscripted into the Army, just say you're gay!"

The class erupted into laughter.

"Thank you, Briony," Mr. Chivers commented. "Always vocal." He moved on to the other subject they had been discussing. "And what did you guys make of *The Monkey's Paw*?"

Briony was back in the driving seat. "The monkey's paw gets you what you want but not in the way you want it because Fate demands a sacrifice to balance out the Universe."

"Once again, Briony," Mr. Chivers complimented, "you're on the ball."

"And monkeys tend to be very mischievous," Briony added as a humorous afterthought, "even in death."

More guffaws from her fellow students.

"Yes, they are, aren't they?" Mr. Chivers acknowledged. "Whilst we're still on the subject, any other gothic works you can think of in relation to their underlying meaning and relevance to modern society?"

"The *Twilight* saga?" someone blurted out from the back of the class.

Briony was on to it like a rocket. "I wouldn't be proud that I like the *Twilight* saga. Utter bollocks if you ask me, pardon my French! It is meaningless and useless, only a way for the author to cash in on teenage misery. Robert Pattinson's centuries-old, unnecessarily angst-ridden vampire harbouring a crush on a teenage girl only smacks of paedophilia. And, as for Kirsten Stewart's character, she just doesn't do anything for me."

"What do you want her to do for you?" asked Mr. Chivers

"Nothing but the body of an anorexic girl desperate to avoid puberty and unconvincingly trying out a heterosexual relationship," Briony said, now in full panning mode, "in a teenage-horror franchise as completely flaccid as the works of E.L. James are to erotic fiction. What's Kirsten Stewart ever done to get where she is? She certainly didn't earn her place in Hollywood. Unlike those poor, old hopefuls at the *Harry Potter* auditions, Daniel Radcliffe only got the role because his mother was the casting director. The same applies to Kirsten Stewart, made famous because of her family connections. Nothing but nepotism, if you ask me."

"Do I detect a hint of jealousy?" Mr. Chivers ventured.

"Oh *purleeze*!" Briony countered, heatedly. "Jealous of Kirsten Stewart? I hope people see her for what she is, just someone undeserving of fame," quietly adding, "and I sincerely hope she goes away."

"Thanks again, Briony," Mr. Chivers replied, "for your emotive deconstruction of Stephanie Meyer's work – or might I say tirade against her work?"

"Criticism," Briony corrected him.

"Criticism," Mr. Chivers said, accepting the amendment.

"Nothing wrong with having an opinion," elaborated Briony, "as long as it's for the better."

Mr. Chivers sounded a little exasperated by his star pupil's scathing denunciation of things, for hogging the limelight. "I'm not sold on the idea," Mr. Chivers said, airing his more liberal-minded views. He looked at Briony hard, signalling for her to shut up. She did not speak. He checked his watch. "For your assignment today, I would like you to write something scary in six words or less…"

"*That's not my hand you're holding . . .*" The other students turned to look at who had come up with that little creepy gem. It was Roden Quist.

"Very good," said Mr. Chivers. "Some use of contractions, but it'll do. Class, that's the kind of example I'm looking for. See how many of these babies you can come up with. Also, I might set a spot quiz upon you, so be prepared."

"Want to hear something even more creepy?" Roden said, summoning up another scary example. "*A dreadnought, a staunch disbeliever of supersitition, died last week after being hit by a number 13 bus.* I know it's not exactly six words."

The students groaned, others guffawed.

"That's quite impress–" Mr. Chivers began, but Roden cut him off.

"Here's another. *There was a picture of me on my phone, sleeping. I live alone . . .*"

The class moaned a shuddery acknowledgement.

Roden was on a roll. "*At first, I thought the knocking was coming from my window until I realized it was coming from my mirror.*"

The class gasped, suitably spooked.

But Roden was not finished yet. "*I begin tucking my daughter into bed when she tells me there's a monster under the bed. I look under the bed and see my daughter, trembling and afraid, who tells me there's somebody on her bed.*"

More disquieting murmurs trickled though the classroom. Mr. Chivers could not get a word in edgeways.

Roden was already delivering another spook-story. "*The last thing I saw was my alarm clock flashing midnight before the succubus dug her rotting nails through my chest and her other hand muffled my screams. I sat bolt upright, relieved it was only a nightmare, but as I saw my alarm clock read 11:59, I heard the closet door creak open . . .*"

The class shared their appreciation again with a low, creeped-out murmur.

Roden seemed unstoppable. "*I awoke to the sound of the soft, soothing tones of a woman's voice comforting our babbling baby on the baby monitor. As I turned over in bed, my arm brushed against my wife, sleeping next to me.*"

"Thank you, Roden," Mr. Chivers managed to interrupt, "for that very creative trip into the macabre. But I think enough for now. Let's see what your fellow students come up with." He dismissed the class. "Oh, Roden – a word . . ."

As the students drifted out of the classroom, Roden watched with a sinking heart Cosmina disappear along with them. Just when he was planning to walk her and her friends home, set up some study dates with her so he could see her more frequently, he wondered what Mr. Chivers could possibly want with him. *Why does he need me to stay behind? Am I in trouble or something?*

"Why do you need to see me, sir?" Roden asked nervously, defensively, when he was alone with Mr. Chivers. "I didn't mean to get carried away." Neither had Roden intended to cement his reputation as a creep. What would the other students think of him now?

"Oh, those stories . . ." Mr. Chivers said, laughing it off. "Don't worry about it – they were good. Extremely impressive. You seem to have a natural talent for that sort of thing." He went on, more to the point: "No, I needed to see you about a completely different matter."

"What about, sir?"

"I notice you carry a camera," Mr. Chivers observed. "May I take a look?"

Roden hesitated for a moment before reluctantly pulling it out of his back pocket. He extracted a vintage compact camera, predominantly silver with a black trim and a red, touchpad-like sensor button and an overall slim, rectangular design that resembled a harmonica, convenient for any back pocket.

Mr. Chivers took it from Roden, handled it, examined it. "I haven't seen one of these babies in donkey's years. A 110 cartridge film pocket camera or as the Germans called it a 'Ritch-Ratch Kamera' on account of the noise the mechanism makes, if I'm not mistaken first introduced in 1973. Flash is provided by a magicube, although later models would utilize a flipflash. You can choose from one of the weather symbols: the Sun pictogram corresponds to a shutter speed of 1/100 of a second and the Cloud symbol selects 1/50 of a second. Its most familiar feature, defining this make and model, is the electromechanical shutter release button hidden under the flexible membrane. It is renowned for the quality of its pictures, particularly for creating photographs as detailed as if one were using a wide-angled lens for landscapes. *An Agfa Agfamatic 2000 pocket sensor.* Still so much better than the pixelated digital photography of today." Mr. Chivers grew contemplative. "Some people prefer to live in the signs of the times, dressing in the latest trends or needing to surround themselves with the newest gadgets. Others get obsessed with old stuff, dressing in vintage clothes or enjoying listening to old vinyl records instead of digitalized music, or collecting and recycling old objects, because they like to imagine the story behind those objects. I put myself in the latter category – you could call me a dinosaur of sorts." He chuckled before continuing: "Don't you think a photograph is like holding a visual piece of history?"

Roden could not help but be impressed – and worried – that Mr. Chivers had taken an interest in his camera. "What does a teacher want with a kid who takes pictures?"

Mr. Chivers cleared up the mystery. "I do photography in my spare time. It's a hobby of mine." He returned the camera to Roden. "You know the discovery of the camera-obscura image dates as far as Ancient China?" He smiled, sharing some of his know-how on the subject. "The camera does not work like an eye, memory does not work like film. For those curious, most human eyes are 16mm in focal length and the pupil can only effectively manage apertures between f/2 and f/11. Personally, I've always gone for the old-style Piccolette strut-folding camera with its type 127 film, just to get that classic photographic look, all dry plate and silver nitrate and emulsion layers, the final product rendered in black and white and those intermediate shades of grey."

"That's kind of cool, sir," said Roden.

"Oh, that's very kind of you," thanked Mr. Chivers, lost in the zone of wonderment. "Ah, the light levels, the shape of the edges, the combination of the lines and the colours, the relative positions and perspectives creating certain forms and the relations between these forms that stir our aesthetic emotions. Vision and memory working in perfect harmony to enable that watershed moment, together allowing you to divine your way to a beautiful photograph. It's all about technique. You choose where to focus. You choose the exposure. You choose the composition. You choose the direction you point the camera. You choose what time of day to take the picture. You choose the exact moment to preserve history. You are making choices as the photographer for the eventual viewer of the photograph. You shoot with intent, make every single frame count, you map the scene and you lock it in your mind's eye forever, and you will have plenty of keepers at the end of the day. With a camera we can create breathtakingly evocative art, a panoply of timeless creations that we cannot imagine the world without. I can identify with those Japanese tourists, snapping everything in sight." Mr. Chivers decided to get to the actual reason for keeping the boy behind class, hunt down the truth. "Why do you carry a camera?"

Roden was struck by the directness of the question. "You as an amateur photographer, of all people, should know why," said Roden, improvising an answer on the spur. "If you must know I keep a portfolio of my own one-photo-a-day project." It sounded all very plausible, except the canny expression on his teacher's face told him Mr. Chivers could see through the lie. An anxious person by nature, Roden's nervousness had a habit of increasing to the point he would tremble, no, *twitch*, if he told an untruth, as though the muscles under his skin were contracting in an uncoordinated fashion. Roden must have realized there would be no fooling his teacher for he asked: "Why did you really want to see me, sir?"

Mr. Chivers disclosed his motives. "The *real* reason?" he began. "Do you know anything about Brexit?"

Roden gave a superficial response, his manner questioning what politics had to do with the price of bread. "Just something in the news that never ends."

Mr. Chivers was looking at him again in that knowing way. He could tell Roden was not being entirely honest. However, he continued: "You must be mystified why I'm asking you about Brexit." Mr. Chivers stared hard at Roden, getting down to the nitty-gritty. "You're new to Becton, to Pemberton College. Your transcript says you were previously enrolled at Woodford High in Oaks Fold."

Roden nodded.

"*I know about you,*" Mr. Chivers announced ominously.

"Pardon?"

Mr. Chivers went on to explain, changing his tone. "You see I had a friend at Woodford High. A very close friend. Worked as the teacher for Media Studies. His name was Alistair Halpin. Ring any bells?"

Roden pretended to innocently ponder the question, where all this was leading to, and Mr. Chivers decided to play along with him. "Yes, I think he was my teacher. Very nice man."

"Do you know what became of him?"

This time, Roden shook his head.

Mr. Chivers knew the boy was still lying. "Apparently, he hung himself on the evening of the Twenty-third of June, 2016, the night the British people voted for

Brexit. Before he killed himself, he told his wife that he believed that the UK Referendum was *not* really about leaving the EU, but the entire British public was voting to decide whether *he* should live or die!"

"That's awful!" Roden uttered with concern.

But Mr. Chivers could tell that Roden did not mean a word of it. "Can you imagine the murder on the nerves, existing in that constantly-deluded, psychotic state?" Mr. Chivers moved to the heart of the matter. "According to his wife, he had developed an obsession with a student of his, fitting your description, without mentioning you directly by name. He was afraid that you'd done something to his mind. Why do you think he would single you out like that?"

Roden tried not to sound defensive. "I really don't know, sir. Madness can make people say and do strange things."

"And, lo and behold, you end up here!" Mr. Chivers exclaimed. "Can you imagine my surprise to actually meet the boy himself, the same boy who once had such a tragic effect on my old friend?"

"As you can see, I'm just an ordinary boy with nothing extraordinary to offer," Roden was quick to reply, but Mr. Chivers could already see that he had shaken the boy. The boy was hiding something. That twitchiness was now much worse, resembling the mild jerkiness of a subacute seizure. And those eyes hiding behind those thick glasses were filling up with a dark fury. "Do you mind–?" Roden asked, bringing his emotions back in check, and aiming his Agfamatic pocket camera at his teacher, clicked an unexpected snapshot.

Mr. Chivers blinked at the spontaneity of Roden's picture-taking. "What was that for?"

"My photograph for the day," Roden responded. "For my portfolio, if you remember me saying. I like to capture reality. For posterity's sake." He deliberately stoked the fires of his teacher's suspicions and his words came off sounding like a less-than-subtle threat. "I'd be very careful, sir. I'd hate to see you go down the same route as your friend."

A new term in a new school and already somebody had begun to suss him out. *I know about you*, Mr. Chivers had declared.

Well, something had to done about him, Roden decided. Shame, because Mr. Chivers was a bloody good teacher, even if he dressed like an overaged teenager, bringing a certain youthful exuberance into his teaching, instilling enthusiasm in his class.

In his dark room Roden stared at the impromptu photograph of Mr. Chivers he had snapped in the classroom, the look of surprise caught on camera.

[I know about you]

In his time on earth, Roden had dealt with everything from fixated teachers to dogged detectives closing in on his tail to online trolls who sent hateful texts and obscene photos. He had once scared the bejesus out of a notorious cyberbully by sending him a picture of him dead. Then it happened in real life, the cyberbully dying in the exact same manner as the photo of him on his mobile phone.

I did it before. I can do it again.

The camera possesses. And Roden had the ability to extend his sphere of influence through his camera. He could manipulate the scene and the subjects within. With such trickery at his disposal, he could establish his power over others.

The camera owns you. I own the camera. Therefore, I own you.

His paranormal photographs allowed him to plunder, intrude, trespass, exploit . . . and quietly *assassinate*.

Jonty Chivers sat at home, pondering the weighty issues debated on *Newsnight*.

Shiver me timbers! He thought he was coming down with the sniffles, but he knew antibiotics weren't always an answer. He believed in natural remedies. Like the generous helping of scotch he'd poured himself as a nightcap. *Yes, time to batten down the hatches!* He let the liquid glide down his throat, appreciating the 'burn'.

Roden's words echoed in his mind: *I'd be very careful, sir. I wouldn't want you to go the same route as your friend.* Roden had threatened him and Chivers didn't accept threats from any student. Roden always kept a low profile, was mostly quiet in class and almost invisible. Yet he had threatened his English teacher. Chivers put aside the threat, unsure as to its meaning, and focused on the news programme he was watching.

The news programme was dominated by Brexit, as it reached a critical stage in the negotiations.

As far as Chivers was concerned, Brexit had been sold to the British people on a lie. The Brexiteers, who had once profited obscenely during the global financial crisis of 2008 and propped up their banking buddies with Taxpayer's money, had made a similar financial killing from the result of the UK Referendum, hiding their fortunes in offshore accounts, investing overseas, some even deciding to live abroad like the detestable hypocrites they were, while minimizing the horrendous impact Brexit would have on the UK once it left the European Union. These hedge-funding, overprivileged Brexiteers, speaking the language of fascism, offered no evidence to support their argument that Brexit would stop foreigners taking our jobs or leeching off the State and thought everything would turn out just peachy for them. The sacrifice would not be theirs to make. They were never going to be affected by the outcome of the Referendum – why would they? – but they continued to refer to the difficulties the British people might encounter after leaving the EU as 'short-term' difficulties when in fact this meant it would affect Trade and the strength of the Sterling and even access to life-saving medications and effectively plunge Britain into a long economic recession where lots of people might actually lose their livelihoods and their jobs. Chivers still couldn't believe the way the old folk had condemned their own children and grandchildren to a life of hardship for generations to come by voting for Brexit. However, any democracy should be entitled to change its mind – that's why it's called a democracy. The British people should be allowed to reverse their decision and undo the Brexit vote, thus preventing a historic mistake, more so now that they realized they had been duped the first time round, enabling them to continue to live peacefully in a strong Europe. Having watched the embarrassing fiasco that had been the Brexit negotiations between the UK and the EU, diminishing Britain's authority and credibility on the world stage, he was certain other European nations wouldn't dare go down the same referendum route and face similar humiliation, even if the Russians oligarchs tried to tip the balance by funding the far right.

But this was neither here nor there.

The Prime Minister had come away with a Brexit deal that the EU leaders had emphasized could be the only logical and acceptable deal, even if the Irish backstop remained problematic. Mrs. 'Dismay' now had to get the miserable Brexit deal through Parliament and already faced a major Commons defeat so had rescheduled the MPs' vote for the New Year. In the meantime, the paper tigers in the xenophobic wing of her party, like Beano and Mr. Peanut, really knew how to put the 'ass' in assassin since they had tabled in a no-confidence motion against their own leader.

Chivers had lost all sympathy for Mrs. Dismay in her onerous task of securing a squalid Brexit deal when once he had felt sorry for her on account of her Diabetes. The UK Referendum had been lost on the playing fields of Eton and now her party's civil war had divided the country, with friends and family members across the nation only just getting back on talking terms with each other and acknowledging the mistake they made in voting Leave after the nationwide exposure of the coordinated falsehoods and barefaced lies of the pro-Brexit campaign. Just as the fight against White Supremacy had been reignited across the Pond, the evils of White Privilege – and Populism – had pervaded the Halls of Power in the UK. Such is the twisted logic of populism that argues that if the Establishment is against them, then it is the Establishment that needs changing, not the strategy. The Conservative Party was guilty on that front. The Conservative Party operated under a misnomer because it did anything but 'conserve'. They used their political advantage to penalize the poorest and most vulnerable in society, overseeing a doubling of those sleeping rough and the tragic increase in impoverished children without shoes or clothes as well as recommending food banks for struggling families, forced to suffer the indignity of navigating Universal Credit, while actively promoting the notion that alcoholism and gambling addiction represent the smart choices for anybody governed by them. Yet, in the same breath, they continued to grant tax advantages to the obscenely wealthiest in society, lying in bed with the tax-dodging bankers and Tory-party donors, who've taken all the covers. They had sold arms to hostile foreign powers and seemed prepared to send our soldiers to their deaths if it made them a quick profit. The Tories had streamlined the education system, leading to schools being unable to fund essential school equipment, and underfunded the police force, causing a rise in violent crimes, including shootings and stabbings and acid attacks. They had sold off the railways, water, electricity, gas, Telecom and Royal Mail in the name of the Free Market while the NHS would, too, soon be gone the way of the Devil, and now the British people had their freedom to travel, to settle and live in mainland Europe stolen from them, too. All so as to keep a party of spivvy millionaires and pig-fucking Bullingdon Boys together, snorting coke and drinking champers and laughing at the gullibility of the British public. He knew the majority of the British people, who voted for Brexit, would not forgive those unscrupulous, lying bastards, who had promised them something they never had any intention of delivering and whose buddies, the currency speculators bankrolling the party, had already bet billions on a hard Brexit, tumbling economy and soaring inflation and rising unemployment be damned. However, the European Court, in its selfless wisdom, had even suggested that Britain could disregard Brexit altogether, simply *cancel* it, as if the last two years had never happened. That, in Chivers' opinion, would be real justice – or maybe force another General Election or, better still, why not hold a second referendum rather than go away with the very real and disturbing possibility of a no-deal Brexit? Why not settle it fairly and democratically with an *honest* People's vote? Why not let the will of the people speak a second time? Lord knows everyone in the British public knew someone who had voted Leave but now wished they hadn't, so a second referendum would most certainly be a Remain landside. And the hard right would surely be remembered as the losers on the wrong side of history. But the Tories had other plans. Not content with their lies and empty promises and cruel austerity measures, they decided, with their usual parochial thinking, they needed an ally to make the no-deal Brexit possible, an outcome that they saw as acceptable, even at a grass-roots level, almost as much as their persistent attempts to normalize state racism. Even entryism was no major cause for concern. Why not bow down to the far right? Why not betray your principles and shed your respectability than lose the chance to stay in power? The Tories did not care – or want to be reminded that they should care. Behaviour without accountability or electoral consequences. Just when you thought the Tories could not stoop any lower . . .

In the meantime, Chivers would have to be content with following a no-confidence vote against the PM by her own party, a political parenthesis, so to speak, in this pathetic Brexit saga.

Pleasantly drunk and feeling sleepy, Chivers was pouring himself another drink and wondering if he should prop his eyes open with matchsticks, turn in once the votes had been cast and counted, see the whole thing through, when he heard a male voice from somewhere nearby: *If you thought the vote of no confidence relates to the Prime Minister, think again!*

Startled, Chivers looked around to identify the source of the communication. Unmarried and unattached, there was nobody else in the house. He sat alone in the semi-darkness of the lounge, idly watching events on the news. "What the hell do you mean?" he dithered loudly, fighting against his rising fear.

The voice came again, impossible to pinpoint. *The Tories are conducting a vote of no confidence not in their leader but a vote of no confidence in* you. *They are voting to decide whether you should be allowed to live or be* put down!

His alarm ratcheted up. Panic engulfed him. Stricken individuals often experience a sudden, inexplicable sense of doom and, in his current panicky state, Chivers immediately remembered his friend and fellow teacher, Alistair Halpin, who had been somehow driven to kill himself during the UK Referendum in 2016, living in constant fear of a perceived notion that the British people were voting on his life. The same thing seemed to be happening to him, presently. Madness could be catching.

And the Tories will be less kind to you, added the phantom voice with a stark, terrible glee. *Have you not seen how little they care about the homeless or the working classes or the disenfranchised – or anybody who ever* defies *their will?*

"This is crazy!" Chivers yelled, his brain floating in a dark cloud of agitation and confusion. "This can't be real!"

Kirsty Wark, the news anchor, begged to differ. She looked directly at the camera, straight at Chivers, and declared: "The Tories do not tolerate dissent, and you, Mr. Chivers, must pay the penalty if you refuse to get with their programme! *The lady is not for turning.*"

The ubiquitous, psychotic voice that had set this lunacy rolling might be frightening for anyone to hear, but receiving a personal, life-threatening warning from the nightly news sent his mind plummeting down a deep well of unimaginable terror – and cataclysmic despair. For, in that instance, Chivers found himself–

–transported to a large chamber that Time itself seemed to have forgotten. And, in this ancient chamber, Time too had forsaken its occupants, who sat in conference, focused on the front table, where sat the Chairman and the ballot-box. Damp permeated the fabric of the oaken walls with the odour of brackish waters, of bubbling rot. The inhabitants of the room would have made the members of the House of Lords appear spectacularly young or that dead sheep, Douglas Hurd, seem like a sprightly teenager. They were the foulest creatures Chivers had ever seen. They resembled cobwebbed cadavers, so emaciated their clothes seemed to weigh down on their skeletal frames, skin shrunk tight across their skulls, crowned by a wispy tangle of hair, hollow-cheeked and dead-eyed. Their grimy, moth-eaten finery and veined, liver-spotted flesh crawled with tiny, nimble spiders.

"The votes have been cast and counted in this session of the 1922 Committee," bellowed the voice of the Chairman, banging his gavel like a judge. In the other bony hand, he held a walking cane, the gold handle of which was shaped like the body of a cat's head with fangs bared. "Let us see what devilry is afoot…"

Chivers did not know when wakefulness ended and the dream began. Except this did not feel like a dream. It was just too vivid to be a dream.

"Damnable days . . ." harrumphed his Deputy seated next to him, playing with his monocle as if it were an ancient scarab. Attaching his ridiculous monocle to his face and puffing himself up like the throat of a bullfrog, bony hands proceeded to open a scroll as yellow as parchment. He delivered the result of the ballot. "ninety-one for, seventy-three against, four abstaining."

Suddenly the room exploded into raucous cheers and applause, raising dust.

"The decision is final!" announced the Chairman, slamming the gavel again on the block.

"Hear, hear!" roared the other Tory backbench MPs, as though Parliament were in session.

"Order, please, order!" the Chairman, using his gavel a few more emphatic times.

The backbenchers quietened down.

The Chairman of the 1922 Committee turned to Chivers, who discovered he could not move from his standing position at the left of the stage, inexplicably paralyzed like a statue. Fresh horror, panic and hopelessness filled him anew. "I'm not quite finished with you yet," the Chairman pronounced ominously, his ancient fingers fiddling with his ancient pocketwatch. He flipped open the cover of the pocketwatch and checked the time. His eyes no longer showed any whites and were now shiny black, reflecting his soul. Because, like his fellow Conservatives in the chamber, it was a *black* soul. It fed on the poor and the weak and the infirm, the slappers and the scrubbers, the chavs and tatts, the liberal gaylords and the tranny sympathizers in a form of soul-ingurgitating cannibalism. *The soul is the most precious part of a person, an exquiste commodity worth plundering.* Bigotry, racism, misogyny, hypocrisy, incompetence, greed, adultery and cruelty *defined* his party, always had and always would. In pursuit of the Great Society of white privilege. "It is time! Your fate has been decided! You shall be *removed* from life – and reality!"

Ghoulish faces grew into states of perverse anticipation, of expectant glee. The onlookers roared their approval like demented demigods.

Bringing this ungodly circus to a close, the Chairman's mouth opened to reveal an old boneyard of tombstone teeth and propelled a gushing stream of black, slithering things, splashing Chivers forcefully in the face, accompanied by a thick stench of carrion-curdled putrescence . . .

Chivers could not escape the nature of his punishment, its inevitability. His friend, Halpin had died by a perceived ballot of the nation whereas Chivers' doom had been drawn by a straw poll of Tory members. He thought he would go inexorably mad.

The horrible, slimy expulsion of serpent-filled vomit obscured his vision for a moment, his arms pinwheeling, as he lurched and fell backwards, and, as he hit the ground, the back of his head suddenly cushioned against–

—the impact was mitigated for he found himself strapped to a gurney in an old, abandoned hospital corridor, terribly decrepit from countless decades of disuse, the part-demolished building probably now sold off to the highest bidder. He struggled fiercely against the restraints but could not break himself loose. It felt like being trapped in a photograph, labouring under the spell of a mephitic mind. Victim of an intelligence powerful enough to cause a normally rational man to fall apart in a matter of seconds.

Rainwater dripped through the broken skylights, puddling the cracks and crevices of the concrete floor. A murder of crows spiralled down through the opening. Wild-haired and screaming, Chivers watched a crow settle on his forehead and tear off a bloody flap of skin. Another crow landed on his chin and began to peck out his tongue. Bridging his fevered mindscape with the real world, a dark figure of small build and wearing thick glasses and a parka, emerged from the shadows and, reaching down, started to pluck his eyes out with a clawhammer...

Enucleated, horribly penned in his figment of insanity, his mental telegraph continued to work for a few more moments as Kirsty Wark from his TV announced the outcome of the leadership challenge, in which Mrs. Dismay had easily managed to secure another year as Prime Minister.

Obliterated by pain, Chivers released a final, agonal gasp.

The last thing he heard was a triumphal proclamation from the disembodied voice: *Checkmate, buster.*

III: THE GIRL WHO KNEW TOO MUCH

The students were surprised to see Mr. Lerner, the College Principal, running English Lit. He had the reputation of a pineapple because he had a prickly face but a sweet centre. Presently, he was banging on about mid-term exams. He was a major proponent of mid-term exams. "All I ask from you with everything in life is you try your hardest . . . there is no shame in failure as long as you try your absolute best," he explained. A rather amusing, constipated facial expression descended upon his face as he gazed somewhere into the distance and he fell back on his favourite spiel. "Ever heard of Robert the Bruce and the spider?" When nobody in the class responded, he continued: "Robert the Bruce was a Scottish king. He had just lost a battle to the English and he managed to escape to the refuge of a cave. Hiding out, defeated and dejected, he was deliberating how he should proceed when he saw a spider next to him spinning a web. The spider would try and build its web, but the web would break, and the spider would start again . . . and again. Robert the Bruce experienced an epiphany that night. His confusion cleared and, the following morning, he rallied his troops together and went on to beat the English army. Moral of the story? The spider taught Robert the Bruce one important lesson: if you don't succeed once, try, try again . . ." He looked at the keen, silent faces of the students. "It's all about positive thinking: conceive, believe, achieve . . ."

The hush continued until Briony spoke up: "Where's Mr. Chivers?"

That all-to-familiar, constipated expression returned. Jonty Chivers' smashed body had been found at the headland. A terrible madness had befallen the teacher. The man had gone crazy and gouged out his eyes and chewed his own tongue, finishing the job by hurling himself off the cliff. He had soiled himself. Mr. Lerner had never pegged his colleague for the suicidal type. No indication whatsoever that he'd been depressed. All this following on from the murder of two members of the college rugby team and the ongoing manhunt for the perpetrator. Mr. Lerner had never faced so much scrutiny. Until the police completed their preliminary investigation, Mr. Lerner would have to be economical with the truth. He would, of course, make a statement when the time came. "Mr. Chivers is currently unavailable. I will oversee his class for now."

He could tell from the curiously dissatisfied silence that his explanation had been insufficient, perhaps unconvincing. Still, they would find out soon enough, and it would be his responsibility as Principal to calm the ensuing panic. He noticed the new boy, Roden Quist, watching him closely, beadily, almost perspicaciously through his thick lenses. As though the boy knew something. There was something oddly disconcerting about that boy and it had nothing to do with his strikingly unattractive, almost rat-like visage . . . maybe he should talk to the boy. But the idea of sitting down with this boy, engaging him in a tête-à-tête, made Mr. Lerner shiver. At that moment, the end-of-school bell rang shrilly down the corridors, and Mr. Lerner suitably ended the lesson with a grunt of constipation. *Saved by the bell*, he thought, immensely grateful.

"Hold up," someone called, catching up with Cosmina and her friends on the way home from College.

The girls turned round and saw Roden Quist, the newbie, the boy who took photographs, hurrying towards them. They had halted beneath the bright circle of illumination of a streetlamp. There was a row of parked cars on either side of the quiet street, deserted of pedestrians, the inhabitants of the brownstones preparing for dinner. The air was cold and damp, mist curling up from the pavement, swirling around their ankles like dry ice. The soft twinkle of Cassiopeia in the dark, unclouded evening sky. Frost expected in the morning. It wasn't so much his spotty, bespectacled presence that surprised the three girls, who were dressed in thick coats and scarves and woolly hats to counter the chill, but what he was carrying. As he approached, he handed Cosmina a bouquet of roses. There was a moment's awe before her two friends started giggling. Frowning, Roden ignored them.

"This is quite the gesture," said Cosmina softly, accepting the gift, feeling the crinkle of cellophane, the moist fragrance of the spruced-up arrangement of red roses. "What's the occasion?"

"Does there have to be an occasion?" said Roden. "After what you've been through, what with Griff and all, I thought I could be the emotional crutch you could lean on."

"You know Briony and Micah serve that very purpose," Cosmina reminded him.

Roden looked distastefully at the other two girls, who wore amused expressions. He knew there was no fooling them. They could tell he was expressing a romantic interest in their friend. Their wide, frozen smirks suddenly made him feel self-conscious. "I just thought I could be there for you . . ." he repeated, trailing off, his confidence waning.

Cosmina had to admit Roden looked and sounded cutely insecure. "How many roses?"

"Twenty-four," Roden replied in educational mode. "Twenty-four roses to represent twenty-four hours in the day. Twenty-four roses to signify the person will think about their loved one at least once every hour of the day."

"That's so sweet of you," acknowledged Cosmina and took another whiff of the roses.

"Be careful what you wish for," Briony interrupted, warning her friend. "If one dozen roses says 'be mine', two dozen roses means 'I'm yours' . . . *whether you like it or not.*"

"Is that so?" Cosmina sounded surprised.

Roden could've killed himself! "Be quiet!" he muttered at Briony with a sulky, petulant look. How dare she? Who made her the source of all wisdom? She was showing him up in front of his girl-to-be.

"Yeah, the game's up," responded Briony, abruptly cracking up into laughter. Micah joined her. This was nothing new. "Don't look so serious. You know I'm only teasing."

Roden's trademark snark did not disappear. "That isn't funny."

"There is no such thing as love at first sight," Cosmina enlightened Roden. "It's something Rodgers and Hammerstein dreamed up one day to rhyme with moon and June."

I can't stop thinking about you . . . even if I know I shouldn't. I think I might be falling in love with you, Cosmina. You are always on my mind, so unbearably beautiful are you, pure as the virgin snow. No wonder all the boys flirt with you. When I say flirt with you, I mean they throw themselves at you. Like them, I've grown to depend on you like a junkie with a habit. Instead, he managed to pluck up the courage to ask: "I would very much like it if you could be my date at the Halloween Ball." He added: "I won't take no for an answer."

Cosmina was watching him now, studying him. She did not like being pressurized, but neither did she detect any threat in his words. She did not speak for a few seconds. She rustled the cellophane enwrapping the roses, deliberating. When she did reply, her tone was kind and gentle, "Okay, you've got yourself a date."

Roden hadn't been anticipating such a positive response – after all, she could get any boy she desired – and he had been expecting to put in more work into her seduction, determine what else he could do to convince her. Least of all, he didn't want her to know he was trying to catch her on the rebound. But when she unexpectedly gave him her consent, having once seemed totally oblivious of him, inaccessible, he was so utterly thrilled, so giddy with ecstasy, he punched the high heavens in joy – *Woohoo!* – and nearly dropped his spectacles. Adjusting his glasses on the bridge of his nose, he said to the girls: "You didn't see that..."

"Because it was so uncool?" remarked Micah.

"We can turn a blind eye," commented Cosmina, "can't we, girls?"

"Yes, we can!" said Briony and Micah simultaneously.

Cosmina regarded Roden again. "Okay, Mr. Quist, pick me up from my house on 26, Ambleside Road at seven on Friday in your best fancy dress."

"It's a deal!" Roden whooped and nearly went to kiss her. His lips managed only a clumsy air-kiss, less than an inch from her face. Embarrassed, he decided he should quickly take his leave before he did anything more cringeworthy. But it wasn't all bad: he was delighted he'd secured a dream date with the girl of his fancies and, yes, there was a real spark between them. *Love is a mystery. Love is like a bar of dark chocolate. Love is misery, bittersweet and forbidden. But, most of all, Love is an exploitable and mystical force. Because I can* make *you love me.* "Maybe I could interest you ladies in a lift home?" He pointed to a black Ford Capri parked nearby.

Cosmina did not fancy a drive in his ratchety, old rust-bucket. "No, it's fine," she replied, letting him down gently. "We can walk. We enjoy the bracing air."

"As you wish," said Roden, slightly disappointed. The girls watched the lovestruck boy get into his car, start the engine and disappear down the street. When he was out of sight, Briony asked Cosmina, "Why did you say 'yes' to his offer of a date? You turned down so many hot-looking hunks for the Halloween bash."

"I can make an exception for him." Cosmina admitted, fighting down her diametrically-opposed feelings, her best friend's concerns and her own sense of duty to the new boy. "I suppose I feel sorry for him in a way."

"I don't think he'd appreciate your charity, if he knew," Briony replied, "or your pity."

"Or maybe I accepted his invitation because as they say: *No Rain, No Rainbow.*"

"Don't you think it's odd that Mr. Chivers pulled up Roden at the end of class?" Briony asked. "That means Roden was the last person to see Mr. Chivers alive."

The three friends were alone at Cosmina's pinkly-decorated bedroom, giant teddies and doggies everywhere, her parents apparently taking in a show at the theatre. Extraordinary how Briony and Cosmina's parents always kept missing each other. News had spread fast that their English Lit teacher had killed himself. Mr. Lerner, the Principal and their English Lit substitute teacher for now, had made the announcement in class. Condolences were exchanged. Inspector O'Hara was convinced this supposed suicide had something to do with the death of those rugger students, but unfortunately the police were stumped, having hit a dead end. Griffin de'Marco was still missing.

"That is something worth pondering over," affirmed Micah. They had all liked Mr. Chivers, and his sudden death, let alone by his own hand, had come as a profound shock to them.

"And what's with that camera?" Briony inquired. "The boy always carries that camera, everywhere he goes. I smell a rat – pardon the pun."

Cosmina and Micah enjoyed spending time with Briony. She was a smart girl, sometimes too smart for her own good. But they appreciated her company and being enlightened by her. Briony had ambition, focus and direction, on course to be the first potential candidate for Oxbridge from Pemberton College for nearly ten years. Hard-nosed, Briony hoped to do Criminology some day, with *C.S.I.* currently one her all-time favourite shows. She would sometimes joke about the way Horatio Caine always delivered his one-liner before putting on his sunglasses at the end of every opening scene or how Gil Grissom often dazzled his colleagues with his remarkable knowledge of corpse-burrowing insect larvae, highlighting his own weird interests. Her parents, on the other hand, were more politically-minded and addicted to *House of Cards* in which Kevin Spacey, before he was fired from the show due to alleged sexual misconduct, played a Democrat but behaved more like a Republican, infiltrating and destroying the Democrats from within in his pursuit of power. As far as Briony was concerned, politics had become a platform for corporate greed. Money was the currency of evil. *Don't you just hate those money-rollers, no*, money-holers, *I say?*

"You think he's dodgy?" asked Micah. "You think there's more to Roden than him just making sheep's eyes at Cosmina?"

"I refuse to believe he's the innocent bystander he makes himself out to be and I, instead, cast aspersions on his motives in photographing the victims," declared Briony. "Griff's disappearance, the unexpected suicide of our English teacher. It's like he's hiding whatever axes he likes to grind and disposing of those who get too close to the truth."

"Wait, are you saying there's more to Roden the Rat and his love of photography and he had something to do with these crazy events?" Micah inferred. "And you base this on – what exactly?"

Briony went on to elaborate. "I did some research. Certain cultures throughout the world fear photographs, their religious belief systems expressing a concern that a soul can be captured, imprisoned or stolen. Photographs have been aligned with the paranormal for a long time. For example, thoughography supposedly disperses a build-up of psychic energy to imprint a mental image onto film. Kirlian photography uses a high-voltage electric current over a photographic plate to get a coronal discharge we call an aura. Early attempts to get pictures at the exact instant of death supposedly showed the spirit leaving the body. Yes, assuming the soul exists, cultures as far and wide as the Native Americans to the Australian Aborigines say a photograph is a window to the soul, a snapshot of life-energy, where the image of the person is independent of the person, just as mirrors – in particular, *broken* mirrors – or graven images – such as poppets or cornhusk dolls or sculptures or runic representations – are thought to endanger the lifeforce of the person, fracture the soul or prevent it from returning to its body. Scrying doesn't just involve foretelling the future but can be about affecting the future of someone in a negative way. That's why there's no pictures of Crazy Horse. A shaman was necessary to restore a person's soul. Just as voodoo practitioners believe that a part of the person, fetish items such as hair, nail clippings, blood or articles of clothing, can create a powerful link to that person, occultists claim that photographic images serve a similar purpose and are regarded as potent tools for casting spells or curses. It's claimed that sticking the photographed faces of exes with pins, burying the photo, desecrating it or burning it should have exactly the same effect on the photographed person in the real world. Taking a picture of a sleeping person might mean they may not wake up. If someone owns your photograph, they can supposedly dwell in you. Some people say it's down to the use of silver on the photographic film since silver is thought to have magical properties – think of silver bullets in combating werewolves."

"I guess that's why it's called 'magic'," observed Cosmina, the voice of reason. "Superstition is an irrational fear of the unknown."

"I know I'm making a leap, but I want you to keep an open mind," Briony said, summing up. "The boy can do things the rest of us can only dream of. Dark, despicable things. He can wish upon a photograph and it translates into real life."

"That's quite the stretch," said Cosmina lightly. "You do know you're telling us to believe in dragons and mermaids and unicorns?"

"These are crazy times, yep, crazy times," Briony reminded her, insistent. [*I won't take no for an answer.*] "He's got a thing for you or had you forgotten?"

"Because he thinks I'm amazing," Cosmina said with mock-vanity.

"I second that," concurred Micah.

"I think you should take this a bit more seriously," Briony warned Cosmina. "You're the one going on a date with him."

A moment's silence as Briony's comment sank in. Cosmina emerged from her thoughts decisive. "I think I'll be alright. I can always call upon the police if I get unstuck."

"The police aren't obliged by law to protect you," Briony informed her.

"It's the Halloween Ball," Cosmina said, undeterred. "What can he possibly do to me when there's so many people around?"

He had heard every word of their conversation. He had been waiting below her window listening in. 'Stalking' was such an offensive and loaded descriptive – he had been 'watching' her in preparation for the big day tomorrow, the Halloween party. Why could nothing go smoothly? Trouble seemed to follow him like a cloud of flies to a stinky caboose. Now that nosy bitch, Briony, had angered him, interfering in matters that didn't concern her, pissing on his parade. Well, not for long.

When the girls decided to call it an evening at nine, voting against a sleepover, Roden took his opportunity. Loading a new roll of film into his pocket camera, he hid behind the bushes and shot a group photo of them as they stood on the doorstep. The noise of the mechanism did not give him away. Then, Briony and Micah said their goodnights to Cosmina and went their separate ways.

He braved the evening chill and stayed behind, feeling a deeper closeness to his love. *Daisy, Daisy, I'm half*-crazy, went the nursery rhyme. And as far as those love songs went: *I will raise mountains for you, swim the deepest ocean.* Roden stayed put until his love had changed into her pyjamas and turned off the bedroom light. *Hope you're fast asleep, my love. Keep dreaming those lovely dreams . . .*

He returned to his own place at the dead of midnight and went straight to his dark room to work on his single snapshot of the evening, coax out an image, grainy or otherwise, from the film. Whereas half the frame had turned out fine, the shape and definition of Briony and Micah captured perfectly by the light of the front hallway, the image of Cosmina had once again come out indistinct and fuzzy, as though on film she were in motion, her face gradually eaten away by black, the surrounding shadows, too, very quickly dropping off to black. Roden could not make head nor tail of these chromatic aberrations. He could not understand how he could have taken such another crude, sloppy picture. A face here, a blur there, a hint of something almost there but not quite. Shadow-copies of silhouette-black drifting off into layers of greyness to lessen the impact. He couldn't blame the viewfinder or the shutter speed since there was enough exposure, with Cosmina sharing the same light intensity as her friends. Wider aperture for lower light, narrow aperture for more light. Field curvature could make it more difficult to control distortions. A shorter lens, or smaller aperture, might result in the image being in focus. *Maybe next time.*

Unless something was preventing him from seeing a photo of his love. What was making Cosmina so camera-shy, so to speak? He had his ways, ancient ways of getting what he wanted. Did it not work with desire, too, with *love? The more focused I become on seducing her, the more unfocused her picture becomes, perhaps maintaining the balance between the natural and supernatural worlds.*

Still, he could bring some diabolical life to the visible remainder of the photo, bind Briony to his will.

Briony tested the bathwater with her toes. Fifty-five degrees. *Perfect.* She slipped out of her bathrobe and gently slid into the bubble-bath, relishing the coddling warmth of the water and the slushy texture of the foam against her skin. She settled into the bath, her naked, curvaceous body largely submerged by the water, her dignity concealed by a frothy mound of soapsuds, only her head and neck visible above the surface, reclining against the foot of the bath, on the opposite end to the taps. A series of tea-candles placed strategically around the bath cast a low, tranquil illumination in the bathroom, not entirely dissimilar to squinting into the setting sun and seeing warm colours splash across the clouds. Comfortable, she closed her eyes, hoping to fully unwind with the bath salts before settling down to a nice milky cup of chicory and retiring to bed. A light nap in the bath should be restorative, curative for her achy limbs, allow her brain to process recent events and conversations and put her on an equal footing with her suspicions. Her mind tolled off fathoms, like Captain Nemo of the Nautilus, as she began to drift off.

I owe you a conversation, a male voice broke through her reverie unexpectedly, following her down into the depths of her sleep.

Her eyes flew open like shutterblinds and she looked around the bathroom, spooked. "Who said that?"

Except she was alone in the bathroom. The mirror above the washbasin was steamed over. The window was slightly raised to let out the mist, the sill decorated with a potted oleander plant. The wind whistled in the eaves outside, making the building creak. Surely, she must be dreaming.

The tea-lights flickered, and the voice intruded upon her again. *Dare you try and cramp my style?*

Briony suddenly became aware of a presence. No, she wasn't dreaming. She didn't know if the voice was coming from somewhere around her or if it was all in her head. Regardless, whoever might be interrupting her bathtime sounded very real...and familiar. "Roden, is that you?"

Girl, that would be me*!* Roden chuckled from someplace nearby.

"How are you doing this?" she demanded with a fierceness that tempered her fear.

Wouldn't you like to know? his voice echoed back. *Or maybe you already do . . .*

Those damned photographs, Briony deduced. Roden must be dispensing some kind of hoodoo on a photograph he must have discreetly taken of her.

Roden appeared to read her mind. *You're a clever one, aren't you?*

"What have you done to me?"

Nothing . . . yet, he responded ominously.

The sharp menace in his voice sent an ice-pick of dread through her heart, despite the relaxing warmth of her bath.

The door handle rattled, jiggled. The bolt was unlocked.

"Mom, is that you?" called out Briony.

The rattling stopped. She watched with growing horror as an invisible finger scrawled a message across the steam of the bathroom mirror: I'M COMING FOR YOU.

Briony had never believed in ghosts, let alone the notion of automatic writing. Until now, that is. The message on the mirror brought fresh terror through her system, but her resilience shone through. "You've got *nothing*, freak! You are not going to scare me!"

I now have you exactly where I want you, promised Roden, sounding as though he was thoroughly enjoying himself, *and the worst is yet to come . . .*

Briony's ears were assailed by a loud stomping from upstairs, like the welter of leaden boots galumphing across the attic. The noise intensified, giving the impression of someone – or something – deliberately banging the attic floor with a heavy object, threatening to break through the bathroom ceiling. There followed a tremendous, bestial growl, not unlike the enraged, demonic utterances heard in haunted houses.

The commotion abruptly stopped. Only the desolate howl of the wind outside, rising to a screeching crescendo. Then, the tea-candles guttered out all at once, and Briony was stranded in darkness. Clutching its sides, she tried to propel herself out of the bath, but something grabbed her ankles. And began to pull her under.

She struggled, panicking, against the immense hold, trying to wrench herself free, splashing waves of water onto the bathroom floor. But the grip was viselike, unbreakable.

As she began to sink, another head began to emerge above the surface of the water between her legs, glistening blackly as an oil slick. Its slippery skin was covered in suckers and polyps and barnacles and it wore strands of seaweed, and the thought occurred to Briony it must possess tentacles instead of hands that had roped themselves tightly around her ankles, using her as a pivot to come up, like some mutant, underwater creature dragging itself out of a swamp. Except, even in the dark, she could see its features vaguely resembled those of Roden, no longer the rat but an obscene, amphibious being – a god of the darkest fathoms. The foul, rotting stench of trawled oceans and bottom-dwellers, accompanied the manifestation. Shark eyes flashed with a red gleam.

Briony's soul-piercing screams were suddenly choked as she was yanked beneath the water by the hideous, swamp thing sharing the bath with her. A black tentacle kept her head pressed beneath the surface. Soon, exhausted by her efforts, unable to come up for air, she was forced to give up the ghost. Water flooded her lungs.

Judy Madigan's arrival in the bathroom, responding to her daughter's shrieking summons, prevented Briony from drowning in the bath. Briony coughed and spluttered, gasping for air, as her mother pulled her head out of the water.

Roden's angry, frustrated response zipped inside Briony's head for an instant, like a trapped insect: *What a bitch!*

Wearing a pink, knee-length T-shirt with the legend, HUGS NOT DRUGS, Briony prepared for bed. It had been an eventful evening, and if it hadn't been for her mother's timely intervention, she would be dead right now. Her mother had assumed her daughter had fallen asleep in the bath and suffered a nightmare, nearly drowning in the process. Rightfully concerned – and frightened – by the incident, the extremely close call, Judy Madigan had given Briony an earful, but Briony decided to leave it at that. She had even declined a trip to the hospital to be checked out, stating she was okay.

Briony could now appreciate how her English teacher had been attacked and murdered by an unseen force, his corpse discovered on the storm-thrashed coast at first light. Neither probably had Griff been himself when he'd slaughtered his closest friends. Forensic psychiatrists defined 'dangerousness' as a product of probability (or risk) and gravity (seriousness). Tantrums aside, Roden took this definition to a whole different level, beyond all scientific reasoning. Highly versed in hypnotism, Roden possessed the phenomenal ability to get inside people's head and conjure up terrors the mind could not conceive, marking out each of his enemies for a grisly demise. Briony had experienced it for herself, been granted a special, hair-raising glimpse of his godless powers, first-hand. He had struck the first blow, but she had not yet figured out his true purpose.

Briony decided to give Inspector O'Hara a call.

IV: HARLEQUIN UNMASKED

It was that time of year again. Even if it was another pagan holiday commandeered by the Catholic Church, like Christmas and Valentine's Day, it remained an important date in the Wiccan calendar, and some of the old traditions of Samhain, marking the end of the harvest season and the midpoint between the autumn equinox and winter solstice, persisted in updated form. Trick-or-treating, the mainstay of modern Halloween, an evening when children were permitted to get a sugar rush from their swag of candy, was nothing less than a variation of 'guising', going door-to-door in costume and singing folk songs in exchange for food. Bobbing for apples was another. Plunging your hand into a bowl of peeled grapes in a darkened room, having been told they were eyeballs, was one more custom revised from old. Those enlightened in arcane wisdom suggested that Halloween night was when the veil of reality was supposedly at its thinnest, when supernatural beings from the twilight world that existed beyond, the dark, alternate plane of chaos, could cross the membrane that intersected reality.

Tonight, the students of Pemberton College descended in their droves on the annual Halloween Ball. They had all come to the dance, but they had unwisely forgotten that Halloween was also the hunting ground of the Bogeyman . . .

She was going to miss her favourite programme tonight, but she could always catch it later. The Madigans did not pay for a TV licence because there was nothing worth watching on the terrestrial channels. The only show even remotely of interest was *Have I Got News for You*, that long-running, British institution of satirical and subversive wit led by Messrs. Merton and Hislop in their honest crusade against pomposity, hypocrisy and corruption which, ironically, Briony watched illegally on BBC iPlayer without getting caught.

The gymnasium had been used to accommodate the Halloween party. Except for the basketball hoops at either end of the court, it had been cleared of all its equipment, its treadmills and horizontal crossbars and wooden vaulting horses, and converted into a dancehall, complete with DJ and disco-lights.

The students were milling in, garbed in their fancy-dress costumes, some wearing dense layers of gothic makeup, others masked to identify themselves with their favourite horror characters; Dracula, Wolfman and Frankenstein's monster formed the majority of getups, but some were dressed as witches and warlocks and zombies and one particularly resourceful student had come donned in the mask of Michael Myers while wielding a rubber kitchen knife. Most of the teachers had foregone their fancy dress, so as to make themselves visible and more easily approachable, and security had been stepped up, various plainclothes police officers located around the gym, watching the proceedings, wary of any sign of trouble. Mr. Lerner had declined Inspector O'Hara's request to call off the Halloween party. It was an atmosphere of a school on edge, and the students needed a release. They deserved to let their hair down. Let them enjoy the festivities, footloose and fancy free.

In one corner of the gym, the nominated DJ, a music student going by the name of Aaron Bentley, was studiously working the mixing deck. Presently, Ed Sheeran played on the speakers, and already Briony was groaning at the 'appalling' standard of the songs. She didn't much care for Ed Sheeran. Nor the conspiracy theories that claimed that he was a member of the Illuminati to explain the speed at which he had shot to fame with his mediocre musical offerings, collecting an M.B.E. in the process. Like Justin Timberlake, total dross. Yes, Timberlake, famous for Disney and dating Britney Spears. Nothing manly about Timberlake's singing, coming across less like a pathetic Michael Jackson impersonation, more like a eunuch. "Are you kidding?" Briony was telling Micah. "It's just seriously weird to hear suggestive songs by Ed Sheeran on the radio when he has absolutely no sex appeal. I mean he still lives with his mother. With a nerdy face like that, he should be on *The Big Bang Theory*. Nothing unique about him, just repetitive and boring and whiny and as gay-sounding as Sam Smith. Where the Illuminati once welcomed the likes of Isaac Newton and Leonardo Da Vinci into their secret society, they really must have gone downmarket to accept Ed Sheeran and Beyonce into their numbers!" An expression of mock-horror crossed her face. "Please don't tell me Aaron's going to play Sam Smith next?"

"Is there anything that you like?" Micah, dressed up like Baron Samedi, asked her.

"Not a lot," Briony responded, looking rather fetching in a Red Riding Hood costume. She carried a gold-coloured staff for rounding up sheep.

"We should make some requests," Micah suggested. "Some Cure or Cult or Siouxsie and the Banshees to celebrate the occasion."

"We could totally do that!" agreed Briony. Bobby Pickett was sorely missed and Briony dearly hoped he'd make an appearance on the decks some time soon.

Amidst the strobe-lighting and the cheery hubbub of her fellow students chatting and laughing and drinking non-alcoholic punch, her eyes caught the arrival of Cosmina and her date. Cosmina had thrown on a black, beehive wig and risqué, dominatrix costume, in tribute to Elvira, Mistress of the Dark. "Hello, my beauties!"

Even if he was clad in a yellow Harlequin costume, stitched in a patchwork of blue diamonds, and his head and face completely covered over by a mask, they knew it was Roden from his modest height and general scrawny appearance. He peered through two holes in the fabric of the mask, likely having replaced his spectacles with contact lenses.

When he saw Briony, he stopped for a moment, maybe out of surprise, more out of does-she-know-it-was-me? uncertainty. Briony was only too glad she'd foiled him. He must surely be wondering how she could have possibly survived being drowned in the bath – all his doing she was sure of it – and whether she had told the other girls. He didn't know she hadn't mentioned it to the others, in case it freaked them out, but she was pleased he would be unaware of her subsequent conversation with Inspector O'Hara. The Inspector could not act at this stage, haul Roden in for questioning, without evidence of wrongdoing. That moment's noticeable hesitation passed by, and Roden was jovial, as if nothing had floundered him. "Ah, the Weird Sisters!" he remarked, amiably enough, appraising their rather *comme-il-faut* getups: Briony, with her silk, red cloak and golden staff, and Micah, suitably attired in black tail coat and top hat and half her face painted like a grinning skull, perhaps befitting her mixed heritage. "What a nice coven we make!"

Briony went directly for Roden without sparing any punches. "Did you watch *Creature from the Black Lagoon* last night?"

Roden immediately knew what she was implying, and his confidence began to wilt. "C-c-can't say I d did."

Cosmina and Micah wondered what Briony was getting at. "What's going on?" asked Cosmina. "Did something happen last night?"

"Why don't you ask Roden?" Briony said, outright challenge in her tone. "Tell me, Roden, did something happen last night?" Roden remained silent but his eyes appeared nervous, fearful of Briony, maybe in case she let the cat out of the bag. At least he knew now Briony knew. "Come on, spit it out!"

The other girls just looked inquisitively at Roden for answers, unaware what had transpired the previous night.

The heightened attention upon him and accompanying tension with Briony caused Roden to avoid answering the question altogether. "I'll go and get us some drinks," he excused himself and walked off.

The girls watched him disappear into the crowd. Then, Micah was straight on to Briony. "So, tell us, what happened last night?"

Briony blurted it out: "He's a childish, murderous coward, selfish and cruel and amoral."

Before Briony could continue, they were interrupted by a couple of boys. "Hi there, ladies . . ." said Steve Capstone, fellow English student and presently dressed as a red devil, complete with horns and inflatable pitchfork. His buddy, Oswald Trise, wore a werewolf costume, the wolf mask in his hand. Steve was already checking out Cosmina. "Like your style. Very vampish. *Niiiice!*" He pointed to the people moving and grooving on the dancefloor. "Fancy kicking back and letting loose?"

When Roden came back with the four paper cups of punch gathered up in his arms, he was met with the sight of three boys crowded around his date, chatting her up and hanging on to her every word. Briony and Micah didn't get a look-in and were standing a slight distance away from the main group.

I was only gone for a few minutes and already my girl has nearly eloped with these testosterone-headed Neanderthals. Such was the effect she had on other boys. *She makes you high with desire, then you crash and weep and crave her. Please cut me some slack, won't you?* For once, he didn't want to be competing with other guys over his girl. He had already dispensed with the official competition, Griff de'Marco. Jealousy was not far away . . . and jealousy always made him dangerous.

Briony and Micah took their drinks off him, Roden conscious of Briony's watchful eye, interested in what he would do next.

Not to come across as weedy in front of his girl, he barged into the group of bigger boys. "Well, well, what have we here?" he said nonchalantly. He offered the punch to Cosmina. "Drink, darling?" He was grateful when Cosmina took it and did not protest being referred to as 'darling'. As a fortunate consequence, it made them seem like an item. "Please, guys, give my girl some room to breathe."

But Cosmina was enjoying the attention lavished on her by these boys. "I'm okay, Roden. Just having a chat and a giggle."

"Yes, she's okay," acknowledged Steve Capstone, rounding on Roden. He seemed to know who inhabited the Harlequin costume. "Now push off!"

"Yeah, get lost, pipsqueak!" said his buddy, Oswald. The third boy, another fellow English student by the name of Linus Cosgrove, merely looked disdainfully at Roden, viewing him as a chancre, someone totally undeserving of Cosmina's beauty.

"Hey, sweetheart," Steve implored, going back to Cosmina, "what do you see in this loser? Why don't you just ditch him?"

Roden didn't like it. He didn't like it one bit. "Get off her! Leave her alone!" he shouted, throwing his drink at Steve.

When Steve realized what had happened, he was furious, and Roden suddenly regretted his moment of impulse. "Fuck off, you little squirt!" Steve pushed Roden hard in the chest, sending him reeling backwards, sliding partway across the dancefloor like a bowling pin, colliding into numerous legs, nearly bringing down the dancing couples, his progress eventually halted.

Nearly winded, Roden got up awkwardly and, not only embarrassed but also mad as hell, charged at Steve, reciprocating the gesture, pushing him firmly and squarely in the chest. "*You* fuck off, dickhead!"

Except Steve barely budged from his spot. Roden lacked any physical strength to move the bigger boy. Instead, Steve just punched Roden in the face, mask and all, and once again the smaller boy fell backwards, landing heavily on his backside.

For a moment, Roden did not know what hit him, but, when realization dawned, he ripped off his Harlequin mask. His nose was bleeding. He rose slowly to his feet. He was shaking. He glared fiercely at Steve, and suddenly Steve took a step back.

Many other students became conscious of the commotion in their immediate vicinity and formed a circle around the two boys, giving them space to tough it out, fight over the girl. Teachers and police officers, standing on the sidelines, too became aware of the disturbance and waded into the fray but were prevented from dealing with the altercation by the sheer number of student spectators.

But it was already too late.

Roden lost his shit. He didn't need his camera this time. His fury was explosive, his wrath far-reaching, infernal.

Roden suddenly raised a trembling finger towards Steve, a gesture that appeared less accusatory, more a hex marking out a foe. Before Steve could react, his two male friends, Oswald and Linus, abruptly laid into him. There would be no respite, as Steve collapsed to the floor in a volley of brutal punches and kicks. There would be no rescue, either, as the teachers were prevented from reaching him by the encircling mob of avidly-watching students.

Always hit a man when they're down, rose a universal telepathic command, and all the students witnessing Steve's beating by his best friends closed the circle, joining in the action, demolishing him with their boots. Their murderous frenzy ended with them stamping on his skull, as if it were a rotten pumpkin, until he had no head left.

Students screamed, some horrified at what they'd done, others still under a terrible, malevolent spell. All hell broke loose.

"I'm worthless," Aldo Grayson, the computer nerd and geekiest kid in the college, said, suddenly sure of this one fact, his self-esteem dropping a hundred points.

The nearest boy, Logan Campbell, a normally level-headed Maths A-grader, sensed an invitation coming on. "Then let me help you," he volunteered, a wicked grin spreading across his face. "Better to stab you in the face than stab you in the back." And, with that, he shoved a fountain pen into Aldo's right eye, thrusting it deeper into the brain.

More screams. More pandemonium.

Another student, Sandy Gould, said hopelessly, "Nobody screws me unless I'm blind drunk."

"Why not do it sober for a change?" Thierry Dacré, her classmate in French studies propositioned her.

"Why not, indeed?" she said, the hopelessness replaced by an irrepressible wantonness. "Is it true what they say about black cocks?" And pulled down the pants of his costume, putting her mouth around his appendage.

The teachers were not immune, either. Mr. Tringham, the Art teacher, told Mrs. Buckley, the Media studies teacher, how much he fucking hated teaching. "I've got some blow. We could snort it together, finish it all off. I know you want to."

Mrs. Buckley did not decline and, grabbing his hand, began weaving her way through the crowd towards the toilets. "Bathroom, pronto!"

Elsewhere, Mr. Rowlinson, History teacher, and Mr. Jeffries, Music teacher, collectively known as 'Tubs and Chubbs' to the student population, were already ripping off each other's clothes. "I want your arse so bad!" Mr. Rowlinson told his colleague.

"I like it when you talk dirty!" replied Mr. Jeffries, syncing lips in a passionate clinch.

A student approached the Principal, who was watching the scenes of carnage with a bemused expression. "I'm going to trash your fucking Jag!"

Mr. Lerner promptly thumped the boy in the face, instantly breaking his nose and flooring him, knocking him out cold.

The plainclothes officers, too, were ramping up the ante, beating up both teachers and students alike. Miss Lissard, the Economics teacher, had hooked herself up with a particularly handsome police officer. "I've got this thing for policemen."

"Maybe I can do something about that right now . . ." PC Denton replied but got nowhere when Mr. Pickering strode up to him and gave him an upper cut to the jaw. Reeling from the force of the blow, PC Denton swayed on his feet momentarily and spat out blood, teeth and a section of tongue.

"She's mine!" Mr. Pickering declared.

Miss Lissard squealed in delight. "My hero!" And suddenly the two of them were all over each other.

Briony stared around her in stark horror, trying to fathom how the Halloween party had quickly disintegrated into indiscriminate libidinous behaviour, mindless violence and death. Cliques dissolved into violent spats. Fisticuffs between individual students and teachers and police officers. Teachers kissing other teachers. People of every age stripping off and indulging in a Roman-style orgy, partaking prohibited delights and pleasures of the flesh, consensual or otherwise. The massacre of students by other students, murdered with impunity, in a variety of ways: strangulations, throat-slittings, stabbings, eviscerations. Carnality and savagery and insanity ruled the day. Briony did not want to believe people were capable of such sick, horrible acts, more so what could make them do these things.

The madness had been contagious, the mayhem spreading like a virus because Roden was like a mind-virus contaminating the minds of the people, bringing out the very worst in them, revealing their baser instincts, tapping directly into their id. The bloodbath was all a distraction anyhow, she realized, because she could see Roden, still in his pantomime dress, already heading towards the exit with Cosmina. Cosmina seemed unable to resist or struggle. He was stronger than he looked. Not content with simply bumping off his competitors, the same powerful influence pervaded the hall full of people and now controlled Cosmina, as his amorous pursuit of her reached fever pitch.

Just as she was about to follow them, two boys approached Micah and surrounded her. She looked positively dazed.

"Sorry to wreck your loveboat," said one of the boys, Gaz Matlock from class, "but I love half-castes, even if I've never fucked a nigger."

"We don't use words like 'nigger' these days," said the other boy, Kev Monaghan. "Too politically-incorrect. 'Jigaboo' is probably a bit less racist and a lot more fancy."

The first boy grinned at Micah. "So how's about it, my dusky princess . . .?"

Micah kneed him in the balls.

Gaz doubled over, clutching his groin in agony

His friend remained unfazed. "Ouch, that must have hurt!" Kev spoke to Micah, disappointed. "You're no fun!" He drew his attention towards Briony, instead. There was rape in his eyes. He grabbed Briony's shoulder. "If I can't fuck chocolate girl over there, I can always go for second best . . . the brainy babe will have to do!"

"Unhand me!" Briony demanded and kicked him in the groin. Kev dropped like a lead balloon, rolling around the floor in pain. "Call it Girl Power!" she told him. Turning to Micah, she advised: "Let's get the hell out of here!"

The two of them moved quickly through the disorientating mêlée, evading the rampaging mob, their safety compromised.

They passed a male student urinating into the punch bowl and drinking a cup. Nearby a group of four girls, wearing hideous masks of rage, had savaged a boy and were sitting on his dead body, clawing and biting him like a pack of starving wolves. The lead girl ululated like a tribal queen and went back to scooping out his pulped brain from his broken skull with a spoon.

Briony had hoped to have left the craziness behind indoors, except some of it had spilled outside. Estranged from their sanity, some of the students had gone on the rampage in the carpark, smashing cars and setting them on fire. The air smelled of smoke . . . and the madness of rioting asylum lunatics.

Briony and Micah wove through the orbit of madness and watched Roden step into a different car, bundling Cosmina into the passenger side first. He had arrived in a Ford Capri and was leaving in a black Alfa-Romeo Spyder. Briony knew it was same car made to look like a different car because it bore the exact same number plate. How he'd done it – created this illusion – was beyond her. After everything she'd witnessed today, was this any surprise?

The Alfa-Romeo drove off, and Briony's heart dropped, as she wondered how she could possibly go after him and save her friend, whom he had kidnapped.

A white Vauxhall Astra screeched to a halt in front of the two girls. The passenger door opened. It was Inspector O'Hara. "Get in . . ." he told Briony and Micah. "He's getting away. We don't have much time . . ."

Inspector O'Hara didn't think the riot looked as if it was going to burn itself out any time soon. He had called for police back-up to restore order to the campus. They would be here shortly, but he didn't want the Riot Squad to suffer the same fate as the plainclothes officers.

"We've lost him," said Briony, disappointed. True, they could no longer see Roden's taillights. "But I think I know where he's going." She gave him directions.

"How come we're unaffected?" asked Micah, reliving the chaos on campus, driven by evil forces, in her head.

"We're protected by the Cross," said O'Hara. "You both wear crucifixes around your necks, I bet. So do I."

It made sense, although little else did. Inspector O'Hara told them that Roden was not on the national database. No social security information, *nothing*. Unless he was using an assumed name, the boy did not exist.

They arrived on Ambleside Road. They disembarked from the car and crept up to Cosmina's house.

The door was open. The lights were still out.

They snuck through the house without meeting any resistance. There was no sign of anybody, not even Cosmina's parents.

But there were signs of life at the bottom of the garden. The light in the shed was on. Was that Roden down there with Cosmina or Cosmina's missing parents?

"You ladies stay back. I'm going in," Inspector O'Hara smashed the Yale lock, stepped into the shed. And stopped in his tracks. Briony and Micah joined his side and realized what had flummoxed him.

The light was coming from a small candle. It cast a glow on the figure held captive in the shed, causing them to loose a gasp of inarticulate shock. It was neither Cosmina nor her parents – or Roden for that matter – but someone they had least expected to see.

Inspector O'Hara and Briony drove through the lonesome backwoods in the dark of night and arrived at their destination, brand new information provided by the unexpected figure in Cosmina's shed. Micah had stayed behind in order to contact the Emergency Services. Inspector O'Hara and Briony now knew where Roden was taking Cosmina.

A place where most of Becton buried their loved ones, generations of dead kin stretching as far back as the seventeenth century. The crumbling tombstones and rotting graves marked fathers, mothers and siblings – even unfortunate children.

Wych Hill Cemetery.

What kind of kid lives in a cemetery? thought Inspector O'Hara. *The kind of kid who's not a kid at all.*

They parked up next to Roden's car, which had somehow reverted back to a

Ford Capri.

"You stay here," Inspector O'Hara advised Briony. "If I'm not back in half an hour, call the police."

"I'm coming with you," said Briony, adamant.

Inspector O'Hara knew there could be no changing her mind. She was in this as deep as him.

They emerged into the blowy, bitterly-cold night, the wind wailing and shrieking, rising and falling. The vapid eye of the moon watched them from overhead.

They followed a path towards a stone building set into the crag of a hill at the back of the cemetery. More steps sent them down into a tunnel. The walls were concrete blocks, lit by ensconced, flaming wooden torches. They moved quietly through the passageway, wary of any sound or activity.

Voices up ahead.

They arrived at a subterranean chamber with its signs of habitation: a metal chair and table, a basic bed with a dirty mattress to sleep on. Except the room contained a collection of antiquities of dark fascination. A leather journal in an unfathomable language. Rusty sexual apparatus that could not have been designed for humans, alarmingly complex and alien and invented for profane lovemaking. Other instruments with inscrutable inscriptions, of equally unholy design and purpose. A dying rose sagged in a pewter vase, like some profound romantic statement.

The room forked off, one side leading off into a makeshift dark room where, Inspector O'Hara had been led to understand from Briony, the kid photoshopped the pictures he took. He hoped Forensics would do a clean sweep of the place. Inspector and College student took the other opening. They crept up to a fallen block of stone, peered over the top, keeping to the shadows. Crouched, they were not spotted.

They found themselves in a vault. The air was cool, like that of a fruit cellar. The cracks in the walls exuded crooked, trickling streams of moisture. Withered rose petals were scattered across the floor. The earthy odour of the place, complete with sprouting fungus and fruiting toadstools, had a dank, unpleasant undercurrent: the effluvium of dead things. Briony spotted a grey, graveyard rat nearby and just managed to stop herself from screaming. It stared at her, bared its tiny fangs. It suddenly detected movement and snatched up a rapidly-moving spider before scampering across the floor and disappearing into a hole in the wall.

This private crypt should have been a place to remember the dead, but, instead, its sinister atmosphere equated to a place of ancient evil where one half-expected disinterred skeletons to stir and rise up from their individual tombs, moonlight painting their gravestone grins and birdcage ribs in a dazzling, white gleam, their black, vacant pits of eye-sockets transfixing one with a blind, feverish stare. Except, as a place of ancient evil goes, Roden's underground lair had been set up like some obscene bridal suite, a stage upon which to enact the blasphemies of love.

The closed stone sarcophagus at the centre of the vault upon which Cosmina lay brought to mind a sacrificial altar. Gagged, she struggled against the ropes tying her wrists and ankles while Roden looked adoringly down at her. Her Elvira wig had fallen off, and her natural bob was sweaty and plastered across her face. Not with fear, mind, but a deep-seated anger. She was spotlighted by a slanted cone of light coming down from the ceiling, a peculiar, preternatural light with a soft, phosphorescent glow, and Inspector O'Hara could not make out its source. Certainly not rays descending from the moonlit sky.

Showtime . . .

"I have always considered myself an outsider," Roden announced. "Like a ghost I am a haunter of these places. Mankind sees me as a devil and fears my attachment to his mortal world. Unlike death gods stalking those destined to die, I deal in passionate ownership and I have acquired you for the Master. Throughout my nomadic existence, I search for love and you are the one that nearly got away..." He laughed, desire mingled with triumph, revelling in his *Phantom of the Opera* act. "Nobody gets away from me!"

He reached down and removed her gag.

"Let me go!" screamed Cosmina, and Briony almost had an urge to show herself and try and rescue her friend. But she stayed put after recalling the sight within Cosmina's garden shed. She wanted to see how this would pan out.

"Hush now . . ." Roden whispered gently to Cosmina.

But his command did not subdue her. Cosmina continued to wrestle against her bonds. "If you do not let me go, you will regret it!"

"You are in no position to make threats," chuckled Roden. "You will give in to me, whatever the cost."

"*Never!*"

A frown furrowed his brow, signalling displeasure, the look of someone who does not like his authority being questioned. Should she not be besotted with him? And if not, why not? "Human skin is so uncomfortable . . ." Roden said dramatically . . . and, without warning, underwent a visceral transformation. No longer did he appear like the scrawny, geeky kid his classmates were so accustomed to. His face rippled, melted, ran like wax. Eyes became small and beady and black like two polished pearls of jet. His nose shortened, nostrils dilated, flared. His skin darkened, tautened, splitting his Harlequin costume to shreds, grew coarse with a light dusting of hair. Strange esoteric markings carved into his chest. He developed several bony, outward growths: a horn, a tusk and a single, white fang. The mouth spread open to reveal . . .

They all beheld a demonic figure with black, buckshot eyes and horn-like protrusions and a cluster of file-sharpened teeth.

Inspector O'Hara should have been shocked by this hellbeast that should not exist. During the course of his investigations, O'Hara had considered Roden to be the prime suspect. Roden Quist was the only new element in the equation. Every tragedy that had befallen the College had involved Roden somehow. But where had been the proof? Now, here it was, in front of his very eyes. The same wolf in the fold that had effortlessly orchestrated the Halloween school massacre. The shock did not materialize because O'Hara had never forgotten his Catholic upbringing. St. Augustine had spoken about faith in things not seen. The words of Jesus were captured in the non-canonical Gospel of Thomas Logion 5: *Recognize what is in your sight, and that which is hidden from you will become plain to you. For there is nothing hidden which will not become manifest.* This canny observation alluded to creatures hiding in the light, beings with paranormal abilities that the human eye could not see or human minds seemed unable to comprehend, where things are right in front of your eyes, but nobody can see them for what they really are. Unless, of course, you are secure in your faith, fortified. Non-canonical because the verses of Thomas, like those of Mary Magdalene, had been deliberately discarded by the Catholic Church, in case they interfered with the pontiff's plans. His ignorance, his loss.

Presently, in this eerie shaft of unearthly luminosity, he could see Roden in his natural form. The thing in its true incarnation. Evil incarnate. The same abhorrent being the hypnotic powers of which left its victims helpless, corrupting minds to kill others or oneself, a consummate practitioner of the half-understood remnants of old magick, of demonology and necromancy and psychic control. O'Hara crossed himself.

Roden in his demon-like manifestation did not have the desired effect on Cosmina. "Am I supposed to be scared or something?" she mocked. "No wonder the girls think you're a creep! They can see right through you!"

Roden couldn't understand why his plan wasn't working. Shouldn't there be fear, cowing and eventual submission. "I have had many girls – thank you! You will love me, and I will feed you to the Master!"

"That's what you think!" Cosmina sounded like she was enjoying herself.

How dare she spurn his advances! Why wasn't it working? "Nobody gets away from me . . . *ever*!" he thundered.

"Believe me, I will *never* be yours!"

"Why not? What makes you so special?" No more bullshit. He needed an explanation. The oily, black orbs of his eyes showed sudden surprise. "What the hell's wrong with your face–?"

And Cosmina revealed herself to him. Corresponding with a momentary stuttering of the shaft of strange light, her transformation was almost instantaneous, resolving itself into something equally repulsive. She metamorphosed into an insectoid shape, of enormous height, segmented and wingless, bearing the swollen, slightly translucent belly of a bedbug but the powerful hooks of a praying mantis. Multiple eyes bulged and shone on the dome of her head, crystalline, cat-irised. They blinked simultaneously, fully focused on him, predatory, *hungry*. Her ropes were redundant. She sat up.

Just when you think you know someone . . . Briony had once said. It was neither Roden nor Cosmina, or either of Cosmina's parents, they had discovered in the shed but Griffin de'Marco, the missing murderer, gagged and trussed up on the chair like a turkey. Except he wasn't the burly brick of a rugby player they were all familiar with. He was *huge*. In the space of a month, he had put on over ten stones and begun to resemble the human equivalent of a whale, a massive blubbery piece of flesh. At the time of his disappearance, Briony had tried to understand why Cosmina never mourned his loss. Was she made of stronger stuff – or was it something else? Now Briony knew. Now she knew where Griffin had disappeared to: Cosmina had been keeping her boyfriend hostage in her shed for a whole month, overfeeding him as though he were some factory-farmed animal. Fattening him up. *For what purpose?* Fattening him up for slaughter? As an offering to this Master fellow?

Griff had spoken, tired of eating, tired of his harrowing ordeal, each word a burdensome effort, too obese even to talk. He had seen things nobody should. He told them where Roden resided. *Roden lives on Cemetery Hill.*

Which house number? Inspector O'Hara had asked, aware of the fake address Roden had submitted on his College application.

No, at the cemetery itself . . .

For Roden, presently, Cosmina's appearance proved an eye-opener and, for the first time, he felt fear. Her not being photographable. It also explained his sudden attraction to her, his unutterable longing, his slavish devotion to a girl who would never have looked at him twice. He had wanted her to love him the moment he had set eyes on her. He had loved her intensely, *madly*, the second she walked into his life . . . and at long last he had thought he had her. Yet she had never really been his.

"We are magickal beings, you and I," Cosmina said, all six-foot-six of her towering over him, her mouth faintly human. "Like you, I come from the same place beyond this world. I'm a creature disguised by daylight, but when darkness falls, I too walk the midnight path."

Two of a kind, thought Briony. Like J.R. Ewing and Alexis Carrington getting together to plot the destruction of society.

"But unlike you," Cosmina continued to address Roden, "I am venerated, *sacred*. You've met me a thousand times. You've prayed before me, worshipped at my altar. My human form, it seems, has deceived you. I am your High Priestess, as lesser gods might speak of me. You have committed an irrevocable transgression."

Roden kneeled down before her. "How was I to know?" he pleaded.

But there was no compassion or understanding in Cosmina's voice, only cruelty. "Know what's unique about black widows?"

"The female stings and eats its mate?" ventured Roden, the demon sounding apprehensive. His fawning manner suggested he knew where this was heading . . . and he sounded afraid.

"They do, right after copulation, because she wants to use him as a form of nutrition to feed her offspring," said Cosmina. *Here's a bit of your dad, kids!* Briony thought drily and remembered the bizarre, alien sex equipment they had passed on the way. "Except there will be no copulating tonight . . ."

"I am deathless," uttered Roden in feeble, trembling protest. "I don't know how to die."

"I can change that." Cosmina pronounced her final edict and, in this confluence of evil, this meeting of two monstrous beings, sprang her muscular, mantis-like front legs into her underling, puncturing him like a balloon, ripping through his demon flesh, horns and hooves and all. Roden deflated and merged with her, sucked up by her, in the same way a dominant twin absorbs the weaker embryo in the womb. Before his essence was absorbed and digested in an act of sexual cannibalism, he had to accept that the weaker, fairer sex, capable of faking tears and orgasms, was deadlier than the male. She was a supernatural being much like himself but higher in the hierarchy of their race. A high priestess, greatly

~ 412 ~

superior to him. He hadn't suspected her true nature because the scent she had emitted, the powerful pheromone of a female in heat, had masked her identity and inadvertently lured him in, leaving him delirious with desire, moonstruck. Only the photos had given her away which he had put down to human error. He had felt helplessly caught in her spiderweb as she cast a web of passion on those around her, including him. She had played the long game. She had played him good and proper. She had owned him, controlled him all along. "May your extinction stretch out into eternity. The Master will not be killing the fatted calf tonight, slitting its throat and dancing on its hot, spilled blood."

Briony actually felt a small degree of sympathy for Roden, imagined him thinking he had been bested by somebody crueller and more ruthless than him. This showdown had led to his destruction. Briony thought of *Dangerous Type* by The Cars.

"I kept to our agreement, Master . . ." his last words echoed in the confines of the crypt before fading away forever.

The subsequent silence was vast and illimitable, unholy in its immensity, as events in the crypt reached a climax and some kind of closure. Until Cosmina – or the hulking, multi-eyed, insectile entity that had once been Cosmina – broke the stillness. Standing within the strange hue of light spilling down from another dimension, this dreamlike limbo between this world and the other, she redirected her attention to the two humans hiding behind the block of stone. Bystanders to a secret feud between two monsters, Inspector O'Hara and Briony realized she had known of their presence all along.

"Don't you know I can anticipate your thoughts," Cosmina acknowledged. "Quite the sideshow you have seen."

Busted, the two crouching human intruders got to their feet, emerged from their hiding place.

"What are you?" Briony asked hesitantly.

"A glimpse into a twilight realm, of terrors lurking in the infinite shadows," Cosmina replied. "You know too much into the existence of things unknown. Therefore, before I report back to the Master, I must make you forget everything that has transpired. I'm sure this will not be the last you hear of me. It was nice knowing you. I will always be watching."

She spared their lives . . . *but not their memories*.

In an instant she was gone and the curious, tinged cascade of light in the crypt vanished with her. Inspector O'Hara and Briony blinked, exchanged glances, perplexed.

"What are we doing here?" Briony asked him with a dazed expression. They had stumbled upon something monumental, something outside the laws of the known Universe, yet whatever it was she hadn't a clue. Recent events suddenly seemed hazy, obscure, inaccessible.

Inspector O'Hara tried to remember, drew a blank. "I'm not quite sure . . ."

The church bell tolled midnight. Something told him this may not be the end.

"I wasn't expecting to see you again so soon," Hank Schofield told his visitor at the door of his Italianate apartment in Oaks Fold.

"I didn't mean to disturb you so late," Inspector O'Hara informed his old acquaintance. He looked around the apartment, the clutter and dust, and sat down wearily on a clothes-free space on the leather couch. "There is a reason I came."

"Forgive the mess, I don't get many visitors." Schofield, a famed local writer, apologized. "You didn't believe me when I told you my story all those years ago. But I'm guessing you're here because it happened again?"

Inspector O'Hara checked his watch. Ten at night. He recounted his tale, distilling his experiences with Roden Quist to the man, who had once shared similar experiences and whose case the Inspector had investigated. Griffin de'Marco had got committed to a mental unit, having gone permanently crazy. The College massacre had been put down to somebody spiking the punch. Referring to Cosmina the High Priestess, Inspector O'Hara told Schofield: "She won't leave me alone. She tried wiping my memory, but my faith made me remember. Now I can't seem to get rid of her. I see her everywhere . . . see her as she really is."

"Frightening, isn't it?" Schofield agreed. "It is said that old magic is the science of tomorrow. They can use the power of charms, hexes, wards and spells against us. Their mastery of illusion to deceive our five, puny human senses. Offering up human souls to the god of dark places. They serve the Master, an alien divinity older than mankind or the Abrahamic god, in a reality co-existing with our world, their dark realm rarely glimpsed behind the thinning veneer, a universe of matter and energy . . . and *life*. Of ancient deities and twilight beings. I don't know what they are, but they come when the conditions are right. I'm thinking she wants something that you have."

"Like what?"

"I don't know . . ." Schofield replied, shaking his head. He paused before adding: "Your nightmare – *our* nightmare – may be far from over, but our faith will always protect us."

September 2018-December 2018

Painted Devils, Vaulted Heavens

Nine Roses: My love for you is eternal.

PART ONE: FIRST IMPRESSIONS

1

She texted me first:

Paul, I know this is a strange thing 2 ask eventho we haven't spoken, but would u like 2 meet me after work 1 day? Heidi

I, Paul Hempston, stared at the message, digested it, tried to analyze it. I knew about this Heidi girl. Although our paths hadn't formally crossed, I knew she was the PA for Marianne Keene, the chief editor and owner of HAMBLEYS PUBLISHING, the publishing house where we both worked in different departments. I knew her because of the rumours. I'd heard she'd been interested in me for quite some time and that she'd been inquiring about me here and there, as a number of my colleagues later attested. Watching me from afar, sizing me up, deciding whether I was worthy – of *what*, exactly? The kind of detached person I am, I'd paid no heed to these rumours. But what mystified me presently was why she should ask me out on a date when, as the office gossip went, she was already seeing someone. Besides, my suspicious, paranoidy mind sensed an ulterior motive behind her request. Did she just want to meet me for coffee, simply get to know me, or was there something more, something yet-unspoken behind why she was now approaching me? I racked my brains, cogitated and speculated, but I couldn't fathom what it could be. I realized I would learn her reasons soon enough. I can't deny I was intrigued. But such is my mistrust of people in general, it took me nearly an hour to reply as I vacillated between the uncertainty of indecision and a curious desire to determine her motivations. I finally resolved to sound casual, nonchalant . . . and run with it:

Fantastic suggestion! Gusto's tomorrow at 7pm? C u then!

2

Heidi Schilling was already at our planned rendezvous when I got there, dead on time. I soon learned she had arrived half an hour before me. Either she possessed excellent time management skills or she was eager – no, *desperate* – to see me. I greeted her, asked her how long she'd been waiting and took the seat opposite her at our designated table.

"So how goes it?" I asked Heidi tentatively.

"Very well, thank you," she replied softly. "Come here often?"

I glanced around the restaurant, took in its cosy atmosphere and noticed it was beginning to fill up with courting couples. Situated in the town centre of Chertsford, with vaulted brick ceilings and wall mirrors, GUSTO'S was a respectable establishment, specializing in Italian cuisine, the perfect place for a romantic, candlelit dinner with one's paramour. A little pricey but worth it. "Sometimes, but it's been a long while since I was last here. I thought you might appreciate the food, friendly service and general ambience."

"And the company, of course," Heidi said with a gentle knowing smile.

"Of course," I remarked, pleasantly. "I promise not to disappoint you."

"I don't think you could ever disappoint me . . ." she said dreamily.

Her comment bemused me. "But you don't even know me. I might turn out to be the most evil man in history."

"Oh, I kinda know you," she admitted.

Some people might have found her disclosure slightly creepy, the words of a serial stalker, but it didn't bother me particularly, not at that moment at least. Except I couldn't help but wonder: who *was* this woman who seemed so damned interested in me? I'd paid little attention to her in the past, but sitting down with her presently, I was able to study her up close and personal. Most men would have found her attractive and I certainly did not struggle to see the appeal. True, she had a balayage of long, dark-blond hair and sleepy, blue, bedroom eyes and, yes, with her slightly flaring nostrils, she possessed more than a passing resemblance to Uma Thurman, and the fetching black dress she wore definitely did justice to her slim, five-foot-six figure, but it was a natural, unassuming beauty, unspoiled by cosmetics. "I know you've been asking about me just shy of hiring a private detective. What puzzles me though is why ask me out on a date when you're supposed to be going out with someone else?"

Heidi seemed unfazed by the question. "You mean Ted from Marketing. I left him. We only went on a couple of dates. Nothing happened. He just wasn't right for me."

At that point, the Maître D' wandered over and we ordered drinks: Heidi requested a mineral water, myself a glass of red wine.

"Don't drink?" I inquired.

"Occasionally . . . but not tonight. I get drunk very easily, get very flirty and disinhibited, so I prefer to be in control of my senses. I know you're partial to Irish whisky."

"That's probably the understatement of the year. You do realize I'm a functioning alcoholic."

"I know," she replied in that same steady, untroubled tone. "And you dabble in a little weed when you're feeling low."

"Heck, you've really done your research!" I exclaimed, genuinely astonished. "So what else do you know about me?"

"You were born in Crouch End, an only child. Your mother died in childbirth and you were raised by your father, who worked for the Inland Revenue before retiring, a belligerent man and strict disciplinarian – you're both estranged from each other these days. You went to UCL to study Literature, but you dropped out in the second year. After a few years in the wilderness, jumping from minimum wage to minimum wage, you discovered you had a talent for writing for other people. Hambleys contracted you as a ghost writer. Unfortunately, you hate the various Z-list celebrities and footballers and egomaniacs whose autobiographies you help write. You smoke, drink to excess, take drugs when the mood suits you. You always wear black. Your girlfriend recently broke up with you and it hit you hard. You're a bit of a loner and you sometimes take companionship in escort girls to ease the loneliness."

"You seem to have captured my life story to a tee," I said, somewhat shaken up by her frank knowledge of me. All credit to Heidi: she'd been thorough, left no stone unturned. My life, even the sensitive aspects of my life, was an open book. There was something rather perturbing about someone knowing your every intimate secret when you knew nothing about them. I was glad when the drinks arrived. "You got me pegged. But enough about me. Tell me a little about yourself."

"What do you want to know?" she volunteered.

"Your name, for instance. Heidi Schilling . . . German?"

"How did you know? I'm half-German on my father's side. Mother's English."

"Amazing," I said, smiling. "So your father comes from the nation that brought us *Schicksalstragödie* and *Schadenfreude*."

"Very good!" she said, impressed, translating these two powerful German words. "Drama focusing on the tragedy of fate and, yes, joy at someone else's misfortune."

"Can you guess what *Straßenbahnhaltestelle* means?"

Heidi laughed. "Tram stop."

"Good girl!" I remarked. "You really are German!"

"And you seem to know your German."

"I find your name strangely aristocratic, regal even. You could easily pull yourself off as Countess Heidi."

"Thanks. But I'm not royalty."

I made another observation. "You don't have a hint of a Teutonic accent."

"No, I hail from Leipzig, but my parents moved to the UK when I was two. I'm as English as the Queen."

The Maître D' intruded again, wondering if we'd decided from our menus. For starters I ordered beef carpaccio with parmesan shavings, a fillet of veal in rich marsala wine and mushroom sauce served with salad garnish and rosemary potatoes as the main course, and tiramisu by way of dessert. I also requested a whole bottle of house red, which I intended to polish off with my meal. Heidi surprised me by ordering just an ordinary Italian salad with gorgonzola and bruschetta, drenched in extra virgin olive oil and balsamic vinegar, when I'd already explained I was buying and she could order anything her heart desired.

"Not hungry?" I asked when the Maître D' had gone.

"I can't eat when I'm anxious," she replied, with a slightly embarrassed expression.

"I'm making you anxious?"

"Maybe. It's just that I'm so excited to be with you."

Never had any girl told me I made them excited. I felt privileged. "Is there anything I can do to relax you?"

"No, I'll be fine. I couldn't manage a heavy meal. A salad should suffice for the occasion. Besides, I have a tendency to burp when I feel anxious."

"Which is why it's important you have a substantial meal to settle the stomach. Otherwise, you're simply swallowing air, hence the burping."

"No need to fret over me," she reassured me when she in fact needed the reassurance. "I'll survive."

I decided to close the matter and get my mind off her bodily functions for the sake of my meal. "So, Heidi, I understand you're an artist in your spare time."

"Yes, I have a degree in Fine Art," she explained, brightening up. "I adore Dalí, Magritte, Ernst and the whole Surrealist Movement in general, although I also have a great deal of appreciation for the Cubists and Dadaists as well. I paint when I get the time. I have a studio at my cottage."

"Sold many paintings?"

"A few. The highest any of my paintings fetched was two hundred pounds."

"That's terrific!" I said, genuinely impressed. "A shot at the Turner Prize, perhaps?"

"Unlikely. The galleries don't seem particularly interested in my work. I've never had the pleasure of a formal exhibition. I can't be that good."

"Don't sell yourself short," I encouraged her. "Your stuff's got to be better than the shit Tracy Emin or Damien Hirst produce. I mean what is it with that stinky bed? Just because Emin slept in it doesn't make it a work of art. Or Hirst's anatomical cross-sections of a cow. Interesting concept but nothing to write home about. Not to mention some other geezer's installation art of an empty room, turning the light switch on and off. The Turner Prize judges must be blind."

Heidi laughed, distinctly encouraged. "Thank you for your vote of confidence. Maybe I'll show you some of my work some time, gauge your opinion. *Painting is something that takes place among the colours, and . . . one has to leave them alone completely, so they can settle the matter among themselves. Their intercourse: this is the whole of painting. Whoever meddles, arranges, injects his human deliberation, his wit, his advocacy, his intellectual agility in any way, is already disturbing and clouding their activity.*"

"Great quote. Rilke, I believe."

"I'm also a sucker for silent German Expressionist cinema."

"You mean *Nosferatu* and all that?"

"Yes, it's dark, romantic and inspiring . . ." She paused before asking abruptly: "Ever thought about getting married?"

I nearly choked on my wine. "Aha! I knew there had to be a motive for your interest in me! This is our first date – we just met! Now's not the time to be talking about marriage!"

"Come on, I'm not asking you to marry me. It's an innocent enough question any girl might ask her date. I just want to know your views on the subject."

"I'm a man's man. I don't want to be tied down with a wife and kids. I'm really not ready to marry, yet."

"But you're forty years old."

"And your point being?"

"Aren't you leaving it a little late?"

"Possibly. I might have already missed the boat on that one or, as they say, life begins at forty. Either way, I prefer the life of a carefree bachelor. Besides, I value my privacy."

"You're stuck in your ways, that's the problem."

Was that really the problem? Did Heidi know me better than myself? "And you, Heidi, don't you want to get married, have kids, settle down?"

"Some day, perhaps," she said thoughtfully, "when the right person comes along. My biological clock is ticking, too, you know. I *am* twenty-nine."

"So you expect me to make babies with you?"

Heidi responded with a laugh. "Of course not, silly. The whole marriage thing really freaks you out, doesn't it?"

"I'd rather you didn't use the 'M' word," I answered in mock-dread.

She quizzed me further, on a separate matter. "From the life you lead, something tells me you're not a religious man."

More prying, more probing, this time into my spiritual beliefs. Still, it was a more neutral, less uncomfortable topic of conversation than marriage. "I had a Catholic upbringing so I experienced a lot of discipline and guilt. I remember going on a school trip to Bayeux Cathedral. And, there, sitting in a side chapel, I found love and peace . . . and *presence*. An inchoate feeling that I suppose needed developing with prayer and supplication. Sadly, I didn't get round to further exploring or nurturing that feeling. Disillusioned by my mid-twenties, I shed my faith. Now, I'd like to think of myself as an atheist, but in fact I'm an extreme agnostic. I believe in the Human Animal, that we evolved over millions of years from more primitive beasts. Unfortunately, I cannot completely rule out the existence of an All-seeing, All-knowing Creator. How do you explain consciousness or self-awareness, for instance – what makes you *you* and me *me*? And how can you ignore Pascal's wager, a philosophical stance that states that a person should live by the notion of God's existence since the infinite gains he receives will outweigh the small, finite, earthly sacrifices he makes, particularly if, in the end, God turns out to be real? Certainly, there's that remote, infinitesimally-small possibility that God truly exists. You never know I might be judged by Him one day and asked to explain why I didn't practise my faith."

"And what would be your answer?"

"I can't get my head round the idea of blind faith when there's so much evidence to the contrary. Why would an omnipotent being create us only so we kneel down before Him and worship Him? Don't you think that smacks of narcissism?" I paused for maximum effect. "Just because you don't believe in God doesn't necessarily make you amoral. The scientist, for example, lives by a strict code of ethics. He makes no less an important contribution to society than a vicar or a rabbi, possibly more so in this Age of Reason, Medicine and Technological Advancement." My mind stumbled across a famous quote. "*In a world without religion, good people would be doing good things and bad people would be doing bad things. For good people to do bad things, it takes Religion.*"

"Richard Dawkins . . ." Heidi mused.

"As usual, you're surprisingly well-informed," I replied, getting into my stride. "Professor Dawkins: the greatest, self-proclaimed atheist of the modern scientific community. He teaches us that we possess a selfish, evolutionary gene and deluded notions of God. We have always had an unending preoccupation with the Meaning of Life because it's in our inherent nature to understand where we come from and where we're going. Except, like any living thing on earth, we are nothing more than complex animals with a unique ability to think and reason, an innate desire to breed and a universal necessity to leave adequate provisions for our future generations so they can carry on our genes. Our insignificant names and memories will fade with time, but it's our genes that ultimately make us immortal. We will always strive to hope there's more to life than the shit we're stuck with, when there probably isn't much else. To quote Hamlet when he's on the brink of death: *I die, Horatio, the poison oe'rcrows my spirit . . . And the rest is silence . . .*"

Heidi did not speak, appeared crushed.

I let my words sink in before continuing. "Consider the monk who lives out his entire life in a monastery, forever searching for God but never finding Him in the end. You could argue that it's a tragic waste of an intelligent life when he could have been doing so much more. A life shrouded in ignorance. But, on the other hand, at least he chose a path he cherished, at peace with himself and the world around them, in life and in death. Monastic life is a great witness to eternity – or that is the hope. I, however, strongly believe Heaven and Hell are on this earth, and perhaps God is simply your moral compass. Or a state of mind."

Heidi remained silent and I wondered if I'd offended her in some way. I hadn't meant to get into a theological debate so early. I decided to lighten the conversation. "I don't know if you know this old joke about a devout Protestant who dies and is met by St. Peter at the Pearly Gates who takes him on a tour of Heaven. As the tour goes on, St. Peter points out all the other different religious denominations that have made it to Heaven: Lutherans, Methodists, Presbytarians, Jews, Arabs, Buddhists, and so forth. As they come to a certain group keeping to themselves, St. Peter draws the man closer to him and whispers conspiratorially: *Now, with the next enclave, we need to tread very carefully. They're the Catholics and they think they're the only ones here!"*

It raised a small smile. Heidi appreciated the joke. I was relieved. I told her about my uncle. "I know a little something about my faith, not just from my local priest when I was growing up but also from my uncle, who was a devout Catholic. He left the Passionist movement to become a postulant at a Benedictine monastery when I was twelve. I haven't seen him since."

"How come?" Heidi asked. "Isn't he allowed visitors?"

"Only once or twice a year and only family members. Apparently, he can only get day leave if one of his immediate family members were dying."

"That's a bit unfair," said Heidi. "Would his superiors discipline him if he just upped and disappeared for a few days to see his family?"

"Very likely," I replied. "Treated as *mea culpa* on his part. His superiors would probably accuse him of not being fully committed to serve Jesus." A thought occurred to me. "And that is the problem with practising one's Catholic faith: you receive only *conditional* love."

"I'm a Jehovah's Witness," Heidi said calmly.

It was a disclosure I least expected. My mouth dropped. I looked at her incredulously. *Dear God, I'm dating a Jehovah's Witness – how crazy is that?* I thought of those sombre people, walking in pairs, who suddenly appear at our doors, offering religious pamphlets and the everlasting salvation of our souls. I also imagined the double disappointment she must be feeling: I wasn't marriage material and that I'd rejected God. Had I said too much? Was she about to walk out on me? Though I wouldn't blame her if she did. I was forced to backtrack, tried to find some middle ground, something positive from all this. "It doesn't matter what faith you belong to. Faith is a powerful thing. I'm sure you've heard of the story of the patient with terminal cancer. The doctor gives them three months to live. And the patient starts praying with conviction to whatever higher power they believe in, in order to ease their dying days. It doesn't necessarily have to be God; it could be Elvis Presley or beings from another planet. They set their affairs in order, make peace with themselves and prepare to die. When they haven't died after three months, they go back to the doctor, who repeats the scan. Lo and behold, their peace of mind has boosted their immune system and caused their cancer to regress. It's rare but not unheard-of. One might argue that their recovery is nothing short of a miracle, actually the work of God, who has rewarded them for their prayers." I felt I also needed to openly re-evaluate my opinion on Atheism, keeping in mind my early experience in Bayeux Cathedral, the sense of a 'presence'. "You could even call Atheism a religion in itself. Even it is subject to an element of faith. Faith in hard, indisputable scientific evidence. One of the biggest criticisms directed at Professor Dawkins is that he preaches Atheism in a fundamentalist manner, in some respects no different from the Evangelical Christians or those crazy Muslim extremists."

I breathed out a long, drawn-out sigh. I hoped she didn't think less of me, now. I hoped I'd balanced the books.

"Nice recovery," she said, apparently wise to my game. "Don't worry about me. It takes a lot to hurt my feelings."

Our food arrived at that stage, by which time I'd already drunk half the bottle of wine. The old nerves needed steadying. *Wine to gladden the heart of man*, I recited Psalm 104:15 as a lame excuse. I tucked into my meal, Heidi only picked at her salad. I thought I should take the opportunity to explore some of her religious beliefs. It was only polite. "So, as a Jehovah's Witness, what do you do?"

"Oh, the usual. Attend twice-weekly meetings at the Kingdom Hall. Go on the Ministry door-to-door once-a-week, spreading the Truth."

"Do you find your work satisfying?"

"I suppose," she said with a tone that spoke otherwise. "You'll be amazed how so few people are prepared to talk to us."

I knew of the reputation bestowed by the public on the purveyors of *The Watchtower*. Intrusive, religious nuts, whose passive change-your-ways-and-save-your-soul mantra was considered a complete waste of time. "That's the problem with the world today. Most people are more concerned with the goings-on in Albert Street or Jennifer Aniston's new boyfriend or David Beckham's latest hairdo to even care about finding God."

"I know," agreed Heidi. "How shallow and empty must your life be if all you look forward to are the miserable, mundane lives of the characters on *EastEnders*, *Emmerdale* and *Coronation Street*? Give me *Sex and the City* any day."

I found her latter remark extraordinary for someone so supposedly religious. I did not comment on it. Instead, I continued my line of inquiry. "Besides declining blood transfusions and not celebrating Birthdays or Christmas, what else can you tell me about your faith?"

"We preach a return to the lifestyle and faith of early Christians and strongly believe society is in its Last Days and under the wicked influence of Satan."

"So when do you predict the End of the World?"

"There's been a whole succession of dates pencilled in by our spiritual leaders, but Armageddon did not happen. These dates aren't set in stone – they're just approximations. The current prediction is 2012."

"Like the Mayan prophecy?"

"Yes."

"You're saying the world is going to end *this* year?"

"Yes, some time soon . . ."

The idea we were fast approaching the End of the World was a fascinating one, if not a little disturbing. But where were the signs? London was busy hosting the Olympics and doing a splendid job. There was a black man in the White House who actually cared about the people. The financial markets were gradually emerging from a global economic recession. Of course, you had the usual ongoing strife in the Middle East and natural catastrophes in the Third World, but these were nothing new. So, pray, where indeed *were* the signs, the omens indicating Judgement Day? I didn't intend to point out the flaws in Heidi's and her fellow Witnesses' firmly-held prediction. No use getting into a heated debate over it. I would believe it when I saw it. I decided to move on. "What about your family – who's at home?"

"Just me."

"How come?"

Heidi grew quiet, as though deciding whether or not to tell me. I thought I might have touched upon a sensitive issue. "I'm an only child, too. My parents liked the high life, buying flash cars and overindulging in material possessions, exuding an illusion of wealth to the rest of our congregation. Except it was a reputation built on a house of cards. Even though my father was an elder, he could not escape his own gluttonous urges, wining and dining in the fanciest restaurants every day. He ended up suffering multiple health complications: obesity, diabetes and heart disease. He would drop dead one day from a fatal stroke. My mother was heartbroken, inconsolable, and too followed suit twelve months later."

Heidi engaged my sympathies. "Oh, I'm so sorry . . . I didn't mean to–"

"No, how could you possibly know?" she said, putting on a brave face against her wavery voice. "It happened a long time ago. I visited my mother daily, but in the end she no longer recognized me. When she died, I used what little funds I inherited to buy a cottage in the woods. I am still paying off their debts."

The mood had turned distinctly melancholic. Here was I smarting over Marcy for ending our relationship on Valentine's Day earlier in the year – *Valentine's Day, of all days, who else can boast that?* – and there was Heidi who'd suffered a string of fatal family tragedies. *Poor girl* . . . my heart went out to her. "It seems you've come out of it a stronger person. It's a testament to your resilience."

"True, I've made my peace with the past," she stated, without losing any of her composure.

We continued eating, although I'd lost some of my appetite, and talking, small talk mostly. I learned that, like me, she was a massive fan of rock opera, such as that dispensed by Meatloaf and Queen. But what I found more astonishing was that her tastes went way beyond *Sex and the City*, and she adored erotic cinema when I plumped for the occasional thriller. She could list *Turkish Delight, Betty Blue, Secretary, Bitter Moon* and *Last Tango in Paris* as among her favourites. I tried to reconcile her love of erotic films with her religious commitments, somehow couldn't. The girl was full of surprises. She spoke of her infatuation with certain actors. Whereas I fancied dating Naomi Watts with a little Scarlett Johansson thrown in on the side, Heidi considered the likes of Jeff Goldblum, Joaquin Phoenix and Robert Downey Jr. as the epitome of intelligence and manliness – not to mention quirkiness. She preferred what she termed 'character faces' as opposed to vacuous, self-involved pretty boys like Brad Pitt and Jude Law.

When we finished our food and our espressos, I called over the Maître D' and paid for our meals.

Outside, our night in late July was hot and sultry. A crescent moon hung in the heavens amidst constellations of twinkling stars. The pavements teemed with people on a night out.

"I can tell you were ambivalent about going on a date with me," Heidi said, as

I walked her to her green Saab 900SE. The car certainly resembled a mechanical goose. "I mean it took you ages to respond to my text. Now that you've met me what do you think?"

"You're absolutely right. I was initially unsure. However, now, I think I made the right choice."

"Can you see yourself seeing me again?"

"Probably," I said, giving her a quick rundown on my philosophy on women. "I don't condone what the Nazis did during the Second World War. The Holocaust, the oppression of weaker nations and the unspeakable experiments..." Heidi gave me a baffled look, wondering where all this was heading. "But if their ideology had come to pass and they had created the Aryan race, *that* would be my ideal woman."

Heidi didn't seem to take umbrage by my mention of the darkest hour in German history. "Blond, blue eyes, fair skin?"

"And German . . ."

"Of course," she said, smiling.

"You tick all the right boxes." *Save for the Plain Jane effect*, I thought but didn't express verbally.

"My grandfather was a staunch supporter of the Nazi party, but my father detached himself from that awful past and married my English mother. He was ostracized by his family particularly when my mother eventually converted him to the faith of the Jehovah's Witnesses. Did you know that Jehovah's Witnesses were persecuted by the Nazis as much as the Jews, the gypsies, the homosexuals and the mentally-infirm?"

"I never realized . . ."

"Yes, Jehovah Witnesses faced imprisonment, torture and execution for our refusal to support the National Socialist Party. Our literature was burned, our work benefits eradicated and many of us were sent to the concentration camps for refusing to renounce our beliefs or for something as little as refusing to do the Nazi salute. Witnesses were identified by the purple triangle they were forced to wear on their prison uniforms. But unlike the fate of the Jews and other persecuted groups, the Nazis were lenient with us, trusting us implicitly to be their domestic servants because of our strong ethics and unshakable devotion to the Bible, even if we continued to refuse to engage in their conflict."

That's awful, I thought, *being forced to work alongside the Nazi scum*. I found Heidi's forthrightness refreshing. But I was still obsessing over the 'ulterior motive'. "There is something I've been meaning to ask all evening. As questions go, it's not about *What?* or *Where?* or *Who?* or *How?* but *Why?* . . . *Why* did you go out with me?"

"I won't lie to you. I think you're a lovely man."

"I'm extremely flattered, but why?"

"You're tall, handsome and mysterious."

"I really don't see it myself."

"Modest, too, it seems. Do you know how incredibly attractive that is to a girl? I can imagine you brooding all alone in some dark, gothic mansion somewhere on the misty moors."

I still didn't understand her high regard for me. I didn't deserve it whatever her underlying explanation. "It sounds like you have a plain old schoolgirl's crush on me." *It'll pass*, I wanted to add but didn't.

"Maybe. You have a 'character face' that surpasses all 'character faces'."

"Are you comparing me to Jeff Goldblum, again?"

"Yes, except you're a hundred times more desirable."

I kissed her then. I put my arms round her, leaned her backwards and kissed her fully on the lips. It might have been pure impulse. Or an irresistible urge to shut her up because I was getting uneasy with her compliments.

When we'd kissed, she looked at me with perplexed, blinking eyes, delicately licking her lips as the moment passed. "Why did you do that?"

"I thought that's what you wanted."

"I do." She smiled. "What's done can't be undone, you know."

I decided to take my leave. "It's been an enjoyable evening – very interesting and revealing. Thank you for your beautiful company. I promise we'll do this again soon. We'll keep in touch."

"No, thank you for that magical kiss," she whispered rather adoringly.

I pecked her on the cheek, said my farewell, lit a Dunhill and climbed into the waiting taxi. I had to admit it had been an unexpectedly successful – and enlightening – first date.

On my homeward journey to my apartment on the outskirts of Chertsford, I received a text from Heidi:

U r beautiful.

3

"What the hell's wrong with you?" Mathis Evangelos demanded to know at my cluttered apartment the following evening.

"What's wrong with *her*?" I deflected the question back at him.

"Why should there be anything wrong with her?"

"Has to be! No girl in her right mind could find me desirable, let alone incredibly attractive!"

"The girl can't do anything right, can she?" he said not without a hint of sarcasm. Of Greek heritage, Mathis was one of the few true friends I had. We'd known each other since our schooldays. He was a travel writer and had recently returned from a two-week trek of the Inca trails; he was a relative success compared to my mediocrity. I'd called him over for a drink and to catch up as well as discuss my present predicament. "Well, you've certainly got that Jeff Goldblum thing nailed," he noted, amused. "Come on, Paul, cheer up. She's obviously smitten by you. Is that so strange?"

"I'm not the kind of smouldering Sex God chicks swoon over or fall at the feet of. That's why I *pay* for sex."

"So when someone vaguely normal comes along, you think she's messing with you?"

"She keeps leaving dirty text-messages on my mobile."

"I wouldn't call describing you as are 'a lovely man' or 'beautiful' particularly dirty."

"You would if she means to use and abuse me before plundering whatever little dignity I have left. She might turn out to be a crazy stalker or a bunny-boiler. She might stab me in the middle of the night with an ice-pick."

Mathis sighed, taking a sip of his Connemara. "I agree that your dinner date might have seemed like a full-on experience, but you've got to remember she's looked past your smoking and drinking and call-girls and hatred of God to still want to proceed with a relationship. You've laid your cards out on the table and she doesn't mind. It's not often a girl falls for you. Revel in it. Thank her."

"She's got an agenda – she *must* have – a secret motive I'm yet to figure out."

Mathis stared at me, his rising exasperation plain to see. "Marcy really fucked you up, didn't she?"

"Come again?" I said at the mention of my ex-girlfriend.

"You ignored my warnings. Once she realized you had nothing left to offer, that evil witch reached into your chest, ripped out your heart and binned it like a maggoty piece of meat! Took you to the edge of a nervous breakdown, destroyed your faith in the basic goodness of humanity. She turned you into a pathetic, insecure, mistrustful, sorry sonofabitch who sees a conspiracy on every corner!"

"That's a bit harsh, don't you think?" I said, slightly hurt.

"Is it?"

I couldn't deny the sucking ruins of my heart. Admittedly, those last few nightmare months with Marcy, when she'd discovered greener pastures elsewhere, for which I had been forced to confront her, had changed me for the worse. I had thought I would never recover. I therefore listened to Mathis's stern bollocking with tacit acceptance in the hope he would inspire me to brighter thoughts.

However, Mathis must have realized that bollocking me wouldn't do my self-esteem any good, so decided to refrain. He lowered his voice. "Paul, if Heidi thinks you're lovely, if she believes you're beautiful, that's how she feels about you. You can't change that. You can't take that away from her. To recite Goethe: *What's it to you if she loves you?*" He poured himself and me another tumbler of whisky. "Here's a girl who's really into you. She made the first move. Give her a chance. You owe it to her, but most of all you owe it to yourself. Seize this golden opportunity. Or you'll come to regret your inaction later."

The man was right, of course, as always. He was a moral and ethical man who, unlike most men, practised what he preached. Despite his rather adventurous lifestyle, which included a little surfboarding, he had personally established the bedrock for a stable marriage and proved to be a kind and doting father. Listening to him, I felt more positive about everything. "Thanks for the talking-to – I guess I needed it. I'll take your sound advice. I'll explore my relationship with Heidi, see where it leads to." *Besides, what do I have to lose?*

"*Thattaboy!*" he exclaimed, triumphant. "He finally sees sense!"

"Couldn't have done it without you, man," I said appreciatively.

"Glad to be of assistance." He grinned at me broadly, as he conjured up a joke. "Hey, what do you get if you cross a Jehovah's Witness with an atheist?"

I shrugged my shoulders.

"*Someone who knocks on people's doors for no apparent reason.*"

We drank into the small hours of the morning, chatting and laughing like the old friends we were. The lounge was shrouded in a fog of cigar smoke by the time Mathis departed. When he had gone, I checked my messages on my mobile. I discovered that Heidi had texted me earlier:

U shouldn't have kissed me. I feel so horny for u right now. My mouth waters and my body aches for ur joystick. I desperately want u in my mouth. Let's run off to Gretna Green and get married! ☺

I wondered if this particular text fulfilled the definition of 'dirty'.

4

I had always thought of the Jehovah's Witnesses as a fringe religion, a cult even, rather like the once-polygamous Mormons or the passive Pennsylvanian Amish communities. I remember to my shame Father Donnelly, who represented the sanctimonious opinions of the intolerant, non-progressive Catholic Church in my neighbourhood when I was a kid growing up, calling the Jehovah's Witnesses *'the lowest of the low'*. I took his vitriolic comments as Scripture for nearly a quarter-of-a-decade. That was before I became wise and decided to do a little investigating into the history and teachings of the Jehovah's Witnesses, largely on account of Heidi Schilling, the girl I was currently dating and who seemed enamoured by me. I wanted to know, like anyone in my situation, what I was dealing with. Rather than bore you with the details, I will summarize my findings.

Charles Taze Russell is credited with founding the Zion's Watch Tower Bible and Tract Society circa 1870, an autonomous offshoot of the International Bible Students Association. He believed Christ had returned in the flesh and would oversee the coming of Armageddon, with 1914 penned as the end of the Gentile Times and the establishment of God's kingdom on Earth. The predicted date came and went with no sign of Christ or the dawn of his thousand-year reign of humanity, although it did coincide with the beginning of the Great War. Another failed prediction was 1925. Russell moved the Watch Tower Society's headquarters to Brooklyn, New York, combining printing and corporate offices with a house of worship; volunteers were housed in a nearby residence he named *Bethel*.

After a period of in-fighting and disenchantment, the Watch Tower Society developed its own clearly-defined doctrines and an appointed hierarchical system called a 'theocratic government' to reflect its obedience and submission to God for He was the 'Universal Sovereign' and ruled over his people from the 'Divine Top Down'. In 1931, under the leadership of Joseph Franklin Rutherford, they adopted the name 'Jehovah's Witnesses' from Isaiah 43:10: *Ye are my witnesses, saith Jehovah, and my servant whom I have chosen.* Jehovah's Witnesses consider their denomination as a restoration of first-century Christianity.

The organization is led by a Governing Body, consisting of a small cabal of appointed males, who professes to be of the 'anointed' class with the hope of heavenly life and believes itself to be the only visible channel through which God communicates with mankind. Much of its funding is provided by donations, primarily from the rank-and-file members, and the Watch Tower Society is currently one of New York's richest corporations, with revenues exceeding one billion dollars. Its overall authority from its Brooklyn headquarters is passed down to its branch offices worldwide in systematic fashion, from organizing international assemblies to overseeing circuits of congregations, where male elders maintain congregational governance within their jurisdiction in accordance with the organization's principles and doctrines and remain wholly responsible for arranging and conducting meetings in Kingdom Halls, while selecting suitable speakers for these meetings, as well as directing the intensive public preaching programme, which includes evangelizing door to door and distributing religious literature, such as *The Watchtower* and *Awake!*. They also sit on judicial committee meetings investigating and disciplining cases seen to violate the organization's strict moral code of conduct and doctrinal breaches, employing their ecclesiastic privilege to hear confession of sins. Baptized followers deemed to have acted unrighteously and refusing to seek redemption after counselling suffer a form of excommunication called 'Disfellowshipping', meaning that they are officially shunned by existing members, including their immediate family. Apostasy, resigning from the religion, suffers the same fate. Disfellowshipped members can eventually be reinstated to the local congregation if they have sought sufficient repentance.

The beliefs of the Jehovah's Witnesses are a cause for much controversy and debate. The organization amended the Bible in 1961, and the *New World Translation of the Holy Scriptures* has since attracted a lot of criticism for its clear bias in favour of Witness practices and beliefs. Jehovah's Witnesses consider their own version of the Bible to be both scientifically and historically accurate, the only literal, inerrant source of 'the Truth'. They consider their Bible to be the absolute final authority for all their beliefs alongside the pronouncements of the Governing Body, who interpret and apply scripture through the Watch Tower Society publications.

Witnesses have always been at loggerheads with the Catholic Church, claiming that after the death of the Apostles, the Church modified the original teachings of Jesus Christ for its own ends and conducted corrupt, ostentatious ceremonies, even if it is argued that Catholicism encapsulates the entire history of Christianity to this day. Witnesses, of course, believe themselves to be part of the one true religion, having restored True Christianity from the grip of the Great Apostasy committed by the Catholic Church. They consider all other present-day religions to be false, identifying them with 'Babylon the Great'. Witnesses reject the concept of the Holy Trinity. God is seen as the Supreme Creator and Father of All Things, an infinite and invisible spiritual being whose only-begotten Son is Jesus. The emphasis is on God – or 'Jehovah', as He should be rightfully called – rather than Jesus. Witnesses believe that Jesus began life in Heaven before being willingly transferred to the womb of the Virgin Mary. Jesus served as the ultimate sacrifice to atone for the sins of mankind and died on an upright torture stake rather than a cross, an alleged phallic symbol in pagan worship. Satan is thought to be a fallen angel who rebelled against Jehovah and was cast down to earth in October 1914 when the End Times began and he became invisible ruler of the world and, together with his demonic horde, the cause of all human suffering and disease. This date marks the beginning of the Great Tribulation, as Satan began to use world governments and the United Nations, supposedly the Eighth King and the 'image of the wild beast', according to Revelations 13, to attack and persecute Jehovah's Witnesses. And it is said that secular society is in a state of escalating sin and moral corruption under Satan's influence as it hurtles imminently towards Armageddon when Jehovah will destroy every government on earth and transform the world into an earthly paradise, similar to the Garden of Eden, free of crime, death, disease and poverty, ruled over by Jesus and the 'little flock' of 144,000 pure Christians who currently reside in and govern Heaven. Only Witnesses, fully-tested and considered to have led a righteous life (the 'other sheep') will be saved and resurrected to populate an earth cleansed of wickedness in the imminent new age of earthly and human restitution under the reign of Christ, the 're-creation', the 'new system of things'. Those humans not chosen to be resurrected to God's Messianic Kingdom, which includes all 'worldly' non-Witnesses and some liberal Witnesses besides, will perish into nothingness (the 'common grave') since Witnesses do not accept the idea of an immortal soul and see death as a state of unconscious non-existence. There will be no eternal damnation in hellfire, either, as this idea is seen as too unscriptural. Supposedly, since only Jehovah's Witnesses serve as 'approved' representatives of God's kingdom on earth, spreading 'God's inspired message' through their ministry work, only through baptism into the Jehovah's Witness faith can the person attain salvation and meet the scriptural requirements for surviving Armageddon. But only Jehovah, through divine guidance, will be the final judge as He cherry-picks a true-to-His-worship, glorified human race for the earthly extension of His heavenly kingdom.

Other traditional Witness practices have caused friction with society and certain international governments. While Witnesses abide by government laws and decrees, they stay well away from public office, avoid voting or entering into politics and refuse national military service or to bear arms, not unlike the Quakers and Seventh Day Adventists. They do not pledge allegiance to national flags or sing patriotic songs, as Witnesses consider these as forms of idolatry. They see their only purpose as to serve in God's kingdom, a literal government in Heaven, where Christ is crowned King. They do not celebrate Christmas or Easter, or observe Birthdays or national holidays, since these occasions honour people instead of Jesus and are deemed to be steeped in pagan origins, encouraging creature worship. They claim even the early Christians did not celebrate Jesus's birth because they considered the celebration of anyone's birth to stem from pagan customs. It is also a recognized fact that the actual date of Christ's birth was never known and December the Twenty-fifth in fact correlated to a celebration of the infant god of light by the Cult of Mithras. Instead of celebrating Easter, Jehovah's Witnesses commemorate the death of Jesus at the Memorial, the most sacred day in their calendar. Witnesses refuse blood transfusions as they consider blood to be sacred to God, equating it with life and expressing their belief that only the spilt blood of Jesus Christ can truly redeem them and save their life. The organization encourages – and enforces – clean living. Gambling is unacceptable. Drinking must be in moderation as alcohol is a poison to the mind, body and spirit. Witnesses are fiercely against smoking tobacco or taking illicit drugs since each is considered a violation of the human body – and soul. Sex before marriage is strictly prohibited and grounds for disfellowshipping and formal expulsion from the religion, as is homosexuality. Suicide is a sin against God. Witness homes generally operate a patriarchal family structure, with the husband considered to have absolute authority on family matters, apart from God.

There are presently an estimated eight million registered Jehovah's Witnesses worldwide, its brotherhood transcending all nationalities and ethnicities.

The thing that fascinated me most from my aforementioned research was the predicted coming of Armageddon. So many failed predictions, so many numerological disappointments: 1914, for instance, 1925, 1975 . . . and now 2012? Why should 2012 be any different? I pondered.

However, even if they had predicted several apocalypytic events that did not come to pass, I could never have anticipated the general ignorance of the world we lived in, including my own ignorance, and the terrible nightmare that lay in store for us . . .

First, though, our relationship would gather steam, move on to the next stage. I took the risk, counting on Mathis's recommendation. Heidi sent me a staggering eighty-one texts that week. My crappy little mobile phone couldn't cope with the quantity, and although I struggled with my knowledge of text-speak, I managed to reply to each text with some patience. Her communications culminated in another personal, forward-minded text I received the day before I would see her again:

I saw this cute baby in Sainsbury's and I thought this is what ours might look like. I'm so lucky 2 B going out with u. I hope we last a lifetime.

I didn't know the woman [yet] and found her texts somewhat daunting. Once again, I responded with my usual, simple text, expressing my bewilderment:

?

PART TWO: THE INTIMACY OF IMPERFECT BEINGS

1

Prompted by Mathis's sage advice, I took my chances and saw Heidi again. Not an expert on relationships, I did everything by the book. She took me to see Rammstein in concert at the O2 arena in London, a unique and thoroughly satisfying experience, rocking to industrial metal. I felt curious inner stirrings of something special, perhaps love, for her that night and I dispensed with my fear of public displays of affection (which she abbreviated to PDAs): kissing, holding hands, etc. Our next date consisted of a long Sunday morning drive through the New Forest, stopping off at a country pub for lunch. Cinema followed that same week, an intense erotic Czech film, the title of which escapes me. I learned that

Heidi had a taste for travelling. She booked us a nice romantic getaway at a place called the Gothic Temple, owned by the Landmark Trust, in the Cotswolds, our first holiday together as a couple.

Our time at the Gothic Temple proved a real eye-opener and set a standard by which all our future vacations would be judged.

Driving up towards it, through the protected countryside, we saw where we would be staying for the coming week, a venerable, old, gothic edifice that stood out from the natural landscape for miles around. The blazing midday sun gave the beige stonework a soft, golden glow.

We parked the Saab in the gargoyle-fountained forecourt and strode up to the main door, composed of solid oak and studded with grotesque, grinning faces. Using keys picked up from the security lodge a mile down the road, we opened the door and entered. Walking into the Gothic Temple was like walking into a late medieval basilica.

Commissioned by an anonymous, eighteenth-century nobleman, the Gothic Temple was essentially a circular building set within a triangle of three turrets. Only one turret harboured a stone staircase which spiralled up to the main tower. The other two lesser turrets housed a modern bathroom and fitted kitchen on the ground floor, each leading off from the circular, mosaic-floored hall, which had been converted into a lounge for visitors. The spiral staircase took you to the first-floor gallery, where you could peer down over the hall from the circling balustrade. There were two separate turret rooms along the gallery, turned conveniently into double bedrooms. The high-domed ceiling, completely visible from the hall, bore painted murals of strange, Pan-like deities and provided perfect acoustics. All the doors were shaped like a bishop's mitre, and most of the windows were arched. Several quatrefoil openings and lunettes pierced the stone walls. If one continued up the turreted staircase, one would arrive at the tower, with its hooded parapet, crumbling battlements and stunning view of the lake and surrounding land.

Legend had it that the Gothic Temple had been originally built in honour of the pagan gods. Apparently, robed figures had conducted dark rituals and secret ceremonies within its walls before news spread across the county of orgies and animal sacrifices and other diabolic practices, forcing the Duke of Gloucester to capture the building and turn it into an armoury during the Napoleonic Wars; what became of the cult-leaders and their godless disciples no-one truly knows, but it was rumoured they fled to France. The property had since been lovingly restored and refurbished and rented out to wealthy paying guests.

I felt, overall, the Gothic Temple looked bigger and far more impressive on the outside than the inside, but I had to admit it lived up to its sinister name since it did, in no uncertain terms, resemble a place of worship and boast a dark history. Heidi pointed out, with her artist's eye, a fundamental feature of its design: it offered the observer something new and unique when seen from a different angle as well as providing a wide variety of picture-perfect views from within.

We settled into the place without any problem, relishing each other's company. On our first night, we dined on sirloin steak and Parmentier potatoes with wild mushroom sauce, washed down with a full-bodied Rioja. As we finished our meals, we raised our glasses to Our First Adventure, clinking them together while looking directly into one another's eyes lest, as superstition goes, we experience seven years' bad sex.

Sex figured a great deal during our stay there, I was to discover, as we took our relationship to the next level.

"So what do you think of me so far?" Heidi was insisting at the dinner table.

"I think I like you," I responded, enlightening her with my philosophy. "Unlike most men, I measure a woman's general beauty on both Physical Appearance and Personality. As a rule of thumb, each factor constitutes 50:50 to the sum total. And I must congratulate you because you score a whopping 74%, which means you qualify as Beautiful."

"Do you have an equation for our Love Compatibility, too?"

"Unfortunately, no."

Heidi dispensed some of her own wisdom. "As a Pisces, I can tell you we get on very well with Cancerians. In fact, together, they have lasting relationships."

"Personally, I think it's a lot of crock," I replied, slightly drunk. "There's no scientific basis for Astrology. Talk about the power of blind faith . . .!"

"You can be such a killjoy sometimes!" exclaimed Heidi, feigning annoyance.

"You seem very keen for our relationship to last," I observed.

"Don't you?" she said, getting worried.

"Perhaps," I said with a small smile.

"Most women dream about having the plushest white wedding and the perfect, curly-haired babies."

I didn't need reminding the way Heidi had mentioned marriage on our first-ever date or her flurry of audacious text-messages. I took another sip of Rioja, enjoying the warm breeze drifting in through the open back door. It was still daylight outside.

"Am I coming on too strong?" she asked.

"A little . . . but it's understandable and manageable." I glanced at her thoughtfully. "You do realize I'm deeply flawed. Tobacco, drugs, alcohol, girls – when the need arises."

"I sought you out, remember?" replied Heidi, puppy love in her eyes. "I see real potential in you, in *us*. We're here now. Let's make the most of our time together." Favouring me with a knowing look, she joked: "I could turn a few tricks for you if you want."

"Tell me about your boyfriends, inquires an inquisitive mind."

Heidi informed me she hadn't been out with many guys. She told me about her last boyfriend from a fortnight back, Hambleys' marketing department's very own Ted Trenton. Big mistake! They never slept together because Heidi couldn't really stand him. The only reason she'd gone out with him was to please her aunt, who was aware he was a Jehovah's Witness and considered him an eligible bachelor and therefore a suitable match for her niece. Except, Trenton was the kind of man who wore hideous, brown Jesus sandals, always reeked of fried onions and BO before a date, would pick his nose in public as a laugh, keep a roll of toilet paper by his bedside for use after masturbating or dilute a curry with water in order to make it go further. Heidi dumped him after a month, just before she met me, and never spoke to him again.

"He sounds like quite a catch!" I remarked, grinning broadly.

She laughed. "I know, doesn't he?"

When the moment of hilarity had passed, I said: "You see the trouble is, as a man's man, when it comes to making love, I can't wait forever."

Heidi must have been feeling genuinely tipsy and somewhat disinhibited for she got up from her chair, padded around the table barefoot and perched herself on the end of the dining table in front of me, spreading her legs wide open. I could see her white panties clearly below the hem of her short, yellow summer dress and they were distinctly wet with anticipation. "Why must you wait . . .?" she whispered softly.

I was completely thrown by the unexpectedness of her invitation. I was speechless.

With Heidi only inches from me, I made a quick study of her. She possessed a distinctive 1930s' face, a face from a television period drama, full of dignity and grace. Yet, there was a dainty, youthful quality to her manner, an expression of girlish adoration, blue bedroom eyes sparkling with excitement.

Without further hesitation, Heidi grabbed the sides of my face and pulled me towards her, propping herself up on the table using her elbows for support. Our lips pressed hard and our mouths locked, our tongues exploring the moistness of our counterpart's. I clutched her slim waist and pulled up her dress. My mouth worked its way down her svelte neck in a succession of sensual kisses before arriving at her modest bosom. My fingers slipped her shoulder straps down below her chest, and I noticed she wasn't wearing a bra. Her breasts were small, milky-white and enticing, her pink nipples standing up pert and proud. I crushed my mouth against her petite breasts, rolling my tongue around her nipples teasingly, caressing, nibbling, gently biting, causing Heidi to writhe and moan desirously. I descended southwards to her damp panties and pulled them down to her ankles, sighting her intimate golden thatch, her glorious Venus mound. I pleasured her with my tongue for a while, tasting the creamy juices running from her pink crevasse of carnal delights as, soon, I undid my belt and opened up the fly-buttons to my black jeans and, with one hand, carefully manoeuvred my throbbing member into her.

I took her on the dining table, Heidi stretched out on her back, half-naked, her smooth, athletic legs astride my waist, myself leaning over her, my impassioned lips alternating between her hungry mouth and her sweet, wholesome breasts. She was tight inside, but the ever-generous lubrication she secreted facilitated my sliding action. Each thrust produced a joyous, squealing exclamation from her, that rose higher in pitch with her increasing state of arousal. At the peak of ecstasy, her back arched and she nearly screamed, lost in abandonment. I came with her, our separate orgasms synchronized to perfection.

I collapsed beside her on the dining table, and we lay there for a while as we each caught our breaths.

We had gone the distance – and beyond. Spent and sweating profusely, I kissed her tenderly on the cheek. "Did that meet with your expectations, my German Countess?"

Likewise hot and sweaty, Heidi stroked my hair affectionately. She sounded fulfilled. "Hark the Angels sing!" She laughed deliriously, reality filtering back into her eyes. "We *have* to do that again!"

"Glad you approved, my darling, little honeytrap . . ."

A local cross-country team came jogging past, the male runners glancing initially in sheer curiosity at us through the open back door before quickly realizing what we'd been up to as they carried on down the country path.

Still starkers from the stomach up, Heidi waved at them as they passed by. One of the gawping runners almost tripped and fell.

So absorbed I had been in my physical, intimate moment with Heidi, I hadn't realized the back door had been wide open. I wondered if she had kept it open deliberately or it had been an absent slip on her part. I soon learned it was the former. "Just so that you do not shy away from your feelings and PDAs," she told me as the fallen runner got up and stumbled away.

"You're a right, raving exhibitionist!" I remarked, marvelling at her brazenness.

"Roger that!" she remarked, unabashed. "I'm a free spirit, if you must know. My body has a lifetime warranty."

"And a very nice body it is, too!" I eventually stepped down from the table and grabbed her arm. "Put your clothes back on. Come, I want to show you something."

Fully dressed once more, we opened another bottle of wine and carried it up to the main tower to watch the July sunset from the battlements. From our high vantage point, it was a view even finer than that from the window seats on the gallery. Presently, we had a complete three-hundred-and-sixty-degree view of the landscape. We surveyed the lake to the north, with its rippling waters and honking geese, and oak and cedar woods to the west, inhabited by squirrels and field mice and hooting, predatory owls. Molehills sprinkled the open countryside. Holding hands, we gazed at the glorious setting sun until it was nothing more than a diminishing, sepia tinge on the western horizon. A bloated full moon rose up, and the stars came out in an unclouded, benighted sky, excellent portents for our time together. I recognized Cassiopeia and the Plough, which seemed to impress Heidi. I smoked and drank in the warm evening air, taking in the inspirational, moonlit vista, with Heidi more concerned with talking and laughing and filling me on the details of her life.

Heidi proved to be an extraordinary girl, a mass of contradictions. I should have guessed from her interest in erotic films that Heidi was highly-sexed. After all, her favourite read of all time was *The Story of O*. Heidi claimed she first reached orgasm at the age of nine. She used cucumbers, handles of hairbrushes and beer bottles to stimulate herself. As she sought greater sexual thrills, she went to dogging sites and watched. She frequented sex chatrooms, helped the perverts communicating with her online get off. I was therefore shocked to discover that, in person, she had dated and kissed only a handful of men, all Jehovah's Witnesses, and before I'd come into her life, Heidi had been a virgin!

2

The week passed by pleasantly enough. With no TV or radio available and only limited Internet access, we spent the days exploring the neighbouring villages and landmarks and the hot, sticky nights drinking wine and watching *Sex and the City* (her choice) and *Californication* (my choice) on the laptop and making slow, sensuous love.

Heidi grew on me. She was insatiable. I found it hard thinking above the waist. I promised her sex on demand whenever the fancy beckoned, and I must say demand was high. Desire struck when we least expected it. We danced up a storm in bed, fucked like bunnies. I called it Epic Sex. In particular, she liked being tied up and teased to the point of almost losing her senses. How could I say no to a girl who, in a manner of speaking, had fallen at my feet? How could one man, as Heidi complimented me, be such an endless fuck?

After our last epic loving session in the Gothic Temple, Heidi professed her love for me, rolling over on to her side of the bed, exhausted and sweaty and sore from the friction of love.

I didn't reciprocate the sentiment since I had my reasons, hoping she wouldn't notice. Instead, I said: "Thank you for coming . . . *twice!*"

She slipped back into her red, silk négligée from Agent Provocateur. I looked into her dreamy, doe-like eyes, as she stroked my groin. "We should do the South of France next week."

"Don't you think it's a bit too soon to be going away again?"

"Not in my book! I know the perfect, little farmhouse in Provence!"

"Okay, surprise me . . ." Of the Gothic Temple, I expressed my thoughts. Not about the cold floors or the bare stones walls, their rich plasterwork or the incredible vistas of the grounds or the simple yet complex design of this historic building, but about what went on inside. Heidi had amazed me by proving she could exist both in a state of sin and a state of grace all at the same time. Her sexual awakening had come as a revelation to me. "I shall surely miss this place. I hope I was decadent enough for you."

"I don't want to be reminded of your previous debauchery," she said, a hint of jealousy in her tone. "I just want you, Paul Hempston."

Checking my watch, I realized it was half-three in the morning. I kissed Heidi gently on the forehead. "Sleep the sleep of the just and dream of fabulous places and fantastic creatures."

"I shall, my love . . ." she whispered back, closing her eyes and drifting off.

I received a humorous text-message from Mathis the morning we were due to vacate the Gothic Temple:

Has your mad, Kraut hotter half stabbed u up yet?

3

Heidi lived in Chapel Mead. I had passed through Chapel Mead on my bicycle a number of times, but I had never really stopped there. Admittedly, the village was a visual gem of eighteenth-century houses and limestone buildings, like jewelled buttons on a coat from a distant past. With its hollyhock-lined causeways and tents of hornbeam hedgerows, Chapel Mead boasted a Norman church, tithe barns, a marketplace and an old, coaching inn called the HOGSBACK. One could watch cricket on the village green on Sundays. The village hosted an annual summer flower show, and one could not help but admire its picturesque offering of follies, grottoes and vistas.

Heidi introduced me to the period stone cottage she owned, THE POSTINGS, some way out of the village high street. It was a beautiful place with a thatched roof, dry stone walls and exposed stonework indoors. Mullion windows and beam ceilings and flagstone floors. The place was big enough to accommodate a large family. The living room housed an inglenook fireplace with a woodburner. The rustic kitchen boasted an Aga. The cottage possessed a separate dining room, office, cloakroom and art studio, crammed with chinoiserie, single-rose blooms in vases, folkloric textiles and oil canvases, strange and surreal renderings straight from Heidi's fertile imagination, including some unexpected paintings of ovaries and pudenda. Upstairs were two spacious bedrooms and the bathroom. Most of the rooms were decorated with oriental rugs. For all its high-bohemian luxe, the place was spotless. Cleanliness was next to godliness, Heidi reminded me. If she couldn't sleep, she would clean the cottage in the middle of the night until tiredness finally set in.

Her garden, too, was a glorious sight to behold. Hanging baskets of begonias and petunias. White roses crawled up the walls together with the pale blue of wisteria. The flowerbeds were in a full bloom of pastel colours. Poppies tussled for space with the peonies. Shrubby artemisia with its silvery leaves. The pendant lights of evening primrose. The drooping bells of foxgloves. Frothy white valerian. Purple lavender. Pink hydrangeas. Clematis, snowdrops, dahlias and geraniums. A wild pear tree stood regally in the middle of the lawn, bearing the ripest, juiciest fruit. A warm tranquillity hung in the still summer air, even in the darkest, inner hollows of the garden. Heidi shared her garden with the bats and wasps and damselflies.

Not only was Heidi an artist of potential greatness, she had proved herself a green-fingered goddess and was in the process of converting her cottage into an eco-friendly home. She could comfortably claim she was one with nature.

In fact, the door to her backyard opened conveniently on to Tangley Woods, a stretch of protected woodland owned by the Chapel Mead Preservation Society and trail-mapped for long evening walks. A veritable arboretum of oaks, larches, sycamores, rowans, beeches, wild cherry and horse chestnuts. Somewhere in this wooded expanse stood a Saxon ring of hawthorns and tucked at the back was an orchard of pleached lime trees. A brook of clear, sparkling waters split Tangley Woods in half. Kestrels and hawks, curlews and moorhens, thrushes and tits, frequented the woods, a birdwatcher's dream. One time, Heidi spotted a kingfisher and I could only gawp at the bejewelled splendour of this native bird. As an artist, Heidi had an eye for detail; myself, I had never paid much attention to such things until now.

Indeed, I acclimatized very quickly to the clean, unspoiled atmosphere of what amounted to a charming rural idyll, half-expecting the entire cast of Farthing Wood to make an appearance. I enjoyed those lazy, hazy days of summer in the company of my wonderfully-chipper, completely-besotted girlfriend. We ate, drank, talked, walked, shut out the world and made love. It was a wondrous place, full of enchantment, the stuff of fairytales.

One particular evening, as we settled into a hot bath together, having dined on roasted wood pigeon with grain mustard mash and burned off the additional calories with a long ramble through the woods, I began assessing my life before and after I'd met Heidi. I rattled off the misgivings of my former life, and Heidi heard my woes with complete impartiality. She was a good listener. She walked with little gay bouncy steps, on the balls of her feet, slipped out of her bathrobe and stepped into the Jo Malone-fragranced bath with me, back turned to me, between my legs. A single, Yankee candle burned steadily on the farthest corner of the rim of the bath, giving the bathroom a pleasant, warm glow. *Glorious* by the Pierces on the small, portable radio on the windowsill quietly played in the background.

"You know my father was a taxman before he retired," I was relating. "You can imagine what a super-moralistic man he must have been, not averse to punishing me if I ever stepped out of line."

"He must have been a good man even if he might have seemed punitive," Heidi replied. "Maybe you should give your dad a call . . . see how he is."

I considered her suggestion. "That's going to be awfully difficult. I haven't spoken to him in ten years, neither has he bothered to ring me."

"You don't have to do anything right now, but at least think about it. You might come round to the idea. Family *is* family, after all."

I thought of contacting my estranged father – hearing his gruff voice, how he would react. "He will be so disappointed with my life . . ." I felt sad. "I never amounted to anybody, in the service of others, writing bullshit about how great my nobodies are." Yes, on the wrong side of forty, I didn't even have a name for myself. I was one of the ghosts of the literary world, forced to work in the shadows. "An average writer makes less than four grand a year."

"I'm beginning to understand your disillusionment with life, with family, with religion," Heidi acknowledged. "Parents can be so hard to please. And parents fuck you up, according to Philip Larkin." She moved on to the crux of it. "But when it comes to our work-life, it's the job we were meant to do. All of us have to earn our bread one way or another." She paused before coming up with an idea. "You could always ask Marianne for a raise."

It wasn't an altogether terrible idea. Marianne, our editor at Hambleys, appreciated the immense effort I put in with so little to show for it. And Hambleys was thriving as a publishing house in her shrewd, capable hands. She also encouraged healthy relationships between her staff. She was aware both Heidi and I were currently an item and thrilled. Such was she our guiding star, she had given us a two-week break to consolidate our romance. She was a kind, caring, generous lady, very supportive of our relationship, to say the least. "I can only try."

"That's all she would expect from you."

"I think you're way too good for me."

"I could say the same about you," Heidi reciprocated affectionately. "You know I would have died for you . . ."

It was a truly dramatic thing to say and I didn't know if she meant it in the literal sense or it was a measure of her feelings for me, figuratively-speaking. "You have rescued me from a sad, lonely life of anonymity: living in a crappy flat, eating microwavable meals, paying for sex when the urge got the better of me. For that I am grateful," I said sincerely. "Although my father would be aghast that I was going out with a—" I just stopped myself from completing the sentence in case it came across as objectionable or shameful.

Heidi picked up on it immediately. Yet, she did not take it as an affront. "You were going to say 'going out with a Jehovah's Witness', weren't you?"

"I didn't mean to sound . . ." I apologized before trying to lighten the mood. "You certainly don't look like a Quaker oat."

"No, it's fine," Heidi replied, unfazed. "We, Witnesses, get that a lot. Part of the Great Tribulation, supposedly. Our hardships are many. The gift of faith in the face of adversity cannot be underestimated." She made a sage suggestion. "Why not bring a little spirituality into your life? Why not accompany me to my next meeting at the Kingdom Hall, get a taster of my faith, tell me what you think? We've got a travelling overseer visiting who's scheduled to speak this weekend."

I didn't mind. No harm in providing a little moral support to Heidi – not that she needed any. "It's a deal." I touched her almost unnoticeable Harrison Ford-style scar on her chin, acquired when she fell off her bike as a kid, and kissed her. She let me scrub her smooth, silky back with a loofah.

After our romantic bath, we made for the bedroom, snuggled up beneath her patchwork quilt. We were inseparable.

The prevailing evening was filled with the trill of birdsong and a croaking frog chorus. I listened to the sound of a horse's hooves in the gloom.

"I crave you so much, my kitty-cat," I whispered into Heidi's ear as slept before I too drifted off into the land of nod.

4

That Sunday, Heidi drove me, as promised, to the local Kingdom Hall in Oaks Fold to attend the weekly service. It was an elegant Georgian building which had undergone a radical modern redesign, transforming it into a sublime architectural hybrid. Apparently, the local Conservative Party had made a generous offer for the hall, but the Jehovah's Witness organization had rejected it, point-blank. Inside, the place was typically functional in character, free of any religious symbols. A plaque on the wall read: *Do not be anxious, for I am your god.* Isaiah 41:10. The dress code of the attendees was sober, suits and ties for the men, formal dresses for the women, although to some outsiders it might have resembled an

Ascot fashion parade.

Heidi's religious acquaintances and the congregational elders were superficially welcoming towards me whilst viewing me with some degree of suspicion and a wariness I found discouraging. Nevertheless, they promised an experience like no other.

"Soz, what's it all about?" I whispered to Heidi as we took our seats near the front of the stage.

"Oh, something about God," Heidi joked, out of earshot of others in our row.

The congregational elders had invited a guest speaker, Dale Ludreau, a tall, gangling, silver-haired individual. After the initial hymn singing, the man introduced himself. "Brothers and Sisters, I have travelled all the way from Bethel to attend your meeting for worship and study of the Bible and current Watch Tower Society literature." Indeed, he bore a slight New York accent. "You may wonder why I have left the comfort of my Bethel headquarters and journeyed so far to be here. But I thought it important to visit your catchment area where we suspect an Anointed One worships." Gasps of awe from the congregation. How exciting was it that there was one anointed amongst them? "We do not know who the Anointed One is – and neither do they – but it brings home the message some are 'more chosen' than others. It also forms our study of the latest issue of the *Watchtower*: unjust treatment, of course, and the need to endure." Dale Ludreau shifted on the lectern before he began his symposium. "It would not be inaccurate to perhaps consider us the most persecuted Christians on earth and our *New World Translation* the most burned book in the world. For many reasons. Our faith is littered with many examples. We suffered at the hands of the Nazis because of our political neutrality. The Catholic Church colluded with the police to arrest those Jehovah's Witnesses who refused to stop preaching and went on to stir up a public campaign of mob violence against us. Just because of our rejection of the Cross and our attempts to convert the worldly to the Truth. Because of our obedience to Jehovah and Jesus, who if you remember requested the Apostle Peter return his weapon to its place and not engage in warfare on more than one occasion, we face resentment and ostracism and oppression from political parties around the globe. Our Brothers and Sisters have been fined, convicted, imprisoned, even executed, for being conscientious objectors, and our own children humiliated, beaten and expelled from school. Our religious activities are banned or severely restricted in such countries like China and South Korea, Armenia and Turkey, Malawi and Eritrea and countless Islamic states. Russia is in the process of outlawing our faith, branding us an extremist organization. And our hearts must go out to those Brothers and Sisters, who will not stop their worship against all the odds, sometimes forced to take their devotion to Jehovah into secrecy. Because we will not succumb to the tyranny of the world. Because we must *endure*.

"Our global harvest work began in 1919, reaping the earth, allowing people to repent, and now we are deep in the End Times, spreading the 'good news' of the Kingdom and awaiting the reward of becoming a new civilization in Jehovah's design. Badness has been around us for a very long time. As Jehovah's servants, we have experienced insult and injury, ridicule and discrimination while attempting to deliver Jehovah's inspired message to the world. You give a tract to someone and, when you look back, they are putting it in the trash. A sailor cannot control the storm, but he can weather the storm by adjusting the sails. Similarly, you may not control the illness or catastrophe that has stormed into your life but weather it with the physical, mental and emotional resources at your disposal. Despite our imperfections and painful humbling experiences or the prolonged illnesses we are forced to endure, we remain focused on serving Jehovah because, as in Romans 5:3, Jehovah sees our tribulations and will never give up on us while equipping us with the strength and the hope to carry on. Our close interpersonal relationship with Jehovah also means our Heavenly Father can bring all unjust treatment to an end in the fullness of time. Do not rise to provocation and fail the trial, fall out and stop Witnessing, lose the privilege of service. Trust in Jehovah and He will reward the loyalty of all Christ's anointed followers. Endure *despite* persecution, maintain your spirituality despite opposition. Never forget the Apostle Paul was tortured for his faith or that David was victimized by Saul. It is so easy to give up, give in to imperfections, all because of Original Sin, the Fall of Man in the Garden of Eden. But we are free moral agents. With our free will, we have the power to choose between good and evil. We may have assured expectation in business or demonstrate our competency in legal matters, but we cannot serve two masters: Jehovah or money and the things riches and prestige can buy. Remember what happened to the Wife of Lot: turned into a pillar of salt. Remember the promise we made to Jehovah. Jehovah is the Great Timekeeper, with jurisdiction over times and the seasons. He controls events any way He sees fit. Jesus was installed as Heavenly King in 1914, the beginning of the end of this wicked system of things. We exist in Satan's world with Satan's standards, and if we are not too careful, we will learn those standards. Believe me when I say, Armageddon will come on time when Jehovah will crush every last vestige of government, and pure worship will be exalted. Faith is a response to evidence.

Belief exists even in the absence of evidence. When we talk of leaps of faith, how do you test a parachute? Jump from the plane and pull the cord, of course . . ."

Faith makes all things possible, but it does not make them reality, I thought. Even if the man was an absolute pro at public speaking, I did not find the message Dale Ludreau preached completely convincing, neither did he totally hold my attention. My attention, like surely of those around him, drifted in and out of his sermon. Soon, to my immense relief, he was riding down the home straight.

". . . When the end is almost upon us," he was summarizing in conclusion, "our global preaching campaign programme will bring many to the path of righteousness and many more still to come. Maintain integrity and joy and humility. Knowledge, discernment, self-control. Put study and meditation into practice. Practice virtue in a world lacking in faith, of degrading moral values, with a determination not to give up. Endure and fulfil the law of Jesus. Your spirit can bear things because beyond the pale it sees the goal. Keep on enduring and don't give up. *The one who has endured to the end will be saved,* Matthew 24:13."

He received a rousing round of applause from the congregation. To those gathered, he had certainly proved a motivational speaker. Fair to say, it was a good talk, and I suppose I appreciated the spirituality of the occasion. The message was crystal-clear: endure, endure, *endure* . . .

After more hymn-singing, I witnessed an *actual* Bible study group, the stuff of Sunday School, as the congregation as a collective cited the power of endurance, grace under pressure, from various biblical sources, laid down in *The Watchtower.*

All nice and godly. But what about behind the scenes?

Dale Ludreau wrapped up the meeting with an important announcement. He stated that the Oaks Fold congregation would be relocated to another Kingdom Hall, centralized to one in Chertsford, and this particular Kingdom Hall would be sold off 'because that is what Jehovah would have wanted'.

Except his explanation struck me as glib.

What a crock!

5

Being in the service of Jehovah was almost like a second job. Some people might say, 'I'm a doctor,' or 'I'm a bricklayer', but a member of this religion might introduce themselves as, 'I'm a Jehovah's Witness.' Like it was some kind of job title. Which I suppose, in some respects, it was. I couldn't deny Heidi was a devout Christian. Truly praiseworthy in her spiritual endeavours. She did all the things expected of her as a Witness. She attended Kingdom Hall meetings twice-weekly at the new hall in Chertsford and went on the Ministry with a colleague around the neighbourhood as part of her regular pioneering work, preaching door-to-door, canvassing the End Times and attempting to start 'Bible study' with members of the public. Remarkably she was not paid clergy, for since Witnesses believed themselves to be the model of first-century Christianity, all baptized members were ordained ministers. Heidi went as far as completing a monthly field service report of her preaching and teaching activities, an accurate record of hours clocked. In her pioneering ways, she completed her seventy hours of ministry a month quite comfortably. Needless to say, Heidi took her religion very seriously.

Except Heidi and I were living in sin.

She struggled to reconcile our relationship with her ministerial work.

I am a writer. Writers may not be Psychiatrists, but they carry out enough research to understand their characters' personalities and motivations and therefore are easily capable of applying this technique to the real world.

I shall begin my takedown of the organization by focusing on its founding father from the 1870s, 'Pastor' Charles Taze Russell. Just as Scientology is based on the crooked, opportunistic teachings of that failed science-fiction writer, Hubbard, the Watch Tower Society was led by two controversial figures in the early days. Russell relied on a dictatorial style of leadership. He was also accused of cheating many of his congregation financially as well as scamming the public with an ordinary strain of wheat he called 'miracle wheat'. His wife, too, divorced him on the grounds of mental cruelty and for carrying on an affair with their foster daughter and possibly several other female members of their congregation. Russell stated the allegations were false and guided by Satan in an attempt to subvert his work as a minister of the gospel. It further turned out he had lied about his own qualifications; he had never gone to seminary school or ever been ordained a minister.

Joseph Franklin Rutherford, meanwhile, the man who shaped Witness ideology, was a qualified lawyer by trade and his strong booming voice with an eloquent grasp of the English language made him a powerful orator. He was also described as brusque and insensitive with a volatile temper and a forceful personality, full of self-righteousness, and a man obsessed by his own overinflated sense of self-importance. Anyone who dared oppose him he regarded as 'working for the Devil', and he is accused, as president, of using *The Watchtower* as a platform for propaganda to attack his opponents, namely the Roman Catholic Church, while autocratically exercising complete control over the affairs of the Watch Tower Society. It was his distaste for Christmas and Birthdays which would be included in Witness doctrine. He believed there was a proper place for women in society and claimed there to be a satanic influence in the rise of the Women's Movement. Rutherford did not engage in door-to-door ministry, despite his assertion that it was a requirement and sacred duty of all Witnesses. He saw it as beneath him, using the excuse that his responsibilities as president did not permit him engaging in this activity. Getting Rutherford to the podium to give public talks also proved difficult due to his inebriation. In fact, Rutherford had a serious alcohol problem. He had cases of expensive whiskey, brandy and beer at his home and workplace and would go from drink to drink, leading to alcohol-fuelled, unjust treatment of his staff, outbursts of anger and vulgar language. Still, this glorification of alcohol at Bethel under his watch did not compare to his extravagant lifestyle during the Great Depression, which included numerous luxurious residences for his own exclusive use, complete with lavish furnishings and personal attendants, and a predilection for flash cars, including a couple of Cadillac V-16s, while at the same time promoting austerity as a part of Witness life. Of the many houses he afforded himself, his favourite would be a Californian mansion called Beth Sarim which he authorized the purchase of, with the claim it would provide protection for him during Armageddon and serve as a house for Abraham and other resurrected Princes during the earthly resurrection. Rutherford summered in Europe and wintered in Beth Sarim. He continued to live with his servants while falsely claiming to be anointed. And his legacy continues to this day under the guise of the Governing Body, who whitewashes its own history and exculpates itself from every hypocritical action originating from the very top of the organization. The Governing Body has received widespread criticism regarding biblical mistranslation and unfulfilled predictions about major biblical events, such as Christ's Second Coming, the advent of God's Kingdom and Armageddon and their failure to report child sexual abuse cases to the authorities as well as alleged coercion of existing members and the cruel treatment of former members, all of which have been the subject of various formal investigations.

Full of glaring discrepancies, the *New World Translation* has been accused of scholastic dishonesty for rewriting the Bible in favour of Witness practices and claiming anyone who doesn't read their book 'falls into darkness' or reverts back to 'ordinary Christianity'. The Watch Tower Society's claims to have an exclusive relationship with God and His Son and advanced knowledge of Armageddon and the establishment of God's Kingdom have, like Harold Camping's outrageous predictions, been repeatedly discredited. From 1966, Witness publications and convention talks built up anticipation of the possibility that Christ's thousand-year reign might begin in 1975. Never happened . . . just another failed prediction, no failed *prophecy*. Yet, in 1995, they continued their apocalyptic message by once again changing their prediction that the End of the World would come when the generation of Witnesses born before 1914 died. Doubts begin to understandably emerge in the minds of those who have accepted and followed every word written by the Watch Tower Society unquestioningly as God's channel of communication to mankind when each day foretold as the End passes uneventfully without any reappearance of Christ and *The Watchtower* prints a 'new Generational truth' to supersede an existing, fundamental, so-called 'truth' – and the Truth surely begins to unravel. Perpetuating the fear that Armageddon is just around the corner (but never comes) will constantly hold a practising Jehovah's Witness firmly in the fold. In 2001, the Watch Tower Society was accused of registering as a non-governmental organization with the United Nations, its so-called satanic enemy, causing a scandal, and once its hypocrisy was discovered, it blamed the newspapers of printing lies.

Adult Witnesses can give an advance directive to disavow blood transfusions but Thank God the law protects vulnerable individuals, such as children, in life-threatening medical situations. Because many Witnesses are reluctant to mix with worldly people, there is an overrepresentation of physical illness in the religion, due to the concentrated gene pool, as well as mental illness, such as anxiety and depression, sometimes hereditary but often driven by the extreme guilt and fear instilled in them by their faith while blaming Satan for their unwellness.

Domestic violence is tolerated because the man is at the head of the household, even if he treats himself to steak every night while his wife suffers in silence and the children fight for scraps. Doesn't that speak of the subjugation of women, who are told to keep quiet in the face of adversity and put up with their husbands, for which Jehovah will surely reward them? Adultery is the only grounds for divorce, forcing women to stay with abusive husbands. Jehovah's Witnesses have, time and again, helped conceal cases of sexual abuse within the organization because of its 'two witness' rule for disciplinary action which requires sexual abuse to be corroborated by a second person if the accused denies any wrongdoing. In the event the allegations are dismissed for lack of two witnesses, the Watch Tower Society's instruction is that the elders will leave the matter in

'Jehovah's hands'. Do you really think you would find another witness to an act of child molestation? Some victims of sexual abuse have asserted that, when reporting abuse, they were ordered to maintain their silence by their local elders, who are trained to cover-up any embarrassments or failures of the organization. Such has been the Governing Body's resistance to change a Watchtower policy that protects paedophiles, it is not uncommon for an alleged child abuser to be reinstated as a Witness while continuing to perpetrate abuse, a wolf in sheep's clothing, and the victim to be disfellowshipped as an apostate, the usual default position of the Governing Body.

It also warns members to avoid independent thinking, claiming such thinking was introduced by 'Satan the Devil' – oh, please, do *not* insult my intelligence! Even attending University is discouraged because the person might actually learn something instead of being spoonfed nonsense. Yes, the Governing Body is hugely invested in keeping its members ignorant. Those who openly disagree with official teachings are condemned as 'apostates' who are 'mentally diseased' – always the fallback – when God gave us a brain so we could think for ourselves. The organization has even urged adherents to delay marriage and child-bearing until after Armageddon – how crazy is that? Doesn't this denial of free speech just smack of nothing but a cult fearing information?

I thought of Heidi's father, who at age twenty-one became a Jehovah's Witness after meeting her mother, and the havoc his conversion would have caused upon his birth family. Late teens and early twenties are the ripest ages in terms of vulnerable minds and trying to find direction in life for cults to take advantage of and swoop in.

Jehovah's Witnesses surely fit the description of a cult in terms of their flawed doctrines and the level of cultic, abusive control the religion has over its members. A cult like any other, just like the Mormons and the Moonies. Let's begin with their claim to be an extra-scriptural source of authority and their view of themselves as the only community that will be saved, with salvation impossible for anyone outside *The Watchtower*. This includes distorting their own information or outright lying about their own history or misquoting outside information to make their teachings appear to be backed up by authoritative sources. They control information at different levels in order to regulate an individual's physical reality, in effect 'micromanaging' the person's life. This is done by denouncing rational analysis and constructive criticism, forbidding all critical thinking about their leadership, doctrines or policies and encouraging spying on other members by implementing a 'buddy' system to monitor the individual and report any deviant thoughts, feelings and actions to their said-leadership, who promotes a culture of naming and shaming and ultimately punishes the individual during confession by withholding forgiveness or absolution. This promotion of feelings of guilt and unworthiness, that the individual is not living up to their potential, means the person is constantly at the mercy of the leaders. Obedience to the organization above all else is demanded, even at the expense of its members' health and safety, practically equating the Watch Tower Society with God. And, like the Scientologists, the Governing Body continues to indulge in financial exploitation of its members.

It was Raymond Franz, who left the Governing Body and oversaw the religion's decline after releasing a book with the self-explanatory title, *Crisis of Conscience*, comparing the religion to a cult by highlighting some of its extreme practices. The book is off-limits to Witnesses by official edict, keeping them in the dark as to how *The Watchtower* runs its ship. Even *Harry Potter* is a no-no, considered by Gileads and Bethelites to promote spiritism.

The pop singer, Prince, may be arguably the most famous Jehovah's Witness of modern times, and Michael Jackson himself once an active Jehovah's Witness until his disassociation in 1987, but Jehovah's Witnesses have been condemned for courting Peter Sutcliffe, the Yorkshire Ripper, who has considered converting to the Jehovah's Witness faith. Repentance is all good and well and every soul should be given a chance to seek redemption, but one can surely guess Sutcliffe's repentance is only superficial, a ruse to be stepped down to a less secure wing of the prison. Not surprisingly, too, since it is a religion that has dispensed with Hell; what must have definitely made it more attractive to Sutcliffe would have been the lack of a Hell to punish him, giving him the message that nobody is held accountable for their evil crimes.

Masturbation is forbidden. Pornography, too, is prohibited, even between married couples. *The Watchtower* refers to oral and anal sex as 'perverted acts'. Even if homosexuals usually come to recognize their orientation during the hormonal turmoil of adolescence, their sexual identity is deemed an abomination to Jehovah since their 'disgusting urges' are thought to be 'under the control of Satan', and their only hope of salvation is to repress their sexuality and remain celibate for life. No wonder the poor teenager becomes invariably depressed and contemplates suicide. Jehovah's Witnesses do not allow their members to have sex before or outside of marriage.

Heidi and I were living in sin.

This was a massive issue for her. She could have hit rock bottom with her crisis of faith, the conflict raging inside her, if I hadn't been more supportive. I do not suffer fools gladly and, for me, the Bible is nothing but interpretation by man and the Witness doctrines total tosh, the workings of a cult.

They say the earthly paradise will be full of Jehovah's Witnesses, Heidi despaired. *I do want to live forever, but I don't want to live forever with Jehovah Witnesses. Our religion is full of cliques and scrutineers, people who preach against intolerance but are themselves intolerant of others, disassociating from them because of the smallest peccadillo.*

Heidi got the invitation to see her congregational elders – and she knew she risked disfellowshipping for dating me. Punishment for seeking love, friendship, intimacy, a glimpse into somebody else's soul.

Congregational elders form a judicial committee to investigate any cases where the baptized member is accused of committing a serious sin – in Heidi's case a charge of sexual misconduct was levelled against her – and to give counsel or administer a reprimand, if the individual hasn't lived up to certain standards of man-made conduct. Perhaps the most stringent, controversial and all-encompassing form of punishment that Jehovah's Witnesses administer is the practice of shunning, whereby the individual who has been disfellowshipped and deemed wicked is disowned, ignored and isolated by family members and friends, the practice of putting the organization ahead of their own family drummed into even the children. It means most active members are forced to suppress any doubts, even against disputing any of the official teachings or organizational policies, for fear of losing their relationships with friends and relatives, and this serves as the ultimate control mechanism. Family forms the foundation of society and when the Jehovah's Witnesses try to convince you that shunning is scriptural – who the hell you kidding when Jesus himself preached love of family not just to provide moral support to the person but help heal them when most in need? – and for your own benefit and a way to bring the disfellowshipped person 'back to Jehovah', a requirement for their own everlasting life, this process is actually nothing more than emotional and social blackmail, something inhumanely cruel and, need I say, *criminal.*

A committee of three elders, including the circuit overseer, spoke to her as I sat in the car. The atmosphere of the room brought palpable emotions of dread and panic. Can you imagine how highly traumatic and petrifying it would have been if Heidi had been a teenage girl confronted by these three older men demanding her to disclose her innermost secrets to them in as much detail as possible? The panel asked Heidi pointed and direct questions about her sex life. Too many Witnesses had seen her holding hands with me in public. Had she slept with me? The judicial committee effectively told Heidi that if she did not stop seeing me, she would be disfellowshipped and, if she chose to leave, then all her Jehovah's Witness friends would shun her. She could either give up her romantic love or give up all her Witness friends. And, if she chose disfellowshipping, she would die at Armageddon because she would have rejected Jehovah.

When she later told me, I was morally outraged at this immense abuse of psychological power, this unethical use of confession, which might be, in a manner of speaking, comparable to an infringement of her human rights. It just went to prove that the basis of this organization was, just like my own religion, *conditional* love.

The elders did not disfellowship her or even counsel her.

Because I had got one over them.

We were living in sin and she risked disfellowshipping. Disfellowshipping would be a bad thing for an extravert like Heidi due to its social exclusion and isolation.

Her dilemma percolated through my mind, filtered a verbal response. *I will marry you.*

Isn't it too soon? she asked honestly.

It's not up for debate, I said . . . and did the honourable thing. She accepted my proposal to make our relationship legitimate under the eyes of God. I married the woman who had once been watching me from a distance for ages. I married her because I had a special place in her life – I was her first, consummating our relationship at the Gothic Temple. She had taken me to a Rammstein concert at the O2 and that was when I think I fell in love with her – and I have loved her since.

The judicial committee stopped in their tracks, gobsmacked, when she showed off her diamond wedding ring. A ton of pressure is put on the happy couple to plan the event that is supposed to be one of the happiest days of their lives. Naturally, the bride and groom want everything to be absolutely perfect – venue-wise, food, flowers, cake, tablecloths, centrepieces, music – and the wedding to go smoothly. We, on the other hand, kept it a simple affair and plumped for a shotgun wedding with only a handful of guests in attendance, all colleagues from Hambleys. Marianne Keene was thrilled and utterly proud of us. Heidi told the committee elders she had married me in a quick ceremony at Chertsford Registry Office, then we'd held the reception in her garden, a wedding barbecue. She finished off her testimony by smugly reminding her elders of Hebrews 13:4: *Let marriage be honourable among all, and the marriage bed without defilement, for God will judge fornicators and adulterers.* The panel of elders had no choice but to bring the meeting to a close, unable to proceed any further. They had nothing.

I moved into The Postings with Heidi and we resumed our new life as husband and wife. So far, the summer had been a revelation, a romantic awakening for Heidi and, for me, I had seen her 'religion' for what it really was. It had all gone in our favour. And the lustrous summer promised to go on forever.

The calm before the carnage.

PART THREE: IN THE SHADOW OF EVIL, THE LIGHT BEYOND THE TRUTH

1

I had only been living in The Postings, with my wife, for less than a fortnight when odd things began to occur. And things only got stranger and stranger.

It started with us waking up in the morning and finding someone – or something – had got into one of the kitchen cupboards, broken into a packet of uncooked rice and transported some of the grains of rice down to the cutlery drawer, piling them up neatly in a small heap. This happened over a number of nights. Always the discovery of a neat pile of rice in the kitchen drawer by the morning. It was mindboggling – and perturbing. Being a religious woman, Heidi began to believe it was a sign. She implicated poltergeist activity. Except, in her teachings, all ghosts were demons in disguise.

It was Mathis who solved the mystery. *It used to happen to me too when I used to live out in the sticks,* he told me over the phone. *You've got mice.*

And, for the first time, there was an explanation to the strange goings-on in the kitchen overnight. We lived in a rural area, an obvious haven for brown field mice. They had somehow got into the house, squeezing through some tiny gap, and their behaviour classically included raiding the cupboards and storing potential food for later – rice was a favourite. It put Heidi's mind at ease from the constant worry that her cottage might have been infiltrated by demonic spirits. We laid a few traps – except none snapped. Either it wasn't mice, or the mice were wise to our intentions of catching them in the act. Once we stored the rice in a food container, the invasion of the cottage by these nocturnal rodents suddenly ceased, although we noticed something had tried to get into the food container – there were tiny teeth-marks on the plastic lid.

Then, there was the other stuff. Innocent enough . . . or possibly not so innocent.

One particular evening, I was typing away on my PC in the study, having started ghost-writing the memoirs of a Page 3 model. I mean who releases their memoirs in their late twenties. Only a football player or a WAG, Z-lister or nobody. It was only when I was taking a short break after a couple of hours of intensive labour that I turned to my left and saw something that nearly caused me to fall off my chair. The light from the single desk-lamp, which was bent at an angle, was cast on a stack of papers on the paper tray resting on the filing cabinet, but the shadow projected on the wall behind the pile of papers had innocuously formed the silhouette of a head in profile. Except the gnarled profile resembled that of demonic figure or medieval witch or leprechaun. Sharp, crooked nose, heavy-set brow and pointed chin. The mouth was slightly open giving the impression of it being filled with needle teeth. I was mesmerized by the image, just an interplay between light and shadow that had, by the laws of chance, created something vaguely recognizable and freakish. And the figure, parallel to and almost at the same height as my own head, seemed to be glaring at me. I swear I could just about make out a small, illuminated hole in its aspect that might have been an eye – or was I only imagining it? Breaking out of my paralysis, I rearranged the papers in the paper tray and the devilish shadow of a head instantly vanished. I thought of Heidi jumping to conclusions and calling it another sign. I didn't mention the occurrence to her. Then, another thought popped into my head, an old saying: *do not paint the devil on the wall . . . or he will appear to you in person.* One could take it literally, but, in a more practical sense, it advised us not to assume the worst of any given situation before anything has even happened. I half-expected to see the shadow of my own head cast in similar demonic profile on the back wall, as though I might be, unbeknownst to me, some supernatural creature hiding in the light, and I think that if I saw something like it, it would have freaked me out no end. I avoided looking at the back wall . . . just in case.

It was the height of summer during which we witnessed Nature at its finest. Cockchafers in flight. The elegant shape and extraordinary mandibles of flying stag beetles. Hornets more concerned with building a temporary, summertime nest under the garden shed than stinging us. A blizzard of butterflies in the brightness of day, moths drawn to the cottage lights after sundown. But it was something as small and twee as a ladybird that brought us crashing down to earth.

Ladybirds visited the house in ever-increasing numbers, getting into the cottage through the open bathroom window. We often saw them crawling up the bathroom window, the larger, darker American species which cannibalistically preyed on the red, common British variety. It was on one occasion when Heidi and I were dressed in bathrobes and preparing to have a bath together that Heidi spotted something above our heads. I looked up and my mouth fell agape. A group of black-shelled, red-spotted ladybirds had formed a word on the ceiling: SUBMIT. It was clearly visible, a product of design, and this time, unlike the episode of the hungry field mouse or the evil silhouette on the study wall, it could not be put down to mere chance.

Submit.

We stared at the ladybirds, how they had somehow organized themselves to spell out a word so perfectly on the bathroom ceiling, as though of their own chemical intelligence or directed by a powerful external sentience. I had seen nothing like it.

Submit.

It was Heidi who reacted first. She grabbed the mop from its bucket and slammed its head against the grouped arrangement of ladybirds. The ladybirds scattered and fled, flying out of the window but not before some swarmed around us, activating their defence mechanism and spraying us with a pungent gas, offensive and a skin irritant.

When the last of the ladybirds had disappeared into the evening, I broke the silence. "Did we really see that?" I could not imagine any naturalist being able to explain what we had witnessed.

"It's happening," said Heidi quietly, preoccupied. "The end is nigh."

"I'm starting to believe you about the end of the world," I said lightly. But I didn't find my comment amusing. The freaky shadow play on the wall, the extraordinary phenomenon of highly-coordinated insect behaviour all pointed towards something dark and imminent.

We got on with our lives for the next few days. Going on the Ministry, Heidi was hearing rumours of bizarre behaviour from the villagers of Chapel Mead. Reports of the villagers sitting at the kitchen table, talking to themselves, at three in the morning, as though communing with the Devil. There were even extreme claims that some villagers had resorted to eating rats, flies and spiders. Events culminated in the local priest going completely insane and allegedly holding nightly orgies at the local chapel. Accused of devil worship, his last act as a man of the cloth, before he got taken away by the authorities, was to drown a baby in the font during baptism. Heidi was distressed and furious at the Devil's cowardly action of sacrificing a vulnerable newborn. It made the headlines. As did the news of a paranoid husband who blinded his wife and five-year-old child and pet terrier before turning the pencil on himself. His entire family died of their injuries. He survived. He didn't know why he did it, except that he didn't want to see what was coming to Chapel Mead.

The dreams came next. Dreams are the mind's way of processing the events of the day as well as the past and sometimes extrapolating the future, sometimes clairvoyantly. Heidi meanwhile had spoken of supernatural signs, dark omens of things to come. Indeed, we both felt as if the village was on the edge of something profound. Both myself and Heidi dreamed the same dream, the same horrific accident: of a petrol-carrying tanker truck overturning in the High Street, catching fire and exploding . . .

I awoke to the whoop-whoop of the emergency sirens fading into the backstreets of my mind. I discovered I had my side of the patchwork quilt over my head in spite of the stifling summer heat. I had created a small gap with the blanket through which I could see the rest of the bedroom. The wardrobe, the dressing table and mirror, my clothes hung on the back of the chair, Heidi's vintage Shirley Temple doll sat upright on the seat, watching me. I thought how the sweetest dolls become scary at midnight, how the Shirley Temple doll's glassy eyes were looking at me with a malignant stare. I lay under the covers with that hole for air, filled with a clammy fear, an unnameable dread. Not just from the recurrent nightmare but due to the ongoing palpable sense of being watched by *something* in the house all the time.

The face of the Shirley Temple doll suddenly appeared in front of me through the visible gap formed by the blanket, the expression twisted into an evil sneer, the feral glow of the eyes burning into me, and I nearly screamed.

I opened my eyes, waking up again. The duvet was pushed down to the foot of the bed, and I lay in bed next to my wife, who appeared to be somewhat restless in her sleep, twitching, as though experiencing an equally-disturbing dream. Daylight came streaming in through the slightly-parted bedroom curtains.

"Holy Christ . . ." I murmured, using the Lord's name in vain, relieved it was morning. *A dream within a dream.*

The alarm clock went off at that moment, causing me to start again, *Sparkling Melody* on Heidi's mobile, a perfect waking jingle for a busybody like her.

That day, when the whole thing kicked off for real, I learned the actual reason why Heidi had chosen me above anyone else.

Armageddon had come to Chapel Mead.

2

We never saw it happen, but we heard about it on the radio. When we switched on the television, we saw the horrific aftermath in the news footage. Reports were coming in that the driver of a tanker truck had apparently ploughed through a line of pedestrians on Chapel Mead High Street, whether intentionally or otherwise, before crashing into the Village Hall, the petrol the juggernaut was transporting igniting immediately on impact, the exploding fireball consuming the buildings around it, dense, black smoke billowing upwards for miles around. The main high street was immediately evacuated by the police while the fire brigade fought the raging inferno and the unfortunate casualties, who had been mercilessly mown down, some killed instantly, attended to by the ambulance crews. But the rest of the onlookers, who had witnessed this dreadful tragedy and the ensuing mayhem, refused to leave the scene of the disaster and stood behind the cordon, watching events unfold with a look of almost symphorohilic fascination. It wasn't so much the unnerving way the spectators stared at the emergency services doing their job or the knowledge that such a thing could possibly occur in this quiet corner of the world and so very close to home, but how Heidi and I had somehow foreseen the whole nightmare in our sleep on consecutive nights in advance. We had experienced a recurring premonition of this terrible disaster – that could, in some ways, be considered more disturbing than the incident itself, as though there were supernatural forces at work here.

We kept abreast of the events in the news and went about the rest of the day without leaving the house. I tried to write. Heidi painted. Then, we ate dinner and prepared to make love, like husbands and wives do. Except we were not in the mood. Our thoughts went out to the families of the victims, some of whom Heidi knew from meeting on the Ministry.

By the evening, the furore had died down, and Chapel Mead High Street remained cordoned-off, a major crime scene. Scotland Yard would be coming to sift through the wreckage for human corpses and clues. Terrorism had not yet been ruled out, except the truck driver had been a hardworking family man with no list of priors. What motivated him to commit this atrocity, drive through a pavementful of pedestrians, was still unknown – we might never know. The death toll now numbered forty, many Saturday shoppers, who had been cut down by the arrival of the petrol tanker, but most of the deaths were of those who had been completely incinerated by the subsequent blast. Several shops and apartments within the vicinity of the catastrophic blaze had either been gutted, reduced to a blackened shell, or totally demolished, razed to the ground.

Heidi made a comment that sent a momentary shiver through me. It was only a quiet observation, mere speculation, but it hit a nerve in me. "It's like the driver just went crazy the moment he drove into Chapel Mead . . . like he got somehow *infected.*"

"Yes, you may be right," I replied in agreement. "Surely, you must *feel* it, having lived here for so long. I've walked through the village so many times now. It's like something's in the air, as though some dark force has pervaded the streets of Chapel Mead and the very fabric of the buildings, and anybody who arrives here from outside and comes into contact with that very evil becomes contaminated down to the soul."

It was at midnight when we decided to turn in for the night. We were still downstairs, about to go up, when we heard the shrill whistle of the kettle. When we checked, the water was somehow on the boil and it had been off the heat all this time – the cooker was still turned off. But we realized it served as a prelude to something else.

The doorbell rang. The sound of the bell was loud and echoey in the dead of night.

Heidi was mystified. "Who could that be? I'm not expecting anybody, certainly not at this hour."

She was about to go to the front door when I grabbed her arm. "No, let me answer it." The radio, which I had muted low, I switched off and I crept anxiously down the hallway. After a moment's hesitation, I opened the front door.

It was dark outside. The electric lamp that should have spotlighted the visitor seemed not to be working, probably fused, so it was impossible to identify the silhouetted figure on the front step. It was not until the August moon came out from behind a bank of clouds and cast its waxy illumination across the land and lit up the features of our midnight caller that I saw it was a man whom I'd never seen before in my life.

He was of medium height and slightly overweight, with a pasty face and a shaved head and a neatly-trimmed goatie. I estimated him to be in his mid-thirties. He was stylishly dressed in an expensive black suit and black, open-collared shirt and shiny, black Oxford shoes, causing him to almost blend in with the night, except for his bald head that seemed to give the impression of having been decapitated. It wasn't so much his black attire or the illusion of his floating head or the fact he wore leather gloves on a sultry summer's night like tonight that bothered me but his eyes, which appeared large and dark and crafty. "Good evening," he greeted me.

"Hello," I replied. "What can I do for you?"

"I have come here to give you a message," he told me.

"At this hour?" I asked querulously.

"There is never a good time to convey this message . . ."

"Okay," I said, "what's this message that cannot wait until the morning?"

"*Submit* . . ." he said simply.

It was that single word that those ladybirds had jotted on the bathroom ceiling. I shuddered. What was the relevance of that word? And how could this man whom I'd never met before possibly know? "Do I know you?"

I heard a gasp from just over my shoulder. I turned. Heidi stood behind me, her face frozen in an expression of disbelief and alarm. "What the hell do you want?" she murmured, addressing the man in the black suit, anger mixed in with apprehension.

The hard lines on the visitor's face softened as his lips curled into a deliciously wicked smile, enhanced by his short beard. "All the better for seeing you, my dear. How I've missed you!" He noticed our wedding rings. "Married, too, I see," he said, amused, "and I didn't even get an invite!"

"Do you know this joker?" I asked Heidi, getting more and more concerned.

"That's Jon Chandler . . ."

I knew who it was. Heidi had mentioned him when we'd been discussing our exes. Jon had briefly dated Heidi before she'd gone out with Ted Trenton. Jon was a used car salesman and a former Jehovah's Witness. He bragged his father was in stocks and shares when his father, in fact, lived in a shitty flat in the Algarve. When Heidi refused Jon sex, he started slagging her off behind her back and going on dates with countless women he'd met online while still going out with her. When Heidi had learned what he was up to, she had dumped all his personal belongings into the street and tearfully informed the congregational elders of his antics. Jon was a bullshitter, gaslighter and manipulator. He had been disfellowshipped for carrying on with a different Witness, a married woman, but rumour had it he was poised to be reinstated because he had expressed repentance, even if he was blatantly lying to the elders' faces. I was glad to have finally clapped eyes on the bastard, even at this ungodly hour.

"I think you better leave . . ." I advised Jon on the doorstep.

His moon-face floated up from above his black suit. "Not yet," he replied, chuckling. "After I've finished with you and, in particular, with *her*!"

I heard his words as a threat, and a distinct fear began to rise through me. "What do you want with us?"

"I have come to claim your *souls*," he told us with a darkly serious tone, "in this, as foretold, the End Times, the Great Tribulation."

"You're just a man . . . a mere *mortal*," Heidi reminded him derisively. "You cannot be capable of collecting souls."

Jon laughed. His black eyes glittered maniacally. "Oh, I'm much, much more. *I am Legion for we are many . . .*"

And that was when I noticed the others. All I had been focused on was this man, who had suddenly appeared at our doorstep dead on midnight, this man with his pale, doughy face hovering above his black garb like a balloon, this man who had once been my wife's former flame, cheating on her with impunity and saying nasty things about her behind her back, causing her unnecessary distress in the short time they were together. This man who presently insinuated he was in league with the Devil, possessed by demons. I did not see the bigger picture until now, looking past Jon's immediate presence into the street behind him. No Four Horsemen in sight, but some of the other inhabitants of Chapel Mead, about twenty or thirty of them, had gathered on the street outside the cottage. The villagers dotted the pavements and the main road, standing still and stiff, watching us with eyes that glowed fiery-red, inhuman. Locked in a deep trance, waiting for something to happen. We were faced with a plague of devils threatening a potential siege, a home invasion.

Whatever slow, insidious evil had taken over the village was now gathering momentum, each manifestation more disturbing than the previous: the indefinable unease we had felt in the lead-up to today, the ladybirds coordinating a message on the ceiling, the priest holding sex orgies in the church and sacrificing a baby in the font, the husband who murdered his entire family with a pencil through the eye, the mad driver of the runaway juggernaut rampaging through the village centre in broad daylight, indiscriminately massacring the public. And now this, the midnight presence of these possessed, lantern-eyed villagers. Our dreams had been visions from another time, warning us of future events. Midnight was when reality was flimsiest, allowing Hell's dimension to spill into our world. And the Devil would take any shape to pull you in, deceive you, before messing with your head.

There are no ghosts, no spirits of the dead, Heidi had once said. *There are only demons.* And Jon had converted the villagers into his minions. He signalled to them and they began to shamble towards the cottage, their burning eyes like tiny, fiery beacons in the moon-soaked darkness of the street.

An icy chill radiated through the highways and byways of my skeleton. The best I could muster was to importune weakly: "Go away!"

Again, Jon burst into cackles of laughter. "Or else?" He grinned a devil's grin before the grin faded and he shoved me violently in the chest. I was catapulted backwards down the hallway by a disproportionate amount of force, as though someone had strapped a huge piece of elastic around me and stretched it to its limits and let go. Except I did not slam into the living-room wall. My flight was abruptly halted in the middle of the room and I was hoisted up by invisible ropes and turned upside down, my head several inches from the ground, defying gravity. My arms were flung outwards, giving me the overall shape of an inverted cross – the Devil's symbol.

The spatial dimensions of the room changed, expanding and contracting, the walls wavering in and out of sight. The floor was no longer made of solid stuff anymore. A rift appeared in the suddenly-malleable stone floor. Hell opened up. I could see the molten hellfires below, feel the terrible heat, smell the eye-watering acridity of brimstone.

Heidi pelted down the hallway, followed me into the living room. She gasped in horror at the sight of me being hung perpendicularly, the wrong way up, my arms outstretched and held horizontal over a fiery, impossible rip in reality.

"To hurt or to heal, to give and take," Jon said, moving down the hallway. He seemed to grow taller with each step, his progress causing the lights in the house to explode. He wandered into the living room. His eyes glowed like a candlelit Halloween pumpkin. "Taze, Rutherford, the Governing Body – all the same, as corrupt as a tent revival preacher or television evangelist, crooked as a dog's hind leg, constantly abusing their leadership and subjugating their own people. The humble servants foot the bill so their leaders can live in the lap of luxury. Your Governing Body is no different from the politicians and the bankers and other organized religions of the world in exploiting your fear of God in order to keep themselves in the position of power they are accustomed to. Every religious organization serving the Abrahamic God is *compromised*. Once reinstated, I too will begin my work to corrupt and completely dismantle your Jehovah's Witness faith from within. Not that I need to do much work, considering those at the top of the hierarchy are doing a fine job of delivering the Devil's manifesto, anyway. Satan claims dominion over mankind. The aristocracies of hell reign over this world, remade in Satan's image." He addressed Heidi. "Do you like being a Witness? A member of an apocalyptic cult? A party-crasher nobody wants to hear or associate with. Coming back again and again with supposed insider knowledge about the future, about everybody's doom."

"Look where we're at, now?" Heidi reminded him. "The earth doesn't belong to Satan. It's always belonged to Jehovah." Her expression told me she wanted to waltz off in high dudgeon, but I could not escape the fear in her eyes, fear for my safety and fear of the demonic being her ex- had become.

"Better to reign in hell than serve in heaven," Jon enunciated, and he grabbed Heidi by the arms, bringing his face close up to hers.

"Leave my wife alone!" I yelled at him, unafraid even from my present vulnerable position. The fires of Hell reached up from below me. The perspiration poured down from me in bucketfuls.

"You should be more concerned with what I'm going to do to you . . ." he said menacingly, then leaned in close to a paralysed Heidi . . . a long, forked tongue, impossibly big for his mouth, extended outwards and licked her left cheek...Then, the tongue snapped back into the demon's mouth as he stepped back, letting her go. "Tastes like wild strawberries." He grinned hideously at Heidi. "Oh, how I do enjoy befouling other men's wives! More of that later, darling!"

Heidi grimaced disgustedly, wiping the dribble of carrion-smelling drool from her cheek. She was shaking. She glanced at me. "Your destiny, your purpose..." she whispered to me.

Jon had violated my wife and I was furious. He had demonstrated every vile quality associated with Satan: arrogance, pride, desire, lust, cruelty. But now was the time to set things in motion. "Is the Devil so fucking stupid he doesn't know he's destined to lose?"

The grin was gone. I had humiliated Satan. Jon fixed me with molten eyes as hot and incandescent as the hellbound furnace waiting to swallow me up. "Do not *anger* me! Or you shall experience such pain and suffering the likes of which you've never seen before!"

I answered my own rhetorical question. "The reason the Devil doesn't acknowledge his long-since prophesied defeat is because he can't see beyond his own intense, concentrated evil, and it is his absolute corruption that is his blindspot, his shortcoming and his ultimate downfall . . ."

"If you believe in God, now's the time to start saying your prayers," Jon threatened me, piercing me with a gaze of hellish fury. He removed his leather gloves to reveal claws. His hand went directly over my ribs, his foul, sulphurous breath in my face. "You have no hope in hell."

I felt him begin to squeeze my heart from outside my chest. Upside-down, unable to move, trapped in the blazing, sweat-filled dark of the room, I held my ground against his threats, his posturing. "There's something I know that you don't . . .." I thought of Saint Augustine of Hippo. "*It was pride that changed angels to devils; it is humility that makes men as angels.*"

Heidi recited Hebrews 1:14. "*Are not all angels ministering spirits sent to serve those who will inherit salvation . . .?*"

Jon ramped up the pressure on my heart, and I pushed against the pain, the very real probability of my heart imploding. It seemed I was to be tortured and corrupted before being sentenced and condemned to Hell. "When you're stuck in a five-mile holdup on the motorway because of some accident somewhere up ahead," Jon humoured me, "don't tell me you've never hoped the driver, whose reckless driving caused the accident, be permanently crippled as a constant reminder of their stupidity, forced never to forget their mistake for the rest of their life, or better still, end up dead, so they will never have to drive again!"

I continued with a stuttery wheeze, hoping our fortitude would save us: "In the name of all that is good and pure on this green earth and the vaulted heavens above..."

I never thought it would happen, what I had in my mind would translate into real life. But it did.

Belief. It was all about belief.

It happened in an instant. A *miracle.* They came down from Heaven, teleporting into the living room from above, like creatures of fantasy from some mythological realm. They gradually resolved into a distinct image. Faceless celestial beings in clear humanoid shapes, neither transparent nor solid, but composed completely of bright, white light, a trailing radiance. The pure, immaculate energy of the two angels was powerful enough to illuminate the entire cottage, lighting up even the tiniest cracks in the wall, without completely blinding the onlookers. Heidi and I received their angelic protection that filled us with a sense of peace and serenity. The vast, ethereal light from the two beautiful, dazzling forms neutralized and banished the pervasive darkness and caused Jon to growl, scream, shrink, cower in terror, his fury drowned by the Holy Power. He was forced to retreat down the hallway, a bested thing, in the wake of his dying scream. We never saw him again. His evil influence was no more, either. The possessed villagers, too, were gone, probably returning to their respective houses, the memory of tonight erased from their minds. One moment, my heart was being crushed by diabolical, psychic forces, a split-second later the chest pain ceased, and I was on the floor, a free man. Even the fiery rip I was meant to fall into had disappeared. I felt physical relief. The angels abruptly vanished, ascending to their upperworldly realm after their flying visit, and the candles on the dining table came back to life.

I got up and held Heidi, my hands over her, her mouth on mine. My entire life had led up to this very moment, the reason why Heidi had sought me out. She had always known. Together, we had the power to summon angels.

"I would have died for you," she whispered to me as a reminder of her utmost affection.

"Wild horses won't keep me away," I promised her, thinking back to the song the radio had been playing earlier, Dean & Britta's cover of *I Deserve It*. I quoted Herman Hesse. "*If I know what love is, it is because of you.*"

We maintained our embrace and kissed again.

We had survived our hellish ordeal by divine intervention. It brought us even closer together. It provided us with a brand new dawn on our life together and gave us a brief glimpse of the chaos and carnage that might yet devastate the earth, for in the words of the German writer, Heinrich Heine: *Wild, dark times are rumbling toward us, and the prophet who wishes to write a new apocalypse will have to invent entirely new beasts, and beasts so terrible that the ancient animal symbols of St. John will seem like cooing doves and cupids in comparison.*

I did not know if it would happen in our lifetime, but neither Heidi nor me would face it unprepared.

3

The world that we knew did not end in the summer of 2012. But, in Chapel Mead, it came damned close. That summer, false prophecy or otherwise, restored my faith in God and the Heavenly Host. Just as the Devil came to Chapel Mead, there were reports of similar visitations around the world, from Sydney to New York, from Paris to Cape Town. We'd been touched by that mysterious hand behind all things, received a blessing of divine grace. You'd think that after what I'd witnessed and endured in that single tick of Heaven's cosmic clock, I'd have immediately converted to the Jehovah's Witness faith, being a non-practising Catholic with the same difficult upbringing and measure of guilt as any Witness.

Not a chance.

Returning to her faith was not a pleasant picnic in the park for Heidi, particularly with what she had experienced, with what she knew. Heidi was promptly disfellowshipped – *surprise, surprise!* – when she discussed her ordeal and disputed some of the false doctrines of her faith. *What gives the Governing Body the right to pass themselves off as anointed?* she challenged her congregational elders. *Only Jehovah knows.*

But there was no room for dissent. She was accused of being an apostate, a recreant, and promptly expelled.

Goes to show what the Truth really is.

Welcome to the first day of the rest of your life, my darling. I told Heidi supportively.

Rejecting her religion didn't prove to be a particularly difficult decision. She never looked back.

There is life after *The Watchtower*, after all, as many have found out. Heidi is one of them. She took the first fearful steps of leaving the religion and found Jesus. Once she had overcome her intellectual struggle with cognitive dissonance and tasted the exhilarating freedom, she never considered choosing the Witness life again. And she was better for it. *The Watchtower* would make you believe that those who leave will become miserable failures, addicted to drugs and suicidal – which, of course, is nothing but propaganda. For many, many ex-Witnesses go on to lead happy, more fulfilling lives than when they were under the Orwellian control of the Watch Tower Society. To a devoted Jehovah's Witness, the world must seem a very dark and terrifying place. Life is not an opportunity to explore the world but a test, and the earth a battlefield where a war against the demonic forces of Satan wages that will end in a global genocide of the supposedly righteous and persecuted minority of the Jehovah's Witness faith. 'Worldly' people allegedly want nothing more than to drag Jehovah's Witnesses into lives of 'sin' so that they, too, will die when Armageddon arrives. Anybody not following the Truth is lost, confused and doomed to die. The Watch Tower Society says evolution is a lie, science is a lie, other religions and philosophies are founded upon lies, meditation opens your mind up to demonic possession and the Buddha is a false prophet.

But Heidi did not feel evil when she left her faith. What felt evil was the way the judicial committee enabled a thousand crimes, such as calling the little girl her father molested a 'liar' when she came forward, because there wasn't a second witness to corroborate her claim. What felt evil was how so many Witnesses lied, cheated and fornicated while many 'worldly' people were very nice people, and the

Governing Body legislated and propagated the irreconcilable idea that God would kill the worldly ones and spare the Witnesses simply because they're Witnesses, with the Governing Body giving themselves a free ticket to Heaven. What felt evil was how the Witness ideology discouraged education, personal improvement or any sort of future security. What felt evil was *The Watchtower*'s strict shunning policy for instructing entire families to betray and isolate their disfellowshipped family member until they returned to the religion while, at the same time, describing the kindness and humanity that exists in the world around them as part of 'Satan's plan'. What is evil is how *The Watchtower* will depart from the truth to support its own doctrine, that it is a religion that uses coercive persuasion to manipulate and control its members, enslaving them through fear and guilt and lies. What felt evil is how, like the Israeli government cries 'Antisemitism!' when someone challenges its massacre of the Palestinians or much in the same way as Queen Athaliah cried 'Conspiracy!' when confronted with the facts of her falsehood, the Governing Body is quick to cry 'Apostasy!' when anybody dares challenge its authority, a diversionary tactic intended to make the other person seem wicked, mentally infirm and unworthy of life. What is evil is how Jehovah's Witnesses claim to be God's only spirit-directed organization on earth today and that nobody can come to God and receive salvation in the grace of Jesus except through them as God's chosen representatives, while failing as shepherds to protect the herd by superimposing themselves between us and God or ever displaying the love that Jesus said would characterize his people. What felt equally evil is the smugness and sense of superiority they exhibited over others with a belief they're better than everybody else, the unchristian, unloving and hypocritical way the Witness faith persecuted the Church, preaching judgement instead of grace, mercy and salvation. The Governing Body was utterly immoral and evil in claiming that it was *more chosen than others* and, as the chosen few, it could do whatever the hell it wanted. We all know that anybody who insists they have the power to get you to Heaven if you do whatever they say is *lying*.

I can't believe I wasted my loyalty on these snakes who will stab you in the back the moment you question their motives, Heidi espoused under advisement, once I'd distilled the dark untruths about the Truth. *The so-called new system is a myth! What my people accepted as the Truth is nothing but a lie! Do not believe the Truth!*

As with any cult, I reminded her, *the power of indoctrination does not make it truth.*

Those poor souls, Heidi said sympathetically, *locked in* The Watchtower, *living not in the Truth but a wholesale deception perpetuated by the Governing Body speaking with a devil's tongue of danger and ruin, deliberately keeping its flock ignorant so nobody may ever learn the* real *truth and choose a better life, one that is more spiritually fulfilling and free of its suffocating influence.*

Heidi made the audacious claim that those who leave the religion are the ones actually shunning the congregation of Jehovah's Witnesses, leaving the false god of *The Watchtower* in search of deliverance from the true God and experiencing the supernatural, life-transforming power of Jesus Christ's forgiveness and salvation – for he is the Truth and the Life and the Way. We enjoyed a close, personal relationship with Jesus, shared a covenant with God, free of interference from any JWs.

I will never forget that spotty teenager, who felt God in that French cathedral all those years ago and now I can make good on my promise. The Bible may say that nobody can see God and live. But you don't need to be physically saved by angels to see His handiwork, in the world around us, in ourselves. It is God who gave us an intelligent, rational brain. We need to tread carefully against those who preach religious intolerance and create God in their own image and tell others that a different creator, perhaps a satanic creator, made them. A wise rabbi once said that religion becomes a threat to democracy if we turn our religion into idolatry. It is essential that we broaden our communities through inclusion. For churches, synagogues, mosques and temples must never close their doors on others.

Despite its corrupt origins to its ongoing contentious practices, most practitioners of the Witness and Catholic faiths are good people, albeit somewhat misled and closed-minded. I do not claim to know the mind of God. But, looking at it from a purely logical and sensible standpoint, using that rational mind He endowed us with, any sane, benevolent god would reward all those people who have observed their faith closely, no matter what religion they hail from, even Scientologists or atheists who've chosen to live by a moral code.

Don't you think that's fair?

August 2012 – February 2013

Indescription II:
Caerdroia on the Hill

"I have been a word among letters,
I have been a book in the origin."
Cad Goddeu (circa 550 AD)
Taliesin

Ten Roses: A perfect ten to represent the perfect love.

The black Range Rover sped through the Welsh valleys, very much alone on the country roads. It was late August and it seemed summer had no intention of letting up. The noonday sun blazed down over the green, verdant vales, floral-rich meadows and sleepy hollows, the sky a beautiful laundry-blue and completely free of any wisps of cloud.

Windows rolled down, the cooling air-conditioning on full blast, the two occupants of the car still sweated against the oppressive heat. "I thought Wales was supposed to be a place of incessant rain," commented Helwyn Dwyer, glancing over at his companion while trying to keep the vehicle within the national speed limit.

"Be thankful the weather's favourable," Stacey Davenport replied from the passenger seat, looking through the window as the world outside whizzed by. They meandered the small roads of Wales, nose to the wind. Stacey's gaze was drawn to the flowering hedgerows and groves of trees as she contemplated the little details of the landscape: the soft, inviting shadows of the glades, the definition of the colours, the swaying grass, a sense of calmness as though the land knew its own striking beauty, its own enchanting greatness. "Enjoy it while it lasts."

Helwyn realized they hadn't passed a single car for miles, feeling his own sense of loneliness take a stronger hold. "Surely, there must be other people who live around here, shouldn't there be?"

"What do you call that?" asked Stacey, pointing to a single-storey dwelling amidst the ploughed fields, possibly a farmhouse, sunlight glinting from its many windows. In the fields yonder gaped the dark mouth of a barn as a combine harvester stood lifelessly next to it. Further behind loomed a lofty grain silo. "Remember, it *is* Sunday."

"I guess you're right," agreed Helwyn. "When you're used to life in the big city, everywhere else must seem as deserted as a ghost town."

"Must be odd, returning to where you were born and raised," observed Stacey. "I can't imagine the apprehension."

"You know that's the funny thing," stated Helwyn, thoughtful for a moment. "I can't remember any of my childhood. I can't recall ever growing up, let alone in Wales. But I must have, at some point, lived here. I must have had family once. Otherwise, why would my uncle track me down to London and write to me, requesting I visit?"

"Maybe this is what you need to stir up some of those dormant memories."

"I suppose this'll be the ideal chance to get back to my roots, reconnect with whatever family I have left."

"And you could introduce me to your relatives as your esteemed ladyfriend," said Stacey with a seductive smile.

Helwyn glanced at her again. Stacey was certainly beautiful, clad in that short, sleeveless red dress . . . and definitely intelligent, despite the countless unkind jokes about blonds. Whereas he was a writer of weird fiction, his latest book, *My Immortal Daemon*, hitting the bestseller list, Stacey was an investigative journalist with *The Tribune*. He'd heard about her long before he'd even met her, having read her newspaper article on John Humphrys, a stalwart as greatly respected and outspoken as Sir David Frost. She had only met Helwyn in person recently when she had interviewed him at his Muswell Hill home over his new book and the dangerous impact it had on certain readers. There had been instant chemistry between them, and Helwyn had asked Stacey out to dinner. Their first date went extraordinarily well, and sparks flew in the bedroom. Later informing her he had received a letter from an uncle he didn't know he had, Helwyn was pleasantly surprised when Stacey invited herself along on the drive down to Caerdroia in the Brecon Beacons. She explained she could kill two birds with one stone: meet his family in a country she had not visited since a school field trip to Borth and investigate media reports of the disappearance of people around the Caerdroia area. His was more on par with a traditional vacation, hers was a busman's holiday in many respects. Motives aside, he believed they were perfect for each other, both emotionally and intellectually. Moreover, he thought he might actually be developing certain feelings for her. And, without sounding presumptuous, he hoped Stacey felt the same. After all, he thought it can't exactly be a bad thing going out with a successful author. "My fair lady, it would be an honour."

Stacey leaned across and pecked him affectionately on the cheek which he greatly appreciated.

They continued to cruise at a steady sixty deep in the heart of the Welsh countryside. They encountered more farmhouses, more tracts of arable land and crossed a bridge over a brook, its crystal-clear waters sparkling silver under the hot glare of the sun.

Helwyn kept the mood light and playful. Not without a trace of mischief, he said: "You must know about the public perception of the Welsh?"

"Sex with a miner?" remarked Stacey, catching the knowingness in his tone. "Rugger bugger?"

Further along, they passed a field of grazing sheep, looking undeniably hot and bothered.

"Ram-raiding?" she added with metaphorical license, and both of them cracked up laughing. On the car radio, Shirley Bassey had given way to Catatonia's allusions to *Mulder and Scully*. "At least they're not playing Tom Jones every fifteen minutes, as I was forewarned."

Helwyn found it particularly odd that their destination wasn't listed on any of the standard Ordnance Survey maps. Nor was the route signposted along the way. Even the Tomtom wasn't much help, either. One might have been forgiven for thinking the place never existed. Helwyn was forced to rely solely on the directions his uncle had sent him. Then, just when he thought of telling Stacey they might actually be lost, the road mounted a rise and, as they reached the crest, the village hoved into view, nestled in the picturesque valley like a precious gemstone in an exotic dancer's navel. He spied the peaked church spire rising above the cluster of gambrel rooftops and chimney stacks. The village was mostly surrounded by pleasant rolling fields with woods visible towards the west and hills to the north. "That must be Caerdroia," he announced with some relief.

"You're an absolute star," said Stacey gratefully. "Leave the navigation to me and we'd probably have ended up driving around for miles."

"That's why men are the better drivers," he humoured.

She punched him playfully on the arm. "Sexist pig!" she said, as if he'd hurt her feminist sensibilities.

"Burnt some bras lately?" he replied, amused. "There's no call for violence."

"Then don't make me, honey bear. Or you'll get more of the same."

"Oh, darling dearest, I love it when you lose your rag . . ."

They continued their mock argument driving down the gentle slope. Helwyn slowed down the Range Rover as they entered Caerdroia.

As they crawled through the cobbled streets, the visitors formed their initial impressions of the village. Most of the houses were slate-grey and terraced, each sufficiently roomy to support a large growing family, unlike most of today's urban housing. The few, more familiar semi-detached residences and bungalows dotted here and there seemed curiously out of keeping with the prevailing old-world charm. Of the small number of locals out and about, there was nothing to distinguish them physically from other village folk anywhere in the country: men walking their dogs, women gossiping with their neighbours, children playing pitch-and-toss. All abruptly stopped what they were doing to watch the Range Rover pass by, probably wondering who these strangers invading their tiny haven might be. For, in the opinion of the two occupants of the Range Rover, Caerdroia *was* a haven, a peaceful rural idyll in a quiet corner of Wales.

Soon the Range Rover approached the village green, and Helwyn eased the vehicle into an empty parking slot. Helwyn clambered out of the Range Rover, followed by Stacey, and went to the back of the vehicle and lifted out their separate suitcases from the boot. They glanced around the village green with its wooden benches, breathing in the fresh country air with relish. The post office, fish-and-chips shop, working man's cafe, butcher's, embroidery centre and hardware store were all closed for business. It seemed even the newsagent's shut at noon on the sabbath. On the opposite side of the village square stood the small municipal building, a blue lantern with the legend POLICE above the narrower of the two entrances, a bicycle chained to the railings outside, as well as offering a second set of doors this time to the administrative offices, with an independent solicitor's firm situated on the first floor. Next door, a townhouse had been converted into a lone-practice GP surgery. Diagonally across was a mock-Tudor inn called THE HANGMAN, the kind of macabre name for a pub, Helwyn expected, one would only find in remotest Wales.

The most impressive piece of architecture, by far, should have been the church the pair of travellers had spotted from the distance, sufficiently capacious to accommodate all the villagers at any given service, fashionably gothic with its own flock of winged gargoyles perched along its walls, its spire pointing proudly up to the heavens. Yet, what was immediately obvious was those very walls were composed entirely of dark granite, giving the church a distinctly sinister feel. Less a house of grace and worship than a place people would be afraid to enter. Even more perturbing were the arched, stained-glass windows: no haloed angels or Christ on the Cross, but hordes of nameless demons crawling up from the bottomless pit. Overall, different, if not downright weird.

Fascinated, Helwyn walked up to the church steps and inspected the programme schedule. Stacey joined him. "Church of Annwn," he read aloud.

"Must be an off-shoot of the Church of Wales," Stacey speculated.

"I seriously doubt it," Helwyn said skeptically. "Go anywhere out in the sticks and, more often than not, you'll find the natives hold strange beliefs. Remember, I write about this kind of stuff all the time." He tried checking the worship times and discovered to his disappointment a sign plastered across the schedule board, informing the public that the church was currently closed for renovation. And, this, just when he had been hoping to sample one of their unique backwaters' evening services . . .

"Admiring our little church?" came a deep, throaty, Welsh-inflected voice from over their shoulders, causing both of them to jump simultaneously. "Magnificent, isn't it?"

Standing behind them was a tall, gangling man, a towering six-foot-four, dressed in a white, open-collared shirt, brown cardigan and grey trousers. Despite his snow-white hair and crow's feet, he didn't look a day over fifty.

"Hello, I'm–" began Helwyn, thrusting out his hand in greeting.

"–Helwyn, I know," said the tall old man, shaking it. "*Prynhawn da.*" *Good afternoon.*

"And you are . . .?"

"You don't recognize me?" the old man said, looking a little hurt.

Helwyn took a wild stab in the dark. "Chetwyn? Chetwyn Dwyer?"

"Call me Uncle Chet . . ."

"Your uncle?" said Stacey, glancing from one man to the other. "I can see the family resemblance."

"And who might this delightful creature be?" inquired Uncle Chet, with a look of mild admiration.

Helwyn introduced his companion. "This is my esteemed ladyfriend, Stacey.

She's a journalist."

"Hi," piped Stacey.

"The pleasure is all mine," Uncle Chet said, kissing her hand chivalrously.

"What's the deal with the church?" Helwyn asked, curiosity getting the better of him. "Who or *what* is Annwn?"

"A place we hold very dear to our hearts," explained Uncle Chet. "Annwn is our name for the Otherworld of Welsh legend, a place of departed souls, ruled by the god Gwynn ap Nudd who appointed Arawn as King and Keeper of the Afterlife. Arawn drew up the laws governing the dead and recorded them in an endless ledger we now universally refer to as *Yr Annisgrifiadol* or, as it roughly translates: *The Indescription*."

The Indescription, marvelled Helwyn. *Could happen only in Wales. As much a crazy title for a holy book as all those confusing Welsh place-names.* "Doesn't sound very Christian."

"We don't complain. Arawn manages to fulfil our spiritual needs. Our pagan prophet is as well-respected as any Christian god around these parts. We follow a tight moral code without proscribing to Christian values."

Helwyn could not fault the veracity of Uncle Chet's argument. A principled, boundaried thing, morality ultimately stemmed from within the individual and did not necessarily need to be dictated by religious dogma. Scientists and atheists were a case in point. If the people of Caerdroia were sufficiently rewarded by putting their faith and trust in this Arawn character, then, by all means, good luck to them! "As the old adage goes: if it ain't broke, why fix it?"

"I ought to introduce you to the rest of the locals," said Uncle Chet with a more affable air. "They'll be gathered in the inn." He left the dark-stoned church behind him and began walking across the village green, trailed by Helwyn and Stacey. "No telephone call, no letter?"

"I tried ringing a few times," Helwyn said, rather apologetically, "but I couldn't get through. All I received was static and hissing and faint voices whispering in a strange foreign language."

"The telephone lines are always playing up," said Uncle Chet. "Never mind, though. The important thing is you made it, with the loveliest of girls in tow. You've got quite a lot of catching up to do."

They approached THE HANGMAN and Helwyn noticed the painted sign. It showed a man, hanging from a tree by a noose, twisting slowly in the wind.

"Queer name for a pub. Must have an interesting history."

"The name harks back to an age when the English tried to anglicize our lands. Our druids were persecuted and hanged, and witches burned at the stake. But we refused to bow down to the yoke of the English oppressors. The inn, like our church, is our connection to the past."

"I see nothing wrong with preserving heritage and custom," mused Helwyn. "From the letter you sent me, I understand you own the place."

"Yes, it's been in our family for six generations," Uncle Chet said with pride. "Best pub in Wales. Some day it will belong to you." He led them through the door, out of the bright sunlight. *"Helwyn, meet your people . . ."*

And, as they entered the inn, heads turned in their direction and all conversation stopped. The patrons – and there were an awful lot of them – stared unnervingly at the two newcomers.

"Everybody," announced Uncle Chet in proper, oratorical fashion, "this is the long-lost nephew I've been telling you about . . . Helwyn Dwyer!"

Helwyn dumped his luggage on the floor and raised his hand in awkward greeting. "Hello, everyone . . ."

Their reaction was instantaneous. Nearly all the pub-goers got up and thronged boisterously around him, eager to meet him.

With Uncle Chet mediating some of the introductions, Helwyn suddenly felt like a celebrity, which in many respects he already was.

"We've all been expecting you," said Geraint Davies the Newsagent.

"Helwyn, good to finally meet you," said Lustig the Country Doctor. "The long wait is over."

"Let me shake the hand of the man who wrote *My Immortal Daemon*," said Evan Carew the Solicitor.

"You read my book?" said Helwyn, surprised his work was known even in the boondocks.

"Of course. You're one of our greatest heroes."

Old Ephraim Jones the Schoolmaster joined in the greetings, with a contented look of nostalgia. "I can still picture you as a child. Never missed a day of school. A worthy scholar, conscientious and intelligent, always writing stories."

"Shame, but I don't recall much of my youth."

"A lot of people don't. Don't worry, we'll help you remember. Soon it will all come flooding back."

Helwyn continued to exchange platitudes and pleasantries, as best he could under the circumstances. Stacey hardly got a look-in, and if she did, it was more akin to a lewd once-over that made her feel underdressed and uncomfortable.

Uncle Chet intervened when he saw Helwyn was on the verge of being inundated. "Give my nephew some air. You'll get a chance to speak with him later. As your landlord, I advise you let him be and get back to your drinks because your drinks won't finish by themselves."

The patrons disbanded and slowly returned to their tables, in lively conversation.

"Thank you for that," said Helwyn, getting a flashback of a recent book-signing. "Uncle Chet, you're a lifesaver. I didn't expect such an enthusiastic reception. I'm deeply moved."

"You may not think so, but you're one of us. We believe firmly in family and neighbourliness. You will never be short of a friend here."

Uncle Chet took the visitors to the plump, middle-aged woman wearing horn-rimmed spectacles and an orange sundress, standing behind the bar. He introduced her as Aunty Myfanwy.

"Oh, Helwyn, you've come back to us after all these years," she said, beaming maternally. She leaned forward and kissed him on both cheeks. "We've certainly missed you." She looked inquisitively and somewhat suspiciously at Stacey. "Is this your wife?"

"Ladyfriend," corrected Helwyn.

"Pardon my ignorance, my dear," said Aunty Myfanwy and placed a big wet smacker on her cheek, too. "Any friend of Helwyn's – particularly one so pretty – is a friend of mine. We must get to know each other."

"What'll it be?" asked Uncle Chet, stepping behind the bar.

"I'm parched," said Helwyn, licking his lips.

"I'll have what you're having," added Stacey.

"Two flagons of your finest ale, please."

Uncle Chet laughed. "This is the twenty-first century, not medieval Britain. We normally measure in pints."

But the pint glasses turned out to be tankards made from polished pewter. As quaint as the inn itself, thought Helwyn, decidedly impressed. Whereas most modern pubs he was accustomed to were often part of a franchise and strove to imitate the bland European model, forever driven by market forces, THE HANGMAN, despite its perturbing name, was your traditional, stand-alone rural drinking establishment, untouched by time, cultivating a wholesome family atmosphere and a strong sense of community. Not a spit-and-sawdust den, either, but a homely place where good, honest, salt-of-the-earth folk could get together after a hard day's toil and make merry. Therein lay its vast appeal. These so-called country pubs were a dying breed with, sadly, only a few of them left in this day and age. Looking around at the animated, bucolic Welsh faces happily drinking and chatting and laughing in pleasant company caused Helwyn to imagine he'd somehow been transported to another time, to an olden and simpler time. The ceiling was low and uneven, the rafters supported by solid oak beams and the lattice-windows thrown wide open to admit some much-needed fresh air to combat the sweltering heat.

"Nice drop of ale you got," declared Helwyn, sipping from his tankard. Stacey nodded in sound agreement.

Their approval produced a genuine smile on Uncle Chet's face. "There are some people who are keen to meet you," he said, lifting the counter and coming out from behind the bar. He led the couple past the islands of seated locals, lost in their banter and laughter, to a table in the far corner of the lounge. Seated at the table were two men, one tall, scrawny and somewhat elderly with a prominent hooked nose, the other younger with a bushy moustache and dressed in a police uniform.

"This is Ivor Griffith, our resident Justice of the Peace and most influential man in the village," Uncle Chet announced, gesturing to the old man with the beaky nose. He introduced the second, uniformed man. "And this fellow is Bryn Trevent, our one-man village constabulary."

"Helwyn Dwyer, I presume," said Griffith the J.P., putting down the book he had been reading.

"That I do be." Helwyn shook hands with the pair of them. "Can I buy you fellers a drink?"

"That's very generous of you, son," said Judge Griffith warmly. "Tot of whisky for myself, please."

"And a ginger ale for me, thanks," added PC Trevent. "I don't drink on duty."

Uncle Chet went off to fetch the drinks.

Griffith eyed Stacey curiously. "And you are, my dear?"

"Stacey Davenport, Helwyn's esteemed ladyfriend."

"Charmed, I'm sure," said Griffith, adding with a weary sigh: "There's so precious few beautiful women in Caerdroia, it would be an honour to have you as a guest."

"Fascinating picture," pondered Helwyn, surveying the large, gilded painting on the nearby wall. A space had especially been created in front of it where one could stand and admire it. Essentially an oil-on-canvas, it portrayed a sinister character possibly from the Dark Ages, adorned in period thick, black garments and leather, behind whom shuffled ghostly figures with tormented expressions in the swirling mist. The powerful brushstrokes gave it a vigorous intensity – a stark vividness – that should have made it a collector's item. Except the portrait was strangely incomplete, lacking any semblance of a countenance. There was a splash of grey where the subject's face ought to have been. "Who's it supposed to represent?"

"Arawn," said Judge Griffith in a respectful tone.

"As in the King of the Otherworld?" acknowledged Helwyn. It made obvious sense since it was this particular fellow the church-goers believed in and worshipped. He wondered as to its outright facelessness. "Why no face?"

"The artist died before he could finish his masterpiece."

"Call it a work in progress," remarked PC Trevent.

"Whose work is it?" asked Helwyn.

"Jermyn Maddox," Griffith informed him, "a painter worthy of the Welsh dragon."

"Never heard of him."

"Not many people have," said Griffith, a wistful look crossing his features. "An unknown artist to most, but also a great artist, much in the Haston Sant-Cassia mould. Both painted the improbable, although Maddox existed a whole century before Sant-Cassia's more modern but demented interpretations of the arcane. One could therefore claim that Maddox was the original master. He will be missed by all."

Curious, thought Helwyn. Griffith almost acted as if he had met the artist in person. He tried to estimate how old the good Judge might be. "So what kind of law do you practise?" Helwyn asked Griffith, grabbing a stool next to Stacey.

"I was a High Court Judge once upon a time in Cardiff," began Griffith, "dealing mostly with criminal law. Retired now, I'm afraid. I now run the village in a purely unofficial capacity as the senior-most figure, a town elder if you will, settling disputes and offering advice on judicial matters in accordance with our ancient village scrolls. We are a simple farming community, after all."

"Not a bad way to spend your golden years, I suppose," said Helwyn, smiling.

"Not bad, indeed," agreed Griffith. "But enough about me. Tell us about yourself, Helwyn. You're a big-shot writer, I gather."

"Nothing fancy," Helwyn replied modestly. "I write horror. I'm very fortunate it sells. Must earn my bread somehow."

"So the prodigal son has returned. Even if horror fiction is considered a humble genre by many, you're seen as a god, a literary giant. Here, you are as popular as Dylan Thomas."

Hero, giant, prodigal son, god, is that what I am . . .? thought Helwyn, astounded at his extraordinary reputation in these parts. *Or are they exaggerating, dishing out the compliments because I'm a homeboy?* "I must confess I've never read any Dylan Thomas. Closest I got to a Welsh author was Louie Knight and his brand of noir fiction."

"Not to worry," said the Judge, not appearing disappointed. "It's never too late to learn a little Dylan." He showed him the book he had been reading, *Under Milk Wood*. "This is a decent read for starters. Ranks as one of his finest works. Poetry in motion."

Uncle Chet arrived with the drinks and took a seat beside his nephew.

"Feeling cold?" PC Trevent blurted out abruptly.

"Pardon?" said Helwyn, not quite understanding the question.

"The black clothes you're wearing – feeling cold?"

"On the contrary, I'm as hot as hell in this get-up. Poor choice of clothes for this weather, I guess. I don't claim to be a fashionista, but I live by the notion that black is the colour for all seasons."

"You'll fit right in," said Trevent, quickly turning his attention to something else that had been bothering him. "From your accent, you've been in England far too long. Lost your Welshness, I see. No offence intended."

The constable was right. Helwyn spoke perfect estuary English. "None taken."

"Don't worry. Stay with us and you'll soon get it back."

"We can only hope," responded Helwyn politely. The oddness of Trevent's manner amused him. Not exactly a people's person, Helwyn concluded of the police constable. Slightly eccentric.

"And you, Miss Davenport, what do you do?" Griffith inquired.

"Oh, I'm a journalist. Sneak around the neighbourhood, break into houses, do some investigating – you know the usual," Stacey joked.

"Investigating anything in particular?"

"The disappearance of people in this region."

It was as if Stacey had opened a can of worms. For a moment, Griffith and Trevent grew silent, stern, staring at her as though she were some kind of troublemaker. Then Griffith spoke up rather gravely. "You've raised a very sensitive issue. We pride ourselves in the fact that there is practically no crime here. Hence we employ only one police officer. But you're certainly well-informed. This land has a habit of swallowing people up. People have been disappearing from Caerdroia and thereabouts dating as far back as the time of the Roman fort of Caerleon when an entire garrison vanished without a trace. The Viking invaders and the Norman conquerors soon suffered the same fate. Then it was the turn of the English feudal barons trying to impose their laws and taxes on my countrymen. Nothing seems to have changed over the passing centuries, those unfamiliar with these lands falling victim. Runaways, gypsy travellers, hillwalkers, nature enthusiasts, carefree holidaymakers whose camper van is suddenly discovered abandoned in the morning. These borderlands even hide many uncharted cave systems from where potholers never see daylight again. But these disappearances do not necessarily indicate foul play, but something much more profound."

"What do you mean?"

Griffith went on to elaborate. "I am loth to admit Caerdroia, and the outlying towns of Tolwyn and Bracken Hill, lie at a crossroads between our world and the one we believe exists parallel to it. People sometimes get a glimpse into that other world and its eternal inhabitants at the cost of their sanity. Caerdroia could be described as a place where all mystic lines converge, where reality is thin and easy to breach. A fragile, broken place, if you will, where outsiders are apt to vanish."

Stacey didn't know what to say. Was this the best they could come up with? The shuddersomeness of his explanation aside, she considered it downright crazy talk from a man supposedly of silk, of authority, justice and reason. Apply a little deductive reasoning, why don't you? Maybe there wasn't a story here, after all. Her readers would surely laugh her off the page if she ever printed this incredible, superstitious hokum.

Helwyn, however, seemed understandably riveted. "You know I'd like to sample some of your culture and maybe explore some of these mysterious places. I might be able to derive enough inspiration for my next novel."

"That's what we like to hear!" boomed Uncle Chet, slapping Helwyn on the shoulder. "We will make you a Caerdroian, yet!"

Griffith sounded equally pleased. "You've both arrived at a convenient time. It's the day of the Harvest Festival. We celebrate it annually on the last day of August. It's a social event. The whole village gets together to give thanks to Arawn for this year's harvest."

"Look forward to it," said Helwyn enthusiastically. He finished off his ale. "I think we should freshen up. It was a four-hour drive from London."

"Take your time. The festivities don't start until four in the afternoon."

Helwyn took another gander round the inn, catching the loud exuberance and sociability of its patrons. The song on the speakers was a cover of *Mama Told Me Not to Come* by the Stereophonics accompanied by of all people, and Stacey's present pet peeve, Tom Jones.

"We will meet again later when we can carry on our conversation," said Griffith pleasantly enough. "Once again, we would like to welcome you both to Caerdroia and hope you enjoy our hospitality."

The infamous incident that caught the public eye and, in particular, piqued Stacey Davenport's interest, occurred several months back. Helwyn had been signing books at an Oxford Street bookstore when one of his so-called male fans lunged over the table and tried to stab him with a letter-opener. Helwyn escaped being seriously wounded, with the blade missing his face by less than an inch. In the ensuing pandemonium, the perpetrator was restrained by store security and escorted away forthwith, but not before frenziedly shouting back at Helwyn: *I can see through your disguise! You're an EVIL man! You must be stopped before you bring about the End of the World!* A little shaken, Helwyn laughed off the incident as nothing more than the paranoid actions and ravings of a mentally-unstable individual. The crazed fan, in fact, turned out to be a religious nut and an End Timer – no surprises there. But his subsequent suicide, from hanging, whilst in police custody increased media coverage of Helwyn Dwyer and his works and led Stacey to interview him.

Not much could be unearthed about Helwyn's past, which was in many respects mystifying as was his explanation that he didn't remember anything of his formative years. He admitted to getting mixed up in drugs as an adolescent which probably knocked out his memories of the time. He insisted he was now a private person, lacked any interest in consumerism and didn't enjoy the current media attention.

Death concerns me, he had confided, at interview. *It's what I do. Each passing day brings us closer to our grave.*

Of the incident itself, he was circumspect and reflective and sad for his would-be attacker's death, stating the man would have greatly benefited from early psychiatric intervention. Helwyn didn't consider himself a particularly good writer to have affected his assailant in the way he did. He was no Salman Rushdie.

One might have dismissed the incident as a one-off occurrence, except for the fact that over the years at least a dozen people throughout England had committed suicide after reading his books. Helwyn didn't believe he should be cited as the cause. People committed suicide all the time, for whatever reason. It was unfair to lay the blame directly at his door when these people were probably unhinged to begin with. It was like accusing violence on TV as being the root cause of violence in society – highly dubious. He doubted his readers had suffered mental trauma from his writings. After all, the themes of the stories he gravitated towards weren't anything special or original. Fantastical tales of Monsters from Beyond awoken from their Eternal Sleep by dark underground cults in order to reclaim the world they had once ruled. In an age when the Japanese were obsessed with angry, vengeful ghosts, the Norwegians Nazi zombies and the Americans psycho-slasher trash, Helwyn's take on the horror genre seemed strangely retro, archaic, *eldritch*.

Still, the whole thing was proving great for publicity. His books now sold – *really* sold. For the first time ever, his books were on the bestseller list and becoming a worldwide sensation. His latest work, *My Immortal Daemon*, the story of a writer taking his girlfriend along in search of his forgotten past, had been translated into twenty different languages. He'd even made a guest appearance on *The South Bank Show*.

Did Stacey truly believe Helwyn's enormous success heralded the End of the World? She didn't think so, and nor did Melvyn Bragg, for that matter. But, in her enlightened opinion, Helwyn was a damned better writer than he gave himself credit for. He didn't boast a particularly large body of work, but he had a way with words and, from what little she'd read, the remote settings and his esoteric knowledge, his use of suspense and his descriptions of the impossible, got under your skin and somehow stayed with you long after you'd closed the book. He shouldn't be writing horror, she thought. He ought to be writing serious stuff and maybe taking a stab at the Booker Prize. Lord knows he was good enough.

As a person Helwyn oozed a dark sexuality he seemed oblivious of and which made him all the more attractive. The over-elaborate hair, the designer stubble and the expressive tribal tattoo crawling up his shoulder to the left side of his neck gave him the air of a recycled teenager in search of his dwindling youth. Stacey had slept with him only once and that had been through pure impulse and a desire to satisfy her own curiosity. In all honesty he had proved better between the sheets – passionate and versatile and considerate – than expected, and their one time of intimacy didn't seem sufficient enough, leaving her craving for more. But she decided to slow things down so she could get to *know* the man before embarking on a serious relationship. Lust was all good and well, but not the end-all. She sought to learn more about Helwyn during this trip, which was why she had primarily accepted his invitation to accompany him down to Wales. Since he was currently Flavour of the Month, she could effectively report back to her boss at *The Tribune* with some useful information about the man, the myth and the magic. The investigation she had been tasked with, involving the mysterious disappearances around Caerdroia, already seemed like a non-starter.

"What do you think about the village?" Helwyn asked Stacey.

They were presently unpacking their suitcases in a twin room assigned to them by their avuncular landlord.

"I'm not altogether crazy about the place," said Stacey truthfully. "On the surface, everything appears normal like any other remote country village, plenty of rural charm, but I've got a horrible gut feeling something's not right here."

"How come?"

"They present themselves as an innocent agricultural people with their peculiarities, strange history and eccentric beliefs, but they called you down here for a specific reason, a motive I haven't yet figured out."

"They're supposed to be family."

"There's more to them than meets the eye, believe me. It's like there's a creepy undercurrent to this place that can easily turn into a riptide and pull you under."

"Always the cynic. I promise I won't let you drown."

"I don't like the way the men leer at me!"

"You're an extremely attractive woman, Stace, very desirable. You're bound to get a bit of attention, even a few coarse stares. There's something flattering about being coveted by other men."

Stacey remained indignant. "It's rude and undignified! I feel almost violated! No wonder they have a reputation of doing indelicate things to wild animals! Haven't they ever seen a woman before?"

"Never fear. I shall protect you, my fair damsel, as long as I live."

His reassurance seemed to calm her. She shivered, despite the heat. "Any more and I'm cutting short my holiday and heading back to London."

Helwyn put a consoling arm around her. "Well, I certainly mustn't allow them to scare away the filly."

"Something doesn't smell right," she reiterated, less emphatically this time. However, she could not shake off her sense of foreboding. "I don't trust these people. I just want you to be aware, that's all."

"Point taken. I'll try and keep an open mind."

"And another thing . . . I don't want you to leave my side."

"I won't let you out of my sight, I promise," he replied, kissing her gently on the forehead for good measure. It disturbed him how this place had already produced a massive negative impression on her, almost a sense of loathing, on someone normally regarded as headstrong and fearless and tenacious in journalistic circles. *You don't often hear of an anxious reporter, except, perhaps, one covering a war zone.* Maybe it was because she *was* a woman and because of the sixth sense women were reputed to possess. In any case, he should heed her warning and stay cautious, even if her fears might prove unfounded. "Now this is interesting . . ." he observed, detaching himself from her.

Unlike the huge, enigmatic oil painting downstairs, the pictures around the white walls of the bedchamber were plain charcoal drawings. There were five pictures in all, each framed behind glass, each bearing closer scrutiny. The first sketch was titled *Ysbaddaden* and featured an evil-looking, fairytale giant in hand-to-hand combat with a brave band of Arthurian knights, swords flashing, heads lopped clean off. The eponymous lake monster in the second picture, *Afanc*, was seen to rise up from the dark waters and seize its prey, a luckless naked swimmer, between its crushing jaws. There was also a watery theme to the next drawing, *Cyhyraeth*, as the crew of a sailing ship were inferred to hear a disembodied, moaning pronouncement of doom, accompanied by eerie corpse-lights in the midnight skies, just before their vessel would inevitably crash against the crags below the storm-tossed waves. *Coblynan* showed a coal pit inhabited by little impish knockers, with picks and lamps and miner's hats, deliberately setting off a fatal cave-in down the tunnel. The final piece of art, *Cwn Annwn*, involved a pack of spectral hounds, with glowing eyes and gnashing teeth, in hot pursuit of a uniformed officer of the law, his expression full of desperation and mortal terror, through the woods.

The menacing delivery of these works could not be understated. Each individually captured a different aspect of Celtic mythology, rendered with a raw-edged power to unnerve. Helwyn noticed from the signature at the bottom of each frame that all the charcoal pieces had been created by the same Jermyn Maddox, whose apparent masterpiece hung proudly in the bar. "Do you think such creatures exist?"

"I don't much care for any of them," said Stacey disdainfully. "The people, here, possess some really questionable tastes."

"I know!" exclaimed Helwyn, unable to contain his awe. "We've hit the mother lode! As ringing endorsements go, everything about this place is so marvellously backward! Can you imagine the amount of material unearthed so far I could use? And we haven't even had time to explore the village or its customs, yet! I can feel a book coming on . . ."

"Don't get carried away," warned Stacey, not sharing his boyish excitement. She lifted the curtain-veil and looked out of the window. The church, gargoyled and granite-black, stared back at her ominously from the other side of the village green. She replaced the veil with a momentary shiver. "Remember what you promised me."

"I haven't forgotten, so take it easy."

"I'll take it easy when we're safely back in London."

"Please yourself," sighed Helwyn, beginning to get a little irritated by her uncharacteristic whining. Maybe he'd made a mistake in bringing her along. God, he never expected Stacey, of all people, to be squeamish. "In the meantime, we've got a couple of hours to kill before the Harvest Festival begins." He hopped onto one of the beds, resting supine, folding his hands behind his head. "I'm taking a short nap. Wake me up when it's time."

Stacey decided to join him and, as she lay next to him on the same narrow bed, snuggled up in his arms, she closed her eyes and, listening to his soft contented snores, tried to get some shuteye.

But she could not sleep.

By the time four o'clock came around, Helwyn felt refreshed and ready for anything. Stacey, on the other hand, looked tired and distinctly worse for wear. He sprayed on his best cologne while she adjusted her appearance with a little last-minute makeup. Neither spoke.

Uncle Chet met them downstairs. He had changed into a black suit and tie and reminded Helwyn of a country squire. The pub was eerily quiet and deserted.

"All set?" Uncle Chet asked expectantly.

"Groomed, presentable and rearing to go," replied Helwyn eagerly.

Stacey merely offered them a wan smile.

Aunty Myfanwy appeared from behind the counter with a hamper. She wore the same orange sundress, but her spectacles were gone. She appraised the two newcomers without any obvious visual impairment and spoke with her usual maternal warmth. "Why, if it isn't the two lovebirds . . .!" She seemed particularly interested in Stacey. "Hello, my dear, now that you're courting a member of the Dwyer clan, ever thought of getting pregnant?"

Uncle Chet laughed. "Myfanwy, please! What kind of question is that? They just arrived!"

"I didn't mean to embarrass our guests," Aunty Myfanwy responded defensively. "It's just that we could use some new blood around here."

"Thank you for your blessing, Aunty Myfanwy," Helwyn interjected, unruffled. "Stacey and I have only just started dating. We both have very time-consuming careers that keep us mostly apart. Babies and the suchlike are a major commitment and can only be a consideration in the somewhat distant future, that's if we're still together." He put his arm round Stacey and squeezed her shoulder affectionately. Stacey smiled again, fraudulently.

"Oh, well, at least I tried," Aunty Myfanwy conceded.

Uncle Chet gestured to the door with the open palm of his hand and a gracious bow of his head. "Shall we . . .?"

They stepped out of THE HANGMAN to be blasted by the shimmering afternoon heat. They joined the procession of villagers, who were carrying picnic baskets of their own and waving banners with such throwaway slogans as YASBADDADEN LIVES, DOWN WITH NODENS and PRAISE BE TO ARAWN FOR HE SHALT RETURNETH. Dressed colourfully in summer dresses and open sandals, the women were busy gossiping with their neighbour while keeping their prancing little ones in check. Musical accompaniment was provided by the husky menfolk, most of whom, like Uncle Chet, were suitably attired in their Sunday best, as they sang the national standard-bearer, *Men of Harlech*, in close, deep-vocal harmony through the streets. The view of the dark church caused Stacey to shudder again, and she was soon glad they were leaving the village green well behind. Helwyn soaked up the sun and the carnival atmosphere, the excitement of the villagers, young and old, on this seemingly joyous occasion, infectious and uplifting and almost palpable. Their journey took them out of the village, northbound, towards the hills.

There was much to enjoy apart from the weather. The native wildlife, for instance, which made up an important chunk of the countryside. Foxgloves, snowdrops and primroses grew in rich abundance, their seductive petals attracting the insect population. Honey bees buzzed about, collecting nectar and pollinating the flowerheads during their many travels. Painted ladies and peacock butterflies danced in the air like orchard blossom in spring. Only the hoverfly proved something of a nuisance, urgently demanding to be batted away. Slowworms slid lethargically amongst the sulphur tufts and shaggy inkcaps. It was even possible to spot the occasional common frog hopping in great bounds along the grass, having inadvertently strayed from its natural habitat, the distant western woods of oak, willow and rowan through which a brook sparkled in the glade and where the minks and bank voles lived. Nature documentaries claimed the grey squirrel had displaced its red counterpart and reported that the recent cull of badgers had greatly affected the shape of the ecosystem. Sparrows flocked the cloudless skies in great, whirling numbers.

The last thing Stacey needed on a hot day like this was Aunty Myfanwy's incessant brand of gossip. Aunty Myfanwy turned the wheel of the rumour-mill with consummate ease and she never let Stacey forget it. The advantage of being the landlady of the local pub, she told Stacey, was that she was always kept informed of all the latest goings-on in the village. It wasn't a great secret that Dr. Lustig had a reputation as a ladies' man and was currently helping the Widow Freeman through the grieving process. *She took it exceedingly hard, as the Bishop said to the Actress as she bent over to pick up her swimming costume from the dressing-room floor.* Stacey listened but did not hear, her mind elsewhere.

Uncle Chet continued to regale his nephew with the history of the village. "Caerdroia is the Welsh name for Troy."

"Troy, as in the legendary city the ancient Greeks raided?"

"The very same."

Ephraim Jones, the old schoolmaster, who'd been walking alongside, got involved in the conversation. "Some believe the events chronicled in the Homer epic, surrounding the erection and deployment of the Wooden Horse, actually occurred on Welsh soil thousands of years ago."

As a self-confessed purist, Helwyn found his wild speculation preposterous. "Aren't you reaching just a little too far? It's perfectly acceptable you have your own Welsh myths, based largely on Mabinogion lore, but borrowing tales from other ancient civilizations and calling them your own does rather stretch credibility to breaking point, practically amounts to stealing. You don't actually believe the so-called Trojan War was fought here, on this very land?"

"What if I do?" Ephraim Jones insisted, growing indignant. "Why shouldn't it have taken place here? Pre-Christian Britain seems a good a place as any."

It surprised Helwyn that an experienced schoolmaster like Ephraim Jones could hold a firm conviction to such a ridiculous theory. He wondered if the old man was going senile. "Classics scholars might disagree."

Ephraim Jones' gentle manner was gone. He was clearly on the warpath. "No need to get all English about it!" he snapped.

"I didn't mean to offend your Welsh pride," said Helwyn rather apologetically, taken aback by the angry outburst.

"Just remember, boyo, you're one of *us*!"

Uncle Chet's intervention couldn't have come at a timelier moment. "Gentlemen, *please*! We wouldn't want you both baring your fists and beating the hell out of each other! Let it go!" He drew Helwyn's attention away from the old man and pointed upwards, to the crest of the hill. "What we're particularly proud of, Helwyn, is our caerdroia."

Shielding his eyes from the bright glare of the sun, Helwyn peered up ahead. Sure enough, a long, green, man-made hedge crowned the hill, following its contours in ever-decreasing circles. The villagers were disappearing through its entrance. "I thought a caerdroia was supposed to be a turf maze, not a ten-foot tall labyrinth."

"That's what makes us unique," replied Uncle Chet. "It's been with us since as far back as I can remember."

Up the hill they climbed and soon arrived at the entrance of the caerdroia. The walls were indeed ten-feet high, the foliage thick and impenetrable and manicured with topiary precision. Glastonbury Tor, thought Helwyn, paled in comparison. "What shrub is it composed of?"

"Common hawthorn mostly," Uncle Chet informed him.

"Must take a lot of work to maintain."

"Our professional landscape gardener keeps it in shape. Coppicing is rarely required."

Helwyn paused briefly at the entrance. "Dare we enter at the risk of getting lost?"

"There are no dead ends to speak of, so you cannot get lost. The caerdroia follows a circuitous route round the hill and eventually leads to the centre."

"And what should we expect to find at the centre of the labyrinth?" asked Helwyn, reverting back to Grecan mythology. "A minotaur, perhaps?"

"No such luck," said Uncle Chet with a knowing smile. "But you might be pleasantly surprised."

With keen anticipation, Helwyn followed his uncle and the other villagers into the maze. The walls on either side provided some much-welcome shade from the late afternoon sun. "And what purpose does this caerdroia serve?"

"It's a popular tourist attraction for what few tourists come here, as well as an important sacred site . . . You'll know soon enough . . ."

His last comment, deliberate and cryptic as it was, intrigued Helwyn. The procession of people followed the course of the labyrinth as it repeatedly circled the hill. A quarter-of-an-hour in and, after a heated debate about the floundering fortunes of the Elements Cefn Druids in the League of Wales, they eventually reached the centre and the hilltop proper.

What struck Helwyn immediately about the summit was how predominantly flat and spacious it was, large enough to accommodate over fifty people. Flat, yes, relatively-speaking, apart from the obvious geological feature on the far side of the summit. Formed of solid rock that jutted up from the ground, it harboured the entrance to a cave – natural or man-made, Helwyn couldn't tell. As the rest of the villagers emerged from the caerdroia and gathered on the hilltop, he noticed them taking up positions in the direction of the dark cave with the same reverence as an imam faces Mecca at the time of prayer.

"What's in there?" Helwyn inquired, his curiosity in the highest stratosphere.

"That, in English, is the Well of Lost Souls," Uncle Chet replied solemnly.

Before Helwyn could ask as to its significance, Judge Griffith stepped up to the front of the cave and brought everyone to attention. The hubbub subsided as the villagers sat down on the grass and listened. "Thank you all for coming," announced Judge Griffith. "Today is an important date in our calendar. As you are all aware, it is our *Gwyl y Cynhaeaf*, or Harvest Festival. But what makes it even more doubly special this year is that we have guests, fellow humans who have come from afar to witness this great event. So, please, give a warm, homely welcome to our guests-of-honour, Helwyn Dwyer and Miss Stacey Davenport!"

The villagers clapped and cheered for a good long minute. Helwyn raised his hands in acknowledgement, a hefty grin on his face, genuinely moved by their salutations. Stacey, on the other hand, produced another detached, ungainly smile.

When the applause and whistles finally died down, Judge Griffith continued: "As is customary on this occasion, food and drink first and some light dancing before we hear a few words from our glorious religious leader. Let the celebrations commence . . .!"

The picnic baskets were raided and emptied of their contents. Aunty Myfanwy unhooked the lid of the hamper basket and produced some fancy plates and cutlery which she passed around. She popped open several containers of food. Seated on the ground, the Dwyers tucked into the feast Aunty Myfanwy had prepared.

Helwyn was impressed by what was on offer. For appetizers, there was chicken in aspic as well as faggots, meatballs made from lamb's liver, and the vegetarian Glamorgan sausage, a blend of eggs, cheese and breadcrumbs shaped like a sausage and pan-fried. The Welsh were apparently famous for their lamb as Helwyn soon discovered, for Aunty Myfanwy had conjured up a tender, succulent lamb stew, the ever-popular *Cawl*. The main dish was accompanied by laverbread, patties of seaweed fried in bacon fat. Dessert consisted of a slice of sumptuous harvest seedcake together with *Bara brith*, a traditional speckled bread made with raisins, currants and candied orange peel, topped off with summer berries and cream. There was even a selection of Welsh cheeses: Caerphilly, Tintern and Pantysgawn. The Black Bomber was particularly strong. It was all washed down with some excellent fine Welsh ales, courtesy of the Felinfoel and Upper Cwmbran breweries. There was Penderyn Portwood for afters, apparently something the French could not get enough of. Helwyn found it extraordinary how this one delicious buffet nearly incorporated the entire repertoire of Welsh cuisine.

Every so often, people would drift over for a natter or try some of Aunty Myfanwy's cooking in exchange for their own brand of home cooking. Helwyn, however, couldn't manage another bite; he had gorged himself silly and his stomach felt heavy and bloated. He glanced around the grassy hilltop, hidden within the walls of the caerdroia, as the villagers shared food, swapped stories and socialized.

"A bloody good feed," complimented Helwyn, dabbing his mouth with a napkin. "Aunty Myfanwy, you are, without doubt, a miracle worker in the kitchen."

"You've outdone yourself again, Myfanwy," agreed Uncle Chet in high praise. "Every year, your cooking gets better and better."

"Stop exaggerating, boys," said Aunty Myfanwy, positively beaming. "You're making me blush."

Helwyn looked over at Stacey, who'd remained on the fringes of the community, silent, preoccupied. He saw her plate, the food on it barely touched. "You're not eating?"

"I'm not hungry," she replied quietly. A ladybird landed on her hand. Stacey didn't seem to notice.

"What's wrong?" Helwyn asked her, concerned.

Aunty Myfanwy put a motherly arm around her. "She must be feeling the heat," she sweet-talked, as though addressing a little girl, "aren't you, my dear?"

Except the heat alone could not explain Stacey's distant manner, for the day was disappearing fast and it already felt markedly cooler. The sun had long since begun its steady descent in the west, the sky layered in deepening shades of red.

The younger and fitter of the villagers were getting up to dance in tune with the beat of the drums, the flowing chords of the harp and the sharp, quirky sounds of the fiddle. *Twmpath dawns* to use its proper name, as Uncle Chet informed Helwyn, a traditional form of folk dancing. Helwyn watched the people get their freak on to the Celtic music. Soon the party was in full swing. New brides and husbands were supposedly chosen on the strength of the person's ability to dance, explained Aunty Myfanwy. Gladys Bowen's three daughters, Petra, Rowena and Lynette, were the bee's knees of the scene, Aunty Myfanwy emphasized, and in search of suitors of their own. Helwyn had to honestly admit they were heavenly creatures, with their perfect white skin, locks the colour of mead and sweet, seductive looks. Aunty Myfanwy called them over, to his slight consternation, and introduced them to him. He had a feeling where this might be heading.

"We would love it if you danced with us," requested Petra boldly.

"Dance with us and we'll wash all your troubles away," promised Rowena.

"Come, let us fill you with passion," intimated Lynette with an outstretched hand.

How could he possibly resist the tempting call of these Sirens? Helwyn glanced at Stacey a little guiltily and discovered her curled up on the grass, eyes closed, apparently out of it.

"Go to them," encouraged Aunty Myfanwy. "Your ladyfriend's tired and resting. I'm sure she won't mind you having one dance. We'll look after her."

After a series of half-hearted protests and even less half-hearted excuses, Helwyn surrendered his will to the three sisters, who grasped his hands lustily and led him to the dance circle. Full though he was, he managed to get into the spirit of the thing. Again, he felt like he had boarded a time capsule and been whisked hundreds of years into the past. Under the watchful eye of Gladys Bowen, who seemed ever-pleased by her daughters' choice of mate, Helwyn shimmied and two-stepped, trying to keep up with the pace and rhythm of the folk music. Barefoot, each clad in a flimsy white cotton dress and wearing a garland of flowers round their neck, the Bowen sisters moved gracefully to the music of the bards, loosing tinkling laughs and flirting unabashedly with Helwyn. He found the experience strangely elating and, for a moment, he imagined himself frolicking in the hay with all three fair maidens as they kissed and caressed and pleasured him, their soft, nubile bodies rubbing maddeningly against his . . . He quickly pushed away this carnal image and decided to return to his aunt and uncle while his dignity was still intact. He had got so close to getting carried away. These divine creatures didn't make it easy for him, and not accustomed to being rejected, the Bowen girls expressed their disappointment with sensuous pleas for him to stay, but he politely excused himself and wandered off. Gladys, their mother, seemed to take umbrage, the frown of someone whose machinations have been comprehensively foiled.

The sky lost its red glow as dusk fell. The temperature dropped, becoming cooler and a lot more bearable.

The celebrations continued for a little while longer until Judge Griffith took to the stage again. The merriment and music ceased, and a hush descended. Everyone paid close attention.

"It is time," Judge Griffith announced, loud and clear, "to hear from our venerable spiritual leader, Father Anwell Melkin."

And then Anwell Melkin was addressing the audience. Helwyn did not know where he had come from, whether he had emerged from the cave like some hermit or had already been among the villagers from the outset. Except he was a person Helwyn would surely have remembered, the reason being Anwell Melkin cut a formidable figure. He was tall, taller even than Uncle Chet, a towering six-foot-eight, in fact. A giant of a man, his face was pocked and scarred from old smallpox, his nose crooked, bent to one side, and his shock of hair dyed as black as his ministerial tunic, less one clerical collar. His beady eyes travelled discerningly across the expectant faces of the congregation and, when he spoke, Helwyn noticed his teeth had been filed down to vicious points like those of some tribal cannibal. All-in-all, he looked more like a dangerous thug than a revered priest.

His voice was deep and oratorical and ageless, resonating ominously across the secluded hilltop. "Welcome, people, to *Gwyl y Cynhaeaf* or – dispensing with Cymraeg for the benefit of our two guests – our annual Harvest Festival. It has been a fruitful year as I'm sure you will all agree. We have laboured long and hard so the earth can give up its riches and prepare us for the coming winter months. We are truly blessed. We have amassed a productive yield of crop and our sheep grow fatter by the day, grazing in our lush green valleys. Thanks we must now give to our Lord of the Harvest. Do, now, as is our custom . . ."

The villagers did, as instructed. Each and everyone, including the children, brought out robes and eased them over their heads, eventually raising the hoods. Robes that were black and unembroidered and composed of a fine material, like silk. The adults amongst them lit wooden torches against the advent of night. The flames crackled and spluttered as the countless torches illuminated the hilltop, isolated from the rest of the world. The torchlight danced and flickered, playing across the faces of the villagers and, for a moment, Helwyn saw only demonic expressions all around him, ancient and twisted and full of malice. Even their robes seemed to shimmer and whorl and move with unearthly life, as slickly as tar. Then, he blinked, bewildered, and the disturbing optical illusion was gone. They were only the villagers of Caerdroia, as human as him.

Stacey stirred in her sleep, suddenly bolted upright. She looked around, took in the flaming torches and black robes and the giant, muscle-bound priest, and a look of understandable alarm crossed her features. "What's . . . what's going on?"

"Sunday Mass," Helwyn informed her, putting a comforting arm round her, "Caerdroian-style."

"We, the first Britons, have reached a significant milestone," Father Melkin continued. "As earthly representative of the Olden Ones, it pleases me to tell you that Arawn himself has returned among us."

"We deliver our praise to the Olden Ones and their sovereign, Ancient One!" the congregation began to chant in unison. "The Lord of the Harvest! The Goat of a Thousand Young! The Master of All Concubines! The Eater of Worlds! *May Arawn know himself!*"

All eyes abruptly turned in Helwyn's direction. He did not like the occult-driven worship or the fact he was now unexpectedly the centre of their dark focus. Was he witnessing the outpourings of a satanic cult? "What is it?"

Then, Melkin let loose a startling revelation. "Today is a double celebration. Not only did we ensure a good harvest, but a special visitor has dropped by our way to reunite with local tradition. *The one who calls himself Helwyn Dwyer is none other than Arawn, Ruler of Annwn!*"

For a moment Helwyn was at a loss for words. He could not process the priest's outrageous claim. "Me? Arawn? Surely not!"

"You have forgotten who or what you are, O Lord."

"Look, I'm just an author. I write cheap horror for a living, that's all."

Ephraim Jones decided to interject. "Most people cannot afford imaginations, but *you* . . . you were writing from past experiences without knowing it. Let us awaken those forgotten memories."

"Just because my memory leaves something to be desired doesn't mean I'm some [*hero? . . . prodigal son? . . . GOD???*] fabled figure from Welsh mythology."

"Are you familiar with Lovecraft?" asked Jones.

"What half-decent horror writer wouldn't be?"

"You should be. You met him in 1926 when he visited Wales while researching his book."

"This is getting absurd." Helwyn said incredulously, turning to Uncle Chet for help. "Can't you stop this nonsense?"

"We were *never* related," disclosed Uncle Chet. "We are your worshippers, Arawn O Great One."

"You are our rainmaker," added Rowena Bowen from back in the crowd. "You sanctify our existence."

It was bad enough these people mistook him for some kind of prophet or deity, and in another life he might have found the idea amusing, even appealing, but his mind was struck by a horrible thought. What did they intend to do with him? What did they envisage as the end-result? "If you plan to make me a human sacrifice in one of your wicker figures, then go on right ahead. I'm not afraid of dying."

"We cannot sacrifice you," Melkin declared. "You were never born and you can never die. You are *ancient!*"

"You don't seriously buy any of this, do you?" Helwyn asked Stacey, wanting a journalist's rational and impartial viewpoint.

He got none. Stacey had been watching this incredible exchange with wide-eyed wonder . . . and fear. Once poised and confident, Stacey's mind seemed to be slowly unravelling through whatever sinister force pervaded this place. "I never realized we were in the presence of a living god," she giggled.

"Arawn! Arawn! Arawn! Arawn!" chanted the villagers for the best part of a minute. "Arawn! Arawn! Arawn!–"

Father Melkin silenced the masses with a raise of his hand. "Let him speak."

Helwyn tried desperately to reason with them. "As a god, shouldn't I possess supernatural powers or something?"

"You are a hollow man as yet," explained Melkin. "You need your Daemon. He is everything you once were. He is everything you will be, again. A bond that transcends the physical."

Helwyn pleaded with the audience. "Listen to yourselves! You surely can't accept his loony talk as gospel!"

"Prove us wrong," Uncle Chet challenged, pointing to the dark maw of the cave. "There, within the Well of Lost Souls, lies your past, present and future. Soon all shall be revealed."

"Your return has been long overdue," Father Melkin stated. "Embrace your destiny. Only *you* can usher in a new era for the world of Man."

"Your loyalty is to your people now," reminded Ephraim Jones.

"We prostrate ourselves at your feet!" uttered the talented Bowen dancing girls together, deliriously, desirously.

"Go, now, into the Well of Lost Souls and find the part of you that you are missing," insisted Melkin. "You will not be the same person when you return. You will return as something much, much more . . ."

Helwyn grappled with the flurry of astonishing information he had received. Commonsense, it would appear, was taking a serious bashing today. He tried to reconcile the deluded beliefs of the villagers with his own genuine curiosity of the cave, the same cave that had fascinated him since arriving on this remote lonely elevation. What did he have to lose? What horror writer doesn't crave vindication of their life's work by venturing into a cave, where supposedly the Rules of Normality do not apply? There was, however, still the small matter of Stacey. He gestured towards her, her expression imploring him: *Don't go, please.* "I can't leave her like this. She's not well." *If it looks like madness and smells like madness, it must be madness.*

"Don't worry about Miss Davenport," Aunty Myfanwy reassured Helwyn. "You've more important business to contend with. Trust us, we will keep her safe."

Helwyn looked hard at the uninviting entrance of the cave and back at Stacey. Aunty Myfanwy was gently stroking her hand. Nodding slowly, Helwyn reluctantly began to walk towards the cave. He grabbed Judge Griffith's proffered flaming wooden torch along the way.

"Our hour draws near . . ." declared Melkin.

"Arawn! *Arawn! ARAWN* . . .!" went the chanting, rising higher in pitch, providing Helwyn with all the encouragement he needed.

Helwyn stepped intrepidly into the yawning mouth of the cave and thought: *This way doth madness lie.*

His flickering torchlight gradually receded to a feeble orange glow, growing fainter and fainter, as he progressed deeper into the cave. Soon it disappeared altogether.

Helwyn realized he was on his own now. In one respect it allowed him time to think, to reflect on the far-fetched reverence his so-called people had bestowed on him. On the other hand–

–*What in Christ's name do they expect me to find down here?*

The walls of the tunnel were smooth and composed of polished rock, in all likelihood man-made and as wide as any mineshaft. The light from his torch picked out prehistoric cave-drawings at set intervals, more detailed than those famously discovered at Lascaux, France.

The pictures were an instant source of fascination for Helwyn. They told a strange story. Basic matchstick figures with spears worshipping tentacled, Kraken-like monsters that fell from the sky aeons ago. There was something powerful yet oddly prophetic about these colourful scenes, particularly with those further down the tunnel. In the later drawings, one could make out skyscrapers in an industrialized cityscape together with vast temples and colossal statues in veneration of the gods of old, an ancient vision of the future that put Nostradamus to shame. The very last cave painting, vividly rendered, predicted the enslavement of Mankind by this globulous race of titans that had finally risen from their eternal slumber, with cities ablaze and millions upon millions massacred in a world ravaged by an apocalyptic war.

The locals should open this place up to the public like Wookey Hole. The history and religious beliefs of their first ancestors are here for all to see. Whoever – Early Man or otherwise – created these prehistoric works of art deserves a special mention in the British Archaeological Honours for their astounding imagination.

The cave continued its steep downward gradient the further he went, and Helwyn realized it would be something of an effort getting back up to the surface, a real test of his overall fitness.

Helwyn pushed forward. He was already fighting a mixture of stomach-coiling dread and deep-seated claustrophobia, but his curiosity kept him going. He needed to know what was down there, in the heart of this very hill. What forbidden secrets would he uncover, what mysterious fate awaited him? Was he indeed, as the Caerdroians claimed, Lord of the Otherworld? Or was he heading straight into an elaborate trap? In the words of Uncle Chet (with whom he wasn't even related), he would find out soon enough.

As he pressed on, his ears picked up moaning from the darkness ahead. He initially thought it was the wind rushing down from the entrance, but the air was still, as verified by the full, undisturbed flame of his torch. On closer listening, he realized the sound was distinctly human or coming from something that had *once* been human. The moans of perpetual suffering, a chorus of lament, and the deeper Helwyn journeyed, the louder grew the commotion.

Then, a few hundred metres further along the passage, Helwyn saw for the first time what was causing the disparate sounds of grief. As he had rightly suspected, the moans came from a gathering of ghosts . . . *actual* spirits. Men, women and luckless children in phantom form populated the tunnel, wandering aimlessly and wearing sorrowful expressions. Their outlines were ragged, undefined, as wispy as mist, and Helwyn passed through them unhindered. They moaned and wailed, begging him to help them end their suffering and restore them to their former lives.

Helwyn understood where he was at. Through some invisible trapdoor between reality and the other side, Helwyn had ventured without warning into some kind of Hadean realm, or Annwn to be precise, the Otherworld the villagers believed belonged to him. This was not Hell in the conventional sense. But it was a hell of sorts, at least for these poor lost souls condemned to an afterlife of misery and torment. Instead of fear, Helwyn felt only pity for Annwn's insubstantial denizens. Was this how the dead lived?

No coin-collecting Ferryman in sight. No Barge of the Dead, no River Styx to cross. No drinking from the River Lethe, either, in the desperate hope of forgetfulness and sweet oblivion.

No, here in Annwn, the dead were forced to spend eternity as slaves to boredom and regret and despair, forever yearning for another shot at life, reduced always to confront their present abysmal circumstances in an unendurable confusion of everlasting emotional pain.

How they must surely envy his physical presence, Helwyn thought, conscious of the fact that he had turned into a 'necronaut', if there were such a term.

Down the tunnel the apparitions stepped aside, made way for him, let him pass.

If you want to give up and turn back, I won't hold it against you.

Helwyn suppressed his anxieties and continued his exploration of the cave system. He passed side-tunnels and by-passages and recesses, but he had no need to check his bearings since he continued to follow the largest tunnel of each branch. He suddenly happened upon a huge, gloomy subterranean cavern. This must be a significant place – a *sacred* place – for it didn't take him long to spot the large tome resting patiently on the stone pedestal in the centre of the cavern. Like the walls of the cavern, the pedestal held mysterious hieroglyphic carvings that Helwyn didn't recognize. This must be journey's end, he thought with a sense of inevitability. The villagers had expected him to find that book, the purpose of his tour through the Well of Lost Souls. The second reason, he presumed, although he was yet to figure out exactly what, related to the massive hole that existed where the far wall of the cavern ought to have been. The aperture wasn't just pitch-black, it represented the very antithesis of light. It drew in whatever light was available, like a black hole in deep space, and possessed the thick, rippling quality of crude oil. The fire from his torch was reflected feebly back from the dense, impenetrable blackness as though the opening were covered by some kind of film, or *membrane*. A hole, Helwyn speculated, leading to the very bowels of the earth . . . or elsewhere, perhaps beyond reality itself.

The mirror of darkness was fascinating enough, but the book was his primary focus.

He wandered cautiously over to the central stone lectern and the huge tome it supported. The embittered moans of the dead, protesting their tortured existence, came from all around him. It was interesting to note that the ghostly inhabitants of Annwn avoided approaching or looking directly into the light-sucking hole in the far wall, giving it a wide berth.

Torch aloft, Helwyn examined the volume, bound in scuffed leather. He blew off the layers of dust and tried reading the title, couldn't. It was in some indecipherable archaic language, the literature of dead tongues. Just when he thought he was getting nowhere, the title morphed into what Helwyn guessed to be early Arabic judging from the pot-hooks and dots and curves. It changed again into the Brythonic languages, first Old Welsh [Yr Annisgrifiadol], then into modern English, apparently for his very benefit, as though the paper possessed psychical properties. Now the title was clear to him:

THE INDESCRIPTION

Chronicled by Arawn

Edited by Gwynn ap Nudd

Uncle Chet had mentioned the ledger when they had first met outside the church. This was supposedly the bible of the Caerdroians and their fellow countrymen, particularly those who had not converted to Christianity but kept to strict, ancient druidic tradition.

Not without some apprehension, Helwyn opened the book. The vellum was old and yellow, and the lettering faded. The contents' page alone consisted of hundreds of chapters, dating as far back as 10,000 years BC when Mankind was a primitive, cave-dwelling species. Helwyn wondered if this might be the oldest book on record. Skimming through the chapters, he learned of the distant past. From what few passages he scrutinized, the pages spoke of the rise and fall of alien gods and the people who came to worship them, the emergence of secret cults and underground sects conducting dark rituals and human sacrifices in order to rouse their sleeping deities and prepare the world to be ruled by them once more. The arcane knowledge of the Olden Ones invaded every great civilization and belief system throughout the ages, in some guise or another, all variations on the same theme. They provided the mythological basis for the Olympians, the Norse gods and the Aztecan sky-gods, even the romantic figures of the Mabinogion scriptures.

This was meant to be taken seriously, as written law, far from the big, cosmic joke he had anticipated.

The craziness wasn't about to end there.

More insane secrets were about to be revealed.

It was only when Helwyn had gone halfway through the ledger that he was struck by a stark realization. It occurred to him that he recognized the long-hand scrawl.

The ancient text was fashioned in his *own* handwriting, and Helwyn knew for a fact it wasn't down to the psychic paper.

Feeling dizzy, Helwyn took a moment to steady himself. Most people didn't know or, if they did, would laugh at this secret history of the world that he had supposedly authored. But their rash ignorance didn't lessen the significance of the disturbing knowledge contained in this book.

The forlorn pleas of the surrounding ghosts could not distract him. Totally absorbed, he whipped through the book, travelling up through the annals of time, glimpsing chapters capturing important dates and key events in chronological order. The disappearance of the Roman legion at Caerleon was chronicled in great detail here. The ledger periodically carried the names of unfortunate outsiders offered up to the gods as human sacrifices as well as a random peppering of dangerous incantations and spells, the forbidden knowledge of the druids.

Then he came across material he didn't expect. All the novels he'd published in recent years were already present in the ledger – his complete works, every word, every sentence he ever put down on paper. Each book compressed into a chapter. One whole chapter was even devoted to *My Immortal Daemon*. Except, according to the date in the ledger, he'd written the damn thing over *four hundred years ago*.

Only I've forgotten . . .

And why is that?

Helwyn remembered what the villagers had told him back on the hill. He was...*incomplete*. He was missing a vital ingredient, an essential part of himself. He needed to unite with his Daemon to make him whole again. The same, separated Daemon-spirit slept silently, hibernating and dreaming, waiting for the day its other half would return.

And Helwyn *had* officially returned . . .

Let Sleeping Gods lie, I say. Never wise to wake them up, or you might find them in a foul mood.

Helwyn didn't have time to peruse the book any further. He detected a new sound.

Above the collective piteous moans of the spectral figures, he heard a distant rumbling, screeching noise, like a braking express train, from the dark rippling chasm in front of him.

Something was coming . . . something big, something terrible.

[*my Immortal Daemon*]

Coming for him . . .

But that wasn't the worst of it. What hadn't clicked before and what had since been tugging at the back of his mind now occurred to him. If he remembered the plot of his latest bestseller correctly, a horrible fate would befall the heroine in the final pages.

And if he really was a prophet, as the villagers claimed, and life imitated art, it meant Stacey was in big trouble.

High up on the torchlit hill, Stacey tried to make sense of the events of the past day.

It had started off innocently enough. A pleasant drive down to Wales with a man she could easily fall in love with. Meeting his family and the people with whom he supposedly shared a kinship. Then things had turned strange and terrible, distinctly alarming. The vulgar looks the men had given her, as though starved of sex, and the unsettling talk of the brittleness of reality and the unseen worlds of monsters adjacent to our own when she attempted to elucidate the village's history should have amounted to nothing more than superstitious nonsense from a bunch of bucolic simpletons. But seeing Helwyn succumbing to the deceptive charms of the Harvest Festival and being coaxed into believing he was some immortal god, so he would undertake a fool's errand into the caves from where he might never return, only highlighted his gullibility and the persuasive power of these crazy people. Helwyn had abandoned her when he had promised to protect her, leaving her vulnerable to the villager's misguided beliefs and whims. Abandoned her, left her to the wolves.

As a journalist – a respected journalist – she knew she was in a tight spot. She could only guess as to what they might have in store for her.

Night had descended, and the countless burning torches brought a sinister illumination to the hilltop.

Father Melkin was presently preaching to his flock. "Helwyn will soon discover that he is Arawn and, as he merges with his Daemon, he will restore the balance of the Universe and set in motion the events that will forge the future in our favour. The gods will rise again from their dreaming and change the world the way it ought to be. Once again, we will serve the Original Masters of the Earth." He spied Stacey, prompting his congregation to turn in her direction, honouring her with ominous looks that brought a dark chill down her spine. "We, of course, have a non-believer in our midst, one who has come from the closed-minded streets of London with her blond ambition, ignorant views and longstanding prejudices, an outsider unlike our very own dear Helwyn." He paused for effect before continuing. "It is the decision of the Council – including myself, Anwll Melkyn, and the Defender of our Laws, Ifor Gryffudd – that we should serve up the one who calls herself Stacey Davenport as an offering for our successful harvest."

Stacey froze. She could not speak. Fear of the worst kind washed over her. It seemed she was to be sacrificed in some cruel, brutal way.

Melkin went on to elaborate, "Our great fourteenth-century poet, Dafydd ap Gwilym, had the right idea. Whether he was glad-eyeing women in church or having intercourse with young girls, one thing was constant: he had unending praise for the sanctity of the phallus. We will therefore have sport with the outsider in accordance with his divine teachings."

The atmosphere turned malignant and the situation grave.

The men feasted their eyes on Stacey.

Stacey looked to PC Bryn Trevent for help, but he was part of the programme, one of them. She saw only sin in his eyes. He joined the others as they advanced towards her like a medieval lynch mob.

Her paralysis broke and she began to back away from them. The manner of her fate was to be more terrible than she ever imagined. "*You can't do this . . .!*" she sobbed, terrified, trembling.

"Heavens-to-Betsy," said Aunty Myfanwy, in a mockery of her motherliness, "no need to fret, dear. Let our men take good care of you. Besides, you have nothing to trade except your womb. Consider your fertility as currency *for your life."*

"We have such high hopes for you," intimated Dr. Lustig. "The doctor will soon be in . . ."

"We must reap our reward," emphasized Evan Carew the Solicitor, hungrily.

"We need to breed," declared Old Ephraim Jones.

She backed into the wall of the caerdroia that offered no escape. And, then, the men were all over her, crowding her, her skin feeling their warm, spoiled breath and drool, their many hands stroking and touching her soft flesh. She could already smell their sweat and their semen. And, beneath their hoods, their features melted like candlewax, eyes narrowing into upturned crescent moons as they transformed into something inhuman. The sight of their drooping, gloopy faces caused her to seek the sanctuary of unconsciousness.

Her Christian god had forgotten this accursed place. Here, Christ had fallen, and they had raised an unholy god. Before she finally blacked-out, she realized there would be no God waiting for her in the end. Punishment enough for messing around in the Devil's playground.

"Take her to the Black Church," boomed Anwell Melkin from somewhere faraway, "where, as your spiritual leader, I shall enter her first . . ."

He stood rooted to the spot. His passion for the grotesque and the weird left him staring into the inky, mesmerizing blackness of the chasm. He meant to see it, he had to know. He meant to see the screeching onrushing peril, the unique immortal Daemon the villagers had promised him.

For Helwyn was now beginning to believe them and the forbidden religion they practised.

Yet, rationality intruded itself into his mind, a flash of fear of the cosmic horror heading his way. He decided he should move . . . and *fast*. He had to try and save Stacey if he could, though he doubted he had enough time. He thought he was probably already too late. Most of all though, he had to evade the Daemon – whatever shape or form it would take – that was hurtling headlong in his direction through infinite leagues of sentient blackness, the hinted-at space between worlds. Helwyn could hear the approaching unearthly screeches of the Daemon, like metal nails dragging down a blackboard. Soon it would break through the nethermost limits of reality, into his world and claim him.

He ripped his eyes away from the black, shimmering mouth of the pit and slammed the ledger shut.

Helwyn began his scramble back up to the surface, leaving behind the majestic cavernous vault. The maudlin apparitions of the dead faded into the ether as though aware of the approach of the yet-unseen, dimension-crossing being. Helwyn was suddenly alone . . . except for the thing that was coming after him.

He retraced his steps, picking up his pace, fighting the upward gradient of the tunnels. The incline was hard going, but his reserves of adrenaline fuelled his flight.

He made his desperate bid to escape as the ground beneath him started to shake, slowing down his progress. Bits of rock and grit showered down from the roof. He worried about the structural integrity of the caves, fearing a cave-in. He wondered if he would manage to return to the surface alive and with his normally iron-clad sanity intact. He wished desperately for an avalanche of sliding rocks in his wake to stop the Daemon in its tracks. Amidst the rumbling and the quaking of the cave system, the hideous screeches of the pursuing Daemon grew steadily louder, beginning to resemble the thunderous shriek of a high-velocity jet through a wind tunnel. It sounded big, immense, utterly unstoppable.

Stumbling, getting up, trying to maintain his footing through the subterranean corridors, Helwyn struggled on, bridging incredible dimensions, leaving behind the sub-reality of Annwn, running up the Well of Lost Souls. The caves lurched from side to side as the seismic waves increased, Helwyn leaping and bounding and scrambling. On the final leg, he passed the previously-intriguing rock paintings without giving them a second look and suddenly, thankfully, he burst out into the open.

The hilltop was strangely silent and deserted and bleached in moonlight. The locals had probably scattered back to the village with their prize, Stacey. Glancing anxiously back at the cave, Helwyn got moving again. He didn't wait to see what would emerge from the so-called Well of Lost Souls, the portal to Annwn and the fathomless depths of the Stygian world beyond, realities within realities, dreams within dreams. The rising crescendo of alien shrieks and screeches told him that his monstrous pursuer wasn't far behind.

Helwyn now had the unenviable task of negotiating the caerdroia. The fire from his torch guided him onwards. He wished he could just run down the hill instead of following the caerdroia's long-winded route. No such luck. The walls of the caerdroia were too high to climb . . . and–

–It was if the maze was *alive*. The leafy walls rippled and undulated, and the branches seemed to snake and move, reaching out for him, trying to trip him up. Helwyn ran at full-stretch, using his strength and speed to rip through the grasping serpentine branches. He did not glance over his shoulder lest he should glimpse the unnameable horror in pursuit.

He was sure it was gaining ground, and Helwyn redoubled his efforts in panicked determination. A sloshing, like thick churning mud, now accompanied the howls and shrieks. And, all the while, the animate, groping branches of the caerdroia vied to upend him.

Helwyn didn't know how he managed it, but after what seemed like an unreal, decerebrate eternity, he arrived at the entrance of the caerdroia.

There was no relief or gratitude.

For the sound was incredibly loud now, sharp and incisive, like the howling of wind-wraiths, nearer still, drawn to him as though through some magnetic pull.

Helwyn tried to make a dash for it, but his right foot struck a rock and he lost his balance. He flew through the air and tumbled to the ground, rolling briefly down the hill. He came to rest a couple of hundred yards from the caerdroia, his torch falling from his grasp, extinguishing. Regaining his senses, he got up clumsily and fell again, pain exploding in his right leg. Tired, scratched and bruised, wincing in excruciating pain, he raised his head and looked back in objective defeat.

He realized he didn't stand a chance. He was in no fit state to carry on. He'd known all along – and didn't need Melkin to remind him – that he would not be the same person once the creature from the abyss caught up with him, but he wanted to savour his freedom, his individuality, his human existence, for whatever short time he had left. For he knew, from everything he had written in his novel, he would lose his current identity and serve as a vessel to a powerful deity, becoming something he would not like but had always been and was destined to be again. Neither would he care anymore. To use an appropriate biblical quote, why gain the world if you lose your soul? He cherished his humanness for a moment longer until the monster finally came over the hill.

For it *was* a monster, a black, behemoth being. A tenebrous, amorphous, tentacled thing of cataclysmic stature, too horrible to describe and one that should never exist. It emerged from the exit of the caerdroia and flowed down the hill towards him like a river of black slime, stewing and seething and bubbling. It stopped a few yards short from where he lay and raised its anterior aspect like some colossal tongue, screeching and roaring in brain-blasting triumph into the night, a mass of writhing tentacles, its ebony-black surface glistening slickly in the moonlight.

As the gargantuan, interdimensional creature engulfed him and its astronomical entirety disappeared into his mouth to occupy his single, pain-wracked human body, Helwyn saw the not-too-distant future in his mind's eye, as foretold in the prophecy, a vision in keeping with the cave paintings he had witnessed earlier. In that frozen moment, Helwyn saw the world's great cities on fire, turning to ash and rubble, buildings burning and collapsing on the frightened masses below as Mankind fought a losing battle with a superior race of alien beings, whose civilization pre-dated his own and who had risen from their sleep through forbidden prayer to take back the world that had originally belonged to them. After all, what was Man in relation to the cosmos but a minute, carbon-based lifeform operating on bioelectrical energy, an ephemeral species whose flesh-and-blood body ultimately died, decayed and disintegrated? Whereas the Olden Ones were eternal – ultra-supreme conquerors of death and time and of fabulous, inaccessible dimensions.

The world was poised on the brink. A new human order sat in the wings, waiting for the moment when the Ancient One would reign over the Olden Ones and prepare for the coming of the Eternal One.

Time to Become . . .

Helwyn's last thoughts before he lost his humanity and became inextricably linked with his Daemon? *Evil attracts evil – there's no two ways about it!*

There were clouds in the night sky where there had been none before. They smothered the moon. Thunder roared like a barrage of cannon-fire. Lightning forked a trident directly to earth.

The doors of the Black Church opened, and a familiar figure entered, his hair and clothes wet from the driving rain outside.

He closed the doors behind him and walked up the aisle, his footsteps echoing ominously up to the high ceiling, his manner calm and eminent like a medieval king back from the Crusades. The villagers, seated on the pews, gave obeisance as he passed.

Candles, in infinite supply, provided the necessary illumination to the church's interior and seemed to bring the demonic creatures depicted on the stained-glass windows vividly to life. They complimented the corruption and deconsecrated nature of this unhallowed edifice.

The newcomer approached the altar, on which Stacey Davenport lay naked, spread-eagled and heavily pregnant, her wrists and ankles restrained by iron shackles. She wore an expression of pure, unprecedented exhaustion and presently seemed completely unaware of her surroundings, giggling at nothing in particular. Then, her eyes fluttered open and caught sight of the newcomer and a moment of recognition dawned. "Helwyn, is that you?" she whispered like a feeble old woman.

"There is no Helwyn here," replied the black-clad newcomer, impassively. "There is only *me*."

And she realized there were no untruths in the newcomer's words. Although in all outward appearance he looked and dressed like Helwyn, the man standing before her was not the same Helwyn whom she had accompanied down to Caerdroia. She could no longer see the humanity in his eyes, only cruelty, eyes that were conscienceless, merciless, pitiless. "What have they done to you?"

"I can ask you the same question," he said in a hard, glacial tone.

Stacey wanted to weep, but her tears had run dry. Hadn't she suffered enough? The men – if they were in fact men – had entered her one by one and she had tried desperately to fight them off. She had struggled and thrashed about, but after a while her resistance had grown weak, and she had let them take her, passively, reluctantly, in the hope they would spare her life. Her unspeakable ordeal, she discovered, was far from over because once the men had completed their gang-rape of her, her belly had ballooned in record-breaking time. These demons – or whatever the hell they were – had impregnated her with their vile, alien seed, causing an accelerated pregnancy. She could feel the gestating embryos floating and kicking inside her by the sacful as they pushed against their human confines, producing an outward effect of invisible knuckles kneading her overinflated belly like dough. She yearned for the sweet release of death, but she knew she would not find it.

Father Melkin, who had been silently watching their verbal exchange from behind the altar, spoke up: "People of Caerdroia, the Transition is complete!" he boomed, triumphantly. "Helwyn has merged with the Ancient One! Our Lord Arawn has returned!"

The congregation rejoiced, clapped, hooted, cheered.

When the delirious babel of joy died down, Father Melkin addressed the newcomer, bowing his head in deference, "Welcome home, O Dark Lord. We are your humble servants. Do with us as you will."

"I desire only your unquestioning loyalty. I seek to galvanize the faithful, marshal an army, prepare our troops for the coming war: the subjugation of the human race."

"As it is written, so shall it come to pass . . ."

Stacey screamed. She clutched her swollen belly, her face streaked in sweat, grime and tears and contorted in exquisite agony. It was obvious she was on the cusp of labour.

An anxious murmur ran through the congregation.

"Her confinement is almost at an end," Father Melkin informed the Lord Arawn. "The impending birth of our new spawn is in honour of your great return."

"Then, get on with it!" snapped the Lord Arawn impatiently, his eyes flashing momentarily like shiny, silver pennies. Then, the effect was gone. "Do you not understand we have work to do?"

"As you wish, your Majesty . . ." Father Melkin muttered like a whipped monkey, avoiding his intense stare. He called over Aunty Myfanwy from the congregation with a beckoning finger. "You will serve as midwife."

"Haven't I always?" she replied cheerily. Dr. Lustig joined her as a matter of duty, to oversee the delivery. Standing on either side of Stacey, each grabbed a knee and widened her legs as far as they could go against the iron ankle restraints, with Aunty Myfanwy clutching her left hand as a supportive gesture. "Push down, my dear."

"Don't think!" advised Dr. Lustig. "Just let it happen."

Not that Stacey needed a midwife or doctor in attendance. The birthing process turned out to be a simple, unnaturally straightforward, albeit chundering affair. Stacey bore down hard, screaming with each wave of pain, and her waters ruptured in an outward explosion of black ichor. Her womb discharged the gestating young, which emerged from between her legs as dark blobs of sticky, animated goo. The tiny abominations oozed, smoothly and wetly, out of her vaginal canal one after another without requiring any form of manual handling or cutting of the umbilical cord, plopping onto the ichor-splattered altar in plentiful numbers.

Aunty Myfanwy gathered up three of the newborns and held them in front of their mother. "Aren't they adorable?"

One look at the sable, gelatinous nightmares she had given birth to caused Stacey to scream. She shrieked like a banshee. A protracted, deafening shriek. It was a godawful sound. Already half-unhinged, the last trace of sanity slipped away. Her repulsed, idiotic screams reverberated around the interior of the church.

Dr. Lustig grabbed a handful of her hair and slammed her head savagely on the altar to shut her up. It worked, Stacey knocked clean unconscious. She was no more use to them now. "Her fecundity though impressive, she would never make a good mother."

Aunty Myfanwy cradled the newborns in her loving arms, the shapeless, black obscenities twitching and squirming with alien life. More of these slickly-glistening, fist-sized monstrosities rolled and sloshed and splashed around in the thick, crude-oil-consistent, partum gore expelled by Stacey, emitting faint, discordant squeals. "I've got the nursery all prepared. Isn't the miracle of childbirth wonderful?"

Dr. Lustig concluded his assessment. "Very healthy offspring. Come from good stock."

"They must be hungry," said Aunty Myfanwy, full of maternal concern.

"Do what we always do. Let our little Broodlings feed on their mother. Our flock has fertilized her, and she has borne more of our flock. Her flesh will now provide rich sustenance. Miss Davenport has otherwise outlived her usefulness. The energy from her soul, shall, like that of those in the Thereafter, serve to power the waking of the gods."

Outside, thunder bellowed furiously. Another lightning stroke pierced the heavens. Rain pelted against the stained-glass windows in thick, torrential sheets.

Lord Arawn, who looked like Helwyn Dwyer, turned away from the abhorrent proceedings at the altar, satisfied with the blasphemous religious practices upheld by his followers, their fanatical devotion. He dismissed Stacey's inevitable doom from his mind. *She used to look good once, desirable even, but now she is nothing. There is no such thing as Love. Love is merely an illusion. Love is the condition of fools.* "I drive to London tonight," the Avatar of the newly-awakened Ancient One announced to his eager acolytes. "I must spread the message through my books. Drive my readers crazy, continue to convert them to our cause, ready them for the ascendancy of the rest of my pantheon as well as the revival of the paragon of the gods, the Eternal One. Bring about the downfall of Man." Again, he foresaw the crumbling, ruined cities of the world, consumed by apocalyptic fires, as the gods vented their wrath and took back what was rightfully theirs, and his eyes glittered scintillatingly like polished, finely-cut diamonds. And, while in THE HANGMAN the once-faceless painting of Arawn that dominated the lounge now bore a perfect likeness to Helwyn Dwyer, his new, complete incarnation in the Black Church presently declared: "Whatever I write shall come to pass . . . because I am the End of Everything."

March 2010 – June 2010

A Loving Wraparound...(concluded)

"*Perfect timing,*" *I tell the woman at the door. The Face that Broke a Thousand Hearts. She has ditched her cap, breeches and riding boots in favour of a wardrobe of haute couture. She looks utterly ravishing, exquisitely dolled-up in a sultry, sequinned evening dress and light-coloured stockings and wrapped up in a brown fur coat and wearing a cloche hat, embellished by a couple of crow's feathers, over her bobbed hair. Her neck is ornamented by several extravagant strings of pearls and beads. I give her a polite, customary peck on the cheek, but there will be no exchange of Valentine's gifts whatsoever, for long since has become the case, both of us have come empty-handed. This invitation is not entirely based on sentiment. Nevertheless, I wonder if there is still life in our long-distance relationship. "Please do come in."*

She follows me into my Parisian apartment. Outside the windows, dusk has deepened into night and the moon rides high in a starlit sky.

"Happy hour," I announce and pour her a dry martini, adding a green olive speared by a cocktail stick.

"Don't mind if I do," she replies.

I raise my martini-glass. "Here's to stolen moments . . . and stolen kisses."

"To stolen moments . . ." she acknowledges, doing likewise, and we each take a sip from our respective glasses while watching each other silently.

She eyes my black ensemble. "Black, again? That's sooo . . . Paris! Or macabrely does it. You're not about to go axe-crazy on me, are you?"

"You can't deny it's smart for all seasons."

"Did you finish the stories?" she finally asks, getting down to business. Whereas Agatha Christie dangled the seemingly paranormal in front of the reader's eyes but provided a more down-to-earth final twist, this young lady's works would resonate with a moodier atmosphere and a sense of dread with subtly-hinted supernatural elements. The literary world would soon fall under her spell, not just because of her wildly creative talents but on account of her devil-may-care attitude that embodied the spirit of the times, looking very inch the flapper.

"Indeed, I did," I confirm. "The tales must be told."

"What about our tale?"

"I'm on the cusp of completing it . . . right now."

"How does it end?"

Worms wriggle around in the skull of Valentine, writhe in the eye-sockets, the daisies having disintegrated. In that single moment, we notice the beheaded statue of Cupid, his bow and arrow also broken, the marble tarnished, covered in moss. The roses in the vase wilt, wither away, now nothing but decayed, desiccated remains — ten, perfectly-corrupted roses for the perfectly-corrupted love. The room is suddenly full of dust and cobwebs, as though the place has been abandoned for centuries, teeming with crawling spiders. Ladytron has begun to spill out of my iPod speakers, encouraging the listener to write a protest song in the absence of one's love and set oneself on fire.

"Between us? Not well . . ."

"It never does," she reflects with a sorrowful sigh. "This hour eternity has given us always ends the same."

"Perhaps one day things will be different," I reply, hopeful

"But not today," she says, sounding a little disappointed, despondent. "As much as I appreciate the kisses, I suppose it's for the best."

I once again appraise her glamorous 1920s evening-wear and gaze deep into her face, as fresh and youthful as that of a Hollywood starlet, and feel myself succumbing to the enchantment of those beautiful, knowing blue eyes. Daphne du Maurier truly is the Face that Broke a Thousand Hearts. She cannot help but betray her bohemian, privileged background. The blood of the French aristocracy runs through her veins. "I'm not letting you go so easily, this time."

"What choice do you have?" she reminds me, cannily observant as ever. "The cosmic window will close shortly."

She is right, of course. We languish in this impossible re-run of eternity, like that phrase you can only utter in French, perpetually at the crossroads of our semi-existence. "In which case we should make the most of our time together," I suggest. "Whatever time Fate has left us."

"No, I don't think so," Miss du Maurier says, finally making up her mind, declining my advances. "Our love was always doomed from the beginning. I mean was it really worth me coming?"

"You want to be alone," I ask, "like Garbo?"

"Who?"

"Maybe a little after your time, I guess," I speculate. "Or are you missing Fernande, instead?" The name of Miss du Maurier's former headmistress from the French finishing school with whom she allegedly had a sapphic relationship. "Or would you prefer to call upon 'Eric'?" Her alter-ego, the boy trapped inside the girl's body.

There is a wistful look in her eyes. "You have your moments . . . as do I."

"*Let's have one of your moments right here . . .*" *I encourage, full of romantic suggestion. But she is having none of it.* "*Do you expect me to bend to your will?*"

Unfortunately, a part of me knows that her presence here is my own doing, an upshot of magical thinking. "*Absolutely!*" *I exclaim cheerily, trying to put a positive spin on things.* "*You can experience a taste of passion, even if for a fleeting moment! Live and let live, I say!*"

"*More like live and let* die,*" she again corrects me,* "*or* love *and let die!*"

How does she expect me to respond? I can find no comeback – she has gotten wise to me. The problem is there is a bigger fault at work. I suppose the saddest thing about Valentine's Day is that if you strip away the schmaltz, all you're really celebrating is capitalism, *and both capitalism – and the media – do their scheming utmost to reinforce an entitlement of desire, propagating the notion that if a man buys a woman chocolates, wine and roses, he should expect certain things in return. Society tells us we are not worthy of love unless we pay the retail market, splash out ridiculous amounts on our true love (or mistress or inconsequential fling) on February the Fourteenth, and, like sheep, we follow the herd. Having just survived the festive season, Valentine's Day comes when we are at our most vulnerable. We are subjected to Valentine's Day chocolates and lame bouquets of roses and insipidly-romantic muzak piping through the department-store speakers, designed to manipulate feelings of desire and make us feel a longing for people who are possibly unobtainable or unable to reciprocate those feelings or just not right for us, setting us up for a great fall and a whole lot of disappointment and hurt. Except love – or sex – should never be owed to anyone just because the man has bought his Valentine's date a fancy dinner in a posh restaurant. Besides, how can anybody truly appreciate a seven-course meal that will only make you fall asleep? Exactly what is romantic about buying a bottle of wine that costs as much as a pair of diamond earrings? What's sexy about stuffing your face with expensive chocolates until you feel bloated – and sick?*

Maybe those who do not conform to these unrealistic ideals and manufactured desires, those who are not suggestible and prefer to be single or alone on Valentine's Day, those unwilling to let go of their hearts or are repulsed by the mere sight of soppy PDAs have got it right *and should rejoice in the knowledge that no such disaster shall ever befall them. Let someone else suffer the consequences of chasing a foolish romantic dream. They can always watch Meg Ryan in* French Kiss *and* Addicted to Love *back to back, as some token celebration of the day.*

"*Happiness is not a possession to be prized – it is a quality of thought, a state of mind,*" *Miss du Maurier, the young lady who would put Manderley firmly on the map, reminds me for the umpteenth time. She toys with the olive in her mouth, consumes it, before putting down her empty cocktail glass.*

"*We will meet again,*" *I promise her by way of reassurance,* "*maybe in another hundred years?*"

"*Don't count on it, Ixidorr . . .*" *Miss du Maurier remarks disagreeably, getting up and heading for the door.* "You keep damning the lovers and killing every cupid that comes to their assistance because you're such an interminable — what is the word I'm looking for? — creep!"

Hack Track Listing

If Music be the Food of Love...

Are You Lonesome Tonight?	Elvis Presley
Black Velvet	Alannah Myles
Piece of My Heart	Janis Joplin
Lay Lady Lay	Bob Dylan
Runaway Love	Alice Gold
Molly's Chambers	Kings of Leon
Cat Scratch Fever	Ted Nugent
Lotus	REM
Fallait Pas Écraser La Queue Du Chat	Clothilde
Bâti Mon Nid	Françoise Hardy
Ce Que Tu Désires	Jean-Louis Murat & Carla Bruni
Devil Woman	Cliff Richard
Moi...Lolita	Alizée
Lolita Nie En Bloc	Noir Désir
Ever Fallen in Love	Nouvelle Vague
People Are Strange	Yodelice
Mulder and Scully	Catatonia
Mama Told Me Not to Come	Tom Jones (feat. Stereophonics)
Dangerous Charms	The Delmonas
Dangerous Type	The Cars
Stop Me	Mark Ronson (feat. Daniel Merriweather)
Burning Up	Ladytron
Glorious	The Pierces
I Deserve It	Dean & Britta

Also by the Author

DAMNATION INN
WEIRD THEATRE

www.ingramcontent.com/pod-product-compliance
Lightning Source LLC
Chambersburg PA
CBHW030923020726
47498CB00001B/87